DEAR DEBORAH,
    NICK WROTE THIS NOVEL BASED
ON HIS PEACE CORPS SERVICE IN LIBERIA
FROM 1964-66. BEST WISHES IN LIBERIA
AND IN YOUR HEALING CAREER.
                    Charley STARTUP

An African Mask

A novel
by
Nicholas Ivancic

PublishAmerica
Baltimore

ISBN: 1-4241-3873-6
PUBLISHED BY PUBLISHAMERICA, LLLP
www.publishamerica.com
Baltimore

Printed in the United States of America

ACKNOWLEDGMENTS

"Rainy Day Women #12 & 35"
by Bob Dylan.
Copyright c 1966 by Dwarf Music. All rights reserved.
International Copyright secured. Reprinted by permission.

"Goin' to Chicago Blues"
by Count Basie and Jimmy Rushing
c 1941 WB Music Corp. (Renewed)
All Rights reserved. Used by Permission.

FOREWORD

An African Mask is entirely fiction and shouldn't be read as anything else. Begun in 1970, the American segments are rooted in the Vietnam-Watergate period. Real events appear only for the purposes of fiction as do the words of real persons.

There are three time frames: Africa, 1964-66; the Midwest, 1966-69; and primitive dream time where past and future merge into an eternal present as intimate as the nearest bird song.

NI
Kipton, Ohio
November, 2006

CONTENTS

PRELUDE

DANCE OF THE MASKED SPIRIT

You! You who wander aimless in the market place! Do you marvel at a slab of wood that speaks? A voice that wears a feral face? A face that counts a thousand scars yet argues love of life? I am hair and bone and breath of hope, much as you and yours…No trade with animal speech? A smile of disbelief? Hear me now! I am Nyamu! Spirit of the Sacred Earth and all that keeps therein! A thing you know but rarely see and then refuse to look! I am I! Sire of the Sunrise! Secret of the deep. Dead bones I melt and forge anew, wet boys I mold to men, watch new species form and die, swirl the seasons in the sky. I orchestrate the ocean's roar! Crash cymbals in the storm! Grind mountains into seas, stretch white beaches where they reach, undulate the trees. I am the secret wishes of the leaves, the soughing wind that sighs for thee. I contemplate the morning mist, give compass to the east. Clouds I call to spacious skies, shade to purling streams. In camouflage I keep. Creep. Leap! Roar! Spook the wildebeests. Put thunder to their feet. Sweetness in the meat. I revel in the kill. Death is but a planter, his work an unborn age. All that is must come and go, I am it that stays. As fertile rain I soften grief, soothe a virgin's sorrow, germinate tomorrow. I am science in the civet's eye, grace in the ballet of springing gazelle, solace in the simmering dusk. I fertilize your dreams. I am darkness. I am rare. I am Silence. I am air. I drink, think, throb, thrive, in every teeming drop of life I hide, every wild cry! Every human tongue! And yours! Though somewhat clumsy in these paper words! But I have the scent! The seed. I will give you lovely juice. Come. Look into this face. Look deep. Do not fear this fearful gaze, these bloodstained teeth. To thee alone I speak as to a dreamer in the arms of night. Come. I will tell a tale how I snared a human heart, kindred to your own.

To the Loma People

CHAPTER 1

NIGHT

Night falls quickly in the jungle. The late afternoon sun relents, breezes die on the leaves, shadows lengthen into wiry figures walking on stilts, smoke settles among the clustered rooftops like a milky blanket, the distant bark of a dog fixes the edge of the world. Then the curtain drops. Crickets ring out the joyous heartbeat of the slumbering earth. Darkness opens its eyes.

There's not much dusk. The reason, of course, is the near perpendicular angle at which the setting sun meets the tropical horizon, that and pockets of rising haze that screen out the last rays of light. But this is daytime reckoning. Night changes the rules. Perceptions fade, relationships get lost, names detach from their objects until everyday realities become shadows afloat in a faint dream calling home the smallest fear that grows in the vacuum. Nothing becomes something; daytime's certainty, a charlatan.

Think of an aching thirst, the scent of fresh water, a long drink and a pause afterwards…then an eerie stillness, a silence that isn't a silence, a cracking twig, a pang of terror, a crashing thicket, the whole sky screaming! Nails driving into gushing blood! Shrieking fury! A snapped vertebra as the grip locks, a thin foreleg pawing the air, slower, now irregular spasms, a tremor, a last helpless spurt and a skyward eye goes placid reflecting a feeble question, What is this? A naked tongue lolls in the dirt, flesh goes limp, and stillness returns to the quiet leaves like water refilling a careless footstep.

Thus Night. And when it does fall, the darkness is as no other. It is tactile, monstrous in its serenity. Its tongue drips on your neck. It has a million eyes, claws, cries of terror and lament—in reality birds and animals as even the children know but also something more as even the adults know, something large and fateful animating the drifting air, whispering leaves, the tremor in the stars, something with big teeth. Then—when darkness itself would bolt the earth—comes the beat of a drum; shy at first, as though another human heart has sensed an impasse asking no more than another drum to keep vigil.

Afraid o' see, not me not me
Afraid o' be, not free not free
Afraid o'thee, not see not see

There's nothing like drums in the middle of the night. They seem a thunderous echo of your own heart, deep, resonant, born of terror, yet defiant. Defiant. There's the key. Another frightened animal—but one doing something about it, working, announcing itself to the universe. Behold mankind. Should there be a greatly advanced intelligence focusing a microscope on this tiny world, the faint record of these feeble utterances might bring a notation to a nightly log. Planet III: Primitive life. Pockets of fear. Rhythmed effort to dispel perils thereof. Possibility of reflective consciousness.

We dream free, comeba me comeba me
Dream we thee, cometa be cometa be
We decree, come be see come be see

If banging on a drum is our first attempt to frighten the bogey man, mustering the courage to touch him comes next. Remember the dark closet in Grandma's basement? The voice in the furnace pipe, the empty squatters' shack after the sheriff ran them off? Later on, the eternal silence of those infinite spaces that struck terror in the heart of a great mathematician? These are the faces of the unknown. They recede but never go away. To go into the darkness then, to seek it out, touch it, constitutes the oldest rite of all, dutifully recorded in all our mythologies making men out of something less than men.

But to live through the night is to meet it on its own terms. So too the dark passage from youth to manhood. The forest itself, it is said, swallows its children, carries them in its belly, then returns them to the human village marked for life by the imprint of its teeth into their skin. It is of course much more than a forest of trees; it's a forest half humanized; a memory, a face, a wild cry, all of these when it materializes into a masked spirit and bursts into virile dance more animal than human. To the uninitiated this is the "forest thing," so awesome its name must not be spoken, and when it appears, it is as though for a brief lapse of time the forces behind the physical world concentrate all their power and ferocity, but their beauty and fecundity too, into one wild release of inspired music focused in this fantastic figure somehow come to life in a vague suggestion of a man.

When it's time for the initiates to go into the forest, "it" whisks into town unannounced—the timing is precise, the last light of day to set the stage. Dancing musicians and human cult members complete its retinue (hauntingly reminiscent of a Greek chorus). The entire village jumps to life. The spirit seems to know its way around, the occupants of houses, their ancestral names. It yields to no one. Like a gust of wind, it sets to work flying from place to place in a show of maternal concern. ("It" can assume either gender, any species, any physical form at the touch of a drum.) "My babies!" the distraught mother cries, "Where are my babies?" The drumbeat picks up. The attendants keep up a steady conversation to discover its intentions, reassure it, console it. Soon a circle of intense faces forms around the drama; the townspeople play their parts as though they've done it a thousand times. No one addresses the spirit directly, only through an interlocutor. It speaks in deep guttural tones with archaic words and double meanings. "The forest sings. Bring to me her babies!" "What will become of them?" "I will take them to my grove."

"When will they return?" "Soon. I will birth them new." This exchange is known like the words of a masterwork. The pain of separation is somewhat eased by the frolic and the theater, but never entirely. Women who cry are sent indoors.

Soon a line of nervous boys files into the waning light. Whimpering, practically naked, they stand apart rubbing their noses, looking for a familiar face, their sweaty hands clinging to a plaything that may be allowed the very young, some of whom understand only that they are to be devoured by this terrible "thing" and surely do not appreciate the symbolism. Quickly they are led into the forest—prolonged good-byes being rare in tribal society. They disappear behind the sweep of the spirit's rafia skirt; the turning dance steps of the retreating musicians close the door to their childhood. A last shout of a father to his son ends the scene. The luxuriant green curtain of the jungle resumes its soft rustling. Should one die before he's reborn, his few belongings are found next morning on his mother's doorstep. She knows her boy will stay in the forest.

"Bush school" takes place in the sacred grove, an unimposing fenced-in compound an easy walk from the village. It's called the *Poro,* which means "Earth," and it at once becomes a spiritual as well as geographic reference point the rest of their lives. Much of what happens here is secret but the general format is well known. We're allowed to know, for example, they learn sacred songs; we're not allowed the words or melodies. While the *Poro* is in session, the entire area is quarantined; there is no contact with the outside world. Betrayal of this or any other rule meant death in the old days. Now things aren't so strict, but discipline remains rigid, the living conditions

Spartan, the day long. The boys sleep on the ground, rise at daybreak, learn the necessities of survival—tool making, house raising, hunting, the arts of war in times of peril. They undergo circumcision and skin carving learning to bear pain with indifference; they go days without speaking aloud, communicating by gesture or eye contact. At night they share a communal meal and listen to their elders speak of lineages, lore, and tribal law, all of which must be memorized in the absence of a written alphabet.

However the *Poro* is not without compassion. One of the human cult members may bring a fatherly hand to a boy who's fallen behind, or a bolder lad may be allowed the secret behind the mask. And there's humor, too. There's a clownish spirit who might be called Mr. Backwards, who teaches etiquette by doing everything wrong, eating with the wrong hand, interrupting an elder. But above all the *Poro* instills strength of spirit, a strong spirit being the best weapon against whatever hell the world can muster.

Think of the one thing you fear most, seek it out, touch it. That is the essence of the *Poro*. In most cases it is the Great One. There are masks and there are masks, but the Great One, the Unnameable, is so fearful, so charged with supernatural power weaker people are said to have died merely by looking at it. It is primeval darkness incarnate. To touch it is to submerge your hand into the waters of death not knowing whether it will emerge human or "other." Only the strongest are challenged to do so—in the dead of night with the knowledge they will be punished if caught.

The entire experience is a spiritual inoculation. They've correctly identified fear as the culprit in all human failure, and to counter it they give the boy a shot of the disease itself, impressed into the quiet of his soul in increasing dosages to build an immunity against the larger trials adulthood is sure to bring. He is made a man by tasting fear and coming through it. He thus learns his true size, his need for his fellows, the limits of his universe. For the time being his ordeal becomes his personal sanctuary; later it will be an invisible trophy secure in the memory of its winning, a core of self worth that will define him as a man, fill the quiet of his days, grow character. In times of need he will draw on it in full knowledge, "I have looked the devil square in the face and did not flinch."

We can appreciate the agony of leaving home, the sting of discipline, perhaps the shock of coming face to face with a spirit (it's somewhat like meeting a wild animal in close quarters) but the jungle at night—on a black night, in the deep of its belly, with its cries and whispers, its dripping branches and snapped twigs resonating like gunshots in a sea of breathing silence—thirty centuries of civilization have fought to banish. There is no frame of reference. Nothing moves. The inward eye senses an invisible hand pouring pure stillness, like ether, from a black vial into an ocean of darkness; warm, tactile, it hisses like a snake, touches your skin; the air moans, something runs down your spine, your imagination whispers things you've never heard. The unknown draws close as though to speak. A shrinking heart weaves itself a useable fiction; a belief in spirits becomes irrefutable arithmetic. The rational mind fights to see but is drowned in fear; its animal twin awakens. This one senses something bestial and reacts in kind. A man is reduced to bare animality. He has only his inner reservoir, the company of peers, a shaken song.

The severest test comes the night they go "hunting." The phrase is for the uninitiated. With uncanny speed, as if by magic, they find themselves in a strange blind outside the grove, abandoned. Not even a fire stick. At last it registers; they must find their way back—a task daunting enough in daylight but under the regency of Night a veritable journey into the supernatural—and by now they know if they fail, the lesson will be repeated until it's mastered. But then something happens. One of Night's oldest laws takes effect. In a real crisis—natural leaders emerge. After the initial shock wears off, the sharper boys hush the whimpering of their smaller mates and direct them to hang on to someone and not let go, a command easily obeyed. It's time to begin. Reason must go to work in an abyss of fear. They listen. A strict word muffles loud breathing. Silence is a friend; sound and smell, allies. A weak rustling directs them to nearby branches. They break off probe sticks and strain to hear beyond the undertone of birds and insects—a dog, an echo, anything. Perhaps the direction of the air can tell them something. Is that trickling water—or a slumbering demon? Where did it trickle like that before? What is the incline of the terrain? Was the grove uphill or down? Did anyone smell smoke? Yes! The scent of the hearth will take them home. Now they move as one, a centipede painfully picking its way through the undergrowth, leaders to the fore, the little ones hanging on with fingers of steel. The terrible voice of Night must be analyzed for meaning. Was that a swallow? Like those that flock to the breadfruit tree in the grove! Listen for that one species among hundreds. Eventually they stumble on a familiar landmark—a water hole, a dominant tree, a human footpath—and its recognition comes in a squeal of delight. They read the path with their bare feet. Sand or mud? Use or disuse? Does it widen or narrow? Now they move with confidence. It widens! Now to hurry home.

Next morning "it" appears in all its majesty; the world seems to abate in awe. They line up in their places scratched and bleeding. "What is this?" it asks, "What has befallen my children?" One of the attendants answers casually, "Gone hunting." Another continues feigning a busybody, "In the bush! At night! Don't know to avoid thorns." Now the spirit intercedes in its native tongue, Dance. Not the wild throb of male passion, but a quiet ballet of undulating rhythms, oblivious to the surroundings, pensive, feminine. Something has changed. Even the slower minded boys sense it. Something subtle. Its demeanor, its movement—no longer dominant, overbearing. But what? Perhaps the slightest tilt of the head, the graceful sweep of the raffia skirt like a kiss on the bare earth. It seems to weep for their hurt, produces a medicinal leaf, applies it to a scratch on one of the weaker boys, examines the others, all in dance, finally settling on the ground in the posture of a trance. A long interlude is drawn out by the buzzing of insects. Then a recovery, and a deep baritone they haven't heard before, but with a new tinge of comradeship, demands, "Where be these hunters?" One of the elders answers simply, "Here. Hungry." Nothing more. The play is ended. Now the experience must be preserved for the rest of their lives. We would take a photograph. They introduce a ritual. "You Hunters!" the spirit cries, "Have you brought me meat?" They recognize the completion of a test and cry out in unison. A sacrificial animal is killed and thus an offering made to the Spirit of the Forest that saw fit to underwrite this transforming mystery.

They carry the memory of that night into old age although they may never speak of it, too much talk is unmanly. They all know who led them home, who wet himself, whose hand held theirs. In their adult lives they gravitate to their proven leaders just as they did that night; these are the men whose words carry greater weight in council though they may not be as eloquent. (Beware of grand oratory in tribal affairs; it's often subterfuge to disguise the real power structure.) Tribal people often keep up a hard exterior but they're quite cordial in the privacy of their friendships. They're capable of great warmth. Sometimes a haggard old man all but broken by a life of trial will betray the tenderest feelings in a few unguarded words when informed of the death of an age-mate. "Ah, yes. He held my hand once, long ago when we were small hunters," a phrase at once lost on outsiders, seemingly a bit odd.

The day the session ends they leap through the compound wall in a ceremony called "breaking the fence." They race back to the village where they dart among the houses brandishing spears, yelling, frightening curious girls back into their houses. They've come home triumphant, ecstatic. Who are these fierce strangers? Even their mothers pretend not to know them. But it doesn't last. Soon the play subsides and they are formally introduced by their new names. Then there is welcome, public and private. Then dancing, feasting, revelry, a carnival atmosphere, maybe a girl for the first time. But dancing everywhere. To the tribal mind dance is prayer. No important event can begin or end without it.

But in the tropics things fall apart rather quickly, sacred groves included. Green creepers grow out of thatch fences, mud walls succumb to fresh moss, and white tourists pay five cents to photograph the dancing "devil" as the missionaries have named it. Nowadays the *Poro* sessions are shortened to coincide with the school year. Children learn to read and figure and drift from the village. They study books that tell them their traditions are backward. Their rites and sacred relics fly to distant universities to be numbered like test animals, and runaways from the old discipline turn up on foreign missions where they become devout Christians in long pants quick to accept foreign rule and denounce the ways of their fathers.

Jump the Atlantic, take a long look at our own youth in the sixties, exchange long pants for long hair and play the drums again. We brave the future only to meet the past.

CHAPTER 2

THE SALT AIR OF NEW ENGLAND

Ten-thirty. Another night shot. The main reading room of the library felt like a mausoleum. The high ceiling echoed shuffling chairs, showy chandeliers hovered over the oak tables, a round clock with black Roman numerals graced the far wall—but someone got to it. McCarthy 68. Bumper stickers everywhere—notebooks, water coolers, hockey sticks; then came rallies, teach-ins, ad hoc committees; but it all seemed so...loud. I was bored with my classes, my students, the prim coeds laboriously crossing their fat legs as if they weren't aware how much you could see.

The war had been troubling me. Though capable of mistakes, I'd always believed America meant to do right. Now...something didn't wash. And the answer? Overindulged brats chanting obscenities. The antiwar movement turned me off; yet I felt myself drawn to it. I felt ill at ease at a protest, but no more than at the National Anthem.

I'd come home to a foreign country. Africa wouldn't let me go. I expected to pick up where I left off but couldn't. Couldn't concentrate. Things had gone sour, commitment became indifference, success a sham, what had been heroic now wore the sleaze of a movie magazine. The gimmicks, the gadgets, the fads, seemed to merge into a nauseating mix of enforced mediocrity.

Old friends had become strangers, even Jenny. Sweet Jenny—first-time Jenny, back home for a visit with her new husband, an accountant with a bright future—asked me if I was on drugs. Was I that far out of it? And my peers? Their glib parties, facile conversation—Marx, Heidegger, a pouch of grass, all smashed together under the hammer of loud rock. Too loud. Bach was all I could listen to anymore. Slow Bach. Was I doing drugs? The old back road by the lake Jenny. No one comes here now. Headlights down. Here's where we turn off. You know the way Jenny. It's dark, overgrown, privet and ivy. We used to pick wild raspberries over there. No one will know

Jenny. Under the dark sycamore Jenny. Only the owls and the swallows. The sound of the water like kisses. And the lights along the shoreline like a necklace that comes off in your fingers. Lithe Jenny. Easy to talk to Jenny. Sweet Jenny.

There was no one to talk to anymore. College kids with the intellectual equipment for calculus but the maturity of twelve-year-olds, they got on my nerves. Little things got on my nerves, like the constant complaining in the cafeteria. The sight of bus boys scraping the remains of untouched dinners into garbage bags triggered memories of shanty town families huddled under flaps of stray roofing hardly sheltering the watery soup bubbling in a rusty can. I had trouble talking about it. I could feel them looking at me...

Another twenty minutes. What made me keep looking at the clock? It was the only thing not making noise. After the quiet of the jungle, the smallest sound grated on my nerves. The blare of car horns struck me the minute I got off the plane. Lawn mowers and radios were hellish; humming ventilators or buzzing florescent lights, static over a symphony that wouldn't play. I missed the jungle—the birds, they practically lost their balance in the act but never failed to bring the wet morning under their spell, the shattering tones piercing the quiet air, reaching crescendo like the opening of a petal, then rising to a note of jubilant victory, oo-oo-ah-ah-ah-ah-AH-AH! Night vanquished. Now the days came with police sirens and screams of jet aircraft; morning with the clang of an alarm clock.

A deep longing to get away. It came like a night thing, a haunting reminder that somewhere people were dancing—the right place, the right music, the right girl, something the airline posters hinted but never captured, a day that would make all the difference. And I was missing it. Oh to get in a car and start driving. But where? How empty the small towns would be, how mournful the echo of their loneliness.

Chris Crieghton sent a postcard from Tenerife. He says it's good there. He has a villa a short walk from a fishing village. You can sit on the veranda and watch the boats come in at night. Miles of beach and fair weather. I'd have to get to the Bahamas first, then a tramp steamer to Las Palmas, a mail boat to the island.

My life was one of quiet desperation. It mocked me in my morning mirror. I slapped on aftershave, tied a neat tie, buttoned my jacket, but felt like a fraud. A perfect disguise. So I left for work and forgot the fraud in the mirror except when I caught myself telling the necessary lies—not the big black lies, I thought I could live with those—the little white ones that get one on in the world. "How are you today?" says the pretty receptionist, "Fine, how are you?" Wouldn't it be better to say, "I'm not fine at all, I'm miserable. If you insist on cheerful dishonesty, perhaps you shouldn't ask?" But it's easier to lip sync the social banalities and get on with the show. Truth takes time. And our world has none to spare.

But the thought of giving in to a life of middle class complacency, beating the traffic to a cubical cell just in time to politely slit his throat an equally harried competitor—I wanted out. I felt like a caged animal being primed to jump into the pit to the delight of rich matrons squealing in the galleries—but when I looked it was only a nest of sorority sisters giggling at the next table, something about a wiener, "winner" mispronounced, meaning anyone not up to frat house standards—probably me.

Ten after. The library closed at eleven-thirty. Back at the office the conversation would be as dull as the March weather and down at *Howard's* they'd be hashing over the latest atrocity in the news, then another debate over the war.

I leafed through some notes. The travelogue was the only thing I could read without distraction. Pure escape. But what wasn't? The actor in the mirror? The house in the suburbs and the soap opera that comes with it? My thesis had something to do with Faulkner—a fall from grace—the whole damn thing no more than a coloring book exercise; the result, I was beginning to hate Faulkner. I could fake it easy enough. My office mates kidded me for taking it too seriously; this, after all, was no more than a gentlemen's debating society.

I had to be in Forrester's office first thing in the morning with "something tangible;" the meeting had been postponed twice. All I had were a few garbled paragraphs and my inadequate bibliography.

"Inadequate," his only comment as his eyes dropped down the page. "What else have you been reading?"

"Bathroom walls."

"Well," he answered sweetly, "glad to hear you're acquiring some tastes."

"No doubt the result of graduate study."

Our meetings weren't much fun. The nameplate on his desk announced his turf, Everett R. Forrester II, pronounced Foster, Mister Foster, which meant Doctor. The informality was facade. He tolerated small freedoms, smoking or a joke, now and then a street expression to let you know he was up to date; he even conceded an argument, but never budged on anything that mattered and I came away like a school boy after detention. He fancied himself open-minded, corrected people politely, pronounced the hardest names, even mine, kept low key under fire, in no circumstance hurrying the measured New England accent he acquired back in his student days at Harvard. Curious how Midwesterners picked up the accent so quickly. Perhaps the salt air effects the vocal chords in some way peculiar to that latitude. But no matter, he never lost his composure, got ruffled; he was never beaten; at most he might remove his caramel-colored glasses at the salient point but without the slightest disturbance to his gray sideburns. He understood ideas and books but not people. Whatever they were, his feelings never surfaced through his tailor-cut style, but you knew they were as impeccable as his diction, as consummate as his tastes. He was so damn correct. If he were damned to hell, he'd book a reservation. Had he slurred a phrase, just once, I could've embraced him. But no, he knew exactly where he was, what to say; he paused for the right word like a matador, precise, urbane, not a glance too strong, a smile too weak. Underneath it all I suppose he meant well. I'd chosen him because he was one of the heavyweights on campus. But my respect dwindled as I began to see a refined tyrant and our conversations turned to polite contempt. Two drunks in a seedy bar would have had the decency to grab the nearest furniture and get it over with.

"Is this all you have?" he asked calmly.

"Yes."

"What about your introduction?" He tapped the pages in place. "Have you begun rewriting it?"

"What else should I be doing?"

"I suppose," he leaned back in his swivel chair, "there's nothing like thinking things through…even if it takes a semester to write a prospectus. When, may I ask, is the great unveiling to be?"

"As soon as you're ready to read something pertinent."

He smiled—graciously of course, "Oh for the good old days when you could ask a student a direct question and get a direct answer. Coffee?"

"No."

"A teaching fellow no less," he mused aloud. "How's your class coming?"

"A few good kids. Most of them have no business in college."

"Which is not your concern," he said curtly. "Apply yourself to the job we've assigned—speaking of which, I've been made to understand you were discussing, again last week, ritual and magic in a unit dealing primarily with American Realism. How that is possible I will not hazard to ask; I'm sure there's a simple cosmic explanation and I've been pushing my luck in that area with respect to your research plans. The task at hand…" he sipped his coffee and sat for a moment looking hard at his desk. Whatever he was thinking, it didn't show. He began in his usual pat-on-the-head tone, "Perhaps if you'd come in out of left field, limit the scope of your research to a more manageable problem. Stick to specifics. That's with respect to your subject matter; as for yourself, you might try…discipline, something hardly to go unlauded in your case and I quote the opinion of other faculty as well as myself. Sooner or later you're going to be one of us. There's no reason you shouldn't have this thing wrapped up in a few months. What then, in one sentence, do you see as the essential problem?"

"You won't let me do what I want."

He sighed. An audible sigh! "I fear I'm going to regret asking, but what…might that be?"

"The tribal folk myth I told you about."

"Oh God not again," he actually ran his fingers through his hair. "I haven't finished my morning coffee." He sipped politely, cuff link upward. My ungodly proposal, a mere ripple in his universe. "Very well." He leaned forward. "Believe me I enjoy having my students come to me with active interests, new approaches—but this—leaving aside the anthropology, in which neither of us is qualified; the absence of a written record, your own admission; the *painful* realization the African continent is somewhat outside the mainstream of American Letters, a simple case of geography; that aside, don't you think dimensions of classic stature in tribal folk tales is stretching things…just a bit?"

"Perhaps dimensions of classic stature in the Classics is stretching things…just a bit."

"Where then, in all the published literature are you going to find support let alone precedent for such a perspective?"

"Nowhere. That's why it's significant."

He pushed himself back from his desk, locked his hands on the back of his head, fixed his eyes on the wall behind me. I could hear it coming. It would begin, "Consider this," or "By definition."

"Right," his eyes remained on the wall, "the minute a scholar begins his work, whether student or established authority, he is subject to arbitrary but necessary limitations, the language itself implies them. To ignore this—" he continued in his precise monotone that made attention impossible. My eyes began drifting around the room. On his desk a framed picture of his wife and two sons, next to a spiral calendar filled with notations. Stone gargoyle bookends held a neat row of reference books, a pipe stand, a stack of periodicals, two foreign newspapers, *Barron's,* a telephone, some mail. Next to his desk a typewriter table with a stack of themes on one leaf, a monogrammed briefcase underneath. On the wall an original nineteenth century etching caught the amber lamp light between the draped window and a luxurious hanging plant. A framed print, *The Fall of Icarus,* complemented it, and in the window against the sash, how careless, a postcard from Maine. On the other wall, a map of Ireland, a photo of an English Manor, a coat of arms, a specimen of Medieval script, probably original, two tiny figures suggesting Giacometti, a photo of T.S. Eliot. An early American rocking chair with a hand made cushion completed the room; his grandmother brought it by covered wagon from Connecticut. An sharp gray topcoat lay neatly folded over the back. Directly behind him, bookshelves, floor to ceiling. Most were old, maroon or brown with gold lettering, a few paperbacks. On the last row, a leather-bound copy of *Walden* waited among the others.

"Well then," he was saying from far away, "if you choose to call a horse a cow, it's your prerogative but you're not going to communicate with anyone. And that's what this business is all about."

"I'm not interested in your semantic parlor games."

"Are you interested in communicating with anyone?" he asked delicately. "Anyone at all? Or one of these fine days am I to find you too decked out in beads and sandals screaming obscenities at me?"

What an opening!

"You don't think I'd do that?" I smiled. "Barricade you in your office. At gun point! Maybe you don't know me as well as you think."

"You'd have to grow your hair much longer," he said pleasantly. "Do you think you could manage the effort?"

"...They're right about the war."

"What?"

"I said...they're right about the war."

"Who?" he was making a notation.

"Our long-haired friends. The uncouth and the unwashed. Their behavior's atrocious. They could use a little toilet training; you should give a seminar."

"Why does every conversation these days invariably end in Vietnam?"

"Because Vietnam—"

"Spare me...your folk remedies for that situation."

"Ah. Forgive me. You haven't had your morning coffee. One shouldn't commence a war before finishing one's coffee."

"Look!" A retort! "It's a dirty world out there. I should think you'd have noticed in your many travels. Fourteen countries? I never saw the Continent until I was thirty."

"I beg your pardon but I'm having difficulty reconciling my reading of the Constitution with what we're doing in Southeast Asia."

"Source?" He interrupted in high pitched boredom, his way of shutting off rambling excursions.

"Bernard Fall, *Two Vietnams;* Halberstam, *The Making of a Quagmire;* Buttinger, *The Smaller Dragon: A Political—*"

"Excuse me?...You're reading *that,* in conjunction with American Studies?"

"Some other things too."

"You're not in the ball park."

"...No we're not. That's the point."

"The point is you can't get all the dirt out in one wash. We pick our spot and fight our own battles. Yours is here. You chose to continue your studies; that says something about you, and along with that choice, if I understand my existentialism, come responsibilities. If one chooses to live outside—"

"Him DIE Keemosabee!"

"That's it," he abruptly pushed his chair back, but quickly broke into a boyish grin. "I know when I'm licked." He placed his hands on the back of his head and stared at the ceiling. "Had I consulted my horoscope this morning, I should have known rational discourse with you is not in the stars. Be that as it may. Let me only remind you," he paused meaningfully, "in my pedestrian capacity—this institution, and others like it, maintains," it was going to be something weighty, "and will continue to maintain," what a beautiful spring day, "what for lack of a less prosaic term let us call," blue sky, dogwood blossoms, "standards of academic performance, perhaps a bit murky out here in the provinces but definitive on a clear day from the third floor of the Humanities Building. In your future labors therefore...may I suggest—"

Sea gulls! Streams of them. Gliding in swift grace, skimming the horizon then rising to hang on the air, fluttering down in wild disorder, clamoring, twisting—and a curtsy—settling on the water, miniature sailing ships amid the squeaking wings of others lifting off. Their cries pierced the gray morning like pagan screams in a Gothic vault. The surf groaned. Its rumbling bass boomed a steady undertone, the madcap chase of white waves tumbled home crashing into blankets of sizzling foam that chased the sandpipers up the beach, and when they rushed back, a wet mirage blushed in the sand. From a fishing pier south to a rocky spit the other way, a lazy pulse bent the shore into a smooth crescent that rose into heaps of littered sand anchoring a line of drowsy palms. When they struck at an angle, the spiral of the breaking waves followed the curvature and carried along a muffled roar that faded out downwind. First the thunder, then the drum roll. Then a lullaby. And in the distance, the sea. And a faint smile behind a blue veil.

CHAPTER 3

SOPHIE'S SMILE

The sunrise hadn't been spectacular. Its colors quickly faded, jet trails crisscrossed it like daggers. Up toward the spit behind the highway, the angular shapes of two stucco houses began to catch the first rays of light and with the help of a "no trespass" sign reclaimed possession of the beach. Soon there were people, diminutive, far enough away to be in a dream. A woman under a wide hat lounged in a low chair, a child played at her side while a man with a big stomach stood off to the side gazing out to sea. Two boys with fishing lines came the other way. A mongrel dog raced ahead biting at the waves in a fit of unleashed freedom; on catching my scent he tested the air then returned to a two-fingered whistle. He chased past them doubling back in a wide circle, his ears back, hair streaming.

Well beyond, a lone man with a gunny sack seemed to be looking for something in the surf; barefoot with an old hat and trousers wet to the knees, he bent down to pick up what must have been a treasure. He studied it, turned his back to the world and concentrated on his work; several pieces of driftwood stuck out of his sack like human arms.

I rolled up my sleeping bag and stretched out. It was late when I woke a second time, the sun up, the day blue. People everywhere. Swimming, sunbathing, sprawled out under portable umbrellas, kids running up and down, a radio, pleasure boats on the water. I took a walk to the end of the spit. The waves leaped and splashed. I felt the lure of the sea, but weakly; it wasn't my calling but echoed something that was. After awhile I dove in and made for the pier.

Didn't quite make it, climbed back on the beach a little wobbly—wasn't in shape anymore—dropped on my knapsack, then rolled over and closed my eyes. A warm bubble broke in my ear and the world came back. Not far away, three girls reclined on a blanket strewn with clothes, bags, popcorn, a book. The tallest was very friendly, asked if I'd keep an eye on their belongings while they took a dip. They walked down to the water, tried it—the short chubby one pulling up the front of her one-piece suit—shivered, then ducked their heads and swam a short way out. When they came back they frolicked in the surf, compared their suntans and tried to look at ease, like their companion, a peroxide blond with a natural tan who looked like she was born in a bikini. This one stood knee-deep in the water, arms akimbo, looking off into the distance, much at home but bored with it all.

After a bit they came back, stooped daintily, took up their towels and began drying their hair, then sat and began forcing combs through it. The blond picked up a paperback. The friendly one checked her mirror, parted her hair letting it fold around her face and over her shoulders. Then she put on her sunglasses and relaxed but quickly remembered something, took up a tube of lotion and began applying it to her shoulders, the strap of her top dangling over one arm, then her back, with her friend's help, elbows, calves, ankles. Smooth. Round sunglasses gave her a flair of style but when she took them off, a tinge of anguish darkened her face as though girlish innocence had discovered a snag in womanhood. A bit later she dug out a floppy straw hat with a light blue band. It looked like something from Grandma's attic but when she put it on—presto, tattered elegance. Wisps of dry hair began to flutter on her neck. Beautiful girl. Pure Hicksville. But with quiet assurance if Hicksville put its best foot forward, New York's eyes would turn.

"Thank you," she said suddenly, remembering the favor.

"Sure."

"You looked exhausted when you came out of the water. I was afraid you weren't going to make it."

"So was I."

"Then why do you go out so far?" the chubby one scolded.

"I don't know."

"Do you live here?" the friendly one asked.

"Yeah."

"In town?"

"No."

"Then you must live along the highway. We saw some really beautiful homes—"

"Did you see that beige split-level just before the marina?" her friend chimed in. "I just drooled."

"I don't know, I kind of liked the little bungalow," the friendly one answered drawing her ankles underneath. "The cute one with the little old man trimming his lawn with a sickle—"

"It looked like he was cutting the shoestrings off his sneakers," the other broke into a giggle.

"Shhh, he might live there."

"Afraid not."

"Then where do you live?"

"Here."

"On the beach?"

"Yeah."

"And do you find it accommodating?"

"Depends on who you room with."

They were from Indiana, a small town nobody ever heard of, down for a couple weeks in the sun. Me? A small town nobody wanted to hear of. The winter got to be a bore up north. It was lucky they knew Jean, the blond, an old schoolmate whose aunt enjoyed house guests. There were lots of groovy places to go nights, but the days were kind of boring especially if you didn't know anyone with a boat. Jean knew a guy with a yacht, but not really well, just a friend, besides he was in Nassau, with the yacht, so that shot that one. At least they'd go back home with nice sun tans. Sometimes you could meet some groovy guys on the beach but you had to be careful. Was I going to school? Karen had gone to college one year. The friendly one helped her father run his lumber business but hoped to have a dress shop someday, nothing *tres chic*, plain styles, things that bring out your real personality, you know, the kind of thing a working girl would wear when her best beau comes home on leave. So what did I do, she asked quite casually as though we were longtime friends. Her name was Sophie.

"Nothing."

"Don't you even have a job?" Karen asked sourly, then sighed, "It must be nice."

"You must do something," Sophie pleaded. "Didn't you have a job once, or go to school or something?"

"I was a imperialist once."

"What's that?"

"It's a little bit like a gun runner only without the guns."

"And of course a gun runner can't engage in anything as degrading as work."

"We got a strong union."

"I don't believe you, you know," Sophie said seriously, "but I envy you. You sound as free as a bird. If I were you I'd just fly away into the wild blue, anytime, anywhere, don't mind me world, here I come," and she enjoyed the thought. Then checking her mirror, "I heard this place used to swarm with college kids this time of year."

"Fort Lauderdale," Jean said without looking up.

"That would be too crowded for me." Sophie continued, "It's bad enough here, everyplace you go—No Trespassing. 'Hi there. Just lookin,'" and she waved at an imaginary land owner. "Do you mind if I ask you a personal question?" she asked abruptly, reclining on her side and catching her hat at the same time. Karen held her breath.

"Shoot."

"Well." She paused, lowering her voice. "You don't have to answer. I mean if it's…well…too personal."

"Am I a transvestite? No."

Karen let go.

"Something worse? A Republican?"

"Shush!" Sophie cried, making to throw something. "This is difficult enough and you're not making it any easier," she composed herself and began, "Your hair. How do you…well…do you set it. Or anything?"

"No."

"I mean…how do you…get it to stay?"

"I dunno. Never thought about it."

"Wouldn't ya know!" Karen turned away in disgust. "You'd think if guys are gonna wear their hair long, they'd have to go through what we do. It's not fair!"

"I kind of like long hair on a guy," Sophie said. "On the right guy, of course. I think it makes them look more…individual, I really do. Yours goes well with your neckpiece. What is it? A magical charm or something?"

"A leopard's tooth."

"It's not very big," Karen said.

"Small leopard. Big ones don't let ya pull their teeth."

"Where d'ya get it."

"In darkest Africa."

"Liar."

"Come on, where did you get it?" Sophie smiled.

"Off a dead body."

"Where did you get it!" Karen shrieked.

"A pawn shop. New York."

"That's better," Sophie said. "You're really a terrible liar you know."

"For every lie," Karen warned pointing a strict finger, "that's one more worm in your coffin when you die."

Jean sat up. After flicking some sand off her legs, she gazed into the distance looking altogether bored, checked her shoulders, marked her place in *Valley of the Dolls* with a comb and jammed it in her purse. She hadn't taken the slightest interest in our conversation.

"Any good?" Sophie asked.

"Kind o' wild," she answered forcing a smile. Then as if she felt she ought to say something, she turned and asked, "Have you read it?"

"Kicked the habit."

"Drugs?" Karen asked practically in a whisper.

"No. Reading."

"I didn't know reading was a bad habit," Sophie smiled.

"The worst. If a man readeth unto gluttony he groweth well-rounded, but full of shit."

"And where did you read *that?*"

"Confucius."

"Liar!" Karen snapped.

"A liberal translation."

"Liar!"

"Actually it was carved on the front of the library—"

"That's one more worm!"

"Do you know what I think?" Sophie said softly. "I think, sir...you are the biggest B-S'er I have ever heard, and I've heard some pretty good ones at my father's lumber yard." And she drew down her sunglasses with the strict look of a schoolmarm.

"I'll bet everything he said's a lie," Karen said in a wide-eyed whisper. "He's probably some rich brat, so spoiled his folks can't stand to have him around the house so they packed him—"

"No!" Sophie cried. "An eccentric millionaire! He owns this whole beach and everything on it, and he's bored to death because money can't buy happiness."

"What tipped ya off?"

"And he's got a mansion with a swimming pool," she continued, "an butler, umpteen French poodles, a sports car, but," in a teasing whimper, "nobody to tuck him in for beddy bye." She smiled, pleased with herself, then thought of the clincher, "And!...a yacht! Ta daaaa!"

"Right. It's parked around the corner."

"You don't park a yacht," Karen scowled, "You dock it!"

"That's the butler's job."

"Why can't we meet some normal guys?" Karen pounded the blanket with her fists. "Just once."

"And what is the name of your yacht?" Sophie beamed. "And it better be a good one."

"The *Everett R. Forrester.*"

"And just who was he?"

"A pirate! The Spanish Main! A real swashbuckler! Patch on his eye, knife in his teeth—"

"That's not even a Spanish NAME!" Karen shrieked.

"He changed it! Evartto del Guano. Try sayin' that with a Boston accent."

"You're awful!" Sophie cried. "You're *really* a terrible liar!" She tossed a towel, missing. Composing herself she reached for some popcorn with feigned elegance but spilt the whole bag. "There," she frowned. "See what you made me do." After brushing it off the blanket, she leaned back, dropped her sunglasses to the end of her nose and changed her tone to a governess when it's time to go home. "Come on now. I'm tired of this game. Tell us who you are and where you're from, why you're making up these tales. I want the truth." She had an easy sincerity about her, a disarming trust in strangers, a warmth that shattered every pretense—and I was tired of the game too. So I told them. Everything. The small town nobody ever heard of, Grandma's farm, her scratchy burlap apron, her stories from the old country, the chickens and the ducks and the collie under the porch, the schoolhouse with creaky floors, college, the village in the bush, the tribal boy who gave me the neckpiece, back home to grad school, even how to pronounce my name. Karen wasn't ready to believe any of it, Jean didn't give a damn, but Sophie mulled it over with real concern, then looking out to sea but without a trace of displeasure, she smiled, "It's too bad you dropped out."

The wind gusted and wrapped her hair around her face. For a split second she looked disheveled, gave me a quick unguarded glance, and I felt like a schoolboy who'd failed his favorite teacher.

"What will you do when you get to Tenerife?"

"I have no idea."

"You gotta have a plan guy," she smiled sadly. "That's what life's all about. If you got a plan, you got something to work on, and if you want it bad enough, if you really want it, there's got to be a way."

"Right," Karen asserted with a nod. "No matter what, just so you want it bad enough."

"So there," Sophie concluded with a soft smile, "now aren't you glad we came along to set you straight?"

"Yes. Thank you."

It seemed they got serious all of a sudden, more than they needed to, but as the afternoon wore on we shared a sandwich, talked some more, no lies this time, plain things, places we'd been, movies, music: Sophie and Karen both liked the Beatles, Judy Collins, I liked Dylan—they said it figured. By and by the shadows began to fall and people got ready to leave. Maybe they'd see me later at the *Beachcomber,* on the main drag. I doubted it. There'd be a band. I still doubted it. After folding their blanket, which took some doing with the blowing sand, they gathered up their things, said it was nice meeting me, turned and walked up the beach to Jean's car, lazily, as though to prolong the last day of summer. When they were out of earshot, Sophie looked back and smiled. With one arm holding down her straw hat in an unwieldy bout with the wind—on anyone else it would have been a disaster, on her, the key to an unflappable grace—the other reached towards heaven, twisted at the wrist and waved a delicate good-bye. She had to be in love. She withdrew into the quiet pleasure of being herself and I felt a warm chill, like that first kiss in the darkened hallway while the grownups were getting their coats. Her smile was somethin' else, surely one of the tender mercies we somehow shouldn't deserve, soft, selfless, it beamed in the radiance of a shared secret, fed on the warmth it kindled, made music; it drew the best out of you, reminded you of home, who you were, the people you knew; it was a quiet wish for the happiness of whatever it touched. It turned out she was married. Her husband was in Da Nang. Beautiful girl.

CHAPTER 4

A CANCELED FLIGHT

After they left the emptiness came back. It always came back, like rubbish with the tide. It moaned in the surf counting out the hours no less oppressively than the clock in the library. The days passed but tomorrow never came. Only the sameness, like a hangover, only I didn't smoke, except that once in Africa. Yet everyone treated me as if I did. The stereotype whispered what they wanted. If I said I wasn't affluent enough to support a habit, they smiled "nice try." The real hangover had nothing to do with drugs; it was a thing of the heart, a feeling of utter desolation in full view of a world throbbing with excitement, a gnawing hunger as we sat down to the bountiful banquet called America.

We've had it too easy. Our whole damn generation. So we enshrine a collection of drug addicts and wonder why we can't get no satisfaction. We have everything but our manhood. We have not gone into the jungle at night—and come out men.

Almost a year now. The beach had become a bore, as routine as going to the office and no less intolerable. The fraud in the mirror had become a fraud in dirty jeans. And tomorrow? I'll watch the passing ships, or buy a paper and read of misfortunes greater than mine, visit the local bar where the marlin on the wall will be the only one smiling while the men talk boats and a barmaid's creamy face reflects the rapture of soap opera. Without missing a beat she'll slide off her stool and ask what I'll have. If I say beer, she'll ask what kind and stand there as if it's a momentous decision. Freedom's become the choice of a brand of beer. Tenerife! Tomorrow.

Something quaked in the stillness! Spooked the tethered demons pulling at their moorings, woke the mother beast shrieking for her babies, all the deadly babies keening for their souls, squeaking in the ground, each footstep makes a creak. There's a shadow in the mist! The bogeyman comes for bad boys, puts them in a sack and takes them far away. A scratchy burlap sack. Something foul inside. There! Embedded in the sand, bubbling beneath the backwash, a face, a savage face worn smooth, eyes picked clean, but lips that move, lips that want to whisper something dear.

"May I have your attention please. All flights to Seoul, Anchorage, and Los Angeleeze have been canceled due to inclement conditioning. All passengers, please report to baggage claims for personal customs. Thank you for flying UnAmerican."

An airplane. And a stewardess in a blue Sophie. Don't cry Sophie Only the owls and the swallows Sophie The dark sycamore by the lake and the water kissing the shore water rushing from the sand washing the face in the sand the face from far away its lips are whispering Pilot error. A funny light in the cockpit Don't open Sophie Don't look now Sophie You got to have a plan You got to have a plan NOW Sophie! Creak. Creak. An old brick schoolhouse with polished floors go creak! When you step they go creak in front of the principal's office you can't get past without him looking up his glasses fall down on the end of his nose he never smiles his face can't smile his lips can't squeak but his floor goes squeak no matter how soft you step there's a doorway a sunny playground all around and kids can run and yell but first the old men on the wall A lie Abe Lincoln cannot tell their faces all embedded in the wall cheeks and noses painted blue they come to catch a bad boy or a gnat catch him in a burlap sack their lips are whispering something dear *I am George from Valley Forge, be brave my dear.*

Fire in the cockpit!
Find...the right...wire.
Many whyers.
Run my darling run!
Something coming.
Stay. Analyze the problem.
Something bad.
Faster! Faster!
Fast as you can!
Something dead.
Find the autopilot.
Something ticking like a clock.
Run to the field!
End of the street!
Hide in the thicket!

Under the peat!
I can't fix it!
Bypass negative circuits
I'm not an electrician!
Reroute eternal power.
"It's not my problem! I'm not an electrician!"

"Ey you! Wha' d' ya think you're doin'?" Two dark forms stood one behind the other, their faces lost in the glare of a flashlight.

"Please don't shine the light in my eyes."

"We got a city ordinance against sleepin' on the beach."

"I couldn't find a motel."

"There's two motels down the road."

"Great. I'll get one tomorrow."

"All right let's see some I.D."

"That light's hurting my—"

"I *said* let's see some I.D.!"

"It's in my—"

"Get this shit off the beach."

"It's just a knapsack."

"I'm talkin' 'bout YOU! PAL!"

The up and down bars looked like teeth. An old black man waited against the cell door with his wrists dangling over the cross piece. He stepped back when the deputy opened it.

It stank. The walls, the air. The john sat in a puddle, brown water, a roll of paper tossed in. No seat. The sink torn off the wall. Two bunks, the mattresses moldy.

The old man sat on the edge of his bunk with his elbows on his knees and his head in his hands. His slim fingers covered his forehead, his face hung down studying a collection of cigarette butts around his shoes. When he looked up, a deformed eyelid set in an emaciated face and the tired movement of his hands betrayed an utter sorrow. Civil Rights had passed him by, but when he spoke his voice came in a deep rolling resonance like the rumbling of waves.

"You frum up Nawth?"

"Yes."

"Dey don' dig tha' long haih shit down heah, boy. Gitch you in a lotta trouble. Wha' dey gotch ya fo'?"

"Sleepin' on the beach."

"You gotta hab mo' nat, man."

"They think I got dope and they're mad as hell because I don't. Now they're goin' through my stuff to see if I got military secrets, as if the dumb fuckers can read."

"Don' try t' fight 'em. Daz jis wha' dey wawnt. Nex' time gitch you down heah t' de traila pawk. Fo' three dolla he letch you sleep on de groun'. As long as you payin' rent, dey can' touch ya." He paused toeing another cigarette into the floor. "Naw. You thenk you go' trouble. You go' nothin' boy." He drew out the word "boy" until it sounded more of sorrow than contempt. A scar ran from under his ear down his neck, his lip twisted, smoker's cough racked his lungs. His troubles weren't to share. He put his face in his hands and went back to staring at the floor.

Another bad dream. My dreams were getting scary. I could remember the sound of something slinking away. A dead face in the sand, whispering, but couldn't make it out. Then an airplane. But it wasn't moving, rather hanging in suspension, and people outside the windows with their faces pressed to glass and their lips moving. And a beautiful stewardess. She looked frightened, held her hand over her mouth trying not to cry. A sickly yellow light in the cockpit. I looked inside. The pilot slumped over, dead, blood dripping from the radar console. A radio transmission. A canceled flight. Then everything went haywire, a knot of entangled wiring fell from the instrument panel. I knew I'd never get it back together. I distinctly remember crying out, "I'm not an electrician!"

Then the pigs. Now this. One more day I'd have been in Tenerife? What to hell would I have done there? Live off Creighton? I rolled over. The stink was worse. "Fuck you," someone had written. "Eat it raw," a little higher up. "Flush the john twice…" the whole wall. "Rebs suck," a swastika in the middle of "Nixon," some in Spanish, the peace sign, "chicken tracks" underneath, practically a running conversation.

"The pig that bust me smoke to."

"Fuck the pigs!"

"Napalm—Johnson's baby powder."

"Fuck you hippie chicken shit!"

"Hippies blow dead niggers."

"Suck my dick honky motherfucker."

"Fuck you nigger!"

"Some hillbilly pissed the bed!"

"What's fat as a sack a shit and almost as smart?"

38

"A redneck!"

"A redneck pig is fatter."

"Wallace," blocked over "Redneck.

"Bama sucks."

"My lawer's a fuckin jew!"

"Faggot."

"Well, I'm a hillbilly and proud of it, Billy Grimes, Wells Hollow, West Virginia."

"Reality is an illusion created by a mescaline deficiency."

Then—in unusually fine penmanship, sharp Roman letters: "How much longer are we putting up with this shit? The Revolution is now! All power to the people!"

"Eat it, commy queer."

"Casserate the queers."

"KILL M ALL!! LET GOD SORT M OUT!"

And over it all following the full sweep of an arm in thick, blocked letters, "KILL HONKY KILL HONKY KILL HONKY!"

One square yard of rotten wall and enough venom for a lifetime. It was all here: Vietnam, Watts, Chicago, a hundred other places. Raw rage poisoning the vessels that carried it. And this merely the stink left behind, they took the "essence" with them.

"Az right boy, you read. You gitch you education in heah, aw right."

At least they tried to purge themselves, unlike some of us whose toilet training required repression. But was it any worse than the six-thirty news? The facile euphemisms of Pentagon press releases? The polite savagery of corporate warfare?

Poverty of the soul. Here in the richest country of all. A pot-bellied kid crying in a squalid alley. There we stand. But how effortlessly we pass it off as affluence! Flaunt our pearls, twirl our ermine, whisk our Cadillacs into mortgaged mansions filled with bored housewives and unruly brats. What a clever disease.

"Wha's a matta witch you, boy? You in heah now, cryin' 'bout it ain' gonna gitch you OUT."

I was wrong. I'd hated America for its arrogance, its greed, war, racism, but I'd mistaken the disease for the victim. These were only symptoms. I'd been kidding myself to think I was above it. The word "pig" had come from my lips as easily as "hippie" or "nigger" from these. The wall was a mirror. My own petty self-seeking looked back at me. Those vile screams were more than mere rage; they were rather the *loud* desperation of an age that lost its way. I'd forgotten the good things, the little things that make the world soft and rare and build up the soul from within, the tender mercies…like Sophie's smile.

"You cain't rub 'at out, boy."

He's right. You can't rub it out. You've got to rise above it. "Got a pencil, man?"

We're better than this…I'm better than this.

"You gotch you som'un t' put on na wall, boy?" he shook his head with a faint sneer.

Where did we go wrong? The decade began with such promise. Where did I go wrong?

CHAPTER 5

DINNER AT *OSCAR'S*

"Welcomb. You look insi'. Cha'lie Numba Wawn, fine sto', largess in all Wes' Africh, many fine itams, make fine pri', you step insi', you see you try. Good evening, sah, welcomb—"

"You see someti' you li'? You co' you try, Cha'lie Numba Twel', I ha' many fine ca'ving, wood, ebony, i-varee, all impawted, zhewelry, all numba wawn con-dishon, Guinea, Abidjan, Tome—"

"You loo' someti' fo' de womah my frie', fine necklass, goool', hond crawfted, so fine, black lady like plenny, *white lady like toooo*—"

"You ma', you wan' fine watsh, sevenny fi' dollah wha' say, esponshon bond, impawted fro' Swizzalon', fifty dollah, you ma' price, fauty, keep fine time, you try you like, thurty, you may be late, tha' wou' be unfawchannat, twenny fi' dollah *Parlez Francais peut-etre?*"

He followed half a block then switched to a man coming the other way. I turned down Randall Steet past two more Charlies—traders in tourist art spread out on a blanket, the number for flair—past an old cripple hunched down in a doorway, her frail arm outstretched for alms, then some closed shops, rogue bars on the windows, men arguing, two bars, the *Moby Dick* and the *Paradise Lounge,* several blocks of two-story houses capped with rusted roofs, siding to match, a junked car on the curb, a battered fence that fell into a vacant lot where barefoot kids played soccer with a stuffed rag tied in a ball. An older boy danced over it challenging all comers, but the nearest dropped off when he saw me, "Gi' me fi' cen' yah? You. Whi' ma'." Not much further the street disintegrated into puddles and broken pavement, a pile of refuse, then footpaths that wound their way to clusters of small shacks, hammered pieces of rusty zinc strung together with lines of laundry, leaning with the wind but never quite falling, all teeming with families, disease, misfortune. Potbellied kids stood listlessly in the dirt, pregnant with worms and hardly the strength to cry as they eyed their healthier mates running up and down alleys vying for discarded beer bottles.

There were always foreigners dumb enough to pay first price so it was easy to ignore the Charlies, not so the kids. If you reached for a nickel, you drew a crowd; there'd be fights, curses, they'd follow you home. If you emptied your pocket, others came running only to be denied and your imagination conjured hundreds more, each with a pressing claim on life. The realization that some were con artists only deepened the tragedy. In the end you had to ignore them. You had to ignore a lot. Look straight ahead. That was the trick and most people learned it, some faster than others.

No matter how pure his intentions an American quickly learned his place—above. His very presence whispered "I am better." The way he walked, checked his watch, the spare change that jingled in his pocket, his complete confidence in a foreign city, the smart loafers that clicked on the pavement as he strode in the broad sunshine with his jacket tossed carelessly over his shoulder, his smile, his offhand manner, the ease with which taxis and waiters found him—all whispered "I am better." Even those who knew and made an honest effort became victims; somehow "equal" became "better," and in the end the natives began to play their part—subservience. For them it was the easy route and more lucrative; rebels were more admirable but stayed poor. Sincerity became part of the baggage to be handled for a tip. Again you had to ignore it but ignoring it only whispered, "I am better." So you learned to live with it, took cabs, wore sunglasses, until you forgot you weren't home and they forgot they were.

And they saw. To impressionable young eyes that looked up from fingering the bottom of a discarded sardine can, the language may have been foreign but the whisper came clear. In some it took root like a dormant cancer. *He* was always right by virtue of who he was, *he* knew the answers, the correct words for the hunger that gnawed in your gut, *he* could afford compassion, calculated solutions. *He* could say, "cultural disparity", and sound brilliant; you could say, "gimmie fi' cen' yah", and sound like a thief. But the cancer bided its time; there would be a day it would speak, and he would listen. During a coup, for a brief flash within the rattle of gunfire, hunger fled, the dry tongue tasted revenge, the whisper stopped; but a day or two later before the dogs finished the last corpse, poverty, the true sovereign, returned to retake its turf. It was the underlying reality that both fed and buried revolutions, but journalists usually missed it for the sideshows—the coups, the clashes, the political alignments. "Tumbo hasn't had anything to eat today," didn't have the smash of a headline, yet it was the most prevalent story, the definitive if dim light behind the shadow play on the third world stage.

Yet—and it was a formidable "yet"—they laughed and danced and believed in life. To those of us who grew up pasting gold stars to grammar school calendars for having brushed our teeth, the initial blow of poverty—its smell, squalor, the embarrassing lack of hygiene, naked behinds and expelled worms—often overwhelmed the sight of anything else; yet life went on. It awoke, it harbored hope. Something subtle manifested itself not in words or things but in a rhythm, nothing audible, rather an underlying ethos that animated everything it touched. Though her colonial past had tainted her indigenous traditions, Africa remained Africa. Neon and asphalt invaded her forests, nylon and lipstick ensnared her women, imported Italian shoes directed the paths of her men, but none of these, not even the profanity of rock music could touch what was by birthright hers—her exquisite rhythms. They were the inner sanctuary of every African, timeless, indestructible, as unintentional as barter in the marketplace, powerful but soft, like women pounding rice for the evening meal. They fed on whatever came near: loud palaver, the clank of machinery, the incessant beeping of taxi horns as the drivers chased each other through cluttered streets like kids with new toys, blaring jukeboxes, quarrels, the whistles of whores, screams of fighting children, the agonizing scratch of a cripple crawling over rough planks, the far off wail of a Mandingo at prayer—all found rhythm, dance. To an African dance is hardly a performing art, rather a running conversation, spontaneous, volatile, inspired of joy, in a language and an urgency they all understood. It drew on whatever moved—loud speech, uninhibited laughter, political passion, a hand shake, all found their way into short untitled dance phrases. The street came alive with it after the sun went down. Even on quiet nights small islands of activity formed under the false light of dingy street lamps accentuating the gesture-ridden talk of men who made jest of the smallest event, their exuberance ready to burst, life afire beneath the shackle of poverty, rich, effervescent—unmistakably African.

It was a mere mile from the Chase Manhattan Bank on the Boulevard to the soccer game in the vacant lot at the end of Randall Street, and only another half mile down a side street and up a dirt lane to *Oscar's Chalet,* a fine French restaurant nestled in a grove of lazy palms, an earshot from the beach where the surf moaned seductively and for the length of dinner you could forget you were in Africa. Inside it retained a Swiss atmosphere but with African fixtures: neat white table cloths, rugged woodwork, framed pictures of the Alps, but tribal candle bowls and an antelope over the bar. I liked to sit by the terrace window where the sound of the surf filtered through the bamboo shades. After months of my own dismal cooking, dinner at *Oscar's* was a real treat; it meant mixing with a clientele of diplomats and foreign businessmen, listening to loud talk and bold plans, but there are times, as my tribal friends urged, when the stomach is better counsel than the brain.

So I ordered a filet, medium rare, a dry burgundy, and tried not to think of the conditions outside—but it never worked. No sooner than my knife touched the juice, I could hear a voice at my sleeve, "Gi' me fi' ce' yah. You whi' ma'," see the imploring eyes, the belly of worms. I could finish the meal but never enjoyed it. The trick was to find a diversion. You rolled up your windows, buried yourself in a magazine and when your car hit the first bump at the end of Randall Street, you proffered the driver a casual observation on "economic problems," checked your appointment book and rushed into the lounge firing a short salvo to the maitre d' before joining your party. During dinner you talked about the Common Market or the World Cup. It was easy. I could do it in the right company, but tonight I didn't feel like company.

I got down to the coast last night after a twelve hour ride from the interior. Today, the usual hustle of a Saturday in town—some small business matters, mail check, haircut, letters home, but later on a good book and some time at the beach. A lazy calm embraced the blue water. Dusk fell, the sun seemed to pause before touching its pillow. It was a delicious new feeling, waste deep in lukewarm water, a bulging orange ball quivering like an egg yolk, westward, in the Atlantic.

After dinner I sat awhile gazing at the sea. You could hear it in the distance, a low rumble like a far-off cannonade, and if you looked hard you could catch a glimpse of surf breaking on the shore under the palm fronds, ghostly white in the distance with no reference to its noise due to the sound lag. It had the rhythm of a sorrowful chant but its fresh fragrance found the curtains and played with the light in the candle bowls.

I ordered a creme de menthe and thought of home. Then they came. Four of them. "Well, look who's here," the first exclaimed, the second waved at the same time mouthing a hello to someone else. The third seemed out of place; slim, demure, she wore a pink chiffon dress, tiny earrings, light makeup over a dark suntan. Brad followed them to my table. Dark haired, rugged looking, he still wore cowboy boots. "Tonight's your lucky night man," he winked, "I got three on my hands." He held the chair for his date while Frances and

Marie seated themselves smiling brightly and straightening the folds in their skirts; both wore comfortable dresses, bubbled with sincere but overwrought friendliness. After the usual preliminaries, he introduced her, Helga Heinemann, a staff assistant at the German Embassy. "West German," he added. "On our side."

"It seems like ages since we've seen you," Frances began at once. "Tell us where you are, what you're doing."

"Upcountry. A Loma village."

"Near Zorzor?"

"Further. Halfway to Voinjama."

"We were up that way a few months ago," Marie added. "Funny we didn't see you."

"It's not very big," I said. "Most people buzz through."

"Another wide spot in the road," Brad mused looking around for the waiter.

"Well, next time flag us down," Frances said happily, "Or better yet come on down and see us. Let us know you're still alive for heaven's sake. Did you hear what happened to Rick Johnson? He flagged down this rickety old car. He said he saw the goats in the back seat but he didn't notice the windshield was missing."

"It's a good seventy-five miles from Ganta," Marie added excitedly.

"You should have seen him," Frances exclaimed.

"He looked absolutely dazed," Marie laughed.

"You remember Rick—tall, blond hair, glasses?"

"Maybe he needs new ones," I suggested.

"He looked like a termite mound with two eyeholes," and she did an impersonation. Helga beamed brightly and Brad cracked up. When the waiter brought the menus, she leaned towards him and they glanced over the same one while Frances and Marie went over theirs in detail reading aloud the dishes that caught their attention. Soon the conversation got going again, mostly gossip, who'd been reassigned, who hadn't, new projects, old problems.

"By the way, who are you stationed with?" Frances asked.

"Nobody."

"You're alone?"

"Yes."

"Yuk. How'd they stick you with that one?"

"I requested it."

"Requested—"

"Oh he's always the loner," Marie teased.

"Likes to be his own boss," Frances suggested.

"Unlike Monrovia," Brad sighed. "Every able-bodied person down here's a supervisor. You can't move a box of paper clips without approval. I envy you."

"You wouldn't if you had to eat my cooking."

"It can't be that bad," Marie said.

"That's what I keep telling myself."

"Well, I don't see how you can stand it up there alone," Frances winced. "What do you do with your spare time, for relaxation I mean?"

"I've got a box at the opera."

"Will you knock it off!"

"Oh he probably likes it up there," Marie said. "You and Chris Creighton, you're two of a kind. I hear he's moved out by himself too."

"Well, I heard," Frances whispered, "The last time he was down here, Mr. Richardson asked him what he was doing and he answered, 'Training a guerrilla army.'"

"He did," Brad smiled. "And for a second he caught the old boy off guard. You know Creighton, looks like he just stepped out of a yoga trance. You had to be there."

"So you can smile after all," Frances mocked.

"You were close in training, weren't you?" Marie asked.

"We roomed together."

"And they got lost in Muir Woods," Frances recalled. "How did you ever—"

"On purpose."

Fortunately the mention of training turned the conversation to other things. We'd spent the previous summer in San Francisco and it had pleasant memories for all of us. I enjoyed listening to them reminisce. Brad and Marie were telling Helga about Sausalito, its shops and artists, the beatniks, the good old days before they sent them back to Berkeley, about the cable cars, the bar with the turtle races, the down-under nightclub where the main entrance was a playground slide—you paid the cover, slid down and wound up on your ass in the middle of a floor show. But no one could remember its name. *The Mill* I thought.

When the waiter lit the flambé, the conversation let up a bit. I ordered another creme de menthe, which Frances had to try, then settled back to listen to the surf again but Helga looked across the table and smiled, "I've always wanted to visit one of the interior villages, but I'm afraid Kakatah is as far as I've been." She spoke with a slight accent, her quiet manner complimented her delicate features, her glance came direct, refined, at ease with strangers.

"You'll have to go farther than that," I said.

"I know," she smiled, "but I don't think I have the nerve."

"There's nothing to be afraid of."

"That's what everyone tells me, you know. But they say such awful things about them."

"About whom?"

"The bare-asses," Brad said.

"Well, I never," she drawled in disbelief.

"Shame on you," Frances hissed at him.

"Don't believe what the educated Africans say about them," I said.

"Then you like them, the…"

"'Natives.'" Brad added delicately.

"Yes."

"And you really like it up there in your…what tribe?"

"Loma."

"In your Loma village?"

"Yes."

"I should think it would be terribly lonely."

"It's peaceful. Quiet. Especially in the evening when the leaves go limp and the smoke's rising. No electric, no radio, only the rustle of palm leaves, birds, the bark of a dog…until white people come and screw it up—"

"Will you listen to him," Frances scolded. "No wonder people talk about you, you know people talk about you? Mr. Richardson was asking about you just the other day, nobody knew anything, no one had seen you. Don't you ever get out and see people?"

"I see people every day."

"You know what I mean. Some of us aren't so bad you know."

"Watch out or you'll wind up like Campbell," Marie smiled.

"What happened to Campbell?" I asked since we were going to hear it anyway.

"Well, first he started giving away his possessions, then he moved into a small hut, no windows, pretty soon he was eating with his hands and God knows what. They finally sent him home."

"And he was living with a tribal woman," Marie added, "which might have been the clincher."

"He was sort of weird to begin with," Brad said, then to me, "Quite seriously though, you need to go in and see Richardson. He's afraid you're going native."

"Maybe he'll send me to Dr. Novatny," I said knowing it would change the topic. The shrink back in training, his German accent and earthy sense of humor had made him our favorite.

"Dr. No!" Frances and Marie cried out together. "Alvays, alvays!" Frances exclaimed in a deep rasp. "My voice isn't deep enough, you do it Brad."

"Vhatever you do," he began in feigned solemnity turning to Helga who held back a smile, "remember ziss. Zomeday. You vill have to come home. So vatch vhat you're doing, or learn to be a good liar."

"You watch what you're doing, too," Helga warned with no accent at all.

"Doesn't she speak great English?" he added with a hand on her shoulder.

"You really do," Marie said pleasantly.

"Comes from hangin' out with us Laramie intellectuals."

"I was one year in New York."

"And," Brad continued signaling the waiter, "*aand,* she does a mean, a devastating…Ella Fitzgerald impersonation."

"How could you!" Helga's perfectly manicured fingers went to her face where a girlish blush at a betrayed secret quickly expired. She regained her poise at once and explained matter-of-factly, "I enjoy jazz. In its place of course."

"Bee bee d'beetly be beep—boammm," he concluded with an upbeat as she beamed her best diplomatic warning in return. "So then," he clapped his hands together, "how 'bout a movie everybody?"

The Rivoli Theater was the finest in Monrovia, its glittering marquee ruled the fashionable boulevard that ran from the Hotel Ducor down to the old presidential mansion in the heart of business district. Stylish shops and two rows of trimmed royal palms lined both sides. Inside, an elegant spiral staircase rose from a carpeted lobby to an air conditioned balcony with two-dollar cushioned seats; but for fifty cents, if you were game, a side entrance opened into a downstairs gallery with movable benches on a cement floor. The audience down here came from the emerging middle class, tribal people turned workers, often younger men new to the city but with the tribal fire still burning, a zest for life that erased the distinction between audience and performer and required visceral belief in the clumsiest monster. Loud, opinionated, with little interest in plot or purpose, they had no patience for art. They loved blood and guts, cheered as the battles raged, screamed as heroes wasted whole armies and it wasn't long until a stray bullet found its way into one of their bellies, the victim falling into the arms of friends who cried wildly and clung to their beer bottles. When the action subsided the gallery did too, but then the commentaries began, sure death to the tenderest love scene. Eye make-up, a little confusing. "See de gree' pai'! She witch-oh. You ma'! You betta ta' ti!"

Tonight we sat upstairs,   though I preferred the gallery. I thought Helga might have enjoyed it for a change but decided not to suggest it. Brad got the tickets while she exchanged greetings with some German acquaintances, introducing us politely before breaking away and mounting the staircase with an ease that suggested finishing school.

The movie stank. Pure Hollywood. The critics down below agreed. The air conditioning felt great but twenty minutes was all I could take.

Outside, the Charlies were busy, taxis zipped by beeping for rides, a gusty breeze kicked over the palm trees hinting rain, the air felt heavy, a bit sultry. *The Moby Dick* was packed. The smell of sweat and cigarette smoke clogged the place. The deafening metronome of *High Life* poured out the open door— a lame attempt to tame tribal rhythms into a fox trot; it didn't work but they danced to it anyway. The latest hit told of a lad from Cape Palmas who lost his girl, sung to the refrain, "Chicken is sweet with palm butter and rice." The crowd spilled onto the sidewalk where men talked and two bar girls moved with the music under the hand painted sign lit by a yellow bulb and strung with Christmas lights. A taxi waited at the curb, its driver patiently palavering some gas money with two friends, "Fo' de ga' ma', two dolla le' go."

I hated crowds—Americans in particular. Half-crocked, expatriate cowboys, their only claim to virility other than having blown the brains out of a cornered beast on a guided hunting trip was that of exposing paper currency in a crowded bar. On a street where five dollars brought a man running, they were big shots. Once they'd offered a kid twenty bucks to stand against a wall so they could knock a beer bottle off his head with golf balls. The boy lived on street savvy and quick legs and easily dodged their drunken pitches—no harm done.

Two more bars and a cook shop, then the noise died down, then another side street, another alley and a maze of zinc cubicles. A block further and a garbage pile buried the curb, a small truckload, stinking and tapering off toward a gutted building but with a thin trickle of rancid liquid running the other way. Two dogs fed on it, their ribs practically ripping through their purple bellies, tongues white with disease, but diligent, like misers, licking whatever the street orphans left behind. They turned their sunken heads but their jaws hung down with mange. Death had already claimed them. Slow, ghoulish, as though a heavy weight were suspended on a thin string, one of them turned to follow, then the second.

The alley followed an open ditch; pee-stained walls to either side crumbled into a maze of broken bottles and rusting utensils themselves overgrown with working filth. The smell, something awful. Then another larger ditch emerged from the mouth of a cracked culvert and ran alongside a warehouse style tenement. The heat and the tightness of the quarters magnified the odor. It ran black, green on the edges, clogged with discarded objects half submerged in sewage. An animal carcass somehow impaled on a dead branch, its teeth and bones beginning to emerge from its leather. Flies swarmed. A little later a single plank bridged the ditch before it broke away and disappeared between some bleak two-story houses leaning windward on squat pylons beneath loose sheets of corrugated siding that peeled off like flaps of dead skin. No glass in the windows. A domestic quarrel. A bawling child. All carried on the dank air. The dogs turned back.

The alley ended in a pile of rubble. A dirt lane continued before breaking up into a web of pathways disappearing in the open spaces between randomly spaced bungalows. The skeleton frame of a junked car lay half buried in the weeds. Foliage streamed from its windows and seats like tongues of flame and refuse filled its hood cavity. Something underneath scuttled away.

Tilley's Lounge—the original owner British, her successors not up to a new sign—nestled in a cluster of drooping palms sporting a broad veranda and a tile roof. It had been a fine-to-do residence, then a business venture gone bad, now a quiet little retreat for those who didn't mind a half mile walk from the end of the lane. Down here things were more open, quite a few palms. Some of the bungalows weren't too bad, tucked away in the shade with verandas and little gardens. Once it must have been a nice neighborhood before urban sprawl began its strangle hold. The distant rumble of the surf regained its voice.

Inside a crippled beggar squatted in the corner. A few people wiled away the time in low conversation. The slow rise of cigarette smoke kept pace in a cracked mirror behind a polished bar. White wicker chairs and small tables furnished what once must have been a spacious living room with a view of the sea, but tonight dull rose curtains enclosed everything, scented candle bowls, hassocks, the Duke of Wellington over a clumsy grand piano. Two bar girls gyrated tiredly in front of a jukebox mouthing the words to a pop tune, their lips plastered red, slinky black dresses so tight the zippers strained. The first backed into me without missing a beat—Oooo, how I need your love—while her friend continued measuring a small circle with one shoulder.

I sat at the end of the bar. A heavy mulatto woman poured me a drink before returning to an involved conversation with younger woman who leaned forward with intense interest. I felt rotten. My book-learned ideals had rotted away in less than a year; the real surprise, the ease with which they went. I tried to explain it in a letter of resignation—still in my pocket—but the words rang hollow; fancy phrases like "cultural imperialism" didn't work. Of course I didn't need a letter; Richardson was pretty liberal about letting people go, a fatherly talk, a few questions, a hardy "thanks for the effort."

A year ago it had been just another word in a book, imperialism, a sidelight before the crucial chapter on World War I. But they missed the point, the books. It wasn't ideological, even economic, but rather…it planted a microbe in the native soul, a disease that lay dormant but invariably took hold until the best of them accepted inferiority without even knowing it. How could they compete against telephones and airplanes? The newcomers were clearly superior, technologically therefore culturally. Fatal mistake. And who were the victors? A superior military force? Not even a gang of hardy pirates. Bureaucrats and businessmen—with a whisk of a pen, tribal integrity became modern servility. Weaker tribesmen were drawn to the cities like game to a baited snare. To the capitalist question, "Isn't twenty-five cents a day better than nothing at all?" their stomachs said "Yes", but their souls went silent. The tragedy ended, the comedy began.

And I was part of it. My very presence was an act of imperialism, a case for my freedom, not theirs. Freedom had been a word in a book too, something handed down on a silver platter, a gift for which I owed a debt. But if I had to earn it, why couldn't someone else? To earn it meant to kill somebody. That was the price. Our most cherished cause rested on wealth extracted from others. For every Madonna adorning a splendid museum, a hungry kid dodged golf balls somewhere in the back alley of the world.

"Buy me drink yah?" She slid to the next stool with her head propped in her hand and her elbow on the bar, seemingly bored. She was dark, very dark, North African, smooth skinned, supple, with piercing black eyes in a cloud of jet black hair. Huge gold earrings and jingling bracelets suggested a Gypsy but her pale dress was very quiet, mauve, off the shoulder. Her smile hardly moved the corners of her lips. "What is your nem?"

"You couldn't pronounce it."

"Are you a Pis Corpse?"

"Corps. Watch my lips…corps. And it's peace, not piss."

"You haff fine lips. What you got to be frown about? Let me tell you something," and she drew near as if to share a secret. "You are crazy. You liff in rich contry, you haff rich family, and what you do? You come in place like this, you work for nothing. Why? You haff education. You could be haff fine closse, fine car. Is nothing wrong with thesse. You are crazy. Do you know what we woult do to get in your contry? We woult giff our *blood!*" She spoke rapidly with subdued fire, her fingers lost in her hair, her eyes sharp, but after a bit she softened up and smiled. "At least you're young. How many years do you haff?"

"Twenty-three."

"You look like sefenteen."

She was twenty-six. Her mother Arabic, her father Senegalese, but she also had European blood in her veins. She had three languages: Arabic, French, and English, "American" English she added enunciating very carefully. She originally came from Morocco but there had been trouble (it was a long story) so she moved here to live with her half sister, but it hadn't worked out. Her sister's husband turned out to be a real "besturrt!" (here she forgot her American accent) so she moved out and got a job, then another, now here, but only for temporary. That was six months ago. She sighed with boredom. It was a long story.

"Are you buying me a drink?"

"Give her a shot o' tea."

"Ey! Where you think this is? Some kinna dife? This is high class place! You got money? How much money you got? If you cannot pay you will be trouble."

"There! Satisfied?"

"Giff me here the bottle," she said to the barmaid. "Okay." She made me smell it. "Scotch whiskey."

"Impawted from Scotchland," I said.

"You never haff whiskey? Of course not." She yelled something in Arabic and the barmaid returned with some water. "You are afraid to drink the water, no? There you see. What did I say? All you do is add shot of whiskey and water is fine. Did not anyone tell you? But is expensive. The whiskey."

"I had a feeling—"

"You know something?…I like you. You are crazy but I like you. Tell me something—just between us," she leaned close, then paused thinking something over. "Come here. We make tete-a-tete." She walked to one of the low tables in the far corner, sat, crossed her legs and zeroed in. Her hair. Pure Night.

"Pretty dress," I said.

"You like?"

"Yes. Just right."

"Tell me something," and she leaned real close. "What do I have to say to go to your country? At your Embassy? To get a visa? They ask questions. I can get money, yes, but the questions."

Oh God not again. The sixty-four dollar question. "Tell 'em you got plans for a nuclear weapon."

"Ey! Do not joke at me. If you joke me I will not talk to you."

"Sorry."

"I would do anything to get out of this place. I am so unhappy."

"I'm sorry. That was a terrible thing to say."

"No mind yah. *C'est un malentendu.*"

"I really don't know what they ask at the Embassy. The truth is it's very hard to immigrate to the United States these days...unless—"

"Come tell me."

"Well, if you're really desperate...marry an American. Then they gotta take you. But you already know that."

"Is okay suggestion," she said thoughtfully, "Thank you," then went to staring at her glass. "If I could get to New York, I could get a job just like that," and she snapped her fingers. Then she changed her tone. Softer. "I was a dancer in Morocco, what's use dancing in place like this?"

"New York's no better."

"You dawn't like? Is fine place. I see in movies."

"Movies lie."

"They do yah? Where were you tonight—before you come here?"

"The Moby Dick."

"Before that?"

"The Rivoli."

"You dawn't like but you go?"

"I like the crowd downstairs."

"You haff money. Sit upstair."

"I don't like it up there."

"But why?"

"I can't stand the stink of cologne."

"You dawn't like cologne?"

"No."

"But you wear it. You are wearing it now."

"Well…aftershave."

She smiled a dark smile. It was getting late. A heavyset black man got up to leave, but first he came around and wished everyone a pleasant good evening. Not long after a gray-headed white man climbed down off his stool and left. The two bar girls sprawled half asleep and most unladylike in two wicker chairs across the room; between yawns they cursed the son of a bitch who promised to pick them up two hours ago. The jukebox finally went silent. The crippled beggar hadn't moved. The barmaid joined us and they began another conversation, mostly Arabic with a word of English now and then.

"Can we have another drink yah?"

"All right."

"You got enough money?"

She said something in Arabic and the barmaid got up. In a few minutes she brought back a tray with a bottle and a steaming silver pot. "Is coffee. I dawn't know how you call in English," she asked the barmaid in Arabic but she didn't know either. "Arab coffee. We take with kahlua and a little piece of cognac. You try." We clinked glasses. Not bad. "It will make your blood warm. You must drink not too fast. That way it can stay long time on your tongue."

"Yah."

"Tonight I am your teacher," she smiled quietly. "You really are teacher?"

"Yes."

"For…*alors…les petit noires?*"

"Yes."

"And they learn?"

"Yes."

We finished our drinks and sat silent for a longtime, I couldn't think of anything to say. The place was empty save the beggar in the corner, the coffee strong.

"Come we play some music." She got up and started for the jukebox. "You got money? Give him something first," she nodded toward the beggar.

"He's asleep."

"Tomorrow. He will need," she said taking a dollar and slipping it into his fingers. "What kinna music you like?"

"Ella Fitzgerald."

Her finger dropped down the list; it had some interesting selections: High Life, country and western, Gershwin, Negro Spirituals, Elvis, the Beatles, Lebanese folk songs, *The Marseillaise.*

"You like Billie Holiday?"

"Yes."

"Come we dance." She put her fingers on the back of my neck and came real close. "What's the matter with you?" she whispered looking straight into my eyes. "You sit alone. You dawn't talk to nobody. You got some kinna trouble?"

I didn't answer.

"Come on. Tell me."

"Nothing…really."

"You think too much. You dawn't enjoy. Soon people will laugh on you, soon you dawn't got friends and you will go crazy in the streets. Believe me. I have seen," she paused then nodded towards the door. "You worried about them? We all got trouble but we go on living."

"I suppose you're right."

"Yes, I am right. You stay alone in your life, you will go crazy in the streets. That's no way to be, believe me. Life is young. We will be old soon enough. Drink. Dance. Make love. You will feel better." Then she put her fingers on my face and buried her face in my neck as if to share a special secret. "Ey? You in love?"

"No."

"With somebody here in Monrovia?"

"No…really."

"You sure?"

"Yes."

"…Maybe that's what's the matter."

She lived in two rooms above a store. A bare light bulb dangled from a crooked cord in a narrow passage, a tiny kitchen opened into a square living room and in turn into a small bedroom by way of a beaded curtain. A French window led to a useless balcony at the side. Several hassocks clumped together over a threadbare rug, a couch filled one corner, an awkward wardrobe the other and a cloth lounge chair sat next to a low coffee table with one leg missing. Clothes and magazines all over the place. The stained ceiling drooped from leakage, the plaster cracked and peeling, but she'd done a nice job making the most of it. A thin tapestry covered one wall and elsewhere she'd put airline posters where they did the most good—a North African village with a beaming stewardess and bearded men in white robes standing proud with their camels. She flicked on a light and disappeared behind the clink of the curtain.

An apricot-colored lamp shade gave the room some warmth. A carving on the table caught my eye. A piece of driftwood. Light gray and worn clean, it had a natural form of its own but someone had carved two vertical eye-openings into its gnarled involution. That was all. But it came alive. The darkness flowed through, a lovely darkness. Its power imposed itself in the space around it; its steady gaze penetrated the room like the presence of another person. It radiated warmth, life, you waited for it to speak. "You like?" she said from behind the curtain.

"Yes. Very much."

"You like...you take."

"Oh I couldn't. I...Where did you get it?"

"A friend make for me."

"I'd like to meet him."

"You haff meet!" And here she laughed unaffectedly for the first time. "The sick man. In the bar. You gave him dollar. When he is not sick, he makes things, whatever he can find. He is...clever in the hands."

It was going to rain. The first drops began an erratic tapping on the window panes as though in warning. I went to the balcony. With the release of the latch, the door flew open and a wave of cool air poured into the room billowing the curtains. The street looked dark, deserted. Wet plops struck the sidewalk below, the cadence quickened, white lines streaked across small circles of electric light that marked store entrances. Then the wind dove into a palm tree next-door and soon a steady shower engulfed us. Splashes of white light flicked on and off on the black pavement, cones glistened on the water. At first the street sizzled, but as the volume deepened, it sounded rather like the prolonged applause in a grand hall. "You like the rain?" She came up behind and put her arms around my waist. "In Morocco we say rain is a lonely herdsman looking for new pasture."

When the wind kicked up again, we went back in and closed the door. The wet sizzling became a muffled drone.

She was quieter now, more relaxed. The affected American mannerisms as well as some of her accent stayed back at the bar, thank God. She wore a shiny blouse, dark maroon with fine blue swirls, open in front, tied simply at the waist with a gold cord, jeans underneath, and barefoot. The two gold earrings remained. Her hair gleamed even in the dull light. She was darker, more subdued, more distant but in an odd way closer, as though we were both fugitive from a common enemy. Her demeanor, less defiant. She lit a candle and sat on the couch; one glance was invitation enough.

"Give me your hand," she said softly. She turned it over and began studying it. "I am a reader of palms."

"I thought you were a dancer."

"That was Morocco. Here I am a reader." She looked up meaningfully, "I have many things I do. Come. You have long life. You dawn't belief, do you? You Americans are so smart, you drife big car, you think you knaw eferything but you dawn't knaw this. It is our science. Poor people. Let me read. The truth is not in your hand of course; it is in your heart. Looking at your palm is only…how you call? A trick, yes, so you cannot see what I am really doing."

"And what are you really doing?"

"Making your heart to giff up its secrets. Giffing me your hand is way of giffing me your heart without letting you know. You haff surrentered it to me becauss you want to know what is there even if you cannot belief. You are very easy to read you know. Because you cannot lie. Go on. Try. You see, you cannot. People like you are easy. Gamblers and businessmen are bat; they are too good at talking one thing and beliefing another."

"What else do you see, since I'm such easy reading?"

"You are secret, you think too mush. I cannot see clear but you are afrait of something. You carry insite your heart…how you call, a diseasse. You will liff long but you will not be happy. You will all the time be carry sadness in your heart. The reason is you are too clever. You see people hungry and you are sorry, this is your virtue but it is a small one. Your sin is much greater, and it is a sin that carries people to hell. You know that people do not have to be this way, hungry and sick, if only they would listen to you, but they do not, they lie and steal and fight like dawx, and you cannot forgiff. But this is the way of life, it is the way of all of us, even you. Do you think you are so perfect you can neffer lie? Then you haff neffer been hungry."

"How do you know all this?"

"Becauss to be poor is the world's best teacher. My grandmother once to say. You haff to be poor to knaw how to be rich. You Americans are neffer poor so you—"

"Not all Americans are rich."

"But that is naught the reason you are sad. But no mind, I will show you to forget." She let go my hand. "You are really twenty-three years? I am twenty-nine. Before…I lied." She rose and went out to the kitchen. After a bit she came back with something in the bottom of an old teapot. Only it wasn't tea. "I dawn't knaw how you call in English. We call…hashish."

How slow the world withdraws. It sighs and something sways, something goes away but stays. Something far away comes clear, whispers in a welcome ear. There's music in forgiving eyes, in the lyre something sighs, a yellow flame begins to glow, the fragrance in the air so slow, in pliant palm boughs bowing low, creaking in their seams, notes on mellow strings, unending as in cradle dreams. Hear the wind, the soughing flow, something murmured low. A psalm of joy, the earth receives, whispers in the sea, the undulating sea. See the sunset's smiling face, beaming colors streaming down, brilliant fire bulging round, maiden fruit, heavy laden, reaching down, setting somewhere where the seabirds cry, winging nightward into purple sky, now to windward, now to lee. A splendid sunset this, simmering day and feral night entangled in a kiss, in earth's most fervent wish, forbidden fruit, ripe with seed, shifting in the leaves, in the movement of the seas. Taste the raindrops. Now the power. The bounty of the bursting seas. So strong the shore responds, so soft the hour. Night cries mimic morning dreams, in weightless flight, winging home through violet light. Dawn is near, eastward, rising, clear. In peace new sunlight sleeps, the earth replete, bejeweled in rising mists, off an earthly altar upward to all the gods that be.

CHAPTER 6

THE LURE OF A SIREN

"There's something unforgettable about a dark woman," Mr. Eddington told me some time later. "Quite inexplicable, but you know it the minute they look at you. And that's why we're drawn to them, oh I'm not talking about people, actually I am, more about cultures, places—India, Egypt, all the god awful rag heaps of the world." He was English, white haired, hazy blue eyes, moustache, a studied air of indifference, a remnant of the old Empire, he looked the part but lost the conviction. A rugby player in his youth, now an importer of hardware and fabrics, we'd hit it off right from the start. I'd called him "Sir" at the onset of a small business arrangement and he invited me to his terrace as he called it, an attractive second-story rooftop with potted palms and white deck furniture overlooking the port where he had a warehouse, the doings of which he surveyed through a pair of field glasses, World War II issue. "I can't really see much anymore, at least they know I'm watching." During the midday heat he retired for a glass of lemonade with a spot of gin, in his case a rather generous spot; by three-thirty he was ready for tea, iced with a dash of Scotch; by four, quite talkative. "Ours have lost it you know."

"What is that, sir?"

"Mystery. The lure of the unknown. Don't get me wrong, I'm not against women's suffrage or anything like that. I'm all for it, vote liberal, but in the process they've lost something rather special. So now they fly airplanes and discuss Kafka and no one has the slightest notion anything's missing. I say, how's your drink? Silence in a woman, in anyone for that matter, is not necessarily ignorance; oh it can be, many times it is, but at its best it's the expression of what can't be put in words, a window into the other world I should say, and once the art is lost it's lost for good. And women are its bearers; they're born with it, men only know it through them. Ice? Better have another, they don't last long. Take Hitler. Contemptible baastard, had he known the love of a dark woman the whole bloody joke could have been avoided."

"World War II, sir?"

"Quite." He looked around for something. "Ah. Here we are. Bitters? I know it must sound astonishing but I sincerely believe there's some truth to it. So much of the world's mischief is due to bungling idealists, so-called knights in shining armour who've never explored the dark side of...of themselves I should say, take themselves so damned seriously as if honor's a helpless cripple. True honor can damn well take care of itself—and in the most unlikely circumstances. I remember a time during the war—won't you have another? Are you quite sure? I was perhaps a little older than you, just married, but quite inexperienced, do you?...of course. It was here in the African sector—"

"Then you were with Montgomery?"

"Monty's Eighth! And we let them know it at El Almein! We stopped the German advance there and afterwards had them on the run all the way back to Tobruk, at least when Patton wasn't getting under foot, the abominable pest, a royal pain in the oss to be more precise—you'll have to forgive me, I'm quite opinionated on this point, I mean no offense to your country naturally, all that we've been through. Where was I? Tobruk. You can still come across the remains of tanks up there, did you know? In the desert, all but buried by now I should say. My unit got sidetracked into a small, half-ruined place. It looked for all the world like a column of armour had driven straight through it. We put in late one night. I was pretty well done in. We'd had a bloody time of it at Almein as you know. I lost a dear friend there. And after Africa there would be Italy, then Europe; there seemed no end in sight, only exhaustion and despair and the next day more of the same. We bivouacked in a blown out telegraph station, some of my friends decided to go uptown, whatever that meant. There wasn't much danger since our unit was at that time in the rear of the advance. I didn't feel like living it up but went along nonetheless. I wasn't up to drinking or whoring just then. I was newly married at the time. Katharine and I only spent three weeks together before I left for Africa. She was a lovely girl and she's been a good mother—we've two daughters, the eldest is with the BBC in Karachi—and I've been loyal to her too, don't get me wrong. I...just that once out in the Sahara.

"I was on my way back to my quarters, alone. Ironically I was thinking about Katharine, how brave she looked when we said good-bye, when all of a sudden, this young thing, a shadow really, darted out from behind some rubbish, quick as a bird. I investigated naturally. I found her huddling in a crooked doorway shivering with fear. I didn't speak much Arabic—still don't, ghastly language—but I managed to quiet her down, gave her some money and a trinket. I thought I should see her home safely, the least I could do. She led the way to a broken-down hovel not fit for dogs. By the time we got there, she caught hold of herself. She took my hand and led me inside. I stayed the night. It wasn't that I took advantage of her, mind you. She invited me in, to stay, do you?...not by anything she said—she hardly spoke a syllable I'm sure. Her eyes. They said everything...dark, piercing, like an animal. I suppose it's hereditary, their women...well, for centuries they've been that way. The darkness speaks for them. You can feel it, their eyes on you, drawing you in, weaving their spell.

"As I said, I stayed the night. We made love. She was young, delicate, but remarkably...adept, not the way you think, something more subtle than all that...communicative, but without language. A remarkable experience—not that I don't love my wife mind you, I do, Katharine and I have had it good, but never quite...perhaps the war, I can't say.

"Next morning I woke in pure sunshine—the bloody hovel didn't so much as have a roof—and there she was. A child asleep, the perfect embodiment of peace, a Renaissance painter couldn't have captured it. I looked at her and for awhile the anxiety that accompanies one in war ceased and I felt overcome with a sense of well being; but all at once it changed to horror as I realized she was just that, a child, no more than...sixteen...well, fifteen, that I was...do you quite follow? Then she woke and with one glance put me back at my ease as though some dark wisdom chose to smile through a child's eyes and reassure me all was proper. No remorse, no accusation. Wide-eyed understanding of the way of the world I suppose."

"Did you ever see her again?"

"No." He looked away with embarrassment. "It happens that way in war; there are many you never hear of again, in fact I never thought of her again. Mind you I love my wife. Katharine and I...it's the kind of thing you remember when you're old, on an overcast day like this, on the spur of the moment, I don't know what dredges it up. You'll find your memory's sharper as you grow older. You relive your youth the way it was supposed to be. Quite remarkable."

"I know what you mean."

"I don't think that you do," he smiled graciously. "When you're as old as me...you may."

CHAPTER 7

UPCOUNTRY

Dawn. A gray sun scarcely lit a dull, drizzly morning. A dense haze lay over the harbor, filled in the empty spaces between the ships and warehouses giving them the illusion of an eerie detachment from everything grounded to earth. The sound of dripping water and the far off groan of a fog horn seemed to come from another world. We finished loading the jeep in silence. Jameson gave a low whistle as he swung in behind the wheel.

The streets were already jammed, the main market a jumble of canvas-covered trucks, cars, overloaded Renault buses crowded with passengers, cargo tied haphazardly on top—spare tires, bunches of green bananas, live chickens in wicker cages. Impatient for the open road, drivers inched their way through throngs of people, laid on their horns; carboys sang out destinations.

"Kakatah! Gantaaah! Le' go! Le' go! Le' go!"

"Voinyama! Le' go now! Do' wa' ti'! Voinyama-Voinyama-Voinyama!"

The marketplace brought the grayest day to life. It glittered in color, eye catching, alive with movement, caught up in simple things like plastic slippers, head-ties, gaudy beads, a national flag sewn into a woman's garment; brilliant reds and purples, golds and greens, bobbed up and down on a sea of high-tempo syllables bubbling from a host of tribal dialects, each an island of swarming activity. The smells of ripe fruit and fresh fish mingled with shouts and beeping horns into a riot of excitement. Agile women eased through the crowd under high headloads, their regal bearing, a model for the younger girls who came behind under smaller headloads, chewing kola nuts and spitting pulp. Vendors and their customers bartered on the curb within arms reach as we passed, others spread out their wares on tables or the ground, small children ran in and out, carboys leered at young girls, impatient passengers leaned out of cars looking ahead for the cause of the delay and offering their opinions in no uncertain terms. Bolts of bright colored cloth beckoned from shop stalls. A picture of the president graced the back of a man's shirt. For three blocks we had to navigate the flow of people and vehicles practically nudging them with the nose of the jeep, but once out of the bottleneck, Jameson pulled into a side street and soon we were downtown where a smartly uniformed traffic officer halted us at the corner of Ashmun and Broad St. A late model American car with the U.S. Embassy insignia pulled alongside. A guy in a neat sport shirt rolled down the passenger window. Not much older than us.

"Boy Scouts Africa! Down for a little R&R?"

"Could be," Jameson observed.

"Let's get back up there and save the world."

"The taxpayers are gettin' their money's worth."

"And let's get that jeep washed!"

"Who the hell are they?"

"What you see my friend," Jameson explained as loud as needed, "is a 1964 Ivy League legacy with a lily up his ass." And he smartly pulled out in front of them. We could afford another dent. They couldn't.

We at once got caught in another bottleneck. Native drivers had no concept of order; a traffic jam came as alien to their experience as democracy to their leaders. Beat-up vehicles cut through gas stations, vacant lots, nosed into traffic wherever they could, some tried U-turns in the middle of thronging intersections, others beeped and lurched, drivers gestured wildly, carboys taunted their rivals, passengers shouted defiance at unfortunate pedestrians caught in the pinch, hobbled goats bawled over a blaring radio— "Chicken is sweet with palm butter and rice." The only cool customer, a sleeping baby tied to its mother's back.

It was over an hour before we pulled into the hostel in Sincor, the outlying suburb. After a quick breakfast and a glance at a magazine, the usual complications began. Someone shouted to check the bulletin board—pick up Scot, wait for Marge and Gary, make sure to bring Stephen's water pump valve, don't forget the soccer ball for Bokezaw, "Forty-two boys are waiting patiently, Peggy." That meant going back into town but Jameson took it calmly.

It was some time before we were on our way again whisking along the wet pavement past the new Presidential Mansion and through some shanty towns that practically leaned into the road as if pulled along in the wake of passing vehicles. The open highway followed the coast for twenty miles before turning inland.

Not long and the rubber plantations began. Miles of trees with splotched trunks bent in the direction of the prevailing winds, the lower limbs cut away leaving only high branches that merged into an unbroken cover, all in straight rows following the curvature of the hills, each tree with a small collecting cup below circular grooves in the bark, each equidistant from the next such that diagonal rows became perpendicular as the jeep sped past, then into further diagonals behind, all giving the illusion of order no matter how you looked.

Now and then the sight of rubber workers walking along the roadside broke the monotony. Heads down and arms outstretched over their shoulder yokes, they resembled tiny crucifixes in the distance but grew to human size as they sped toward us under the weight of their burdens, two shiny pails that rose and fell with their gait as though they walked a treadmill. What really struck me wasn't the surroundings but the inevitability of it all, as though the whole damn thing were scripted, each word, each feeling. What was it about her? Not just her looks, I wasn't *that* green. The lure of a siren, the stark honesty she'd tell any lie to get what she wanted, the ease with which she shattered all pretense. And the music. *Solitude.* I could still hear it. There was something terribly wanting in my soul and she'd found it, something more than the need for a woman.

"Can you take me straight to school," Marge said all of a sudden. Kakatah. Jameson pulled into a side street, around some shops and backtracked down a dirt lane to a low roofed, five-room structure with a flagpole. Marge got down, hitched up the strap of her shoulder bag, wished us a sympathetic bon voyage and crossed into the schoolyard where a swarm of delighted kids surrounded her.

Kakatah looked like it got kicked bare-assed into the twentieth century. Thanks to the surrounding rubber plantations cramming a major crossroad square in the middle of a tribal village, it quickly bloated to unnatural size spreading a new helter-skelter pace of life, a new Africa. Downtown everything squeezed together—people, shops, an outdoor market, a theater, two-story frame buildings tilting on poor foundations, electric poles, a church, advertising, beer bottles, and no place to pee.

The saddest of all, the sight of a tribesman hammering a Coke sign to the door of his mud hut. Sometimes it kept out the rain; more often the bright color seduced the tribal eye, the thermometer and the invitation to "Have a Coke" being of no consequence to people who had neither money nor "book." Soon battered and rusted, it grew into the dismal surroundings like mildew. You had the unshakeable conviction it had been there, in that improbable place, unmoved, unreported, at least a millennium or two. The bleak drabness spoke of time immeasurable; the very coil of the dog asleep in the dirt seemed etched in stone. But another part of you objected; there weren't any Coke signs a thousand years ago; someone must have brought it here at some point in time, but that event, though done on a whim, had to have been a monumental break in the rhythm of their world.

As soon as we got out of Kakatah, the rows of rubber trees resumed their march. The morning remained wet. A dull grayness engulfed everything. There were only four of us now, Jameson and Scot up front, Gary and I in back. Gary looked entirely bored; he stared vacantly out the window oblivious to everything he saw but hating it just the same. His only comment the entire morning had been a sour plea not to pick anyone up. "I don't mind the fall fashions, but I can't stand their choice of cologne."

The paved highway came to an abrupt end not long after the president's country estate, which wasn't far past the American plantations—which said something to those who listened. The road was especially bad for several miles as the pavement deteriorated into mud; the chuckholes deeper, harder to miss. Several times the sudden thud lifted us out of our seats sending pencils and cigarettes flying off the dashboard while a chain clanked to the floor in back. "Try takin' 'em *real* easy man," Scot pleaded. "I got ten cc.'s in each cheek and I'm sensitive to begin with."

"You're about as funny as a case o' crabs," Gary sneered.

Upcountry roads were the source of endless jokes; they called this one the Bong County Parkway. They were constructed in the only feasible way— bulldozing trees and leveling off the laterite base which gave the surface a ferrous color and in time broke up into loose gravel, but herein lay the trouble. During the rainy season surface water took a good part of the road with it leaving crevices that changed configuration practically over night such that a driver couldn't count on finding the same wheel track a day later, and the ditch at the side became a small gorge that ate into the shoulder leaving a crumbling cliff at the edge. In low lying areas it turned into a wallow of mud that lay there until it evaporated, then hardened into narrow wheel tracks that defied all efforts to steer. The body of a vehicle pitched and dipped squeaking like a strained vessel. But that was the worst of it, often it ran smooth for long stretches; sometimes a pole with a scrap of cloth marked a warning, or a rusted wreck lay bottom up in the leaves, stripped of every usable part.

Then came the more gamey drivers whose faith in magic outweighed mechanics. Their favorite sport was to shut off the motor at the top of a hill and allow gravity to find the bottom. You had to give way while they sped past, dust whirling, the driver a picture of cool confidence, his riders wild with excitement, their arms reaching out in the air until he popped the clutch and took them on their way, a bright colored shirt or two flapping in the wind.

Now and then it wound through rice farms where we saw people working in the fields or in the shade of a thatched shelter; sometimes we could see them fishing with wide nets or washing clothes under a bridge. Whenever a river ran near a village, there were sure to be children playing in the water. The sunlight gleamed on their wet backs, set them off in sharp contrast to the tawny current sweeping around their black bodies as effortlessly as through reeds in the bank. They splashed and ducked and paddled with their skinny arms, their delighted screams as much music as the water rushing over shallow pebbles. When they heard us rumbling over the bridge, they paused to wave.

We had a stream just like it in my village and on torrid days when the zinc roof crackled in the heat and sweat ran down our backs, they began fidgeting with their pencils, watching me. On the first syllable of "Go quietly," they shot from their benches, through the door, the windows, overturning chairs. In a flash they were across the road and halfway down the bank where books and trousers dropped to the ground only an instant before their naked bodies split the water in the middle of wild, running leaps, one hand holding their noses, the other their genitals, while those already in the water screamed laughter at the slowpokes.

The kids. I couldn't quit. I could explain it to Richardson but not to them. What did they care about imperialism? It was something best left down on the coast. I was a friend. We played soccer, told stories. Up here a friendship was no small thing.

We made Gbanga in good time, dropped Gary off, picked up Ernie, then sprawled out on some coffee sacks in the shade of a storefront while the attendant cranked the gas pump. Jameson pulled out a *Time Magazine* and turned to an article about a troop build-up in Vietnam. I bought some oranges and dry biscuit.

We backtracked to the turnoff. The main highway continued to the iron mines in the Nimba Range, but a branch broke for the deep forests on the Guinea side with lots of space in between. "Okay," Scot cheered as we suddenly found ourselves in the bush. "*We're on the road again.* How 'bout some travelin' music now that our upcountry enthusiast is departed, what's eatin' him anyway?"

"He might be goin' home soon," Jameson mused.

"What a ya mean!" Ernie sang. "We *are* goin' home! And a one, and a two—

Goin' to Chicago
Goin' to Chicago
Sorryyy can't take you
Nothin' in Chicago
Girl like you could doooo

"Hey man, where's the uke?" Ernie cried. "I could use some accompaniment."

"I gave it to a kid," Jameson mumbled.

"You *what?* That was a gift, I paid two bucks—"

"He learned to play it in ten minutes. I was impressed."

"Wow! Three yards and a cloud o' dust and he fumbles the ukulele! How 'bout that sports fans!"

"Shut up and drive."

"You really play football at Ohio State?" Scot asked.

Jameson mumbled something under his breath.

"Injured. Spring practice! Junior year! Third string right linebacker!" Ernie was merciless, he pulled down his Michigan baseball cap and went into his sportscaster mode. Like Creighton and I, he and Jameson were assigned roommates back in training, the theory being you had to learn to get along with the least compatible person. "He breaks open! He's at the ten, the five—"

"Where's yer grass skirt?" Jameson countered. "Ya can't play the uke without a grass skirt."

"You knew that! Woody would be proud o' you."

"I shoulda busted it over yer head. That would've been music."

Ernie got carried away as he drove, sometimes going into his disc jockey mode or ad-libbing a Beverly Hills travelogue, but mostly he sang, anything that came in his head, *Motorcyle Mama,* the Michigan fight song, and Jameson countered by stuffing cotton in his ears which he carried with him for that purpose.

Ten miles out of Gbanga and we were in better spirits. The morning mists lifted, two small showers came and went, the sun began breaking through; as it climbed in the sky, cloud shadows began drifting over of the land like herds of lazy elephants. It was going to be a nice day. After Gbanga "upcountry" meant something, a new slant on things, a subtle change of mood. People like Gary didn't give a damn; those like Helga didn't dare; but for anyone who cared to look, it never failed. All the crap stayed behind. Careers. Politics. Didn't mean a damn thing up here. Poverty reigned, true enough, but some surprising things grew from it—forbearance, independence, camouflaged in the same grim faces so easily mistaken for failures. But they didn't see themselves as failures—and that made all the difference. Unlike their educated countrymen down on the coast, they had not the whore "progress" with which to compare themselves unfavorably.

Life was simpler up here. Daily occurrences separated it into two basic components, joy and pain. The doubts that haunt us in the guise of educated abstractions vanished; ideologies boiled down to getting along with a neighbor; success came in the completion of daily tasks; friendships, in the sharing of a bounty. If a hunter had two birds and gave you one, he gave you half his net worth. Both the bird and the friendship tasted of it. Living poor reduced human existence to its barest necessity, the bone-bending labor of hacking out a living from an unyielding forest and making payment with the days it took from your life—but the struggle took on quiet dignity. There was no time to think about life; you lived it, you died of it, and danced in between. On a primitive level all existence is a dance, a celebration of the passing moment over everything that is not life, a victory of joy over hardship.

I loved the ride home. The low hills of the coastal plateau gave way to a higher, more rugged terrain where the unchecked jungle grudgingly let us pass; the road wound through a dense wall of leaves straight up on each side, a fresh scar in the wet earth as though someone tampered with Eden. Green was dominant, every imaginable shade in every imaginable shape. A healthier green. The far off hills emerged in robust energy rising like islands when our view wasn't obscured. They came on apace, a hint of organic purple in the faded olive-gray. Perhaps the deeper colors were due to better soil or the shade from the towering mammee trees. More of them now. It was rare to see them in their entirety but even in part they were magnificent, like somber giants. In contrast, the white trunks of smaller trees were the bones of a skeleton, their thin lines jagged in the pervading half-light. Within, a second parasitic jungle infested the first slashing up and down through the lower stories clinging to whatever it could with groping tendrils, fighting upward to saplings that grew out of crooks in the branches never knowing the earth; and from all of these, intertwined in knots, pulling against each other, a profusion of vines, decay, dismembered branches, lichens and ivies and now and then a flower seemed to float in the air like debris caught in a net. Sometimes silky mosses swept to the floor as effortlessly as stately drapes. Or a ray of sunshine touched a clump of dwarf cecropia reflecting sparks of translucent green light, its minute leaves shimmering like a mirage. Otherwise stillness prevailed. Each leaf hung poised in mute perfection, each blossom held its breath; and when the wind stirred, new life coursed through the green blood of the slumbering Titan. The sound of a single car horn became a sacrilege.

Of course all this wasn't visible from the road. From a moving vehicle the jungle looked as impenetrable as people thought, its detail lost in a blur of motion. Driving through it wasn't enough. You had to walk it—not just once, but often, and in different moods until one day the moods matched, Mine and Thee; you had to walk until the vibrations of your automobile engine stopped buzzing long enough to be replaced by the resonance of birdsong, until your senses acclimated to the flow of moving air, the whispers in banks of lambent leaves, until everything in your mind shrunk in importance leaving it free to penetrate the stillness—and be penetrated. Then the jungle took on a life of its own and spoke to you, like a work of art, telling new tales each time. You had to walk it with enough time on your hands to lose all track of time, until the noise of your life died down and the pool of your inner spirit cleared, until the sounds of dripping water and murmuring leaves took hold and reshaped an inner vision of inert matter on the verge of life; and from there it's but a short step to a feeling for the spirits that animate the trees, the wind, the water, all that speaks to the primitive heart. To know the jungle without the animism within is like knowing a man solely by the writing on his tomb.

Sometimes you came to the hollow of a sheltered clearing so quiet you could hear the housework of a chipmunk. It was like walking in on an intimacy; you felt like excusing yourself and tiptoeing away. Then the light brightened and new patterns unfolded; a new awareness dawned on the dullest eye and yellow butterflies, like flakes of sunshine, flitted away as if to entice a lost soul to a brighter promise.

Six months in the bush, people said half jokingly, and you'd believe in the supernatural—and it was true. It worked on you. You started to see things in a different light, hear voices where others heard noise, not as an alien in a foreign land but a native returned from a prodigal mistake. I'd never believed in the Supernatural. The Judaic-Christian tradition drove a wedge between Nature and the Supernatural, the latter becoming a separate country to be won through conquest, people venturing there returning a bit touched, veterans of foreign wars. But here the rift was unknown. Nothing was more natural than the Supernatural; nothing more supernatural than Nature. Hence the agonizing problem of whether the one produced the other didn't exist. There was an interplay of perspectives, a dance. Depending on your disposition, perhaps the angle of the sun, you saw terror or beauty, savagery or grace, all in the same furry face. Nature held fast its motley kingdoms, intimate secrets, its power, subtlety, its frail beauty built on petals of silk strong enough to conquer mountains. Deep in the forest, after your eye acclimated to its dark stirrings, the two visions married like waters of a singular stream. A birdcall was more than just a bird; a gust of air, a spiney trunk, no longer nature denuded into laboratory specimens but life incarnate; a quiet conviction in its endurance entered the soul. The distinction between birdsong and human language vanished. Only to put it in words. But something said "nonsense", perhaps the ghost of thirty centuries of civilization. But you listened anyway. And there was music. And this could only happen deep in the bush. It vanished like a dream the minute you stepped out on the motor road. You felt a little silly. You looked back at the overbearing presence of the forest, its bleak solitude, impenetrable shadows, lush fertility, and there was nothing to say. You hoped no one was watching. You'd touched forbidden fruit.

What a startling revelation. The entire pageant of existence inside my very soul framed in a human cast. Hence the human-faced god rather than the deafening blow of silence. The trick was to forego gods and men, learning and language, to banish remembrance and swim unbodied in the waters of forgetfulness. The immense silence before which modern philosophers quailed was not the devastating godlessness they imagined, rather the most eloquent speech of all. But these thoughts were difficult to share, they verged on mental strain, as easily spooked as herons off a sleek lagoon.

Time itself moved slower up here. Simple events measured its passing— the drone of insects, the trickle of water, motes of dust revolving in a shaft of sunlight. Things came and went of their own accord. A missed chance was not irreparable, it would come again; no need to press into the future, it could be lived just as well in the past. History unraveled into the fragments of a dream stored in the recollections of old men, dreams took on the duties of revelation, eternity became a day's labor. But once you acclimated to the new order, reality opened like a flower, the problem of existence became nonexistent. It made for the unsettling impression life was unconcerned with its own fate. At first it piqued the nerves—something seemed amiss. You were late but there was no place to go; the world passed you by but you hadn't missed a thing. Then something fell in place, like a pebble in a quiet pool, and when equilibrium returned, you drank of forgetfulness and understanding came as balm to a broken heart. A stone lifted, a tethered spirit slipped its moorings to find the drift of the lazy current, direction in the dreamy sweep of passing boughs, soft smiles in dimpled eddies receding in the stream.

Still the road wound toward us, the villages more isolated, smaller, poorer. Here the task of carving fields out of high bush with machetes and axes discouraged all but the strongest. For long periods we hardly saw a sign of human presence—now and then an abandoned habitation with its roof pitching out of the leaves as if it were afloat on a green sea. Sheer desolation. But then a clue, a meandering footpath beaten into the shoulder of the road, faintly at first, then more visible as it dodged the chuckholes alongside the wheel track. Returning from a day's work on their outlying farms, people followed it back to the village single file in perfect posture under high headloads. As we came up, they would stop and turn against the oncoming blast of dust and air. Sometimes they would smile in spite of it. And a minute later their village rushed past before the dogs had time to bark.

Later on, along a lonely stretch of road, we saw a single human figure moving in our direction. Small, squat, he carried a cutlass tied to his waist, its flat blade flapping against his hip marked the quickness of his pace. He labored under a headload that made him look like an ant; its weight settled around the top of his head exposing only his straining neck muscles. Ernie slowed down to pick him up. (It was against the rules. Insurance liability.) His short legs beat a youthful pace as we pulled alongside. But he turned out to be old, the muscles on his gaunt face drawn taut, his eyes fixed on the earth in front of him like a pack animal. Jameson, a two hundred pounder, struggled to get his load into the back of the jeep. He gave a low whistle stealing a glance at me.

The old man turned childishly awkward the minute he got in. He had trouble finding the door handle, Ernie had to reach back and close it for him. He tried to tell us something in Kpelle while his crooked finger pointed in the general direction of the dashboard. Despite the impasse, he was much delighted with himself and kept repeating whatever he was trying to say, perhaps the name of a village. Six miles later, at the next sign of human habitation—two houses and a shed—he let go a barrage of meaningless syllables as the entire population of five people, a goat, and two dogs surrounded the jeep and made us understand he was going further. As we pulled away he kept laughing and pointing up ahead; he finally said, "Zawzaw," another sixty miles, and repeated it five times as though he just thought of it.

He was old. Tribal society respected age not so much for the wisdom that's supposed to come with it, but as a tribute to having survived—which is a kind of wisdom in its own right. He sat on the edge of the seat in back eagerly watching the road ahead and marveling at how fast the trees flew by. He wore only a sweat-stained T-shirt and a pair of tattered canvas trousers ending in strings at his knees and tied around his waist with a strip of bark, the same that laced his load together. The bottoms of his flattened feet were thick as leather and imbedded with grain-sized pebbles. His arms and legs were scarred but muscular. Only the kinks of white hair betrayed his years. When he laughed his lower gum showed pink with most of the teeth missing and the skin on his face folded into deep furrows. A stubble of white beard grew on his cheeks, his eyes were deep set with wrinkled skin hanging underneath, but within, altogether contrary to his outward appearance, something shined bright. A tough little cookie.

That's what I liked best about them, the upcountry tribes; diseased, ragged and dirt poor, but inside they retained a spark of something rare, a *joie de vivre.* Not always of course, they could hate and deceive and burn with anger, but these violent eruptions emptied themselves as quickly as afternoon thunderstorms. I never saw that unyielding look of burnt-in hatred from our ghetto streets back home. Despite conditions we would call intolerable, they weren't mad at life; they revered it. Its misfortunes they accepted with stoic resignation. Outsiders saw it as weakness; thus their oldest strength turned against them, condemned them to accusations of Uncle Tomism by their educated descendants. The happy-go-lucky Negro too dumb to know he should be angry. No. Something deeper animated the tribal soul. They were a match for their fate, they had penetrated human evil and come out on the other side of anger. Their laughter came with experience, their resignation with the knowledge today's master will be tomorrow's clown. But resignation to what? To the simple truth men are small and the forest great, that our best efforts will come to grief. Or perhaps the gleam in the old man's eyes was the dark fire of life itself, that dogged, damnable persistence that drives men to hang on when every humanitarian rule in the book allows them to lie down and die.

I remember seeing it once before, that dark fire. Walking home three miles below my village, alone, near dusk, I saw what I thought was a black dog. It came towards me trotting easily along the edge of the motor road and at first nothing seemed amiss. But it seemed big for a dog. I looked again. A cat? Then it registered. A black leopard! We both froze—no more than thirty yards apart, it with its forepaw poised in the air, for a split second, eye to eye in the full glare of its awful beauty. Then like a shot, gone! Across the road, two strides up the bank, a crash in the thicket, and pure silence like darkness filling a room after the light's turned out. I never saw a living thing move that fast in my life.

She had the look of a predator—that was it. Not in anything she said or did, rather in the penetrating gaze. That she'd be in the same bar tonight tempting the next likely candidate for a ride to New York, I had no doubt. No, what made the thought of her so startling was the realization there was something memorable in what should have been a weekend fling.

We got to sleep at dawn just as the shopkeepers were opening their stores, woke with the rain in the early afternoon. I went out on the balcony for a minute feeling a bit lost. Soon I felt her slip her hands around my waist resting her chin on my shoulder. "What are you thinking?"

"I was thinking how upcountry rain makes people happy, here it makes them sad."

"You think too much," she said with a kiss. "You remember what I said last night? I wawnt to get New York. Can you help me?" She was giving it all she had. "I hate this place. More today than ever. I haff money."

"Can you get back to Morocco?"

"Is impossible. I cannot explain."

"I'm sorry."

"I didn't think so. You dawn't know how to lie. You're too young." She released her arms and turned back. "You will never he happy," she added with an awful coldness.

We had lunch at a native place down the street. Walking back the world seemed more dismal than ever. The rain stopped but buildings and trees still dripped and weak rivulets ran along the curb. The air got oppressively humid, swollen in the dank scent of the city. Nothing stirred.

We stopped at Charlie #1's. The boss himself was there, a silent Mandingo who remained aloof to the world even as he rode to work in the back seat of his 52 Chevy. I wasn't in the mood to barter. Seeing this, and her, and what was between us, he continued in discreet silence pretending not to see but in reality seeing everything and knowing all along he'd make price on whatever she chose. A simple necklace. She could have taken me for more but didn't. Why in the world had she—

"OW! GOD!" Scot eased back in his seat in real pain this time. Jameson who'd taken over hadn't seen a deep crevice on the right and drove straight into it at a pretty good clip. Like an explosion, the front wheel dropped in, the shocks hit bottom, and the entire chassis lurched to the right lifting us out of our seats and in the opposite direction. Scot landed on the edge of a wooden box wedged in between the two front seats while Jameson fought to keep control. After he came out of it, he downshifted, then leaned forward gripping the wheel with both hands. "Sorry," he winced. All the time the old man giggled with delight slapping his knees with both hands.

CHAPTER 8

MARRAKECH

They hurried onto the platform just as the train pulled in. Both wore coats and ties despite the heat; one carried two suitcases and a cloth valise, the other a heavy canvas bag with electronic equipment. The first dropped his bags and dashed back into the station, the second remembered something and made to go after him but then turned and asked, "Going to Marrakech? Could you keep an eye on our gear?" Soon they were back followed by a porter with a push cart loaded with more equipment, some packed in crates, the rest tied in bundles. A slight hassle over one of the duffel bags followed; they insisted on keeping it with them and after a tip the station chief conceded. All the hurry for nothing; there was still time for a cigarette. "You're American?" he said offering one. "Been here long?"

"About twenty minutes."

"I meant Rabat. You look quite at ease."

"A couple days."

Conversation came without effort and by the time we got ready to board, he casually turned and asked, "Won't you join us in our compartment? We'd enjoy your company."

"I'm afraid I've got a second class ticket."

"We'd be happy to make up the difference; it's the least we can do."

His name was Paul, originally from New Zealand presently in London doing advanced study in geology. Brisk, serious looking, his sandy hair fell loose over his forehead as he placed one foot on a crate and checked something in a pocket notebook. Sidney was a geologist too, a native of London, a blue blood. They were headed for a remote research station in the Sahara where they were engaged in some field work.

Inside they loosened their ties, kicked off their shoes and settled back in customary first class comfort. Soon the steady ka-klunk of the wheels began marking time as the country-side swam past the window. Occasional trees dotted the fields, fresh crops sprouted from the dark fields with a hint of light green and the impression of springtime. A skinny boy in a gray robe took time from minding his flock to mooch a cigarette by lifting two fingers to his lips.

"I expected to see desert up here," I said gazing out the window.

"Actually you're nowhere near it," Sidney answered. "From Marrakech it's at least two hundred miles over the mountains, another fifty to our camp and that's only the edge of it."

"Too bad."

"Good Lord why?" Paul asked.

"I wanted to see some desert."

Sidney looked at me curiously before going back to *The Times*. He sat back uninterested in anything out the window. His distinctive accent seemed aloof at first but mellowed after awhile. He didn't look very English, nor the type for field research. He wore caramel rimmed glasses that disappeared into full temples of dark curly hair, his lips were full, with color, perhaps a bit girlish, the same as his light complexion. If it weren't for his heavy eyebrows and square forehead, he might have looked Italian. I wondered whether I should call him Sid, being a blue blood and all, when Paul said, "Sid and I will be spending most of tomorrow rummaging around for supplies. Perhaps we'll see you again. We won't be leaving until the day after."

"I'm sure we can get together over dinner," Sid added. "I'd enjoy hearing about the Sub-Sahara. I've never been in the bloody jungle."

"It's no place for a geologist," I said. "Take up botany."

"Where exactly is your station?" Paul asked.

"About three hundred miles north of Cape Palmas."

"Then you're practically on the equator?"

"Eight degrees north."

"What are you doing here then?"

"I'm on leave. Thirty days, but not enough money to last that long."

"And what precisely will I find," Sid continued, "if I do take up botany three hundred miles from Cape Palmas?"

"Bush. A few small villages."

"You actually live in a tribal village then?"

"Yes."

"How small?"

"A football field, maybe a little more."

"What's it like?"

"Quiet. Unencumbered. The bare basics."

"Which means?"

"Subsistence."

"Ah."

"No electricity or plumbing I take it."

"Oh no."

"What do you do for...the facilities?"

"The facilities are somewhat informal. I'm not sure what you'd call it in London. I call mine an outhouse, solid little structure, mud with thatch; I'm quite fond of it. For bathing you find yourself a shady spot on a secluded stream or a bath fence in town—a small enclosure of sticks with a gravel bottom. You take a bucket of warm water, sit on a flat stone and pour it over yourself a cup at a time. If you're married, one of your wives might assist. If she's a good wife, she may hum a song. Tribal life has its moments."

"Ah for the life of polygamy," Paul mused.

"I don't think I could enjoy polygamy," Sid pondered matter-of-factly. "One of my ancestors was a polygamist actually. It complicated legal matters for three hundred years."

"But you've all had your baths," Paul observed.

"How does one acclimate to such a life? Yours?"

"Shut off the radio."

"Seriously."

"Try to forget the outside world, let the ritual of the seasons run its course."

"I should think the first necessity would be some sort of contact with the outside world, a radio or something."

"I decided the first necessity was some sort of contact with their world. I figured for every modern gadget I could to do without, I'd be one step closer. So I didn't bring a radio or a camera or a record player, later on I gave away my watch—still got my Swiss army knife."

"I notice you carry quinine tablets," Paul added.

"And I take my shots."

"And how far have you got?" Sid continued. "I mean how far is it possible to escape the twentieth century?"

"Well...I went a whole month before I found out Johnson beat Goldwater."

"Really."

"The Superintendent of Public Works passed through one day—they love their titles. He asked what I thought of the landslide; I thought the motor road got washed out again."

"That's intriguing," Sid remarked after a long pause. "I should think it's impossible to isolate yourself one hundred per cent, do you agree?"

"Of course. I'd be flattering myself to think so."

"I'm still curious," Paul said. "About the election, surely you could have flagged down a passing vehicle."

"I chose not to. You're quite right; it's really impossible to isolate yourself. The present has a way of seeping in the tiniest cracks."

"But surely," Sid was getting agitated, "the ancient superstitions are pretty much intact, do you agree?"

"I suppose. The kind of thing you're talking about, I seriously doubt if they ever change."

"I see. Then even if you do succeed in isolating yourself," he said pushing the argument further, "you can never really experience primitive life as they do?"

"No."

"He's only trying to come close," Paul said.

"Quite," Sid mused, "I'm not disparaging the effort. I'm only interested in whether cultural relativism is fact or if the entire species is homogeneous. You suggest a culture's total isolation is impossible, yet you talk as if it weren't which only begs the question, can a primitive culture exist intact these days or not?"

"Their days are numbered."

"How do you mean?"

"They'll become auto mechanics and secretaries but their culture will die out. And we'll miss them."

"Really? How exactly?"

"It's hard to put into words. They teach us we're a part of nature's ritual, not its master."

Sid bit his fingernail then countered, "But isn't this contradictory? You say they're dying out, then you speak of their ritual as if it were eternal."

"I think so."

"Then modern society proceeds on ritual?"

"Yes. Certainly you don't take the modern world that seriously."

"He doesn't," Paul interjected.

"Good God man," Sid exclaimed, "Will you listen to what you're saying? If this train moves according to ritual, primitive culture has hardly died out. It's dominated."

"I think what he means," Paul said turning to Sid, "is once these cultures die out, we won't be able to make these comparisons." But Sid was deep in thought and the conversation died there. He was right, I never thought of it that way.

It was late when we got to Marrakech. We checked in at a hotel across from the station, had a nightcap then turned in. Next morning they were gone when I got up, but the desk clerk handed me a note.

How about dinner? Sid's still pondering last night's discussion. I'd like to hear more about the Sub-Sahara. Hope to see you later. Paul

I slipped it in my pocket and walked out hoping to avoid the self-proclaimed tour guides—didn't—and wound up taking a taxi to get away. The driver suggested I see the city grand style, in his cab; he'd take me to the Medieval Palace. Madam Kennedy had stayed there once and for that reason I had to see it. He was visibly disappointed when I asked for the marketplace. I spent a morning of aimless wandering in the company of a young boy who quietly became my guide without my knowing it. He knew his way around and seemed genuinely pleased with three francs. We had lunch together on a roof-top restaurant overlooking the main boulevard; at first they wouldn't let him in but we prevailed. The view was stunning. Snow-capped mountains loomed above the city like a blue mirage wedged between the desert and sky; they gleamed in the distance seeming to come near in the bright air. The snowcaps looked altogether out of place in the sunny surroundings of whitewashed palm trees and tan adobe with the golden dome of a mosque in the background.

"Did you have a pleasant day?" Paul asked from the lobby where he relaxed in a lush sofa while Sid sat opposite buried in a newspaper.

"Yes, thank you. How did your preparations go?"

"Well enough. We have everything we need, the Land Rover's packed, so it looks like we'll be off in the morning."

"What's your research station like?"

"It's no more than a series of reference points. We've a small shed for equipment but otherwise everything's portable. We sleep in a tent."

"Then you'll be moving around?"

"Definitely."

"Do you come back to town often?"

"I'm afraid so. With all our equipment we can't take enough supplies to last over several days."

"Do you think I could go along," I asked on the spur of the moment. "I'd like to see the Sahara. I'll try to stay out of the way."

"It's not the desert as you're thinking of it," he smiled. "As for our work, it's no great secret. It's up to Sid of course; you'd have to ride in back on the baggage—"

79

"We'll make room," Sid interrupted putting up his paper. "We're not drilling for oil or anything quite so exotic, merely ascertaining where the Atlas Range begins. At present we're attempting to measure the slope of underground strata leading up to the primary surface eruptions, the most tedious part of the job actually."

"Also the most important," Paul added dryly.

"Right. It wouldn't do for geologists to be theorizing in thin air. It's been done before of course—the measurements—but I just can't trust the results. I've a hunch whoever took them originally must have had a girl here in Marrakech—throws the readings off."

"You know what they say," I said. "Great discoveries are made on the way to lesser ones."

"Good God who are you quoting? Sounds banal enough to be British."

"I can't remember. I really can't."

"You're welcome to come along," Sid added after we had our laugh. "But don't be surprised if you're bored."

"I won't be. Who knows, maybe I'll see a mirage."

"Probably not," Paul smiled. "At least not where we're going."

"To a sane man," Sid explained, "a mirage is merely an optical illusion, only when you're delirious does it take on some sort of psychic reality. I met a man once who said he'd experienced such a thing, but he'd pretty well run amok. By the way, we're having dinner at a little pub up the street—"

"A tourist trap," Paul noted.

"I'm afraid it is," Sid agreed. "But they do have a fairly proficient dancer. You probably won't be bored."

"Oh really." I couldn't help smiling.

"It's a bit expensive but don't worry about it. We're on an expense account and you're not. I understand you chaps are supposed to be living in poverty. I never met anyone who willing chose poverty."

"That wouldn't be me. Real poverty's when you can't afford an invitation to see…a fairly proficient dancer. Only I hope she doesn't throw your readings off, I'd hate to learn the Atlas Mountains begin somewhere in India."

"AH!" Paul let go a shout of laughter, more like a cry of pain. Sid grinned amiably.

The place was nearly empty. It must have been early. A frail man in a fez ushered us to a row of plush leather cushions behind a low table in a not too spacious room, done in maroon with ornate bronze trim; another promptly appeared with menus and a matching bronze centerpiece. Sid ordered in Anglicized French and we waited a long time listening to the haunting strains of Arabic music from four musicians who sat cross-legged on a richly carpeted platform framed with slanting tent poles beneath luxurious cones of red satin. People began coming in in twos and threes, then a large group of businessmen; waiters moved among them like dark apparitions. After dinner Sid wiped his lips and tossed the napkin in the wine bucket, then he leaned back and belched. A little later he ordered a bottle of champagne. After a sip, he leaned near as if to share a confidence. "I say…a gloss of champagne…it wouldn't…"

"Oh no."

She appeared at the click of a beaded curtain off to the side. Neither musicians nor music took notice. Quickly to the center, she captivated the room at once. Calm, as in a trance, one foot flat, one knee flexed through shiny gold strings, arms arched above her head, tight bracelets squeezing warm flesh, wrists crossed, fingers coming to life in the clinking castanets, eyes downcast, pensive in a cloud of waste-length sable hair embedded with rubies and pearls, radiant even in the low candlelight, her top thin as gold leaf, filled tight, gleaming on dark skin, liquid and young—she was desire incarnate. Slow, sedate, she completed a single revolution in weightless perfection, head to the side, faster, barefoot with arched back, tingling bells from tiny ankle bracelets, double dimpled in the lower back, round hips, supple thighs, faster, dazzling within a whirling shimmer of silk, and all the time the deep serenity of her lovely face governed the room in soft radiance high above the pounding rhythms.

There was nothing but to yield.

"Actually," Sid began reflectively—he'd loosened his tie and relaxed, "this has to be the subtlest art I know."

"Then you've missed the point my good man," Paul countered, also relaxed, "art is never subtle. It's straightforward. You should have learned that years ago."

Sid remained unfazed, "You're quite wrong you know. Subtlety is everything. This girl for example. She's an artist because of it. Suggestion is the essence."

"If you choose to live in fantasies, I suppose that's your affair."

"Rubbish!

"Cheers."

"You and your bloody mathematics."

81

"Mathematics and art are quite the same thing as every school boy knows—precise, proportioned, stimulating to the imagination, one is never left...groping."

"The numbers tell the story," I suggested.

"Exactly," Paul added.

"Then you're a classicist?"

"Clossicist my oss," Sid grumbled. "Why don't you just fix your bloody seismograph to her navel and sit back and watch your bloody needle jump? Cheers."

"It could be done," Paul said mildly. "To your health."

"And hers," I added.

"You, sir." Sid frowned severely. "And just how will you explain your presence here should your superiors require...an accounting?"

"He's on leave," Paul complained.

"We have a standard response," I said. "'The taxpayers are getting their money's worth.'"

"Taxpayers?"

"To the taxpayers."

"Right. The bloody taxpayers. Cheers."

"Cheers."

Here the musicians picked up the tempo and she went into another mood, quicker, with rattling beats and rapid steps, not so distant, now with girlish caprice, friendly smiles, teasing, full eye contact, fleeting but filled with language, palms outward, shoulders thrown back, way back, her face laughing at the sky, hips twisting, fingers over her face like a veil, slowly pulling apart, her navel drawn in, now in a dance of its own beating a muted rhythm, skin shimmering like water, mellow, very quiet, then a fresh burst of sharp drumbeats and she responded at once, twirling on twisting tiptoes, round and round, hair streaming outward until she ended on the floor bowed over her knees. After that she visited all the tables one by one, passing quickly between them, her hips leading the way with steps of their own. At ours Sidney adjusted his glasses and she obliged with one hip, beating a furious rhythm, higher and higher, tassels flying, closer and closer, looking down in triumph, then to Paul, straight on, shoulders twitching, wide-eyed delight, bright smile, music in every pore, inviting, fragrant, girlish, now me, oh boy, a wild flourish, savage, robust, the drumbeats came from deep within her hips, showers of joy from a pagan spring, naked excitement, but something softer too, a quiet lyric deep in the grace of her soul, billowing, sentient, hidden on wet lips, dark, delicious, with a hint of forbidden promise, but disciplined, subdued, now eye contact, (oh my God...t' hell with the taxpayers) steady, penetrating, demure, unequivocal in the language of desire...'To you alone I speak as to a dreamer in—'

"Vous etes tres gentil."

She backed away, smiling, found another table, lit another flame.

"Did you know this dance was originally performed only in the presence of women?" Paul asked. "Some sort of puberty rite."

"I didn't know that."

"Do you enjoy books?" Sidney asked next morning from the front seat of the Land Rover. Soon we were out of town and moving comfortably along a paved highway winding through an olive grove with the mountains in the background. We made a good start, though not as early as they hoped. I sat in back on the right behind Paul who was driving. Sidney sat with his arm draped over the seat on what should have been the driver's side. Both wore heavy shoes and khaki work clothes, it looked natural on Paul but a little odd on Sid. "Yes, I do," I said. I couldn't get used to the driver on the right.

"Read anything good recently? Or have you given away your books as well?"

"No, but I don't get much reading time."

"And when you do?"

"Well, I finally got through *Crime and Punishment,* reread *Walden,* started *Ulysses,* but I don't think I'll live long enough. I did come across a little book by Jacob Bronowski recently, an essay really, can't remember the title; anyway he went to Nagasaki shortly after the war and oddly enough came away with a renewed dedication to science. I found it—"

"He's British you know," Sid remarked casually. "I heard him once at Cambridge."

"Wow! What a small world! Tell me about him."

So for the next two hundred miles, save when the view of the mountains overwhelmed us, the conversation rambled on from science to the wilderness and back again. We didn't conclude anything terribly significant but got to know each other. Sid suggested I might find *Two Cultures* interesting. My friends were right; it was good to get out.

They had not exaggerated the remoteness of their station. A single Quonset hut waited beneath a burning sky, minute in the barren surroundings, surrounded by clumps of dry shrubs and scattered crates with two faint tire tracks ending abruptly alongside—the end of the road literally. From the distance it looked bleak and diminished on the empty horizon, like a plaything; up close a picture of abandonment. Had there been a human skeleton, it wouldn't have been out of place. We unloaded the Land Rover and quickly pitched the tent. A Moroccan boy put on water for tea. The three of them went about their work without the slightest notice of me. Good. I felt like taking a walk.

Tan and dull olive, the predominant tones. The mountains had lost their majesty—had crossing them done that?—now they were dark and forbidding, brooding gray with a sense of having turned their backs. The sun-baked earth radiated dry heat. No trace of animal life, rock everywhere. No trees, only dry shrubs with sharp branches that scraped my pant leg, brown grasses and thin-stemmed creepers spread over the ground like disease. Very little green. Small pointed leaves clung to seemingly dead wood. I picked one and bit off the end. Not a trace of moisture, no scent, only a pungent taste to spit out.

I looked back. The camp had quickly receded into the distance. The Quonset hut and the Land Rover looked like toys set off sharply in the late afternoon sun. The vast expanse had grown into something alien, predatory. I went further. There wasn't much chance of getting lost. I had the mountains behind me, clear sky, there would be stars later. But the emptiness began to take on a life of its own, no longer shadows and sky and wind moaning as it kicked over the shrubs, but all of these commingled into a forbidding companion.

CHAPTER 9

THE LADY AT THE CARROUSEL

On the horizon! A tent! Streamers flying in the wind. Banners with big letters. Carnival! One day only! It can't be! Balloons! Orange, yellow. It...I'm not...a monkey in red trousers! White ponies pulling a wagon! Yellow wheels, a spotted leopard in a cage. And a carrousel! Three rows of leaping stallions, black hooves, racing round and round, silver bridles up and down, lights flashing on and off whirling faster and faster. Oh for a ride. Just once. I'll clean my room, I'll drink my milk for a week.

There's a girl! Golden hair streaming in the wind, her face in a magical trance. But not a sound. Only the creaking of the wooden floor and the lift bars turning in their sockets and every time she comes round she has a different face, first white, then African and Indian and Chinese, even Eskimo like the boy in the story but all the time it's the same girl. People everywhere. Jugglers! Acrobats! Clowns! One with a big red nose and fat yellow shoes. And a hurdy-gurdy man with a little dog. And an elephant! He's bigger and bigger and a man with a towel on his head sitting on top and a ballet lady with pink underwear standing on a horse. And grownups with little glasses with good things to drink, men in black coats and white shirts their mothers must have ironed all day, and fine ladies in shiny dresses and furry things crawling on their shoulders and they smell like the stuff that comes out of the funny bottles in Miss Wilkensen's store, and music from an ump-pah-pah machine, the drum banging and the cymbals crashing. And one of the ladies is taller and taller her dress is just as tall as she is and she looks right at me every time and knows all your secrets, but doesn't say anything, she's not like the others, her dress is all shiny and dances when she walks and tiny pieces of glass hanging from her ears blinking on and off and tied around her neck like tiny mirrors you're not allowed to play with and bunches and bunches of golden hair with swirls the way Grandma makes the frosting on your birthday cake you're not allowed to touch until she lights the candles and then you take a big breath and try to blow them out. And there's a man and he's the luckiest man in the world all he's got to do is ride the merry-go-round all day and not go to school, swinging in and out between the pipes and push a drop of oil on the squeakies, he's bigger and bigger like a motorcycle man with a black beard and fat arms with pictures of snakes and he smells like the stuff that makes the motor go and a red handkerchief around his head and greasy pants with a monkey wrench in the back pocket so he can fix the ump-pah-pah machine and he's not allowed to smile cuz he's tough and he'd squash anybody who said he wasn't, you can hear him whistling when he collects the tickets and he knows I haven't got a ticket, and it's real quiet like the wind in the window when it's nap time and the curtains play tag, but now there's music and it's the sweetest music anyone ever heard and the man wants to sing and it's the same song as the ump-pah-pah machine and it's the most beautiful song anyone ever sang like the opera man when he sang in church and Aunt Rosie said he tried to break the windows but if he breaks the windows he'll have to pay and the words are far away but they sound so close like the voice down in the furnace pipe, the one that knows everything even your birthday.

> *The Danube ain't blue*
> *It's brown. It's brown.*
> *These ladies ain't true*
> *They've been. Around.*
> *The diamonds ain't fake*
> *They cost. A mint.*
> *And silk ain't O-paque*
> *You get. A hint.*
> *They come from up town*
> *In lim. O-sines.*
> *Their names are renowned*
> *Like French. Cuisine.*
> *Oh why can't you see*
> *can't you see*
> *can't you see*
> *What I'm trying to…*

And the music's coming from all around and people dancing and popping big green bottles and a man with a shiny silver dish with good things to eat and he's not spilling even one and paper streamers and confetti and a man whispering something in a lady's ear and it's taking him a long time and the birthday cake lady smiling like sunshine and fire crackers shooting in the sky then big flowers falling down BANG and people looking up and the white pony scared and the ump-pah-pah machine banging its drum like crazy and the floor turning faster and faster and the horses leaping higher and higher and lights flashing brighter and brighter and the monkey wrench man swinging out from behind the horses. Oh for a ride. Just once. Please just once.

> *They Pow. der Where. it's Round.*
> *And they Per. fume Up. and Down.*
> *And a French. man Fits. their Gowns.*
> *But their daddies you see*
> *Are Harry Yett and Browne*

Please Mr. Monkey Wrench Man. Just one little ride on the merry—

> *Their Hair. comes From. a Sink.*
> *And they Flaunt. a Lit. tle Mink.*
> *And so sure. ly Do. they Think.*
> *As they strap on their rocks*
> *Their dirty socks don't stink*

And people whirling and laughing and more green bottles popping and white stuff fizzing over the top and more big flowers up in the sky BANG like somebody turned on the lights and an ump-pah-pah band with red coats and gold buttons and the players with fat cheeks blowing their horns and people with their arms around each other kissing and crying they're so happy and the man still whispering to the lady only her eyes are closed and a man fell off the merry-go-round but jumped right back up and another man helped him and one of the fine ladies fixed his tie and the Birthday Cake Lady smiling like sunshine. Oh for a ride on the merry-go-round. I'll never ask for anything again as long as I live. Please just once.

> *In Dain. tee Sil. ver Shoes.*
> *They eat Li. ver Wurst. and Booze.*
> *Take a Drug. to Get. en Thused.*
> *Oh your life must not be*
> *As frivolous as this*

And now the Birthday Cake Lady is standing next to the Monkey Wrench Man and she's holding his arm just like in church, only he doesn't look like he goes to church but she doesn't care and here comes the music again, only not the ump-pah-pah band, some old men in shiny black coats and white shirts their mother's must have ironed all day and they look like they're at a funeral and someone is singing but very far away, only the Monkey Wrench Man isn't singing and neither is she, only it feels like she is and it's the softest and sweetest song in the world just like when mama sings at bedtime.

> *Oh why*
> *Can't*
> *You*
> *See that you're scaring...the crown*
> *wearing...a frown*
> *world's upside down*
> *Oh my love let's try to turn it around*
> *The trick is to dance when you're down.*

And now the Monkey Wrench Man is standing behind her and they're both looking down at me but she looks so sad, like when you're sick and the doctor says stay in bed and the song is even softer and sweeter than before, like an angel in heaven who hasn't got anybody to play with and the Monkey Wrench Man is looking down and feeling pretty bad like he wants to cry only he don't cry cuz he's tough and he'd squash anybody who said he wasn't and she's looking at me and smiling so soft and the singing is coming from her and she's telling me to be brave and go to bed now, only I DON' WANNA GO TA BED!

> *Oh*
> *Look*
> *At those tear...drops run right on the ground*
> *down on the ground*
> *making no sound*
> *Oh my love let them fall all over town*
> *The good earth will surely abound.*

I WANNA RIDE THE MERRY-GO-ROUND! I'll take my medicine. I'll go to bed.

> *ROUND and ROUND!*
> *And AROUND!*
> *Like a turning top*
> *Like a burning plot*
> *And AROUND and AROUND!*
> *All you have to do*
> *Is watch Harry Yett and Browne.*

Now there's another kid and he doesn't have a ticket either. Lots of kids! No shoes, and their clothes all rags and dirty and they look sad like when people think you've been bad and you haven't, one's black and one brown and one Chinese and another one his belly's sticking out but he's skinny and looks old and yellow stuff coming out of his eyes but he isn't crying and another little girl has an empty pan and it's chipped and dirty like the one Grandma keeps in the barn to feed the ducks.

Well
Then
Child why are you wearing a frown
When the music and laughter abound
And those teardrops keep running right down
When the merry-go-round goes around

Give me something to eat. My head is hurting. My eyes burn and my knees hurt. There's an animal in my stomach with sharp claws. Please something to eat. A piece bread, please before I die.

Oh
Tell
Me why are you skinny and weak
When there's pate and plum sauce and meat
Simply feed your poor worms some of these
Just say pass me the caviar please

But they can't hear us. The noise is getting louder and louder and the ump-pah-pah machine faster and faster and the horn blowers redder and redder and the man with the stick madder and madder and the singers higher and higher their mouths open so big they could swallow double-decker sundaes and they're all getting ready for a big bang at the end and if they break the glass they'll have to pay.

TOO! DAMN! BAD!
Just because
YOU! CAN'T! PAY!
So you've
GOT! NO! DOUGH!
Don't you know
It takes a buck to get into the
TOO! DAMN! BAD!
YOU! DON'T! RANK!
You GOT! NO! DOUGH!
You come back when you've broken the bank!

It stopped! Quiet. Real quiet. The whole place abandoned, only the sand sliding over the dirt and the wind crying low, flapping the tents and it's dark inside like the mouth of a giant sleeping and a paper bag tumbling across the street and someone's coat tied to a scarecrow, an empty shoe and a half-eaten candy apple. The platform of the carrousel half-buried, the horses broke, the pipes all twisted, the big drum smashed. Wires hanging out of a rusty box on a light pole, one of them with sparks. There's the little girl on the merry-go-round, maybe she knows what happened only her hair's all white. And she's dead! And her teeth are hanging out of her face! I wanna go home.

Run my darling run!
Faster and faster!
Fast as you can!
Run to the cellar!
Under the house!
Hide in the coal bin!
Keep like a mouse!

CHAPTER 10

MISSION IN THE DESERT

Ghost town. A shabby storefront. Movie posters, *La Dolce Vita,* advertisements, Dr. Quigley's patented foot powder, a faded red gas pump leaning off center with a cracked bowl—high test supreme with no-knock additives.

"Can you direct me to the Mission?"

"But this is it."

A tonsured monk finished filling a wine bottle with gasoline, came forward extending an arm of welcome; he wore a Notre Dame athletic jacket over a brown robe, a dirty white rope around the waist, wooden cross. "I'm so pleased you've come," he said, "You don't know what it means when old friends come back." He's talking as though he knows me; I've never seen him before. "And how is dear Professor Marcos? Does he still dabble in taxidermy? Would this younger generation were as careful of lost souls as he with stuffed rabbits."

A dirty flap of canvas covered the dark entrance, like the mouth of a giant sleeping. Something's wrong, he's too friendly.

"Come inside," he said.

A great vault but open sky. Gray clouds and circling birds. Vultures! A bombed-out cathedral! Gothic. The stained glass gone, open windows crisscrossed with lines of laundry, statuary crumbled, roof beams fallen in. Small fires smoldered in dark recesses, wraith-like forms sulked in small groups around bubbling kettles. Weeds, heaps of refuse, broken bottles, rusted cans, old tires, a scrapped washing machine—and a scrawny crab apple grew out the side of a compost pile in the nave, its upper leaves reaching for light but overcome by poison ivy that jumped to the wall and spread like a fan. Dogs slept on the altar, chickens scratched in the dirt, but the stones held, unmoved by whatever blast gutted the place; a real shame, it must have been elegant in its day. Deep strains of Gregorian Chant resonated in the background, strong, masculine, like cool water on a stinging cut. Behind the chancel, three hooded monks labored dismally, lowering a gilt-framed painting into a hole. Carrion dogs sniffed the air. A masterpiece.

"Fifteenth century Florentine," he answered.

"The Madonna?"

"Perhaps."

"Why are you burying her?"

"She's immoral."

"You mean immortal."

"Try to understand. Madonnas…eat a lot."

"Why are you wrapping her in burlap?"

"Burlap is chic,"

"You mean Cheap!"

"Inexpensive. Please lower your voice."

"BURLAP IS SCRATCHY!"

"We are under severe budgetary restraint!"

Still the Chant—deep mournful, far away, like the voice in the furnace pipe the one that knows everything, even your birthday.

We walked along a dirt path. The voices seemed to follow us in pure fidelity. I thought I heard a flutter of wings. We came to a makeshift scaffolding built over the altar. Electronic equipment, speakers, loose wiring tangled and taped leading to an overloaded fuse box hammered into the choir wall. A hand microphone off to the side.

"A rock concert. We try to keep up with the times."

Up above a grand theater marquee hung over the pews complete with nymphs, cherubs, golden trumpets, its running lights dancing on and off, yellow and white. A workman in a cherry picker placed square red letters into a white frame: COMING ATTRACTIONS. TONIGHT. DIRECT FROM LAS VEGAS.

To our right someone had fixed a wooden beam across the far end of the southern transept. A single strand of homemade rope held a chain pulley from which an automobile engine swung dangerously over the open hood of a small coupe, its front end up on blocks. A wiry young man in greasy jeans and longish blond hair struggled furiously under the great weight. A tattoo on his biceps. Mother.

"Billy Grimes. One of the neighborhood kids. He's been in a little trouble."

"What's he doing?"

"Restructuring his vehicle," he whispered.

"He's trying to drop a Cadillac engine into a '36 Ford Coupe. It won't work."

"He needs more power."

"It's not going to work."

"Have faith."

"He's gonna need more than—"

He turned and smiled. "Do not feel badly if you cannot fathom the intricacies of esoteric matters. Theology does not lend itself to the casual acquaintance of the lay public, nor bear on the day to day commerce of the lay world."

The Chant strengthened.

"How many voices do you have?"

"A hundred and twenty."

"Where are they?"

"We have discreetly placed the speakers out of sight."

"Speakers?"

"Yes, we have a complete stereophonic system with floating turntable and eight track feed. It brings out the bass rather well, don't you think?"

"But why hide the speakers?"

"As long as people *think* there's a real choir, that's all that matters. What they don't know won't hurt 'em. Once again may I suggest you do not trouble yourself over ecclesiastical concerns."

"Then I've—"

"Been listening to a recording."

"All my life—But where do you get your power?"

"…Underground," he said furtively.

"You mean—"

"Shh. We can't be too careful. With Rommel and his accursed tanks chasing back and forth—"

"Rommel? Tanks? But the war's been over—"

"The war is never over my son." And he clapped a fatherly hand on my back. We approached a small lean-to at the back of the choir. He genuflected then pulled a plastic cover from a turntable resting on a bust of St. Jerome. His Master's voice. A frail monk with boney feet and his knees drawn up to his ears sat next to it dutifully watching the needle rise and fall with the warp of the record. "Brother Knute is thus serving penance for playing with his base balls during vespers," he explained rather severely as the other went contrite with shame. "And that's twice!" he added with a smart rap across the knuckles. Behind the turntable two thin wires, red and black, ran along the ground then straight down into the earth. Something seemed to be ticking— not really ticking, more like a tiny heartbeat. Like a bird.

"Can you hear it?"

"The Chant? Uplifting isn't it?"

"Shhh." It's getting stronger—like a pecking within an egg. "Not the Chant."

A look of concern came over his face, "There could be a short in the system."

"Not the stereo." It's getting louder. Throbbing. Distinct from the Chant. Not Gregorian. Very old.

"Perhaps a loose tube?"

"Listen! Can't you hear it?" It's clear, growing. Definitely not in the Chant, but with a life of its own, rising, louder.

"But of course," he said looking heavenward as if struck with the solution, "there must be a scratch—"

"It's not the record."

"Perhaps a grain of sand," and he bent low to blow it off. I grabbed him by the cowl and gave it a yank.

"It's not in the record!" He looked shocked. "Forgive me Father." It's getting louder. "I know I've been less than exemplary." Now a rhythm. "And you've made sacrifices on my behalf." Repetitive. A simple five beat rhythm, happy, joyous. "Do you hear it?"

The pulse kept getting stronger, defining itself. We stood straining to hear. He kept looking behind him. Only the dismal walls, thin wisps of smoke like strands of witches hair rising off the rubble. His face went from curiosity to concern. He kept looking at me.

"Drums."

"But Gregorian Chant has never used percussion accompaniment to my knowledge."

"Under the Chant. Very faint. They must be in the forest."

"Forest? This is Desert. People have seen these visions before."

"It's not a vision!"

"Believe me they are unnatural."

"It's not unnatural!"

"But this is the twelfth cent—"

"Twentieth."

"Yes, twentieth. Miracles don't exist."

"It's not a miracle."

"Try to be calm. Can I get you a sedative? Brother Knute is remarkably skilled with herbs and chemicals."

"No."

"Perhaps if you spoke with Dr. Novatny—"

"No!"

"These…these imaginings are the work of the Dark One."

"NO!"

"The Dark One has powers—"

"I'm sick of your damn supersti—"

"DO NOT TOY WITH THE DARK-_."

"SHUT UP!"

"I beseech you—"

"It's NOT something bad! Can't you see what I'm trying to—"

"I see you're sincere in your conviction. This is commendable. Only let me remind you—"

"I gotta get outta here!"

"It is forbidden to leave these walls."

"Forbidden?"

"Yes, once safely inside, why go out? It's madness."

"Well, if you never go outside, how the hell do you know what's inside?"

>*Drum! Drum!*
>
>*Drum a can o' sun!*

"They're drowning everything out! ARE YOU DEAF?"

>*Run! Run!*
>
>*Can a drum o' sun!*

"Come my son. We'll check out the wiring—oh God have mercy look at what you've done now!"

"Well, you tripped over it!"

"Look at what you made me do! You've defiled Our Most Holy—"

"Nothing's defiled! You don't need that stupid toy! You've mistaken the technology for the music!"

>*Drum a ton! Sun'll come!*
>
>*From a drum a son'll come!*

"The forest! They're in the forest!"

>*Never mind the holy see!*

Here's the only sea for thee!
In the frothy foamy feline sea!
Holy lady waits for thee!

"Forgive me Father."

"No! You'll be lost forever!"

"LET GO! Damn you let go!"

"You'll never find your way!"

"Forgive me Father."

"There are demons and deceivers!"

"Good-bye Father."

I looked back. The whole place receded into a dream. I could see it as though through a curtain of gauze. There he was, kneeling before his beloved idol lovingly watching it revolve while its frozen passion sang of spring. He never heard the drums. Maybe he was hard of hearing. Forgive me Father.

Outside a fierce sandstorm. Clouds of dust, wailing banshees, sand stinging like snakes. Where am I? Why did I come here? Oh to be home again. The long driveway with the drooping elms, the swing under the cherry tree, the key to the back door under the eave. Buster would bark then catch my scent and swish his tail. What's that? In the ground? A black face with wisps of sand moving over it, filling the eyes, but the lips are moving, whispering, "Lost." I know I'm lost. I need to find...There! Sticking out of the sand. A big pipe with a ball on the end. A little house. Iron wheels. A German Panzer! Half-buried in the sand, iron cross on the side, tracks gone. Climb up. The hatch...light as a feather. Jump down. Dead German! Teeth laughing. Skull covered with cobwebs. Sand running out of his head. Get out of my...Here's your hat. Afrika Korps. An officer. Must've got lost.

Lili Marlene. A radio! Wow! Some kind o' reception. Wait a minute! 57 Chev! Just like Skip's before he wrecked it. Garter over the mirror, two Trojans under the seat.

"Vhatever you do Mien Herr, remember ziss. Zomeday, you vill have to come home."

Faint. Fading out like an electric banshee.

"It's sunny and mild, seventy-three degrees with offshore breezes ten to fifteen knots on a very pleasant Sunday afternoon here in downtown Cleveland. This is Jeff Masters playin' the favorites for you and you alone here on Radio WERE twelve forty on your dial where you'll find easy listenin' each and every day twenty-four hours a day, so if you happen to be cruisin' down Shoreway Drive with your best girl by your side, lean back, relax,

traffic is light to moderate, slight congestion at East Ninth, and to keep you company here's Bobby Helms, You…Are My Special Angel."

Push button tuning.

"All flights to Seoul, Anchorage, and Los Angeleeze have been cancelled due to high level interference. All passengers are cordially reminded the cocktail lounge is now open. Thank you for flying Unavatican."

Five stations.

"Do not touch…the last button."

What can be so bad about…the banshee again. Try the knob.

"Mission accomplished! Let's take 'er home Jack!"

Not you. The other…far away…like the voice in the furnace pipe.

"The information you are requesting is classified. Unauthorized personnel—"

Screw you.

"Under the dark sycamore Jenny. Only the owls and the swallows Jenny."

Almost had it. I know you're in there.

"Why die boys? You know you can't win. The Imperial Japanese army will gratefully accept your surrender…"

I'm close. Real close.

"Sand bunker…early…trucked in…five a.m."

Yeah.

"Nervously…field glasses."

That's it.

"Horizon…streaks of dawn…"

Come on Baby. Don't fade out now.

"Secrecy…told only…reaction…within the hour…"

I gotta know.

"Witness…own eyes…unalterably the course of human history. Robert J.—"

Oh no.

"Mutual Broadcas…"

No.

"July sixteen, nineteen forty-five, Alamogordo, New Mex…"

CHAPTER 11

DAWN CANTATA

Dreaming again. There'd been an accident. The night Skip wrecked his car. 57 Chev. Hottest thing around. I went for help but couldn't find anyone. Strange.

Early. Birds singing. Sun up. Outside the village was beginning to stir, familiar sounds sang in the morning air—the soft rhythm of women pounding rice, a clank of a metal pot, roosters, the shrill cries back in the bush. The crescendo had passed. It came every morning like a reliable clock peaking precisely at the first hint of light, shaking the trees as it swept through the jungle like a tidal wave, smashing open the deepest sleep in celebration of a new day—and accurate too. I timed it. Why did they sing so violently at daybreak? I never bothered with questions like that before.

Now human voices too, shouts, greetings, kids about their chores, men on their way to their farms, doors opening, water tossed out. The absence of mechanical noise amplified natural sounds and at first they made my nights uneasy, but with time I learned to trust them. I stretched a bit and thought about the coming day, the trip, the chicken hutch, a story for the third grade. Perhaps Nanook now that he's old enough to hunt the great seal—

"Teacha! Daydobah pooling you roostah tai'!"

"Teacha, da lie!"

Their cries came from the other side of the mud wall only a few feet away; they played there every morning often waking me with their soft chatter. Constantly under foot, eager, hungry—they were always hungry—they lived next door and tried to help, anything for a "dash," usually a banana or an orange. Jacob was ten, maybe eleven—they didn't keep track of birth dates—but an undernourished body made him look younger; Daydobah wasn't in school yet, but had already picked up enough English to deny his constant mischief which I tolerated more than I should have, at least it was a sign of health. The last two survivors of six children, which wasn't unusual, they stuck together out of fear, more so since the recent death of an older brother, and if one got in a fight, the other struck at once as though their fate were one.

The day was up. Dawn rose from within, like water filling a well, unveiling the green jungle from its thick mists. Now the first beams of pure sunlight were pushing through, a sure sign the day would be bright. My bedroom had only a small window facing east. When morning came, a dark gray apparition began to materialize until it defined itself as a window and framed the lower branches of a drooping palm at the edge of the jungle fifteen yards away. It had been scary at first. That first night I hadn't slept. It seemed morning would never come. When it did, it brought the sight of a dense mass of alien foliage so savage it might have been another epoch. It struck home then, as it never had, just where I was. But after awhile the palm tree got to be familiar and I looked forward to seeing it every morning. Now the sunlight filtered through, first on the sill then the wall where it set the uneven surface in relief exposing the hand prints of the builders who'd squeezed wet mud into the skeleton of sticks and vines, some of which stuck out like ribs, one had even taken root, a tiny green leaf bathed delicately in the sunshine. My house was alive in many ways—a dull gray fungus clung to the ceiling mat (the roof leaked) and by putting my ear to the wall I could hear termites, like a small electric motor.

The furnishings were spare. The bed, a crate serving as a night stand, a dresser made of more crates lashed together, a footlocker, and beside it under the window, my one real luxury, an adjustable cloth bottom chair with a footrest—the village carpenter made it for me working only from the memory of a chaise lounge he'd seen at a *qwi* house in Zorzor. Six dollars. But a solid success; I usually read a little before retiring. *Ulysses* lay unfinished; couldn't get into it. Junk cluttered the rest of the room, a machete, an axe, a flat soccer ball, mosquito netting—I couldn't get used to sleeping behind a curtain of gauze, it felt like a cage. A shiny red clock lay on its back like a fallen soldier. A clock was an encumbrance up here. People got up with the sun and went to bed at dark. Originally I used it for school which was to begin at seven-thirty sharp and proceed by orderly forty minute periods, but one day I was late; so not to screw up the schedule, I set it at seven-thirty. Nobody noticed. Soon I realized it could be seven-thirty whenever I wanted. In fact the first order of the day was to wind the clock and set it at seven-thirty, the kids vied for the privilege until John Tellywoiyea snapped the spring. What a relief. Never late once. The taxpayers were getting their money's worth. True, the Mandingo storekeeper had a clock but purely a status symbol and rarely on time. And once Taanu, a young man about my age returned from Monrovia casually wearing a new silver watch high on his wrist. He was quite the dandy until his friends found out he couldn't tell time. After that he didn't wear it again.

Now the sunlight stretched across the opposite wall. Then it dropped a bit and touched a peg half way up. Time to get up. Only two new mosquito bites. One good stretch. It sent a small house lizard scampering up the wall onto the screen. My jeans hung from a branch I'd found in the bush; it grew in the perfect configuration of a three-pronged coat hanger. I took special delight in these small discoveries. It wasn't the five cents saved on nails but the thrill of finding something familiar in place so alien. Coat hangers and a good many other necessities grew perfectly formed; only it took a new way of seeing to find them. Spooky really, as though something out there knew you were coming. Likewise I'd entwined a fragment of broken mirror with strips of bark and fixed it to the wall. Needed a shave. My tan was deepening. Some of them joked I was turning black. After checking for spiders, I pulled on my boots and yawned. It was going to be a fine day.

When I opened the back door, Daydobah bolted from the doorstep. "Goo' moni' teacha," Jacob said pleasantly. I took down my toothbrush from a peg above the rain barrel. Daydobah inched his way back. He wore only a single garment, a pair of faded red breeches two sizes too big. Continually pulling them up into his armpits, he was always ready for a chase, his quick eyes and one adult tooth enhanced an impish appearance.

"Teacha, he teenk you comi' to catch heem," Jacob laughed.

"Why would I want to catch him," I mumbled still brushing, "so he can kick me again."

The three of us smiled remembering the time he tumbled into the privacy of some bigger boys. They caught him and tied him to my clothesline by his breeches. When I answered his screams, I found him swimming in midair and he fought like a cat thinking I would punish him further. Not all his mischief ended so easily. Once he'd really frightened me after I realized what happened. He'd found a bee's nest, got stung of course. When they brought him in, I hardly recognized him; his face was swollen so far out of proportion that the bridge of his nose looked like a second forehead separating two half closed walleyes. The skin on his lips had puffed up smooth, his distinguishing features lost. But he was taking it like a man, ignoring the laughter of the older boys, hurt but not crying. Then somebody brought a mirror. It began innocently enough, just to show him how funny he looked. While he gazed at himself someone said something in Loma. All at once the veins on his neck bulged, his mouth gaped open, violent convulsions racked through his body and the piercing screams seemed to be coming out of the jungle, not Daydobah. Jumping like a shrew, he banged into the wall shrieking uncontrollably. Then he pressed both fists to his forehead while two streams of tears raced down his face and around the new tooth gleaming in his lower gum like a splint of raw bone. "Teacha, he teenk de genii do i'!" Telleywoiyea cried. Then I understood. When he didn't recognize himself in the mirror, he thought someone had "witched" him. The evil process was at work changing him into something vile, a lizard or a toad. He went wild with fear. I could feel it when I took him in my arms. There was nothing to do but wait until his own exhaustion calmed him down and he stood there shivering, tears all used up, his shrieks weakened into dry moans. Then he coughed till he threw up. What monstrous voltage of terror must have shot through that frail body. How swift the strike of the supernatural predator. "There are many things in the bush," they were fond of saying, and they weren't talking about coat hangers. Uncharted powers lorded over their misty world. Witchcraft reigned. Yet they survived. In three days the swelling went down and he was up to his old tricks again. I loved these kids.

I splashed some water on my face and Jacob was right there with a towel. "Ey Daydobah," I sighed ruffling his hair. My backyard consisted of one dead tree stump, a small garden not doing too well, a few square yards of "lawn" then the wall of the jungle shot up like a fortress dwarfing a small chicken hutch underneath. I'd put it there to take advantage of the shade but it proved a mistake. Within days young tendrils reached down and took root in the thatch, the jungle reclaiming its turf. I walked back and peed in the grass. Jacob checked for eggs. None. There hadn't been any for a month now. Why? Rhode Island Reds were supposed to be a hardy breed. It had to be the climate. But that was the whole idea, "To develop new strains of domestic poultry capable of withstanding tropical conditions." So said my bold objective, written in ink and by now filed away somewhere down in Monrovia. I smiled at the thought of it. Not that it was a bad idea, only up here paper objectives soon gave way to real needs and my new strains had a way of winding up in soup pots before they had a chance to reproduce. Chickens were meat, meat was food—so went the logic of hunger. Still I kept the project going, perhaps a growing fondness for the crowing of roosters at daybreak, but I could hardly put that in a progress report. I dreaded going in to see Richardson. He'd be sitting behind his neat desk beneath a photograph of Kennedy, exuding confidence. At his right, a detailed map with a colored pinhead at each project; at his left, the flag; throughout the office, American superiority unchallenged. If I told him my project was a failure, he wouldn't hear of it. Failure was unacceptable. I'd get a fatherly talk, some advice on how to word things in a progress report, and presto!—one stroke of bureaucratic witchcraft and failure becomes success. We're winning the battle, he'd assure me. But it didn't work for me. Up here no eggs for a month meant no eggs for a month.

The foot path from the main part of town passed beneath my bedroom window then disappeared into the forest through an opening in the foliage that resembled the mouth of a cave. As if to hesitate, it dipped gently beneath a medicine post, two sticks supporting an overhead crossbar bearing a light bundle of vines wrapped tightly around something that was supposed to keep out evil; but in time, the whole thing began to droop, overcome with ants and lichens, looking more a part of the forest than anything man-made and people passed beneath it paying not the slightest heed. It brought to mind a Civil War statue in the town square.

I decided to take a walk before school. My one diversion. Surprisingly they understood—perfectly; the white man's way of communing with the spirits he left behind. So it had been at first, but after awhile "home" took on an added meaning. Before long, Jacob and Daydobah came skipping up behind me, the latter holding up his breeches with one hand stretching the other to Jacob who gave him some paca nuts. After a few yards the jungle closed in behind us smothering the familiar sounds of the village. Now the bush. Only our footfalls to mar the spell. How abrupt the transition, the stark savagery of entangled limb and thorn. Immersed in pure silence. To hear it, rather to feel it, was to drink of the river of timelessness. I couldn't explain it, but it never failed to shore me up for whatever hassles the day would bring.

The wet trail wove effortlessly through green lushness hanging in dumb profusion while powerful limbs thrust upward through taut lianas and knots of undergrowth bursting with life. Somewhere within, the low drone of insects continued in perpetual undertone like a motor propelling the universe. Bird cries pierced it like audible lightning. After awhile I asked, "Do you ever dream at night?" It was considered foolhardy to tell your dreams in public, but the rules didn't apply to kids. I didn't think they understood so I explained, "You know, when you're asleep and you think you're somewhere else then you wake up in your bed."

"Teacha, I know," Jacob responded eagerly.

"What do you dream about?"

"Las' ni'. I no drea'." Neither had Daydobah.

"But the last time you did, what was it about?"

He thought awhile keeping his eyes on the path, then began. He spoke in a bubbling, high-tempo accent elongating vowels, dropping final consonants, creating the rhythms of his own language, the language of drums. I'd given up trying to correct their pronunciation, a task as hopeless as correcting the birdsong and just as absurd. "One ti'," he said spitting out paca nut pulp, "I ca' drea' we be comeeng i' de bwush, me a' Daydobah a' da boy Dwoiyou, he not attendi' to schoo'. We see Isaac Kezelee faddah, he be skinn' de re' deah. De ton' falleeng o' de grou', de eye beeq. Plenny mea'. He say, 'You boy! You he'p me coddy i' tow'. We he'p heem coddy. We see da' o' lady, she no' go' de tee', she loo' li' di'," and he made a toothless smile, "She be cleani' de mea'. We ea', we ea' plenny."

We smiled at Jacob's dream. Their dreams usually revolved around food just as mine with being lost. That was it! Lost. I came to a deserted gas station to ask directions only it was a monastery. A monk invited me in; we got into an argument over some trifling affair. It seemed I knew him. Father Marcos! Once he caught me playing with my baseball cards during instruction. He asked me what I'd give for two DiMaggios. I asked him what he wanted. He said a Christian, and I knew exactly what he meant. He died my junior year. I never had the heart to tell him I'd left the Church.

After a bit we turned back. Soon a file of women came toward us, an elderly lady with dangling breasts led the way greeting me in Loma; she walked with gentle ease under the strain of a headload turning only her eyes in greeting. A younger, full-breasted woman followed carrying an equally heavy load tied up in a porcelain pan. She remained silent. Tribal women had to be careful about keeping the correct social distance; they couldn't be too familiar with strangers but the proper greeting was essential. Two school girls came after them and greeted me in English; they both carried headloads on their way to the outlying farms where they would work and have a bite of breakfast before school.

"Teacha?" Jacob questioned after they were out of earshot, "You be drea'—i' de slee' ti'?"

"Oh yes…I dreamt I was at a fine celebration with many fine ladies and gentlemen, music and dancing."

That's it. A formal affair but I wasn't invited. I wanted so much to be like everyone else. Then a beautiful woman, like an actress, way out of my league.

And a mechanic in greasy jeans. Couldn't place him. He was whistling a tune. What was it? Right on the tip of my tongue. Then he was singing, as though he were giving me directions, but it sounded like a nursery rhyme. Then drums and a big explosion. It must have rained last night.

When we got back to my house, John Mulba and Moses Y. had the teapot boiling. We'd mercifully shortened Yakparwrodlo to Moses Y. the first day of school after a brutal contest trying to pronounce each others names. "Wha' you do-eeng I' de bwush?" he asked in mild amusement.

"Taking a walk," I said.

"Dose o' ma' to Quolidobu' sto', dey be loffing o' you. Dey say you go' de medisan', every morni' you go loo' see."

"No medicine, taking a walk."

"They are superstitious old fools," John said severly.

John Mulba, my best student, already a bit of a rebel. Where was he getting it? Surely not from me. I'd made every effort not to rock the boat. Slim, taller than most, but with perception beyond his years, about sixteen, he quickly became my confidant. And in tribal terms he was a marked man because he'd cheated death. A few years back, he'd suffered a prolonged case of hepatitis that steadily sapped both flesh and spirit until they'd given him up—the drums of the dead had begun, he remembered them himself. But his mother, a frail but bright-eyed woman and hardly a rebel, snatched him from the medicine men, who to this day thought her touched, and in desperation started for the Mission in Zorzor, thirty five miles away, at night, with John tied to her back. Somehow she made it. There, recovery came slow and he was moved from the hospital to the home of an American missionary family where he began picking up English more out of gratitude than anything else. During his convalescence, he witnessed what must have seemed miracles to a tribal boy who'd never been out of his village—his own blood cells under a microscope, voices coming out of a radio, words frozen into print. By the time he returned, he was dedicated to the idea of educating himself. "To know book" had become his passion and more than once he got me out of bed in the morning to confirm something he'd read. His mind turned slowly, but once it grasped an idea he never let go. His English for example, it was forced but unusually articulate, only a slight accent. On learning a new word, he would repeat it once, then carefully store it in his ordered memory. Accordingly his thoughts followed the same pattern, deliberate, well-reasoned, intense, always the reliable John Mulba, even when his feelings got the best of him as he related one of the tribal superstitions in half anger, half shame. Physically he had a youthful face with smooth skin over soft Negroid features that usually carried the serious expression of early manhood but easily changed to a boyhood smile when his mother beamed with joy to know her son excelled at school. Anger rarely ruffled his quiet surface, but once aroused, how quickly it became the proud vessel of African Nationalism, and an apt one at that for he had the inward qualities to match—sensitivity to his heritage, integrity, fierce pride—all of which, I feared, could easily make an unyielding revolutionary if future circumstances should choose him. Even so, he had difficulty fitting back into tribal life after living on the Mission. People said he acted like he wanted to be white and some took it as an insult. They looked askance on his mother's intervention and his recovery as unnatural acts. In his dilemma he turned to me for friendship. We were remarkably open with each other. He even confided to me his most secret desire, to go to America to study medicine, speaking of it with the conviction of a pilgrim seeking Mecca. I hadn't the heart to tell him his chances were nil. Christ he didn't have five dollars for the trip to the coast.

He sat cross-legged in the chair, poised, holding the tea cup in his index finger as taught on the Mission while Moses squatted on the floor with his back against the wall holding his between the palms of his hands. He wore no shirt, his skin carvings came up his chest and branched out to his arms. "Did it rain last night?"

"Eh, my frien'," he smiled in sympathy, "you canno' see de watah?" Right. My rain drum in back had been full to the edge. They noticed things like that. I didn't.

"I thought I heard rain last night."

"Firs' ti' you co' you canno' slee'. Now you slee' like o' ma'."

"I'm surprised you didn't wake up," John said politely. "Pass the pineapple please."

"It sounded like drums," I said, "you know, on the roof. Or maybe it was drums."

Yes! Drums! Now I remember. In the dream. I heard drums but everybody thought I was hearing things.

"Did you hear drums?"

They stole glances at each other, then John spoke in a low voice, "Yes, there were drums."

"Well then, I'm not hearing things after all. Good tea. What were they for?"

Again stolen glances, again John answered low, "When drums play at night, do not ask what they are for."

"Ah, *The Poro?*"

Their silence told me to be careful. It was bad form to ask about *The Poro*.

"It's our law," John smiled.

"Dey ca' ma' medisan on us," Moses added. "Fo' we talkeeng." Though they could joke about it, both still believed in medicine. I knew Moses did and beneath his book learning, I suspected John too.

"Well, whatever it was," I smiled, "they were awesome. I'm beginning to like your music." At this they both laughed. "Well, I can at least enjoy the music can't I?" They looked at each other, paused, then burst out laughing.

After breakfast we cleared the table and went out on the porch. Across the road smoke curled upward over the rooftops. The round old-style houses with inverted clay pots over thatched peaks predominated, but the newer zinc roofs which required square frames had begun their assault on tradition. The two styles did not compliment each other in the least but they reflected a culture in transition. They also made for a quick index to the wealth of a village if zinc were tallied against thatch. We had thirty some thatch and six zinc—the chief, two elders, a rich Mandingo, Jacob's father, and mine, but I paid rent, the only one in town who did, and Jacob's father worked on the section gang, the sole wage earner for miles around.

I had three rooms, a bedroom, a kitchen, and a narrow study with a separate entrance from the side. I called it my study, but it served as an office, a clinic, library, and a ready gathering place for the kids when they weren't in school. A few steps beyond the porch, the ground began falling away until it leveled off at the edge of the motor road that cut through town like an empty canal severing my house and two others from the rest. I was never part of it, but from my porch I could see the entire width of the village, only the compass directions seemed wrong, the reason being the northbound road formed an S beginning several miles back and by the time it got to town, it actually went south. Thus east became west, and given the fact the sun kept to the northern quadrant half the year, I never did get my bearings.

The village had already come to life, work being less strenuous now than in the crushing heat of midday. Women were pounding rice. They beat it with smooth poles in wooden mortars filling the air with a soft rhythmical thumping, so soft it often put to sleep the babies tied to their backs. Men walked briskly about their business sometimes stopping to examine a leg of fresh meat or a bunch of green bananas hung from a rafter for sale, kids chased each other in and out, goats rummaged in refuse, chickens scratched in the dirt, the sound of metal on a whetstone came from the blacksmith kitchen. Now and then men or boys came to the steep embankment and urinated into the ditch below. There were no streets, no design nor spacing of the buildings; they seemed to grow out of the ground, different sizes, facing different directions, sometimes in clusters bound together with flimsy fences. There were "quarters" but they had more to do with family lineages than street plans. And beyond the housetops, no more than a hundred yards away, the forest once again rose straight up, silent, inscrutable, with a desolate beauty shrouded in mists as though behind a curtain of gauze.

Across the road old Quolidobu dragged open the rickety doors of his one-room store, an enclosed porch tacked on the front of his house. He carried the usual stock of cloth and kerosene, trinkets and candy, lanterns and soap, but also a rare item or two, a tin of Norwegian sardines or a tiny vial of cheap perfume which seldom sold but became the talk of the town when it did. Men gathered there to meet their friends and get the news. Indeed the old Mandingo even had a radio which he played sparingly, batteries being dear upcountry. One event they never missed was the local news broadcast each morning in a host of tribal languages. When the magical box began to speak in Loma, they crowded round sometimes gesturing in response. But before that, at sign-on, when the morning gloom seemed grayest, it broadcast a few bars of a Viennese waltz, and the contrast to the surrounding environment could have been no greater had an Austrian princess stepped out of a carriage and six. Whatever I was doing, I paused to listen and forgot the century.

Nor was it unusual to find a modern gadget uncomfortably fixed to something from their world—like the prongs on my birdcage. It hung from a rafter, empty now, woven of twigs and raffia fiber, and in true tribal fashion of making do with whatever you had, the builder had fashioned, for a door, a three-pronged copper electrical switch—God knows where he got it. It came with a bird, a rare bird, silvery gray with a band of green turning black on the wing tips and tail. I bought it for two dollars, cage and all, and tied it to my porch rafter. At first it flourished and sang of hope, "Sing song SWEET," but after a few weeks it seemed to pale in its dismal surroundings, "Song ring WEAK." Then one day I opened the switch and let it go. Soon I had a small scandal on my hands. They talked about it for days; some laughed and shook their heads, others thought it an extravagant display of wealth, Quolidobu that his goods were defective. A rare bird was something to display, only a moron would let it go. Two dollars! Even John Mulba found himself hard pressed defending me. I apologized and they smiled their acceptance, but for weeks they continued to regard me with a sense of disbelief, except Old

Zubah, the town eccentric, whose penetrating stare met mine with a intensity I wanted to think was not disapproval.

I was in my study going over some school work when they brought her in. About Daydobah's age, she wore only a threadbare strip of cloth tied around her hips. Two older girls eased her through the door. "Teacha, de gir' go' de ba' so'," Mary Kolu said. They needn't have told me. The putrid smell of jungle rot preceded them. A puncture, a scratch, even a mosquito bite and the infection set in. Rotting began as soon as the bacteria entered; they fed in the open ends of capillaries sealing them off. Hence no bleeding. In time yellow puss gathered in the crater that grew each day, sometimes to a diameter of two inches and nearly deep enough to see bone. All you could do was swish away the flies and watch your own flesh disintegrate. We took her out on the porch and set her down with her ailing leg stretched out on the ledge. It was in the calf just below the knee, tied with a strip of stained cloth, the excess liquid running down her shin like tears hardening into a wet paste then into yellow flakes. She looked at me apprehensively. "What's your name?" I asked in Loma. "Kalya," she answered shyly. When I asked where she got it, she looked to the older girls for help. The fire had bitten her. I dampened it with warm water but when I removed the rag, she flinched as it tore open the scab. A clot of puss came with it. The other children stood by unabashedly fanning the air in front of them; Daydobah, under foot as usual, right next to me quietly holding his nose. Mary and Elizabeth Ziamoe looked away, too ladylike to show an outward sign of offense. The odor was overbearing. I fought to hide my revulsion. She braced herself when she saw the bottle of alcohol. When the cotton touched open flesh her leg jumped but she gave no outward cry. Amazing how they accepted physical pain. It seemed they saved their loudest cries for mental anguish, like Daydobah's. Flies buzzed around settling in it and on my fingers. This one showed no sign of healing; cleaned out, it looked like an empty eye socket. After dabbing it dry, we packed it with sulpha powder and wrapped it with clean gauze. "Tell her to come back tomorrow."

By this time the school kids began to gather along the motor road. When they saw me come down the path, two small boys darted to the blacksmith kitchen to ring the assembly bell. Some went on ahead with their books balanced on their heads; others dawdled, dancing in place or chasing each other in a halfhearted game of tag. They sensed books were something special to me so they vied to carry mine hoping the power would rub off. Though still in the elementary grades, most were in their teens, the school having opened only five years ago. Despite the late start, those who came, usually of their own choice, already knew enough English to converse with each other, unlike the townspeople, most of whom knew little of their country's official language.

The schoolhouse was about a half mile out of town, away from distractions, an altogether pleasant walk in the morning. It didn't look much like a school, rather a crumbling mud structure with sagging rafters and a leaky zinc roof that became a griddle in the noonday sun—you could hear it ping in the heat and I was afraid a good wind would bring the whole thing down. Nor was its existence as an institution less fragile. If they ever decided to walk out, I would have been left holding the chalk and we all knew it. Compulsory attendance was the law, but back in the bush that didn't mean much. I would have looked ridiculous trying to enforce it. Still our school had something others didn't. Those who did come, came with a desire to learn, and that made all the difference. They didn't save tough questions for outside of class and they challenged me every time I said something that defied their reason—like the existence of germs, for them as unseemly as us believing in spirits. The battle raged for weeks. Finally I borrowed a microscope from the Mission and the excitement lasted all day. Even some adults came to look. One in particular, an elderly gentleman much learned in the ways of the jungle, peered through the glass for the longest time and when he lifted his face, his eyes met mine, and for a brief moment an unspoken understanding spanned the ages that separated us. He said nothing, but I couldn't forget the look in his eyes.

Soon Quolidobu's store disappeared in the papaya leaves, the motor road gently fell away from town, swept over a culvert and climbed a steady grade for another half mile before curving into the bush. The culvert consisted of two corrugated steel pipes running side by side under the road. High enough to stand in, just right for playful boys when the stream allowed; every morning they hurried ahead, broke off down a path on one side, ran through the pipes screaming, then reappeared scurrying up the opposite bank. At night however, it became a rendezvous for those bold enough to recognize the silhouette of a sweetheart in the dark shadows with only the sound of trickling water and their own whispers.

"My padagra' eez abou' de leopa'," Peter Kpudumah cried as he came running up.

"Great."

"Spe' me leopa'," John Zubah challenged.

"Ella—e—o—p—a—ah—d! Leopa'!"

"Das fine boy," Zubah taunted patting him on the head.

"Ah you zee! Teacha, I wi' konk his head-oh!"

In a flash they were chasing each other back up the road. "Where's Akwoi?" I asked, turning around just in time to catch Mary Kolu mimicking my walk. They all had good posture from carrying headloads. I slumped forward and it struck them as terribly comic.

"You rang, sir!" Akwoi. Right behind me all the time. He and John Mulba were my two brightest students. Although he lacked John's seriousness, his mind ran just as quick. Language came easy; he spoke with practically no accent and well enough to mimic others, including me. Jokes, tricks, spontaneous bursts of dance, he never failed to brighten my day. Mimicry was his specialty. His on-the-spot interpretations of "White Man Walking Barefoot" never failed to bring the house down.

"And just what are you supposed to be?"

"I am your butler," he answered strutting along in exaggerated dignity before launching into a mile-a-minute explanation. "You must pay me twenty dollar all right okay ten dollar and I am at your service, as you see I am okay five dollar I will be—"

"All right what have you been reading?"

"Okay, all right, I have been reading a sublime mystery about an English man who had very great plans only his butler was not discreet, vaddy bad guy, and now it is a most interesting case for Mr. Sherlock Holmes and Mr. Doctor Watson. So you see my good man—you boy! Do not interrupt as I am talking to teacha!—you will pay me okay all right two dollar and I will be discreet."

"Discreet! There's nothing to be discreet about for two hundred miles." They loved our sparing matches and leaped with delight when I shot back. "And where did you get those spectacles?"

"They are to help me read important words!"

"They are to help you make monkey out of me." Again a cry of approval. "I do not wish to see them inside the school, sir. Where's Kwokwoiyea?"

"Heah he," Moses said.

"How you doing?"

"Teacha, I feeling fine."

"Good. I'm going to be taking a bush trip, wanna come?"

"Teacha, whe'?"

"In a few weeks, after exams."

"Teacha, wha'?"

"To Kpodokpodo."

"I' fa' oh."

"I know. But I've heard it's a fine town, next to a mountain, and not many people go there anymore."

"But you don't know the way," John Mulba responded eagerly.

"We will have to ask the old men. I will try to make a map. Will you go with me?"

"Thank you." They were always ready for an adventure.

"What about you?" I glanced at Akwoi. "Could I impose upon you to join us? If I'm not being…indiscreet." Another squeal at the sight of him caught in his own net. They loved repartee. I'd scored one on their champion and they danced with delight. He answered with an exaggerated rooster strut but quickly broke off and ran back gleaming with excitement.

"We will find it! Do not worry! I have also heard it is a fine town, but it is far-oh." The "oh" at the end of an expression meant a silent exclamation to convey excitement when a shout would spook things away, an old hunter's trick. "We will carry good things to eat in your knapsack, yes?"

"Sure."

"I comi' i' schoo' today," John Telleywoiyea announced as he ambled up tearing a strip of sugar cane in his teeth.

"What's the occasion?" I asked, but he didn't get it. "It's a good day for hunting isn't it?"

"I co' so I ca' know some de boo'."

"Glad you could make it."

Telleywoiyea was the biggest boy in school, like a tree, solid, immovable. The size of his fingers and the angular bone structure of his face hinted at the great frame from which his heavy limbs hung like crossbeams. Among us he came to the forefront due to sheer size rather than anything else. Everyone knew better than to try to change his mind. At first I was afraid he'd hurt somebody if he ever got mad but he never did. He came to school occasionally but didn't progress. He was intelligent in his own way, handy with a cutlass, surprisingly graceful at soccer; but school work, especially reading, the words played tricks on you, one day they said one thing, the next day another. Just the same he eagerly waited his turn to read. When he did, he coiled over his book gripping it like an anvil, his great hands driving it into the pit of his stomach while his calloused toes dug in the dirt. His muscles flexed, his forehead knotted, his eyes darted from word to word. The harder the words, the harder he clutched, closing his head to the page as if the words had to be cornered like fish in a trap. His face twisted into agonizing shapes as he tried to formulate sounds totally foreign to his tongue. He stumbled through the second grade reader grunting the words one by one with excruciating effort. And no one dared interrupt.

"Tommy…had…a…pet…labum."

"Lamb. This time the "b" is silent."

"Laaama. Whe' Tommy wen' to schoo', Judy—"

"Jeremiah."

"Jadamadda…wou' try to…"

"Follow."

"No! Jadamadda. No! You…ca' no' co…i' schoo'.""

When he finished, his muscles relaxed and he looked up for approval. If I said, "Very good," his face broke into a great white smile and his eyes danced. If I got on him for something he should have known, he answered with the same great smile and I was quickly ashamed of my impatience. He was incredible! Primitive man's first attempt to enunciate himself. A living specimen of an extinct species. To watch the concentration in his face as he squatted on the ground cracking palm kernels was like watching a cave dweller run his thumb over a sharp stone. I fancied him my "noble savage" though he was hardly a savage. He wasn't really very noble either; he had a fine collection of dirty stories and a fondness for bouncing slingshot pebbles off village dogs. A child in a Herculean frame, reasoned effort came hard, planning or discipline not at all. He lived by pure impulse. When he did the right thing, it came on a whim; if it were wrong, he seldom understood why later on. Dictated by whatever excited his fancy, his deeds followed a life of their own. Once something set him in motion, there was no telling how it would turn out. He might stop to clear a neighbor's cassava patch of intruding goats, but it could just as easily turn into a fiasco as he ran behind yelling and kicking their legs out from under them. He could share food with smaller children but also box them on the ears if they got in his way and the next minute turn his attention to deriding the plight of a toothless old cripple. When he laughed he practically squealed and when he cried, like the time his father's youngest wife unjustly accused him of stealing, the tears rushed down his face in open streams.

CHAPTER 12

WHISPERS IN THE DARK

Outside night burned black. A single kerosene lamp lit my study. Its bright globe cast eerie shadows on the mud wall, gnats orbited the chimney, sometimes a moth. Familiar objects seemed to draw closer together—the steel medicine cabinet, the table, tottering bookcase next the door, makeshift shelves on mud bricks bearing odd specimens of shells, bird nests, bones, even a rooster egg—the beginnings of the natural science museum—only the beginnings, nothing ever got finished. *The Encyclopedia Britannica* grew green mildew; faded posters gave the far wall some color, a castle on the Rhine, the Seine at dusk.

The evening meal over, my study became a hangout for the young people of the village; they took to me at once—I don't know why, I'd never been very popular. Their loud play went unchecked and my loneliness drowned in a bubbling undercurrent of chatter and excited giggles, wide eyes and bare feet, protruding navels, round heads, all jammed into one room overflowing onto the porch where conversations turned to shouts and arguments to wrestling. The activity seldom stopped, never went stale; there were challenges, wavers—yes a railroad engine could pull a ship and a ship could carry an engine but an airplane couldn't. The smaller children enjoyed picture books. They sat on an army cot under an outdated map of Africa, cuddled together with their bare arms dangling over each other and their legs not quite reaching the floor, quietly leafing through the same books time and again, turning the pages together and pointing things out to each other. They looked at Hong Kong and Rio, watched Lap children drive reindeer across the tundra, hardy fishermen haul in a net of herring, a Sioux bowman take aim at a stampeding buffalo. Sometimes they pressed their hands against the pictures as if to feel the life within.

"Teacha, who di ma'?"

"Long John Silver."

Sometimes they took up an encyclopedia and pretended to read.

"I ca' rea' yah!"

"You lie!"

"No yah!"

"Teacha, de boy telling stodies'."

"Okay, you boy, wha' da wo' say?"

"He say a'pla'."

"What di wo' say?"

"A'pla'."

"You lie-oh."

"No yah!"

Tonight things were more lively than usual. We were making final preparations for our trip to Kpodokpodo. Originally planned for last March, put off twice, Creighton egging me on as though it were something momentous, it was now or never. Tomorrow John Mulba, Moses Y., Akwoi, Kwokwoiyea, and myself would leave at the crack of dawn. Kwokwoiyea and Moses practically lived in the bush. On the other hand Akwoi's gift of gab would see us through should we encounter a different dialect. He already knew Kpelle and taught himself to transcribe Loma phonetically.

With Kwokwoiyea quietly looking on, Moses squatted on the floor carefully fitting sardine cans into my knapsack. Akwoi beat back the little ones trying to help. We agreed to travel light but when it came to food they ravaged my cupboard for everything they could carry, canned fruit and "fish cup" were delicacies. They studied the packs trying to figure out how to fit two more cans when Telleywoiyea thrust his head in the door and reminded me I owed him twenty-five cents. I reached in my pocket—no change.

"How 'bout a can o' herring?"

"No!" Akwoi shrieked. Too late. Telleywoiyea pounced. One sweep of the paw, argument over.

"The packs are full," I said. "We'll kill ourselves carrying them."

"We will carry them!" Akwoi snapped, "Not you."

"Your back can hurt too."

"We canno' tiah to caddy goo' ting to ea'," Moses explained.

"Well, we won't starve."

By now Telleywoiyea was opening one of the cans. Not bothering with the key on the bottom, he squatted on the floor punching the edge with the tip of a machete; when he got halfway around, he carefully bent back the jagged cover, took one out, smiled, threw back his great head and dropped it in. He chewed it with the tail hanging out of his wet lips; that disappeared too and a drop of oil ran down his chin while he licked his fingers. "Teacha is swee' so," he smiled happily. "Telleywoiyea, gi' me so' yah?" Elizabeth Ziamoe asked pleasantly. He gave her one, then six more excited voices cried out but he silenced them with a sharp grunt. With that he turned and went out on the porch, found his friend, Taanu, and offered him one.

Taanu was a year or two older, but aptly described by the ancient Greek expression, "No longer boys, not yet men." Although technically "men" after the rites of *The Poro*, their behavior up to the time they took their first wives remained that of unfettered youth, much to the chagrin of their elders. Taanu had recently taken his first wife, a shy young girl who raised her eyes to her new husband as quietly as a pilgrim at prayer; yet he still hung out with his younger friends. After the incident with the wrist watch, he was forgiven his one flight of vanity and quickly returned to the personable friend we knew. I had the suspicion he would have liked to come to school, but he was Mandingo (Muslim) and they weren't allowed. I tried to explain I wasn't a missionary, but their headman only nodded amiably in complete misunderstanding.

We took a quick inventory, decided we had everything and were about to go over the map when Telleywoiyea boasted that he too would soon marry. Ignoring him, we bent over the table. "Well, this is it," I said. "I worked on it all afternoon, it's not to scale but it'll have to do."

"We canno' lose a way yah," Kwokwoiyea said politely. He didn't have much faith in maps.

"Okay. Here we are and here's the motor road. First we go to Goseh's farm, take the trail to Yiamah, so far so good. Peter Kpudumah's father is chief there so he'll help us find the way to Bworpu. Maybe he will give us a guide."

"We do not need guide. He will eat too much."

"Teacha, Telleywoiyea say, I' he no fi' womah, he wi' maddy da o' lady, she ha' one eye loo' di way, oddah eye loo' da way."

"After Bworpu, Dawawoli, then Kpodokpodo, then Bolahuhn and out to the Voinjama motor road. But between Dawawoli and Kpodokpodo, that's where it gets interesting. We know Kpodokpodo's on a mountain, so the Lofa River has to be on this side. So there has to be a bridge. But where? Did you ask the old man?"

"Yes," Akwoi said. "He has been to all those towns. He says there is a town between Dawawoli and Kpodokpodo but one day back track."

"What about the bridge?"

"He say, there is a bridge."

"When was the last time he saw it?"

"It be long time. He is very old."

"Did you ask the others?"

"Do no' worry, my frie', we wi' fin' a way," Moses said quite calmly.

I smiled. "There's no reason we should get lost, but your bush has a way of defying reason, doesn't it?"

"Kpodokpodo canno' move i' de bwush," Kwokwoiyea added quietly.

Just then an explosion of laughter out on the porch scattered them in all directions. Taanu staggered down the hill doubled over, then David Beyan and Isaac Kezelee, last Telleywoiyea ambling after them licking his fingers and dodging small boys at the same time. Flumo James practically fell in the study; he had to hold on to the door frame to keep his balance. "Teacha...Telleywoiyea say..." He grimaced as if lifting a great weight, "Telleywoiyea say...if he no fi' womah...he wi' maddy wi' de goa'." Then he dropped to the floor into the middle of a checker game.

"You boy! "You stupi'!"

"You moof fro' da yah!"

But he couldn't, he rolled over shaking while the checker players tried to shove him off. Moses carefully stepped over them and shouted from the doorway, "Telleywoiyea ma'! You crazy!"

"I hope he has many fine sons," I said putting up the map. Akwoi quickly relayed the message in Loma and there was another outburst, followed by goat sounds and further taunts. Telleywoiyea answered by throwing back his furry head and dropping two more herring into his powerful jaws.

I'd gone back to the checklist when all of a sudden the noise shut off. Old Fawkpa's massive form filled the doorway. When he saw me he knocked verbally, "Pok-pok," then stooped under the doorframe moving very deliberately. The checker players scurried out of the way and Flumo James got up and went out. The old man looked at them severely but didn't say anything although he must have thought their behavior impertinent and me indulgent for allowing it. He couldn't understand sparing the rod. When one last giggle escaped, he wheeled around ordering them out with a single syllable more like a bark. He stood glaring after them, then, very slowly, his outstretched arm lowered and found the inside pocket of his robe.

Our meetings were awkward, our friendship grotesque. I respected him for his strength and generosity, tribal virtues, yet he seemed to be embarrassed by them; and he respected me for my literacy which he somehow associated with respectability. We didn't know enough of each other's language to sort things out; I couldn't get across to him it wasn't necessary to call me "sir." Once a "so-so big man" from the District Commissioner's Office came through town with a written directive for the chief who happened to be away. Since his time was valuable, he gave the letter to Fawkpa, the chief's brother. That day I learned the awful burden of illiteracy. With his eyes staring at his bare feet, the letter kept turning over in his hands as if by its own volition as he told the man in pidgin English the business would be attended to. When the man turned to go, he remained in the same spot without lifting his eyes.

Fawkpa learned his pidgin English down on the Firestone Plantation where he'd gone to work as a young man. There he gave eleven years in exchange for his keep and a token wage. One night there had been drinking and an altercation outside the barracks. As someone of his stature, he stepped in to break it up, a jeep pulled up, a white man got out; they were summarily fired on the spot. No questions, no appeal. He went away in shame bearing a guilt that wasn't his, bearing it quietly for years before returning to his native village with nothing to show for his labor but the deep scar in his pride. He'd lost face—and nothing hurt more to a Loma man. When he spoke his "small English," he did it with downcast eyes and when current rubber workers passed through town, he retired to his compound. Yet when the village built its first school, he cut the timber himself. The day I arrived his first word was "Sir."

That he should call me "sir" after the injustice he suffered at the hands of Americans, I couldn't explain—he, the brother of a chief, returning to his native village pennyless, without news, in the back of a cargo truck with coastal ruffians for traveling companions. Perhaps his silence was just what it seemed, the sign of a strong character. I'd never know. Talk didn't come easy for him. Whatever the reason, he paid for it by losing the esteem of the younger men. And he must have known. Whatever the news, he faced it in the same stoic reserve ingrained in the deliberate movements of his tired limbs, his downcast eyes going white with cataracts.

"Goo' evey sah," he said quietly.

"Good evening. How are you?"

"I feely fi'."

An awkward silence followed. I took out my chair and set it in front of him. He looked like he would have preferred standing but didn't know how to decline, so he took it and sat ill at ease in the middle of the room, his massive legs folding around the sides. He obviously had something to say but waited for me to begin. "I see you have some carvings." A crocodile and a bird in fine detail. He would want me to sell them for him knowing I had "connections."

"Tomoddow, you go Voinjama?"

"Yes, but we're going through the bush, Kpodokpodo and Bolahuhn, then Voinjama from the other side."

"Ey my ma', you takey de lon' way."

"I know. I want to see Kpodokpodo. I've heard it's a fine town." I thought of showing him the map but remembered the letter.

"He fa'."

"Then you've been there?"

"He be lo' ti'. Befo' motah roa'."

"Is there a town between Dawawoli and Kpodokpodo?"

"Eh, no."

"Is there a bridge...over the river." He looked confused.

"Dey Loma peopo. Dey wi' he'p you—"

"Teacha! Telleywoiyea say—"

John Zubah. Not realizing Old Fawkpa was there, he came barging in, either sent or suckered. You just didn't interrupt an elder. The old man rose in fury.

"Aieee! You no see de ma' talky busy!" He meant "talking business." A low giggle leaked out. He nearly turned over the chair, clearing the room with one sweeping gesture, then stood like a statue leaving only Moses and Kwokwoiyea who kept respectful silence but stole glances at each other. Very slowly, he turned back around, his huge arm found its way inside his robe and he settled back in the chair. "Dee schoo' boy dey frisky," he snapped. "Dey no ca' respe'."

"I know," I said trying to put him at ease. "You should hear them when I speak Loma." Big mistake.

"YOU MU' BEA' DEM!" he boomed.

Again an awkward silence. "How far to Kpodokpodo?" I asked hoping to turn the conversation.

He thought awhile then held up some fingers. "Fo' schoo' boy, ta-dee day; fo' you, fou' day. To Dawawoli, da one o' ma'. He na' Zobodu. You asky. He show you de way."

Zobodu was an old friend; they'd hunted together as boys. I thanked him in Loma and when he got up to go, I walked with him as far as the motor road. He said good-night and disappeared as quietly as he'd come.

As soon as he was gone, the kids came flooding back, noise, paca nuts, jibes. Telleywoiyea came last, "How you say da one, you clean you fa'?"

"A razor damn it! And tell Zubah no barging in when I'm with an elder! Same rules as in town yah!"

"De razah," he repeated. Out on the porch he straddled the ledge and began opening the second can of herring. How two? He must have swiped it when we weren't looking. Not long and another outburst rocked the place. Again they danced away falling over each other. And again Flumo James scattered the checker game.

"You stupi'!"

"See de ma'!"

As they wrestled someone's foot struck the end of the bookcase and one of the shelves came down along with a healthy clump of mud. When the whole structure started to tilt, Moses lunged for it just as Jacob Jallah's father stepped into the doorway deftly reaching up to catch the top while David Beyan rolled out of the way. The older man seemed amused with it all. Then from outside a shrill voice sang out, "Telleywoiyea say, if he no fin' womah, he wi' maddy wi' da ma'.

"Telleywoiyea ma'! You crazy!" Jallah shouted into the din, then to me, "I te' you teacha de ma' crazy."

Eventually they steadied it long enough to tie the top to one of the rafters. Then he tested it, examined the knot, and finally turned to me. He needed some vitamins.

"For you?"

"My bruddah chil'."

"Where is the child?"

"To Kotitown."

"Why does he need vitamins?"

"He ha' de waddum."

"How do you know he has worms?"

"We see. He belly beeg, li' so," he gestured with his hands. "He sma'-sma'. He ea' bu' he aw-way hungry."

"Okay. I'll give you a bottle of vitamins, but they don't cure the worms. Do you understand?"

He nodded. "Vitamon maybe hep him be strawn'."

"Maybe, but they don't cure worms. You must take the child to the Mission for treatment."

He nodded assent as he took the bottle raising it in a gesture of thanks. I wasn't sure about the vitamins. They seemed to think anything that came from a bottle could cure what ailed them, that the effectiveness of a medicine resided in the person administering it. One old woman swore I cured her toothache—with vitamins.

I'd quite forgotten what I was doing. The map. "We're going to make it," I said to Moses brushing a cobweb from his back. We took a last glance at it. Pretty shoddy. Then I folded it and shoved it in the knapsack. It was anywhere from three to six days to Kpodokpodo, one more to Bolahuhn plus another to hop a ride to Voinjama and back. I estimated a distance of eighty-five miles but maps could be deceiving. Bush trails had a way of taking their time, testing a man before showing him his destination.

When it was time they started filing out of the study, yawning as they said good-night, the little ones first then the girls. I blew out the lamp and followed. Outside I found my favorite post, the one that fit the small of my back where I enjoyed taking in one last breath of night before retiring. Across the porch Telleywoiyea had the other post, Taanu sat on the ledge chewing a strip of dried meat, Flumo James and Isaac Kezelee slung out in the hammock. The others sat where they could, their low voices close in the growing stillness. The crickets in good form.

"Teacha, you ca' belie' da one?"

"Which?"

"Dey say," Kezelee began, sitting up in the hammock. A bright-eyed delicate boy, he loved telling stories. "I' da town to de Guinea si'—"

"Nwegutown," Taanu said.

"Dose peopo stupi' too much i' da town," Telleywoiyea cried.

"Da ma' he com i' tow' he walking backword."

"Da no' how de stody go."

"I telling de stody!" Kezelle shouted. "De ma' be walking li' di'. He got up and demonstrated. "Da ma' say, 'I am genii, you see me, you no see.' De peopo stupi'. Dey no loo'. He stea' da trousa, he ru'."

"Da no' how de stody go," Zubah said as soon as Kezelee finished.

"How does it go then?"

No one spoke. Rakish glances shot back and forth. It was going to be a good one. All the girls were in town by now. Flumo James said softly, "He no' go' de trousa."

"What?"

"He no' go' de trousa," Telleywoiyea said out loud.

"You mean he came in town—"

But I couldn't finish. When it settled down a bit Telleywoiyea continued, "He co' I' tow'—"

"I moofing fro' heah yah."

"De peopo see heem. Dey see he bu' wa' re'," he ended with a grunt. The porch convulsed, the crickets stopped.

"How many times do I have to tell you. Pronounce your final consonants. HiS buTT waS reD! Not, he bah wah rah."

This time their cries sent the birds scattering. Kezelee tumbled out of the hammock, Matthew Zawlaw stumbled over a dog. Still, Telleywoiyea wasn't through. Straining, he continued, "He see de womah. Dey look 'is bu'. He say, 'Excuse pleese, I go' de deesontoddy.'"

One last shot rang out, loud enough to spook another nest of birds. With that the porch emptied. As quick as wind they were down the path and up the opposite bank, Telleywoiyea and Taanu leading, then David Beyan and Daniel Zizi, Flumo James running doubled over, John Zubah, Kezelee, the others close behind. Their dark forms darted between the houses and disappeared. Kwokwoiyea and Moses said good-night and started down the path, their amusement more subdued. "Tomorrow morning yah," I said.

"We see," Moses smiled turning around and walking backwards effortlessly.

With that, he too scampered up the bank and disappeared. A soft serenity gathered in their wake as though Night were settling in her nest. Rice birds came fluttering back to their favored tree. A plaintive cry came from somewhere down the road. Then the frogs, buzzing insects. And the crickets. Right under my feet! A pulsing concerto in effortless rhythm unperturbed by the flapping bats above the rooftops. And when the wind stirred, the leaves whispered, "Yes," low and silky, like a mother's face descending to a sleeping child for one last kiss.

A sea of darkness engulfed the entire village. I stretched my arm upward around the post and gazed across the road. Night smoldered, thick as velvet, diffused into the empty spaces between drab objects that faded into dull gray ghosts, their edges softened, identities lost—how quickly a half-buried car frame with a naked steering column became a Trojan chariot with a one-armed driver, or the forge in the blacksmith shop a cyclops lifting its head out of the faintly glowing ashes. What light there was reflected dimly off the houses and the surface of the motor road as it wound into the trees like the body of a great serpent; otherwise it took a different kind of seeing to learn the different tones of night, blue where the breadfruit tree dried strips of red cloth, pitch where the wall of trees surrounding the village etched itself onto the softer black of the sky defining the horizon only by the absence of stars, ebony on granite. Seeing meant touching the liquid black in the rain barrel. It meant knowing the Southern Cross by its upper two stars where it lay on its side in the treetops behind Quolidobu's store, sensing a round moon where only a sliver hung low in the sky like a burnt out candle—

"I left the light on in your room." John Mulba. He was standing behind the screen door, silent as a shadow, probably worried about me. He'd taken me as a friend and a friend was something you cared for, you read his thoughts, felt his sorrow. "Here is your book," he said stepping out.

"Keep it until you're finished. I forgot you were inside."

"I was reading. It's too noisy out here."

"I know."

"Why don't you use the whip Fawkpa gave you?"

"I did not come here to whip people. Help them understand that."

"I will try."

"Thank you. Good-night."

"Good-night," he said starting down the hill.

"See you in the morning."

"Yes," he turned, smiling, "don't let the drums keep you awake."

He carefully picked his way down the path, crossed the road and climbed the bank. At the top he stumbled. I worried about him too. His passion for educating himself was alienating him from his own people. He read hungrily, by firelight when a lantern wasn't available and already his vision was going bad; not only that, he was getting a little absent-minded, always thinking about what he read. To a people who valued grace of movement, clumsiness and daydreaming were both laughable. But none of this seemed to bother him; nothing could dissuade this teenage Quixote from his quest. We were going to have to have "a little talk." It meant separating him from his dream. Go to the United States to study medicine. Jesus. He wouldn't listen of course. When he finished the book, he'd be back for another. He'd already read *Huckleberry Finn,* although he couldn't understand why Huck didn't like school. When I suggested a day of hookey spent on a raft was forbidden fruit, much like a day of reading in his case, he looked intense but the next day came back smiling. He said he understood. Later he asked me if I liked forbidden fruit. I said yes. He said he'd help me find it. He always had questions. Once he asked, "What is a nigger?" Right out of the blue. The words fell from his lips as easily as, "What is a bacillus?"

A few more steps and his white T-shirt disappeared like a light. I continued gazing across the road. It took awhile for the eyes to acclimate to the dark, to read its language, pick out its shapes; without fail they materialized out of the murky stillness like old friends. The charioteer for example. Now there were chickens roosting on it. Nobody could remember how it got there; it seemed to be growing out of the mud. It couldn't have been older than the motor road, eight years, yet the axles were half-buried and it looked like it had been there forever. So did the thatched roofs, smooth as combed hair, sweeping over the walls almost to the ground, sheltering the mud ledges where goats slept with their heads tucked into their sides; the entire village looked like a clump of wild mushrooms growing unmolested in an open grotto nourished by the warmth of the wet earth and whatever light the stars could spare. And all the time voices of night things resonated in the stillness as though in concert with the animism beneath the solidity of the world. Human endeavors shrunk small; the universe dilated wide. Were it not for the half dozen zinc roofs and the Coke sign on Quolidobu's storefront, the sense of a dwarf town would have been complete. When the moon came out, the whitewashed walls sparkled white; but tonight they were weak apparitions ready to flit away at the first snap of a twig; they mingled with the deeper shades of gray in the great tree trunks that stood like colossi keeping vigil at the outskirts of their world. And within, a fuzzy-toned darkness reigned supreme soothing over the rough edges of human handiwork as if Night herself wished to correct the errors of her children by blending the sculpture of the village into the natural growth of the forest. So complete the envelopment, it could not be discerned where the apparition of light ended and the reality of darkness began, where this night stopped and eternity resumed.

Night. How silent she comes, in mists and fragrant breezes. Edison and his infernal "fire-in-the-bottle" have blinded us to her beauty. We put up lights but make the world darker; she answers by drawing tight round her threatened child, civilization's unmanageable twin. But what if civilization turns out to be the work of children afraid of the dark? What if God is but a fanciful storyteller who keeps a shotgun under the bed?

I slapped a mosquito on my arm. The houses were quiet, the fires out. The air soft, sibilant, feminine. It couldn't have been later than nine thirty, quarter of ten. My lamp was always the last one out; my door the last to open in the morning. So my days passed, one much as the last, each blending into the next. But tomorrow would be different. Tomorrow we'd try the forest. And ourselves. Had to do something about the chicken hutch. Talk to Mulba. His dreams were getting out of hand. Study in America. Where was he getting these crazy ideas?

Where was I getting mine? To see an interior village forty miles off the motor road. It was going to be just like all the others, poor and tumble-down with hungry kids and open ulcers. There aren't any Shangri-las anymore.

Now they sleep. I envy them their freedom from the world's bright lights, their forest, their loud laughter—how could they laugh in the midst of such poverty? They aren't afraid of the dark, hence no need of a street light—nor a jail—nor an asylum. The drums. Who could be playing them? Deep in the forest while the village sleeps? There's nothing like drums in the middle of the night. No wonder they spooked the early missionaries. Kurtz too. Maybe if he heard the "music," he wouldn't have screwed up. Darkness is not an enemy. Like a sleek leopardess she comes slipping through the leaves to check her cubs. You have to look into the abyss until it answers in kind, opens the inner eye, releases the hypnotic spell of daytime illusions as effortlessly as smoke rising from burnt offerings, hissing "this is best." Here she is. Sweet Darkness. Shimmering through a misty veil, barefoot on the stair, on the soft footstep of a bride returning to her chamber prepared for love. "Yessss."

"How now my wayward. You too would know the secret of a stolen kiss, why the stars still whisper when they twist, why for all its ill the world persists. Touch me now and know. I am darkness, I am rest. Win me with a soul on fire, so small a price, so sweet a prize. Come home and realize. You too must hear what's in my heart, what's in the book of time, why the earth spins in its nook, how the music rhymes. The answer's in the speech of these, the forest and the trees, the ease with which they find the breeze. Tomorrow then we'll smile when we meet. For thee I keep, in the fortress of the deep I seethe. Forbidden fruit by dark decree, I save for thee. Win me once and see. For one caress I give you this, hear the air swim through the leaves, close your eyes and wish. Hear the drum make love to lyre, the warm night whisper, Yes. I'll show thee fruit you've yet to press, here in the softness of a fragrant breast. Come ripen thy desire. I am fire. I am blest. Darkness sweetened in a secret nest. I am laden. I am other. I am maiden. I am mother."

CHAPTER 13

INTO THE JUNGLE'S KEEP

"Why are we going to Kpodokpodo?" John Mulba asked from up ahead. His voice broke the spell of our footsteps slushing along the wet path.

"Do we have to have a reason?"

"No. But if country people take a long trip, it's for a reason."

"I want to learn about your people."

"No. That is not the answer."

"It's not?"

"That is what you can say in town, to the women and children. Here in the bush we cannot be telling stories." He meant white lies.

"I suppose it's my way of going hunting," I said after thinking about it. "You know—bush school." I could feel them smiling. "Okay?"

"Teacha, yes," Moses said.

"But what should I say when we get to Kpodokpodo?"

"Tell them you want to learn about our people."

"How if I tell them I came to see the sunrise? I've heard you can see it—"

"Tell them you want to learn about our people."

We continued in silence. For the second day we'd made an early start setting a quick pace at first but after awhile falling into a long distance rhythm; for the second day my jeans were soaked by the dewy grass, the same that bathed my friends beneath their knee-length trousers. In the rainy season it took the sun several hours to rise high enough to melt the heavy mists. Until then the entire forest lay shrouded in dripping gloom, its branches buried in layers of floating cloud as though the bottom of the sky had fallen to earth splashing fountains of wet leaves in the air, like surf, in silent suspension. Up above heavy limbs were fogged into gray forms suggesting shadows, a shade darker than the mists in which they swam; the straight trunks of the trees melted into gray billows much as masts rising into the bellies of swollen sails.

Ahead, Kwokwoiyea led the way passing in and out of visibility as the trail dipped and rose.

We'd started the day before. A soft "pok-pok" outside my bedroom window woke me earlier than usual. "Teacha, de sun is wake up." Then the usual bustle of last minute preparations, two jungle-rot sores, a gulp of tea. By the time I scampered down the path to join my friends, they were impatient for the road. A hundred yards past the school, the entire village vanished in a thick fog. Some small boys came with us part way but turned back as soon as the excitement wore off. Only Peter Kpudumah and his small brother remained; they were to go with us as far as Yiamah, their home village. The first leg of the trip took longer than expected. Once off the motor road, the trail became a slick ditch tiring us after only half a morning; and after a short side trip to Peter's banana grove, which he insisted on showing me, we didn't make Yiamah till mid-afternoon. There Peter's mother promptly sent for his father, the chief, who was at work on his farm—it would have been rude not to greet him properly. So we waited. Peter beamed with pride. Though one of the quieter boys in school, here he was a chief's son and he acted the part inviting us into the palaver kitchen and sitting in the chief's hammock himself. When the old man (an informal but permissible title for a chief) arrived, he asked if we wanted to eat at the same time ordering food prepared. We wound up spending the night. I should have know better than making a schedule.

Yiamah was the smallest hamlet I'd ever seen, trees straight up all around, only enough open sky for the sun to cross in two hours. Three round houses, two smaller ones, a dingy rectangular shed with ribs showing through the mud, three kitchens—meaning a separate, thatched-over work area open at the sides but not necessarily a cook kitchen—a medicine post, a bath fence, three chickens scratching in the dirt, a sleeping dog—that was it. Other than two women fanning rice in the shade of a papaya grove, the only activity came from the blacksmith kitchen where the measured breathing of the hand bellows and the sporadic clanking of steel tolled the slow passage of time. I threw down my knapsack and watched the red tip of a cutlass take shape on the anvil, an old engine block, while Peter pumped the bellows and the blacksmith worked, oblivious to time and onlookers, each movement carefully paced, his aged hammer arm slow to rise but his aim keen. Our talk was brief. Someone asked if there were blacksmiths where I lived. I wondered how they got that engine block in here.

As usual, a collection of small lanky-armed children gathered round, curly heads and bare navels, vacuous eyes and longing faces inching closer and closer, warning each other not to touch, fingering the rings on my knapsack, flicking flies, touching my skin, hair, devouring every movement I made. After the novelty wore off they found other amusements but when I took out my journal, two came back to the click of my pen. I took down their names, Dwoku and Kwibah, which they studied with amazement. What would I do with this? I said it would help me remember them. For how long? As long as I lived. They beamed in response.

Alone at last, I took off my glasses in fatigue and pinched my thumb and forefinger into the inward corners of my eyes only to look down and see the gesture perfectly mimicked by a ten-year-old boy squatting in the dirt. I recognized myself at once; he even conveyed an inward want that he couldn't have understood—yet there it was, as in a mirror. Was I that depressed? Was he trying to tell me something? When he caught me spying him, he broke into a wide grin that I returned but feebly.

Suddenly a peal of laughter. Akwoi of course. Busy ingratiating himself with the women. Talk came easy as they prepared the evening meal. Always the flirt, he delighted them with his impromptu pantomime, "White Man Eating Hot Peppers." Clutching his throat he staggered sideways in feigned agony. Hot peppers he explained could drive a white man crazy; therefore he would taste the soup (the sauce) just to make sure. What a salesman.

The evening shadows had fallen before the meal was ready. The chief himself served it on his porch after seating me in his best chair, a tree stump with cloth stretched between two root members, the curvature of the trunk fitting perfectly the small of your back. First rice then a sauce of palm oil, cassava greens, peppers, and meat—some kind of ground hog. I had to force it down. After dinner, a smoke and the usual talk, hunting or someone's trip to the coast; but then, before retiring, with his voice coming straight out of the dark, he briefly conveyed through John Mulba his pleasure at the prospect of his son learning English. A small, quiet man with muscular limbs and a quick step, he was entirely a gentleman. His name was Tomah.

So we were already a day behind. Bworpu still lay ahead. To the tribal mind the hurried efforts of foreigners seemed ludicrous, our frantic comings and goings a direct affront to their less formal but carefully defined etiquette. I'd been guilty myself of not taking time to say hello properly. To their reckoning if Tomah's kindness cost us a day, well, a day was a small price. Time wasn't money, hospitality was; we were all rich or poor depending on how people spoke of us. And they were right. I felt much better for the day we spent in Yiamah, more relaxed, more in tune to the tempo of the moving mists, less anxious about getting lost.

It was so easy to get lost, totally lost, and only a shout off the road. The dense entanglement often lied, the slope of the underlying ground never kept true, a swamp could look like a pasture, sound echoed off tree trunks at strange angles that turned you around and overhead light often revealed a thin spot in the cover rather than the position of the sun.

But this morning I felt eager for what lay ahead. Kwokwoiyea's quiet confidence was taking hold. He continued to lead, a shadow on the edge of the mist, the silent one, forever alert. Behind him, Moses, Akwoi, John, and me last, in single file as dictated by the narrow path, often no more than a cavern cut through two walls of dense leaves with a leaky ceiling to boot.

After a bit we stopped to switch loads. Our gear accounted for three bundles and two small sacks. We would switch off as needed converting the headload to a shoulder pack when it was my turn. This idea didn't go over real well; it was time consuming, inefficient—each time the weight had to be redistributed, balance being critical to a headload—and they were more than willing to carry my share. But I insisted with a stubbornness they couldn't understand. They hadn't seen the swashbuckling Hollywood heroes hacking their way through merciless jungles (if you had to do that you were lost for sure) with hardly a drop of sweat, porters in the rear, artless caricatures of an African that never was. "Bwana." The truth was somewhat more humbling. Ten yards into the bush, they were the teachers, I the schoolboy. With a boost from behind I swung into my knapsack and we were on our way. I noticed they took tufts of soft leaves and twisted them into a doughnut-shaped cushions to soften their headloads. I tried it under my shoulder strap. It helped.

I kept my eye on the back of Akwoi's neck. At the right distance you could read the trail from the movement of the person next in front thereby stepping over rocks or fallen limbs without looking down, which you couldn't do with a headload, or breaking cadence, which you could do but it made the load heavier. For them it all came naturally. Akwoi walked along humming or jabbering to himself, sometimes grabbing a blade of grass to make a whistle. His over-sized trousers made him look shorter than he was, hand-me-downs tied high on his waist over a faded maroon T-shirt. Julius Caesar in imperial purple. At school he followed the usual practice of adding an English name. First, John, then John Kennedy Akwoi, then George Washington Akwoi, but the novelty soon wore off so he tried Julius Caesar Akwoi and thereafter changed names as fast as he read new ones. In one month he went from Caesar Octavian to Richard the Lion-Hearted, finally Sir Francis Drake Akwoi.

Fortunately his flamboyant handwriting gave him away so I played along. Now he kept a journal too. My every faux pas would be recorded, but his greatest entry would be the midget we were to meet in Dawawoli, the first any of them had ever seen.

"When we come Voinjama, we will drink Coca-Cola yah?"

"I promised didn't I?"

"Ha ha," he cried almost tasting it. "With small ice?"

"Yes. With ice." Ice was a luxury upcountry. Ten cents a cube.

"All he can think about is his belly," John Mulba said coldly. My two sharpest students, they were bound to become rivals—but so far friendly.

"I thought a man's belly is supposed to be his friend," I said.

"Whe' he fu' insi', he you' frie'. Whe' he emp'y, he no' you' frie'," Moses added, no doubt from experience.

"All right. Okay." Akwoi fired back. "When we come to Voinjama, me and my belly, we will go to a Lebanese store and say, 'You! Mr. Storekeeper! Bring us *two* Coca-Cola yah! One for me and one for my belly. And don't be wasting our time!'"

"He will eat all your money," John warned.

"Baa, if I eat all his money, he can write a check and the storekeeper will give him all the money he wants."

"Then why don't you write a check?" John asked.

"Only white people can do da one!" Akwoi snapped.

"I' da one fo' true teacha?" Moses asked.

"Of course not!"

"But I see. One day to Zawzaw, me an' Davi' Beyan. We insi' de sto' looking to buy de kni'. Whi' ma' co'. He buy many teeng'. He wri' dow' de yellow papah. De Lebanee ma' gi' heem an' so' money agai'."

"That was his change. He didn't get those things for nothing. A check is a different kind of money, that's all."

"I' da one true, only whi' ma' ca' wri' de sheck?"

"No. A black man can write a check but he has to have money first."

By midmorning the mists lifted. I never caught them in the act. It seemed something told you to look up and presto! The gloom was gone. A new day that never failed to brighten the spirits. Today was no exception. The sky had opened, clouds of bright green leaves undulated in a breezy whisper with patches of dazzling blue breaking through and the sun blazing off to one side. No wonder the birds sang.

Soon the outlying farms fell behind, the path narrowed into a thin wrinkle of mud and the forest began to reclaim its own. Generally there were four designations of bush—swamp bush, farm bush, low bush, and high or virgin bush—with transition of course.

Interior villages were islands of bare earth in a green sea. Immediately surrounding them the coloring was a shade lighter, low bush, once slashed and burned for farming, but after the soil played out and the farmers moved on, the jungle reawakened and vast networks of vine and leaf ran riot in the absence of high cover; a dense thicket of interlacing branches grew unchecked as though surging in a raging sea, thrusting skyward, leaping to the listing masts of the former vessel. Where once a farm thrived, all lay covered, the man-made contours reduced to vague forms. Trees too were quickly engulfed, betrayed only by peaks in the green blanket, like tilting poles under a sagging tent, and if they broke, the tent sunk but never fell. It righted itself, rose to the sun, growing new skin over fresh scars.

We passed through Bworpu uneventfully. Custom required we pause for the necessary exchange of news and greetings. Unlike Yiamah we were at once strangers. People asked what news as though they were expecting something bad. Nor was the chief as cordial as Tomah. His only interest was in the gifts we brought. Leaning forward on the edge of a low stool, he greedily poked in my knapsack with a stick, found two cans of sliced peaches, a can of pork n' beans, but that wasn't enough. He saw a can of sardines in the side pocket and asked if I'd brought it for him. I gave it over although I knew my companions held it dear. He offered a boy of about twelve to guide us to the next town, but Kwokwoiyea politely declined. As we left kids came running alongside, asking questions. Did we have cigarettes? Did I beat them in school? But outside town, as though coming to an invisible barrier, they stopped and turned back. At the riverside women washed clothes on the rocks but didn't look up. I got bad vibes. We all did. It could have been an old animosity none of us knew about or just a bad chief.

After an hour or two we found ourselves in fairly deep bush. It closed in on you, took away your horizons. The wall of foliage became the edge of your world, forced you to look inward; you learned an intimacy with simple things, the squish of your own boots, the scent of stale mud, fallen petals. The sound of pebbles clicked like dice before your footstep; the undertone of insects measured out the hours forging them into years and eons; an eerie quiet slept in rapt suspension as though every bough, every leaf, hung in exactly that way, in precisely that place since time began.

Then something quaked in the stillness. A savage eye gleamed for the chase, a bird screamed, the thicket crashed, and high above jabbering monkeys telegraphed the event from tree to tree beneath a luminous blue serenity held fast in utter desolation—repose without an Apollo. So too the massive gray trunks, they gave a hint of Grecian columns until you noticed spikes growing out their sides.

At first glance everything seemed out of sync; complete chaos, fertility mad with its own freedom, fighting, falling down drunk, so robust it spanned its own mistakes growing them over with new life, moss over dead logs, stranglers over broken limbs. Anarchy reigned. Order, propriety—banished. The presence of a human ego mattered not at all. No master, no Kilroy. Pure wilderness!

Nor did the so-called law of the jungle apply. In here you saw it for what was, the outside world's rationalization of its own aberrations. True, predators killed, but the fittest didn't always survive, unless you defined "fit" as "trickiest at overcoming unfitness"—humans for example. Evolution seemed to plod ahead without a purpose, to stumble into an ill imagined future by the most devious pathways—seeds through alimentary canals to fertilize the hillsides, moments of mad passion to propel the species through the ages. To say nature favored one tactic, strength, seemed remarkably narrow; she also favored craft, cunning, cooperation, delicacy, even deceit. Tenderness too, as though the thinnest tendril were there to overcome the sharpest thorn, groping as quietly as Adam on the Sistine ceiling. Forever groping. But what perceptive blindness, to culminate in a human brain bent on putting order back into chaos.

Nature means to stay. She brings a strategy to every obstacle, a tooth to every tactic. She favors both mighty and meek. These last thrived in the shadows, mindless of the unlettered law that spoke the sacred word, "Live." It wasn't at all unusual to come across a carcass of a once mighty survivor picked clean by the tiniest predators with butterflies dancing in the hollow rib cage. There was room for beauty too, and quiet, and music, with all creatures moving to their own rhythms, abiding in their own worlds; all struggles but momentary perturbations in a greater undertaking—to see that life went on in whatever vessel, to color every eye, herald every sunrise.

But to every extinction a chit. You felt a tenacity, an inevitability. Worlds die but the show goes on; you felt the endurance of the earth, the littleness of men, that if we're stupid enough to exterminate ourselves, some new radiation-tolerant species will crawl out of the rubble and call to its kind in a different tongue.

As frightening as it was, the thought of annihilation kindled a strange faith, not in doctrine nor divinity but in the simple efficacy of life, in the blind persistence of living creatures to carry its flame to the next generation. Here in the quiet, countless species cried for life and life responded; you felt its dictate in every flowering stem, every liquid eye. And from this dumb faith grew a conviction, from the conviction the courage to go on.

Nature wasn't meant to be understood. That was the key. When you thought you had it, the equation of life, it receded out of reach like a capricious spirit. There always lurked a thing unknown behind the next thicket, a gloom on the far off hills, a sense of strangeness in a hallowed solitude, a savage serenity in the heart of the fray.

Thus the exquisite enigma, the intimacy of decay and generation. Beneath the dull patina of gray lichens and dusty moss lay the vitality of living sap as one bite of an axe testified; through mists of immense time, the vibrancy of eternal youth babbled aloft in a thousand tongues; within the alien cast of an alien world lay a startling immanence, bright and dazzling, sunny and pure. From Paleocene to present, eternal recurrence spun its tale in the alternating throb of a beating heart. A cry of fright, a call of wonder, a dearth and a revelation; vision and understanding, followed by indifference and despair. Each followed in place; and in the eye-blink of an epoch the sibling came home to a lullaby faintly remembered. It took your breath away at first, but when you gained confidence in the certainty of the next cycle, you fell in step with the harmony of existence, its exquisite rhythms, its remote silence in whose deep well virgin energy began to swirl, sculptured by time into matter, consummated into life. And after awhile an order emerged. A certain reed sighed in a certain way. A leaf twirled as only that leaf could. Water trickled over pebbles in the language of water. Things took shape, spoke their names, asserted their presence. The dance of life began—in awe-struck silence with the hum of insects as witness, galaxies of them buzzing with life in the maw of nothingness. What gall! No trumpets, no hosannas, only a dull drone over a stagnant pool in utter disregard for the gravity of the event.

Yet...something smiled. You could never isolate it; you could sense it only by the sounds within, the flutter of a leaf, the clunk of a frog, the swish of a wing. Here is the door! But the key locks out the hand that holds it. What an ingenious fortress.

To pass the time I began a conversation but never expected it to lead where it did.

"What was our village like before the motor road?"

We'd found a steady pace, the trail fairly smooth. "None of us spoke English," John answered. "We did not go to school. If you wanted to go to Zorzor, you had to walk."

"Do you remember when they built the road?"

"Yes. Everyone was excited."

"De motah roa' co' I' ninetee' fiffy eigh' yah," Moses added in a tone of assurance.

"How do you know?"

"Da one whi' ma', he be woiking o' de roa'. He na' Meestah Haddytah."

"Harrington?"

"Yes," John said, "He was an engineer."

"He wa' frie' wi' de peopo," Moses continued. "We be he'ping heem, he be teach us small English."

"Do you know where the creek goes under the road?" John continued. "Before they brought the pipes, it was a mess of mud. The Jeep could not go. The tires turned around but it would not go. One day we cut palm branches and laid them down so he could drive across and that was the first time a car came in our town."

"Some of the people were afraid and ran away," Akwoi added excitedly.

"Children?"

"Beeg peopo, too," Moses added. "Aftah he dri' ova de watah, de jee' co' into tow'. De peopo loo' see."

"They made a circle around it but did not want to touch it," Akwoi continued. "And one old man was poking it with his cutlass to see if it would jump."

"Meestah Haddytah see heem bu' no ongry, he be loffing and shaking han' wi' peopo. He gi' de chie' de seekah."

"Cigar?"

"Yes. And he had a cigarette lighter," John said, "We never saw one before. He took it out of his pocket and put his thumb on it and fire jumped out. I thought it would burn him in his pocket."

"And he gave the chief a ride!" Akwoi remembered. "When they came back everybody danced."

"That's incredible," I said.

"And there was this crazy woman!" Akwoi cried. "When she saw the bulldozers coming, she started to cry. She said this was the end of the world."

"What was her name?"

"Zia," John said.

"How do you know she was crazy? Maybe she was afraid of bulldozers."

"She was long time crazy," Akwoi said.

"No yah," John challenged, "only since her baby died. She was old, past the time for babies. The baby came, very tiny. After it died, she would carry it with her and be talking to it. It began to smell bad and the men had to take it from her. She fought them. They buried it but she dug it up. They had to bury it again where she couldn't find it. After that she was crazy."

"But you were just a small boy yourself?"

"My mother told me. I can remember how Zia would sit on the ground and be talking or singing. People didn't pay attention to her."

"What would she say?"

"Crazy things."

"It would make nonsense," Akwoi said. "She would say things that were not true, only she was not telling tales."

"What things?"

"She said the bulldozer had eaten her baby," John said.

"And when the bulldozers came close to town and were knocking down big trees, she got bad crazy and they took her to another village."

"Was she a witch?"

"No. Just crazy."

"So you had your Cassandra."

"What?"

"Nothing…"

"We all of us afrai' fuss ti' we see bowdozah pooshing dow' de beeg tree," Moses said earnestly. "If we say 'No,' we lie. But only Zia getteeng crazy. Myse'f, I be dreameeng I' de nigh'. I drea' de bowdozah co' into tow'. I look ou'si', I' sitteeng dow', nex' my house. I' wa'…eh yah, how you ca' da one?" and he said the word in Loma.

"Breathing," John said.

"Breeding—"

"No. Breathing," I said.

"Breazing. De bowdozah wa' sitteeng dow' breazing li' beeg anima'."

"I'll bet after awhile you were climbing all over it?"

"Dose ma' o' de roa', dey tell us bowdozah ca' ea' peopo. We do no' belie' da one bu' we do no' go loo' see. One day, many day agai', we comeeng back I' tow' fro' de fa'm. Nigh' ti' come. Dey finish woiking. Bowdozah sitting dow' on de roa'. Me an' Davi' Beyan. He tell me, 'Pu' you han' insi', you afrai'.' I say, 'No.' He say, 'You lie.' I say, 'Okay. You mo' come, too.' He say, 'Okay.' I pu' my han' o' de whee'. He say, 'You mo' put insi'.' So I put insi de motah. Fiah bite my han'! I say, 'Aheee!' We ru'! We do no' stop to we insi' de house."

"How long did it take? To build the road?"

"It took them a long time," John said. "Sometimes water would carry away the ground where they lifted it up. Mr. Harrington said he was going in hell and high water, but we would see the road finished."

"But none of you spoke English then, how do you know what he said?"

"There were Kpelle people working with him. They would tell us. Later on we started to catch some English. After the road came, we built the schoolhouse; we never thought a white man would come and live with us."

"One ti'," Moses continued, "to Kotitow', de jee' fa' dow' i' de watah.' He try. No. He try agai. No. We poosh heem ou'. He geef us ri' ba' to tow'. Da was furs' ti' I ride insi' de ca'.'"

"Really?"

"Fo' true."

"He try to joomp ou'," Kwokwoiyea reminded him, delicately.

"Jump out? How?"

"Eh yah, how you say?"

"It was not like a car," John said. "It was a pickup truck."

"Why did you try to jump out?"

"I was afrai'. De motah talkeeng, Mmmmmmmmm. We go. Now de motah vex. We boomp. I fa' dow'. De roa' running fass, de beeg trees ru' fass. Everyt'i' joomping up an' dow'. I try to joomp ou', bu' o' ma' Fawkpa, he catch me an' hol' me. Dose ma' be loffing o' me."

"How 'bout Kwokwoiyea, was he laughing?"

"I no' loffing da ti'," he said softly.

"Was it the first time you rode in a car, too?"

"Teacha, yes."

"Did you try to jump out?"

"No. I do no' le' go. I was afrai', too."

We walked in silence awhile. I tried to imagine what must have gone through their heads back then. To outsiders they must have fit the stereotype, spooky and superstitious, but to them the sight of a bulldozer knocking over trees must have been something from Mars. What would we do? How many of us would go crazy? Would I have the nerve to touch it, the monster from another planet—after dark?

"Were you afraid first time you rode in a car?" John asked.

"I must have been very young," I said. "I don't even remember."

"Was you afrai' whe' you across de ocea' in de adaplon?" Moses asked.

"Well…not really. I'd been in an airplane before. My people aren't afraid of machines. We grow up with them, but it doesn't mean we can't be afraid."

"What does make you afraid?" John asked.

"The time I was most afraid in my life was the first night I spent in your village. I did not sleep at all. Everything was so strange. The trees, the bush, sounds I never heard before. And it was so dark. I thought what if an animal comes. Then the crickets stopped singing. I thought, now something is coming for sure."

"Big animals never come in town!"

"I know. And I knew it then. I suppose I was afraid of you more than anything else."

"Us!" They cried in disbelief.

"I know. It was silly of me, but that's what happens when you're afraid. You didn't believe the bulldozer would eat you, but you weren't in a hurry to find out."

Akwoi laughed loud and maliciously. "What's the matter?" I said. "You never been afraid?"

"No! Never! I can never be afraid!" he growled in feigned bravado.

"Bah!" Moses sneered. "I' dey pu' you dow' insi' his country, you be afrai', too."

"Inside a big city," John took it up, "big buildings and big trucks going fast and many many people, only white people, no Loma man to help you—"

"I would call a taxi! I would say, 'You! Mr. Taxi Man! Take me to Chicago!'"

"You loo' da one I' da boo'!" Moses cried. But it didn't faze Akwoi, he started singing:

> Goin' to Chicago
> Goin' to Chicago
> Sorry con' ta' you
> Not'ee' i' Chicago
> Gur' li' you cou' do

"You stupi'!" Moses retorted. But Akwoi ignored him, kept humming the tune, then gave us one more chorus at the top of his lungs. He got the words right, but the *blues* evaded him. They weren't of his world.

High bush now. We hadn't expected it for another day. The war for sunlight went on eighty feet above where the dense leaves screened the harsh rays leaving the floor beneath a shade cooler, a tone darker, heavy jades in a sea of deep gray. As the day burned above, yellow shafts streamed through the treetops growing in diameter as they reached the floor, a minuet of yellow spikes seeming to revolve in the floating motes of dust. Outside their span surprisingly dark shadows fell at midday, deeper than the purple of late afternoon. The light could play tricks too, hiding the true time of day or suggesting the approach of a storm. Everything hung calm, bathed in a soft hush. A beam of bright sun sometimes put the spotlight on something insignificant, a single blossom bowed in the sun bravely flying its colors as though to declare, Beauty Lives! Life everywhere, and in the absence of a seasonal cycle, new leaf grew as the old fell. Spring and autumn on the same branch.

The first thing that struck home in high bush was the uncanny feeling of being indoors. The dense cover shut out the breezes. A thick carpet of permirot covered the ground; the scent of decay hung heavy. You got the sense of a quiet morgue. The sharp screams of birds pierced the inner ear; a cracked twig recoiled like a gunshot. Great trunks powered their way to the upper tiers like rockets, their buttressed root systems, sculptured into an upward thrust. Long lianas hung down, in knots, looped, taut, draped over limbs like fat snakes or cradling a falling tree on its way down to earth. Air plants clung precariously where they could, often to weaker branches, their own streaming upward then down in luxurious abundance like springs of water. It wasn't unusual to see a fairly healthy tree rooted in the limb of another thirty feet up. Mosses fell like silk scarfs, spent blossoms exuded musk. Brilliant throated birds trilled fountains of notes, rotten logs sprouted virginal colors.

It wasn't that the trees were higher or the leaves greener. Something else. One look at the unchecked orgy, bristling spikes, the mesh of living and dead, the cries and the screams, and something said, "Turn back." The reach of civilization ended here; human presence ran headlong into a wall of dumb immensity. The only comfort—yet there is something unconquered. And high above, moving air stirred listless leaves from their sleep rattling them like the harsh breathing of a slumbering beast. This and strangler limbs twisting into fat muscles conjured up an impression of a sleeping giant, a green phoenix feeding on itself and we, Lilliputians, walking ant-like before it.

After awhile we came to a hill where the trail became a staircase of interlacing roots. Sometimes a trickle of water came down the path the other way. My friends carefully picked their way up assisting each other verbally while they snaked back and forth under their headloads. I drew a breath and set to work concentrating on the footholds, grappling my way up pulling branches and slipping on mossy rocks. I had to make it. I didn't want them to see me beaten. When I looked up they were waiting for me at the top, Akwoi suppressing his amusement, John serious, Moses sympathetic. "What t' hell's so funny."

At the bottom of the second staircase, we stopped beside a dark pool where a small break in the undergrowth left enough room to throw down our loads. We propped our backs against a fallen log and stretched out. They were tired too. The trail behind dropped down the side of the mountain like a jagged scar; near the base it skirted a great tree, a good five yards in diameter not counting its buttresses, then leveled off over the sandbar where we now rested. Younger trees grew from a framework of roots, or out of the rocky hillside, their trunks splotchy gray, serpentine, as though molten wax were poured from above and solidified into a death grip around mossy boulders. Upward thin yellow moss covered the limbs like hair. Between the sandbar and the outcropping of root-laced rock, a shallow pool formed in a low depression collecting the run off from a small spring somewhere behind. We could hear it dripping behind a crevice before washing down the side of a clean rock that looked like it was bleeding green moss. A shiny matting of black leaves lined the bottom while the surface reflected the treetops high above, sharp as a mirror. A dry leaf floated in the middle without disturbing the picture. Up behind us the cover didn't quite blot out the sky; the pool caught traces of blue but softened them into azure and jade. Thick layers of fungi, bright orange and yellow, grew out of the sides of black logs; splotched lichens stained living bark like white leopard spots.

After we rested a bit, Akwoi began to fidget with one of the loads. "Have one," I said. They began undoing the strings. While they busied themselves, I climbed around behind the pool, refilled my canteen, then sat on a sagging root overlooking the mirror. Before long, they were bickering over food. "Why don't you each have one?"

"What do you want?" John asked.

"Peaches. I'll split one with you."

He opened a can, poured half in a tin cup, sliced a banana on top and passed it over. Soon a veritable feast: sardines, peanut butter, Slim Jims, fruit cocktail, candy, then they split open a fresh pineapple. Akwoi picked up a sardine can and began licking out the last drops of oil with his finger. Then he tossed it in the pool and broke the mirror. Concentric circles widened through the reflected treetops then returned as though to reclaim a lost tranquility. I watched it floating on the water, spinning slow. A sacrilege. I took off my boots and went after it. I knew they'd laugh. I could feel them looking at me.

I sat back down and laced my boots. It seemed like late afternoon but it had to be earlier. They didn't seem in any particular rush.

"Who was Cassandra?" John asked.

"She lived a long time ago. She told the truth but nobody believed her." They didn't miss a beat.

"Di' she liff to Amer'ca?" Moses asked.

"No. When you were telling me how the jeep came in your village the first time, it reminded me of a story. Only they had a horse, not a jeep."

"Tell us," Akwoi said eagerly.

"It's a long story."

They loved stories; I wasn't going to get out of it.

"Teacha, yes," Kwokwoiyea said.

"Ey, yah. People were fighting a war. Long time now. They couldn't break in the door so they thought what to do."

Now questions, rapid fire.

"No not in America...far away...in Turkey...yes white people...They lived in tribes the way you do...they made a big horse out of wood, big enough for the warriors to hide inside its belly...No it didn't have a motor...I don't know how they got it up the hill, maybe they pushed it...I'll tell you about it someday."

"Tell us now," Akwoi snapped.

"I'm not sure I can remember."

"Tell us about Cassandra."

"How dey be hideeng insi' de...'orrus?"

"The horse. That part comes later. Okay let's see...I suppose it begins with Helen. Helen was the most beautiful woman in the world. Not just to look at...but to imagine. Understand? Good. Otherwise you won't understand the story, my people don't understand it anymore, old men read the words through thick glasses but they can't see her face. We don't believe in things like that anymore. Her smile keeps the sunshine warm, the women beautiful, the children happy. Her voice makes a warrior weep, a wise man stumble. When you look at her you understand what it is to be Loma. You carry the memory of her in your heart wherever you go, it shows you the way, how to be brave. If she looks at you, you are strong; but if she looks to your best friend you will fight him; you will strike your own brother. If someone steals her, there will be war. She's not...she's—"

"A hot number," Akwoi piped up.

"Where in the *hell* did you hear that? You didn't hear that from me!"

"We have a word in Loma," John Mulba said in great solemnity after the laughing died down.

"You always do," I smiled. (Making a fool out of myself again; I forgot how seriously they took storytelling.) "Well, what is it?"

John Mulba, old reliable, looked at the others, then at his feet, then me.

"...Well?"

"Gbwolu."

They shot devilish looks at each other.

"Okay then," I said. "We got that part. Only it's not just about...you know...there's more to it than that. Okay. There were these Greeks. Agamemnon was chief, Menelaus his brother. Menelaus' wife was Helen. Helen was...*gbwolu.* Did I say that right?"

Akwoi cracked up. The others, too. "You say it right," John laughed, "but your grammar is wrong. In Loma we do not say, Helen has *gbwolu,* we say, *gbwolu* has Helen."

"...I never thought of it that way. That's good. Well then, there was this boy...Paris—"

Once I got going I surprised myself how much I remembered. So with Achilles in his tent and the Greeks backed up to the long ships, we took up our loads and were soon sloshing through a low swamp. We'd get back to the story; with luck it would last the rest of the trip. The path was no more than a thin hump of wet earth inches above the water, remarkably clear for swamp water. Ferns everywhere. Dark branches of piassava palms shot out of the surface like artillery explosions, dead fronds falling into the water while fresh green grew out the tops, still others like heads of unkept hair half submerged. Birds of paradise tossed their orange heads in the sun while their fat stems fought for every inch of muck at the sides of rotten logs. Deformed stumps decayed into dwarfs. The swamp widened, the sandy trail became lengths of bamboo level with the water squishing underfoot. Soon we were ankle deep, before long knee deep in a field of lily pads that covered the water reforming their pattern behind us without a hint anyone had passed. Insects ferocious. I finally asked if we were still on the trail. Laughter.

Less cover now, more sky, pure blue, now and then a wisp of floating cloud. Dead stillness. A world under glass. All of a sudden rent air. Taut wings! Storks, maybe herons, lifting off, then an entire flock filling the air with checkered patterns, a squawking madhouse bursting into bright color, white, purple, orange, rising slowly to the contour of the lagoon and flying off as one.

At last the trail rose out of the swamp. We made good time for an hour, forded a small stream, then another, skirted a hill, then came to a narrow ravine with a log across. They made it with ease, almost running. Barefoot. That was the trick. I took off my boots. Bare feet could feel the curvature of the log much easier. On the other side the damp ground felt good so I strung my boots to my knapsack. A human footpath, a mere wrinkle in the wet earth but it defined the true size of our species. We leave a path eight inches wide.

Now we were getting into virgin forest, this the deep forest the hunters sought. Nothing moved. The deeper we penetrated, the quieter it got. I got the uncanny feeling of trespassing, as though we'd passed into another realm, the silence deafening.

Suddenly a human voice called out. It startled me. People were coming the other way. A man led, followed by two women, a boy and a girl. He bore a shoulder yoke with two palm wine gourds that sprang with his step. They greeted us warmly as we turned out of the path to let them pass. The younger woman and the boy stared at my feet from under their headloads. The man stopped and asked, "What news?" Moses told him our destination. From their answer I gathered they were from Dawawoli and we were on the right trail. Then the man set down his gourds and disappeared in the foliage. I didn't know what to make of it. He reappeared with a fist full of straws. Handing one to each of us he invited us to try his palm wine. Quite sweet. With that we shook hands, clicked twice, and they were gone as quickly as they'd come. I wondered what they were about, perhaps a great journey they'd talk about for years, and a barefoot white man in the bush. I put my boots back on—didn't want to be the stuff of legend.

By late afternoon Kwokwoiyea hurried us along; he said he smelled rain. The trail showed greater wear, branched off now and them, signs we were approaching a village. Then we saw a peak of brown thatch seemingly afloat on the foliage. An outlying farm, they were usually an easy walk to town and much alike, a thatched work-kitchen under a clump of shade. As we passed we could see them watching us, a frail old woman inside and two younger ones at work in the field. Moses cupped his hands and called out. The town was far and we were welcome to take shelter if we wished. "De rai' wi' beat us in de bwush-oh," Kwokwoiyea urged in his quiet way. A herd of charging elephants and he would urge quietly. We took quick counsel. Right now it was clear but a wind was kicking up and gray patches of low clouds were outracing flimsy white cirrus feathers high over head. We stayed.

Off the main trail a slim path no wider than a human foot wound its way to the kitchen; it jumped fallen logs, dodged a burnt-out stump, threaded a steep hillside dropping straight down a sharp ravine where it became so faint only detached footprints remained. A thin green snake slithered across. On the high side we saw the torsos of two women wading waist deep in waves of undulating rice. A boney-ribbed dog tried to bark but without much luck. Inside the old woman sat on a low stool before a tight little fire straining palm oil into a pot of boiling cassava greens. It smelled good. A second pot of rice steamed under a cover of banana leaves. She remained seated extending her hand to us as she rasped her greeting to each in turn. Her worn out body strained in the effort. Crooked limbs, hands calloused, feet scarred, she looked awful; her dried up breasts dangled on her rib cage like flaps of old leather. She was blind too. Glaucous pupils stared helplessly in front of her, white as clouds, yet, like so many elderly Loma women, she retained the bearing of a lady. Something about her. What could you call it? Gaunt refinement? The ghost of youth not wasted? As she spoke the wrinkles in her old face danced bright and her toothless smile framed a real "Welcome." On touching my hand her voice rose a pitch, *"Ouikwiligee?"* (White man?), then chuckled with pleasure when I answered in Loma. With great effort and Kwokwoiyea's assistance which she solicited without the slightest hint, she rose to her feet and began to feel my face. Her boney fingers moved like tentacles, remarkably sensitive as her eyes stared into space over my shoulder. She was looking deeper too. "He is beautiful," she said—a compliment I was not accustomed to. Her name was Kdubahwhatah. John pronounced it for me slowly, accent on the last syllable.

I didn't realize how exhausted I was until I threw off my knapsack and stretched out on the floor. Not much furniture. Two stools ankle high. A small girl inched her way back to the ledge; about three with carefully braided hair, naked save for a string of thin beads around her waist, she'd run away when she first saw me. Now she scratched the dirt with her cherub toes but careful to keep the post between us. Kdubahwhatah called her but she turned and ran again and the old woman laughed dropping her withered arm in her lap.

Outside gusts of wind kicked up the dust. It was comin'. Beyond the work area the farm sloped down and away towards a low ridge at the edge of the forest where a wall of leaves poured into it like a breaking wave. It wasn't very big, maybe five acres, hacked out of the forest with hand tools, crisscrossed with dead logs lying where they fell with willowy rice growing around them. Otherwise every clump of soil was put to use. Cassava grew well down into the ravine, oil palms spared by the axe dropped sparse shade, a grove of bananas flapped their wide leaves like elephant ears. No fences. It didn't look like agriculture, rather like the jungle had taken a break. Behind the kitchen, peppers, herbs, a few stalks of corn, papaya, and a brake of sugar cane. Two log mortars stood out in the sun, one on its side, the other with a hammer inside.

The gathering storm came on apace. The two women in the field made their way back to the kitchen. They greeted us but kept the required distance. One carried a baby piggy back while she worked, her breasts full from feeding; the other, though much younger, showed no expression in her face. She took a notched log from the floor, put it to an opening in the center of the matted ceiling and carefully climbed up watching the opening above while her toes felt for the notches. She tossed down two blankets and a plastic tarp; the other woman handed up a heavy porcelain pan wrapped in leaves.

It begins with a slight darkening of the sky above the windward treetops. The next time you look—black, forbidding, angry, an invading army amassed. The sounds of the forest subside, animal life huddles low, the whole world battens down. The leaves hush, but with a slight trembling. Everything waits. The air hangs heavy but a light rebellious breeze seems to defy caution and charge toward it like backwash before a breaking wave. It's far away. Now the first sound, like the whine of swarming insects. Soon you can see it. Gray bars of slanting rain wedged in between fat clouds and the cowering forest. Then the hum of an electric motor. Distant objects recede into obscurity, the hills farthest away merging into gray sky. Now a truck motor climbing a hill, a steady rushing waterfall marching closer. The horizon shrinks. The volume turning up. Now a steady drumming on the flat leaves, each beat lost like a single hand clap in the applause of a great human gathering. It's near! First the avant-garde. Cavalry. Heavy drops plop in the dust kicking up tiny craters. Treetops dip into the wind and recoil violently, all their tiny flags flying. Leaves of grass begin to twitch like keys on a player piano. Blue is vanquished. Gray is victor. Then black, thick unnatural black, not night, but an oppressive weight dropped to the earth to serve notice, daytime is suspended. Even after it's come, the surroundings remain dry for an instant in a show of defiance, but all at once everything turns dark, glistening wet behind swift white streaks of water, like lances, knifing into the forest as it hangs its head in submission. The bare earth sizzles, washing down brown water in running rivulets, splashing, tearing soil, stealing earth. Ravines ravaged. Footpaths erased. Nearby trees blotted out. Everywhere gray, opaque. Down. Down in blind rage. Billows of white mist rolling through. The wind roaring, shearing clouds, unfurling the undersides of naked boughs, bending down great limbs, hurling them back, splintering them off and dashing them down in murderous fury. Palm trees, springing their rubber trunks, throwing their heads windward, exposing clean tourniquets at the back of their necks. Lightning! Now a thunder roll in the distance. In town the houses would be islands in a sea of mud with no signs of life save the goats huddled to the lee, with the wind lashing, whipping solid walls, tearing thatch from roofs, flying it through the rain until it catches on something. If one is unfortunate enough to be under a zinc roof, he lives inside a drum.

When the crescendo of crashing cymbals passes, the storm subsides spending its last fury in a steady rush of falling water. The clouds empty, the sky lightens up a bit. Overladen leaves hang heavy to earth dripping steady streams. High limbs bend low. Birds flutter their feathers. The scent of fresh water drifts with the cooler air. In town the drip from thatch to puddle awakens a lighter mood. Kids are the first to come out; their naked bodies recoiling in the chill air, but they soon find their play splashing in puddles and ditches, bathing under running eaves, screaming delight. Dogs stretch themselves then shake off. Adults appear in doorways looking out into the lingering drizzle.

Sometimes the storm is gone as quickly as it comes rumbling over the hills dragging off the sound of rushing water, thin wisps of lacy cloud trailing behind like the white silks of frightened wayfarers, forever drawn to the peregrine spirit, the gray god of rain, seducer of maiden forests, crusher of trees, migrant bull dominant in his skies, loved by his paramours, Wind and Water, master of fertile forests, his forests, father of running waters, life maker. And if the day is not yet done, the sun with his permission reappears to draw the chill from shivering bones, rewarming the earth, his earth. A titillating freshness tingles in the air. The earth smiles.

But today it wasn't to be. Its fury past, the storm seemed to be letting up, the wind died, a light shower fell straight down, sunlight began to glow behind layers of bleak cocoon; but just as we thought about leaving, the assault renewed, full power, naked hordes of wind and water, unleashed savagery slashing limbs and trunks shrieking like a banshee; and when it seemed the sky could give no more, it recoiled and struck again pounding the earth with the weight of a thousand Niagaras. When it seemed the tempo peaked, it rose a measure more, past all limits, past the last boundary of the natural world into the nether-realm of something unnatural. It whipped and snarled and whirled. A white maelstrom. Cataracts without a gorge. East and west, up and down, the time of day; all destroyed. Fear beat its drum; something inside you said, "It will let up, it will," but without the slightest conviction. Then it roared louder, fierce, rampant. Lightning! Lit from below. The underbellies of heavy clouds bulged fat, ominous, bestial. Huge limbs swirled at the bottom of a waterfall. Thunder cracked! The wind drove trees down; they rebounded, fought for their upright positions smashing into each other; it tore them from the earth, hurled them down with a great cracking rumble, crashing to the soft earth in a shower of debris, the undersides of their leaves white, the dirt on their roots—now a sudden ripping right over our heads! By the time we looked up, we saw only a gray opening above the matting. Downwind a good piece of our roof, still laced together, tumbled away at the speed of a car over the carpet of rice bent horizontal in the wind. I looked up. Bamboo rafters seemed to be floating in gray mist with rain slicing through. Moses climbed the ladder and covered the trap door but soon it began to leak. Thunder and lightning raged; one cracking flash and the nearby crash of a tree gave us to understand in no uncertain terms our true place in this world, a small troop of animals huddled in fear.

The child clung to my knee when her mother went to mind the fire—they built a little tent around it—but then she went to the old woman who took her inside her shawl and pressed her head into the hollow of her neck. Throughout the hour Kdubahwahtah had been magnificent, perfectly calm, resigned, pure grace in the eye of the storm. And it was contagious; her very presence calmed me somewhat. Now and then she coughed blood and spat into the fire. Kwokwoiyea unrolled his blanket and we drew it around his shoulders. John and Moses followed suit, then Akwoi and I. Thick billows of smoke rose to the ceiling, flattened out, found their way to the eaves and out into the cold where they were sharply blown away dissipating after several yards. Still the rain sliced through the trees. Just outside a solid layer of clear water covered the bare ground moving diagonally towards us before reaching the ledge and running off. No sign of letting up. The god was angry. Little by little we inched toward the red coals drawing our blankets tighter until we had something like a collective tent. I pulled my collar up. Mists of pulverized rain swept along the surface and through the open kitchen. The sound of gorging water come from the ravine. The fire miraculously alive. Again! One, two—Shhhrack! A tremor shot up the dog's spine. Pure electric. It lit up the black sky with an ungodly glow, like a floodlight in the deep of hell.

CHAPTER 14

RALLY FOR PEACE

"We come here today, this lovely autumn afternoon, to express our dissent over the ever widening war in Vietnam. Like our counterparts who later this week will converge on Washington to dramatize the growing opposition to this tragic mistake at a mass rally in front of the Pentagon, like our fellow students on hundreds of campuses all over the country, we come from different disciplines, different backgrounds, we are young and old, teacher and student, our moral and religious philosophies may vary; but in our distaste, disbelief, and utter horror with what we read in the papers and see on the television, in our shock, indignation, and inability to fathom the foreign policy of the present administration and the untold violence it has visited on the peoples of North and South Vietnam alike—we are one."

His voice dropped but on a note of quiet conviction. A dozen or two people stood in front of a hastily constructed platform on the mall of the inner campus and answered with sporadic clapping.

"As the carnage grows, as the death tolls mount and the end recedes further into the distance, our delegated role of silent onlookers becomes increasingly unbearable."

A loose-knit crowd began to orient itself to the modest voice that caught them a little off guard. Something about him made an audience of those who listened, the intangible quality of moral sorrow perhaps. By himself the boyish-looking botany instructor looked more a student than faculty; he casually leaned over the microphone with one hand buried in the pocket of his corduroy jacket, no tie, open shirt despite a brisk October wind that disheveled his hair and rattled the loose papers on the bare podium. Now in his second year, he was finishing up his doctorate and already one of the promising young men on campus, which left the grapevine to wonder why he'd come here in the first place, the Midwest being the graveyard for such hopes. After the first year doubt set in, then disbelief, cynicism; but not this time. He kept his commitment. His soft-spoken, self-effacing manner won friends, made him popular with students and unthreatening to superiors; he kept up-to-date and exhibited a more than a passing acquaintance with matters outside his field. And he listened to people, responding to them on levels far below his own without selling out. In the absence of anything that could be called faculty leadership, he stepped into the vacuum and soon found himself center stage.

"But once we break the bonds of silence, no matter how loud the cry, mere words will hardly—"

At this point the PA system went haywire and a long-haired student hurried onto the platform to check the mike. Wilbur, Phil, and I stood off to one side on the steps of West Hall, an old women's dormitory, one of the original buildings on the inner campus long since converted to faculty offices—graduate assistants in the basement. Just then Dr. Bainbridge came out the door behind us. "What's this?" he asked.

"The long awaited peace rally," Wilbur said turning to him with folded arms. "They're going to demonstrate. Exactly what, remains to be seen."

"Their own moral superiority," someone sneered.

"The feasibility of electronics," Phil smiled.

"A new Renaissance of political awareness," Louis mocked, dashing up the steps with a yellow legal pad under his arm.

Dr. Bainbridge smiled without interest, lit his pipe, and started down the steps to the faculty parking lot. He carried a neat briefcase. When the wind gusted a cluster of maples and oaks showered dry leaves across the mall; it drove them whirling and scraping over sidewalks that crisscrossed the worn grass where a growing crowd, now maybe a hundred, waited or sat on the ground in a rough semicircle opposite the platform. Across the way the sandstone columns on the library caught the late afternoon sun. A few cardboard placards began to appear, "US Out of Vietnam, Peace Now, Draft Beer not Students," a red fist exhorting "Power to the People," a skull and crossbones with a military hat, "Pentagon Prince," or "Price," I couldn't quite make out, and way in back, real radicalism, "Read the Constitution." Hand drawn flowers and marijuana leaves sprouted from denim jackets, the peace sign everywhere, buttons, head bands, long hair, round-rimmed purple sunglasses, psychedelic tie-dyed shirts—a sense of a cause coming of age, a deadly serious task but a carnival atmosphere. A barefoot girl in a straw hat and torn jeans, handed out leaflets. A tall gal with a blue peace sign on a red shirt waited at parade rest with folded arms. A few sympathetic adults looked on from the perimeter. Way in the rear two senior citizens sat in lawn chairs shielding the sun with folded newspapers.

"I do not believe any peace effort will bear fruit unless there is a genuine, commensurate effort to take our cause away from the confines of the academic community to the public at large. As long as so many people remain disinterested, indifferent, or unaware of the suffering we daily instill, not only on the enemy and ally, but on our own young men as well, as long as people continue laboring under the illusion we are defending our shores against foreign aggression and fail to look carefully into what I think are at best specious legal and political justifications for what we—not they—are doing, then we might as well not march in Washington or anywhere else. Without the support and good will of the general public, the quest for peace will remain quixotic, fragmented, ineffective; representative government will wallow in high sounding rhetoric, the Pentagon will get its way, the generals will dictate policy—and history, I think, amply illustrates where that leads."

The applause lasted longer this time. People were settling in. A definite mood of defiance was asserting itself. The young botanist stepped to the side of the platform, bent down to whisper something to a young woman who made a "can't find them" gesture. When he returned to the microphone, his audience was waiting.

"In this respect we hope our small rally is a beginning to a wider awareness both in the community and on campus. In fact, I'm happy to report, three carloads—let us hope they're not Volkswagens—carrying twenty people are at this moment on their way to Washington." More applause. A few whistles. "I hope this proves we're not as apathetic as some people say. However we do not—" Again the PA system went haywire, wailing like a banshee. Someone jumped to the platform with another microphone; surprisingly they got it hooked up in a jiffy. "Can you hear me back there? I'm not going to do the old Testing one-two number so if you can't hear, come closer." Nobody moved; those who wanted to heard, others went about their business. Two coeds with tennis rackets casually strolled past deep in conversation. A touch football game went on as usual behind one of the dorms across the parking lot.

"We do not advocate violence. Nor do we disparage the sorrow for those who suffer loss. We ask only to be heard, that you consider our objections, think about the problem. If you agree with us, you are invited to join our cause." He took a scrap of paper from his pocket. "Do not expect anything too organized," he smiled. "I'm afraid our agenda this afternoon is as makeshift as the audio equipment but if you'll bear with us, we'll hear first from Dr. Jorgensen in the History Department who will read a paper, 'Historical Roots of the Civil War in Vietnam.'" Wilbur grabbed his head in pain. "Bob Rayburn from Philosophy will talk about, 'Necessity of Empire: The End of Freedom.' Next, Professor Powell from Political Science has the topic of 'Power and Foreign Policy: Myths Past and Present,' and after him I'm told someone from the student coalition will be here. I don't know who this person is or what he plans to talk about…is he or she here yet? No. Okay. Lastly my good friend, Oliver Lester from the English Department, has graciously consented to share with us some thoughts on civil disobedience, entirely extemporaneous he assures me. When we're through, we plan to throw it open for questions and discussion, so without further delay, and if our sturdy platform isn't blown down, we'll hear from the first speaker."

"See you later," Wilbur said.

"Walking out on a fellow historian?"

"Contrary to popular opinion 'historian' and 'masochist' are not synonymous. Let me know when Ricotelli gets here."

Ricotelli was the leader of a small but noisy clique of campus radicals—so they liked to think of themselves—often going out of their way to keep up appearances. Or the lack of them. They took great care to look shabby. Torn jeans were essential, patches the labels of distinction, dirt the sine qua non of "cleanliness"—it could almost be called etiquette if not costume. Denim, khaki, sandals, beards, psychedelic colors were in; neckties, creased slacks, dresses, cologne, and make-up were out. You had to use profanity, smoke grass, hate pigs, deride the university, and distrust the government to keep in good standing. Ricotelli at once stood out among his friends thanks to a healthy head of wild, bushy, hair. Caliban in dark-rimmed glasses, a headband, red, he always appeared in the same pair of threadbare jeans, a T-shirt with a message or even the flag, a leather vest decked out with pins, "LBJ, how many kids did ya kill today?" He'd organized the local SDS chapter if "organize" is the right word; they were a loose collection of dissatisfied kids who gave the impression of having just come from an argument with impossible parents. Their meetings—I attended one—resembled a high school study hall without a teacher and things got done, motions passed, due to healthy lungs more than radical intentions. Yet they managed to hit where it hurt. Why did so many people react to them so violently at the same time perceiving them as ridiculous? A local businessman got wind of their "master plan" from the FBI itself, over J. Edgar Hoover's signature, and took it on himself to warn the entire city of this "menace of a few" in a series of patriotic letters to the editor.

Today, rumor had it, Ricotelli and his coalition were planning to demand equal time, a coup the guys in the basement of West didn't want to miss. Voicing our own repressed curses at the right volume if the wrong direction, he'd become our anti-hero. Rasputin was too removed, Ginsberg too literary; we had to take what we could get.

Ricotelli wasn't a bad kid. Pleasant enough when he could "let his hair down," he had fair, freckled skin over narrow facial lines, quick eye movements, a sense of humor, and more than his share of girl friends. Their soul brother, they said. Academically he didn't show much, but he was savvy, knew the ropes, where the brains were. His fiery arguments were often imaginative, but ended in quick answers to hard questions. His papers lacked documentation, hence low marks, and when I sympathized, he showed me the marginal notation, "bibliography?" He spoke the revolutionary jargon, idolized Che, read the required Marxist literature, but knew it as just that, literature, not as the desperation of hungry bellies suffering real oppression. He turned me off altogether when he started complaining about the shitty food three times a day.

But I liked his underground paper, *The Liberator,* known affectionately as *The Lubricator* in the basement of West where it was avidly read for its athletic style and guerrilla assaults on the English language. Rarely more than two mimeographed sheets stapled together, it had a remarkably eclectic audience. The front page cartoon invariably portrayed the body of a prone student crushed under the heel of an antiquated university policy, but inside Ricotelli's spirited editorials gave it its character. Wilbur would hurry into the office tossing copies all around, excitedly drawing on his pipe while he read, then groan out loud, "Karl would shit." Yet Ricotelli addressed himself to what I thought were pertinent issues, not for their magnitude but for the principle. His enemies, all fascist pigs, were not badly chosen. I think that's what I liked about him; he saw enemies where we were supposed to see friends.

"I see the president of this institution is nothing more than a fascist mouthpiece," Phil said placidly. "Surely you can't take issue with that."

"Pure balls," Wilbur noted without looking up.

I couldn't see Ricotelli's boyish face mouthing a rock tune or rolling a joint. The picture of a revolutionary became ludicrous. He used the rhetoric, but the hardness wasn't there. That's what intrigued me; it was as if he were playing a role, saying what was expected of a young radical because the community which so branded him wouldn't have understood anything else. But isn't that just what they want? As long as they can identify the war protest with long-haired radicals, it isn't a threat. That's what the botanist was getting at.

"I don't understand—"

"Neither does anyone in the English Department," Phil cautioned.

"I don't mean that," I said. "I don't understand why he can't say what he wants without all the theatrics. He might embarrass the opera lovers so what do we do, we deftly nudge him into an absurd radicalism so no one will notice. Wasn't it common in the old days if an unclever heir stood between you and the throne to have him committed for lunacy if you couldn't kill him outright?"

"Nudged by whom?" Wilbur said relighting his pipe while he put his feet up.

"By us. Laugh if you want, but I think there's an honest impulse beneath the bad grammar."

"You think so?"

"Yes, sir, I do."

"You're giving him more brains than he's got," Phil said.

"I'm not talking about brains.

"Then what are you talking about?"

"…Aesthetics maybe."

"But without," Wilbur paused staring at the ceiling, "for lack of a better term…rational discourse, what have you got? Your aesthetics soon go astray and you wind up with bomb throwing pacifists."

"I think you got it turned around. Without aesthetics reason goes astray."

"Talk about reason going astray," Phil said. "How about, 'In order to save this village, we have to destroy it.' I read that the other day. I can't believe they actually said that!"

"Worthy of *The Liberator*, wouldn't you say?"

"You still here?" Wilbur said coming up beside me. I'd moved down on the grass a little closer to the crowd. "How was the paper?"

"Jorgensen? As tedious as it was objective."

"Did he go all the way back to the Middle Ages?"

"I didn't pay attention. See those guys up in front. They don't like what's going on. They've shouted back at him several times, the tall one in the nylon jacket with the collar up, next to the stocky chap in the crew cut."

"Yeah. They're the same guys who ripped up the antiwar literature in the Union last week. Returned vets. Where's Ricotelli?"

"He's around."

"Wearing his beret? He means business if he is."

"I think so. But one of his chicks ran off with it."

"Did she have her ouija board?"

"Let's try to be charitable."

By now Powell was in the middle of his paper, not sympathetic to the war. When the wind gusted, it flipped through the pages causing a short interruption until he found his place again; once it ripped several pages loose sailing them out into the crowd. He went to the edge of the platform and waited patiently until they were returned, thanked the person politely. "Ever notice how fast these old guys get lost without something to read," Wilbur said. Now and then people passed by on a sidewalk that cut through the back of the crowd; sometimes they paused to listen or say Hi to someone before moving off; others took no notice at all. A couple strolled by holding hands, the guy carrying a portable radio blaring out rock music. Another couple leaned out an open window on the second floor of the library. A small group stood well off to one side, attentive but separate. The afternoon classes over, several faculty made a point of showing up and mingling. The touch football game continued.

With the wind ruffling his gray hair, Powell went on tracing the development of American involvement in Southeast Asia from 1954 to the present, placing particular emphasis on the fact our troops had originally been deployed solely in an advisory capacity. He pronounced the word "advisors" like bad tasting medicine each time with increasing sarcasm until it started sounding like "aggressors"—especially to the vets. They answered him with angry shouts but without the aid of a microphone, the wind carried away their words leaving only the vehement gesture. Several others joined them though there couldn't have been more than seven or eight. Their dress set them apart. One, a handsome chap in a stylish jacket and tie seemed to have something to say and repeatedly tried to get the speaker's attention. Finally Powell quoted the present troop strength as being close to "a half million ad-vi-sors, many of whom presumably scored as high as "D" in high school civics—"

That was it.

"How do YOU know!! YOU been there! You wanna tell ME what's goin' on over there!" The husky crew cut lad shouldered his way through the crowd, to the edge of the platform where he stood pointing an angry finger at Powell.

"I see we're going to swap war stories," he said dryly.

"You been there!"

"I served in the Pacific in World War II, so you see I do have some acquaintance with the machinations of the military mind."

"You BEEN THERE!"

"No. I haven't," he smiled.

"Lemmie tell ya somethin'! You don't know what you're talkin' about! You wanna find out? GO!"

"Can't argue with reasoning like that," Powell said coldly and went back to his paper; meanwhile, the stylish young man in the tie excused himself through the crowd and now stood next to Hank, the crew cut. It turned out he, in the tie, had been a communications officer; Hank and his friend in the nylon jacket, platoon leaders. Hank won a medal. The communications officer charged Powell with avoiding the issue and insisted he give them a more specific basis for some of the things he said, namely what in his own experience enabled him to condemn their work. When Powell answered, "I base my argument on twenty-five years experience in the field of international relations," Hank turned away waving both arms in disgust, but then he abruptly spun around pointing at Powell, but this time in a conciliatory posture, almost pleading, as he tried to make his point, "You don't know what's goin' on over there. You don't know everything."

Powell smiled unpleasantly, "Certainly you're not suggesting the military would deliberately withhold pertinent information about...what's goin' on."

Hank started shouting again, something about a dried up old fool, but his buddy calmed him down and by this time the moderator, seeing the impasse, came forward and asked that the paper be finished, at which time they, the vets, were invited to the platform to express their views. They yielded.

Powell finished his paper. It got doctrinaire enough to be harmless, but at the very end he took out a full page magazine photograph showing the charred bodies of Vietnamese children face down in the dirt. "I suppose when all our arguments are exhausted, this is the final word for why I oppose this war. I hope it's 'specific' enough for everyone here." The reference wasn't lost. The vets pushed their way through people, more adamant than ever, "How do YOU know WE did that! You take the PICTURE!"

Instantly things disintegrated. The crowd became a disorganized mob, people shouting and gesturing at each other, a few obscenities, some raised fists. The fellow in the nylon jacket tore himself away from someone in violent anger. People in back stood on their tiptoes to see. The botanist, already in the midst of it, gave up trying to restore order but now stood to the side, with the vets, listening patiently with his head cocked to one side. When it quieted down somewhat, they insisted Powell apologize to them for insinuating they murdered civilians.

"That's not the word he used!" someone shouted.

"He might as well—"

"It's your word!"

"Don't tell me how to—"

"Take it easy—"

"No, let him speak!"

"Who d' hell are you to—"

"I'm not saying," Powell broke in from the microphone sensing things were getting out of hand. "I'm not saying you did this personally," he said cautiously. "I am saying, it is at best, the indirect result of American operations, the definite and unequivocal result of American foreign policy." That was hardly an apology. The shouting started again. Accusations. Threats. One of the placards whirled to the sidewalk. Another grabbed and torn. Someone pushed, another pushed back. Friends stepped in between. The botanist climbed back up on the platform and took the microphone, "If you...IF YOU gentlemen would care to state your case in the form of a rational argument, I promise to give you the time here on the podium. This shouting match is getting us nowhere. Will you meet us this far?"

"All right! One question! Answer one question!" the man in the nylon jacket shouted at Powell. "How do you know we did that and not the enemy?" Powell looked away in disbelief.

"How do you know you didn't!" a woman's voice rose to the necessary volume, equally intense. It seemed to catch them by surprise. They turned to look, one confronted her gesturing, "I was there."

"And your fellow troops? Can you account for all four hundred thousand?" She met him face to face.

"Look, we...we got intelligence..." But he broke off at exactly the wrong place, and a small wave of derision rose from the people around him. A few mean snickers. Then he tried again, "Reports. We just don't...recon patrols..." but he realized his mistake, people were watching, he was center stage to an unfriendly audience, and he started stammering, "patrols...they...we know a village ain't friendly...we..."

"And how do you know they're unfriendly, because they run from your reconnaissance patrols?" She crossed her arms over her chest. Dressed modestly save for a turquoise brooch and a tiny silver earring in the shape of the peace sign, she wasn't backing down.

"Miss," the communications officer said coming between them but it was clear right away she wasn't impressed with style, "that picture he showed you is more likely the work of the Viet Cong, not us. He can't prove who did it. Do we look like we'd do that? I know war's not very pretty, and I don't like it any more than you, but we've got to do our job, all of us. They'll be in Hawaii if we don't stop them now. The least we can do is show some respect to the guys fighting it, some pride in our country." She looked away without the slightest interest until he turned and resumed his sales pitch with someone else.

Not far from her a young man stood silent, seeming not to notice. He looked lost, hadn't said anything, didn't seem to be a vet; he looked strikingly different from the others both in manner and appearance. He wore a beard, longish hair, jeans but with a neat shirt. New loafers. He seemed detached but after awhile abruptly started speaking to her, quietly, looking at the ground, a nervous cigarette in his hand but his eyes unblinking as though the words weren't his. "You can't...you can't...They're jerks, but you can't judge them by your standards. It's not a rational choice. You can't...know...what it is to scoop up the insides of your screaming buddy in your bare hands and try to get him on a stretcher in one piece. Your best buddy. You...and it's your fault, you should have noticed but you...it's not a matter of...of parliamentary debate for Christsake. You just want to get your hands on the son of a bitch that did it. You would too. The next day...black under your nails. It's him. Everything else is bullshit. The army's bullshit. This rally's bullshit. You feel like others don't have the right to talk about it. You can't...you can't know."

"We're here today because you didn't have to go through that. Do you want others to see what you saw? When it's not necessary for our safety?"

"These guys are jerks."

"Which guys?"

"All of them." And he turned away.

"No you're *not* all jerks. No one said that." And she confronted him again, face to face, with something he hadn't seen much—compassion. "What are you trying to tell me?"

"The smart ass, he don't...he never, fast talkers never...they don't see...at least the jerks."

"The officer? What didn't he see?"

"He don't know…"

"Don't know what?"

He looked at her full in the face, calm, unblinking, with a chilling serenity.

"He never tasted blood." Then he quietly turned and walked away, head down.

The rally broke up into small private discussions. On the platform the botanist tried to iron things out while people pressed for his attention all talking at once. When things settled down somewhat, he went to introducing the next speaker, but a hardy-looking, silver-haired man now stood forward insisting that his colleague from the political science department present us with some specific rational proposals for ending the bloodshed instead of mere criticism for past policy since he, the political scientist, obviously dealt in rational arguments. The challenge voiced, he stepped back.

"Very well," Powell said stepping back up to the platform, excusing himself as he stepped in front of the botanist. "It's a fair question, and I'm not trying to avoid it. I agree with you, sir, criticism is easier than a solution…which will not come easy, the reason being, past mistakes are irreparable; however, as the situation stands today, in the fall of 1967, we do have some alternatives although they decrease each day. It may take a blow to our national prestige, but I think we still have time to extricate ourselves with minimal political losses. There will continue to be bloodletting; I am not so naive to think, given the history of this struggle, it will stop after we leave. There could conceivably be a blood bath. But that's exactly what's going on now. Will we be in a better position a year from now? Five years? I think not. We must begin, and begin now, to take some positive steps to bring an end to this sad affair with a minimum of losses on both sides. First, we must negotiate a cease fire. Only then came we hope for a successful troop withdrawal, but before either of these, we'll have to demonstrate our good faith—and it may take some imagination on the part of our leaders—by making some gestures in the direction of peace, a cessation of bombing north of the DMZ is one of the more obvious. As the diplomatic climate changes, we may find ourselves in a better position to design some further alternatives. A lasting peace will not come of our present hard-headed attitude, we will have to make some concessions, certain points they consider essential, such as—"

"Excuse me!" The silver haired man now stepped to the open space before the platform, the vets directly behind him. "Excuse me, sir! I'm sorry to interrupt but what you're saying is pure BUNK!! My name is Demerest, I'm in the Department of Health and Physical Education and although I haven't been in the exulted field of international relations for the past twenty-five years, I have studied history as a student and as an adult and I would like to remind you, sir, of a man called Neville Chamberlain, who, like yourself, stood on a platform waving a piece of white paper in the breeze speaking of concessions and peace in our times and thanks to whom six million Jews died in Nazi gas chambers!" He caught his breath and continued, "And now! Only thirty years later, you, a full professor in political science, you stand up and tell us to concede to a totalitarian dictatorship all over again!" He finished waving the palm of his hand contemptuously in Powell's direction then stormed off towards the Ad Building, the crowd making way for him as he shot through it, some of them chanting the school fight song in derision.

"How much longer are we puttin' up with this shit! If it weren't for militarism, there wouldn't a been fascism in the first place! Are we gonna let 'em make fascists out of us! Well, are we!" Ricotelli. He'd slipped onto the platform and grabbed the microphone before anyone noticed. A few screams of approval from nearby. But then the deluge.

"Sit down BUM!"

"PUNK!"

"GET A HAIRCUT HIPPIE!

The botanist came forward to relieve him of the microphone in the midst of further shouts but also some robust cheering. He jumped back down without an argument and joined his friends.

"DON'T FALL IN A SEWER! YA MIGHT GET CLEAN!"

It came from two inches behind my right ear. I could feel the moisture. One of the custodians. He'd come out to watch, but the minute he saw Ricotelli he couldn't restrain himself. When we turned around, he grumbled apologetically, "Jesus Christ he hasn't changed his underwear in a month."

Down front a short scuffle broke out as Hank tried to get to Ricotelli, but people came between them in time, including the woman who'd spoken earlier. But now they turned back on Powell. They had new fuel. They clung to the word "concession," as he had to "advisors," and when they pronounced it, it came out, "cowardice." Powell retreated, "All right, let's use another word."

"YOU used it!" they shot back in unison.

"You're giving it connotations I didn't!" At last he was getting riled. "All right, let's define it then."

"That's right! YOU define it! Tell 'em how you're gonna concede to the VC!"

Powell drew on his pipe irritably, two clouds of smoke dissipated on the wind. "I'm not interested in drawing analogies between Nazi Germany and Southeast Asia, another time maybe. It's not the same situation. Check your facts. Okay, concessions. What do I mean? Political efforts, calculated risks if you will, new initiatives to get the peace process—"

"You're usin' one fancy word for another! Let's hear how—"

The botanist sensing another tempest came forward. "What's your name?" he said curtly looking at the communications officer.

"Jenkins, sir."

"Mr. Jenkins, since you seem to be the spokesman for these men, I invite you to take the platform and express your views. I'm sure Dr. Powell will yield. I offer this "concession" in hopes that once you state your case, you'll allow the rest of us to continue."

Jenkins took his time walking around to the steps. Powell checked his watch. Although things weren't going according to plan, no one seemed to mind; in fact the crowd was growing. Another thirty people stood on the portico of West Hall, more on the steps of the library, others drew closer. Many uncommitted. Jenkins was smooth, composed, looked you straight in the eye; he'd been in front of a microphone before. He could have passed for a salesman in an exclusive men's store. Of course he couldn't speak for everyone in the service, Hank and Larry could add to what he said if they wished, and naturally he was grateful for the opportunity to speak. Freedom of speech was the greatest; he and his friends should know, they fought for it. A rally like this would be quickly suppressed in the communist world. "Then why suppress it here!" someone shouted—over the mike. Jenkins ignored it. Real smooth. Dictatorships, history had shown, were all alike—ugly, deceitful, thieving, and worst of all, impoverished. To preserve our freedom, they had to be matched rifle for rifle. Appeasement, or whatever you chose to call it, could never work with people like that; their leaders had made robots of them, they were not Christians, they did not have souls. (People looked at each other in disbelief.) They must be made to understand they could never succeed in their designs and the only way to do that was with superior armed might; anything less was tantamount to surrender. As for the people of South Vietnam, they were bravely struggling for their freedom; they sincerely wanted peace, as we all do, but not without democracy. Their resistance proved it. They welcomed and appreciated our help because "They know what communism is. Believe me…it's bad, the absolute, most vile thing on earth and anyone who tells you otherwise cannot be taken seriously. Thank you sir."

He nodded to the botanist and agilely sprang down from the platform. Walking casually with his head turned to the side, he left the rally behind him, confident in his certainty, indifferent to the sparse clapping, aloof from the glances that shot his way. He had said the last word. No one could possibly add to it.

Wrong. Ricotelli was on the stage again waving his arms for attention. He was met with a wise crack or two, but mostly loud cheers and his friends chanting, "Equal time! Equal time!" A short discussion followed. Old Mr. Lester patiently waiting his turn at the side of the platform yielded heartily. Wilbur looked at me drawing on his pipe.

"I guess you all know who I am," he grinned into the microphone, hands in his pockets, sneakers with the sides split open, no socks. The custodian turned and spat in the grass before walking away. "I jus' wanna say…How much longer are we puttin' up with this shit! There are people dyin' out there! This minute! While we stand around listenin' to propaganda straight out o' the fucking Pentagon! While the fucking racist imperialist media tell us what t' think! While the fucking capitalist pigs on Wall Street decide what we wear, what we drive! How long you gonna stand there suckin' your thumbs? This might as well be a fraternity bed race! You might as well be ballin' under the tables down at *Howard's* like the rest of the sick apathetic protoplasm on this dead campus—"

"Apathetic protoplasm," Wilbur whispered. "Did you get that?"

"I think he means us."

"A campus of nine thousand students. Nine thousand! And what do we got? Three hundred? Four hundred? Man, that's real involvement! Man, that's commitment! And three car loads goin' to Washington. Wow! That's twenty more! And our august student leaders? Where are they? Up in Watson's office playin' parliamentary procedure. Heavy shit, maaaan. And where are the other eight thousand six hundred? Takin' Mickey Mouse courses, wow, brownin' up fer grades, wow, thinkin' 'bout their future, 'bout that two-car garage, 'bout all that bread till there's no time left t' think anymore! Well, we got news for Watson! His wart farm ain't what it used to be! We're gonna wake this campus up if we have to drag people out by the balls!"

"What about the chicks man!" a feminine voice sang out. Ricotelli had an answer ready but the botanist somehow got him stopped. However as he ushered him off the platform, a black student in sun glasses and a black power T-shirt jumped up in front of the vacant mike.

"I jus' wanna say to the soul brothers and sisters…keep cool. An' don' furgit, our fight's right here in the streets not ova tha in Nam. We KNOW what it's like to be down. We don' need no white dude tellin' us how BAD communism is ova tha when we already KNOW how BAD racism is right HERE. So don' tell us 'bout dictatorships and fightin' for freedom. We already been EDucated. Long time now. Mississippi court houses been our CLASSrooms, policemen with DAWGS been our teachers, the ghetto been our LABoratory. Stay cool. We gonna git inVOLved. We gonna git what's OURS, or you gonna git the biggest bonfire you eva SAW!" He thrust his fist into the sky then jumped down and trotted over to a half dozen black friends who'd been yelling "yeah" while he spoke.

At last, with effort, old Mr. Lester, now retired after thirty years teaching and little gardening, carefully climbed the three steps with the botanist's help, calmly surveyed the audience over the rims of his bifocals, then through them, turned the wrong way, then the right way, found the microphone and began his extemporaneous comments on civil disobedience which, he admitted, were a bit anticlimactic. But no more than himself. However he found it refreshing to learn extemporaneous speakers apparently had not gone out of vogue. "It's good to know," he rasped from under a tuft of snowy hair, "it's good to know…you're not out of vogue," and the two elderly people in the lawn chairs clapped, one brandishing a rolled up newspaper. After a few pleasantries on the weather and the high cost of haircuts, he reassured us in the gentlest manner but with the soundest conviction, in an aged but ageless voice, that what we had heard today was a healthy thing. The first amendment, he told us, "Guarantees neither truth, nor wisdom, nor the triumph of a cause…but only a chance…to shout into the wind. The best way to defend it," he continued, his voice almost musical with the strain of age, "Not by fighting over it…but by practicing it, exercising it, strengthening its muscle." Not much applause. "The best way to lose it," he intoned as though from over the centuries, "not by giving it flight…but by trimming…its wings." The gal with the blue peace sign gave a mighty two-fingered whistle, but by this time no one was listening; people were walking away in small cliques talking among themselves. A pity. Here again grace in the eye of the storm, but lost in the babble of the moment. He made the drugstore revolutionaries look like choirboys. Civil disobedience? His the most radical of all—he refused to get old.

160

Wilbur and I were nearly out of earshot when it began. We heard a scream, then some people running. One of the placards went sailing through the air, another cracked in two. A coed had either fallen or been pushed down on the sidewalk. About thirty people converged into a dense mob at the far end of the mall. Someone tried to wrestle away one of the placards but a young woman resisted. We heard more screams, shouts, a few curses. Two more people shoved down, a fistful of leaflets hurled into the air. Then I could see the back of Hank's neck, his jaws moving as he shouted something straight into Ricotelli's face. Others ran up. Hank's heavy arm went for his shoulder; he dropped back a few steps, but the second time he tried to parry it away. Two campus security officers hurried in. The first went straight for Ricotelli, grabbed him by the elbow jerking him around while Hank got in a free push, then walked him away in a half arm lock lecturing all the way. The second watched, put a fatherly hand on Hank's shoulder and nodded assent to whatever he was saying. Meanwhile Ricotelli's face broke into a smile of disbelief, which brought on a tighter arm lock, while his friends tried vigorously to explain something. After awhile they let him go but stood nearby keeping him under angry surveillance, totally ignoring his alarmed friends, oblivious to the scuffles still in progress. At the very last Ricotelli offered a gesture of "forget it man" in Hank's direction.

Wilbur and I walked up to the mail room and checked our boxes. Down in the basement they were already talking about it. We could hear them in the laundry room—we still called it that though long since converted to a group office for six grad students and as many others as could get in when a hot topic raged. The wall posters reflected the political divisions. Karl Marx looked down on the proceedings rather severely, Mao kept his secret, Gary Cooper confused, Gandhi uncritical, the knight from *The Seventh Seal* grave, Olivier's Hamlet serene, Sophia Loren...there was no word in the OED. Meanwhile Miss October remained safe behind a white church on an insurance company calendar, and Lyndon Johnson...kind of hangdog high on the far wall where three strong shots pinned him to a dart board.

We met Wilma Winters on her way out, an armload of materials as usual, glowing, very attractive, but all business. Navy and gray with a splash of orange. Nice perfume. "Are you getting back from the rally?" she asked eagerly.

"You're not suggesting we've been working," I said.

She caught herself, smiled, then asked softly, "I heard there was a scuffle".

"They roughed up Ricotelli," Wilbur said. "Don't worry, he's made of tough stuff. Then the untouchables rushed in and saved the day."

"Really?"

"It got tense for a minute."

"How so?"

"Some people wanted it to go ugly. The cops didn't have a clue."

"Wanted it to?" she asked intently. "What gave you that impression?"

"Nothing substantial. I thought it was interesting the way they went straight for Ricotelli. No questions. Zap."

"Otherwise was it that informative?" Neither of us said anything. "What was the most telling thing you saw?" She turned to me. I thought a minute.

"The touch football game behind the dorm. They didn't even notice the rally."

"Really?" she exclaimed with one of her eager smiles, "Well. That's interesting. See you tomorrow."

We watched her walk down the hall and out the door. "Speaking of untouchables," Wilbur said wistfully.

"Nice outfit," I said.

"Untouchable but not unfathomable if we may trust the researches of our distinguished colleague in the German Department," Phil observed.

"You mean our Marxist in resi—"

"Shh."

"Wie geht's."

He rushed in beginning his spiel before his briefcase touched the floor. "Look at this, incredible, life in the basement of West, the world's out there burning, we sit here vegetating, I don't believe it, I don't believe this campus."

"Take it easy Murray," Louis said.

"We're living in the sixteenth century, a guy gets killed in the parking lot and everybody stands there watching."

"Murray, what happened?"

"Ricotelli! The rally! Ten yards away! Nobody knows what I'm talking about?" He sat on the edge of his desk palms upward.

"They said there was a scuffle," Crandall recalled.

"A scuffle? Somebody gets beat up you call it a scuffle?"

"Who beat up whom?"

"Ricotelli got his ass kicked, the living shit beat out of him, broad daylight, cops right there watching, Jesus; who? The Delts, as in 'Daaaa did

I do good, coach,' the whole damn house on top of one guy, people actually thought it was funny, ha ha, ten yards from Walton's office, you know, the real world, planet earth."

"We didn't see anybody get beat up," Wilbur said.

"There you are, did I tell you?"

"Murray, no one's saying it didn't happen," Cathy smiled. They only said they didn't see it."

"Oh they didn't see it?" he mocked. "Well, I'm not surprised, eagle-eye spent two years in Africa and didn't see poverty. Talk about a perception problem."

"Let's not get into that again," Louis pleaded.

"Excuse me," he ignored him, "I must have a slight hearing problem or was it your twin brother maintaining we are the oppressed not the Third World?"

"You have a slight problem with the English language Murray," I said.

"Whoa!" Louis and Phil cheered. Crandall launched a dart, then someone in the next office started banging on the wall for quiet.

"I wasn't talking about economics."

"Ah. Economics has nothing to do with it; a mere coincidence these countries are living under military dictatorships, supported by American arms, a mere accident American Corporate interests do business there, a mere—"

"Murray! Slow down," Cathy said.

"It's not a deliberate master plot," I said. "We make mistakes; we're not degenerate."

"Not de—" he leaned back on his desk smiling, "a half million men to prop up an artificial police state, just a small miscalculation." Great chess player, my move.

"It's a serious mistake. We're not inherently wicked."

"A mistake? That's beautiful," he beamed framing my face in his hands like a movie director. "Don't change a thing. I love it just the way it is, the name, the space, the century—eighteenth wouldn't you say?"

"Murrr-y," Cathy crooned.

"Periwig and powdered hose!"

"Murray!" she scolded. And someone banged on the wall again. Louder.

"Okay Murray, you win," I said. "Nobody can beat you...talking."

"Touche!" Crandall cried.

"Or should I say Camelot without a Kenndey?"

"Wanna get a beer?" I said to Dan.

"Maybe later," he said out in the hall. "Don't mind him. All rhetoric. He quoted you the other day."

"Did he now? Anything to win an argument."

"He makes you *think* he's won," he said pointing his pipe stem. "Remember that."

"Say…that bit about Wilma? Are they…you know—"

"So the grapevine has it."

"…Lucky man."

"Well, now. Has this rivalry gone beyond ideology?"

"Oh no. She's way out of my league. See you down at *Howard's.*"

CHAPTER 15

DOWN AT *HOWARD'S*

Howard's. Originally a small neighborhood bar, eight or nine stools and a ball game in black and white, then the students took over, now the oldest, dirtiest hangout downtown—also the busiest. It started expanding down a side street, first a barber shop next door, then a vacant doctor's office, an antique store, until it found itself halfway down the block with three entrances. The owner didn't dare make improvements. Students liked it, the rattier the better. The scent of spilt beer never quit, the stools had long since come loose, floor boards creaked, flaps of linoleum covered soft spots, peanut shells crunched under foot, the walls and windows cracked, the tables carved, chairs unmatched, the school mascot over the bar sported a garter belt and bra, the john walls abounded with art and literature, the help overworked and lied to, ashtrays stolen, the clientele loud, obscene, the jukebox box full blast—and when they turned on the lights at one o'clock your hangover began at once.

But the last two tables at the south end were special. You went through a back room and down four steps—it helped to know there were four—past the stern faces of several tintype portraits somehow surviving the antique shop, and plopped down in the favorite gathering spot of the local counterculture, Bohemians without a whiskey cellar. Serious discussions vied with the jukebox box and sometimes won, ardent rebels led strange chases through Western Civ, everything from St. Francis to Fellini, Lenin to Lennon.

> *Well, they'll stone ya when ya try to be so good*
> *They stone ya just like they said they would*

The rally. Why was I so worked up? The old man was right. There was something healthy—also something sick. Jenkins frightened me. I felt bad for the vets, they got the shaft goin' and comin.' But after the shouting they didn't have much of an argument. Defending democracy were we? South Vietnam

165

in no way qualified, they themselves often relating the gross incompetence of that country's regime; the analogies to World War II didn't hold either, which left them with "my country right or wrong." But is blind patriotism really patriotism? As far as shutting off dissent—unconscionable. The real war had nothing to do with Vietnam; it raged within ourselves; the real danger, not the Third World but our own arrogance.

It wasn't about ideology. Ideology didn't mean squat back in the bush. I kept coming back to that. Third World uprisings were nationalist in origin—and they weren't a threat. We'd fought the first war of national liberation, but when similar aspirations arise, they become Marxist before we know it. The die is cast, the same old story, a petty tyrant decked out in a grand uniform to halt the march of communism. Anything to stop it. The use of their methods, the betrayal of our own best principles; the result, their best men withdrew and the worst came forward. In the name of fighting communism we were serving it. Why weren't we in the vanguard of these movements? Was there any law that said they had to be Marxist? Was it possible to support them before they turned red? Or was that the point, to make them red? Was it naïve to think otherwise?

> *They stone ya when you're walkin' on the street*
> *They stone ya when you're tryin' to keep your feet*

Why do we always support the dictators? I kept coming back to that. It's like looking into a dark closet; you know what's there but you're afraid to turn on the light. Was Murray right? Was I that naive? Perhaps the real naivete is to think you can play with dictatorships and not get dirty.

> *They stone ya when you're walkin' on the floor*
> *They stone ya when you're walkin' through the door*

We make mistakes, we're not degenerate—two years ago I wouldn't have put it quite that way. We make mistakes—no qualifier. Are we really degenerate? Was he right? That shitass Marxist sneering at everything I said. I hadn't seen poverty had I? He had all the answers—now Wilma. The lucky bastard. What the hell did she see in him?

Then they blew in, three deep, loud, aloof but dying to be noticed. One even had a book; another a "Fuck Authority" button on the lapel of an army jacket. The others went with what they had, tight jeans, straggly hair, heavy mascara. They crowded in, joined two others, dragging up their chairs like cowboys. The one with the book fired first.

"Jesus Christ I don't believe this. This is so fucking incredible, man, our landlady; what an incredible bitch. Jesus Christ, I hate her like she's threatened to have us evicted because it's against house rules, like we got two cats they're both housebroken, like man we'd have one that isn't, but the real reason Randy Wilson blond freaky kinda cute stayed Friday night, like he needs a place to crash, slept on the floor after what Baker told me I wouldn't let him near me the bit about Daneen and him doin' it in the cemetery like on the grave stones and everything so the old broad thinks we had an orgy she says she heard our record player going all night Jesus Christ it's going all day like she's gotta be deaf this is so fucking incredible man so this morning she goes and calls the Dean's office she says she wants to make sure he's enrolled she doesn't want anything to happen to us Jesus Christ I hate her—"

"I don't believe it!" one of the listeners exclaimed in wide-eyed disbelief.

"This is unreal!" another screamed crashing an armful of bracelets to the table.

"Where's Baker?"

"Oh she's tripping," the evictee answered with boredom.

"Shit!" the other answered in overwrought surprise.

The celebrated "Movement." Well…the foot soldiers. Shopping mall Marxists manicured hand and foot, if they ever did an honest day's labor it'd be slapstick comedy. They couldn't clean their rooms, get to class on time, find their books. At least the Lost Generation knew it was lost; these couldn't find America in the middle of Iowa.

What if they won their damn revolution? Did they ever consider the possibility? The morning after? Somebody'd have to get up to open the pastry shop, preferably before two in the afternoon. They'd expect bonbons in a soup line. A line! They'd have to form a line. They couldn't last five seconds in remedial dodgeball.

They stone ya when you're tryin' a make a buck
They stone ya and then they'll say good luck

But they're right about the war. What a tasteless revenge on the tragedies of the past.

But I would not feel so all alone
Everybody must get stoned

They'd had it too easy. Their parents had struggled back in the thirties but for some reason went to great lengths to save their children from anything of the kind forgetting it was that struggle and their coming through it that made them what they were, gave them leave to speak of it with reverence. What would these have to speak of in their day? How they suffered a whole hour at the police station because daddy was late with bail.

Peace and love. And a barefoot flower child handing out daisies in front of the Union, she often picked me for some reason, presenting it without a word, meeting my scowl with a child's smile and lowered eyelids. Why did she fluster me? If I accepted, I felt like an idiot; if not, like I'd kicked a puppy.

"What d'ya say, man."

Jeff. He drew up two chairs, "When's the big bust man? We gonna sneak up on 'em 'r we goin' in like gangbusters?" One of my students, a light complected black with an Afro, wire rimmed glasses.

"Shut up." He leaned back smiling maliciously. He had a girl with him, sweater and jeans, straight hair, a bit distant but bright-eyed; she smiled too, but from far away. His reference was to the time one of the perfumed paupers asked me if I was a Narc. He wouldn't let me forget it.

"It's okay folks," he announced over his shoulder, "he used to work for the government but he don't anymore!" then under his breath, "I don't believe how it blew your mind."

"It didn't...*blow my mind.*"

"I can just see you standin' there, kind o' faint like a kid who juss learned there ain't no Sanna Claus. You should o' played it cool, man. You know, like snapped your fingers, 'Don't bug me chick, this is my thing.'" He kept snickering. "You look like somethin' out of a back-to-school catalog."

"My hippie suit's at the cleaners."

"Honey we gotta do somethin' about that tie," she said drawing close. "Here let me. We don't want Howie to think you're the liquor inspector. Nice shirt. Let's see now, how about a head band?"

"No!"

"Yeah!" Jeff laughed leaning back. "And some war paint!"

"You don't wanna pass my course very bad."

"Nothing out of character," she teased. "How 'bout an ascot—"

"No thank you."

"Well, I'll just keep it safe then," and she put it in her bag.

"Wow! Captured live at Howie's Wild Safari!" Just then he lost his balance, shot forward, grabbed the table tipping over my beer just as she jerked out of the way with a scream, a dish of peanuts flew to the floor, and next thing somebody threw a soggy rag from somewhere across the room. It came like a baseball, hit the wall, I missed it on the rebound and it flopped down on the floor in front of her. She picked it up and started sopping the table. "You okay?" she whispered. Soon a beefy chap in a football jersey and a bar towel came forward to retrieve the rag. She dropped it on his tray like a dead rat.

"Three fish," I said. "Next time let's see your fastball."

"Thank you," she said arranging her sweater. She was plain at first, but then her placid face opened like a flower and a faint smile began to glow; her eyes gleamed, her waist-length hair, straight and silky, on her neck a tiny pearl on a thin chain. We sipped our beers, the jukebox blared but not enough to drown her warmth. People danced, checked out the possibilities.

"I didn't see you at the rally," Jeff said in a more serious tone.

"I was there. How's Rico?"

"Don' know. What I'm saying is…I expected to see you…up on the platform."

"What was I supposed to do? Give another speech?"

"Look at the hypocrite. Talks about involvement, then the real thing happens, he stands there watchin'."

He was baiting me. The girl looked interested. Conversations with him had a way of turning hostile real quick. Beneath the wire rims and fair complexion, he harbored an vengeance beyond anything he'd suffered personally. It only took one word. The bubble pricked, his anger exploded, the fight against prejudice became prejudice. He carried a terrible hatred within, saw people in rigid stereotypes, pigs or Uncle Toms, never budged, and we, good liberals, had to acquiesce. He even had to have a new name, often pumped me on African names, (I thought of Jefferson Akwoi). Massa Jefferson had kept slaves, didn't I know? When I suggested he also kept the flame that extinguished slavery, he sneered contempt. He saw everything black and white, took every criticism personally. Racism was his cause, he thrived on it, went out of his way to find it, without it he was lost. He fancied himself a revolutionary but had trouble getting up for eleven o'clock classes.

"I can't get excited about causes anymore."

"I suppose you've heard the old saying, 'the best way for evil to triumph is for good men to do nothing.'"

"Or something worse in their bungling haste to get on the six o'clock news."

"Jeff tells me you were active in the early civil rights marches," she smiled. Who was she?

"Early? Six years ago."

"What did you do?"

"Things were different then. People's faces."

"What do you mean?" She was taking over. "Come on, out with it."

"I remember gleaming faces eager for the future. We stayed up nights painting slogans on cardboard placards, next day if the weather was nice we walked up and down clean sidewalks singing *We Shall Overcome*."

"Aand."

"The good guys were gonna win, just like the movies. There were unquestionable truths, like granite. The American brain could overcome any obstacle, pay any price, bear any burden, all that bullshit."

"What specifically made you change your mind?"

"Specifically?"

"What *melted* the granite?"

"…It's hard to put into words."

"Try," she whispered.

"Let's have another beer."

"No let's not have another beer."

"Nothing specific."

"Then let's be abstract."

"I can't think of—"

"Yes, you can."

"…There was a beautiful village," she wasn't gonna let me off, "back in the bush, off the beaten track—"

"Did it have a name?"

"Kpodokpodo. No Shangra-La but not shanty town either, nestled on the shoulder of a mountain, a sacred mountain. Then one day a bush pilot flew over and noticed his compass going haywire, then somebody else tried it, then three guys took a little hike, dug a few little holes. Their sacred mountain turned out to be sitting on top of the richest iron ore deposit in the country. By now it's a filthy mining camp, with all the amenities of civilization—drunkenness, whores, VD, blaring radios, servile labor, chiefs who look like paupers. That's where your goddamn noble causes get you. What we've done to that village is criminal."

"Not to choose is to choose," she said softly.

"By the way," Jeff said, "this is Sally Butler. My American Studies Prof—and he's a fake, goes around pretending he's a conservative but underneath he's a red-eyed radical."

"Make that a teaching fellow. What year?"

"Junior. School of Art," she said extending her hand. She looked me full in the eyes, so deep it gave me a start. "Jeff tells me you're interested in the Occult."

"Not if you call it that."

"Then what should I call it?"

"Why not art?"

"Art?"

"Isn't there something magic at the core of every great work?"

"What do you mean...magic?" she said drawing up her chair. Gray eyes.

"You better watch yourself now," Jeff warned.

"What do I mean? Oh boy."

"Come on. You said it."

"...Okay. The only difference between an ordinary Joe and a master is the master's dumb enough to believe he's got some kind of magic going. How's that?"

"But magic is the suspension of natural law," she smiled, "the transmutation of matter; an artist isn't interested in changing the substance of his materials, only their form. Good art doesn't cheat."

"Neither does good magic. When your artist alters the form of his materials, doesn't he also alter the feelings of the person who views it? There's the magic."

She thought about it then Jeff said, "What she wants to know...is...do you, or do you not, believe in witchcraft?"

"Of course. Take nuclear fission. Now there's the last word in witchcraft, transmutation of matter, not to mention the mentality of those who come under its power."

"Damn!" He pounded the table. Then to her, "You know what they call him behind his back? 'Space.' As in, 'Space, the final frontier.'"

"You really don't wanna pass my course very bad."

"Okay, let's try it again. You ready? Can some evil dude back there in Africa stick a needle in a Barbie doll and some dude on Madison Avenue fall down foamin' at the mouth?"

"Of course not. That's ridiculous. There, you feel safe now?"

"Then what do they believe?" she asked.

"In the secret forces that spin the atoms; we see numbers, they see spirits."

"But isn't that just what keeps them down?" she asked.

"Yes. Only they don't see it that way. We master; they abide. You pays you money you takes you pick. Just like art."

"You're not suggesting that we—"

"No."

"All right," Jeff said. "Let's think this out. Here's what you do. Tomorrow morning you go down to the dean's office, make an appointment, don't go bargin' in like you come t' liberate the place, be cool, let the receptionist show you in, then you tell 'em you wanna do your thesis on the existence of evil spirits."

"I might as well be."

"Then you're working on your—"

"I don't want to talk about it!"

By now some others joined us, two girls then a guy. They sat down and one threw a peanut shell at Jeff. Soon they were absorbed in another conversation.

They stone ya when you are all alone
They stone ya when you are walking home

I remembered I hadn't written up my class notes for tomorrow. No matter, we'll talk about the rally. But how? Without it turning into another shouting match?

They stone ya and then say they are brave
They stone ya when you are sent down in your grave

Then a small ruckus across the room, an ill-balanced jock staggered up the stairs, "HEY! Where's d'ass wipe? Felton! You took it! Ya t'ink it's a sugar doughnut!" He grabbed for the loose banister, pulled it off the wall before falling sideways on the steps much to the delight of his friends. One of them yelled, "Hey, Howie! Film for da Brownie!"

But I would not feel so all alone
Everybody must get stoned

"Wanna dance?" Sally said. "It's good medicine donch ya know?"

Out on the floor the magic she didn't believe in came to life; something superior to the surroundings and all its eyes came out of camouflage and spread its wings.

"Pretty gross in here isn't it?," she smiled.

"At least it's—"

"Wanna come up to my place?"

She lived in two rooms above a garage on the far side of town, the key in a rotted knothole in the railing. The steps creaked. A musty black walnut scratched the roof, but the loft above was spacious enough for a studio, at least if you ignored the linoleum. An ugly skylight at the peak, like a little greenhouse, bare beams, two paintings, another on an easel draped with a towel, and a skinny black cat stretched out on a dusty sofa in regal luxury.

"What's her name?"

"Camille. Cammy, sweetheart. Oh I see, new guy in town. She likes you, I can't believe it, she hates guys."

"I have a way with courtesans."

"She's NOT a courtesan! Poor baby, donch ya listen to 'im. Tea?"

"Sure."

"Comin' right up. Put on a record."

The kitchen was off to one side; the bath and the bedroom behind a partition of Japanese panels strung with clothing. Everything in disarray— rolled canvases, paints, brushes tucked in corners. An handmade rug lay in tatters over stained green carpeting beneath a rocking chair with one spoke missing; against the wall an ornate oak desk with globed feet, records and magazines, a climbing vine intertwined in the bricks of makeshift bookshelves, a candle set on a ledge, burnt down and giving the place a feeling of parted company. A black and white photograph, herself, *au naturel,* in soft tones and alienated boredom. Up above, in a deep niche between two posts, a narrow vase with a single dry thistle in burnt yellow glass. And pinched in a mirror, another snapshot, her, hitchhiking, somewhere out west. Jeans, hike boots, red bandanna, a knapsack covered with patches, Cammy perched on top, the same spirit that conquered the mountains a century ago.

"You actually hitchhiked—"

"California."

I was incredulous but something made me believe.

"It's very close to the soul of your generation—that photograph."

"My generation? It's yours, too, isn't it?"

"No. The cars don't stop for me."

"That means you're one of us, buddy. Read the pundits. Our generation's screwed up, you're screwed up, that makes you one of us, just because you can't go about it like the rest of us, don't think you're foolin' anybody! No Bach fugues."

She whirled into the room, two tea cups in one hand, Cammy in the other, singing a Joan Baez tune—you don't like my singing?"

"I didn't—"

"O where have all the—you hate my singing, very well, I'll stay barefoot and pregnant," with that she plopped into the sofa, one leg over the armrest, "Hey. You gonna find a record in the near future?"

"No, I'm gonna stay barefoot and out to stud."

"Oh. Nice choice—the record. How 'bout a candle?"

She jumped up, fumbled for matches, then dropped cross-legged on the floor. Her hair curled into her lap while the candle light caught her face in a glow that changed the mood at once, mine too."

"It works better if ya take your shoes off."

"I know. That's why cowboys don't do yoga…the spurs."

"You really should give your sense of humor a chance. How's your tea?"

"Fine thank you."

They she leaned forward, wide-eyed, intense.

"Tell me about Africa."

"Oh God."

"Come on, loosen up. You're doin' just fine."

"I really don't—"

"What am I gonna do with you? Hellooo in there," she whispered, tapping my skull. "Come out, come out. Whoever you are."

"What da ya wanna know?"

"Why'd you go?"

"I…"

"Come on, just like havin' a baby. Push."

"It was 63, Kennedy was alive, I was an idealist. I suppose there are worse crimes."

"I'll bet your superiors found you highly frustrating."

"I rarely saw them."

"But you saw Africans. How do they see us?"

"With loose change in our pockets, shoes on our feet, strangers who eat every day but never work. They have their misconceptions too."

"If that's an American, what's a primitive?"

"Someone who can look at the sky and see a beautiful face."

"I knew this guy once," she said drawing her knees under her chin. "A real brain. He told me when he was little he loved to go out at night and watch the stars, but after he took up astronomy, all he could see was equations."

"Right! That's the whole point. I was trying to get that across to that imbecile Forrester."

"Imbecile?"

"He should have a propeller on his mortarboard."

"Didn't get your thesis approved, didja?"

"I don't want to talk about it."

"Why don't you scrap the whole idea and start over. Do it on Thoreau."

"How in the—"

"I do my research," she winked.

"…I couldn't do that to old Henry. He's sacred man."

She got up and turned the record over, switched off the bathroom light, then came back and reclined on the rug with her head in my lap.

"You're too…bottled up. You need to let it come out. You're really good when you get off the track. You know the one thing that bugs me about you? You don't seem to have noticed the poverty."

"Oh God, not again! You sound like Murray Weisenbaum."

"Relax, will you." She smiled softly. "There aren't any Marxists in here."

"Poverty's there. If that's what you're looking for, you can take a bath in it."

"Will you *please* relax."

"Most people don't look for anything else."

"But they are hungry?"

"And sick and barefoot and poorly clothed, but they survive. And laugh."

"Laugh?"

"Yes…A sense of humor they've got. It bugged me at first. How they could laugh in the face of such poverty? But they did."

"But they always look so…so ferocious in pictures."

"They don't trust cameras, tighten up just before it clicks; they think it's trying to capture their souls, which is exactly what a good photographer does. Afterwards they loosen up."

"But they still believe in witchcraft?"

"Some do, some don't."

"But those who do?"

"…Are only trying to change things."

"Isn't that what you tried to do?"

"Yeah. Maybe I didn't shake my rattle hard enough."

"But at least you tried. Not trying, that's the crime."

"Thanks."

"You ever see a witch?"

"Oh yeah."

"A real one?"

"Yes."

"Tell me about her."

CHAPTER 16

HOT MUD AND OLD DAN TUCKER

"They say she's a witch!"

"Who?"

"The old woman," Mulba whispered excitedly. "Kdubahwatah."

"How do you know?"

"Mr. Freeman told me when you were taking your bath. You and I, we will go back there tomorrow, it will not be a good day for travel."

"Why not the others?"

"No! Akwoi will laugh at her. She will not speak."

"Let's think it over," I whispered back. "We'll decide in the morning."

Dawawoli turned out to be a dismal cluster of twenty houses huddled together in the gloom like a drove of sick cattle. Only two zinc roofs. And those bent up and corroded. The thatched fared no better, clumps of healthy grass grew in rotted places, several showed signs of repair, fresh palm fronds hastily strapped over leaky spots or flaps of tarp tied down with bush rope. Some didn't even have dome pots, nor whitewash; splotches of gray lichen grew unchecked. Heavy clumps of mud had fallen from several walls leaving dirty niches and wooden ribs exposed to the weather; where fresh clay plastered them over it looked like leprosy. Debris from the storm lay everywhere. Low limbs, like intruders, swollen with rain, hung well into the village dripping fat drops straight down across the grain of slanting drizzle that appeared like white gauze in the blackened doorways.

After the storm we had a hard two-hour hike over treacherous trails. At last we stood alone in the middle of the village, drenched through, spattered with mud while rivulets of ground water washed over our feet. The place looked utterly abject, desolate, bleak. A feeling of total depression came over me. What in the hell was I doing here? I ached to the bone and started to shiver. A wet night was coming on. Then a solitary figure with his head bent forward under a flap of yellow oilcloth came around a corner, extended his hand, two clicks, then turned back uttering a single word, "Come." Dawawoli's hospitality was to completely contradict its apparent poverty.

He showed us to a round thatched house, much like the rest save for a rectangular porch, attached awkwardly, itself open on three sides. There we found the chief sitting in a worn, raffia hammock with broken threads stringing to the floor. He sat humbly over a bowl of rice which he held on his knees wearily lifting each bite to his lips with slender fingers. The skin of his face worked painfully as he chewed his food with failing teeth, but his working muscles were strong and the soles of his feet thick as leather. He wore a threadbare denim robe, more like an apron. Under the hammock, a pair of unbecoming yellow plastic slippers. His name was Kpadehmai.

He motioned us in. His son, who'd met us, cleared the porch of goats, ordered chairs, then stood quietly at his father's side. Without looking up the old man saw our discomfort and ordered hot bath water. Painfully working his food between his gums and lower lip, he asked what news. John answered giving our destination. He listened absently, observed we were taking the hard way and asked for our patience. A *qwi* man was living in town and would see to our needs as soon as he returned from his farm.

The curious now came to greet us despite the steady drizzle; two men, an old woman, and several young men our age. The small ones kept a cautious distance as usual, eyeing me from behind the others but never missing a thing, the simple act of wiping my glasses drew great interest. They only moved to swat insects or scratch themselves. Goats tried to force their way back on the porch and had to be removed, usually with an deft kick.

Two wide doors behind the hammock opened into a one-room store that Kpadehmai ran as a sideline. The size of a closet, lit by a single lantern, a warped plank served for a counter in front of a row of half-empty shelves: palm oil in beer bottles with rolled up wads of leaf for corks, kerosene, also by the beer bottle, a jug of cane juice, a box of rifle shells, homemade soap, a row of bright colored head-ties, a jar of hard candy—and many items gathering dust. Most of the trade came in nickels and dimes, the proprietor often declining to change large bills for fear of being taken for a rich man, which usually meant trouble.

Whether for decoration or to protect the wood, someone had plastered the doors with magazine clippings and old newspapers, the city page of *The Baltimore Sun,* worn through in spots but legible, August 8, 1961. Amazing. Yellowed and stained from the leaky roof, they became a perfect collage.

Large colorful pictures slapped on top one another with no apparent order conveyed tribal tastes. They loved color, health, good will: a hardy stevedore with a bottle of stout, a sultry model with a pet black leopard and a bottle of liquor, a white woman sitting happily before a sewing machine, bright faces with fresh products, cigarettes, Aunt Jemima with a stack of pancakes, a black traffic officer with a soft drink, and a soccer match with the goalie in horizontal flight, and in the lower corner partially hidden by another picture—it was the first thing I noticed stepping onto the porch—the cover of an American movie magazine. Incredible! Here in Dawawoli, a good thirty miles off the motor road, Liz Taylor and Richard Burton were having their troubles. Exclusive photos. And the inevitable question, "Is Liz cheating on Burton?" They're never going to believe this back home. Any Romantic notions I had about finding an "untouched" village died right there.

When the chief's son saw my interest, he joined me taking pleasure in pointing out details. Were these my tribe? Oh, yes. Were they of my village? No, I didn't really know them; I knew about them, but he didn't get the distinction. You either knew somebody or you didn't. The football players? European, my people played a different kind of football. He paused to clear a cobweb. How long would it take a man to read all these words? An entire evening I thought. He hummed approval. Did I know them all? I thought so. He hummed again, then asked abruptly, where did the words go when the paper is destroyed? How easily the tribal mind traversed the trivial to the profound. That was a good question, I said, but I didn't know the answer. I suspected the words were like smoke from a sacrificial offering; they disappear into the air and whether or not they find their destination we never know. He grunted assent. No mistake about the movie mag.

He ducked behind the counter to get my candy, two cent-two cent, more expensive than back on the motor road, but asked that I not give it to the children where his father could see. The old man had rotten teeth thanks to fondness for candy and it pained him to see the little ones follow his bad example. Then why keep it around? The *qwi* man, who would come shortly, had brought it from the Mission in Bolahuhn. He spent "many time" there working the grounds and praying God, but when he returned here to his native village, he brought many fine things: magazines, pictures of God, praying beads, worm medicine, and candy. He even had a radio. And here on this wall a very strange device, he pointed to a calendar, with all the days divided into square boxes, one day in each box and it told you how to pray on that particular day. How could they know in advance? And how can you divide a day into a square box? A day is round. The sun draws a great circle around the village each day. *Qwi* people believe strange things.

The word *qwi* originally meant "foreign" but somehow acquired the connotation, "civilized," which in turn came to be measured by the most mundane things, a few words of English, a pair of shoes, a tiny cross on a gold chain. A job for pay outside the tribal economy helped make one *qwi,* but the position of elder or chief did not. With luck the novice hoped to be assimilated into the emergent middle class, but without it he often returned to his native village wearing a haughty indifference with a store-bought shirt. But not always; sometimes the pull of tribal loyalties overcame the magnetism of civilization. The chief's son obviously had a keen mind, but not for candy.

Two old women emerged from a low doorway carrying two pails of steaming water. At last! The bath fence was shoulder high, open at the top under a clump of banana stalks with the opening facing the forest. Inside, four flat stones set on a bed of gravel with a little ditch leading out. I threw my clothes over the fence and sat down. You poured the scorching water over your body from of a long handled gourd. No soap. The heat, they said, removed the rain's cold hand. I liked to begin on the shoulder blades, across the chest, over the arms, down the spine. It was important not to hurry. I was half way through the first bucket when I heard a noise behind me. One of the old women reentered with another smaller bucket. I expected her to leave but she started applying something to my back. I put my washcloth where it did the most good. Hot mud! It felt good. Her experienced fingers worked it into the muscle where it retained its heat. Oh it felt good. Suddenly she left without a word. Apparently she only did backs. I dipped a handful and rubbed it on my legs and chest.

By this time Moses came in carrying his bucket, then Akwoi, already cracking up before he could set his down.

"You could have warned me, you know."

"De chie' he te' dem, ta' de ma' some de clay baff," Moses said.

"And you stood there like dummies."

"He de chie'."

Night had fallen. Lanterns winked and the dull glow from the evening fires filled open doorways. On the way back to the porch a young man about my age in long trousers and a Hawaiian shirt casually stepped out of the shadows warmly extending his hand.

"Good evening, sir. My name is Jeddiah W. Freeman. I regret I wasn't here to greet you earlier."

"My pleasure, sir. You come from Bolahuhn."

"That is correct, sir. I am working there most of my days, but I come here to Dawawoli when I am getting free time. I have a farm to mind, and of course my relatives."

"I have friends in Bolahuhn, Clara Sharkey and Rob Fellows."

"Yes, of course, I have made their acquaintance. Mr. Fellows has instructed me with the principles of soil management. Are you ready to take dinner?"

He led the way to one of the two zinc-roofed houses, the inside of which came as a bit of a surprise, a living room with lace curtains. When we first saw Dawawoli, none of us could have expected it, nor the kerosene lamp with an ornate crystal chimney. And more. A cushioned chair, a metal coat rack with an umbrella hanging from it, a bureau with an oval mirror. How in the hell did they get it in here? Crosses and holy pictures covered the walls concealing holes—a white man's trick, crumbling walls would have hardly embarrassed a tribesman. A framed picture of President Tubman dominated one wall, otherwise a warped black and white photograph of a tribal family standing rigid for the camera gave the room its soul, but the most telling of all, at the back of the bureau, a rosary draped over a bottle of Old Spice.

In the middle of the room the table was set, a low wicker affair, no chairs, but five places each with a porcelain plate and a spoon on a fresh banana leaf. When he saw my interest in the photograph he pointed out the people in detail, his father, two mothers, brother, and their wives. He tried so hard to be casual about entertaining a guest but his pride came through. When my friends came in from their baths, he excused himself. He had already eaten; the evening meal was considered a private affair. A woman entered with a generous bowl of steaming rice followed by a very attractive girl of about sixteen, with beautiful full breasts. She set a pot of soup on the table with an aloof indifference to our presence, the usual bearing of Loma girls before marriage, in total contrast to their behavior among themselves. My friends stared at the floor. For all their bravado in the bush, now they were lambs. "Thank you," I said in Loma as she hurried out. "What's the matter, you cannot tell the girl thank you?"

"Her father will not like it," John said.

"How will he know?"

"She wi' te' dem," Moses said.

"What will she tell them?"

"She will tell them we are making advancements," Akwoi snapped in a low whisper.

"She will tell them we're a bunch of hicks who don't know how to say Thank you. Don't pretend you didn't notice."

But no one felt like discussing it. We busied ourselves with the food: palm oil and cassava greens with meat, over rice. Moses and Kwokwoiyea ate with their hands, John and I with the silverware, Akwoi tried the spoon, but when he saw the others getting ahead he gave up. They knifed their fingers into the rice mixing in the sauce first. The trick to eating with the hand was to keep the food on the finger tips drawing them over the bottom lip with a quick turn of the wrist as the head drew back. They rarely spilled any. Dropping food back into the bowl was bad manners, so was speaking with your mouth full; licking your fingers wasn't. I tried it several times out of necessity but never got the hang of it.

After dinner we moved back to the chief's porch which seemed to be the center of life; the conversation, light, enjoyable. A single railroad lantern cast a dim glow making apparitions of the nearby houses, projecting the slightest human gesture into grotesque pantomime. They talked of hunting, remembering a kill from several seasons back much as an avid sports fan might relive a crucial game. They were exact with respect to the individual animal, the location, the terrain; but differed with respect to the first shot, some maintaining it could have been taken much sooner thereby limiting the chances for the animal to escape; others that it could have come later at a closer range thereby shortening the chase. One school emphasized the stalk, the other the chase—liberals and conservatives. Both agreed the ideal was a clean kill with the first shot, but that was rare with the weapons they had, a rude collection of hand-me-down pieces doctored over in blacksmith kitchens and fired with whatever ammunition came available, everything from muzzleloaders to sawed-off shotguns. However the most prized were World War II weapons that had somehow filtered down from the North African theater, especially German. They could not distinguish German from English in language but they knew a German piece when they saw it. Hunting was a way of life, a necessity, a passion. The most renowned hunters enjoyed great prestige; they were the cowboys and adventurers but also the PhDs, their knowledge vast, their reputations wide. And there were artists too. One fine old gentleman from the village of Litisu foreswore all firearms; he continued to hunt, successfully, with a homemade spear, working alone, living off the bush, rubbing his body with animal dung to kill his scent, camouflaging himself in the brush near a water hole, chewing paca nuts and drinking the drip of leaves until game appeared. After the kill he would whisper his thanksgiving in the dying animal's ear. He maintained the noise of a single gunshot disrupted the flow of game for three days afterward. They had a saying, "the hungrier the hunter, the sharper the spear."

When the chief retired for the night, Jeddiah took his place in the hammock dangling one leg over the side while he held the rope with one hand and a glass of whiskey with the other. I expected to see the chief's son take his father's place, but there were subtleties I couldn't have known. Or perhaps not so subtle. What if Jeddiah were also his son by an older wife? Still the older brother should come first. Or the chief could be allowing him the hammock only to disguise the power structure.

By firelight Jeddiah fit into the surroundings easier than by day, the Hawaiian shirt notwithstanding. He was a preacher of sorts. Someday he hoped to build a church right here in Dawawoli; already he'd sent two younger brothers to the Mission for their schooling and Christian instruction. Had I ever been to Bolahuhn. It was a fine town on the side of a great hill where the boys played football just the same. The Mission there had a great steel bell carried all the way from the coast on poles by sixteen men and the grace of God—in the days before the motor road. It was indeed a miracle. Not a single crack. When it rang in the morning it could be heard far away in the bush. It was God Himself speaking to the poor illiterate people of this country telling them He was no more than a day's walk away. He paused for a sip, then continued staring into the darkness. Bolahuhn had a fine market, on Saturdays, the very best country cloth in the entire county. Many white people. Another sip. Then there was Bishop's Hill. Surely I'd heard of it. No? It was a great hill upon which the church itself stood high above. Many years ago a real bishop, an old white man with eyes the color of the morning sky paid a visit. He walked many days without complaint but when he came to the place and looked up at that great hill, he decided it would take more than faith in God and consented to be carried the rest of the way. It's been Bishop's Hill ever since. He refilled my glass. It obviously pleased him to converse with someone in English, however several Loma conversations went on simultaneously. He toasted the president and set forth again. The boys at the high school had a fine football team. One of them, a certain Elijah B. Washington could dribble the length of the field and no one could steal his ball. They'd beaten Voinjama 2-0 and were soon to have a rematch which promised to be even better since the Voinjama chaps, sore losers that they were, had sworn revenge after accusations of witching the goalpost.

The curious eyes of children stared like owls from the edge of the darkness. The talk subsided when a woman passed by. After the necessary exchange of greetings, the older men's eyes might follow her as she moved off while their juniors exchanged devilish glances. He filled my glass again this time toasting the Pope and then the memory of President Kennedy. I toasted the gentleman from Litisu. I must forgive him, Jeddiah said, for stealing all the conversation. He was certain I had many exciting stories to tell. Did I enjoy football? I did indeed. In fact I was improving my game rapidly. Moses smiled at the floor. "I can mind the goal," I said, "since I'm more accustomed to using my hands. I kept these so-so players scoreless two games in a row, without medicine, until hot shot here scored on me—and a freak play at that."

That was it! Moses couldn't take it anymore; he loved the game with a passion. He leaped to his feet reenacting the play in the middle of the crowded porch. "No! See de ma' telling stories. I ta' de ba', foo' de ma' di way, ki' de ba' da way. Goal! Now he say I cheating! Bah!"

"He got lucky."

"No! No! See de ma'!" And he spun around kicking an imaginary football into the bush. For the moment his outburst caught everyone's attention. Jeddiah sat back in amusement taking pleasure in being a good host while Moses and Kwokwoiyea enjoyed an insiders laugh. Akwoi stood under the lantern writing something in his journal.

"What are you writing?"

"Is privahte yah!"

"Not if you're writing about me, yah."

Sir Francis Drake Akwoi, Esquire
My Diary November 16, 1965
In the town of Dawawoli Teacher drank three times of Old Dan
Tucker Imported Kentucky Bourbon and was laughing and feeling
happy.

"I'm always happy," I said.

"Not like tonight."

"Imported is it?"

"It says on the bottle. Smooth as silk."

Jeddiah launched into another football yarn, how they beat Kolahuhn in the last minute and the whole town ran on the field; meanwhile a stout, stub-bearded man with muscular hands demonstrated his method of gutting an antelope with three easy cuts using a frightened little boy as a model. Now and then a lantern winked out and the darkness crept closer. One by one they said good-night and left for their houses. Before we knew it, Jeddiah, the chief's son, and ourselves were the only ones left. They escorted us back to the house where we'd eaten, wished us good sleep and retired. Jeddiah gave us his own house, all to ourselves; he would stay with his wife's father. It seemed they hadn't made a complete Christian of him after all; he had a wife on the Mission and two more in the bush.

The bedroom was bare mud all around. A cumbersome wooden bed set in the middle; deep inside it we could see fresh rice straw beneath separate burlap bags stuffed with grass and sewn together for a mattress. The only other furnishing was a steamer trunk with the radio on it, also a bible and a *Watchtower.* Cobwebs laced the edges of the matted ceiling; it sagged badly; otherwise the room retained the spare simplicity of a monastery cell. The face of a black Jesus looked down over the bed from a simple cross carved by a tribal hand, but on the opposite wall, a white man with a halo carried a lamb amid a flock of pure white sheep with his sandaled feet blessing the earth beneath a flowing blue robe. The picture had a serene unreality to it, a forced separation from the harsh surroundings. Sheep were never that clean.

"I' da one true?" Moses asked.

"Which?"

"Two whi' peopo canno' slee' insi' one be'?"

"Of course not. How do you think we get so many white people?"

"Eh yah. Two ma'!"

"No, men don't sleep together."

"Country peopo, we ca' slee' fou' someti' fi' insi' one be'."

"Well, it looks like we're going to have to do just that."

"But it's your law," John said severely. He kept looking at me. They believed everyone had a personal law which was the basis of personal prestige and ultimately other people's opinion. They took theirs quite seriously and now sensed I was about to break mine.

"Look the floor's damp, it's wet outside, we can't afford to have anyone get sick—we have no choice. It's not a big law." Suddenly loud music broke into the room. "I don't think we should play the man's radio, he might not like it."

"He said we could," Akwoi answered.

"Well, turn down—the other button!"

They drew near and watched with intense interest as the signal rose and fell like the wail of a banshee. He got lots of static, more wailing, an evangelist, finally the VOA. It seemed so close.

"President Johnson today promised to ask Congress for legislation to prevent injustice to Negroes in the South. After citing the progress already made in the civil rights field, he concluded, 'But we must do more. We will do more.' In Santiago Chile where he was on an official visit, Senator Robert Kennedy said he would not seek the Democratic nomination for president in 1968 because he fully supported President Johnson who, he added, was doing a fine job. And on the world scene the United States this week increased its troop strength in South Vietnam in response to further communist aggression from the north."

"See if you can find BBC," I said.

"Ca' we heah anypla' o' de earff?" Kwokwoiyea asked.

"No, just Africa. This side."

"Whe' de ma' talking?"

"Freetown. Maybe Dakar."

"How many day?"

"A good many."

They finally got BBC. "The man talks funny," Akwoi grinned.

"It is a different accent," John explained patiently.

They watched the red needle intently. Kwokwoiyea's placid face came within three inches of the dial as he studied the mysterious dim light that seemed to carry the heat of life. Where there was voice, there had to be spirit. They were attracted to the magic noise with the same wonder that drew me to the silence of the forest.

Dead tired. I tried to get comfortable but couldn't. Every way I turned, I bumped into somebody. It was like sleeping on a pile of old rags; I kept falling through to the boards underneath. The burlap smelled of pitch. Scratchy. Then something bit me on the back of the neck. Lice. "Be sure to shut it off before you go to sleep. The batteries will die." Liz cheating on Burton. They'll never believe it. Had to get some sleep. It began to rain again. Gentle, steady. I thought I heard singing. Far away and in a foreign language, a forbidden language, soft, sweet…as though…

"All flights to Seoul, Anchorage, and Los Angeleeze have been grounded due to ultratonic frequent sees in the afterlearner. All passengers please remain unbored."

Can't sleep. Burlap's scratchy. Like grandma's apron. With stories in the pockets. Never could figure that out. What was that song she sang at nap time? If she'd really forgotten my birthday, how come the voice in the furnace pipe knew?

"How now my Wayward. Can't sleep but for a bedtime story? Let me think. Shall I make a silken gown of a burlap sack? A lullaby of Grandma's

love? Remember the story of the little prince who lost his bike and rode on a donkey's back. Remember how she held you on her lap, how she sang in the forbidden language and pealed June apples around her thumb? And in the oven a tart for her little kitten? Here is food for what ails a weary soul. Bright lights and bangles are not for thee, the human heart bears sweeter fruit. Let this smile be thy guide. You saw it first beside a carrousel not so long ago. I have another ticket in my purse, will you ride around the world once more? While the music sings, until wild horses soar?"

CHAPTER 17

THE WITCH OF DAWAWOLI

Next morning we breakfasted on oranges and stale candy. Outside we took quick counsel. The sky didn't look promising. Kwokwoiyea yearned for the bush, Moses agreed, but Akwoi wavered. The way would be muddy, the loads heavier; undecided, he gave his vote to me. (You could give your vote to a friend but only if it didn't work against family interests.) That settled it. I told them I thought a day's rest would do us good, "Besides," borrowing their favorite expression, "Kpodokpodo will not move in the bush." So we stored our baggage and parted ways. Moses and Kwokwoiyea would try their luck with the chief's son, hunting. Akwoi hoped to do some trading. He carefully unwrapped a bag of homemade trinkets he carried for that purpose, smiling roguishly. Moses looked at me, something was fishy.

"Teacha, de ma' say, he wi' make da womah praganon' an' giff it on you."

"Oh, he will, will he? Well, when the baby comes, it will talk like its father—fi' dolla okay, two dolla wha' say."

Soon John and I were backtracking along the wet trail. I had a slight headache.

"You call her a witch," he said, "but the English is not correct. She is not a bad person. You will see. We call her a zo, it means someone who knows about medicine and many other things."

"What other things?"

"The things your people laugh about," he said. After awhile he added, "There is not a word in English is there?"

"Doctor."

"No, she is not a doctor. You will see."

"I thought you didn't believe in superstition."

"I do not, but I knew you would want to see her. She wanted to see you."

"How do you know?"

"The way she was feeling your face."

We found her just as we'd left her the day before. The same low stool, the same fire, the same kitchen but with half the roof ripped off. She sat there patiently picking seeds off a thin branch, her quick fingers dropped them into a pan between her knees while her whitened eyes stared into space. She rarely missed. A pile of stalks lay at her side and empty shucks sprinkled her lap. A young boy cracked palm kernels, rhythmically flipping them onto a flat stone where he crushed them with a hammer stone, now and then stopping to brush away the shells. Outside a woman with a baby on her back worked at the mortar. Two chickens scratched the dirt. "You've come back," she said before either of us spoke. The sound of my boots must have given us away. After finding himself two flat stones John sat next to the boy and began helping him. I sat with my back against one of the posts wishing I had something to do when she sent the boy to fetch something. He returned with two more flat stones.

She was happy we'd come. Someone to talk to made the work more pleasing she said. And she would have known, her people knew well how to weave conversation into work until the two complimented each other like song and melody. The soft thumping of the mortar and the clicking of the stones marked the time and her fingers searched the slender stalks as if she played a lyre. Then in the most fluent Loma John said he ever heard, she began speaking to us of the lore of her people, pausing now and then for him to translate where I couldn't follow. The language fairly danced on her withered lips, its exquisite rhythms flowing in youthful ardor like a bubbling brook off a haggard mountain.

She told us of life and the village, of work and its doing, storms and their passing and the mending of farms thereafter, how a great pestilence came over the land when she was a girl, how fear had stalked the world making sorrow of the sweetest fruit, filling its ghastly maw with the bodies of many victims and the cries of many orphans. Without a hint of pain she told of the death of two sisters as well as her mother who carried child at the time. She'd wandered a waif from farm to farm for many days eating roots and leaves until a man caught her and took her to an old *zo* woman who took her in and taught her many things including the cause of pestilence. (And what was that?) It was wrought by a clumsiness of the world (imbalance in nature?) trying to correct a previous clumsiness. White people think the world is a wise old man but that is not so; the world is a child learning to walk. It falls many times. We have yet to see it stand and smile. (Then is there nothing we can do in times of peril?) But of course there is; we can try to understand there's nothing we can do, a difficult task but an empty stomach (pure heart) can sometimes master it. To hear the stirring of life in death's outgoing cry takes a keen eye indeed.

She told us of a time many years ago, she was already old, but before the hospital at Zorzor, when men from the coast speaking a strange tongue carried a white man to her as a last resort; snake bitten and delirious, he promised to buy her anything in Monrovia if she had medicine for snakes. He died anyway. She shrugged a what-to-hell expression. So he would have bought her a piece of fancy cloth; it would have looked absurd on an old woman, didn't I agree? I did not. Besides, he was not clean of heart. He had been in the bush digging for money stones, a truly evil endeavor. The "powers" certainly saw and killed him for it. (But surely he died of the venom?) So he had. But what was it that made him step on the snake in the first place? These were mysteries no one knew. Besides, with the thought of riches in the brain, he may not have been alert. Who knows? The snake may well have been placed in his path. (By whom?) You never know, perhaps a powerful *zo,* perhaps the spirits themselves. These are rather arcane matters. (How do we know if someone is clean of heart?) That was indeed a skill that took many years learning; it required "outside" help. Only if "they" were willing did the knowledge come and often without clarity.

She rested her barren arms for a moment, gathering her thoughts. Then she smiled. "I see you come to learn of these matters. That's a fine boy." (Is it wrong then to dig diamonds?) "Yes." (Gold?) "Yes." (Iron?) "Yes," with authority, but of course many people disagree. (But why?) It is unclean (like menstruation) digging holes in the Earth herself, throwing up the mud, spoiling the roots of young leaves, crawling inside a pit. Why, the diamonds may be God's very own baby teeth His mother has hidden away. It is distasteful to even talk of these things. (To whom?) Why, to the spirits themselves. (Then why is it not wrong to dig the earth to make farm?) That is something different. Tilling the soil is combing Earth's hair; digging for minerals is violating her privacy. It causes great shame—like digging up a grave. Earth is God's mother. She gives you of her basket but not of her hearth. (Her fruits, not her secrets.) What she keeps hidden is for another day, for your children. You must always save something for the children; they are always hungry. The rice and fruits and herbs are given like milk to suckling babes; so, too, the unwatchful animal as target for the hunter's skill. This is the way of things, even the animals understand—had I not seen the wary look of a deer that knows it's being stalked?—but digging minerals is different, violating the Earth, walking into her house and touching her personal things. It can only lead to trouble. (But her people dig iron from the earth to make knives and spears?) So they do, but only after elaborate sacrifices prepared by a special *zo* with special knowledge of these matters. (What sort of sacrifices?) She did not know. It is not for a woman to talk of such things; they are the proper domain of blacksmiths who guard their secrets well. (Why blacksmiths?) She did not know. It pertains to the impregnation of the Earth herself. She did not wish to speak of this and hastened to change the subject.

But was not this the way of my people, too? She continued in a lighter vein oblivious to what just passed. (How so?) Well, when someone dies your holy men say he comes from dust and returns to dust. I have heard them. Surely then, digging in the earth must be offensive to your ancestors? Digging up a grave would be, I said, but not digging minerals...our gold diggers have no concern for anything sacred. I see you are unhappy with your elders, she said with concern. Do not speak too wantonly. Take time with your words, they have a way of coming home with sharper teeth than when they left. Once she heard a holy man, one of ours, tell how God made the world—she believed the opposite, the world made God, but no mind—and then all the animals and people. He clasped his hands and looked up into the sky as he spoke and she honestly believed him possessed by one of their own spirits. She saw the spirit in his eyes and expected him to leap up and dance but he didn't. We all had a good laugh over that, hers ending in a fit of coughing. She spat into the fire then coughed again. I am surprised you speak so well of missionaries, I said. And why should she speak ill of them? They may be too well washed but they are God's children too. They bring us trouble, John said forcefully. Now they send black ones, our own, these are worse, they can curse an old woman like you for not believing them. Take time young man, she said objectively, they are merely carriers like children in the time of pestilence; they pass the disease but are not its source. (What disease?) The disease of knowing God too well. (What is it's source?) Its source is not for us to know. God keeps his secrets to keep his life. Long ago when they first came, the missionaries, people wanted to kill them but I do not think it would have done. What need rob Earth's nest of even her ugliest fledglings? We would have been killers and killers have forever to listen for the footsteps of their victims. (Avengers) What a dismal way to go through life, never time for a song. There are many complexities in these matters. They are only clear to diviners possessed, and after their return to normalcy the answers becloud themselves like dreams.

John rose to sweep away the nut shells. At her bidding he gave her a bowl and water and she now set to making a paste of the seeds she'd gleaned. I stood to stretch hoping she hadn't tired herself with all this talk. She hadn't.

"We have a story about how God made people too," she said with renewed energy, "but it is different from yours."

"Tell us," John said reseating himself.

"It is a silly story, the kind women tell little children. Perhaps your friend will not like it."

"He will like it," he said without hesitation.

"Well, I have heard it said that people, men and women alike, once grew out of the ground like trees. There were many different kinds of course: tall, round, skinny sticks that bent in the wind, and great towers that conversed with the passing clouds never bothering themselves with things of the lowly earth; but they all had one drawback, where they grew, they must stay. They could not lie down or move about. Birds brought them their food.

"Now there was a boy, a young Kdabubu tree who grew on a hillside among his brothers and sisters. Not far away a young girl grew in a valley beside a stream. She was round and laden with fruit, but since neither could move, she could not share her fruit with her lover, nor he his strength with her. So they cried. Oh how they cried. Especially in the evening as the sun beckoned behind the hills and the mists settled softly like a blanket over the slumbering earth. They would call out to each other. First the boy, then the girl. At first everyone thought it was the spirits, but soon they knew the truth. The boy yelped like a puppy on a rope. Soon the crying became sighing and the sighing became wailing and the air filled with a commerce so impassioned that maidens had to walk with eyes downcast and young men stole longing glances into the forest. And it went on, day and night, night and day. People couldn't sleep nor concentrate on their chores. Birds flew away, game became scarce.

"Even God Himself heard them one night as He sat down to eat His rice. He was not pleased. "How am I supposed to take my evening repast with all this racket going on?" He thundered. "Then why don't you do something about it?" snapped His senior wife as she busied herself about the fire. "I suppose I must," He answered. "This world gives me no peace," and He took up His great cutlass and strode into the forest scattering flights of birds as He passed.

"When He came to the boy He started chopping furiously at his trunk. The splinters flew in all directions. When He finished, the boy was about to come crashing down, but God caught him and helped him to stand up like a man too full of palm wine. Now God began to feel sorry for him so He lay the boy down gently and sat down to think. Soon He jumped up with a plan. From his roots He fashioned the boy a pair of feet cutting away what wasn't necessary, then He gathered a bundle of twigs and pushed them into the ends of the feet, five in each one. When He finished He took a handful of wasted splinters from the chopping and fastened one onto each toe. These were the toenails.

"When He finished with the boy, He hurried through the forest and freed the girl in the same manner. Thus it is lovers have divine feet so they can run to each other."

"That's a lovely story," I said. "Thank you."

We paused awhile, each to our own thoughts.

"May I ask a question," I said. She hummed approval. "If it's improper please say so." She hummed again. "If the world made God as you say, and the Earth is His mother—who is the father?"

It was not an improper question. She answered in three words but I didn't understand. I looked at John. He didn't know either. He questioned her, she responded, he questioned again, then again; she responded patiently, then explained something in detail. When he finally understood, he was at once embarrassed. After a pause she reminded him I was waiting for an explanation.

"God's father is a white fungus that grows on dead trees." She coaxed him forward. "And they look like the ears of white babies. If we see them we must not touch them, a dust will come out and it is very poisonous."

"Understand?" she said in Loma. I said yes. (Perhaps she was teasing or could it be a subtle warning, something not to touch?) These were not simple matters. She coughed, spat in the fire and continued as though addressing two preschoolers—which she was. "Are you surprised that something beautiful issues from something ugly? Well, look around you. It happens all the time."

It was late afternoon by the time John and I got up to leave. The day remained overcast, rain threatened again. "I thought the rains ended in November," I said, sad the time had passed so quickly.

"But look at him," she said. "Do you think you can make the rain obey your calendar? We would say November begins when the rain ends. I know who you are now, you are the clever monkey who would stick his fingers in the flame to see if it tastes as good as it looks. Well, it doesn't."

"If I am the clever monkey, who are you?"

"A puppy too dumb to eat from a master's hand. We are all dumb puppies back here in the bush, but we know no master. That is our 'book.' Don't make them too clever in your school."

We gathered up our things and said good-bye. We each shook her hand which she extended once again while remaining seated. Her fingers were very soft, warm with feeling. When I turned to go, she surprised me by sending John ahead. "Stay," she said very quietly. She was working on another bowl of paste; it turned out to be a base for soup.

"Something troubles you," she said after he was well down the path, but without the slightest interest in pursuing it. Her silence invited me to leave if I wished. It wouldn't have disturbed her in the least; her inward mastery ran deep, unruffled by the mere passing of another stranger; tomorrow I'd be another curious memory in her vast collection.

"I sow seed. But nothing grows."

"Oh you do, do you," she whispered as if to a child. "Well, look around you. The forest grows without anyone sowing seed. We are sojourners for a passing season, no more. We strike a path, and age soon overgrows its purpose; be certain yours will be overgrown, as well." She coughed again and spat into the fire. "The forest cares little for human paths or the shouts of human pride. Ours is not to master, but to ripen to our time. Nothing fine is wrested from the world in violence. The weight of ripe fruit bends down the branch to the hand that waits in patience. If you would know these things, forswear haste, forfeit fine words. Forbearance is stronger than iron. You are young. The forest bears fruit you have yet to dream of. Go to your friends; they wait on you down the path. I see they like you. There is fruit for now."

I caught a last glimpse of her from the edge of the farm. She was incredibly ugly, like a corpse someone forgot to bury. There she sat, upright, teeth missing, a gaunt oracle speaking blindly through the darkness; the ghostly cast of her whitened pupils lost in the emptiness behind a coil of rising smoke. But what music. The delighted cadence of a little girl talking to her favorite doll. What subtle witchcraft. She made the gray day bright, cleansed our spirits, warded off our troubles without our knowing. What a great Lady— young, vibrant, ready to smile despite her pain, stately in her wrinkled elegance, vigilant in her death mask. Africa's richest gem sparkling in the dirt. And the gold diggers missed it.

CHAPTER 18

THE McCARTHY KIDS

"This morning," I said closing the door, "I'd like to talk to you a little bit about motivation, revolution," God what a morgue, "and white rats."

I dropped my notes on the desk and walked across the room. Down below two bundled figures forced their way along a frozen sidewalk, a gust of snow swirled against the frosted windowpanes. My own notes never said what I wanted anyway. Something didn't feel right. I didn't mind the manicures in the second row, the paperback novel, the jocks dozing off, the audible groan at the top of an assignment, the volley of clicking ball-points at the hint of an exam. All they cared about was material ease, beating the system. Anything else—they didn't give a damn. That's what I minded.

"Suppose we have an organism—any organism, doesn't have to be a white rat—a pigeon, a primate, a behaviorist; I prefer the latter, they're easy to obtain, economical, they don't bite."

Here we go again. Miss Ninety-seventh Percentile exuding boredom like high priced perfume, Mr. Data Digest waxing superior once he identifies a name or an "ism," Mr. Fraternity Row practicing board room demeanor, Goodie-Two-Shoes taking it all down.

"Have you ever wondered what it's like to be a white rat at a *nouveau riche* dinner party?"

College was a ticket to a wealthy suburb, a consumer's license.

"How 'bout a dry martini for openers."

They'd as soon be in some damn bar doing drugs.

"An olive of course."

We blew it, our generation. Fate tendered us a rich jewel; we chose a ball of dung.

"An *hors d'oeuvre,* a sip of punch, a raw oyster."

I couldn't get through to them. The world was alive, exciting; it throbbed with art, ideas, men who'd challenged the inertia of their times.

"Now the main course."

I had no rapport with these kids. I would have given them Verdi; they wanted the Beatles. In their eyes I'd always be a square.

"Roast suckling pig with an apple in its mouth, garnished all around, walnuts, bamboo shoots, candied yams, creamed succotash, cold calves liver, broccoli bulimiase, zucchini yuccanini, a glass of *Haut Briand,* sawtayed escargoats, pickled pigs feet, a slug o' wodka, a chain o' Hungarian blood sausage with a splash o' Cajun sunshine, a keg o' three-two—now dessert, pizza! With ice cream! Chocolate syrup, chopped nuts and a maraschino cherry on top, sour grapes for the ill at ease, a thimble of Turkish coffee, a mint for proper etiquette and champagne for everybody! *ALORS!* You've arrived. You sit expectantly on an Early American sofa contemplating the ambience of the situation with Henry Mancini in the back ground, a Mustang in the driveway, *Playboy* under the mattress, Marcel Proust on the shelf, Jackson Pollock on the wall—can art be the mirror of your inner feelings?— two gas guzzlers in the garage, a dune buggy for junior, a pretty wife to decorate the lounge, a bikinied secretary to warm the pool, your senior partner pontificating at the punch bowl, a plump pubescent daughter heavy into mascara, khaki, and combat boots slamming the door in gratitude, MOTHUUUUUUR!—can something be wrong in paradise?—and you try to remember what you're doing here only you can't think because the raw oyster can't decide whether he prefers the inside of your esophagus or the outside of your lapel, but then! A social activist sits down beside you, crosses her legs and asks what you think of the fauve movement and you want to make a good impression only the words won't come because the oyster's decided he's leaving the party, a real pity, the only intellectual on the guest list, and you don't want to make a scene by bolting for the bathroom, you just saw your boss go in there with somebody's wife and you think you might try the aquarium but the precocious little monster they sent to bed early keeps a pet piranha, but wait! Here's your hostess, busting out all over, leaning down in front of you with a silver platter cooing, 'Would you like to try a piece of my cheesecake?' What do you say to the lady? This is the critical moment. The oyster demurs. Your career hangs in the balance."

Sally was sitting in again, way in back with the jocks. When I asked why, she smiled one of her devilish smiles, "Maybe I like jocks."

She just got back from New Hampshire where she'd been working for the McCarthy campaign, a field representative, door to door. And they pulled off a stunning surprise. Forty-two per cent. She was jubilant. We all were.

Students sensed a direction. Hope ran warm despite the March winds, a purpose crystalized, McCarthy buttons began sprouting like crocuses. I wore one too but not to class. I felt that would have been unprofessional and she conceded, but a few days later practically mobbed me, right there in the library like a teeny bopper at a rock concert, knocked my glasses off.

"I beg your pardon, sir, I'm terribly sorry—"

"What in the—"

"Here let me straighten that tie, we can't be looking unprofessional—"

"She kept brushing my lapel in exaggerated seriousness, humming *On Wisconsin* under her breath.

"Knock it off!"

"Wanna come?"

"Where?"

"WHERE? Wisconsin! April second! Planet Earth! Ah do declayah, whayah have you beeun? Come on now you were doin' so good stuffin' all those envelopes, lookin' so hip behind the info desk, ewwww that button turns me on like a ten cent tea pot."

"Sallyyy."

"How 'bout a another bumper sticker?"

"My car's not running."

"A poster? For your office window? Facing out, so people could see it from the mall?"

"I don't think tha would be appropriate—"

"Too baaaad."

"What do you mean?"

"Walked by your office lately?" She flashed a winning smile batting her eye lashes like mad.

"You're coming to Wisconsin then?"

"I've got a class to teach; they pay me to do it."

"My special friends call me Butch, donch ya know? Daddy wanted a shortstop, he got this," she pulled out the front of her blouse. "Sorry dad. But you can call me Butch. So he did. You can call me Butch too."

"I prefer Sally."

"Suit yourself. My daddy was the greatest. I didn't see much of him, he was always on the road, a salesman, then after the divorce only once a month. My mother hated daddy because he never had enough money and because I loved him, couldn't wait till Sundays. I'd go crazy the minute he pulled in the yard, fly through the house dancing and driving her nuts, she'd start right in bitching at him and I had to practically pull him out of the house. For one afternoon, one glorious afternoon, I was in heaven, as though some fairy godmother gave me a momentary reprieve from my dull life, my cruddy house, my cruddy school, of course my mothuuur. As soon as we were in the car he'd be smiling at my mother in the window and he'd snitch out the side of his mouth, 'Been keepin' away from the sailors, Butch?' I was only *twelve!* I was so happy. He had a convertible and on sunny days we'd put the top down. I'd let my hair stream in the wind, I knew I'd get hell when I got home but I didn't care. Then we'd stop in some dinky little town with a gas station and soda bar; sometimes he'd get emotional and try to tell me he was sorry, but I'd tell him to shut up. He wasn't without his faults. He chased women. Once I found a compact on the seat, but I never told. I'd have taken a beating first. My mother always tried to get me to spy on him, but I'd act dumb. When he brought me home it seemed like an eternity till the next time. After he left, I'd stand on the lawn waving, beating the air to pieces even after he was out of sight, then trudge off to my room and not come out till morning."

"Cogitate the cheese," I said, leaning back against the blackboard.

"This is Skinner again," the smart ass in the second row sneered in complete boredom. He had a name, an angle—game over.

"You can't have cheesecake without the cheese," I said severely. "But remember. Cheese only works if the organism's hungry. What do we do for the white rat who has everything? Pretty soon the whole world looks like cheese, smells like cheese. We live in it, bathe in it. A culture of cheese, *L'Age du Fromage.* Our goals become our masters. Cheese becomes the stimulus to run away from cheese. In our hearts we know something's missing, but our heads can't tell us what. We look for a counterculture. But where? Anywhere, as long as it violates convention. But soon the violation becomes convention. We've sated our temporary hunger, but paid with a permanent hangover. So we pop a pill to kill the headache, only to get addicted to the drug. We run to the glittering marketplace, but Wall Street's jittery and the flight to freedom's become a panic in a maze and whatever you may have wanted in the first place has been lost in the ensuing competition to secure it and, therefore, no longer problematic. In our mad dash to win the rat race, we lose the human race. We—"

The bell rang. Instantly, thirty sliding desks answered, then the scuttle of feet, and the room was empty before I could check my watch. I'd been rambling again. I knew I had a point, but it never came out the way I wanted. No matter. Nobody gave a damn.

"Hi," she said softly. Three McCarthy buttons.

"Hi."

"Don't look so depressed. Somewhere the sun's shining."

"The bell rang," I said blankly.

"Shall I start salivating?"

"No, but you're supposed to clear the room in three seconds. Wanna get a coffee?"

"Where's your coat?" she asked outside on the walk.

"I must have left it in my office."

"Not a good day to forget your coat," she said under her muffler. "Gimmie an arm."

"Not in there," I groaned as we went by the Union. "They think I'm a Narc. Stupid little broads."

"Well, where—"

"Faculty lounge. Fringe benefit for teaching fellows, coffee's twenty-five cents."

"Ah ame so imprayussed."

"But no scenes."

"Duh, Wha' d'ya mean, coach?"

There weren't any empty tables by the windows, so we waited in the hall checking out student paintings. "Yours?"

"No, but we're having an exhibition next month. You're coming of course."

"I don't know anything about art."

"Good. We'll tell 'em you're a critic."

"There's a table."

"Why do you have to sit by a window?"

"So I can hear the surf. Two coffees please."

"You look out the window a lot when you're talking to your class, when you're not staring at the floor."

"Is it that bad? My class?"

"Bad? An insomniac's delight! Why not pass out pillows and hot water bottles?"

"Then why do you come?"

"To see you suffer."

"You get your kicks watching people suffer?"

"Only white rats in button down collars—"

"What specifically—"

"You specifically. Look at you. Scholarly, dry, distant, a walking bibliography. In a word, *straight!* As in straight jacket, as in good, gray, conservative. If your tie worked, you could pass for a frat brother. You look like pure establishment. That's what confuses people; they see the outward package, not the inner rebel. You gotta let it come out hon. Try to be a little more...well, Bohemian. Wear your leopard's tooth."

"I'd look like a hippie."

"No you wouldn't. It would show people who you are."

"That's revolting. Why do I have to wear beads and sandals? I'm against war and racism too. Do I have to become a drug addict to prove it?"

"Let's not get overwrought."

"Wear a goddamn hippie suit and spout four letter words—do you know how counterproductive that is? Do you know what a small-town family with a kid in Nam must think when they see that on TV? The Pentagon couldn't have *planned* it better! It plays right into their damn *hands!* What to hell does long hair have to do with a moral conviction? Do you know how childish that is? Do you think I'd be a different person if I changed my pants?"

"Shhh," she said with feeling. "The faculty lounge. We don't want a scene." Then an intense whisper, *"Yes!* You'd be a different person, a more honest one. People would know where you stand. Look at you. Errrh." She shivered. "You've got to live what you believe," she said with growing excitement. "You're such a contradiction. People look at you and they don't hear what you're *saying.* Today in class you were using the pronoun, 'we', again."

"So?"

"You were talking about 'them.'"

"A slight grammatical error."

"Well, keep working on your grammar. In the meantime loosen up, tell a joke, the one about the white rat was good but they didn't get it."

"Do a nightclub act?"

"If it works! You'd make a great stand-up comedian. Tell 'em about about life at a *nouveau riche* dinner party. Scream! Swear! Throw things. Screech your nails down the board, pitch the lectern into the blackboard. When smarty pants contradicts you, sock him where it hurts! When Miss Hauteur opens one of her trashy novels, slap her across the face like a lazy whore."

"Oh Ann wouldn't like that. All A's. And I'll give her another. Do you know what she wrote on her midterm? 'You're question is one of opinion having no basis in empiric data; I can therefore answer only on purely intuitive grounds.' Purely intuitive grounds. Jesus. If she'd ever come down from the ninety-seventh percentile, I'd like to get to know her."

"Maybe she'd like to get to know you."

"I doubt it."

"I think you should take her to bed."

"I'm afraid that would come under the rubric of fraternizing with undergraduates."

Her dark hair folded around her shoulders, her eyes danced, she leaned forward to listen, looking right at you, now and then smoothing a stray wisp of hair back in place, always probing, bright, alert, conscious of her youth, her strength. Otherwise she dressed down, jeans, a dark turtle neck with a vest, or a man's shirt with a scarf, sometimes a frilly blouse, always a leather bag like a boxing glove on long strap, an accent of bright color, maybe a floral swirl or Navajo turquoise on a brooch. Other days a loud clang—silver dollar-sized earrings and sunglasses, boots and a miniskirt—even in winter. Nor was she without contradictions. Behind the zest, an echo of loneliness, a hick town girl watching a sleek convertible zip through her sad life without a chance of catching a ride.

"Are you still going with Jeff?" I asked to change the subject.

"We're still friends." She looked out the window absently. "You can't imagine the bigotry in this town."

"Yes, I can."

"All you have to do is walk down the street with a black guy and you can feel them gawking at you. I might as well be wearing red satin with a slit up the side."

"I'm surprised you let the bigots break it up for you."

"I was determined not to, but then I realized it was just as bad to prolong it out of spite. Jeff's a great guy, but he's hung-up on racism, he's married to it. I wonder if I'd be any different, to know people hate you not for what you've done but for what you are, the way they look at you, talk to you, and there's nothing you can do. That's what would kill me."

"He hasn't slain his dragon."

"What?"

"That's the primitive way of putting it. We each have a secret beast in the pit of our souls. Until we overcome it we're not free."

"And have you slain yours?"

"I haven't had the pleasure—"

"Oh yeah, smarty pants, what would you do if you—"

"I don't know."

"You'd bore it to death. Then you wouldn't know what to do with the carcass. Hey! Gotta run. Thanks for coffee. Don't forget the exhibition."

"What exhibition?"

"In a couple weeks, after Wisconsin."

Wisconsin. Another victory. Fifty-six per cent. And two nights before, on national television, Lyndon Johnson shocked the nation by withdrawing from the race. I couldn't believe it. Four years ago he'd been the hero of the left, the peace candidate, and now, as he went down in defeat we saw a gaunt old man trying to save face before a country that had passed him by. They'd unseated a president. A bunch of kids.

The antiwar movement was gathering momentum. The McCarthy candidacy was taking root in middle America, gaining credibility. Dissent now wore a necktie. Students were finally getting it through their heads the hippie-style theatrics, the foul language and red fists were counterproductive. She agreed and did a complete one-eighty insisting I dress properly; she even went out and bought me a tie, the wildest one she could find—psychedelic yellow, purple, red, mandalas and peacock tails. I refused to wear it. So she broke into my apartment, through the back window while I was taking a turn at the local headquarters, stole every tie I had and left hers with a thank you note from the campaign—on official stationery. My class actually woke up for five minutes. Things were getting heady.

"Which of the celebrated faculty artists are exhibiting themselves?" I asked outside the gallery under a bright banner proclaiming the annual Student-Faculty Spring Art Show.

"Can it buddy," she growled, "er ouch ya go," and she hiked her thumb over her shoulder.

"Then why did you bring me?"

"Artists are never judged by their art, donch ya know, only by whom they bring to see it. I gonna blow deir minds wit you, baby. Just remember you're not down at *Howard's.*"

She was all dressed up today, but a little nervous. I'd never seen her this way. She wore a light blue business suit, heels and hose, light make-up, a white blouse with a high ruffled neck, a small cameo in front, her hair folded in a neat chignon but pinned at the side with a silver brooch matching a pair of tiny earrings that caught the light and made you notice wisps of loose hair on her neck. I'd worn jeans thinking I was going to a Bohemian affair. When I reminded her, she drew up and whispered close, "You're the Bohemian."

"Then what are you?"

"Do you think you're the only one who can play it straight?" she asked turning down the first aisle, but then, suddenly serious, she grabbed my hand and whispered in a breath of fear, "They're ghastly."

"The paintings?" I'd made up my mind to keep still. "I don't know what they're trying to say."

"They have nothing to say," she smiled brightly.

"Is that a crime?"

"No, but there is in assuming god-like grandeur in consequence. Who's your favorite painter?"

"Van Gogh."

"Egad. I knew I'd regret asking."

"You don't—"

"No," she said delicately, "nor the other post-impressionists, nor impressionism per se. They would make life one great Elysian field, la dee da, pastel pig sties; you can't escape into idyllic pastures anymore!" then between clinched teeth, "Try reading the headlines!"

"I like the colors, the way they dance. Underneath there's a sad song that knows the headlines just as well."

She turned in disbelief, "The way they dance? Real good. Sometimes I really worry about you if you should ever inadvertently wander into the real world." Nervous. Why was she so nervous?

"Who's your favorite painter then?"

"I pick them up and discard them," she answered whimsically, stopping to study at a small composition of line and shadow, "like men. Right now I'm studying a Russian, Kasmir Malevitch. He did this fantastic little painting, a soft white surface with an off white rectangle superimposed but off center, almost a square but not quite, almost pure white but not quite; it's called *White on White* and it's not so exceptional until you notice it was done in 1918 when other Russians were filling large canvases with grandiose revolutionary themes forcing the union of worker and artist practically at gun point; yet this statement is so simple, unpretentious, it becomes a revolution within a revolution."

"That's interesting."

"Yes, but only if you know the circumstances. You've always got to consider an artist's surroundings," then as an afterthought, "if they don't crush him first."

"How do you like this one?" she asked stopping before a wide gray canvas with four lines in sharp detail in front and a faint undertone of maroon in back.

It looked like gray clouds with a suggestion of a horizon, but I wasn't sure. "You don't like it, do you?"

"It's yours, isn't it?"

"You don't like it at all, you can't hide from me little boy."

"It's abstract." Her fists clinched. (Shouldn't have said that.) "It's so gray...and your so bright."

"IDIOT!"

"Shhh—"

"What do you want from me! A bloody *wheat field?*"

"No!"

"Then just look at the goddamn thing and stop trying to be a fucking critic!"

"I told you I don't know anything about art!"

She ground her teeth, walked away a few steps, came back. "What do you want to see?"

"I don't know."

"Liar! You want to see me in the **nude** I suppose!"

"For God sake take it easy—"

"Well, go ahead! Ask!"

"Try to calm dow—"

"Did I ever pose in the nude!"

"Shhh—"

"YES!"

"How about this one over—"

"One of the art instructors. All he could see was the charcoal. Men. Never any luck."

"Okay let's get out of here." She was really upset.

"You're right," she said suddenly, quite calm but far away. "I need to get out of here. These paintings. Resumes for the same job."

"I want to like it, your painting, I really do. I wish I could like a lot of things—rock music, pop lingo, the latest fad—I wish I could fit in, be hip, but I'm old fashioned. Okay?"

On the way out she introduced me to some of her friends, all serious, absorbed, engaged in light shop talk with one of the art instructors, a corpulent, sloppy-aged family man with a brood of unruly kids and a seeming disinterest in his own work, at least on Sundays.

"I didn't like my painting either," she confessed on the way home. "Thanks for not patronizing me." She was crying. "Who am I kidding? I have no talent."

"Maybe you're kidding yourself right there. Wouldn't that be—"

"What do you know about—"

"I told you I don't know anything about—"

"That's the whole point! Art should touch people like you, not the damn dilettantes. You're right! My painting's so confined."

"I didn't say—"

"Restricted. Just like me."

"Shouldn't a restricted soul be an apt subject for art?"

"I'm so…so small town. God how I hate that word! Whenever I stretch a canvas I confine myself to my lily white rectangle, my personal sandbox. No matter how I begin my frame excludes everything I want to paint and I wind up with another exercise in futility."

"Paint the futility."

Suddenly she jumped out of the car at a traffic light and started running. I parked around the corner and found her sitting on the steps of a wooden bandstand in a run-down park. Pigeons stained the benches, some elderly folk perused the local paper, a dowdy mother pushed a young child in one of the swings. I sat down and kept still.

"I can't wait to get out of here," she said. "If I stay within five hundred miles of this place, I'm going to wind up with a station wagon and eight kids. It's too gruesome to think about."

"Welcome to the club."

"As soon as I graduate," she went on suddenly excited, "—and don't you dare tell anyone—I want to go to New York. I know it sounds naive, small town girl, big time plans. But you wait and see. If I fail…that doesn't frighten me. What frightens me is the thought of living out the rest of my life knowing I never dared. I want to paint. That's all that matters, getting out, working, seeing other painters, what they're doing, seeing them when they're down, watching their work in the raw before it gathers the mystique that comes with success." When her excitement ended, she added, "I couldn't be a loner like you. I need people."

The days were longer now so we took a drive in the country. Lilacs bloomed in the hedgerows and dandelions dotted the front yards of farm houses, shirts flapped on clotheslines and children stopped their play long enough to watch us pass. The scent of fresh earth hung on the fields; in the woods last fall's blanket of dirty leaves showed sparks of green. The sun beamed bright. Rivulets sang.

They won in Pennsylvania. We won. (My grammar was improving.) Seventy-one per cent. She went at her own expense, worked sixteen hours a day, slept on the floor, lived on a jar of peanut butter and a bag of apples and cheerfully accepted menial tasks. She cut a week of classes in the process informing her instructors beforehand but not asking permission. In my undergraduate days, that would not have been done. The times they were a changin'.

The botanist from the rally last fall agreed, said it made him feel old. He was twenty-nine. He came to my office one afternoon and invited me to dinner. They lived in a century-old farmhouse out in the country, he and his quiet wife who guessed I was a farm boy because I came to the kitchen door. She had a old-timey manner, a soft glow that suggested early pregnancy, her eyes confirming it the instant he took her hand—her first. After dinner we listened to Walter Cronkite read the weekly body count, paused in embarrassed silence, then talked about the consequences. They made me feel right at home, showed me some quilt work from Peru, a cutting of wild anemone, asked about my family, my work in Africa. They told me they felt uncomfortable with politics; there were so many distasteful things, compromises etc., but the nightly news left no alternative. The conversation kept coming back to Vietnam—there was no getting away from it. They asked me questions in complete confidence as though they'd known me for years. Did I think we could divorce—his word—the antiwar movement from radicalism? I said I didn't know but that was certainly the key. Then...out of the blue, would I have a talk with Murray Weisenbaum?

"His efforts aren't helping," he smiled sadly. "Marxism doesn't play well in Peoria. For some reason it takes eastern intellectuals a little while to catch on."

"We're hardly friends," I said. "In fact, Sally's way off base on that one."

"He's your peer."

"Alas."

"I don't think I should try," he said. "He'd see me as faculty."

"And I'm supposed to have the perception problem."

"You'll do it then?"

I said I'd try.

"Thank you," they answered together.

"Only I've never enjoyed great success talking to people who know everything."

"He might listen to you. You're not very threatening—and I don't mean that in a critical way. Perhaps you could remind him this isn't New York, give him a little dose of middle America."

"By the way," his wife smiled as they saw me to the door, "it wasn't Sally's idea." And reading my confusion added, "Wilma Winters suggested you."

"…Now that one hit like a brick."

CHAPTER 19

THE DEVIL'S WIFE

Summer finally came. Sally and I had more free time. On Sundays we took a drive in the country—if my car was running. We enjoyed getting lost on back roads, flipping a coin at deserted junctions then stopping to ask directions of the most unlikely stranger. Not just anyone, finding the proper Hermes became our great delight. Businessmen or people with book larnin' were out, kids on bikes okay, little old ladies in white shoes only in a pinch, an old man with tobacco juice down his chin—the jackpot. She had a knack for talking to people, put them at ease, won them in a trice.

Once we took a dirt road along a lazy creek and stopped at an old iron bridge. Tires and beer cans littered the place, but upstream around a bend, past a fisherman and his dog, a fairly clean sandbar stretched out in the sun. Nice view of the bridge. It angled upward from a man-made ramp to a shale cliff smothered in foliage; a round sugar maple commanded its edge, down below sycamores and poplars lined the river bed. I thought it would make a nice painting but decided to keep quiet. The June leaves were on; young, vibrant, the scent of green sap; a twinkle of sunlight on the water. We lay back and watched the clouds. Thin, white, not much drift.

"Was it this quiet back in the bush?" she said.

"Quieter."

"But there's not even a breeze."

"See that jet up there? You can hear him."

"Not very much."

"But without him it's quiet, like Africa."

"Well, I like him up there. Maybe he's taking a small town girl to New York."

"Or a small town boy to Vietnam. How awful it must be to put your boy on that plane...a bunch of hippies protesting."

"We're trying to keep him *off* that plane damn it!"

"I know."

"Let's leave it alone today."

"Okay."

"What did you do in Africa on a day like this?"

"Took a walk."

"On a quiet evening?"

"Read a book."

"On a wild Saturday night?"

"I had a box at the opera."

"Oh great! Real good. You had a—Hellooo in theeere, come out come out wherever you are. Honey you gotta share those little secrets. Peck peck peck, make a little hole in that shell, 'Hi there I'm havin' a great time, come on in.'"

"...I'll tell you about it someday when you're in the mood for a bedtime story."

"That a promise?"

"Yeah."

"Cross your heart and hope to die?"

"Yeah."

"Okay, let's talk about something more...intellectual."

"Okay."

"Who's Jenny?"

"Jenny?"

"Oh come on if you're gonna be a hotshot woman handler you gotta long way to go buddy my old man was a I know all the tricks! I SAW 'ER PICTURE!!"

"Shh. The pilot up there's trying to concentrate."

"In your apartment," she said very soft. "When I broke in to steal your revolting conservative neckties."

"So it was you?"

"It is standard procedure," she continued in a secretarial tone, "to remove such materials from view when a second lady is granted invitation to your domicile—"

"Invitation? Breaking and entering—"

"It is recommended you discreetly stash said articles under the bed, in the laundry, OR! Oh I'm so clever," and she clapped her fists, "on the bookshelf, inside an inconspicuous copy of...Nietzsche!"

"She was my high school sweetheart."

"That was…quite awhile ago."

"Yeah."

"Now she's married?"

"Yeah."

"With kids?"

"Kids, station wagon, house in the suburbs, PTA—"

"Then she got what she wanted?"

"What her parents wanted. She was…she was—"

"Oh Christ. I'm sorry I brought it up. I was only…come on, loosen up, guys forget their high school sweethearts by the time…you gotta bury the past hon."

"…'The past is a field of weeds.'"

"Who are you quoting?"

"'We cultivate the surface/ It sends up brambles while we sleep.' I dunno."

"Okay let's talk about something else. When you were little, what did you want to be?"

"An explorer."

"Aaaand!"

"I wanted to go where no man's gone before."

"But you got to go to Africa."

"Yeah, but everybody's been there. You wouldn't believe some of the things you find back in the bush."

"Like what?"

"'Is Liz cheating on Burton?'…a movie magazine."

"Back in the bush?"

"Yeah."

"That's not possible."

"I knew nobody'd believe it."

"You saw it?"

"Yeah."

"All right, I believe you."

"What did you want to be?"

"A model."

"Ah."

"Ah? AH!! Is that all you can say?"

"What am I supposed to say?"

"You're supposed to drool! You're supposed to go stark raving insane. Whyyy—you osk. Because I am elegant, sublime, irresistible, I am the darling of every magazine cover, the *catch* of the century. Princes beg me to dirty their palaces, maharajahs squash revolutions to cast their wealth at me, goddesses slash their wrists in jealousy. Can't you see me! Glistening in slimy satin, oooozing sexuality, that sly come hither stare, eyelashes a foot long, gallons of mascara! BUCKETS of jewels! MEN! Thhh-ROWING themselves off balconies! Cr-AWLING through snake pits! To DIE! At my feet!"

"…Ah."

On the way home we stopped in a small town with a white church. A Civil War statue graced the park and a silver pullman car converted to a café set in a bed of pansies. Behind the cash register, a freckle-faced boy counted his change beneath the warm smile of a fat soda jerk, Norman Rockwell. We looked at each other in malicious delight, ordered two sodas, counted our change, and she played a cry-in-your-beer country tune on the jukebox.

"Can I pick 'em, er can I pick 'em," she grunted.

"You shore can Ellie Mae."

She spun around, a perfect vamp, threw open a shoulder. "Gomer. Put down that soda and come dance with me."

"All right but don't start—"

Of course she started singing. The proprietor looked at us oddly, folded up his newspaper and went in back a few minutes, then his wife came in and checked us out through bifocals. Sally waved and she waddled back.

"Hey look," she cried as the screen door slammed behind us, "there's an inscription on the monument. Let's go read it. I love to read the news in these lonely places; they're so far from the bright lights but they try so hard to be part of it."

"They're the whole of it I'd say."

"What do you mean?"

"I think America's one great big small town," I said. "We get in trouble when we forget that."

"You're from a small town aren't you?"

"Yeah."

"Me too, but don't tell the maharajah. What was it like? You're town?"

"Small."

"…Oh that's precious. Real good. Nothing like an exhaustive description, don't wanna wear out that tongue—"

"They had a carnival."

"Aaand…"

"I was five. Things weren't pleasant at home just then so they packed me off to Grandma. She had a small farm down a dirt road, forty acres and a John Deere B, chickens and ducks, pigs in the apple orchard, an old horse who couldn't work anymore, a hayloft that smelled like heaven, a shallow creek with crawdaddies. And Buster, a collie; he liked to chase groundhogs, but never really wanted to catch one. There was a small town a mile away, an easy walk through the woods."

"Aaand. Come on, it's not gonna hurt."

"They had a carnival, The Camden Township Firemen's Carnival—two tents, a snake oil salesman and a carrousel, all on a vacant lot next to the railroad tracks, grain elevators in the background. It was the grandest thing I'd ever seen, the carrousel, the horses rearing back and straining at their bits, the lights, the color, the music from the ump-pah-pah machine. And a greasy guy with a tattoo on his arm collecting the tickets, he swung in and out between the horses as effortlessly as a monkey in the trees. I thought he was the luckiest guy in the world. Well, I didn't have a ticket, but I wanted to ride so bad. You know how it is? You can't thrust your fists deep enough in your pockets. There I was, fighting back the tears, watching the horses go around and the music playing and kids holding on with both hands or waving to their parents and the whole world seemed to be bright lights and laughter—but not for me. All of a sudden, this fine lady was standing next to me; she had shiny golden hair, a hat with a veil, fine clothes, a bit much for a country carnival, a perfect stranger. She smelled like the apple blossoms and when she stooped down she had the softest most understanding smile I'd ever seen. Then she reached in her bag and guess what? Out came a ticket. A gift from heaven. I ran up the plank and chose a black horse."

"A black horse? That's interesting."

"I was so excited I forgot to say thank you—you're supposed to say 'thank you' to a lady—I could see her every time I came around, the kind of bearing that could make a burlap bag look like a satin gown. Maybe she didn't have a boy. Or maybe he died. She was so beautiful. I thought she had to be someone very important, an actress or the fireman's wife. I never saw her again. But I still remember the smile, that sad smile."

"And for those of us who can't change burlap to satin?"

"Ooooooo, tough question. First you must destroy your jealousy of those who can, that's your dragon—and it's not a small one—but once you do, it'll come, the smile, the feel of satin, the gleam of shared sunshine."

"You know...sometimes I really want to believe you...or else you're the biggest—"

"Only me and my hairdresser—OUCH!"

"That's just what I mean! You say something and I'm digging it then you go and throw crap on it!"

We didn't see much of each other the rest of the summer. She got busy with the campaign, taking on more hours, writing letters and knocking on doors in some of the unlikeliest neighborhoods. She even did a radio interview, sounded so professional they invited her to national headquarters but cancelled the last minute. I dove back into the library hoping to knock off my thesis once and for all, but it only became more irrelevant each day. Then one night I found a note under my door. Her handwriting. Come at once, an emergency.

When I got to her apartment, she said she was ready for a bedtime story. What kind of an emergency did I think she was talking about?

"Put on some tea water, I'm going to change."

A poster trimmed in green hung from one of the cross beams, the candidate himself, the fatherly smile. He didn't look the part, maybe that's what scared people. And Bobby Kennedy's smart ass remark that he wasn't fit to be president?—an unwitting compliment to the better man.

Cammy rubbed against my ankles, a cloud of dust lifted in the air when I sat down, the sofa a dustbin of cat hair, spilled popcorn. Albums everywhere. God what a mess. I couldn't resist, "Did you hear what Hoover did?"

"What?" she gasped sticking her head around the door.

"Invented the vacuum cleaner. Gotch ya!"

She ducked back in the bathroom, gave something a vicious kick. Out it came, rolled half way across the room, hit a steamer truck, stopped with a clunk, then an attachment, and another. One landed on the bookshelf and knocked over a potted plant. Then the cord. Cammy jumped in my lap.

"You're so smart, fix it!"

She wore a Japanese kimono, plain black, slinky, a purple sash around the waist, her hair down, a devilish scowl. She took up a karate stance circling her hands.

"You said I needed to loosen—What are you—"

"HOOOOOOOOOOOOOOOOOOOOOOOOOOOOO!"

She landed on top of me with a shriek, the sofa went over backwards, the cat jumped, an ashtray hit the floor.

"Now then," she hissed. "We're going to get some answers. I've just about had it with this conservative crap. Ya voted for Goldwater, dinch ya?"

"I didn't come here to talk politics."

"But politics make strange bedfellows donch ya know? You voted for Goldwater, admit it."

"You're nuts!"

"There are ways of finding out you know," she faded into a far away whisper. "Most unpleasant. No one can withstand torture indefinitely. They always talk in the end. Let's see, what'll it be? Chinese water torture—drip, drip, drip, first like little peas, then pebbles, plink, plink, boulders, BOOM! BOOM! BOOM!"

"Stop it! Are you—"

"Or the Commanche snake pit, eeyew! A barrel full, thick as spaghetti—"

"There's the tea kettle."

"How 'bout—sooo, I'm so subtle—the Rawshyun—"

"I didn't vote for—"

"Nut CRACKERRRR—"

"Uhhh God, ya broke my—"

"Tea tiiiime! British rules. We always stop for tea." She got up and ran out to the kitchen. "What would you like, peppermint? Rosehip? Nothing like a spot of tea to perk up when you're down an' out I always say. Hey! Pick up the couch! Let's see now," she opened the fridge, "how 'bout...pizza! Angelo's '64, that was a good year, last week's chicken salad, ewww, green bread, half an oatmeal cookie, *or*...a nice piece of cheesecake for the white rat who has everything."

"Just tea."

"Okaaaay if ya don't like my cooking go 'head and break my heart. Mind if I sit in your lap?"

"You ruined my lap."

"Comfy? Let me—oops, forgot to light a candle. What was the most exciting thing you did in Africa?"

"We're gonna talk about Africa?"

"You think I invited you here to talk politics?"

"I thought—"

"Do not zink, juzz anzwer zee gwestions."

"Took a bush trip."

"The most exciting thing you ever saw?"

"The sunrise."

"Heard?"

"Music."

"You are naught anzwering zee gwestions broberly!"

213

"**OUCH!** Drums."

"Aaaand."

"I heard the devil's wife singing. Well, the spirit's wife, but the early missionaries of course saw them as devils and it stuck and in a sense they're right because it's the part of ourselves we're afraid of."

"The spirits…have wives?"

"Of course."

"I see."

"One evening, Old Fawkpa came to my house and told me to shut my door and windows and remain inside. She only came at night and no one was allowed to look. They said she was so beautiful no man could control himself if he saw her up close and that means just what you think it means."

"So what did you do?"

"Closed my windows and put out the light."

"Did you peek?"

"Certainly not."

"Didn't you want to?"

"I was curious."

"Couldn't you have taken just a little peek?"

"That would have been unthinkable."

"Just an itty bitty, tiny peek?"

"You didn't have to peek, the music said everything. It started with drums. Everything over there starts with drums. First a muted finger rhythm as they made their way into town from the cult compound, *pa-pa whom pa-pa whom*, restrained, consonant, rather like a beating heart before the start of the hunt. Then closer. A little louder. Other instruments, wood blocks, chimes, then a low humming chant, male voices, *Mnum bwoi yo kdum ba nah.* I have no idea what that means, maybe nonsense syllables. But then! In the middle of the everything (and I can't impress on you the effect of the jungle at night, the utter abandonment of everything familiar, the other worldliness, the presence of something bestial, its warm breath on your neck, a soft murmuring like an alien monstrosity ready to leap, crickets singing, bats flapping, all muffled but immediate, dreamy but close like whispers in a well) and then, in the middle of all this, the spirit's wife, *Wai,* in heavenly solo, pure melody. To the uninitiated it's a bone flute, but to those who know, it's *Her,* singing, sublime but clear, exciting, almost liquid over the murmur of the finger drums—and so out of place, like a blues sax in the middle of an Bach requiem, alluring, suggestive; but despite the culture gap you knew at once it had nothing to do with blues—that's what it became on this side of the water."

"What then?"

"Fertility. I never heard anything like it. It moved in and out through the village then faded off in the distance. She never came back—just that once. Next morning the kids were excited, asked me if I heard. I can't tell you how out of place it sounded, not African at all, not even human; it was the most incredible thing I ever heard. Almost a lullaby…but sexy. Think of a Parisian model in shimmering silk walking through a mud wallow"

"And you didn't peek."

"No."

"Did the crops grow?"

"Yes."

"And the women were fertile?"

"Yes."

"And you?"

"I couldn't sleep."

"And you're not allowed to see her ever?"

"No."

"But she—"

"She's only a melody. If you saw her she would dissolve in the air. You have to use your imagination. She appears to you as you desire her, black if you're black."

"So she could be white?"

"Sure, they're quite sophisticated about these things."

"And how do you imagine her?"

"That's…difficult to say."

"Come on. You're doin' real good. Let's go all the way. Fantasize!"

"Me!"

"…Try."

"That would be…"

"We're waiting."

"Kind of childish."

"Oh no you don't! You're not giving me the run-around! Not this time Buddy! This is crucial! A matter of life and death! The triumph over Communism! The survival of—of—If you don't tell me everything! This very instant! I'm not speaking to you ever again as long as I live! Besides," she continued sweetly, her eyes dancing, "if men don't tell us how they fantasize us, how are we, poor dears, to destroy those fantasies so they can finally grow up?"

"Are you sure you want to destroy every fantasy?"

"Are you sure you want to grow up?"

"I do. Okay, try this one on. It has nothing to do with hair color, clothing, the brand of lard on your face. You can't get that through your heads, can you? How do I imagine her? With an understanding smile, a tinge of sorrow. I think there's always something sad in true beauty as insane as that may sound in our exalted age."

"Like the lady at the carrousel?"

"...Yes, come to think of it. That's an incredible connection! Strange. That you should see—"

"Renaissance painters too."

"It's as though the earth can't bear such radiance so they give it a little smudge to make it human. Beautiful women are always sad—if you look hard."

"Pssst. Maybe they know it can't last."

"Or that it can. And does. Only nobody's watching."

"Not if you're in your little shell with all the windows boarded up. I just can't imagine you out there. It sounds so…You're so…How'd you ever come back alive?"

CHAPTER 20

A BOX AT THE OPERA

"The jungle's not as unfriendly as you might think, nor as impenetrable. It's oppressively hot, musty; houses reek of mildew, clothes stick like spider webs, people stink of sweat, fatigue comes quickly; in the rainy season it's a nightmare of mud and a person has to make a conscious effort to keep up his spirits not to mention his health; there are ungodly diseases, ill-kept latrines, open skin ulcers, blood sucking insects, lizards and vermin, snakes, squalor, hunger, rage…yet, once in a great while, it seemed when least expected as though a reminder not even misery is sole lord over things, a benign spirit would smile and this inhuman place would give up a rare glimpse of a rare thing: a sunlit orchid, wild fruit in ripe profusion, a clear spring and a long drink of water, a green parrot in a tuft of leaves an arm's length away, leopard cubs at play in the mirror of their mother's eye, a dominant mammee tree half asleep in the evening mist then all at once a houseful of clamoring monkeys, or else a sudden explosion of screaming color, pink, white, purple, a deluge of beating wings, stretching necks, pure chaos forming into a flight of waterfowl spooked off a slick lagoon, rising, spreading out like a thin cloud, now an arrow, swift on the skyline, gray then white as they veer into the sunlight. These things have their purpose. They are seeds and a man's memory is a squirrel. If he's to survive he must store them against future miseries.

"For example there was a storyteller in our village. One night a five-year-old boy took me by the hand and led me to him, a gift I could never repay. I can still remember our shared delight. We were quite a pair, the boy and I. For the first time in my life I was beginning to despair and for the first time in his the world was beginning to open in all its wonder. I'd learned the world held more misery than I ever imagined; he'd learned there's no sure way to pick up a porcupine.

217

"A feisty little hornet—his name was Ramses Tokenu. Unlike some children, he never begged; he'd take me aside and tell me, man to man, he needed some rice. He liked to show me things. When he had a fresh set of insect bites, he'd hike up his shorts and proudly point them out; or else he'd spread out the remains of a dead bat on my kitchen table like a set of architectural plans. But that night, with the usual 'come see' look in his eyes, he led me in and out among the sleepy huts to a gang of age-mates sitting on the ground before a haggard old man in the middle of a story. He was quick to see he'd found something I liked—the dead bat had not been a success. After that every time the storyteller appeared, so did Ramses. He'd march right into my house, all three feet of him. The older children found him amusing because he hadn't learned the impropriety of barging in on his elders in the middle of the evening meal. He'd climb into a chair at my kitchen table, terribly pleased with himself, no doubt thinking the laughter was in approval."

"Do you need some rice tonight?" There was no point asking; they were always hungry. The mere mention of food changed a child's face to an adult. "Did you wash your hands?" He knew he hadn't. As he thought what to do, excited whispers coached him from behind the screen door. He hurried out. There came quick instructions, a shuffle of feet, a loud splash in the rain barrel—they must have dunked him head first—then he reappeared dripping from the waist up, hurriedly wiping his hands on his shorts before climbing back in his chair. He took up his spoon clutching it in his fist like a crucifix, stared at it intently, then without a hitch carefully set it aside and began feasting with both hands, one to hold the bowl, one to dig, all the time watching the few kernels that fell to his lap or the floor so he could get them later. When he finished, he promptly delivered the news.

"Da o' ma'. He teddy tody."

"Telling stories?"

He nodded yes.

"Tonight?" Another *yes* and he was down the steps and gone at the slam of the door. When I got up to clear the table, the porch screen came to life with voices offering to wash the pot in exchange for leftovers. Two of them came in at the sound of their names. On the way out I checked the study, the usual beehive of Loma and English rattling on like market day; the quicker of them soon caught on to using weak constructions to their own advantage. The simplest phrase had a way of twisting into an indecent remark; heated invective took on stiff formality. "Get to hell out of here!" became, "To the abode of venerable ancestors please to make haste." New words sprang up like weeds, skoobwoigee (schoolboys) and motarrow (motor road).

Out on the porch stray goats settled in for the night, their heads tucked into their sides, their feet under their bellies. Two small boys sat on the steps playing a game of herdsmen with straws and live beetles. Another watched quietly chewing a stalk of sugar cane, the juice trickling down his chin and onto his pot belly. Across the road in the village the evening fires gave up their smoke as if in offering to the mercy of the coming night; it rose feebly, then spread out in a soft white layer like a communal blanket amid the pointed rooftops. After the day's work everything settled earthward; thatched eaves seemed to reach for the ground, tools with undried mud in their teeth leaned against door posts, fresh game lay limp in the dust, stragglers undid their leaden headloads and sank to their rest in the same motion. Now and then a clear sound resonated through the gathering dusk: the clank of a metallic pot, the bark of a dog, a song lifted in prayer from the Mandingo quarter—all vibrant, sonorous in the heavy air. Open doorways framed dark silhouettes huddled in the smoldering firelight, the scent of wood smoke and burnt palm oil wafted outward. Sometimes a burst of laughter. But more often than not for a short time after the evening meal, nothing moved. Maybe a slight rattle of dry palm leaves, the murmur of air in the high treetops, or a night thing might dart across a patch of purple sky.

Night muted the loud colors of day into an abyss of deep shadows swallowing everything but the whitewashed walls and the conical rooflines. And behind the quilt work of thatch and mud, the outline of the forest loomed vast and immobile, a slate cliff scarcely distinct from the rest of the night as though the heavier part of the sky had sunk to earth. This dumb immensity was the one unquestionable fact of existence, remote, obscure, but very much alive. As nighttime fell, the forest came awake. The air seemed to hold its breath. Each leaf hung poised; each snap of a twig betrayed a silence that wasn't a silence. A sixth sense knew this thing but the eye was never quick enough to catch it. So it went without a name, a fleeting memory that never quite materialized, forever outcast by the prudish laws of reality. But as an outcast it thrived. It prowled in the imagination, haunted a troubled sleep. Now and then it deigned to parrot a human sound, but only in its own time, and in between these dark utterances, an awe-binding tranquility weighed the emptiness and communed with a black sibling among the stars. In these depths a human scream was a transient thing, as easily absorbed as a drop of dew. There was no question who the lord and who the poacher. Yet…this cunning indifference, this deliberate snub of all effort to penetrate it, is just what gave it a soul. An aura of deathly calm betrayed life; the very inhumanity of this place made it human.

"Teacha dress my so'."

"Ask John Mulba. The sulfa powder's in the medicine chest."

"Wha you go-eeng?"

"I'm going in town." And then from down the path, "Watch the lamp wick and no wrestling in the study!"

Across the road men gathered at Quolidobu's store where they exchanged the day's news with quaffs of cane juice and draws off a communal pipe. Kpedah and Wsiogi were examining the teeth of a crosscut saw. The others looked on—Zubah, Taanu, Young Kpoimu, Kokulo, whose three houses and six wives made him one of the wealthier men in the village, his brother, Koiyo, who farmed far to the north often remaining there for weeks at a time, and Gbodo the blacksmith, a reticent man. When they saw me they invited me in for a drink. I accepted because I had to. The distillate of sugar cane was considered ripe when it made the hairs in your nose bristle. They enjoyed watching me try not to grimace when I swallowed. As soon as it was down Gburulu offered me another but I refused. He insisted the second shot followed its elder sister into the stomach without hesitation—and he would have known, having been "well met" back in the bush on more than one occasion with his wine gourds swaying from his shoulder yoke as he sang his way home. They said he'd once fallen from a palm wine tree a full thirty feet to the ground without ill effect, but I refused to believe it.

I excused myself and left them to their talk. They hardly noticed, another topic caught their interest and an animated gesture set the lone lantern squeaking as it dangled from a piece of twine. Outside, Night had quit the forest and entered the village, sleek as a leopardess settling among her cubs, oblivious to both lanterns and the humming beneath them as if they were fireflies. Up above a crescent moon was no more than a faint blemish behind twirls of wooly clouds. But despite the insignificance of our fires, the village continued its social life for a few hours between mealtime and sleep. People gathered on porches or outside houses, kids ran in and out, adolescents kept to their cliques centered on a leader or an interest—in the case of unmarried girls a rather singular interest. If an eligible male walked by, darkened doorways came alive with chatter and soon one of them seemed to dart out protesting she'd been pushed. Teenagers seldom came to hear the storyteller anymore. They'd heard him as children, or else they preferred Akwoi's racy accounts of the same tales, that is if they weren't engaged in more clandestine affairs, such as a rendezvous in the culvert under the motor road where the slightest whisper became an impassioned plea. For the old and the sick however, life wasn't so friendly. They stayed inside mostly. After a joyless meal and fits of coughing, bathing their rotting feet and moaning fatigue, they sat alone by their burnt out fires and watched their flesh yield to diseases they didn't know by name; these and their bodies had long ago learned to live with each other like a bad marriage. If they were able they could crawl onto mud ledges against the inside walls of their houses and hope for rest; it would come like a beast, their breathing heavy, their jaws ajar, worn limbs rigid against the hard earth with skeletal fingers clutching blood spattered covers. If they were lucky, they would sleep. Tomorrow would bring them heavier ache and the night thereafter lighter rest.

The storyteller's house graced the edge of the village, the old round style, small enough to suggest a hermitage. Its conical roof leaned off center in disrepair, no windows, no porch, but a small fenced-in workyard. Wet thatch bore the musty scent of wood smoke. Two boards nailed into a makeshift eave trough and tied awkwardly below the round roof line filled a five gallon can aslant in the mud. In back a rickety bath fence practically melted into the ground, but a solid work table set up on sawhorses under two shady palm fronds showed signs of use. A fair sized lime tree grew alongside a clump of papaya and shreds of okra and Guinea pepper circled the edges of an ancient compost pile. The only sign of life, one rooster who hadn't won many fights thoughtfully scratching the loose dirt, and not far behind the black cloak of the forest hung in majestic stillness like a curtain in a theater while busy voices within prepared for opening night.

I took my seat on the ground in front of the doorstep, a little to one side. Two small boys sat down beside me. Then two little girls with a twelve-year-old chaperone. Slender, slow witted Dwoiyou stood out in the open like a giraffe grinning with delight as he tried to watch three separate games of tag revolving around him. When one of them snuck behind his back, he giggled brokenly then turned around to find out why. Gradually we came together in a loose semicircle of rags, bare feet, protruding navels, small round heads and flashing eyes eager for adventure but not quite ready to go after it.

I thought it odd such a fine storyteller drew only small children, Dwoiyou, and myself. Odd, too, because his stories, though childish in the beginning, often took some not so childish turns. He made no attempt to narrate on their level; Loma children were not brought up on pabulum. Perhaps the answer lay in the informality of the art. In the unhurried pace of tribal life, stories were never in the way; there was always time, during the rain, or on a trip to shorten the distance, or while at work to ease the strain. It was their way of taking a break.

There were stories and there were stories; everything from dirty jokes to full epics. They were the mortar that held things together, more pervasive in their world than the press in ours. They prepared the young for life, the old for death; they were a way of taking leave, of bringing news, striking a foe, giving medicine; they were the spice in a political speech, the meat in a celebration; they came with moral teachings, comic relief, budding rebellions. Whether on the trail or in the marketplace, their blossoms always bore fruit. There were few people who couldn't tell a story and none who couldn't enjoy one— and enjoyment was the key. No matter how grim reality, it became palatable in the form of a story. They were escape, they were therapy. Above all they were fun.

Suddenly a clamor of cackling hens! The tag players froze. Already learning the ways of the hunter, they peered into the shadows. "Da Daydobah!" they cried in unison pointing at him. "Teacha da lie!" one of the shadows shouted back. Then a scolding adult sent him darting toward us. I lunged for him but he spun away and scampered off to the edge of the darkness where he danced in place hitching his oversized shorts into his armpits daring me to come after him, a chase we all knew I'd lose.

"You wa' we catch heem?" his mates asked excitedly.

"Not now. I will catch him someday."

"You wi' bea' heem?" They knew I owed him one for the time he put a centipede down my back.

"I will do him one better," I said. "I will rub his belly with palm oil and tie him to an ant hill." They screamed with delight as he edged closer, out in the open but ready for the chase.

Then a burly shadow not ten yards away grunted disapproval. It seemed to materialize on the spot. Old Fawkpa. Without a word his presence sent them scattering, except Dwoiyou who stood in dumb befuddlement. "Sah," the old man said gravely. "You mu' ta' de cha'."

A low stool hung from his hand. He stood perfectly motionless, a bit uneasy possibly suspecting I preferred the ground. But that he could not allow. This was his village, there were accepted standards, an adult guest without a proper place could not be condoned. I took it inquiring after his health, which wasn't good. He often came to my house late at night after the children were in bed asking for something to steady his hand or ease his breathing. To ask of someone's health often invited a lengthy tirade in which the enemy disease was thoroughly disgraced—but not Fawkpa. He only clicked his fingers showing an open palm in a desolate gesture of, "It is no great thing." His bearing forbade discussion on the matter. Without a sideward glance he turned and disappeared as silently as he'd come.

Whenever I came into town, he saw to it I had a chair. If one wasn't handy, he brought a wooden crate. I called it my box at the opera. It got to be a private joke whenever my own people got too nosey about what I was doing or why I didn't keep their company in the cocktail lounge at the Hotel Ducor.

Then a dry creaking and the door of the storyteller's house opened. He stepped out ducking his head, seemingly aloof to the game of tag, now dissolved into a lewd dance that ended abruptly only a few steps away. Nor did he take the slightest notice of his audience. He seated himself, set a faint lantern on the ground at his feet, coughed wearily, folding his soiled robe around his knees. He was a descendant of the renowned warrior, Weedor, who fought in tribal wars and against forced labor, and this lineage alone enabled a man to sit in council, a privilege he practiced rarely and without enthusiasm. He'd been around, traveled widely in his youth, something rare for jungle folk, seen the seacoast, Dakar, the camel market in Kano. Somewhere he'd acquired the trade of a carpenter, lived on a mission, but converted back to Loma belief. He was old now, his children gone, his wives lost. He lived alone with an older sister who swept his house and cooked his rice, but more often scolded him for his apparent disinterest in worldly affairs. By day he farmed or did odd carpentry jobs, and to see him then, he looked stern and detached, hardly the kind of man who had a need to sit on his doorstep telling stories to small children. His motives were his, alone. Even as he spoke, his inner self remained a mystery and just when it seemed he would at last reveal himself, he'd withdraw into one of his characters. No one really knew him. His name was Kpoodu.

He was thought ugly by his own people. He had the face of a bloodhound, an excess of skin that hung in folds over a slight head, several missing teeth, a nasty scar on his collarbone, bags under his eyes, long ears, and a thin neck that made him appear to be straining to see over things, but as you got to know him, his oddities diminished and left behind the revelation of a subtle spirit that mastered every deformity nature had given him. He made good use of this malleable face twisting and knotting it into the weirdest forms, and his animal "impersonations" won instant recognition, the little ones crying out in unison. He demanded, and got, full attention. The slightest annoyance, any monkey business at all, and he was known to rise without a word and disappear into his house. The sound of the door closing behind him meant no more stories for many days.

He cleared his throat and spat into the dirt—he was subject to coughing fits. He paused, gathering his thoughts as his audience settled in. I sat on my stool flanked by Jacob Jallah, John Frumo, Abraham Beewoh, Joseph Ziamoe, Ramses Tokenu, David Bawkumah, and Dwoiyou, whose gaping mouth suggested hunger for a brain that couldn't eat. Daydobah decided to sit at the opposite corner, facing me, with open space behind him. At the last minute two more girls hurried in and sat on their folded legs with their lappas drawn around their ankles. Kezelly and his brother stood on their knees behind the others so not to miss anything. The semicircle drew tight. The little ones huddled together with their arms around each other rubbing their eyes, fondling each others hair, pinching bugs, or swatting at passing insects. Dwoiyou dug in the dirt with his big toe. I tried to forget everything I knew of literature and art.

Kpoodu was illiterate—and that was his good fortune. Printed words would have frozen his fertile waters. At first his voice ground like a rusty hinge but after several turns he found his rhythm and began his journey; he swept us along as a current carries a boat of revelers. Indeed he knew his art as a river knows a lagoon. In time the eddies died, the water cleared, and the deep mirror of his wisdom reflected a timeless truth in bright fidelity.

I suspected he didn't always know the exact endings of his stories when he began and I was certain he invented anecdotes as he went along—often in passing reference to a scandal the whole village knew—drawing on a vast store of myth and folklore, animal characters and human conflicts which he wove into speech as fluid as a friendly greeting, into stories within stories, impossible predicaments, fantastic escapes, fatherly advice, and when he was in the mood, a line or two of song ensconced in a gravel monotone. But even as he sang his vacant eyes searched his listeners for new stories.

Usually his expression showed no sign of involvement with his narrative which seemed to race along without his help, but at the same time his hands spoke of the silent forces behind the appearance of things and that gaunt face told still another story—perhaps the only story there is—of the human soul's fight to be free. There were times too, when his eyes crossed mine, I got the distinct impression he was speaking to me alone, that he knew what I knew. We listened like hungry waifs. Guinea hens roosted on a sawhorse under the eaves, the low light of his lantern cast eerie shadows on the wall behind, bats flitted above the rooftops, a chorus of crickets sang in the grass, the occasional "klunk" of a frog responded from the creek, a plaintive cry from far away warned of the world's immensity—all of which he used as sound effects sometimes waiting for their response. And of course the presence of the forest loomed larger as Night deepened. Its seeming silence never let us forget where we were. We would have spoken with it but it wore a black cloak, a lone sentry on a distant outpost, its brooding thoughts far from the ant-like doings of men.

CHAPTER 21

HIS STORY

HOW WICKEDNESS CAME INTO THE WORLD

Once, when I was a boy, I lived in a village not far away and spent the summer of my days much as you do now. I and my age-mates, we raced about the town darting in and out like gnats about the evening fire. We scattered goats and guinea hens and ran in turn from barking dogs. But none could catch us. We challenged imaginary foes, cast toy spears at toy phantoms—but stopped at the forest's edge. But soon thereafter we ventured into its shallows. We hunted birds and squirrel with slingshot and stone, learned the secrets of its cries and whispers, its terror and treachery. Stealth and patience became our friends. Sometimes we would go down to the waterside to look for fish and turtle, and if none were there, we would splash and shout until the water turned tawny brown. These are the halcyon days of your youth. Store them in the tree trunk of your memory where thieving squirrels cannot burrow. They will feed you well when Old Age comes to figure his arithmetic in the lines of your face.

One day as I was coming back into town, I saw an old man sitting in his hammock, bowed above a young girl who knelt on the floor consulting cowrie shells. Slim as a young sapling, she had a refined style, superior but not arrogant. I thought it odd because I'd seen them in that exact posture before, several times in fact, so I asked my grandmother who was a learned woman in matters such as these. She told me the old man's son had long ago been caught and taken away, and now his daughter was trying to divine his whereabouts, a task involved enough, but when the diviner weeps over the shells and the grandfather over the diviner, the answer as you might expect cannot come clear. The shells may say "Fernando Po" or "Port-au-Prince" or "Carolina," but these words ring hollow in our ears; they whisper of a loved one lost, beyond the ken of cowrie shells, with naught but futile hope on the face of a hopeless girl and deeper sorrow on that of her father's father.

I asked my grandmother why there was such wickedness in the world. She smiled a smile for questions that come too soon. Then she looked up from her work and gazed into the forest, but when I followed the path of her eyes, I saw only trees and sunshine sleeping in the leaves. What was she looking at? I see, she began in earnest, the time has come to talk of grown-up things. It is true the world is rife with wickedness. But it was not always so.

There was a time long ago, she said, when animals and people all lived together in harmony. Birds too. All spoke the same language, shared the same fire and ate the same food. They worked together and lived in peace. They sang the same songs and danced to the same music. (That is why even today some people remind you of animals when they dance.) Society refused no one, regardless of the twist of a tail or the tone of a beak. None quarreled nor fenced his compound; none stole or swore profanity. Not even a rat suffered want of food or drink. The village had never known strife. Animals that are the bitterest enemies today would stop to greet each other on their way to market. "How do you do Mr. Fat Lamb, how is it with you this fine morning?" And Mr. Lamb would answer, "I am very well, indeed, Mrs. Skinny Lion. It's so good to see you up and about." Sometimes they even intermarried and bore children. Such was the case of the Great Grandsire (Spirit) of the village, the revered elder who spent his days in a shady hammock contemplating what had past and what was yet to come.

But then something happened. Ill fortune, perhaps witchcraft, no one can say, drove the Old Man (Great Grandsire) from village affairs due to a loss of face brought on by the immoderation of contending sons. Wives he had eleven, all properly endowed, upright in bearing. Though the youngest was his favorite, (he knew he couldn't disguise such things, unlike some inexperienced young persons in this very village) he treated them all with tenderness, always buying them combs and colored cloth when the itinerant merchants came to town, and they returned his kindness as befit their stations. As the seasons passed Age began to stalk him, but this tireless hunter was not to taste the meat of a quick kill—not yet. The man grew old, true enough, but he did so without haste. This made the hunter pause to think, "How's this? Surely he knows I stalk him, yet he does not bolt for cover!" And as the hunter paused, the old man lengthened his years. He busied himself with small tasks during the day, unmindful of the cotton gathering on his temples, and in the evenings he listened to the passionate talk of young men remembering those same fires from his youth; but in the afternoons, when the overbearing heat of the sun drove everyone into shade, he sat in his hammock, a solitary figure with his favorite at his side, and contemplated the sunny days. He studied where other men saw nothing. His face was placid water but his thoughts were forever in flight—like clouds up above.

Do you know how great white clouds move about on a bright day? Have you seen how they turn around inside themselves? Have you looked when mountains of white forests move across the clean blue sky? They may seem motionless but if you look well, you will see they are forever working, tossing about, never asleep. They are Heaven's brain and when you see them working, Heaven is thinking, thinking about what she is going to cook for her little ones when the harvest grain is spent; and when she thinks so hard sweat forms on her brow, it will soon rain because the brow of Heaven is very great.

Now the Old Man, as I said, had many fine sons. Some lived in nearby hamlets and had fine sons of their own, all of whom treated him with appropriate decorum. But since the world at this time knew neither fear nor peril, they seldom sought his counsel in matters of state. In his native village however, he had only those of his youngest, fairest wife, his favorite. They were four: Leopard, Spider, Goat, and headstrong, young Moonface Monkey.

Leopard was eldest. Silence and stealth his trademarks. Prowling the forest with cunning and ease, scarcely stirring the leaves, he never returned to the village without something good to eat. He was a hunter and that brought him the highest esteem. But as an aristocrat and man of the world he brooked no sham, his wide unflinching eyes saw deep, even into the night where others could only guess; hypocrisy and cant melted under their awesome gaze like mists before the morning sun. Fear and Solace met like clandestine lovers within the orbit of their terrible glare. What he knew of the world, he did not say, but it was surely profound, and because of this his acquaintances knew him to be wise and warned others never to cheat him for retribution would come swift and severe. He was handsome too. He moved with fluid grace; the powerful muscles beneath his sleek coat were like smooth rocks submerged in rushing water. He could drag weights equal to his own; his straining neck would hold them off to the side as he trotted along. All this, and not a sound, not a whisper. With a single thrust, he could bound into the lower limbs of trees where he enjoyed taking his leisure. There he surveyed the world without comment, now and then twitching his tail or licking his paw, and satisfied things were as they should be, he would blink his eyes—like this.

Mr. Goat was next eldest and like his brother, Leopard, came of select stock. Strong, steady, though not as swift, his fine forehead and horizontal nose at once announced aristocratic birth, although his speech unfortunately suffered a slight stutter, which his friends quickly excused as the mark of a passionate soul. When he lowered his head in his work, it did not rise until the task was done. His great driving shoulders took him through any enclosure, his swift head-butt broke the strongest granary door, the twist of his fine horn tore open the thickest sack, but nonetheless he could be remarkably gentle when he rose to ram his friends in sport. He was well-liked not only for his learning, but for the kindness he bore the aged and the sick. Forever the good soldier, his days were filled with sensitive ruminations and when he was not otherwise occupied, he enjoyed browsing in secluded gardens.

The third brother however, was of a different hue. Spider's teeth were red—red from greed. His bowl of rice was never full. He could never get all he wanted, whether of rice or riches or the talk of men, and if any of these were within reach but not in his possession, he could not rest. The bounty of others gave him terrible worry and made him forget his own. So he went about forever conniving, scheming, hurrying back and forth from one enterprise to another. Once he tricked Dog into giving him his fleas—a sad bargain for Mr. Dog who thereafter he had no one to tell him where to scratch—and another time he dared creep into Crocodile's mouth to steal his supper, no sooner out than his quick tongue was back at work hatching further intrigue. Of course his masterpiece had been the time he diverted the highway of Driver Ant into the barn of Mr. Ant Bear, excising a small consideration per capita. His fingers went like this—never at rest, forever stepping about, inspecting everything, first ahead, then back, upside down, always in feverish haste. When something came into his grasp, he would coil around it with his entire body, dancing over it as he rolled it to his house. Up in his loft, he cached his prize where no one would find it. Even so, he could not be satisfied; he slid down his rope and hurried outside to check his traps. Unlike Leopard or Goat, Spider had no time for leisure or sport, and in all the world there was only one person as devious as he, and that was his wife.

Last came Moonface Monkey, the youngest and in many ways the cleverest. His hands knew many skills and his tongue many fine words. He could climb into the highest trees, laughing and chattering as he did for he enjoyed being up above everyone else. From this high place he saw how small his fellows were, how stupidly they gawked, how easily they fell under the sway of the moment, what few words it took to inflame them to passion. How he despised them. Other times he was quite the jester; he would feign falling to frighten everyone below, but always caught a thin branch just in time to swing into another tree, as easily as stepping off a porch. He turned somersaults to make the children laugh and on market day, he played the dummy as he bartered for his rice. Yet, his cleverness bore him bitter fruit; it made him headstrong and "quick to vex" as is so often the way of young men. His moods varied like the sky; with a slight shift of the wind, comedy turned to disdain. He found the conversation of his fellows foolish and unrewarding. He cherished only his self esteem which he carried about as if he were headloading a jug of palm wine filled to the brim. He respected no one and sneered at all who warned him of his vanity. However it was rumored in the village, were it not for the stubbornness of his ways, his father would have loved him best.

Now the four brothers cleared a great farm and planned to divide the harvest. After careful deliberation and the necessary sacrifices, Leopard chose a fine spot on a hillside sloping to the east so the growing rice would face the young sunlight rather than the burning heat of afternoon. Mr. Goat felled the great trees. Everyone knew it was he for the steady speech of his axe did not cease until they all lay on the earth with the undersides of their leaves facing outward like the bellies of fish on a riverbank. All four worked diligently. They burnt off the creepers and the underbrush. Moonface Monkey trimmed the branches and Spider ran up and down and sideways over the entire farm as the brush piles seemed to stack up without his help. Soon they built a shelter to store their tools and dry themselves when it rained. Moonface constructed the frame and laced it tight swinging back and forth while he worked as if he were climbing in trees, and Spider wove the thatch. When the farm was prepared, the women came to sow the seed. Their work chant and their hoes combed the wet earth in unison. And all the time Leopard kept alert, watching the forest for game.

With the coming rains the rice grew thick. The wind sent shivers through it from one end to the other where thin blades died out in the shadows of the forest. At season's end each stem flowered into grain. The hanging heads clicked and rustled on each other in a song of joy to those who've tasted hunger. In the last weeks, Mr. Ricebird came to see how things were progressing, but boys with slingshots drove him away. As he flew off he cried, "Fee phree, fee phree, take pity on meee!" but you must never believe him. If he eats one, he will eat two; if he eats all, you will eat none.

The women again sang as they worked their way across the field cutting half circles into the waving grain and dropping neat bundles behind them. The sun was their overseer. It pressed down on their bent backs drenching them with sweat as they rose and dipped with each stroke of their knives across fistfuls of yellow stalk. Their hands were like the forearms of grasshoppers.

The four brothers gathered the bundles and tied them together. They carried their bounty back to town in the good spirits of the harvest already hearing the drums of thanksgiving in their hearts. Though the loads were heavy, they were not so heavy as an equal weight of hunger. Spider carried prodigious loads, back and again, some so large they covered his entire body, only his wiry legs visible as he picked his way along the trail.

But then, although the harvest had been plentiful, there was palaver when they began to divide the bundles. Spider claimed he had not been given his fair share; he was admittedly smaller than the others, but his work had been equal to theirs. His quickness and fervor, he argued, more than made up for his strength. Moonface sneered contemptuously. Had not the others worked too? And where would the harvest be were it not for the strong axe of Goat or the wisdom of Leopard, or for he himself whose exacting work had raised the kitchen and kept them dry, or yet the women whose backs were bent for many hard days? And what of the boys with their slingshots? Had they not done their part, Mr. Ricebird would now be singing thanksgiving. Of course everyone had worked, Spider conceded judiciously, so everyone should accordingly get an equal share, and his share, he concluded triumphantly, was decidedly smaller than the others—and especially that of Mr. Moonface. Any fool could see as much. In tones of unbrotherly scorn, they argued the entire afternoon and when evening came, the stillness carried their voices throughout the village. Everyone heard. Neighbors quietly remarked on the fury of the brothers' words, words loud enough to challenge the harvest drums.

Do you know how wind races through a smoldering fire? Have you seen the red ashes brighten till they burst into flame? Even so, the argument grew. It seemed to die over night, but rekindled itself in the morning even before the roosters called to the rising sun. It began as the clatter of monkeys in the treetops but soon waxed fierce as the snarl of a boar. And all the time the Old Man with the cotton on his temples sat motionless under the shade of his leisure kitchen, his face calm, seemingly undisturbed by the shouts of his contending sons.

By midday the heat of their passions rose to a crackling blaze. First Spider appealed to the dispassionate gazes of their unbelieving friends. Had not his work, in truth, been equal to that of any man in the village? It was an outrage

231

to think not. And had not his share been equal too? Moonface shot back. Then they began to hurl insults. "You are a fool!" Spider shouted, "Too stupid in your headstrong way to see the injustice before your very eyes!" And he spat into the ground as the muscles in his neck grew taut with rage. "And you are a thief!" screamed the monkey. "If all the rice in the village were yours, you would yet howl for more, like a mad dog!"

Now that was an insult—to call someone a dog. Leopard and Goat, fearing the worst, came forward to separate them, the latter suggesting that Spider take some of his rice and be satisfied, next season they would clear a greater farm and there would be plenty, but Leopard, looking sternly at his youngest brother, let him know without a word, he would suffer no one being called a dog; otherwise he remained silent, like the Old Man in the hammock.

As the day wore on, the argument became as oppressive as the afternoon heat. There was no quarter. Insults came as thick as flies and stung like hornets. In a final fit of anger Moonface Monkey took up a handful of his rice and hurled it in the dirt at Spider's feet, a further insult not only to Spider but to all who worked the farm. "Mad man!" cried Spider. "Glutton!" screamed Moonface.

Until this point the chief noted the gathering storm but refrained from intervening in deference to the Old Man in the hammock with whom he had gone hunting long ago; but now, as he saw the argument grow out of hand, he came forward and appealed to the four of them asking that they remember the civility of brothers. But Moonface paid no heed answering him with a sneer, "My brother asks for his fair share, let him scratch the dirt for it among the cackling fowls."

Now although Spider indeed wanted all he could get, it was out of the question that *he,* a gentleman, should pick it out of the dirt. He would have lost face. However, seeing that his brother's violent action had offended the chief and townspeople alike, he devised a clever trap hoping to win them over to his side since further argument was useless. Spider was very good at this sort of thing. He calmed himself and in a voice devoid of passion, casually remarked to his neighbors, "See how my brother walks among men yet displays the manners of a beast. We must forgive such rash behavior my friends. Nothing more can be expected of his kind." Then he walked away as softly as one leaves a sick room, seemingly in pity of his beaten brother, all the time reassuring first one neighbor then another, "Nothing more can be expected."

People stared at each other in disbelief. The chief nonetheless followed his duty and ordered Moonface to pick up the wasted grain for it was an abomination to the ancestors to throw rice to the ground in anger. Now the jester began to see his shame in the eyes of his fellows, but instead of quelling his anger, it only deepened it. "You are a fool too!" he shouted at the chief. The chief who also dared not lose face called after him in kind, "Pare the thorns of thy temper Headstrong! Or you will walk a stranger among men!"

Spider had won. But he did not know how well. The young acrobat had fallen from a very great height. Like a thin branch, restraint had broken beneath him and this time there was not a single twig he could catch to save himself. He knew he was wrong, but he could not see what to do. He slinked into a dark corner as abject as an old elephant looking for a place to die. There he sat brooding the entire night. His only wife—a mere sapling chosen for him by the keen eye of his father whose many years had taught him the wisdom of seeing ripe fruit in the first blossom—remained with him but huddled in fright. He did not speak to her, nor she to him.

Have you seen how a young sapling bends to the same arc as its mate because they respond to the same wind? Have you noticed how new leaves dance and dazzle under the same breeze? How a thousand boughs give their color to the same forest because they thrive in the same sun? It is the same sun that shines on you. This is a lesson you must learn if you would be a husband or a wife.

Morning found guinea hens scratching in the dirt where Moonface had thrown the rice. Everyone expected the rash young fellow to make amends to the chief for his impertinence the day before, but when they came to his hut, they found him tying his remaining possessions in a neat headload. His young wife fluttered about as nervously as a bird in a cage. She tried to help but he would not allow, and the cool detachment with which he worked frightened her all the more. He packed some food in a pot, tools for making fire, a knife, a cutlass, his hunting spear, and a personal talisman. That was all.

Had he really hated them, his brothers and the village, it would have been easy to go, but in truth, he secretly loved their esteem. Like two mean dogs fighting over a piece of red meat, first pulling one way then the other, neither daring let go for fear of losing the prize—so it was in his heart. Warm memories of the saplings slender fingers on his shoulders, her lips as she pressed her face into his neck, pulled him softly back to the village; but soon, other, fiercer thoughts of revenge and the monstrous wrong he suffered tore him back the other way. And unfortunately, when it comes to war between love and anger, it is the law that anger must win. So it was with poor Moonface, sad-eyed Moonface. His heart was overwhelmed by something base, while the gentler power of love kept silent in the shadows of his darkening plan.

"What are you doing?" asked Leopard.

"Since I am not welcome in the sight of men," the Headstrong answered calmly, "I will go my way."

"Make amends to the chief first," warned Goat who liked him well despite his ways.

"No," he answered softly, his fury spent.

"The news will travel," Goat said earnestly. "When they hear of your transgression in other places, you will lose face there too."

"I seek no other village."

"No other village?" Goat asked in disbelief as Leopard's eyes widened. "But where will you go?"

"Into the forest."

"There are many things in the forest my brother," Leopard said with great unflinching eyes. "Only a fool goes into the forest alone."

"Then call me a fool," the fun lover jested as he gave his brother a playful cuff behind the ears.

"To be driven from your village is punishment imposed for wickedness," Leopard mused, "but to willingly choose it?" Then, seeing his argument was to no avail, he drew near his brother and gently rubbed his head on his shoulder like a cub in play and whispered one word, so low no one else could hear. "Stay."

Now even Spider did not expect so rash a result as this, and when he heard his wife gossip of his brother's intentions, he too hurried out to offer counsel. He knew as well as anyone the need for community. One cannot satisfy one's greed in an empty village. "Make your amends," he said, though not as earnestly as the other two. "Do not be," he paused for the right word, "unreasonable."

But the Headstrong paid them no heed.

The rage of the bygone day was done; his face showed calm like the forest after rain. He walked to where his father sat in his hammock to bid him good-bye. They looked into each other's eyes for as long as it takes a hawk to fall on its prey and they needed no words. On his way out of the village he wished his brother, Leopard, good hunting and said a warm good-by to Goat, who had always been his favorite, giving him a scratch between the horns, the way he had done when they frolicked as boys. Then the Headstrong turned and left. His troubled footsteps carried him quickly from his native village. He did not look back.

Suddenly! There came a rush of movement like the beating wings of a bird fresh from a cage! The Sapling! She made bold to go after her husband, her eyes were wild like a cornered animal, but Leopard restrained her. She fought and scratched but he held firm his grip and she fell exhausted when he set her down at his father's side. In time, she would take a new husband, an older man who would treat her well, and in greater time she would become a revered elder herself, but even then, not once would she speak of the one time in her life when the passions of youth drove her to recklessness, to her mad attempt to follow her mad husband—and surely she remembered. You have to remember something like that in order not to speak of it.

After setting her down, Leopard turned his gaze upon the empty path that had swallowed his brother. "He will be back," Goat said pawing the ground with his forefoot. "Being alone will kill his pride." Leopard considered his brother's words. "Perhaps," he observed, "but if he would challenge the forest alone, it will leave its mark."

So too thought the Old Man who now sat passively in his hammock—as he had throughout the heated argument, hearing every poisoned word, as indeed everyone in the village had—and who showed no visible sign of pain at the parting of his lost son; he knew even better than Leopard or Goat the Headstrong's anger was overwrought, not the usual anger of men who reclaim good spirits much as the sky after a storm. Although his senses were failing him, he saw this more clearly than anyone; his son's pride was a badly thrown spear lodged in the belly of a beast—the greater the pain, the greater the struggle, and again more pain. After many days, he confided to his senior wife, "He will not be back."

The Castaway walked all day forgetting to tire in his anguish, and when night caught up, he built a fire and cooked wild cassava. He journeyed for many days deep into the forest, away from the sight of men and their foolish jabbering to where the hardiest hunters go. His way led north where the sun had gone to keep house for the season; and there, from her porch, the yellow eye of Heaven watched him each day like that of an old woman bearing down on her needlework.

Once Heaven had had two eyes like everyone else and her fair face had been beautiful beyond imagining, as pleasing as a young wife during the first days of marriage; but a jealous warrior, slighted at her disdain and in the rage of a rejected lover, cast his spear mightily all the way into the sky where it lodged in one of her shining irises. She made not a sound, but when she removed it, all her sweetness drained to earth in great drops of sunshine that melted on human skin like sugar on a child's tongue. That day was the most brilliant ever. People had to put down their work and hurry into shade; even shadows ran away and sequestered themselves in caves. In time, her injured eye turned sickly white and became the moon. Now, during the daytime, she turns her good eye to earth to watch us toil, but at night when we are asleep, she turns the sickly one, and with the other weeps for the beauty she lost so unfairly.

Moonface remembered the story with a faint smile. So the world of men with its two unequal eyes had become ugly to him. He alone had looked it full in the face and seen the truth. It could no longer be beautiful, not even his wife. The barbs of his brother's true words had pierced the eye of his soul and the memory could not be plucked out so easily as a well cast spear. The sunshine of his soul had drained away leaving a sickly white ghost that accompanied him deeper and deeper into the forest, further than he had ever been. No longer did friendly landmarks reassure him, only the sullen echoes of his own footsteps and the fear he did not allow himself to admit. Yet, as he looked about, the heavy arms of trees seemed to point the way, moving clouds seemed to beckon. The song of the forest lulled him. He did not know he was but a hungry beast on the scent of a baited snare.

For many days after he left, Leopard and Goat kept an eye on the empty trail that had given their brother to the forest. "He will be back soon," Goat reassured him but each day with less resolve. Finally Leopard could resist no longer the urge to go after his brother and bring him home. He sought his father's counsel. The old man agreed. Leopard, after all, was the most likely to succeed.

So Leopard too left the village. He assured everyone he would not be long, but that was not to be. The forest is greater than anyone knows. Leopard searched for many days. His silent footsteps carried him farther than he had ever been, away from the doings of men. The search did not go well. There were conflicting signs and as the days passed, he began to lose his bearings. Soon he grew hungry. He could not hunt for himself and seek his brother at the same time. The two scents led different ways. His hunger grew and gave him no rest; it waxed fierce and wailed within. In the morning it rustled like dry palm leaves on the floor of his stomach, at noon it begged like a piteous waif at a merchant's door, but at night...at night it came inside and tore his guts like a monster foetus with poison claws. Yet no game. He dragged his weakened belly against the ground; the pain within became a savage law. Many have claimed to be the rulers of mankind, but the only true ruler is hunger. Do not forget that. Leopard could not, nor could he stand the agony. He screamed aloud. Then trembled at the inhuman shriek that came from his own throat. The entire forest went silent.

After waiting many days, Goat asked his father's permission to go in search of Leopard. Of course Spider did not volunteer to join him; he remained in the village, closer and closer to the inheritance he coveted. Spider's traps can be very clever indeed. Sure-footed Goat did not waste time however; rough terrain meant nothing to him. He searched and searched and when he grew hungry, he munched on leaves. Leopard could not eat leaves but that is another story. After many days Mr. Goat came to an open spot by a watering place and bethought himself to sip a drink and maybe dowse his ears, but he caught sight of something crouching in the grass. Two…silent…pools. Wide as Night. Steady as flame…Ready as flight. "Of all the…" Goat smiled to himself as he recognized his brother sporting with him as he had done so many times in their youth. And he ran forward to greet him. "Brother!" he cried. "It is I!" But before he could say another word, Leopard, driven by a hunger that blinded him to his own brother, sprang upon him **LIKE THIS!**

So it was that the best of brothers became permanent adversaries. Mr. Goat did not go in search of Mr. Leopard again. Nor did Mr. Leopard and his clan, nor Mr. Moonface and his, ever set foot in the human village again. Nor did any wild animal acknowledge his human ancestors and vice versa. They were not to share a fire, or laugh together, or speak the same language—ever again. Strife had come into the world.

With many days wandering behind him, the Castaway at last came to a spot he liked. He surveyed it remembering what his father taught him, and as soon as he made his decision to stay, he began building a shelter ignoring the necessary sacrifices the occasion required. The work went well, however, and he was pleased with his own efforts. Clearing a farm would be difficult without the help of his brothers, but then he would not need so large an area since he had but one mouth. So he passed his days and felt no pain, but he could no longer see his own face. He had not the mirror of his fellows.

Do you know how rain carves gullies in the earth? Have you seen how they grow deep and jagged? Even so, the Castaway's excessive contempt wore lines of anger into his face. His scowl became his permanent companion. When he laughed, it was a mean unhealthy laugh. When he thought of his village, he thought of how there would be accusations of witchcraft and how his brothers would deny it. A man alone must be up to no good. But let them think so. "Let them think I am a sorcerer. Every time evil befalls them, I will get the credit." And he laughed aloud.

Unknown to him however, a spirit was living in this very part of the forest. Spirit-in-the-Form-of-Jinni had the nose of a cow, the eyes of a fly, the wings of a bat, the body of a turtle but with much longer legs for running, the tail of a crocodile, and two big teeth—like this. They were so long they dragged on the ground as it walked; thus it left marks on the earth wherever it went. When it ran fast, its teeth would turn the earth like a hoe making a line as wide as a footpath, and when it stopped short, they would separate and appear to make a fork in the road. You must beware of these false roads when you are in the bush. Perhaps the Castaway had mistakenly taken one.

Of course the spirit knew of his presence, but it waited to find out what would become of him. Perhaps after several days, he would weary of this mad venture and return to his own kind, if he were not eaten first, and it would be rid of him without having to betray its presence, a rather burdensome undertaking for an aging Jinni. Yet, as the days gathered into seasons, the young village dweller showed no sign of weakening but continued his ways with dogged persistence. The spirit was truly puzzled. "How can this be?" it wondered.

The very next morning Spirit-in-the-Form-of-Nosey-Bird circled the village dweller's farm before alighting on the rooftop where it studied him for the rest of the day. It turned its head to one side and watched out of one eye, then out of the other. The newcomer seemed to know what he was about; there were signs of a permanent residence. He had already built a clever catch basin in the bank of a rivulet, but something was amiss. The bird rose and flew away.

At its house Spirit-in-the-Form-of-Jinni scratched its head with the point of its tail, like this, walking back and forth muttering to itself. "Village dwellers! Ptooh! Strange lot. Can't mind their own business. Nosey. Always meddling. And right in my own backyard! It's an insult! Me! A terrible Jinni! Ptooh!" Of course the newcomer did not hear this. To him it sounded like the chatter of birds in the treetops. It takes an unusually keen ear to hear the voices of spirits.

Something had to be done. Next day a crippled old woman painfully made her way to where the newcomer worked, picking her way along the path as she worked her gums from side to side. Of course it was Spirit-in-the-Form-of-Old-Woman. As the newcomer paid her no heed, she asked for water. He gave it her without comment. As she made to leave, she told him of a terrible

Jinni who lived not far away—not far indeed. Moreover this very part of the forest fell within its jurisprudence and strangers would be unwise to disturb the tranquility of its domicile. The newcomer laughed wickedly. No Jinni could match the evil of men. The old woman shuffled away on her walking stick. The spirit was truly puzzled. What a strange fellow.

Next day the old woman appeared again. This time she warned him in no uncertain terms of the Jinni's displeasure at being taken so lightly, and the possibility of unfortunate consequences if the situation were not rectified. The newcomer, sadly still within the clutches of his own self importance, only turned on her in wrath cursing her ugliness. The spirit drew back aghast. Bad enough to ignore its warning, but to insult its beauty—unspeakable!

Now greatly vexed, it went back to its house to prepare medicine for this latest abomination. It kept many such in a dirty bag and they were potent indeed. For this rude fellow however, there would be a special touch. The usual fare of rat eye and lizard's bile would not do. Oh no! Change him into a snake? Kid's stuff. The occasion called for…well…imagination. A human snare, ah yes, a headstrong snare, the unsuspecting victim would be the agent of his own undoing by applying the medicine to his own wound. Perhaps the awakening of remorse in a heart of stone, the flowering of human refinement in a pair of bestial buttocks. The spirit jumped with delight! And with devilish speed, Spirit-in-the-Form-of-Soaring-Bird flew up to the sky and removed a bead of sweat from Heaven's ear, just one, then sailed home carrying it in its beak. This was special medicine, headstrong medicine, and with great care Spirit-in-the-Form-of-Spider placed it delicately within the strands of a beautiful web that glistened in the sunlight and fit the contours of the leaves like a heavenly glove. What symmetry. There, on the very spot young Headstrong was sure to pass. And so he did.

As he came walking along, it smacked him in the face. His flaying hands fought the silken ropes, he cursed his brother the Spider, but as he did, the bead of sweat, Heaven's own, broke on his fingers. The strands of beautiful web clanged like iron in the blacksmith shop but to hear it you had to be a spider or a gnat. The sanctity of his person was broken. It had happened. He was no more a man.

After some days he went to his catch basin for water. He paused a minute to spy himself in the mirror. Savage eyes glared out in terror! Hair grew out his face! A cloud of insects orbited his head. A wild thing! Its lips uttered fantastic noises when it tried to speak. Eerrruoo, eerrruoo. He ran away. When he overcame his fear, he went back and looked again. Eerrruoo,

eerrruoo. He bent down. A stranger looked back at him in wonder as if he, the thing in the water, were curious about the strange creature on the other side! He bent down closer, then he saw something else. A bead of sweat had formed on the inner corner of his eye. As he watched, it grew and fell into the water. The mirror wavered. What a strange feeling came over him. He looked around. Everything seemed strange. Where were his brothers? His father? The tender Sapling? How he missed them. Oh to sport in the sun again, to cuddle together at night. Oh for the human village where kindred spirits draw nourishment from each other refilling the source as they drink. Yes, a well-nourished spirit makes a man a man. Now he understood.

He neglected his farm. He spent his days wandering about or carving trinkets. He ate moss and wild roots and spoke aloud of his misfortune. Eerrruoo, eerrruoo. Then one day he saw a stray goat quietly chewing the tender young rice stalks that remained. "You! Mr. Goat! Yes, eat the young rice. That's right, pull it up by the roots! Have some of my cassava too! Do you not remember me? I am your brother. Do you not remember how we sported and played in the sunshine? How you rose on your hind feet and butted me, how I feigned a somersault? Come, let us play again!" But when the goat saw him, he turned and ambled lazily away with a tuft of rice stalks in his mouth. "Do not run away!" he called after him. "It is I! Your Brother!" But the goat was gone. "You who liked me best! Do you not greet your brother? Do you not remember how I found you the sweetest palm nuts?"

At last he understood what it means to be alone—to no longer speak the same language as your brother. Then one day as he sat in his tumbled down shelter he saw a solitary spider carefully picking its way up a single strand of web. After all these seasons. Surely the rancor that separated them would now be forgotten. "You! Mr. Spider! It is I! Your Brother. Yes, climb into my attic and take my stores. Carry all you can! And weave your web in every corner. Here! Carry away my trinkets too! They will fetch a fine bargain on market day!"

But when the spider saw him, he hurried up his rope and hid himself in the thatch. And again a bead of sweat appeared at the inner corner of his eye. Do you know how drops of water cling to a thread and glisten in the morning sun? These are Spider's riches and if you disturb them Spider will come and bite you. Things of wonder are not to be disturbed. Well, when the Forest Fellow—for he was no longer a village dweller, nor a castaway, nor headstrong—touched them, they melted on his fingers, and a strange feeling came over him. How came he to be alone?

Again the seasons passed; what seemed like days were really years and he wasted them prodigally singing aloud and conversing with imaginary persons. But unbeknown to him...someone was watching. There at the edge of the farm...crouched low in the grass. Two...Silent...Pools. Quiet as Flame. Wide as Night. Wet as rain. Ready to bite. Can you guess—

Yes. Mr. Leopard calmly surveyed the situation in elegant silence. But something was amiss. This Forest Fellow did not behave like common prey; he was supposed to run from his enemies, instead he greeted them in the hardiest terms inquiring after their friends and loved ones. Leopard crouched ever lower, like this; he made himself as a patch of sunlight dappled with the shade of undulant leaves. He studied intently, carefully assessing the delicate nuances of the problem. He tested the air. Not a trace of fear. A strange case indeed. As his hunger was not at this time overwhelming, Leopard waited...the way that leopard's wait. The end of his tail twitched once but he had no say in the matter. A cat's tail obeys a law of its own.

Then one day Moonface—for the Forest Fellow now remembered his name—saw the patch of dappled sunlight and recognized it for what it was. And he remembered his boyhood too, their favorite game, how his eldest brother loved to crouch low in the grass and then bound upon him and roll and tumble until they came to rest against their mother's side.

"Mr. Leopard! It is I! Your Brother! Can you not see?"

But Leopard saw...what leopards see.

"You who have the great unflinching eyes that gaze into the night and never sleep? Do you not remember how we ran and sported in our youth?"

But Leopard remembered...what leopards remember.

"Come, let us share a gourd of palm wine. We will have a merry conversation."

But Leopard did not speak. As the unabashed fellow came forward, Leopard smelled...what leopards smell. And as he came closer chattering all the time, Leopard heard...what leopards hear. He dug his claws into the earth, back and forth, like this, the way that leopards do when such a good chance oh such a good a chance comes along. Still the fellow came closer and closer. He wanted to play, but it wasn't time to play. It's never time to play when hunger comes to stay. And as the fellow smiled and jumped for joy...Leopard thought...what leopards think. The two great eyes locked on their target. What's this? Moonface froze! Something was amiss! He caught the scent of something—! A voice shot through his blood! "Run my darling run!"

"I am your Broth—!" Too late!

Leopard did......what leopards do...

They jump on you and eat you!

On finding his favorite tree in the heart of the darkening forest, Leopard ascended into its branches with one swift bound, his fresh prize dangling beneath his powerful jaws. He found his favorite limb, stretched out in leisurely fashion, yawned, and lifted his handsome face to the current of the evening air. After a bite of dinner, his gaze returned to the earth below and his favorite musings returned like old friends—the memory of his childhood lair, his mother's loving muzzle, fields of jumping game spread out like a dream in dazzling sunshine. After indulging in these familiar desserts, he licked his coat, sniffed his succulent prize, and lifted his lordly voice in regal triumph. How the forest went silent at his tone. He often wondered why. All existence, like schools of silvery fish in a sheltered pool, swam in response to his bidding. He considered the possibilities but they were endless. Then, on a sudden whim, for he was reticent to speak on matters such as these, he remarked aloud, to his brothers the Forest and the Purling Stream, upon the beauty of the Whispering Night.

CHAPTER 22

THE SUMMER OF '68

"Sally."

Cold.

"Sally? You there?"

So cold.

"Hey Butch!"

Two bolts on the door now.

"It's freezin' out here man."

She wasn't the same anymore, the bright eagerness gone, her good will more guarded, her smile muted. She cleaned her apartment now, went to class, didn't push; she still believed in the cause, our cause, but it wasn't the same. I liked her better before.

Things had gone sour after Chicago. The euphoria of spring had dissipated in the reality of summer when it became apparent the system would win. Welcome to the big leagues, they seemed to say; if we can't win, we cheat. Although she'd been warned not to go, she went to the convention anyway and came back with eight stitches above her right eye, the eye itself swollen shut, half her face black and blue, a stiff jaw and two cracked ribs where she'd been shoved to the pavement—deliberately. To the last second she didn't think they'd do it. But she wasn't bitter, smiled bravely, more mature, more committed than ever, her quiet resolve more secure although there were some changes, like the two bolts on the door.

"Compliments of the mayor," she had explained.

"Oh my God."

"It's all right. Come in."

She sat on the sofa drawing her legs up. Cammy jumped in her lap. "I'm all right," she said intently reaching for my hand. "Talk to me."

"I...I..."

"Oh you're such a baby. I'm sorry, that wasn't a good thing to say. Sit down. I'm going to be fine, as soon as the swelling goes down. No missing teeth, no brain damage, Peter Piper picked a peck o' pickled peppers. See. Everything still works. Talk to me." She was made of tougher stuff than I thought.

"I don't know what to say. I'm ashamed."

"Of what?"

"Some of the things I said."

"What things?"

"About you and your—"

"Our! Correct grammar please. Our what?"

"I can't—"

"Yes, you can. Say what you were going to say only begin, 'We.'"

"We're...revolutionaries who can't wipe our noses."

"You're right. We are. I need somebody to talk to, I'm not ashamed of that anymore. You know the damnedest thing? At the first aid station—"

"They had a first aid station?"

"Yeah. Just like a war."

"Jesus."

"Remember that tune you used to sing every time we got lost? For some insane reason it kept running through my head—blood running down my face, people screaming. Sing it for me?"

"What?"

"Something about Chicago. Please."

"...I can't...okay.

>*"Goin' to Chica go*
>*Goin' to Chicago*
>*Sorry...can't take you*
>*Nothin' in Chicago..."*

"Hey. I'm supposed to be crying...not you."

"All right. I'm not John Wayne. Something's wrong, something's very wrong in this country and if they're going to start beating up women in the street, the tough guys aren't as tough as they think! They're chickenshit! Sick despicable...cowards!"

"Sit back down. Look at me. I'm not going to turn into a bomb throwing radical! You were right, that's just what they want."

"What they..."

"If it turns into a violent confrontation, violence wins. You really called that one."

"I did? So have ten thousand other people only…"

"What did you say?"

"This country's…"

"Speak up. You're mumbling again."

"Not in danger. We're runnin' scared. Where's the threat? The third world? That's ridiculous. Our own kids? A bunch of rock 'n' rollers? Something's wrong. So we manufacture a fifth column, we construct—"

"Psst, *they.*"

"Yes, they construct this elaborate FARCE to find a communist bogeyman under every bed! We no longer believe in our better angels. We're blowing it, everything our fathers worked for."

"You know the most sickening thing about it?" she said after a long pause. "They enjoyed it."

"What?"

"The pigs, they really…enjoyed it."

"So did a lot of people watching on TV."

"You saw it then?"

"The whole damn country saw."

"Stop pacing, you're making me nervous."

"Enjoyed it. They're sick! Pathetic men! That whole damn macho mentality. Violence…violence is the love life of a coward. They have go to great lengths to prove their manhood…you know why? Because deep down they're scared and theirs is the worst kind of fear—the fear of facing any kind of weakness, and of course they see any kind of tenderness, empathy, as weakness. They secretly perceive themselves as failures. They're to be pitied—"

"Pitied? You wouldn't be so conciliatory if you had a lump on your head?"

"I'd be blind with rage. I'd wanna kill 'em. And I'm afraid I wouldn't have a friend to stop me."

"Then stop being such a loner. I'm glad I have a friend to talk to. I'm so afraid things are going to get ugly. They really know how to hurt, you know, where to hit, they must give it a lot of thought. They didn't even hesitate, wham! As though they had a green light. Somebody, the mayor must have—"

"Higher."

"What?"

"I don't think the mayor would have acted on his own against his own party, the green light came from higher up."

"Where?"

"I don't know."

"Jesus that's scary. What's happening to this country! We're becoming a police state!"

"I wouldn't have believed it. Even last year—"

"I wouldn't have believed it either," she said staring at the candle flame. "I learned a lot in Chicago. About the world, myself. I can take a billy club in the tits as well as the next man...woman. Remember when I told you I wanted to go to New York and live in the village? Well, I learned more in one night than I could have in ten years in New York. For the first time I understood why I'm protesting the war, and when that two-hundred pound bully let me have it, I was one of the oppressed of the world, their cause became mine, right there in Chicago, but at the same time I was in Prague and Siagon and Selma and a thousand other places. Suddenly it crystalized; I knew what Piacasso felt, what Malevitch endured, why they painted, what drove them, their agony, their rage, but ultimately their victory. Now I think I know what it's all about, art is the permanent war against war, the human scream against everything inhumane. But first it must accept the reality of evil. I never understood that; I was a complete fraud groping for a workable illusion to hide my own insecurity. The first thing I did when I felt better was to trash all the crap in this place. I may never be a great painter, but I can fight oppression in my own way and that's good enough for me...I'm sorry I was so pushy."

"You were never pushy—"

"Not that—will you please sit down. What is it out the window? I'm over here! I tried to force you into a mentality that doesn't fit you...I was wrong."

"Maybe you saw something I didn't."

"Or maybe I only thought I did. Stay with me tonight."

That was last summer, during the crash course in democracy before we rolled up the posters and tossed our buttons in our trunks. We gave our place in the Student Union to the Humphrey kids, nice kids with clean haircuts but another generation entirely. McCarthy had been the perfect symbol of our aspirations. The prince of lost causes. And we?...we'd hardly amount to a footnote.

Now it was winter. And cold. So cold. But what a year. The modest beginnings in New Hampshire, the taste of victory, the coming of spring, our cause rampant, then two assassinations, King and Kennedy, like shots in the dark and another dizzy summer of war and riot, protest and counter-protest and Russian tanks rolling over a Czech playground. Then autumn and further sorrow. Isolation. Defeat. The call of an alien wind and a solitary voice in the school paper lamenting the tragedy of Richard Nixon as something to haunt our generation the rest of our lives.

But then, in December, with the winter snows snugly in place and Christmas decorations twinkling on the light poles, the flight of Apollo 8, almost lost in the tumult of the times. They actually encircled the moon, two-thirds a century from Kitty Hawk. What an incredible achievement! I never gave much thought to what the earth must look like from out there; I suppose I'd thought of it as a schoolroom globe, but the photographs, they struck me at once, the entire earth encompassed in single shot. What stunning serenity, solitude. Wilderness in repose. A lustrous jewel in the deep of Night. The sheen of the atmosphere like silk over glistening snow. And the cloud formations! Veils of bridal white over blue oceans, imperceptible motion over the rumbling of the sea; and if you looked hard you could imagine the equally imperceptible march of history (the ant-like doings of men) like the silent twirling of a broken record, all our wars and passions muffled into perfect silence. The ancients were right. She is a woman, the earth. A virgin lost in a starry abyss lavishing her youth on a black expanse with neither a mirror nor a suitor. But now! A human eye to open on a lover. And the quiet glow of motherhood to smile back.

"How now my wayward? Cold and aimless on a starless night? Night beckons. Her voices whisper, her virgin moon so soon to be kissed walks atop the winter woods, alone, down casting dappled leopard spots on polished Grecian snow. Dare to look beyond the woods, beyond the world's fast changing moods. Dare to go alone. Love your lover's freedom beyond your own. Sorrow is but next year's passion rising in the blood. The window opens once. Be brave my wayward."

"Butch it's freezin' out here!"

"Who is it?" she said faintly behind the door.

"It's me." Two bolts snapped, the door cracked with a sliver of light, a pause, then a chain unlatched.

"What on earth—it's two o'clock in the morning. Are you all right? You look terrible."

A gust of chilly wind caught wisps of loose hair around her face. Her eyes were puffy with sleep, but the scar had healed leaving only a slight trace on her cheek bone. She yawned slowly, found a knitted shawl on the rocker and threw it around her shoulders, walked tiredly to the kitchen and put on tea water. Then she dropped on the floor in front of the sofa, yoga style, fumbling with a book of matches. The candle lit, she switched off the light and sat staring at the flame for a long time. Cammy came out from behind the trunk, climbed in her lap purring.

"You're gonna do it aren't you?"

A record was still revolving on the turntable. I reached over and shut it off.

"When are you leaving?"

"Tonight. Supposedly."

"Supposedly? Jesus. They don't talk like that where you're goin', honey. 'I cuttin' out, man, I don't dig this shit, man.' What about your class?"

"They won't even notice I'm gone."

"Some of us WILL!"

"Don't worry, the assembly line will crank out another mild-mannered—"

She reached over and stopped me, "Maybe the new model won't be as brutally serious...if you could only learn to smile." Suddenly her face broke into wide-eyed delight, "But this is insane! Where will you go? What will you do? First thing, get rid of that revolting straight jacket. Pitch it! Stomp on it! You'll hardly need it where you're going. Let's see, where will that be? Hmmm. The French Foreign Legion! A desert outpost! The call of the bugles, the gleam of the sabers, the memory of an unrequited love in a tiny locket over your heart...too Romantic. A guerrilla commando! Elusive as the wind, bronze chest crisscrossed with bullets...too quaint. A tropical island! Bare-breasted slave girls. You're lord and master but mercilessly strict, make them read their Dostoevsky, but if they haven't...can paradise be flawed? You...you..." Suddenly her excitement vanished. She stared blankly at the candle. "You're really going then?"

"I—"

"Shut up. I'm still trying to imagine...it's not easy at two in the morning. You! A dropout. That's gonna draw some comment in the faculty lounge. Forrester's pet. Well, the GREs can't tell you everything. Did he really tell you to get a haircut?"

"It's not that."

"Well, did he?"

"He intimated I should. Telling me would entail taking a stand; you never do that. I intimated he's a jerk and that's how the game goes I can't stand it anymore, the pettiness, lies, ass kissing, the whole damn—hypocrisy, infighting, these are supposed to be educated people. Wallace was right, they can't park their bicycles."

The tea kettle went off.

"How 'bout a cup o' tea," she said slapping her knees. "Must be hard work fighting windmills." She went around the corner to the stove. "Come on, out with it."

"What t' hell does it matter."

"It does matter damn it! You think you can barge in here in the middle of the night and...and?"

"...I'm scared."

"Of what?"

"I don't know. If it were a burglar or a bear, there'd be a focus; it's a thing without a face, a sense of having missed the main event. I didn't want it to turn out this way."

"How about a cookie with your tea," she smiled settling back down and drawing her shawl around her shoulders. "Sorry about the nightgown...it's warm."

We rapped for hours. One reminiscence led to another. When the candle began flickering, she cracked it loose and held it to her face before blowing it out and for one awful instant she betrayed a feeling so alone, so far away it could have been another century; but as soon as she lit another it revealed someone I hadn't seen before, a little girl with downcast eyelids ready to cry.

"Have you been painting?"

She smiled wistfully then drooped her eyes again. "I've been cleaning my brushes, mixing my pigments, applying color to flat surfaces—no, I haven't been painting."

"Don't give it up. Go to New York. Live in a garret. Paint the unthinkable."

She clinched her fists then tapped her forehead with the heels of her hands, "Will you listen to yourself? Have you taken up counseling? A fine occupation for a goddamn dropout! Oh you're a gem. If I wanted to paint you, I'd paint a lone lighthouse at the end of the world and its keeper sleepwalking on a promontory. Why are you doing this to yourself?"

"I don't know."

"Have you been having any more bad dreams lately?"

"Eh."

She smiled. "You're the only person I know who can go tripping without popping a pill."

"Well, don't tell the cops; they'll be twice as outraged."

"Tell me about the last one."

"I can't remember."

"Yes you can, damn it!"

"It's always the same. Someplace deserted. I'm in a car, Skip's 57 Chev— my high school buddy, I did his homework, he drove on dates—or an airplane. I go up front, there's no pilot but the radio's on. The signal's faint, or in a foreign language. I've been warned not to touch it but I do anyway because it'll tell me what to do, the key to the equation, then it starts smoking or bleeding or else it flops in my lap with sparks and bare wires all over the place. I know I've got to get it back together only I don't know how and there's not enough time."

"Can't you see it? You wanted to be an explorer, right? No pilot, no radio. You need to get your bearings, find some direction in your life. Look at the compass for Chrissakes…my God what am I saying, I'm nagging again. I might as well be trying to tie you down to a house and kids. You really need to get away."

"You need to get away, too."

"You'll be glad to know, sir, I've already made plans to share an apartment this summer with an old friend not too far from the village. He says starving artists never turn out their own, so I'll find out if I'm for real; I need to know what others think about my work. If I do some good work I plan to stay."

"You'll do fine. And don't worry about being a small-town girl; New York's full of small-town people hiding behind sunglasses."

"What about you?" she said staring into her tea cup. "Where will you go?"

"I don't know. I just want to find a spot where I can plop down and listen to the surf and not think about the time it's costing me."

We both stared into space. The candle burnt steady.

"You know what I really want? I wanna build a cabin with my own hands. And when it's done I'm gonna sit on the step, watch the sunset and sleep like a baby—no nightmares."

"Where you gonna build your shack?"

"I don't know. Someplace warm. My sophomore year I had a chance to go to Ft. Lauderdale—that was the place to go back then—only I stayed home and studied. I've always regretted it."

"A shack on the beach in Ft. Lauderdale. That's a gem." She looked at the ceiling in disbelief.

"I know you can't build a shack there for Chrissakes! I didn't mean—I meant I've got to start somewhere. Maybe I'll make it to Tenerife, back to Africa, I don't know. I've always wanted to see a French cathedral, something built by people who really believed. I want to visit a Greek island, the pyramids, Tibet. I have no idea what I'll do when I get there, I only know if I don't go now—"

"Escape! Pure bloody escapism! Can't you see what your dreams are trying to tell you? Dead pilot. Canceled flight. You can't excape from yourself!"

"You're right. But there's only one thing worse—not to go, never having dared, that's what real death is, to wake up one morning and find out you've grown old and missed your only chance. Do you have any idea how many good people in a moment of weakness will admit they wasted their youth? I don't want to be one of them."

She got up. Morning was breaking. "Sooner or later you've got to choose, doncha know?"

"Where's it written I've got to play by the rules?"

"You must," she said with a fierce squeeze of my hand.

"Must I?"

"You must."

At the door she handed me my jacket with a warm smile, not a trace of misgiving.

"I thought you said I should get rid of it."

"You'll need it awhile," she said following me out. "Brrrr, it's cold. When you get to your desert island, you can burn it. Have you got your leopard's tooth?"

"Yes."

"Give me a hug." She wrapped both arms around me in a long embrace brushing my hair in place at the end. "Take care of yourself."

I walked down the steps into the driveway. She stood on the landing with her arms folded over her nightgown shivering lightly but with a warm smile.

"You look like a lighthouse keeper's daughter."

"You look like a lighthouse without an ocean."

"I love you."

"I love you too," she said following a few steps along the landing. "If you ever slay your dragon…come back."

CHAPTER 23

SHOULD HE DIE IN
A FOUL-SMELLING PLACE

Our village sprang to life like church doves at the crack of a rifle. Startled shouts ripped the late afternoon air, dwarfed replies echoed farther off. The blacksmith beat a piercing danger cry on his anvil. I ran out on the porch. People emerged from doorways like dazed phantoms, their fearful faces looking to each other then to the slash in the forest where two silhouettes, now a third, darted into the darkening shadows. Their play ended, children looked around with adult faces. A robust man stepped from his doorway with a dipper gourd still in his hand and food in his mouth; he stopped chewing with a quizzical look towards the edge of town where old Fawkpa hurried down the embankment shouting directions. Then a wild, inhuman scream. A woman ran from a door and threw herself against the wall of the neighboring house with force enough to knock mud loose. It ended with a groan as her fingers tore at her hair. "Zawloe," intoned a grizzled old crone, coming up the path. "Dey coddy heem i' tow' now oh."

Zawloe. I hardly knew him, yet he always greeted me briskly. Now and then he came to Quolidobu's store where he heard the evening news but retained his distance. Men like that built their farms deep in the forest where they could disappear for days on end although it meant a long walk back, the price of freedom from the meddling traffic of the motor road.

Today they were on their way home—five of them, himself, Woiyea, Kpadeh, his brother, and two school boys, David Beyan and John Sumo, his son. They moved with ease, single file, in tired silence. Their cutlasses hung at their sides and their headloads bore produce and two wild hens for market day. Zawloe led. Inside the forest dusk had already fallen. He must have taken his eyes off the path to wipe a bead of sweat, perhaps to take in the beauty of the falling twilight. He stepped squarely on its back—a soft, wet stick that came to life under his bare foot, rolled with his step, coiled, then an open throat, two darts, and a kiss of lightning straight into the instep. One fang broke off in his foot an inch deep. Knowing it must not break off again, they removed it with the tip of a hunting knife while Kpadeh sat on his brother's leg to hold it firm.

"Was it a cobra?" I asked the men in the motor road. They didn't know. A young Mandingo said it was a mamba but others warned him not to make up stories. How quickly darkness came. A few lanterns began to gleam in open doorways; now and then a human form stepped forward to whisper a quick question. One syllable came in reply. The eye of the village fixed itself to the footpath where it dipped out of the forest to join the motor road. The screaming woman had been subdued by her neighbors and the gentle words of the headwoman, the elder Yasah who now came forward to join the men on the bank; a small child clung to her lappa with one hand, a broken chip of coconut in the other as tears streaked down its face. And away from the others, like a shadow under the eaves, Kpoodu the storyteller stood in calm detachment although his eyes too followed to the spot from where they would come.

Of course many snakes weren't poisonous, but the fright that shot so savagely through the village told us this one was. After bringing the news, Sumo had gone back with three others. They had a long way to carry him.

Now a voice. Male. From the far edge of town. A song. Low, subdued, without words, a steady expiration of controlled moaning as though the Forest herself were crying aloud, "Forgive me my children, all that transpires is not of my design."

I turned back to my house. Down in the ditch two figures seemed to be gently pawing at each other. The slow witted Dwoiyou stood with his feet together in the mud where the men urinated, his hands over his face, crying like a three year old while John Mulba tried to take one of his arms and lead him away. He kept drawing it back.

"What's the matter?"

"He's made water on himself," John said. "Help me take him away from here. They will not see him."

"Let him keep his face covered." We got him to my study bawling all the way. "Light the lamp, I'll see if I can find something dry. After we got him changed, he stood in the doorway whimpering, digging in the dirt with his big toe. He had no father. Zawloe, a distant uncle, had taken him in and even bought him a school bag so he could be like the other boys. Now he sensed a monstrous danger.

"Do you have medicine?" John asked.

"No. I told you before."

"Impossible," had been the doctor's curt reply when I asked for antivenom. "Too dangerous, you're up there alone which means you'd have to inject yourself and that could be a tricky business since we can assume you'd be...a little on edge. All you have to do is hit a vein. Frankly I'm more concerned about—" and I got the usual lecture on household hygiene, a smile and, "Don't get bit." I thought of buying some on the black market but that would have been risky; you never knew what you were getting.

"I wish we knew what kind of snake," I said taking down a book.

"I don't think it was a cobra," John said. "One fang stayed in his foot. A cobra would not have done that; his fangs are smaller. They come out after a bite. I think it was a cassava snake because it has three fangs. When they struck it off, the top two came out but the bottom would have broken."

"How do you know."

"Sumo's grandmother. She was in the house when he came with the news."

"A cassava snake?"

"He is fat and very slow. The only way he can bite is if you step on him, but when he does..."

Tropical African Snakes, a book I'd read with some care. "Gabon Viper, *Bitis Gabonica,* poisonous. Bite can be fatal if not counteracted with antivenom. Length, two to three feet, coloring, tan to brown. Glands, duel, separate, upper hemotoxic, lower neurotoxic." Oh God. A picture too. "Is this it?"

"Yes."

It was horrid looking, a flat triangular head, turned up nostrils, protruding horned eyes over a wide snout suggesting a prehistoric monster. A row of serrated scales stood erect along the spine, but blended with light gray and brown splotches. Good camouflage.

"We've got to get him to the hospital." We should have been out on the road right now. What was the matter with me? "Let's go, we've got—"

"Dwoiyou!"

"Oh no. Where is he?"

"DWOIYOU!"

"Look out back."

"Here he is."

He was standing behind the rain barrel whimpering.

"Get somebody to watch him. We've got to watch the road. If a car comes, flag it down. Tell the others."

The embankment in front of Quolidobu's store gave the best vantage point. If a car did come, getting them to take him to Zorzor, away from his family, at night, entrusted to the care of strangers…it was going to be touchy.

Night had come. An uneasiness piqued the quiet air. The entire village felt tense, like prey at the point of flight. But also a sense of submission. We waited.

Then it came. A crash of leaves. Two figures in the road. Shouts. Faces. Taanu, Kwokwoiyea, David Beyan. A swarm of people engulfed them. Yes, he coming, only a short distance. The bite was bad, real bad, as John Mulba thought, a cassava snake.

Then noise. Confusion. A final surge of effort, as though the Forest fought to keep her own, and they burst sideways into the middle of the motor road carrying him in a quick-paced running walk amid a flurry of cries, shouts, orders to give way, then further confusion as commands got tangled and a mob mentality took over. They forced their way through, stumbling forward under the light of several torches, fear and determination etched in their faces, sweat streaming down their bodies; Kokulo led, carrying him by the ankles, one on each hip, then Sumo and Bwomah, one on each side supporting him with makeshift ropes running underneath, and Woiyea last holding him under the arms while Kpadeh ran awkwardly along side, trying to support the back of his head as it rolled from side to side. Now they had more room and with help they raised him to shoulder level and bore him along as on an invisible bier. Across the road the procession mounted the bank like a caterpillar. They wound their way between the houses, scattering chickens and bystanders, alike. Frightened children cried. Curious dogs sniffed the air.

Now his wives burst from their house like Furies. The youngest who'd thrown herself against the wall, and by now in near hysteria, raced straight at them with the same inhuman wail, this time with open hands as if she'd tear the misfortune from his very heart. Old Fawkpa caught her mid-stride lifting her in the air as she kicked and flayed, carried her to a neighbor's porch where several others tried to calm her down. His senior wife too, a heavy middle-aged woman, took one look, then grabbing two fist-fulls of hair, turned her back and began an inhuman moan, rising into a roar, straight into the trees. And an elder aunt, a toothless old crone who had cared for him as a child wandered aimlessly between the houses emitting a low rasping from her sickened lungs while she beat the side of her hip with a toy rattle she must have taken from one of the children. The chief who'd already ordered them to stay put, wheeled around with a sharp monosyllable. Two women ran up to them speaking softly.

They brought him around back to Kpadeh's house and carefully lowered him through the door, again in a barrage of shouts and directions. Inside they lay him on a mat on the ground next to the fire. The swarm of faces closed in but the chief came between asking them to yield, though not as harshly this time. After advising that he did not expect to be disturbed, he lowered his head and went in. The older men moved away talking among themselves in lowered tones; some gathered in the open blacksmith kitchen a few steps away where an unfinished cutlass lay in the deadened coals. No one went far. John Mulba and I waited a little while then asked permission to enter.

Inside, dark as a cave. No windows. Three lanterns and a central fire splashed unsteady light on the walls reflecting the entire night's misery in grotesque shadows that spoke in pantomime. Half-hidden faces peered out of dark corners, disembodied whispers hovered in the air. On the floor they were preparing to suck the bite. Kokulo did it back on the trail, but now he stood out of breath looking a little ill. Soon he turned to leave and we could hear him retching outside against the wall. Old Fawkpa appeared in the doorway, made his way to the fire where he stood sullen and hunched over with a fistful of fresh leaves. He gave them to Kpadeh who stuffed three or four in his mouth and began chewing briskly while he watched Bwomah bathe the instep with hot water. The bitter juice of these leaves caused a slight numbing inside the mouth, probably a mild antiseptic. He spat the pulp into the fire and knelt at his brother's side. The bite was clearly visible even in bad light. Two round punctures, like drops of red ink, high on the instep meant a perpendicular angle and deep penetration while the third, on the side of the foot and well below, measured the size of its mouth, four inches; this one bled where they'd cut it to remove the fang. It had already begun to swell. Kpadeh turned the foot to him, furled his lips around the bite, and pulled with all his strength. The muscles on his neck drew taut. Then he spat hard into the pan without swallowing; small droplets of blood dispersed into thin red clouds as they touched the water. He chewed another leaf and returned to the bite.

Zawloe wasn't fully conscious, but he wasn't unconscious either. He didn't seem to be in severe pain, but his head rolled back and forth on the mat and once or twice he gasped a broken phrase. The whites of his eyes were more exposed than usual and when they spoke to him it didn't seem to register. He seemed a little feverish, beads of sweat formed on his face but no more than the rest of us. Humid, probably rain again. I'd never seen a snake bite. I couldn't tell how serious. Perhaps the venom was killing him right now; perhaps he was in shock. They were tough. Many had survived snake bites. The only sounds were Kpadeh's sucking and Zawloe's occasional groans. I began to feel helpless. Their faces went silent. The chief sat forward of the others on the only stool; he watched with concern. On the wall our shadows stood dumb. I remembered I had some oral antiseptic in my medicine cabinet but it probably wasn't much stronger than the leaves.

We had to get him to Zorzor. It would be a long trip. Bouncing over that road wouldn't do him much good. Would it aggravate the condition? I didn't know. Of course he was strong; they were always stronger than they looked. Perhaps he'd pull through by morning…that was dreaming. The damn thing broke off an inch deep. And his head rolling from side to side out of control. We had to get him to Zorzor.

Convincing them to do it—that was going to be the trick. Many of them distrusted *qwi* medicine not for its internal merits but for the high-handed way we usually administer it sneering at theirs in the process. Their medicine was intimately tied to their spiritual lives and an indulgence in anything that mocked it meant disrespect, a loss of inner strength that often brought on further maladies. Our medicine cured the flesh but left the spirit to heal itself; theirs proceeded the other way.

A trip to the hospital meant raising a fist in God's face. But better insult their beliefs than eulogize a dead man. What if he died on the road? Or in the hospital if the antivenom weren't in time? The cause would be obvious—a white man's irreverent meddling.

It was going to be touchy. Most of them would be against the idea. To carry a man thirty-five miles in the middle of the night, bouncing around in the back of a truck, just to stick a needle in him—only a white man would be dumb enough—but there were always surprises. Once I saw a man order a sick wife to the hospital saying he wanted no part of that nonsense, tribal medicine.

Asking the chief wouldn't do. We were distant. I didn't want to give the impression of trying to influence village affairs, nor he of being too familiar with an outsider; hence our meetings were strictly formal, usually confined to the business of school upkeep. Although I would not have been there without his permission, I got the impression he would as soon not be bothered by either a white man or a school. Yet both his sons and one daughter attended, the eldest studied diligently occasionally asking my views on some rather delicate matters.

But in the end, I was a mere boy in their eyes and we all knew it, untested in the rigors of manhood, no more worthy of counsel than a woman. If I pushed for taking him to Zorzor, they, and especially the chief, would be in the awkward position of taking instructions from an outsider.

Of course there were the younger men of the village with whom I was on more equal ground. And the older school boys: Kwokwoiyea, Moses, David Beyan. John Mulba, too, only his close friendship with me weakened his position with them. And Taanu! The newly married Mandingo. Over a year ago now, I'd been startled out of my sleep in the middle of the night by his frightened whispers as my back door. When I let him in he stood shaking with downcast eyes for ten minutes before he was able to speak. He wanted medicine for Gono. I was surprised he knew the word, but then he described the symptoms. When I asked if he'd been to Monrovia his subdued shame said *yes*, and only after I promised the strictest secrecy did he finally admit he'd bought a girl for fifty cents. Next day on the pretext of doing an errand, I sent him to the Mission with a sealed letter to the doctor. The treatment had been a success. I knew I had only to drop a hint and he'd do anything I asked. Pure blackmail. A card I didn't want to play.

But what about Old Fawkpa? He's seen a little bit of the world, hypodermic needles included, and when the U.N. smallpox team came through, he'd gone from door to door telling people to bring their children! And he was the chief's brother. Good Old Fawkpa. Yes.

But he'd gone out for some reason. Maybe to get more leaves. I got up and went out too. Nobody noticed. John Tellywoiyea's huge frame blocked the light in the blacksmith kitchen. His jovial face gone, he looked blank, his eyes probing but devoid of pity or grief. He hadn't seen Fawkpa. I started back to my house to get my army blanket. Night had become a sea of fear. Something seemed to say, "All your books and you don't know the answer?" The lamp mantle in my study had burnt black; I had to fumble in the dark for another after cracking my knee on the edge of the desk. I found the blanket. Soon John Mulba was walking alongside. He seemed to sense what I was up to.

Kpadeh's door was closed tight. Kwokwoiyea came up to warn me away. We could hear a low chant within. It seemed unattached to human lips, an emission from an unearthly source. Then silence. I found Fawkpa at the forge.

"We must take the man to Zorzor."

"Ey my frie'. Da be no ca' di ni', he ca' rainy now."

"But if one comes. We must take him. The injections." He stared into the ground. I wasn't sure what he was thinking. "What do you think?"

"We ca' try," an idiom that meant, 'We'll see, but don't bet on it.'

"Will you tell the men inside?"

He nodded assent and turned to go hunching his heavy shoulders together as he bent to enter. Old Dawseh sat on his haunches next to the fire. The senior practitioner of tribal medicine, he looked no different from the others, maybe a bit chauvinistic about things Loma, otherwise unthreatening although the younger upstarts knew when to keep their distance. He was close to the chief and confidant to the blacksmith. That meant power. They probably all belonged to the *Poro,* but that wasn't discussed. Nor his practice; when asked about it, his face became a study of evasion. It was said he once brought a dead man back to life, but many people in town doubted it. Like other men his age, he bore the scars of a hard life, but unlike our stereotype of a savage medicine man, he now sat humble in the face of death. I wish I could have got to know him better but he kept distant. He looked up without malice when I stepped around him.

Zawloe still lay on the mat, but with a fresh smear of white mud on his forehead where the medicine had been applied. He was quieter now. I wasn't sure if that was good or bad. Kpadeh knelt behind him holding his head in his lap, now and then wiping his mouth with a cloth. He looked up an instant but his eyes immediately fell back to his brother. But in that brief flash he'd asked for help. We lifted Zawloe, drawing the blanket underneath. He seemed to be losing consciousness. The fever seemed higher. I felt his pulse, then put Kpadeh's fingers on it. "His heart is strong." Several men grunted approval. Kpadeh at once went back to holding his brother's head in his lap as he knelt behind him gently rocking back and forth, the movement so slight it could only be seen in the shadows on the wall where it appeared like a continuous bowing before an immense indifference. Then it started to rain. The first drops crackled like fire on the dry thatch.

In his own good time, Fawkpa finally put the idea before them. The ploy of using him didn't work. They all knew whose idea it was. Now I looked even weaker for not having spoken myself. His words met the usual murmur of grunts, their way of accepting something for consideration, then a long silence as each thought it out. By now the thatch was soaked and several heavy drops came through to the floor. Kpadeh looked up studying the underside of the charred bamboo ceiling. Sumo slid forward and nursed the fire sending a charge of fresh smoke upward around the drying hamper. Could we not take him tomorrow, someone asked.

"No. Tonight."

"There will not be a car tonight."

"But if there is, we must stop it."

Again silence. No one looked indignant; even Dawseh crouched by the fire deep in thought. Then, without addressing anyone in particular, the chief abruptly announced the decision lay in the hands of the man's brother. Kpadeh remained silent. Then he looked up. Wouldn't the trip give him pain?

"Yes. We must wrap him in blankets and tell the driver to take time."

"You mu' do da one," a voice said right behind me. In English! "Ta' de ma' Zawzaw. Dey gi' heem eenzhectshot, he be life. I see many ti'. Dey pu' needo insi', poosh medasee insi'. Feenish." I turned around—Jallah, Jacob's father, in his red rimmed officer's hat. I hadn't seen him for weeks. Now he was repeating it in Loma gesturing as he spoke. They listened in silence— even a few grunts of approval. But then another voice—in Loma. It came from the shadows; I couldn't see who, but the words came clear, unemotional, not without eloquence, "Should he die in that foul smelling place in Zorzor, his spirit may never come home." Again several grunts of approval, including John Sumo and David Beyan, two of my better students, but over all no stronger than those in favor. And the Loma voice may have defeated itself. The mention of death struck Kpadeh with a new awareness, one he may not have admitted to himself. I watched him. He was desperate. If dealing with the devil offered a chance, was not a brother saved worth the transgression? The ancestral spirits would understand; they could be appeased another day. He looked up with pleading eyes looking from face to face in deepening anguish. Two world's had spoken to him. The first had voiced the laws of the ancestors; but the younger laws had spoken too. "Live."

"We will take him," he said softly.

Then from out of the darkness where he'd been sitting silent, a frail old man made an effort to get up, bumped his head on the hanging lantern that sent a start through the shadows on the wall, muttered to himself, and with effort found his way to the door. After some time the lantern stopped squeaking and the shadows steadied themselves before he returned, again making his way with effort. At the end of his journey he stood before me looking down with an aimless face. He was very old. Slowly, enough to try the patience of the younger men, his unsteady hand found its way into the folds of an oversized robe and came out with a dirt rag bound in a tight ball. His leaden fingers worked the surface, opened it, then began unrolling a strip of cloth that began to have clean edges eventually becoming white. Inside, a yellow vial! Antivenom! Ten c.c.'s. Middleton Laboratories, St. Louis, Missouri. Effective against any poisonous snake in North America. Keep under refrigeration. June 1956. They were all looking at me. Kpadeh's face, subdued hope. No. I shook my head. They just kept looking. Damn it what did they want, a miracle? "No good. Spoiled." I gave it back to him. Bwomah took it and examined it by fire light. "We fix fo' de so'. He be figh' de sna' sma'-sma'."

"Okay, but he must still go to Zorzor. He needs a doctor." Bwomah opened it with his thumb nail carefully pouring several drops on the instep, visibly swollen now, where he softly rubbed in into the skin with his forefinger. They all watched intently. When he finished, Kpadeh took the vial and began smearing some on his brother's forehead after the fashion of their medicine.

"You mu' pu' heem o' de so!" Jallah explained impatiently, but Kpadeh ignored him. He continued smoothing it into the mud patch on Zawloe's forehead and they murmured approval.

"Their medicine doesn't work that way," John Mulba said in Loma. "It must go in the blood."

"Let it be," I said. If we started arguing, it might end in Kpadeh's changing his mind. "Let's go watch for a car." Jallah was getting uneasy watching something he knew was wrong.

At Quolidobu's store a crowd gathered, huddling out of the rain under the light of the single lantern. The rain fell straight down and steady. It would last the night. Overhead the zinc roof sounded a light drumming, the runoff washed into a gravel channel along the wall and down to the ditch. A forlorn dripping marked the passage of time as sharply as a clock.

"We watcheeng," Fdumo James said.

"Someti' whan i' rai'," Isaac Kezelee said, "dose driva dey say 'No.' Dey slee' dow' i' some tow'."

"Teacha!" Tellywoiyea broke in. "Sonti' dey be no pla' to slee', dey kee' go, eeva' nigh'ti."

"I remember hearing cars at night," I said.

"Dose privot ca' yah!" Kezelee snapped.

"Well, private or not, we're stopping it. Even a truck. Understand?"

"Dose beek tru', dey no stup noteeng!" Kezelee cried.

"We'll try. If we all get out in the road…we'll try."

We waited again. It wasn't any better here than in Kpadeh's house. The coming of a truck meant life or death. They were beginning to sense it too.

It happened so quick I didn't understand till it was over. A small boy, about four, understanding only that we wanted a truck, decided to give us one. It was easy, all the small boys could do it, begin humming low down, very softly, then louder, they could even shift gears but he never got that far. Adult anger caught him, then a stinging slap and the piercing bawl of an unjust punishment. Now they were busy trying to quiet him down. Quolidobu finally gave him a candy stick. He rarely did that.

The talk turned to wishing. There was a man in Bawein who had medicine for snakes; he wasn't afraid to touch a live one with his bare hands. Several swore they had seen it. If only he were here. If only a car would come. If only—then a cry for silence! A stir of bodies coming alert. Something coming? We ran outside. They peered into the darkness listening with all their strength. "Heah de motah talking," someone whispered. "Shoo," came the answer. I couldn't hear a thing. Others appeared from between the houses and stood motionless in the rain, all fixing their attention in the direction of Zorzor. That meant we'd have to talk him into turning around. I thought I heard it! A low drone. Far away. Not unlike the medicine man's chant—or the little kid's imitation. Yes! Coming on. Now it downshifted at the hill, less than a mile, the motor grinding steadier as it climbed.

The porch cleared. People sprang down the steep bank landing on all fours. Adults, children. I jumped too, hit a soft spot and went over. Normally it would have been a riot but nobody noticed. If the driver were white, the sight of another white man would stop him. Forty of them, half the village, women holding baskets over their heads to shield the rain. At the top of the hill, the first eerie glow, then the dip, another shift of gears, then a groan up the final knob and the rise out of the forest before rattling into the final curve.

Now the hint of headlights, faint and ghostly with a touch of unreality, soon brightening into a white beam angling upward and quivering against the wall of trees as it bumped forward, rounded the final turn and burst into two monstrous eyes, one slightly off course, bearing down on us with devilish speed. It came on like a beast. Only the distinctive squeaking of its rusty frame betrayed an earthly name. Renault.

They started walking then running towards it waving their arms, some giving the palm down signal to step on the brake; and way down the road, some two hundred yards, a lone figure with arms outstretched, fists clinched upward, raced directly at it, top speed, an athletic black silhouette aslant the white lines of rain. Tellywoiyea. The driver crammed on his horn but no. His great surging stride carried him closer, straight into the headlight beams, his shirt flapping, they could see his teeth, until the last instant JESUS close enough to make me cringe, he spun like a matador from the onrushing fender that must have missed him by inches, the horn blaring in mechanical rage.

When the driver saw people in the middle of the road, most of them not as crazy as Tellywoiyea, he slowed down. Then they began running alongside slapping the fenders; he braked enough for Moses Y. and Fdumo James to catch hold the canvas flaps and swing aboard. When he poked his head out and shouted they jumped down. Seeing he was about to stop Fawkpa and Jallah hurriedly motioned the others away. He ground it into first and pulled to the side of the road scattering people in front like a school of fish. It set there a moment, idling roughly, the lights dimming under the strain, one wiper jerking back and forth across the cracked windshield on the driver's side until the motor finally expired with a cough.

It was a Monrovia bus direct to Voinjama. Most of the riders were Loma but the driver wasn't. Not good. And even worse—next to him on the passenger side sat a corpulent soldier in a helmet and khaki uniform, two stripes, and the final arbiter of the coming discussion, an American M-1 with the butt resting on the floor and the muzzle pointing straight up.

Upcountry soldiers had a notorious reputation. Often of tribal birth themselves, they held themselves aloof from tribal feelings. Adventure or poverty originally carried them down to the coast where they joined up as soon as they ran out of money, which wasn't long. Soon they saw their first pair of boots. The M-1 came later. They were here to keep the peace—it hardly needed keeping until they arrived—and when they weren't so occupied, they spent their time carousing and mooching and flirting with women until ordered to inspect cargo trucks or collect the five dollar hut tax which they did in small towns like ours with great airs of superiority especially if people were watching. They weren't so bad when they didn't have a rifle in their hands but if they did, their new found power, suddenly greater than a village chief, was too much too soon; and if they were drunk, it was best to go hide.

At least he wasn't drunk. He sat back with one knee against the dashboard staring blankly out the window wanting to be seen, affecting all the boredom of a seasoned traveler, an impossibility after the ride he just had. His cold eyes no longer found anything of interest in a tribal village; they were only half visible under the rim of his helmet that he wore rakishly forward over barber shop sideburns and a heavy dose of aftershave. His ringed fingers toyed with the muzzle of the rifle. Then he looked at his watch exhaling a plume of cigarette smoke with an exaggerated impatience, the inconvenience of stopping might get him to Voinjama after the bars closed, both of them.

The circle of people drew tight around the truck as if to prevent its running away. The rain pelted us. They shielded themselves against it as best they could with a raised forearm or hunched shoulders. Some held banana leaves or flaps of cloth over their heads and Gburulu, though as wet as the others, stood erect under the torn shreds of a broken umbrella. Fawkpa and Jallah approached the driver trying to explain; it appeared he didn't speak Loma but several of his passengers became visibly agitated on learning the news indicating they understood. The chief joined us now. He stood near, watchful, wearing a dark stocking cap, but said nothing.

"You canno' see I going Voinjama!" the driver cried in English.

"Yes, we know," I said. "But we have a serious snake bite. He must go to the hospital in Zorzor." The soldier gave me a cold, hateful glare as he flicked a cigarette butt out the window. It landed in the crowd.

"We caddy heem Voinjama," the driver offered curtly.

"No! He needs a doctor!"

"We have clinic to Voinjama!" the soldier shouted at me then looked away sighing in disgust. The Voinjama clinic was out of the question. An understaffed show piece, closed half the time.

"Yes, but there is no doctor in Voinjama. The clinic closes for the night. At Zorzor he will get the proper treatment."

The driver wavered. I took off my glasses to wipe them off and Gburulu thrust his umbrella over my head but the water dripped off faster than rain.

"You see I ha' many passengahs." The driver gestured. "I canno' ma' dem go ba' Zozo." He was softening. On hearing this Jallah began speaking in Loma to the passengers who hardly needed convincing where tribal blood was concerned. In fact many were busy inquiring who and what family. When asked if they objected to going back to Zorzor, they answered with dead silence; their fear of the soldier kept them from saying more. The driver was probably afraid of him too. One man in the back of the truck ventured to say he would be pleased to visit some relatives in Zorzor and there were several quick grunts of approval. A clear message! But the soldier sensed it at once and turned on them with a sharp glare as they stared into the floorboards. Satisfied he returned to his bored composure, casually spat out the window narrowly missing a man, lit a cigarette and flicked the match into the crowd looking the other way as if he were posing for a camera; then after adjusting his helmet, he said something in a coastal dialect through a plume of blue smoke. The driver who appeared not to be listening fumbled with his keys before turning to the open window. The rain kept coming harder. "Bri' twenny dollah yah," he said quietly.

The usual fare to Zorzor was seventy-five cents, a dollar for white people who couldn't bargain. Even with the inconvenience for turning around, he shouldn't have asked more than two, three at most. A Loma driver would have been gone by now. Some of the people around the truck moaned disbelief as Jallah tried to negotiate. "De ma' say twenny dollah!" the soldier snapped.

I ran up the hill to my house. I never kept much cash around. I got my supplies down on the coast and paid by check, otherwise everything up here was small change. Had I spent fifty cents on a Saturday night I would have written home. A five and two ones in my wallet, some change on the night stand, nothing in the other jeans. The school treasury. I ran back to the study. "Wha you looking?" Moses said.

"For some money. You got any?" He didn't. I emptied the tin can on the desk.

"You taking de schoo' money?"

"Yes." Three seventy-eight. "I'm not going to have twenty dollars."

"Dey wa' too mush."

"It was that good-for-nothing soldier! He told him twenty dollars," John Mulba cried in visible anger.

"I know it's too much. We've got no choice."

"But we're his country, not you!" He was practically in a rage. "And he spits on us!"

"Zawloe. We got to think about—"

"WE ARE NOT—"

"Take it easy."

"HE IS BLACK MAN—"

"Mulba!"

"That shitman! Crocksucker! He's not..." He groped in English then found words in Loma. Moses said something very low. He got quiet but turned and rushed out slamming the door. We could see him sulking along the path as a file of his mates ran past him.

"Where's Tellywoiyea?" I said.

"Heah he."

"Where's the two dollars I lent you?"

"He ea' da one," Daniel Zizi said.

"No yah!"

"Do you have any of it left?" His silence said no. I took the school treasury can and we went collecting. Small change. It didn't add up. When Zawloe's kinsmen learned I was short, they disappeared into the village. While we waited several passengers climbed down over the tailgate and walked down the road to pee in the ditch talking in low tones as soon as they were out of earshot. The driver stayed in his seat fidgeting with a rearview mirror that hung from the door like a broken limb, but the soldier only stared away, irked at the delay.

When they came back they had six dollars plus change but on handing it through the window some coins slipped from nervous hands and fell in the mud. Luckily Jallah had a lantern but as we knelt for the coins, the soldier again spoke to the driver in the coastal dialect. Now they wanted thirty. A gust of whispers shot through the crowd. Jallah raised his hands in the air in utter dismay. Old Fawkpa hurried around to the passenger side. There was no doubt who called the shots. The old man was on fire. He protested the extra ten dollars with all his force, gesturing wildly, slashing his strong arms through the rain as he bellowed a torrent of monosyllables that cried for decency but fell pointless on the soldier, many years his junior, who not only didn't understand but found a perverse pleasure in the old man's rage. "Ole roostah ca' dance yah." He smiled, savoring the moment, before spitting again, this time missing by inches and dropping it at the feet of the men standing behind. Humiliated once again, Old Fawkpa turned away, staring blindly into space, still shouting and gesturing as if he were rehearsing a part for a play, then he found Gburulu and Taanu and took up the argument with them forgetting they were on his side.

"Who are you! What are you doing to us! We are equal!"

John Mulba! On the passenger side, shouting right at him. Perfect English.

"You're not blacker! Big shot!"

Jesus! "Mulba!"

"You're not better—"

"Mulba. No." I grabbed him around the waist and he started threshing like a cat.

"You damn you—"

"Listen to me. Help me. Don't—"

He kept slashing. Then our feet went out from under us and we fell on top of each other in the ditch. "John. It's me. For God's sake John NO!" He tried to get up and we went down again with a splash. I lost my glasses. "He'll hurt you. He's—" Now Moses and David Beyan had him. "Get Tellywoiyea. I'm sorry John. I'm so sorry. Take him up to my house. Don't hurt him." Still he struggled. The three of them dragged him up the bank, he slipped and slipped again but each time got up screaming, "Damn you, man! You, damn you! So, so, big man!" Then he switched to Loma and we could still hear him after they got him in the house.

Fortunately, the soldier ignored him. A tribal boy who aspired to speak English was below his contempt, as Mulba found out.

"I'm sorry," I said, approaching the window. "He is my student. I take full responsibility for what he said. I will speak to him tomorrow."

He blew a stream of smoke straight in my face, not hiding the pleasure he took in our little wrestling match. "My friend, we really don't have another ten dollars."

"You whi' ma', you no go' ten dollah?" He laughed viciously.

"I have ten dollars, of course. But not on me. Take the twenty. It's all we've got." He sighed boredom. Another cloud of smoke. He looked at the driver showing impatience. "Please take it. What do you want from me? I beg you to take it." He caught the phrase at once, savored it, then snapped around triumphant.

"De ma' say thurty dollah! You canno' unnastan' English whi' ma'!"

"Let me write you a check."

"Bri' thu'ty dollah! Thot iss correct fa' undah the sacumSTANCES!" Then in glory, "You canno' clea' de du't fro' yoseff? Look a' you! Iss thot how you teaching my peopo? TO ATTACK SUPPIYAH OFFICAHS! Look you! You SHIT!"

"It's drawn on the Chase Manhattan Bank in Monrovia," and under my breath, "Fifty. You can cash it as soon as—"

"No checks! By ti' I go da, you will sen' stawp payment!! Thu'ty dollah undah the sacumstances!"

"Let me write you a promissory note. Take it to the Lebanese in Zorzor. His name is Akil, he—"

"You a' westing my time," then to the driver, "Le' we go ma'."

"NO! Wait!" The driver had become more serious as the argument worsened. I addressed him, "Don't you think I'd give him the lousy ten dollars if I had it? You think I like arguing in the rain! You know—"

Not condescending to even listen, the soldier turned to spit just as I was leaning forward to see the driver. Got me in the shoulder. I heard a collective shudder behind me. An awful pause. I didn't know what to do. But then he said, "No min' yah," in bored apology. Then somebody was wiping off my shoulder. Old Fawkpa. With his robe. Then he was between me and the window, speaking to me softly in Loma, making a good target himself, challenging him to do it again. The old man's arms were still strong. And he was in a rage. If he got one around the guy's neck...but if not...I took a few steps away from the truck—and with them went his chance. He'd have to swallow one more humiliation. "Do you think we can find ten more dollars?" He looked into the ground.

There had to be more than that in town, but impoverished people were funny about the little money they did have; they hoarded it to the end often burying an entire life savings in a deep hole under their mud floors returning to dig it up only in emergencies. This emergency was Zawloe's and only his immediate family would be expected to give up so great an amount on such short a notice—if they had it. Even so, flashing the extra money in his face might well send the price up again.

We heard a yell. Sumo came racing down the bank with a crisp five dollar bill. He held it to the soldier but he didn't even condescend to notice. Then he took it around to the driver who took it quietly—a good sign—folded it and put it in his shirt pocket. Then another hand. Quolidobu who'd quietly closed his store when he first saw the soldier, discreetly passed him several large coins. The driver was getting restless. He was deep in Loma country and should he have to cross it again, without a soldier, whether tomorrow or months from now, it could turn out to be a very long trip—and he knew it. Word would travel, not on wheels but fast enough. And there were Loma people down on the coast. After carefully counting the money, almost twenty-eight dollars now, he turned to the soldier, "Le' we ta' de money ma'." But the latter didn't budge. He kept staring contemptuously at the windshield neither answering nor taking the slightest notice of the driver who, after a long pause with only the soft drumming of the rain on the top of the truck, turned and said quietly, "Bri' de ma'."

A cluster of running legs dashed up the bank. Shouts rang out to bring him. The driver turned the key and began grinding his half dead battery. It wouldn't start. Oh no. It kept grinding slower and slower until it barely turned over. "Shut your lights off!" They'd been on all the time; now only a hint of life glowed in the dirty headlamps weakly answering the pull of the starter. Then they expired. He tried again but this time it ground dead. Jesus! Why'd he leave his lights on? "You ca' gi' poosh yah," he said sticking his head out the window.

We lined up alongside and behind and pushed with all we had, slipping and yelling for more effort. Some of the passengers jumped down to help and when I looked around John Mulba crouched next to me against the tailgate. Once off the soft shoulder it went a little easier, the grade leveling off before falling away. After we got going, he popped the clutch, it coughed, backfired a shot of blue smoke, and lurched ahead in several jerks leaving us behind. At the bottom of the grade a quarter mile out of town he stopped. We could hear the motor racing. The headlights came on. Then he just sat there. Then an awful chill went down my spine. They had our money, the motor running, the lights on, Voinjama straight ahead. They had no reason to come back. They were discussing it now. That Bastard! It must have dawned on all of us at the same time. We broke into a dead run. All of us. When we caught up we slowed down surrounding the truck. The driver paid no attention. He sat there trying to grind it into reverse, looking a little worried. Bad clutch. Damn near gone. I walked up to his window.

"We ca' dri' de ca' yah!" the soldier screamed at me. He knew exactly what we were thinking. I put my hand on the driver's shoulder and ignored him.

"Let up on the gas, small-small." He had the engine roaring. He was scared.

"De motah wi' die oh."

"No it won't. That's it. Real easy. When you feel the gears jump, push." He finally got it. It jerked backward several times before smoothing out. With people running alongside he steered for the wide spot in the center of town, stopped, ground into first and swung into the bank driving half way up. The revived headlight beams shot upward through the slashing rain into the thatched huts and the trees behind catching them in a ghostly pallor as though a lid pried off a tomb. People too, it caught their fear as though they were outsiders in their own village. He fought again to get it in reverse. When he did it jolted back down the bank, splashed through the running water in the ditch, now a small torrent, lurched sideways with a flap of the sidecurtains, and promptly sank into the soft mud on the shoulder where the spinning tires cut a clean trench in slippery clay. It came to rest with its rear deck flat on the ground, front wheels up the bank, and the ditch water purling merrily underneath.

A cry for help went up. Again people descended on it trying to push but the angle was bad, so was the footing, and the confusion of shouts and directions only worsened things. Now everybody got out, except the soldier who casually flicked another cigarette butt into the crowd of straining bodies—this one landed with a sting on Borku's back. He straightened up slapping it like an insect but realizing its source went back to work. The driver shouted those in front out of the way, "You move fro' da ma'!" When they got the idea, he ground into first and gunned it. The squeaking frame listed and lurched from side to side fighting like a fat animal, splattering everyone behind, the engine racing like a beast, the headlights jarring up and down. When he got as high as he could, he stopped and I noticed a slight knock in the engine. After motioning us around front, he tried again but his back wheels found the same trench with the same result—only deeper. He shot forward digging a deeper trench. "You got to get out of that rut!" I shouted, but he buried himself again, this time to the lug nuts. He thrust his torso out the window to look. A half dozen gathering lanterns showed only a few feet further to the hard part of the road. Now people came running with armfuls of sticks, palm leaves, some torn fresh from nearby trees with the thorns unstripped. Once more forward, mud splattered everywhere, a fury of shouts, Old Fawkpa, standing alongside a row of straining bodies shouting encouragement. He didn't get so far up this time. Again he leaned out and surveyed the trench, as they ran forward to fill it with sticks, handfuls of gravel, clumps of hard clay torn from houses. "Di way ma'! Di way!" he cried as they lay the sticks lengthwise; yes, across the trench. Not enough. More palm branches. Men ran off in different directions. The chief shouldered a thin plank, which Fawkpa laid across the ditch like a bridge in the path of the wheel. Then another but considerably shorter. The path laid, he paused to plan his next shot. Another failure and he'd be up to the axle. He revved the engine. "No. Take it easy till you get your wheels on the boards, then gun it." The soldier cupped his hands lighting another cigarette, match out the window. "That's it, real easy. Wait till—that's it. Is the other board good?"—"Teacha, yes!"—"Get ready." We surrounded the truck on three sides grappling it like wrestlers, the older men instructing the younger while others slipped down the bank and squeezed in where they could. The truck had become a centipede. Onlookers shouted advice. "Real slow now till we're on the board." It began to crawl backward. "Okay." He gunned it and dozens of legs drove it back. Then a volley of shouts! An explosion of broken sticks and flying palm leaves. A cloud of white smoke. A solid jolt as wheels caught the hard clay with a painful squeak. Yes! In the middle of the road, the engine running. Facing Zorzor!

A swarm of jubilant faces milled around it. Old Fawkpa picked himself up off the road where the turning front fender had placed him and gave the Loma victory cry. The chief retrieved his planks, one half way up the bank where it narrowly missed two boys who dodged it in midair. The soldier sat back unconcerned. Passengers climbed back in. Now they dropped the tailgate and two women punched a rotten mattress onto the floor between the side benches. Mud splattered the entire vehicle; the soldier examined a spot on his sleeve. I walked to the driver's side and told him I was glad he was behind the wheel tonight.

Now they brought Zawloe. They carried him slung in my army blanket with Kpadeh running awkwardly alongside holding his face in his hands like water. He seemed conscious but groaned heavily. They took time descending the gutted bank with helpers supporting them by grabbing their loose garments, then lifted him into the truck carefully placing him on the mattress as Kpadeh sprang in alongside not taking his hands from Zawloe's head. Zawloe grimaced and looked around in terror as if he thought it were a grave. Sumo and Woiyea spoke to him in whispers as they jammed a bundle of cloth under his head. He kept moaning. Good sign I thought. Stephen Bwomah jumped in and others were about to follow but the driver said no. The other passengers were already jammed tight.

Someone drew up the tailgate as it started to move. Picking up speed on the downgrade, he shifted at the culvert, easily enough this time, we could hear the engine take the load as it climbed the slope in front of the school finally disappearing around the bend, a dirty rag stuffed in the gas port. No tail lights. The glow of the headlamps quivered in the surrounding trees then died as the stark black wall closed behind it. Then an awful silence. Only the dripping rain and the torrent in the ditch.

I felt a chill. People turned to go. Several voices conversed in low tones in front of Quolidobu's store. I climbed the hill to my house shivering, heated a kettle of water and ripped off my clothes. They were plastered with mud, I had a cut on my face. Not bad. Worse, the thoughts that started to weigh in. I began to feel ashamed. I'd been so sure of myself. My resolve to live on their level blinded me to an emergency like this. Of course I should have had thirty dollars. I was white. It was expected of me. Why! Why hadn't I thought of it. I envied Dwoiyou; at least he knew how to cry. That soldier! That bastard! That arrogant bastard!! And Mulba! A rebel all of a sudden. Where was he getting it? Another thirty seconds he would have tasted the butt of a rifle. An M-1 of course. And they will have noticed. Long live the arsenal of freedom! Pay any price, bear any burden…**Bullshit!** We arm…the thugs!

During the night a car passed; it hummed through town as sweetly as in a dream—towards Zorzor. I couldn't get to sleep. I kept hearing that voice in

271

Kpadeh's house, "Should he die in that foul smelling place in Zorzor." And if he did? I'd interfered. Against my own "law" as they called it. Later on a truck. The same way. Its motor quietly groaned into town then sang away into the distance as if a leitmotif to the mechanical indifference of the modern world to this out-of-the-way place.

Can't sleep. Something more than tonight's incident. Something underlying it. The modern world and all I was teaching them, there it was, staring at me through the face of a uniformed punk stinking of aftershave. I'd preached nonviolence. But tonight I wanted to grab the son of a bitch and throw him out of the truck—and they all knew it. They couldn't read, but they "read" that.

That foul smelling place in Zorzor. Surely the devil's workshop—sawing people open, sewing them up again like stitches on a sack of palm kernels. Yet they'd gone along with it! They'd turned their backs on tradition, bribed a bully and ate his dirt. We all had. There went the last flicker of Camelot. The jungle brooked no Romantic projections of itself. Its deadly fangs struck like lightning out of cloudless sky. The rule was pain and hunger and want. The noble savage would have sold his soul in a trice for a moment of ease from this unremitting horror. Hadn't we all? Isn't civilization just that? What the hell are we doing here? Everything we touch turns to excrement. What in the *HELL* am I doing here?

I woke up. A bad dream. There'd been an accident. I went to my medicine cabinet. Someone had awkwardly hammered a three-pronged electrical switch to the side, blood dripped down. Out on the porch the bird cage was empty. Then I was in the middle of town. An eerie feeling came over me. It was deserted, the medicine post overgrown with poison ivy. No fire in the forge. Then the hollow sockets of the headlamps in the junked car started to glow. Sickly yellow. I turned and saw him lying on a mat. Two tiny mouse eyes on his instep. But the skin on his foot was transparent. I could see inside. Some sort of mechanism with gears and ratchets and a condenser with red and yellow wires submerged in liquid. Somebody help him. "I'm not an electrician." I looked around. No one there. A wall of darkness.

CHAPTER 24

THE IMMORTAL *BAO*

Next morning the kids came for school as if nothing happened. People were up and about. They took to their work pounding rice, sharpening hoes. Men with shoulder yokes and cutlasses stepped briskly along the way to their farms, some by the same trail Zawloe had taken. The little ones got under foot. The radio in Quolidobu's store played a lively march. The rain had stopped, leaves hung laden with water. But then, long experience had taught them the art of swallowing humiliation and bouncing back.

John Mulba knocked softly two times, his calling card, and came in as I bandaged my scrape. He was his old self, polite, refined. "You dropped this last night," he said handing me my glasses. Not a speck of mud. He must have washed them. Then he put on a kettle of tea water and sat at the kitchen table looking over a magazine. Soon Moses and Akwoi, Kezelee, Zizi, of course Jacob and Daydobah, and all the regulars, curious to see what I'd say, or do.

In school the morning dragged. We couldn't get into our lessons. I was edgy, they sensed it and got edgy themselves. Dismissing them wouldn't work; back in town the waiting would be worse. Last night after all the ruckus, Zawloe's absence hadn't sunk in. Now it had. He was gone and we all felt it. I slapped some work on the blackboard and looked out the window; they dutifully copied it down then looked at me. Waiting.

Normally school wasn't such a drag. It had been at first; I even had a set of lesson plans before the termites got to them but after I stopped going by the book, things livened up a bit, learning became a hunt, game to be taken by whoever got there first, often with a shout, like the first time the littles ones found our old friend Mr. Crocodile in the encyclopedia. We even made up a song: "He walks in style, he dines with a smile, does sly-oh, Mr. Crocodi-oh."

It wasn't long till I realized I had the greatest biological laboratory in the world ten yards out the back door. Soon we took walks and collected specimens. They brought me flowers and butterflies; I brought them books with pictures. And when words and the specimens didn't hook up, folklore filled the gap. Soon we sensed a common cause, a feeling so subtle I couldn't name it, how in the final count we all rely on mythology when the Forest withholds her fruit. There were stunning surprises, like the time I'd been wrestling with a definition of Nature. So I asked them, and one of the shyest girls in the fourth grade, Mary Bwoli, answered in one sentence, "What mama no allow in house." There it was, through the eyes of a child as though Nature herself had smiled on my feeble groping.

They especially relished spirited encounters between "African Science" and "Book." These were our greatest days. The first came on a dreary morning when I walked to my desk and found a rooster egg. I'd strenuously denied any such possibility only a few days earlier. They twinged with excitement. But the greatest blow to Western Science came by way of a remarkable African cricket named Bao, the immortal Bao.

It began one night in my study when Johnson Kwiogi decided to become a scientist. It came on him like a fever. He read all the science books with zeal often asking pertinent questions. Then came the Encyclopedia Britannica. He privately told me his intention of reading all the science articles. An aardvark was an earth pig but looked like an ant bear. Good start. The book covered his entire lap; I broke the rules and allowed him to take it home—something between the two of us. He carried it on his head and read it in conspicuous places, his personal trophy, no one could take away.

Inwardly he must have seethed at the laughter of his fellows. Turning from spirits to science was no small matter. He looked small for his age because of a birth defect that left him with a deformed leg and a wall-eye. Some said his handicap was due to incest, others that he'd been half castrated in an unsuccessful attempt to fix his leg at the Mission; otherwise he got on well enough although his schoolmates called him "Toad," a name he learned to get along with but countered by defiantly renaming himself after the president of the United States. At school he quickly learned his handicap was nothing at all; unlike the bush or the football field, he was equal to anyone, even the great Tellywoiyea who stumbled through books like an infant. Once his confidence came, he read with tenacity, his good eye darting along the line while his wall-eye stared off into space as if it were thinking about what the other one read. He improved each day radiating pleasure at each "well done." No one laughed. The toad had become the leopard.

His study of science soon took him to experimentation. He proved water evaporates, tadpoles are frogs, the earth turns, and when I mentioned oxygen was essential to life, he took the challenge. We'd test the theory. We caught some ground crickets and chose the two hardiest. Each went into a jar, equal water and grass, but one lid had air holes, the other not. Kwiogi wrote it all down.

Next morning the cricket in the control jar lay belly up; the other—very much alive. Not only had he retained his color, his energy—he was singing. We'd repeat the procedure.

The second day we hurried to school only to find him healthy as ever—in magnificent form. I never had much luck with science. The damn thing looked air tight. And he knew what he was doing. "I sing my song, I breathe no oxenjohn nor contemplate its magic theory."

"We pu' heem insi'," Abraham Dworlu cried, "We say, 'You die oh,' he say, 'No!' Le' we gi' heem na' Bao." It meant "no" in Loma and at once became their symbol of defiance.

The third day they were up at the crack of dawn. I could hear their bare feet as they raced down the bank, up the road to school—I lay awake listening for the roosters, roosters that do not lay eggs—then back to town, up the path and beneath my bedroom window where they couldn't contain the gleeful news. "He lives!"

They practically danced all the way to school, the little ones running on ahead clicking toy rattles and their seniors a little more frisky than usual, Mary Kolu chasing Akwoi all the way from town. Even John Mulba enjoyed the fun. But Johnson Kwiogi took great pleasure in being the author of it all. The men at Quolidobu's store waved as I went by and the women at the culvert looked up from their laundry with bright smiles. We pushed our faces into a circle around the jar. Yep. Nothing to do but let him go.

"You wi' ea' heem?" Mary Kolu cried. One of her favorite tricks was dropping a live grasshopper into her mouth and munching deliciously before darting away to her friends. "No!" It was going to be a long day. "Okay, take him back where you got him." In a flash they were gone, out the windows, the door, down the bank ahead of Kwiogi who ran sideways on his bad leg holding the jar up with both hands. I picked up an overturned chair. They stopped at the edge of the ditch, jammed together as he untwisted the lid and shook him out. They waited. Backed way. Then a shout and they bolted back to the school filing past me in the doorway suppressing a sea of delight.

It got real quiet as they waited my surrender. I was glad the giants of Western science whose portraits usually decorate schoolroom walls weren't there to watch. "Something must have gone wrong," I said. Already they were hiding their faces. "Don't give up on science just because one experiment goes wrong. Hundreds of experiments go wrong but we always learn something. Science doesn't have all the answers but if we ask the right questions—"

"You told us not to believe everything in books." The opening shot. Akwoi. Who else?

"That's right! That's why we experiment. This time it went wrong. Next time—"

"Da Afrikon Sciants!" Fdumo James cried.

"Science is the same for everybody, science does not discrim—"

"Bao he no rea' de boo'," Telleywoiyea whined. Then the roof came down. They lay their faces on their desks and pounded the undersides. Some leaped out of their chairs. Even Tellywoiyea had beaten me. I thought of another tack.

"Or else," it wasn't gonna work, "there's been some foul play. Somebody snuck in here and—" I couldn't finish. They leaped from their chairs shaking books at me.

"No! No! No! See de ma'!"

"Eh yah yah yah yah yah yah yah!"

"See de spidah running backsi'!"

"Bao Bao Bao Bao!"

"See de ma'! He see he fineesh! He say we chea'!"

"Tellywoiyea did it. Look at him hiding his face."

Today even the memory of that wild morning couldn't raise a smile. Bao's empty jar set on the table next to butterfly collection, a grim reminder that a kinsman's life lay in the hands of the same science they so instinctively defied. A car came through after some time, but no news. John Mulba snapped a yard stick on the second graders' table to get them back to work, and a little later when Peter Kpudumah and Abraham Dworlu started tug of war over a shared book, I sent them for the football.

Of all the legacies of colonialism, this had to be the finest. Empires come and go but the sun never sets on a soccer ball. They took to it like ducks to water, their passion for it matching that for hunting. While we waited, Moses and Fdumo James entwined fingers and chose teams. The older players stood confident until they heard their names, the others hopefully around the perimeter, but if they weren't chosen, sulked off and eventually joined the little ones who played in the mud behind the school where the girls drew concentric circles on the ground for their favorite game, *jumba,* a one foot

hop-dance where players tried to toe a pebble into the innermost circle
without stepping on the lines or breaking a chanted rhythm. One miss, you're
out.

The sides chosen I turned and walked back to the goal. I had the high side
of the field where the going was a little cleaner, but not much. None of them
liked playing goalie; that was for the weakest. The other team chose Jacob
Jallah. He protested but went grudgingly; he knew if he didn't he'd feel the
weight of Tellywoiyea's paw on the back of his head. He walked back, head
down, cursing them under his breath in a rather advanced vocabulary but
checking over his shoulder to make sure they weren't coming. He sat down
against the goalpost with his back to the field, but his rebellion wouldn't last.
He knew if somebody scored on him like that, he'd be in trouble. Outraged
teammates once chased a daydreaming goalie all the way to town where he
had to take refuge in his mother's house—a lesson I did not forget.

Now they lined up. Meanwhile Jallah climbed up on the sagging crossbar,
hung upside down, while Daydobah jumped for his loose arms. They
continued their game as long as the ball was upfield, but the first time it came
near, he'd be ready. He played with a vengeance. His eyeballs popped wide
open, his skinny head darted in and out like a shrew, his fists clinched, kicking
and swiping and flaying, stealing the ball before they could line up a shot,
then smashing it right back in their teeth if they weren't quick enough to duck.
And when someone did seem to have a clean run, he had an uncanny talent for
being in the wrong place at the right time. The hardest shots had a way of
ricocheting off his frail body like sling shot pebbles off a taut rope and if they
tried to lob it over his head, they more often beat themselves by sending it into
the bush, but no matter how high it sailed over the sagging crossbar, it always
went over Jallah's outstretched body, as well—all fifty inches.

As soon as the game started, the tension broke. The first kick sent the ball
skipping along the ground and a collective yell echoed off the wall of
surrounding trees as though the forest cried back in joy at the universal ring
of children at play. They ran and bumped and jostled each other all the time
watching the ground where a dozen bare feet grabbed at the ball while names
and commands flew up like sparks.

"Fdumo!"

"Koiyo!"

"Sen' de ba' ma'! Sen' i'! Senni! Senni! Senni!"

"You move fro' da ma'!"

"Tellywoiyea!"

"You juke me ma'! I juke you two!"

"Tellywoiyea ma'! You canno' pass a ba'!"

"Di way ma'! Di way! Di way!"

The ball shot upfield and back and sideward as they responded to it like leaves to the same wind. They raced ahead excitedly, sometimes anticipating, more often reacting to its unexpected flight.

Fdumo James was our best, he played with calm detachment chewing a blade of grass while he danced over the ball never removing his eye from the flow of the action. Tall, agile, deceptively quick with long graceful strides that overtook the most errant pass, he covered both sides of the field, always at the center of things, ready for a quick dart, a steal, a spin, a half step over the ball and...good-bye. He had a natural feel for the game that seemed to sense opportunities as well as his rival's presence, usually Moses whose savvy and muscular limbs synchronized into powerful grace, always a match for Fdumo—if he could catch him. Now the two of them raced full speed behind the ball watching their mates up ahead, each knowing the book of the other's moves, both well aware of Tellywoiyea with his furry head down and his great elbows threshing the air as he bore down on their heels giggling like a three-year-old.

Whether opponent or teammate, Tellywoiyea's presence had to be reckoned because of his recklessness and complete inability to grasp the game. He had no concept of teamwork. None. He'd just as soon bounce a shot off a fellow player or a stray goat than go for the goal. Sometimes he came into battle with a short stalk of sugar cane which he carried in his fist chewing it from time to time, but even when he got knocked to the ground with a thud, he always bounced up giggling and chased the action with a renewed strength going directly for the ball.

He alone wore shoes, tennis shoes, but they flopped like galoshes and quickly came unstrung. Not realizing they came in sizes, he'd bought the first pair he saw and when his huge foot wouldn't go inside, he chopped off the toes with a machete. After that he had to bind them to his feet with strips of cloth which he did with great ceremony at the beginning of the game but to no avail. They always came undone and he kicked them off rather than miss the action. When he butted the ball the dust flew.

The game wavered back and forth. Beads of sweat trickled down my face. A slight breeze half-heartedly tussled the leaves but hardly enough to drive off the inverted ocean of heat. They didn't seem to notice; they played in it naturally, untiringly, unmindful of their drenched bodies. If caught in an unexpected shower, they threw off their trousers and played in their loincloths and when the sun broke through, their wet backs gleamed like bronze. They looked like a swarm of hornets following the central prize while the smaller boys kept to the perimeter hoping for a stray pass. Of course the sick and the lame didn't play; they either sat in the windows or watched from the sidelines. Gwoibo had a clubfoot but hobbled close to the action; so too Johnson Kwiogi, Daydobah, holding up his oversized trousers with one hand, and sundry small fry who made up the defense but often took to their heels when the game bore down on them.

Today we played in mud. Last night's rain filled the shallow puddle ten yards across half way up the field. The first time the ball splashed down, afloat in a neat spin, the ripples scarcely formed before they were on it, Fdumo James first, tiptoing delicately, then the mob right behind clinging to each other to keep from falling but knowing if one went down, they'd all go. "Ta' time ma'! Ta' ti'! Ta' ti'! Ta' ti'!" Soon the ball was bobbing atop a maelstrom of brown water, kicking feet; high pitched screams sang out, splashes of mud leaped in the air, excited faces turned away, one eye shut while the attached leg kept kicking. When it finally squirted out, Akwoi kicked it right back in. "You stupi' ma'!" Tellywoiyea cried ready to swipe him but no time. They both jumped back in the caldron. Fdumo James and Moses and Kwokwoiyea and Zizi and Kezelee, all ahold of each other by the arms or elbows like a bacchic dance. "Le' go ma'! You wa' you t'row me dow' ma'!" Somehow, someone got a solid foot on it. It came out like a shot, caught Johnson Kwiogi trying to duck, too late! Splat! Square in the back. Tellywoiyea liked the effect, got the rebound and gave him another. A rubber stamp! Paid! And at once the trees rang with the echo of wild delight as Tellywoiyea came back down to earth after a marvelous leap of pure athleticism. Kwoigi stood still trying to look over his shoulder with his wall-eye, saw the imprint on his back, swallowed his hurt, reached down for a clump of mud and took after him. He let go a wild throw, missed badly but caught Daydobah right in the mouth before he could dart away. He ran straight to his big brother who, already swearing revenge on Kwiogi, stopped long enough to wipe his face with his arm before sending him down to the creek to wash off.

The ball had become an unmanageable glob of slick leather squirming like a wet fish. Still they fought for it. No one thought of stopping to dry it off. A miss, a slice, "dammi'," then a lead pass dead center. Beautiful. It looked like an easy goal—but no! Jallah shot out of the goal like a cat, met it square, a solid smash straight back at the charging stampede. It grazed the side of Kwokwoiyea's head, flattened Zizi's ear, slapped Moses' shoulder, still with a sting, lodged between the jammed bodies, came to rest for a split second between Peter Woiyea's hip and Fdumo James' mid-section. Then came Tellywoiyea's monstrous foot thundering through the thicket of slashing limbs, a hollow thump, a grunt, the ball rocketing straight up and Fdumo James crumpled over with his arms clamped over his groin. "Tellywoiyea ma', you stupi'. You stupi'." It came down with a clank on the schoolhouse roof, bounced the other way and the small boys shot after it. While they were gone the others checked their scratches and took a breath. "Tellywoiyea ma'!" When the girls saw Fdumo on the ground grinding his teeth, they darted onto the field, taunted him mercilessly, then ran back shrieking in delight as the ball bounced back into play. They were after it like a shot, hurdling Fdumo before he could get up.

Later on Moses scored on me on a break away, my defense abandoning me for a game of skip rock. As he came on, the ball seemed to lure him after it, he lengthened his stride, looked up, smiled—I knew I was dead—faked right, shot left, and followed through with a half leap as the ball sailed through. Then he turned and ambled back up field, several teammates ran up and touched him for luck, the scoring team made a few lewd signs, small boys mimicked my sorry attempt to catch it. That was it. Normally a goal brought on a carnival of frenzied delight. But today—all business.

The game was on again. It vied back and forth but without further scoring. Fdumo James, more cautious but always dangerous, missed wide with a sweet shot off a wicked fake, Telleywoiyea sent two cannonballs into the bush but nothing more. He couldn't get it in his head no matter how hard you kick, if they don't go in, they *don't...count.*

Then they stopped dead—the ball spinning free at their feet. A car! Out of Zorzor! We listened. I could hear it too. Across the stream, up the hill, down the grade, just like last night, up the long hill and around the first bend. An awful emptiness came over me. Into the last bend, just around the corner, now a metallic elongated horn, the driver laying on it, a rush of motion, another Renault, healthier than last night, speeding down the grade with flapping canvas. And Sumo! The upper half of his body thrust out the side with outstretched arms and an exploding white smile splashed across his radiant face! Six inch headlines! HE LIVES! It tore into town scattering a brood of hens, slammed on its brakes almost sending Sumo into the ditch as people came running alongside grabbing at his shirt. They swarmed it as it came to rest very close to where the other one stopped last night. "We go-eeng i' tow' yah!"

The field cleared. They ran down the path, others jumped the bank with graceful leaps, then up the road. The girls too. Mary Kolu clutched her skirt hip-high and shot past the boys like a springing gazelle; after them, the slower runners, the small boys beating the dirt with their bare feet like chubby little guinea hens, the cripples, a stray dog.

I looked at the oil palm across the road. I thought of it as my special tree because I could see it out the window from my desk. In dark moments I drew strength from it reminding myself darkness doesn't last. One day Ramses Tokenu's father climbed it to harvest the oil but the bounty it gave me remained. There it was now, arced like a graceful bow, splendid in the lifting breeze.

I gathered up my books and followed down the path. The morning mists had risen. A new day broke, awash with the innocence of children, forgetful of past wrongs, opening its vast blue depths to whomever paused to drink.

By the time I got to the edge of the schoolyard, Jacob and Daydobah came racing back, "Dey say de ma'—okay." With that they turned and darted back skipping all the way to the plank that bridged the ditch where their spindly legs broke the orbits of butterflies hovering over the mud. Then Jallah threw back his frail head until his face touched the sky, stretched out his skinny arms sideward, and danced down the road to his own music, pirouetting like a falling leaf, squealing with delight at the trees whirling around him as Daydobah excitedly tried to catch his flying shirt tail until it all ended in a pile of giggling arms and legs in the middle of the road. The day was theirs. They salvaged victory where I could only see farce—the guy could have died—they could dance while I could only torture myself with the poisoned darts of my own conscience. What if he *had* died? Whose fault? Whose fault the soldier? The fiasco with the thirty dollars? The whole damn thing was a farce. Their whole damn country was a farce! A complete unmitigated...yet they danced. Their friend Zawloe was alive, and to be alive was a thing of joy; grief would have to wait another day. It was that simple. They could dance because they knew joy could only be savored once, the moment it came, like ripe fruit.

Perhaps my palm tree knew the answer. It had witnessed the entire comedy. If it could speak perhaps it might say, "You're right of course. This is a farce and a rather poor one at that but we take our cue and laugh when the play allows. The only difference, we know our world's a farce; you think yours an exulted tragedy and therefore cannot spare so much as a stolen smile."

Daydobah chased Jallah all the way to town, up the bank and through the agitated gestures of men talking on the step of Quolidobu's store where Sumo and Woiyea were the center of attention as they described the trip to the hospital. Gburulu stood near listening intently and two old women not far away danced back and forth on their heels, slowly, dipping to and fro from their waists. Shouts rang in the air, naked toddlers sat in the dust unattended as their mothers paused a minute for the news, dogs got up and stretched. Life resumed.

Back at my house John Mulba held the door open for me, "They say he will live."

"I know." The screen door slammed and the usual crowd came in. I felt like having something to eat, a cloud of red ants floated out from underneath yesterday's bread.

"How do you know? You walk in town looking in the ground. Those men at the store are laughing at you."

"He loo' someteeng' o' de roa'," Moses jested.

"Sumo told me," I said. They looked quizzical. "With his teeth. I never knew he had so many."

"I'll get some new bread," John said going to the cupboard.

"Dey gi' heem eight eenzhection," Moses said. "Two li' so, two mo' o' de leg, one heah, one heah, two I' de ardm. His foo' eez...eh yah," he finished in Loma.

"Swollen," John said.

"His foot is swollen two times," Akwoi said excitedly. "He cannot walk, that is why he must stay there. But the sickness is past." Then he added, "Cannot you be happy for the man?"

"I'm happy for him," I said. But they laughed.

"Why you canno' dansse?' Kezelee snapped.

"It is not my way. But I...well...I'm still vexed at the man last night. The soldier."

"Eh yah," Moses sighed. "De ma' ma' troubo one ti' two ti'. I' we bri' twenny dollah, he say thahty, I' we bri' thahty, he say fawty. You canno' see da one?"

"We should have beaten him," Mulba muttered.

"Oh, hell yes. The guy's got a gun in his hands, you want to start a fight."

"You will speak to him now?" Akwoi grinned. They hadn't missed it. I told the soldier I would speak to him.

"I *am* speaking to him. Never attack a fool with a gun in his hands. If you do, make sure you got a bigger gun. Is that satisfactory, sir? Would you care to add anything? Good," I smiled at Mulba, "Let's have some lunch."

"Tellywoiyea say, he wi' go Monrovia, be soljah," David Beyan said.

"I know."

"You wi' te' heem No?"

"I can't tell him what to do." I couldn't imagine Tellywoiyea in a uniform. "I will miss him."

"Dey gi' heem am wah?" Beyan asked.

"What?"

"He said, 'Will they give him an M-1?'" Akwoi said.

"I don't know." I knew they'd get to it eventually. They knew. They knew exactly where it came from. The thumb print of American Foreign Policy. No use denying it. "Yes...that was an M-1."

"Look at Mary Kolu!" Akwoi cried pointing out the screen. "She's dancing the hunter-bring-meat dance!" We all took a look. "The girl is frisky yah!"

"She beat you guys back to town, didn't she?"

"Eh ma'. De gur' ca' run," Moses smiled. "Only Fdumo Ja' fastah. Co' we go i' tow'."

"I'll be over later."

"Eh yah. Do no' be looking i' de grou'."

"Do I look that bad?"

"YES!" they cried in Loma.

CHAPTER 25

A BEETLE ON THE DINNER LINEN

The rain outside Akil's store fell straight down, slow and mournful, striking a broken bottle in the drip ditch with the measured resonance of tiny bells. This rain would last. Not the loud adolescent testing its lungs, but an unrelenting gray melancholy come home to stay; it drew its strength from the immense weight of the leaden sky, hopeless as a brooding lady alone at her curtainside waiting the return of an unloving husband. It would linger for days with intermittent moods, calm drizzle, sad gusts of spent breeze that whispered false hopes of clear skies. And it would continue at night, dripping through rooftops and into the thoughts of those who lay awake, much like the night we loaded Zawloe into the truck.

Akil leaned across his counter looking out into the wet squalor past the faded red gas pump growing atilt out of the mud like a totem pole from another world. Water dripped from its crank. It came with the motor road, traffic gathered to it like beasts to a water hole, stores clustered to the traffic and eventually pushed the good Christians on the original mission another two miles back in the bush. An orange tree grew nearby, gave sparse shade on sunny days, but no less out of place. A rivulet cut around its roots, joined another, ran along a narrow street stealing mud from under the rotted steps of a row of zinc-topped sheds that leaned on each other like drunks, found a wallow then a ditch, eventually the swamp the edge of town. Now and then a thatched cone rose above the rusted zinc to remind people this too had once been a tribal village.

He kept staring into the deserted street ponderously shifting his weight or scratching a purple tattoo on his heavy arm, seemingly unworried about the lack of business. I liked him because he didn't say much. Years of looking over that same counter had hardened his exterior, lessened the pace of his thoughts until they fell in step with the surroundings. Not that he was without

284

wit. When pressed, he showed surprising savvy; his was the merchant's wisdom that left his listener with a purchase but himself the profit. Nor was he without humor. He enjoyed telling of the unusual events that transpired in the arena beyond his gas pump—like the time many years ago when automobile travel was still a novelty; an old patriarch came down from the hills to take his first ride which began in child-like delight but ended with a headlong dive out the back window when the beast began to move. Nor without feeling. When old Warbah, a leper with no feet, shoulder muscles contorted from pulling himself along the ground on two wood grips, would struggle up the Mission road into town on sunny days, Akil grinned as if the old man were his infant son taking his first steps.

It didn't look like there'd be a ride. And this the county seat, downtown Zorzor. Akil couldn't understand it. I got up to get another beer, slapped fifty cents on the counter and resettled on the burlap sacks in time to catch his vacant comment on the scarcity of dry wood. Then Jim Philips came bounding up the front step stomping the water off his feet, fighting a red and yellow umbrella that wouldn't close; sneakers, jeans, an Arizona State jersey, and a cigarette dangling from his lips set him off from the surroundings as drastically as the cardboard girl on Akil's tobacco display. "Goddamn rain," he grumbled giving up on the umbrella. Then with a agile step he lifted himself to the counter, swung behind, "Got any dry matches?" Akil hardly noticed as he fumbled in a torn box.

"Well, well, what's this? Something they dumped off with a load of coffee?"

"Shut up and get a beer."

"He speaks."

"I'm buying you a beer, dammit."

"Where the hell have you been? Richardson's been—"

"I have a busy social calendar."

His blank expression changed to a slow grin. He shook his head. Two townswomen silently disappeared down an alley under covered headloads seemingly afloat in the rain.

"The old boy practically had kittens the last time you skipped his little pep rally." He turned and looked out the door. "Whatever you're doing up there," he got dreary again, "it's not going to make a difference."

"I know."

Now he stood in front of me like a schoolmaster.

"So go down to the coast. Wash this place off. When was the last time you went to Monrovia?"

"Before school."

"Jesus," he groaned in disbelief. "Well, go again! You don't feel good. You need a physical."

"I got one last time."

"Well, get another one," he smiled. "You can't be too careful."

"How's your swamp rice?"

"Constant guesswork. We can't figure the drainage, too wet, too dry, by the time we make the adjustment the seedlings spend their strength outgrowing the error."

"I think it's a good idea."

"Yeah," he sighed dejectedly. "Swamps are funny. Come over if you don't get a ride."

"I'm invited to dinner."

"The Mission? Esther must have been very persuasive."

"I think she likes me. Damned if I can figure it out."

"Dinner at Esther's. Wow. Needless to say Greg and I won't be joining you. We're *persona non grata* out there. Somewhere she got the outlandish idea we're using the jeep for immoral purposes. It doesn't have a back seat."

"You should have pointed that out."

"We did. Then she really got mad. Oh well, if God meant us to propagate, He'd have given us organs. Come over afterwards."

"Okay."

"And mind your manners."

The Mission road slipped out of town and disappeared in a swamp. In the rainy season setting water reclaimed it leaving only half submerged ridges at the sides, two wheel tracks in between, distinguishable only by their unbroken brown surface and curved flight to the other side where a maze of tire tracks gutted the earth like scars. There it banked hard following the contour of a low hill. Out in the swamp bushy piassava palms looked like unkept dwarfs lording it over pastures of decay. Dead logs lay face down in tepid water. Green slime covered everything. A place you gladly consigned to vermin, yet a stillness spoke of an ungodly permanence. Then came the first sign of the Mission itself, the drone of the diesel generator mercilessly out of tune with the jungle, casting off a foul vapor like something from the bowels of the earth. A knot of wires emerged from a block building, fixed themselves to aqua knobs, then a row of wooden poles, each with a crosspiece, dismal crosses ready to fall but following along the road to the hospital and the leper colony, all the way to the chapel set like a tarnished dollhouse on the highest vista where its bell could call the converts over the whine of the generator. Beneath its door five acres of hillside opened like a book, grass-covered and shorn of natural growth, with the forest receding a polite distance as though unwelcome in this man-made Eden. Living quarters dotted the perimeter. Neat, cement block buildings stood secure under the rain; square lines and planned spacing, all strung together with the magical threads of dripping wire like a company town in small-time America. Then came a school, a soccer field, a pair of tennis courts, rectangles of shiny mud with water trickling into the grass at the sides, a radio antenna, a lawn mower.

I ran into Phyllis Roy coming the other way. A crusty old nurse who'd spent over twenty years in the bush, much of it before there was anything resembling a hospital; her overcrowded schedule reduced all conversation to an exchange of facts. Rumor had it she once performed an emergency appendectomy in the doctor's absence but no one talked about it. Loma women trusted her, men feared her, young doctors sought her advice. She said a curt hello without breaking stride.

"Thank you for treating the man from my village." She stopped abruptly, looked confused. "The snake bite."

"Which one? Had two last week."

"About a month ago. Zawloe."

"The one the soldier brought in? Good thing they got him here when they did."

The pastor met me at the door. A six footer in a crew-cut and T-shirt, shorts, sandals, he didn't look like a missionary; he loved western movies and fly fishing—though African rivers weren't amiable—read modern novels, spoke fluent Loma, but his conversations were usually a bore. Everything turned on Christian charity. He had his pet projects, Mission branches in outlying villages and vaccinations for school children, but a patronizing attitude towards "his flock."

"Here he is dear," he said removing his pipe.

"Be right there!" Esther sang out from the kitchen.

"Don't worry about the floor," he said. "Here let me take your jacket."

"Marion, are you making him comfy?"

"Yes, dear."

"Munchies on the coffee table!"

"Yes, dear. Here let's sop that up just a—"

"Lord." Esther gasped. She stopped in wide-eyed disbelief under the arch to the kitchen.

"The buses weren't running dear."

"You came through the…"

"I told you he'd come."

"We could have sent a jeep."

"Nonsense," the pastor interrupted. "What's a little water. There we are. No harm."

"Through the…swamp?" she whispered very low.

"Yes, dear. Nothing to fret ourselves—"

"I felt like walking," I said.

"I told you," he chuckled.

"You felt like…"

"I like to walk in the rain." I thought I'd try humor, "Helps cleanse the soul." But she wasn't laughing.

"Well." She gasped, a little breathless. "I guess you've come to the right country. You didn't let him drip on the rug did you Marion?"

"No Pigeon. We've just about got him wrung out."

"I have dry clothes in my knapsack," I said.

"Probably a good book too," he smiled.

"Well…yeah."

"There ya go. A little light reading for a rainy day. Lemme guess? Kierkegaard? Kafka?"

"Marion! You're making fun of him. I won't allow it."

"It's all right," I said. "Now I can comment on his fishing stories."

"Well," she finally acquiesced. "I suppose there's nothing like being prepared? You can change in the den."

After the slight jolt, of which there were no doubt many, she regained her composure without a trace of misgiving. Her sweetness was hard to figure; it left you beaten if you didn't respond. I told her, plainly enough, I'd left the church but she only got friendlier, inviting me to visit, sending clippings. I'd put her off so many times I felt shabby, but since I couldn't find a ride I gave in. She was said to be an excellent cook.

Were it not for the sight of the forest out the window, the inside of their house put a guest back in the States. Precisely arranged furniture, framed pictures, a bookcase, covered sofa, easy chair with a reading lamp, potted plants, a short wave, phonograph, magazines, lacy curtains, a set of china in a polished cabinet, doilies on the arm chairs—no wonder the tribal people who saw the pastor's house spoke of it as a thing of wonder not realizing it counted as a hardship post to his friends back home. Even a machine for opening cans.

"I can't tell you how wonderful it is to see you," she practically sang as I joined them in the living room. "You're a godsend. I'm so delighted I sent Marion to town, otherwise he would have missed you."

She sat on the sofa, ankles comfortably drawn in, completely at ease, ever the perfect hostess even as she busied herself with her needlepoint. She looked well despite the climate, wore a floral print dress, a prim hairdo, an ivory cross around her neck, but her warmth more than anything attracted people; always gracious, glowing, her smile never wavered, her words never harsh.

"I hope you're hungry," she beamed. "The gravy needs a few more minutes. Do you like Danish meatloaf? New recipe," she twinged with excitement, "I've been itching to try it out on someone."

"We ran out of guinea pigs," the pastor added dryly.

"Marion...please. We don't know him that well."

"Don't worry," I said. "After my cooking..."

"Well, I never," she exclaimed. "Haven't you learned to cook yet?"

"I just can't get the hang of it."

"Well, all you need is to curl up with a good cookbook—in fact," she got up and went to the bookcase, "I thinnnk I may have something for you."

"And if that doesn't work," the pastor added, "try boiling it over low heat...with a little salt."

"Listen to the gourmet," she laughed. *"Chef d'une canne openaire."*

And the table. Wow. Center piece of swamp lilies, tall candles, banana leaf place settings, sparkling white tablecloth with matching napkins, delicate coffee cups in saucers, shiny silver, nothing an inch out of place—and me used to eating out of a frying pan. The pastor said grace. He thanked Jesus for sending them a welcome friend and asked for the strength to lead our black brothers out of darkness to the light of Christian knowledge. As soon as he finished, they cheerfully began passing brimming dishes of food: the meatloaf sprinkled with walnuts and mint, a light gravy, scalloped potatoes, broccoli hollandaise, pickled cassava greens, fresh rolls, real butter, a fruit salad with papaya and avocado, lemonade with a sprig of something green. The hungry season was over. Esther opened the dinner conversation (Henry Mancini in the background), "Tell us what you're doing. You must be up to your ears in work."

"No more than you."

"How's school? I marvel your schoolhouse is still standing. It seems to lean a little harder each time we go by. Come, have another. Don't be shy. I'll bet your children love soccer?"

"They certainly do. We're not quite world class but we're making strides."

"Making strides," the pastor chortled. "I warned you, he's got a sense of humor."

"Marion please, the fork is not a conversational aid."

"I'm making strides too," he winked.

"Well," she responded brightly. "I guess we're all making strides then. It's so easy to let things slip back here in the—Marion there's a little creature on the—thank you. Do your children enjoy school?"

"They're not really children. The fourth and fifth graders are mostly in their teens."

"Quite common in small towns dear," the pastor said.

"Our school's only five years old; they got a late start."

"But you have little ones too."

"Yes."

"How do you keep track of everything?"

"I farm out the little ones to the big ones, an old tribal trick."

"Just the same, I worry about you. I wish they hadn't put you way up there all by yourself."

"I'm okay," I smiled.

"Of course he is," the pastor chimed. "Nothing fazes this guy. He's the only guy I know—"

"How do you do it?" she whispered intensely. One of her rare interruptions. "Tell."

"...I...I try not to sweat the imponderables."

The pastor threw back his head. "That's a good one," he snickered getting back to his salad.

"Well, next time you're not...sweating," she said very precisely in spite of herself, "I wish you'd come for a visit. You can't be...I mean what's there to do up there?"

"I've got a box at the opera."

"Box at the...oh no," the pastor roared. "I warned you...he'll sneak up on you."

"You *are* a godsend! I've never met anyone so at home in the bush. I do wish you'd let us in on your secret," she said with that winning smile. "You know what I mean? It's so easy...to lose one's sense of humor up here."

"I don't know any secrets. Maybe I'm too dumb to be cynical."

"Why that's a splendid thought," she reflected. "Become as a child again. Yes, I like that. More meatloaf? Go ahead. Splurge." And she twinged with pleasure.

"It's really very good," I said. "Thank you for the care you've put into this lovely dinner."

"Why thank yoooou. You're very kind. By the way," and she leaned forward with her warmest smile yet, "I've been meaning to ask, Marion and I were discussing it just the other day. I know you're probably sick of the question but…how do you pronounce your last—Marion. Marion! On the vase! OH NO not again! One of those…damn water beetles! Ewwwoooo! OH PLEASE! Please be careful! It's a BIG ONE, tooo! Do something! I told Dworba OW NO NOT MY NEW TABLECLOTH! Hurry! GET IT out of here!"

Fine specimen. Two inches long. Jet black. You could see the barbed legs and mandibles in detail on the white tablecloth. The pastor eyed his prey, put down his fork, discreetly picked up a napkin. Pinching it tight, he got up and went out. She squeezed her napkin to her nose, squirmed horribly, shivering all down her spine, eyes like a terrified animal. When the outer door slammed she reached across the table and grabbed my hand. Her fingers trembled. When he came back he slipped behind her, put his fingers to her shoulders, kissed her, then she shivered once more and dried her eyes. Her face turned red with embarrassment. "I don't like the big ones," she whimpered.

"We can handle the little ones," the pastor explained, "but when they get as big as turtles—"

"Marion…please do not exaggerate," she said calmly, making a gallant effort to compose herself. "I'm sure the good Lord knew what He was doing when he made those awful things…but I don't want to know why." And she fought back the tears.

"Are we going to make it then?" the pastor asked.

"Yes, darling. Thank you."

"Isn't she a trooper?"

"Yes, she is."

"Well," she exhaled deeply, overcoming her embarrassment, "Now the floor show's over, shall we get back to dinner? Do you like the salad? Isn't it grand? Quite seriously, you should get out more. At least let us know you're all right." A sip of lemonade. "Some of your associates, and I won't mention any names, think nothing of taking the jeep and disappearing for the weekend. Last time they didn't return it until *after* Service. We had to carry the choir chairs on our heads. Not so much as 'Thank you.' The good Lord knows where they went with it."

"They couldn't get into that much trouble dear," the pastor assured her.

"Just the same, they could show a little courtesy," then to me, "Both Greg and Jim belong to our Church? And how many times have they come to Service? Once."

"The dedication," he added.

"Make that twice. And the little McMullen girl, such a sweet person—"

"They're just young dear," he said patiently. "Frankly I wish I had the energy to keep up with them, to visit some of the out of the way places—like yours."

"You do well enough, dear."

"I understand you had a snake bite?" the pastor asked.

"A month ago."

"He recovered?"

"Yes. Fortunately we got him to your hospital."

"Never hesitate. Make sure your people understand they are all welcome. You must have done some fast PR work."

"No. I think they brought him in desperation. The real flap came over the extra ten bucks."

"Bad show huh?"

"It got ugly. I never knew a man's life came so cheap. There was this soldier—"

"Armed?"

"Yes. I don't keep a lot of cash on hand—no thank you I'm finished—there's no reason to…I made a bad mistake. They expect a white man to have cash. I wound up begging that…oh my…I almost said a bad word. I beg your pardon, maybe I have been up in the bush too long."

"It's quite all right," Esther said reassuringly. "I'm sure he was whatever you were thinking."

"I always carry an extra twenty in my boot," the pastor said. "An old army trick."

"Marion, you never told me thaaat," she said very low.

"In case of an emergency dear."

"I never begged for anything in my life," I said. "It left a bad taste. I never really understood the humiliation of being impoverished; it's the humiliation that would kill me, not the want of money."

"Did you hear that Marion?"

"Yes, dear."

"Marion is also of the opinion there is more to poverty than material want."

"Grace," he said intently as though solving a mathematical problem, "that's the key."

"Well," Esther smiled, always a little out of breath, "I see we're about finished. May I suggest coffee in the living room where we're less likely to be attacked by whatever form the devil takes next."

When we rose from the table, I remembered to compliment her again and she beamed a ready response, her universe back in joint. Outside, a bell chimed six o'clock and treated us to a screened view of the chapel with its yellow electric light dangling over the door. Quiet drizzle. The conversation turned to the more immediate world of the Mission. Had I seen the marvelous woven baskets from the leper colony? Imagine the effort. What did I think of the people to people program? Did I know they were planning an eye care center at the hospital? Only the talking stage.

"More coffee?"

"It's not a new story," the pastor remarked lighting his pipe. "Your soldier. He's typical, they wander down to the coast, see all the pleasures that money can buy. Next thing he's out for the quick buck."

"But we've imported the notion of the quick buck."

"Indeed we have!" he said pointing the stem of his pipe at me. "That's why we've got to import the notion of Christianity to counteract it. Your soldier reminds me somewhat of Washington Cooper, about your age, fine boy."

He was launching into one of his interminable stories. If I didn't bail out now...

"Gee, I hate to—"

"Nonsense," Esther crooned. "Your friends will be up till all hours. Besides you haven't had dessert." Then with real delight, "Shall we tell him dear?"

"Wait until you hear this," the pastor beamed.

"Strawberry shortcake!"

"Strawberries?"

"Yessss! With whipped cream."

"...Esther. That's too big a temptation for a sinner like me."

293

CHAPTER 26

A PILL TO SWALLOW

Doc's note came several weeks in advance reminding me I was due for a thousand mile check up, an appointment I didn't dare ignore, and couldn't, since Akwoi, Lancelot du Lac Akwoi, had appointed himself my personal secretary pestering me every morning with a list of "engagements." The weekend of the twenty-first, Gbanga. Doc didn't like driving upcountry so we'd meet halfway, see some old friends—call it R&R.

The ride to Gbanga began with a rickety truck bouncing to a stop in front of Quolidobu's store and a gang of small boys scampering up the path to announce its coming. A cloud of rolling dust caught up from behind releasing a fit of coughing from passengers. The dry season. The road had become a river of dust. Passing cars made swirling eddies, trucks stirred it into a fog that settled on every surface, leaves turned ferrous brown halfway up the forest wall. From the distant hills, their path could be traced by plumes of reddish cloud that shot up from within the trees as invisible devils darted to and fro. Streams ran shallow. The earth hardened.

Inside, each bump struck a discordant drumbeat, each lurch threw people into each other and edged the slushing kerosene drum closer to the front, nearly onto the gasping chickens that lay on the floor with their feet bound. The bed was stacked with cargo—sacks of palm kernels, bundles of cloth, palm oil, pans of unshucked rice, a sewing machine, green bananas. Two goats knelt under the side benches. Twenty people jammed together where there should have been twelve. They sat uncomfortably but without complaint knowing the pounding they took was the price of going to town. What money they had, they carried in handkerchiefs clutched in their fingers; they carefully unfolded the corners before removing their fare one coin at a time. Small children hugged their mothers' knees while plump babies suckled in peace. Ten years ago the sight of an automobile would have set them bawling, now they rode in complete ease, old hands at it.

Wrosurlu drove, an altogether pleasant chap who enjoyed people and often stopped to flirt with women. When he stepped down to walk about town, he was again a Loma man, greeting people in tribal fashion, sometimes backing away in a short dance phrase of delight; but when he swung in behind the wheel he was all business, "Fiffy ce' ma', no palava, le' go!" In the cool mornings that attended the dry season, he wore a leather aviator's cap and chewed oranges to cut the dust. When he came to a hard piece of driving, he cut a mean figure with his angular face set in concentration, both hands gripping the wheel, bare feet pumping the pedals, the orange clinched in his teeth and the flaps of his aviator's cap flying in the wind.

Going to town was a luxury. When the day arrived, people were ready hours ahead, they wore their best clothes, sandals and a store bought shirt for men, lappas and head-ties for women, shorts, maybe a white T-shirt for kids. They climbed in, men first, then the women who very properly ignored the leering carboy who lowered the tailgate. Someone handed up their belongings amid excited shouts of advice and last minute requests to go along.

We bumped and lurched and choked for most of the day, but now and then the road leveled off and we rocked back and forth on the benches as we passed through small hamlets and alongside farms where people straightened up from their work to answer the horn. When he came to a village where he had a relative, Wrosurlu thought nothing of stopping for a friendly chat. There was always time; that was the key to their way of life. In the larger towns, he stopped to take gas and the passengers climbed down to stretch their legs. If the kids were lucky, they got a penny candy. Little things were luxuries. After mooching a cigarette, Wrosurlu beeped his horn and we were off, cruising town, beeping for fares. At the outskirts he shifted and pulled away from a troop of racing boys who tried to keep up while the carboy shouted challenges. A carboy attended the driver and collected the fare—if he could be trusted. Most enjoyed notorious reputations, bragged of their exploits, of impregnating multiple women while the driver relieved himself along the road. A favorite trick was to hang on to the tailgate and swing aboard while the truck gathered speed.

It was late afternoon when we pulled into Gbanga. It too had been a tribal village, Kpelle, but the coming of the motor road had effected a transition so rapid it must have suggested witchcraft to the tribal mind. The clatter of merchandise, growls of engines, drunken brawls, even the voice of choirs had shattered the quiet pool of tribal life.

Shadows had already begun to stretch across the road and up the whitewashed walls of the American compound. The buildings were well-kept, all white, secure, dry beneath sharp rooflines struck with square and plumb. Palm trees grew in perfect symmetry up and down the driveway, their trimmed trunks painted white halfway up, not a broken limb to rattle its dead leaves in the wind, grass cut with a lawn mower, indigenous plants manicured to match, maroon leaves with red veins spreading their color over the lawn like water lilies. And sidewalks! Square, no time to meander, the shortest distance a straight line. Only the electric lines sagged. Ample shade. Dappled sunlight. A grapefruit tree. It would have been altogether American were it not for a ghost or two, the native groundskeeper lazily swinging a machete for no reason he could see or Charlie #6 sitting cross-legged in the shade with his array of wares spread out on a mat.

Doc's jeep and two others were parked on the grass next to a bungalow-style guest house. The screened-in porch buzzed with a half dozen conversations—the usual subjects: the awful climate, inept natives, red tape, but all with youthful energy and a swig of beer. Jim Philips and Rick Ekleberry were well on their way.

"Late as usual," Peg smiled without looking up from a book.

"Got a bucket o' water?"

"The shower's inside. You're in the big city cowboy."

Afterwards I saw the doctor. He set up shop in an adjoining room. It was clean with drawn curtains and an overhead fan, but spare, except for a table, two chairs, a refrigerator. Doc had a great sense of humor. "What kind of dysentery? Diplomatic or Kamikaze?" He maintained there were three ways of contacting VD—toilet seats, bar stools, and doorknobs, the latter extremely rare, only two cases in medical history, the most celebrated back in Henry VIII's time. Tall, lean, in his fifties, he was a World War II veteran with thin hair pasted to his neck with perspiration; his skin very light, scarcely enough to hold the lines. He wore shorts, hike boots, a pullover shirt which didn't look very professional, but his hands gave him away; they had a life of their own moving quickly outside his conversation, flashing a shiny silver watch with a second hand no wider than the sandy hairs on his forearm. But in his serious moments—and they came without warning—his light gray eyes betrayed a depth beyond the scope of general practice. "Have a seat," he said matter of factly. For some reason he never joked with me. "So then," he said looking up from a manila folder. "We don't see much of you, do we?" Probing already.

"It's a long trip." It was hard being evasive.

"Been taking your aarlen?"

"Yes." Especially if he had you alone.

"Good. Let's have a look." He unwrapped a tongue depressor and examined my throat, then ran his hands down my neck, "You're tense. Relax," tapped my chest and back, finished with a quick look under the eyelids and in the ears. "Experience any fever? Passage of blood? Nausea?" I said no and he began preparing the shots. "Hear you had a bad time of it not too long ago," he said casually with his back turned, "Snake bite was it?"

"The guy lived. How'd you hear about it?"

"I got a long grapevine. Okay, let's find a spot." He swabbed my arm and inserted it with scarcely a prick. "Somebody spit on you." It wasn't a question.

"Oh that." How did he know? "It washed off. Rained that night."

"Good. Here, hold that a minute." He went back to the table. "Lots o' work huh?"

"Yeah."

"This one goes in the hip." He went about his business as though talking to himself. "Work can be good for you. But it can be a dodge too."

"So I've heard."

"That's it. You can button your shirt. Sit down a minute." He looked at me hard for what seemed a long time. "You look a bit glum," he said quietly, with eye contact.

"It's a pretty hard ride. Dusty."

He shook his head with a faint smile, "Dust washes off," then looked out the window. "Just like spit." I didn't like evading him. "Bad show eh? Must've been one of those army tough guys. Who was it said, "'Inside every tough guy there's a little girl crying for her teddy bear?'"

"He wouldn't have appreciated the humor."

"But that doesn't make it any less true. Well then. You're in pretty good shape otherwise. Keep taking your aarlen." Then, right out of the blue, "I've heard talk you're going native. As a rule I don't pay much attention to talk—"

"But you repeat it when it serves you."

"'Deed I do…You can't be one of them; you can't go all the way, remember that. A little thing like aarlen keeps you connected to your world; I always get nervous when people stop; it's not the malaria, we can treat that; it's the other ailment, the one we don't like to talk about."

"I'm having…" It didn't feel good dodging him. "second thoughts about what we're doing here."

"Ah."

"Whether we have the right to inform our conception of freedom onto others."

He leaned back staring at the ceiling, hands clasped on the back of his head. "Philosophical ailments. Worst kind. We can't seem to come up with a pill."

"We teach them to read, but the books tell them they're backward; we arm them against tyranny, but the guns wind up with tyrants; we advertise the good life but we have no idea what it is."

"You can't fix all that," he said softly.

"No but I'd like to keep from adding to it."

"Of course," he went on as though musing to himself, "you could come down to the coast sometime. I know a tolerable little French restaurant; I wouldn't mind listening to a cum laude analysis of the good life…oh don't look surprised. I have access to your complete file." He eyed me steadily. "Your old man worked in a steel mill."

"Yes."

"Mine worked on the railroad…Baltimore and Ohio, thirty years, wanted me to do anything but railroading. I don't know why. I always loved trains. The old steam engines, you could hear 'em whistlin' down the tracks on a clear night with the stars twinkling in the snow and the steam drifting off in the dark; it's the loveliest sound in the world, mournful, like a big iron baby cryin' for its mama. Bet your old man didn't want you down in the mill?"

"He wanted me to wear a white shirt and drive a Buick."

"Can you blame him? Poverty's not a lot o' fun…is it?" He looked away, uncomfortable. "You know when you finally grow up, the hardest thing has to be the realization the old folks aren't as stupid as you thought."

"I'm beginning to see that in our tribal friends."

"Think about it."

"About what?"

"Dinner."

"I'm afraid it wouldn't be very interesting. I don't have any bright answers anymore."

"Maybe that's good. Admitting your ignorance is the beginning of wisdom. Check Socrates on that."

"Now that's a rather sizable pill, wouldn't you say?"

"Yes, yes, it is. Most people gag on it."

"Well, I'll try not to," I said getting up to leave. "By the way you got one helluva grapevine."

"My colleague at Zorzor. We talk. Boring dinner conversation is my specialty."

Out on the porch people were in a party mood. Two cases of Heineken in a tub of ice, a tray of snacks, fruit punch, spiked, the Kingston Trio. I took a bottle and settled down in the corner. The others sprawled out around two wicker chairs, a footlocker, a hammock. The conversations ranged from swamp rice to third grade math books, now and then a comment about Vietnam. Some of us rarely saw each other: Scot, Rick, Barry, Andy, Jim and Greg from Zorzor, Jameson and Ernie, Ohio State and Michigan at peace at last with a quart bottle of Club Beer between them, Larry, a black from South Carolina and veteran of the early civil rights marches, Vladimir, a young Lebanese who found easy acceptance in this age group, Warren and his wife Laura, Shelia, Lizzy, and Peg, a tough little customer behind a plain appearance—she'd killed a rabid dog in her schoolyard with a machete.

And of course Maureen Brubaker. Given the climate women soon gave up on fashion, cut their hair short, junked their make-up and took to loose dresses—slacks or shorts being unacceptable. But Maureen kept up the good fight. She wore her hair long, well-managed, which took some doing, eye shadow and a fragrance noticeably out of place in the surroundings; her snug dresses were always properly pressed, often above the knee, not unusual in itself if it weren't for her missionary zeal, wide-eyed interest in native culture and an airy aloofness to everything else. She sang her way through life, oblivious to the unperfumed world and its many eyes. She'd written a letter to her hometown paper. "Each day I'm surrounded by a sea of poverty but I'm reassured by the gleam of hope on bright faces eager for the future." She actually wrote that—but neglected to mention the gleam in the eyes of her male companions. Rumor had it her native supervisor chased her three times around his desk before succumbing to the heat, but that may have been the stuff of legend. Incredibly she took a shine to my buddy Mark Creighton who didn't match up with anyone; yet she persisted until he moved out to the bush, which confused people even more. I chose not to ask him about it.

"Need a place to stay?" Jim asked innocently enough.

"Sorryyyyy," she sang out. "I just don't trust myself." And she waved "Bye-bye," backwards over her head gliding out on a cloud. Warren and Laura followed, she with a sympathetic smile to Jim, he with a "tough luck guys," to the rest of us. They had to step off the walk to avoid Rick. He stood ill-balanced trying to shake the flowers from an earthen pot—needed an ashtray. A clump of mud fell to the ground just as Maureen aligned her Italian sunglasses. "What's *that?* " she asked with exaggerated interest. He looked at her, swayed upright, "Doc's gonna take a collective urine sample instead of a mental health questionnaire. You're first!" And he thrust it at her. "No thanks!" she exclaimed and continued her exit unfazed, undulating, one elbow rigid at her side and the other hand at rest on the strap of her shoulder bag, the perfect model as she studied something in the distance.

Suddenly Jim scrambled out of the hammock. They hurried to the screen to watch her get in the jeep. High carriage. Easier to get through the mud, but no way to keep your skirt on your knee when you climbed up.

"I never thought it would come to this," Greg sighed.

"Someone up there's punishing us," Andy said.

"We never covered that in divinity school," Barry remembered, his favorite expression when things got rough.

"You guys are sick!" Peg snapped from across the porch. "Take a cold shower."

"Easy for you," Barry countered, "you don't sleep in a tent." He trudged back to his seat, all five foot of him, the bearded scholar beaten again.

After they drove off, Rick yanked the screen door open but it caught him on the rebound and he dropped his ashtray shattering it to pieces. "Ekleberry," Peg snapped, "will you sit down before you fall on your ass! And for God sake zip up your pants!"

"Excuse please," he said in dialect, looked down to check, caught his balance, fumbled and gave up.

"Oh forget it," and she went back to her book. Somebody threw a broom but he didn't get the message. Sheila continued her needle work checking him over her glasses.

"He's treating a case of parasites," Andy whispered. "He thought he had 'em licked but now they're alcoholics."

"Oh yeah, what's your excuse?" she asked.

"Mental strain, and there's only one known cure but the Doc won't gimme a prescription," he answered eyeing her while stretching a leg over the side of the wicker chair. Jim chuckled from the hammock, his arm fell lazily to the floor where he fanned through the pages of an old *Playboy.* Scot flipped an empty bottle into the shrubbery, Vladimir fingered a native drum. Then they pulled up a footlocker for some poker. Sheila dealt; a wicked player despite the knitting in her lap, she called Jacks wild and eyed Scot with a vengeance. Rick plopped down against the wall with his legs spread in front, drunkenly scratching a match several times. A lacrosse player at college, he'd lost weight—we all had—and now looked much older in his oversized clothes. His clear rimmed glasses with a band of tape at the bridge hung askew. He probably did have parasites. Jameson sat down next to him and said something private. Lizzy took the tray and went out to the kitchen.

Just as it looked like things were quieting down, a jeep tore into the drive sliding to a halt in the gravel. The driver was out and around the side before the dust caught up. Larry beamed a bright smile. The others perked up. "And here he is!" Larry announced triumphantly holding the door open. "Champion of the Meek! Wheelhorse of the Inept! Renowned Driver of Jeeps! Ladies and gentlemen I give you Raymond! Anthony! Orley!"

"What's this you sit around ya got nothin' betta to do gimme a beer."

Ray always livened things up. Larry started to sing, Ernie too, then the others. The lyrics were Ray's.

> *Hah Vah. Havah tequila*
> *Gee I can feel ya*
> *Quick, gimmie the salt*

Without missing a beat they draped their arms around each other and stepped into a lusty folk dance:

> *This is how we circumcise*
> *This is how we serve six wives*
> *Mama mia be precise*
> *The ending must very* **YOUCH**

"What's this Alcoholics Unanimous I've seen betta posscha in the palsy wawd."

"Posscha! You think you're in an Italian Restaurant?"

"We got comedians? This is Las Vegas?"

"What j'ya do with the prepuce Ray, make an arm band?"

"I hear they make good slingshot—"

"It's getting just a little bit gross in here guys," Peg intoned.

"We never covered that in Divinity School."

"I have no idea what they're talkin' about," Ray gaped apologetically to Shelia who didn't believe a word of it.

"One more verse Ray, aw come on, the fans are waiting."

"Come on Ray, the taxpayers want their money's worth."

"What's this? I drive a hundred miles I put in a hawd day—"

"Ray! Does gin work as well as tequila?

"Don't ask me I only drink boiled watta."

"Been in the bush lately Ray?" Vladamir cried.

"He means with your jeep of course."

"I got a clean drivin' recud. Everybody knows it."

"That's right!" Larry thundered. "Bashin' in the front don't count! It's only an accident if you crack your coconuts!"

"One scratch!" Orley yelled in disbelief. "One scratch! Now you wanna make a federal case you think you're in Selma you should be in Bellvue all of ya looka this shit twenny miles up the road you live like—"

"Tell us about it Ray."

"Ya can't even find the john—"

"Simply ring for the butler Raymond."

"Butla? I'd be satisfied with a papah bag, ya gotta drive thirty miles, then it's out in the woods you should see Sandas'. Just down the path he says, just down the path you're in the Gola Fawrest I expected to see wild animals."

"You're a long way from New Yawk Ray," Shelia said sweetly.

"I thought I'd neva find it, the leaning towa of Pisa, termites ate the foundation ya can feel it give. Will he dig a new one? That's too easy, aw you ready for this he takes a machete wacks a hole in the side runs a vine through you're supposed to sit an' hold on t' the vine. Inshawance. The Teutonic hero waiting the Fall of Asgawd and when you're done there's no paypa. What d'ya suppos'd to do go look for a soft leaf, with all those wild animals watchin'—"

"Sounds like a chance to practice your Tarzan yell, Ray."

"Yeah, Ray."

"Just once," Shelia wheedled.

"I can't do it with gentile ladies present—"

"Come on, Ray,"

"Yeah Ray. Just once—"

"Tawzanne was a rabbi, ya didn't know that did ja—"

"RAYMOND!"

"Okay, heah goes I'll have to stand up who's that out in the yawd?"

"Nobody!"

"Come on Ray," and this time she blew him a kiss.

He let go. The birds outside went quiet.

"It's an old Hebrew folk song, 'O come ye Gentile Maidens.'"

"Ray if bullshit were music you'd be a brass band," Lizzy quipped as she stepped in from the other room with a fresh tray of sandwichs.

"What's this where'd she come from how many maw' ya got locked up?"

"You're in polygamous country Ray."

"So ya jus' sit tha why didn't ya say somethin' you know I'm a sensitive person I'd never say anything impropa in front of ladies."

"Will you look who you're sitting next to?'

"Who? Hatchet lady? She can take ca' of herself as for the rest of ya you're ignorant I don't even want to discuss it Hi Doc how's your VD?"

Doc had quietly come into the room, helped himself to a beer and sat on a crate, his back against the wall. He was the only one who could keep up with Ray and now everyone came alert. The first punch had landed. The Doc took his time, studying the bubbles in his beer.

"Probably benign now in the dry season," Scot mused.

After a respectful pause the Doc pondered aloud, "It's been a long dry season." Then as an afterthought, "Hasn't it Ray?" He knew something. Orley groaned.

"How's that Doc?" Shelia asked.

"Nothing. Nothing at all," he hesitated, savoring the moment. Shelia cracked up. "A short time ago I happened to visit a little restaurant down in Monrovia and who should I see parting with his hard earned money like a farm boy in the big city."

"Foreign aid, huh Ray?"

"I have no knawledge—"

"Now Raymond, we don't keep these things secret."

"Ray, a date in this country—"

"A date! You mean—"

"Wow, a date, I almost forgot—"

"Come on Ray, the suspense is unbearable—"

"Who was the young lady Ray?" Lizzy asked with extreme finesse.

"None o' yaw business—"

"RayMOND!"

"It was Maureen," Shelia giggled.

The room exploded.

"I don't believe it! I don't believe it!" Jim screamed, fighting his way out of the hammock.

"She finally went out with somebody!"

"I thought she had the hots for Creighton."

"Does she know you're not Catholic Ray?"

"You actually took her out?"

"Once," Doc said with relish.

"Details Ray? Details!"

"Runs, hits, errors. Anything!"

"And afterwards, a quiet drive through the pawk."

"Dancing at the Waldorf."

"What does this mean as far as your Orthodoxy is concerned Mr. Orley?" It was Barry standing on the footlocker but still shorter than anybody in the room.

"Get back in your music box," Orley sneered.

"Well, IS IT TRUE?"

"How was I supposed to know the CIA was watching!"

"Well, do we have to wait to read about it on the society page," Lizzy cried pulling up a chair.

"Nothing happened!" Orley shrieked in desperation.

"They probably talked shop," Doc suggested.

"Come on Ray," Larry pleaded. "The old skills, ya never ferget, just like ridin' a bike."

Ray decided he'd better get it over with. "All we did was talk about povaty. Everybody's but mine." The room exploded again. "Extend the balance of payments, attract faweign capital, a lawn mowa mota in a new Fewawri and James Bond three tables away talkin' in 'is shoe." Doc sat back with a poker face twirling the beer in his glass.

"Have another beer Ray," Shelia winked at him. "They're all jealous."

It was late before things started winding down. The Doc spun a couple World War II stories, Ray advised on the availability of textbooks, always a hot topic and he was remarkably deft at getting around bureaucracy, Rick passed out on the floor, Jameson threw a sleeping bag over him. Shelia and Scot were the first to leave, then Barry and Peg, which raised some eyebrows, then Vladimir. The others got ready to spend the night at the compound. I thought I'd slip out easy enough, but the Doc caught me at the door with a sharp glance. "Take care."

CHAPTER 27

INCOMPATIBLE FRIENDS

Outside, darkness smiled. It fed on the feeble light of electric bulbs dangling from dirty lines, on the whitewashed tree trunks, the raked gravel in the driveway. It came to the window when you blew out the light, then deepened, emerging from its lair to claim its own. Vague forms seemed to grow out of the black earth, shadows died. The surface of the motor road reflected an eerie emptiness in stark contrast to the muted luxuriance of sleeping leaves. From the top of the slope behind the compound the entire town began to sink into the surrounding sea, soft flakes of yellow lantern light swarmed about the outskirts like moths to a mud hole, then settled at the edge of the solitary street where the Lebanese stores defined "downtown." Now and then a rooftop winked in the feeble moonlight. Over a crest in the road, only a dozen steps down the downgrade, the jungle closed in snuffing out rooftops and windows, compounds and churchyards—a change as abrupt as diving under water.

The jungle never sleeps. A soft flame burns black in a bottomless well. A shroud falls. She swirls her silk. The leaves murmur a savage lullaby, *comeba me,* reeds beckon the wind, *unto thee,* tree trunks clunk their upper limbs, *drumba see,* a night thing etches a silhouette on the sky. Deep in her belly a foetus moves.

Suddenly a horn shrieked. The glare of onrushing headlights tore open the night, the forest went rigid, its white limbs froze before the insane eye of the beast. I dodged into the ditch. An engine growled, a blast of dust rolled over into the leaves.

Chris lived two miles out of town down a side road. My best friend—yet I hardly knew him. He was a loner like me, the hermit of Gbanga, constantly in hot water with our superiors. Rumor had it he was a spoiled brat from a ritzy prep school, lived with a tribal girl and talked like a Marxist. People didn't like him for his brash indifference to protocol—once he'd walked out of an important reception in Monrovia when the talk turned to "our backward cousins in the bush." But for some reason he took to me. Whenever I felt uncomfortable with an idea, I tried it out on him. If wrong he'd only shake his head; if right he'd brush it off as too obvious for comment. Seeing him meant staving off futility another day. He never had smart answers, more often no answers at all. His damnable inattention forced me to say out loud what I could hardly say to myself. No matter how low I sunk, he managed to put it in perspective with a spacey non sequitur, "The universe unfolds exactly as it should. Who are you to throw a monkey wrench?" When we agreed things were hopeless, he got out his guitar.

We were roommates in training. San Francisco State. It seemed so long ago, the scent of eucalyptus and ocean air, banks of fog in and out like clipper ships, the Golden Gate piercing clouds. I could still see his bright face the first time he looked in the door.

"Hi. I'm Chris Creighton. Nice campus."

"Sure is," I said. "I don't know how they study out here."

"Did you hear the latest?" he smiled boyishly. "Somebody came up with the bright idea of putting the least compatible people together as roomies. They put a jock from Ohio State with a ukelele player from Michigan."

"It's a test."

"Of course."

"What do they want?"

"To see if we'll kill each other."

"And if we don't?"

"Then we get to go to Africa and pass on the skill. I got an idea. Let's do something together to see why we're incompatible. May I suggest a long walk on the beach."

"Excellent. I love the beach."

The next weekend we took a bus to Muir Woods, jumped a fence, found a fire trail and later the ocean which met us with a thunderous roar and a brisk wind. He took his shoes off and slung them over his shoulder; I did too. It was the first time I touched the Pacific. Ice cold.

"Who's your favorite composer?" he asked casually.

"Bach."

"Artist?"

"Van Gogh."

"Slugger?"

"DiMaggio."

"No. He's mine."

"Okay…Ruth."

"He was before your time."

"What's this another—?"

"Look," he said with concern, "if we can figure out why we're supposed to hate each other, maybe we can get on with being friends."

"Right. Great. Well, who's your—"

"Tschaikovsky, Andrew Wyeth, and a tie between Dimaggio and Ted Williams."

"I really like the desolation of *Christina's World*," I said. "It's like a homing call—"

"Shut up. I didn't ask for a critique."

"Right. I really don't know much about art. How do you feel about them telling us who's not supposed to be compatible?"

"They can play their games, but when they're done, I'm gonna decide who I like." He picked up a handful of pebbles. A sailboat fought the wind about a mile out. Beautiful day.

"What book made the most difference for you?" I asked. He wound up and pitched at a rock. Nice form.

"The Tao Te Ching."

"Walden."

"How so?"

"I think it's very close to the American soul."

"Try one."

"I can't pitch."

"Yes, you can. Aim high, let the wind bring you back. Do you like opera?"

"I love opera. *Carmen.*"

"Aida. Let's go some night!"

"On two dollars a day?"

"Right," he winced. "I guess we won't be hearing much opera for a while. So what do you like on pizza?"

"We can't even afford that. Anything but anchovies."

"Favorite jazz musician?"

"Benny Goodman."

"Miles Davis. Existentialist?"

"Doestoevsky."

"Euripides."

"He was before your time."

"This is getting us nowhere." He pitched his last pebble. "Let's see. Women. How many should a man have, ideally?"

"I'm basically conservative."

"Just give me a number."

"No more than fit under a bear rug on a winter night."

"That's sounds liberal."

"A matter of semantics."

"Then you really are…conservative?"

"Yes."

"Goldwater?"

"Not that conservative."

"Give me—"

"Adlai Stevenson."

"…We'll get back to that one. Let's try something else. What do you think of the situation in Mississippi?"

"Great idea. Why stop in Mississippi?"

"Where then?"

"Leningrad. Never heard of Russian Freedom Riders? Does that tell you something?"

"Okay hotshot. Let's see what color you really are." And he came up face to face, dead serious. "Do you advocate the violent overthrow of the United States Government?"

The sailboat, they were bringing her about. She fought the head wind then found her tack. Her bright sails billowed in the wind and a row of portholes gleamed along a sleek hull. "No," I said looking at him. "Yourself?"

As if pushed by an invisible hand, she dipped into a trough and came up smartly. We could see people on deck, her name on the bow but too far to read. "No," he said softly, "I shouldn't think so."

By and by we found a rock to climb, enjoyed the view but getting down took some doing. Then he showed me how to throw a curve ball, off the side of the forefinger to get the right spin. But in the middle of the next windup he stopped dead. "I almost forgot. There's one thing I should warn you about. I vehemently detest rock 'n' roll."

"Eine kleine schiesse musik?"

"No jokes. It makes me ill. This is it, isn't it? I can see you're not smiling. Well…there's always a monkey wrench. I'm warning you if you ever play that stuff in my presence I may do something violent, smash the stereo, throw it out the window. Oh, well. At least we'll go down with our guns blazin'."

"My good man. Allow me to inform you, I utterly abhor that vulgar noise and if you should feel so moved as to throw a radio, or the musicians themselves, out a window, I will assist you anyway I can."

We had a good laugh, pitched more pebbles, enjoyed a small lunch as we walked back—two bagels and a bottle of water. The sun never beamed more bright. It sparkled on the water with a fair wind in its reach, a pacific wind that tousled our hair as if in blessing of a new friendship at the beginning of a bold adventure. Though we wouldn't have put it quite that way, the world was ours to win. To a small town boy first time to the big city, that day, that glorious summer day had been the peak of something grand. The little incident in the Gulf of Tonkin was less than two months away.

I thought I heard a guitar. Very faint, miles away. His house nestled native style next to a clump of plantain, a dark silhouette with one window of orange lantern light a little off center and its stringy thatch resembling tail feathers. He sat on the back step, one leg extended, his pipe in the corner of his lips, lost in his music. The notes were of the forest, preserved in living wood; his fingers only released them like drops of water from a wet branch. One touch and they mingled with the crickets, found a new chord and rose to seek their kindred in the whispers of the teeming wilderness.

Oh but this magnificent night is worth retrieving. Her starry deeps and velvet whispers, static and spectra. How unabated the lust for life, her shadows and inscrutable dreams, her fair moon falling off to sleep. Are not these harbingers of something better? Yes, but we thrust our steel probes into living flesh and wonder why the heart stops. Me too, I thought my efforts might help; now it was clear they didn't. My education had prepared me for practical things, not the questions that come in the night.

Suddenly his fingers stopped. He put up the guitar and began refilling his pipe. "Need a place to crash?"

"What we're doing is all wrong!" I blurted out. "Christ I saw a kid in Zorzor with an 'Elvis' T-shirt! And Vietnam! The same damn thing on a grander scale. Where did we get this damn Louis XIV complex? How is it we get on so well with corrupt regimes? We don't believe in our...beliefs anymore. Damn you, are you listening?"

"I think so......wanna smoke?"

"No I don't want a smoke!" I snapped realizing I got carried away.

"But this is the pipe of peace," he said intently. "What's a matter? Don't you believe in peace?"

"I don't—where in the hell—"

"Don't ask," he whispered staring into the distance. "That's your problem. You ask too many questions. Stupid questions. 'Is the universe Hegelian?' Never anything anybody can answer. 'Where do I go to get laid?'"

"That's two different disciplines."

"They're all the same. Life revolves around the irrational. If you insist on going to hell, take the freeway."

He passed it to me but I coughed on the first draw. How could they inhale that crap? After a bit he spoke again as though to the trees, "Wanna see somethin' wild? In my room. Go on. There's a lantern on the table."

There it hung! Magnificent, an aura of deathly calm tilting downward. Wild terror. All the demons of night held in suspension. The polar opposite of a Grecian god straight from the reptilian brain. Yet…something familiar. In the sparse light it seemed to come to life. Even in the darkness, it betrayed another darkness, a silence that wasn't a silence.

A tribal mask! A real one! I'd never been this close! And alone with it. A soft black flame drifting outward from the protruding eye holes. I walked up close. Hair, cloth, nails, scraps of wire, raffia mane, all over an oblong base of blackened wood. Rough irregular lines suggested an unskilled hand but fell into asymmetric compliment in the emerging form. Angular shapes of the snout and cheeks, the uncoordinated lines of sight, even the rank untidiness defined it in space, but its stare, that penetrating fixity, that glare of recognition gave it its depth, its life. It just hung there, inert, secure in the secrets it held. It radiated sheer animality, a living spirit cast in rigid wood. Cracks in the grain, very old, yet smooth to the touch. Cowrie shells embedded in the…skin. Sticky. And a tiny bell under the chin, out of sight. The scent of the forest. The feel of—

"You…dare…"

Ouch!

"Touch…this sacred face."

No!

"What? Can't speak? Cat got your tongue? Am I a beetle on the dinner linen? Come. Never touched a wild thing? Yes, you see me as I am; you are one who wears a mask. Well, go ahead, scratch my hair, no one's done it for some time. Yes, I speak as in a dream but stoutly to those who do not flinch."

"Who are you?"

"A voice…a human voice behind a slab of polished wood. Such are gods and kingdoms made. My name? Names are but trinkets to trade with strangers. In Kpelle I am Nafu, in Loma, Nyamu. I have so many I cannot *remember; they are as leaves to the passing seasons. Yes, I speak your tongue. I speak a thousand tongues, I yield a thousand ages. I am darkness primeval; I am the terror behind the seventh seal, the void you cannot fill. So then. God is dead. You no longer believe in yours nor mine in me, you cannot sleep nor I awake, and here we meet at a loss for words lest our whispers echo back in laughter. A fine day indeed."*

"This...I...this entire...conversation—"

"'Constitutes a psychotic episode' is the crude terminology, and your medicine men understand it but crudely; they would encage the human spirit in a spate of words and publish it in a book. Nay. The human spirit is not a billiard ball that dances to a man-made law, it is neither measured in an inkblot nor purchased for a pound of gold. Its essence is inverse to the flesh that probes it; it forever rejects—this very moment is rejecting—all efforts to understand it. It lives in darkness, yet feeds the sunshine. To know its highest reach is remembrance of its foulest depth. If you would know your sacred soul, know the darkness from whence it came. A psychotic episode indeed. You who flaunt every convention your world requires, cast your elders in the role of fools, mock tradition in ribald songs—worried about so small a trifle as a case of madness? I could smile had I not this face of wood."

"I cannot...believe in the supernatural."

"But nature and myself are twins of a common conception. There is none more natural than me, nor anything so supernatural as the mystic revolutions of mindless atoms. You are a child of your time, so young, your country a paltry two hundred years. You are spoilt children in a house of clever toys yet to know a purpose from a prince. My years are in the thousands. I was old before Egypt saw the Nile, before your virgin continent felt a human foot."

"I...I shouldn't be talking to you. Who are you?"

"I am Nyamu, Spirit of the Forest and all that moves therein. I am power, I am lust. Of mighty mountains the upward thrust, I curl an orchid's color, abide in the lingering breeze. I sing in every sunrise. I marvel at the howl of wolves in the hollow of the winter wood. I am of a time when men and beast were of a singular stock. I have stirred the virgin mists over a green and girlish earth, struck Promethean fire, shaped a million lips to the edges of a prayer, sucked forbidden fruit, thrilled to the scream of the kill!...What is true abides, beauty wastes no smile on grief. Change is but an eddy in the daytime air, the weight of night holds firm these minuscule revolutions, its starry deep burns not for nil."

"Who are you?"

"*I am the voice in the furnace pipe. Remember? Your third birthday at Grandma's? You froze in fear yet asked my name; and Grandma found a birthday cake then a story in her apron pocket? A little kitten lost its way, nursed at a potato sprout and went to sleep in Nanny Goat's ear. I spoke to you then, or must I tell tale of a cold and wordless hired hand who stoked the furnace by night and cried within for the son he never had?*"

"How did you know that?"

"*Is not one fiction as good as the next? Do you think you can live without such tales? I am the teller of all tales. Are not such fictions children of the human brain? Is not this brain a child of natural law? Can the rumblings in its basement have less right to life than neutrinos or supernovae? Nay, I am the very Fiction that sired Truth. Know me and she will beg to tell her wildest tales.*"

"How do I know—"

"*I am Nyamu, Spirit of All that Knows. I am Silence. I am Wonder. Every whisper, I absorb; I hear every feather that falls of a storm. To every rhythm comes a life, to every hurt a use; even hunger has its work, it keeps sharp the hunter's spear. To give him charity is to take his edge. You've come to see your philanthropy as a devil in disguise. Indeed. But do not give in. Make whole your singular spirit. It is the only safe refuge you will ever know. It will encompass tragedies as great as mine. You are startled that I speak with such resolve? When you bemoan your lack of it? Do you take me for a slab of wood? I have flown with eagles, traded horses with unlettered Fausts. I forever find new ways to speak, even through lips as pale as yours. Mark me well. Your false face will one day crumble too. And without it where will you be? A naked soul. But a naked soul is virgin earth. There you hear the mountains slumber, sunlight sleeping on a blushing leaf, these the most natural things of all. Every insect knows as much. Yet you! You deny the magic. Do not play the dummy with me! I know very well you hear voices, you needn't deny it me, you deny it badly enough to your friends. Shall I tell them you converse with the evening breeze and inquire of Mistress Night? And your doctor worries about your 'health.' You are a curious lot. Why does the word 'magic' send tremors through your heart? I've yet to see a white man give it due. Perhaps if magic exists your machines will betray you? So you make a world without it to keep them running, which is to say you've given them a power greater than their own, a magic touch indeed. You believe in love and joy and numbered law, even in the power of a written word to fly a thousand years and blossom in a foreign brain, but not the magic of a single sunrise. If you weren't so naive, I'd call you biased. Hear me now! Magic is the heart of all that is. It does not allow things afloat in air; rather holds them down to earth. It is natural as the deep of night. Magic makes every birth a virgin birth, every sunrise sacred. Here is touchstone to the rarest gem, the human invention most practical of all. Yes, practical! How else could we have endured all these wretched trials, these hungry aeons you scarce imagine? Try migrating north to meet an ice age coming south. Do you suppose we survived by chance? Are you arrogant enough to think you can survive on wealth alone? Is nothing sacred to you? Will you replace this primal need with mindless escape! What bumpkins in Broadway suits. Will your gadgets save you! Machines more vile than demons in the deep of hell! Oh, yes! I have watched the 'progress' of your war machines in our deserts to the north. I have felt the point of tempered steel piercing naked flesh, marveled how the human juice is squeezed from living screams, how the stumps of arms enmesh in tracks of burning tanks, I have sniffed the charbroiled flesh, heard leg bones snap like kindling sticks, run in terror from screaming bombs, pitied the howling babies in their headless mothers' arms. I have shivered in the mud at Ypres, walked unseen at Austerlitz. I have pondered the ungodly mushroom clouds. Now to abort the babies to save them from this holocaust. Oh, yes! I have looked into your brave new world! I am much distressed with what I see! Yes, I! The blood stained savage! Have witnessed all! And I...your kindred spirit...have gleaned my own demise. I can no longer endure the frenzy of whirling wheels. My time is near."*

"Surely...you cannot die."

"All that lives must die. And you! The weakest of all, will be the death of me. I have withstood the scourges of time; I cannot withstand your humanity. Fortune hunters took our riches, slavers took our sons, but you! You! Would have our hearts and minds! Today the young men look to you. They read your books and forget their ancient rites. You! With your talking ribbons and easy friendship. They think you have the stronger magic and follow without a thought. And what will become of me? An anachronism on a museum wall? Know that your most splendid works will one day grace a foreign museum too, perhaps not far from me."

"Forgive me."

"Rubbish! Do not fall prey to guilt; it is deadly poison. Stand straight. Do you think I want the world to know my mortal foe slumped at the shoulder? Cast your eye to the future not your shoetops. You are the victor! Start acting like it! My time has come; this century is my last. So be it. Yours is the hour

to speak. Fate has cast you forward on the world's stage. Do not miss your cue. A victory cry is but prelude to the next decline. Meet both with grace. Keep circumspect this law—nothing vital comes with ease. Calm your heart with understanding. Know that life is not perpetual youth. A thing of beauty can never last—but it can be born anew. Do not hide from sorrow, but break out the prison of its keeping. Temper your spirit with tears but feed it with joy. Stay a child. Listen to the wind. Mark the rhythm of the years. There are songs you've yet to learn. In the caldron of your troubled heart dare perform the magic rite...transmute hatred into love."

"Why are you talking to me?"

"I talk to those who listen."

"You are not of my world. This is the twentieth century. I cannot believe in evil spirits."

"I am not evil."

"You are everything science has overcome."

"I am everything science cannot overcome."

"Five thousand years of civilization have driven you away."

"I have driven five thousand years of civilization to fruition."

"You are alien! You are everything my learning forbids! If I talk to...I will be...people will say...all is lost. Very soon men from my country will go to the moon. Can you appreciate how far we've come?"

"Nay. Can you appreciate how far you've yet to go?"

"What do you want of me!"

"I want you to bury me in the past as you claim to have done. But to do it you must be strong—only without me you are weak. Come then, since you are so bold as to penetrate the sanctity of my space, do not stop half way. Dare to look the devil in the face."

"And if I don't?"

"Hear me well. Fear is not the enemy you take it for. Follow it to its source, it will show you truth as in a mirror. You will know the essence of my heart, you will embrace my very wife. You have nothing to fear but fear itself as your venerable ancestor has said."

"I would know what you know."

"The ugliest thing of all?"

"The mushroom clouds."

"Indeed. The 'medicine' of Alamogordo. I trembled in the warmth that morning. The idea was to transmute the troubles in the human heart, not the elements of the earth. Now see what black magic you've wrought? Can you hear the babies screaming?"

"Yes."

"And their mothers?"

"Shrieking."

"And they will make my savage rites—"

"Look like child's play—Help us. I fear the future. You're right, we're children in a house of dangerous toys. I don't know the answers anymore, I don't know where to look. We're lost."

"The answer is in your heart. Not on the moon."

"Help me find it."

"Would you know your very heart?"

"Yes."

"In the deep of the darkest night?"

"Yes."

"Do you know what that entails?"

"Tell me."

"Prepare…for an arduous journey."

"When?"

"It has already begun."

"What do you mean?"

"You always wanted to be explorer, let me assure you there are uncharted regions you've yet to visit."

"What will I find?"

"Me."

"But I already—"

"Not in my natural element."

"Where…would that be?"

"In the heart of darkness. If you touch me then and do not flinch, you will find what you seek."

"Touch you? Is that all?"

"Hell overflows with those who've failed."

"Will I survive?"

"Perhaps."

"Will we meet again?"

"Perhaps."

"How will I know you?"

"I will say hello."

"And if I fail?"

"I will walk our favorite haunts alone and contemplate my shoetops."

Next morning thick bars of yellow sunlight came streaming through the porch screen like brilliant rivers spreading fields of dewy jewels in the grass while torrents of birdsong lifted upwards as though in answer. Why do they sing at the sunrise? In the distance, two low hills like islands in the mist. Nearby an open field and people already at work, a thatched shelter, a drawn out call met three children coming single file the other way. One carried fire. He walked quickly, his eyes fixed on a tin of smoking coals. A dog stretched, then lay back down.

Chris's hammock hung diagonally across the porch overlooking a wobbly table cluttered with papers, specimens of soil, a typewriter. Behind it a brick and board bookshelf sagged under the weight of plumbing tools, a pump, labeled samples of drinking water. Rain gear and a shovel in the corner, spilt tobacco and a paperback on the raffia floor mat. Virginia Woolf. Airline posters, a bull fight in Spain, some children's drawings on tablet paper, two games of tic tac toe penciled over the whitewash.

I had a dream. I met an old friend—couldn't place him. Then he spoke to me in a foreign language but I understood every word. Strange. I had the feeling he'd fallen on hard times. He gave me hell about something, something insignificant I thought, but then we talked about taking a trip.

I unwrapped my blanket and rolled out. "Want some breakfast?" Chris asked from out in the kitchen. I went outside and splashed some water on my face. I had to have another look.

It was altogether different. Daylight robbed it of its power. It looked harmless, dusty, old—very old, as though it had lain in a trash heap for years. I walked up close. Termite holes on the snout, mold in the crevices, dirty, dead. Yet something remained. An emptiness that wasn't an emptiness, a faint memory emanated from the eye holes staring listlessly into space like a stuffed teddy bear in grandma's attic. How far away. Once it struck terror into the hearts of believers, molten spirit flowed through its form. And now? A curio for a voodoo shop.

"Tea?"

"What? Oh. Sure."

"Did it speak?" he smiled.

"Yes. No! It has a presence don't you think?" I said coming back to the kitchen.

"I'd call it personality. Sit. Grapefruit?"

"Where did you get it?"

"Toast? It's different by daylight, isn't it?"

316

"Yes. And you're right, it has a personality, a strong one. You never have to ask who's wearing it, it absorbs the person behind it."

"You still trying to figure out their metaphysics?"

"I can't get a handle on it. Our entire tradition is based on clarifying an unknown, reality behind the appearance. They don't have to do that. I can't understand the relation between an outward mystery and an inner compulsion to leave it alone."

"That sounds like a good place to start."

"It's not. I keep trying to understand. The idea's to not understand. Is that burlap? The lining?"

"Raffia maybe. Why?"

"My grandmother had a burlap apron, I didn't know it was so…universal. Where did you get it?"

"Monrovia."

"Monrovia?"

"It's a long story. Originally it must have been stolen by someone who, shall we say, lost his tribal sympathies. After several years it showed up in an art shop on Randall Street. Somehow the cult found out, which isn't extraordinary with all the tribal boys down there. The weird part is how they found me. One night I'm playing my guitar and these two dudes—how shall I put it, they would've been a little out of place at the country club—are standing there like fence posts. They had a younger man with them, about our age; he spoke fairly good English. They asked me to help them get it back. So I went down and bought it."

"How much?

"Eight hundred."

"Eight hun…where in the—"

"Don't ask," he said in his familiar way. "I couldn't stand the thought of it winding up in some damn 'collection.' They haven't come for it yet. Did you know in the old days, the artist who executed it was himself sacrificed after he finished? And he must have known. It kills the first thing that touches it. You believe in God?"

"No. Do you?"

"No. But I envy those who do. Their storybook Eden can't stand a day against modern science but once you leave, as the man said, you can't go home again."

"But if you stay you never grow up."

"One day we were talking about God, the kids and I. There was this little guy, about five, he pressed his fists into his eye sockets so hard I thought he'd hurt himself. God was something he wasn't supposed to see, that's all he knew. That little boy believed. Ourselves, we've traded God for technology. Maybe we've been had. When I touch it, it's just a piece of wood. That's what God has become."

"Why don't you try talking to it?"

He looked exasperated then smiled, "I come from a rational tradition, math and physics, quantify it or forget it. I suppose we all inherit the sins of our fathers. If I spoke to it, I'd only get the uncomfortable feeling of doing something unhealthy. I lack your…cosmopolitanism."

"I'm no better than you."

"But you stare at a piece of wood half the night?"

"I guess I'm not a clock watcher."

"What do you see?"

"Where?"

"Where the hell ever you're looking!"

"Nothing. Same as you."

"Does it speak?"

"No."

"But you listen?"

"Yes."

"What do you hear?"

"Silence."

"That all?"

"Maybe that's God's most eloquent speech."

"But you don't—"

"I believe in silence."

"Tell me about it."

"That would break it."

"Ever hear of Heisenberg?"

"Who?"

"Werner Heisenberg. When we attempt to observe something very small, like atomic particles, the system is so delicate the probe itself may alter the structure of what we're observing. We can never be certain what we know is entirely objective or something we've in part created. We observe an observation. As far as the external event, we only approximate it with higher probabilities of certainty, which means there must be uncertainty as well—as a constituent of reality."

"What's that got to do with the availability of safe water in Gbanga?"

"I dunno. But we keep probing. Gimme your canteen."

He filled it at one of three filters he was testing while I got my things together. After packing his gear, he flipped open the screen door and ambled down the steps.

The sun was up. People were about. Women worked at their rice mortars and kids played in the dirt. There were two other houses I hadn't seen, a hamlet of five altogether. Someone shouted from up ahead, two kids ran to catch a car on the motor road. We could see the dust but he called them back and took a footpath through the bush. We walked awhile in silence. It was going to be another inferno.

"Heard about your little protest," I said.

"The placard? Just a reminder."

"What kind of reminder?"

"This dignitary was supposed to come through. The locals wanted to make an impression so we lined up, military formation, the whole damn school, sick, lame, everybody. In the rain! Half hour, forty minutes. Ca' we go insi' yah? Oh no. They finally came through like a bat out of hell, motorcycle escort, scattering people like leaves. I only got a glimpse of him asleep in the back seat with his head buried in a stack of white pillows, probably passed out, windows rolled up, private chef in the next car, totally oblivious to the potbellied kids standing in the rain."

"But the placard?"

"Just a piece of cardboard."

"What did it SAY?"

"'You're late.'"

"That's all?"

"I didn't have a lot of time, in fact I had to flash it at 'em like pit crew at a racetrack."

"But the guy's asleep!"

"Apparently someone wasn't. A couple weeks later I get a note from Richardson, drop in for a little visit. I'll say this. That Caddy came by a hummin'. They sure know what to do about these potholes back in Detroit."

"Richardson pissed?"

"He took it pretty well. Kept his composure, offered me some of his pipe tobacco. I didn't offer him any of mine. 'I can appreciate your frustration,' he says. 'Under the circumstances I think I'd have acted no less impulsively; however'—and the 'however' came out like a switchblade. He asked about you. Wants to know if you're going native."

"What *in the hell—*"

"Hear about the congressman? Right here in Gbanga, the hub of the world. They were carting him around like a diabetic in a candy factory. 'You're doin' a fine job!' The dumb ass wasn't even out of the jeep. So he stands there pumping my hand, I could've been preaching Marxism for all he knew."

"Can you keep a high level secret?" He looked at me with a sinister grin. "I'm going to try to make it to Kpodokpodo. I've heard it's beautiful. Isolated."

"And they're going to have the answer in Kpodokpodo?"

"No. Probably just another mud hole. I heard some boy scouts tried it last year and damn near got lost but good."

"They were experienced back country people and Richardson *did* lose his composure over that one."

"They were overloaded. A rubber raft? Jesus."

"Got a map?"

"Sorta."

"A compass?"

"…A compass is for somebody who's already lost."

"Of course. You'll navigate by the flights of birds."

"Even better, I'll have Moses with me in case we come to a wilderness…one of my students."

"When are you going?"

"Midterm."

"How are you going to get across the Lawa?"

"The Lofa. There's supposed to be a bridge."

"Says who?"

"The old men."

"What if they're wrong?"

"They say they've crossed it."

"What if you can't find it?"

"…You ask too many questions. Stupid questions. How do I get across? Never, What's on the other side?"

"What if the bridge no longer exists!"

"That's obviously a bridge I will not cross when I come to it." His face softened into a weak smile, then a devilish one. "Take me with you," he whispered.

"Can't…Richardson mustn't know about this one yah?"

We parted ways at the edge of the marketplace, already a hubbub of loud horns and high headloads, shouts and orders, children darting about, goats bawling. The barrel-chested Lebanese traders watched in ponderous detachment from across wooden counters of adjoining stores jammed into a hundred yards of frontage along the one dismal street mesmerized by the wail of Arabic music from Japanese radios, loud enough to drown the fiercest tribal bartering. Chris made his way up the street in the midst of it all, stopped, turned and spread his feet Dodge City style, switched a matchstick in his teeth, "I said sundown Billy."

CHAPTER 28

TROUBLED CROSSING

We got to it by early afternoon. They gave a shout, put down their loads and started running. We'd had a hard morning trudging through another murky swamp. I was beat. I slipped off my knapsack trying not to rub my raw spot. We had spent an uncomfortable night in Dawawoli; it had rained again, the roof leaked, lice in the bed. But now! Right where the old men said it would be. I felt a little silly for doubting them. Akwoi and Kwokwoiyea were already scampering across.

Made of the bone and sinew of the jungle itself, vine and raffia, two great cottonwood trees anchored it on either side, each with a bamboo ladder and rope handrail leading to crow's-nest twelve feet up; there a round foothold resembling the bottom of a wicker basket narrowed into an elevated footpath eight inches wide swaying effortlessly thirty feet over the water. Two support vines underneath. Several strands of braided root the thickness of a man's arm ran parallel but wider apart—handrails. A vertical mesh of raffia rope dropped to the foothold forming a V. Towards the middle at irregular intervals heavy support vines flew up and disappeared into the high branches over the river. Not a crack of sky. Not so much as a ruffle in the anchor trees. It stretched across like a spider web, yielding to interior stresses, absorbing movement like a diaphragm. It had the resilience of living tissue, yet two of us couldn't take up the slack on one of the supports. If something pulled one way, it drew taut the other. Only the absence of green leaves suggested it wasn't alive. And it responded to the slightest touch like an empty canoe, listing in the wind, then taking the weight. Walking on it gave the impression of being aloft. Movement sent a shiver up and down its length; the rushing water beneath, the illusion of flight. You had to focus on the foothold, one step at a time. Quick if you bore a headload.

I made my way to the middle testing as I went, lost balance once or twice but quickly learned to pull on the handrails in the opposite direction. Like a swing. Fat tree limbs felt your mistake and pulled you back. Signs of repair alternated with signs of use, fresh vines spliced into old, knuckles of knots worn smooth. A beautiful spiral cobweb in one of the joints moved in perfect unison with the rest of the structure. A blueprint! But no trace of Spider. Perhaps he went to market with his wife. I found a comfortable spot, leaned back with my arms outstretched along the rail and eyed one of the suspending vines as it vaulted into the leaves twisting under tension until it ended in a noose around a high bough another thirty feet up. After you acclimated to the movement it was quite comfortable, like riding in a boat.

It undulated like a wave when they came running back beaming with excitement. This, one of the highlights of the trip. Akwoi jumped up and down trying to make me loose my balance. When it didn't work he tried another tack. "Is our Brooklyn Bridge. You want to buy? I make you sweet price. Twenny fi' dollah. Wha' say?"

The others laughed but didn't get it. Where was he getting this stuff? We relaxed a bit, enjoyed a few more jests, decided we were hungry and climbed back down. "Think you can find some dry wood?" While they were off, John and I washed out the cooking pot. Then we unpacked some cups and a bottle of cooking water. He smoothed some powder on my red spot; I checked his skin rash. At the base of the bridge a clearing of bare earth surrounded a fire pit and two bench logs. We got comfortable. Soon Kwokwoiyea was back with a length of hollow log that would be dry inside. He split it with his machete and after sending up a cloud of white smoke, we finally got fire, musty but enough to heat a pot of soup. I felt better now. Then we broke out two cans of chocolate pudding for dessert, a luxury we'd been saving for the right time.

Afterwards we sprawled out. Moses cleaned his teeth wit a sharp stem, John and I lay back and studied the treetops, Akwoi took out his journal and began sketching the bridge. Kwokwoiyea edged down the bank by himself and squatted next to the water peering down its course or following a floating stick, sometimes adding one.

He and the river shared secrets. Both were careful thinkers, always on the move. He hated waiting without a good reason and since he knew the ways of the forest well enough to hunt with the older men, consenting to this trip, to the likes of Akwoi and myself, was an unexpected compliment. Without words we confirmed him our leader the first day; yet he didn't look the part, rarely spoke, never raised his voice. When he stopped in his tracks, we did the same; when he hurried, we fell in step. His quiet manner inspired confidence.

When he paused before a fork in the path and took a road less traveled, I felt a chill but soon a solid faith; he read the "signs" with ease and I followed him, a man of sixteen, remote as a lost language but in the bush close as a brother. He never said much. No bravado, no jokes; an inner strength spoke for him. Always gentle, circumspect, never a curse, his eyes were set in narrow slits oriental style, but the wide gaps between his wide teeth formed an easy smile; otherwise his smooth skin covered his feelings like a blanket. He came to school occasionally, usually on rainy days or when we played soccer. He was good at figures, enjoyed books with pictures of animals, but never took part in discussions, rarely asked a question and read aloud only with prodding. His was the mind of a hunter; it belonged in the forest. Unlike the others, he kept his one tribal name politely declining a surname out of a book—he didn't carry excess baggage.

"What are you looking at?"

"Eh no," he answered with a soft grin. So much for his meditations on muddy water.

"Is it rising?" Maybe a practical question would coax him into conversation. But no. Moses came to his aid.

"Eh yah, you see de watah brown. He caddy sma' woot. Whe' he do dah one, he coming beeg. Whe' you see insi', clean watah, he go-eeng dow' to slee'."

Kwokwoiyea was right. The day didn't encourage conversation. The lazy sweep of silky water said "Forget it." Upstream it muscled around a broad bend sliding out of the trees like a sleek snake. The rains had worked it into creamed coffee—smooth, thick, effortless considering its bulk as it pushed through the forest pulling at strings of rubbery branches, ripping broken roots out of the bank, upturning them with clumps of mud in their teeth and fresh leaves in tow as they shot under the bridge betraying the true speed of lazy water. Upcountry rivers rose with surprising suddenness. Knowing when they'd reached their peak required a sensitivity to the bush that came from being a part of it. Mud-blanched leaves marked the previous high water, a full six feet above our fire, and even above that, debris clung to the crooks of branches. Not a good place to spend the night. We'd have to be moving in a bit.

Up above an intricate green city, streets and avenues of arboreal life, houses and parks, sirens of birdsong and hardly a chink in the roof, a world unto its own with no thought of the heavens above or the water below. Had the river torn off its support, it would have repaired the breach in a single season.

So strong the upper network, sometimes a fallen tree stopped halfway down, held up by its hair, while the water washed dirt from its exposed roots until it could send down new—thus seeming to walk along the bank if seen from a century away.

"Wha' you looking?" Moses asked.

"Nothing." I lay flat looking straight up.

"You as' de ma' wha' he see i' de watah. Wha' you see i' sky?" It had been a silly question.

"I see a big city with streets and houses, a minute ago I saw a small squirrel running along one of them." They came alert searching the treetops. Moses drew his slingshot from his hip pocket rising to his feet in one smooth motion, his fingers searching his belt pouch for a pebble.

"Whe' he?"

"He's gone now."

"Eh yah," he sighed in disbelief. "De ma' see mea', he canno' opah 'is mouff."

Meat. I forgot again. They were hunters. By and by Moses put away his slingshot but kept searching, Akwoi tossed a stick in the water and after we settled back again, his voice came floating through the air in mock civility. I was to pay for my mistake.

"You! Mr. Fat Squirrel! Good afternoon yah. How do you do. Mr. White Man send you greeting—" He couldn't finish. Their shots of laughter rang out like artillery. Moses drew his knees into his chest in agony, John hid his face, even the immovable Kwokwoiyea shook at the shoulders as he grinned the other direction. Akwoi revelled in his—

"There he is!" A reprieve. Despite the noise, it was back, scampering along the same limb. This time my finger gave them a target. Instantly all four went creeping along the bank picking their way through the underbrush. The squirrel had their total attention. It went about its work without the slightest awareness of its pursuers; however it was over the water. If they got him now he'd fall in. So they waited. Kwokwoiyea and Moses squatted in the mud halfway down the bank, their slingshots ready, eyes fastened above. Akwoi stood erect, motionless; and John coming up behind stopped mid-stride, his back heel off the ground, face upward, quiet as a candle flame. Moses chewed something. They spoke in pantomime, understood each other at once. Then he turned and motioned me to come. Perhaps too much silence wouldn't do; but no, it kept jumping to its business. John's eyes danced with delight. He gestured the handle of his slingshot towards me. Now I understood. The etiquette of the hunt required the first shot to the first sighting—if possible. The others didn't seem to object, which was a little odd. We all knew I'd miss. But tradition was strong. I took it and pointed the handle at Kwokwoiyea. He acknowledged by lifting his.

After a bit the squirrel ran along the limb, jumped to another and darted inside a knothole before anyone could get a shot. Now it was over the bank almost directly above. They backed off for a better angle. Soon it was in the door of its nest but a hit would have knocked it back in. No one moved. Not long and I started to tire but they seemed to thrive on standing perfectly still. But the waiting finally paid off; it squirted out of its den and paused in the crotch of a limb just below. But that brief pause and Kwokwoiyea's pebble met as one count of a larger sequence.

It fell in a graceful dive. But when it hit the ground, the jolt must have brought it back to life. It quickly scurried for cover in a deep thicket at the base of another tree. Now no need of silence. Their shouts went up as they descended on it. Moses called for his cutlass. John ran to get it while Akwoi danced about shouting orders and getting in the way until Moses showed him a fist. They burrowed like pups. Kwokwoiyea chopped furiously at the thick brush; they all tore loose leaves out of the way. As they worked they addressed their prey in controlled pleasure. "You fine, Sqwaddle. We wi' ea' you oh." Their voices bore no perverse joy of killing, only the thrill of victory. They spoke to it lovingly, as if to a friend. "I comeeng to catch you now, oh. You Sqwaddle, you no' run 'way yah? Whi' ma' watcheeng. He see you. He see everytee'."

The end came quickly. They cornered it, Kwokwoiyea thrust his arm into the roots of the thicket. His eyes looked away while his fingers searched. He grimaced then pulled it out by the back of the neck holding its teeth away. Moses handed him a cutlass and he calmly struck it with the dull side at the base of the head. As we walked back he held it delicately between his fingers while he sucked the bite on his other hand.

They had it dressed in no time. John did the honors while Moses squatted before the fire blowing into the smoldering coals. Akwoi went for wood. They divided these tasks without comment. It would set us back another two hours but what the hell. Fresh meat was something special, dessert. It looked young, hardly worth the effort. They skewered it to a stick, fixed it over the fire and watched intently as it began to crackle in the stream of smoke. "It doesn't look like there's very much meat on it," I said.

I knew it the instant my words were out. Another faux pas. They shot glances at each other. As I was to learn later, eyes wide open I'd walked into the oldest hunting joke in creation. If anyone found fault with the catch, the impropriety called for a standard riposte: "Then you may eat the tail." And to the hunter making the kill went the honor of silencing the critic. Now they looked at Kwokwoiyea. He stood motionless with his mouth agape, caught in the embrace of the moment. His polite restraint would make it all the more devastating. Akwoi fought to hold it in. Finally he spoke, in the shy refinement of a gentle soul, almost in sweetness, "My frie'—" but Akwoi started giggling. Moses threw a stick at him. "My frie'…you may ea'—" He didn't get it out. They shrieked in unison. Akwoi leaped into a wild dance threshing his arms and mounting imaginary she devils. John dropped his knife and started jumping up and down as if trying to drive a post into the ground. Moses doubled up and fell over. They didn't stop. Akwoi kept circling the fire like a mad man. John looked at me, then started pounding another post. Kwokwoiyea remained in the same spot, face uplifted, beaming his joy back to heaven. He would have this day for his grandchildren.

Eventually the noise died down and they got back to minding the spit. How the day had changed, the fatigue of the dreary morning vanished. To a hunter the kill was more than a mere acquisition of food; it was a revival of faith. They had a special dance to honor the event.

At last Akwoi took up his journal and began writing furiously. The worst was over. So I relaxed a bit and enjoyed the revelry but soon felt myself getting drowsy. "I'm going to take a little nap in the hammock."

Barefoot, the bridge responded to the slightest touch. It swayed a little as I knelt and stretched out. With one foot locked in a vertical support, the opposite arm around another, I found my balance. In a short while it resumed its natural motion; the entire structure rising and falling with the soughing of the high limbs. Though motionless to the eye, I could feel each breath of air. Looking down on the rushing water gave the illusion of a mad flight. Clouds of blue smoke rose from the fire. Not long the floor of the bridge lifted to another footstep. John. He got the idea, balanced himself, then looked up and smiled as if to say "not bad white boy."

Now sunshine came streaming through the treetops in thin slivers, widened into taut stripes revolving against a green curtain. With the slightest movement in the upper tier, they sprang to new patterns, jumped from stem to flower until they found momentary rest on the muddy bank or the surface of the mocha water where they became floating leopard spots. Ferns and elephant ears on the ground seemed to hold still for them like fat pups having their bellies tickled. Up above oceans of tiny leaves kept in constant motion, green registers of the passing day, and the soft pitch of heavy boughs, though earthbound, answered the pull of the sun undulating upward and down like a ship at sea. At the edge of the direct glare they fluttered like tiny black flags between jewels of white flame; downstream their undersides turned up in the wind, silver fishes swimming in the air.

So here is the heart of darkness. Sunshine and shadow dappled on a sleeping earth and a peace so fragile one word will shatter it; the movement of water like a lullaby to a slumbering brain. No savagery. No drums across the river. And the natives? Hardly restless—lounging before their barbecue amusing themselves over my breach of etiquette.

The only sounds were the exhale of air into leaves, as soft as steam coming off a pot of cooked rice, and the more immediate lapping of the water as it washed around fallen logs or licked the bare earth on the bank. Then came a deep wooden creaking, like a cradle rocking, loud enough to resonate in the trees as invisible lines of force cracked in rapid succession to the upswing of a limb. And the creaking of the vines as they twisted in tension then twisted back. I could feel sleep coming. There really wasn't very much meat on it.

"Sleep my child come what please; let dreams like winter rivulets flow. These are bridal riches from a locked trousseau, secrets to the jungle's keep. And once you taste these fruits so hard forbidden, how in sunshine will I sing, like birds to newborn spring. Hush. None must speak but I to thee. This life so frail is like no other. I am maiden; I am mother. You will know me in my splendor soon. First you must see me in my tomb. "

What happened? How did it get dark so quick? Fire's out…but a strand of witches hair rising from the ashes. Where'd they go? Kwokwoiyea! Moses! Abandoned. They left the squirrel. That's strange. There it is still on the spit like a little red foetus. Something coming! So quiet. Deserted. Yellow electric lights strung up and down. Sound of city traffic. Something's wrong. What's that? A heavy burlap sack, sewn shut with potato sprouts growing out. More sacks. Hundreds. Floating in the river. When the bogeyman comes he catches bad boys and puts them in a sack. The actress! There she is! The carriage of her head. Jewels. Satin. How it dances when she walks. She's going to cross the bridge. She's scarcely touching the ground. Eye contact. Music. Where's it coming from? A phone booth! Here at the side of the trail with a faint red glow inside. Antique, polished mahogany with two bells like eyes and a black mouthpiece. Like a face, but mechanical. A copper switch, three prongs, handle "up," implanted in the side, blood dripping onto the pages of an open directory. The 'S's. Shepherd, Smith, Sophocles. Wonder if it works?

"All flights to Seoul, Anchorage, and Los Angeleeze have been temporarily delayed due to computer infidelity. All compilers please reprogram to archaic crypto-Sweetish. Reroute all nonsensual circuits. All systems...close your eyes and think of Jenny."

Jenny. Under the dark sycamore by the lake Jenny...only the owls and the swallows Jenny...First time Jenny. Sweet Jenny. Lithe Jenny.

So quiet. There! Half buried in the sand. Down to the fender skirts. '57 Chev. Headlights down. Velvet dice over the mirror. Someone in the back seat! A black veil.

"Jenny! Don't cry Jenny."

"The sycamore has fallen into the lake, the water's polluted, they drop trash over the bank. You wouldn't recognize the old place. Remember how beautiful it was back then, the cliff and the footpath, the lights from the harbor, the rock where we carved our names...I have two children now, a boy and a girl, I'm active in PTA and I hope to run for the School Board. I need...we both need to forget the past. It was my choice too. The first time is always something special to a woman; the lake never sparkled so soft, the moonlight, the water; I felt like dancing on the beach afterwards but you thought we should get home. I wanted to go through with it you know...but that's all past. You have an arduous task ahead of you. Why they chose you of all people...I wish you...I give you all my love. And for the sake of my children...Please do not fail."

Must have dozed off. The sun beamed in the treetops, still dazzling but moved over, the soft wash of water under the bridge seemed to freshen up. Late afternoon. We had to get moving. They were all on the bridge now. Moses and Akwoi stood cradled in the handrail with their arms twisted around it, their feet braced opposite. Kwokwoiyea sat sideways with his legs dangling over the side and the leather pouch of his slingshot hanging out his back pocket.

"Why didn't you wake me up?"

"You were dreaming."

"I thought you didn't believe that stuff."

"I don't," John said. "But in the bush..."

He didn't finish. A phone booth of all things. And the stewardess again. All flights canceled. But we were already aloft. I could feel the drift of the airplane. Then I ran into an old friend, someone I hadn't seen for years; we had a chat about the good old days. But I woke up scared.

We had no chance of making Kpodokpodo before nightfall; with luck, tomorrow. So we kept pushing. The fatigue of the last five days came back with a vengeance. I'd fallen asleep on the bridge only to wake up stiff. We were past half way, but where? I had no idea. The map was useless. The trail wound in and out, around scum covered pools, thickets, fallen logs, some of them shoulder high, through standing water, alongside feeder streams to a fording place, up slippery banks with nothing to grasp but mud and rotten sticks and back again on the other side to the main trail where the path cut further into underbrush to avoid widening bogs, and back again for a net gain of a hundred yards—a half hour gone and leaden feet heavier than before. It didn't take much of this to bring on a sense of futility. I'd heard of a white man who'd gone momentarily berserk flaying the bush with a machete after becoming entangled in it. I was too tired for anything like that. When the going straightened out, the raw spot under my shoulder strap reminded me I was walking upright again. So did the sweat and the stinging and the spiders. And the possibility of being lost.

Tonight, for the first time in my life I would sleep on the bare earth away from the security of civilization with no possibility of chickening out and going home. That alone didn't bother me—I'd slept out before—what did was the uncomfortable feeling I hadn't thought it through. I began to feel uneasy. We knew all along we'd have to spend at least one night out, but now that dusk was falling, the realization took a different coloring. Thinking about it made it worse. I knew very well we weren't likely to be attacked by wild animals. But with the growing shadows assuming other identities, the conviction carried less weight. The idea of burrowing into the ground didn't sound so silly after all, only one direction to defend. I tried to concentrate on finding a good campsite, dry and open. Two impossibilities. A snake bite in here was something I didn't want to think about. But what if a larger animal happened on us by mistake, a territorial animal. There was no effective way to disguise our human presence, so said the old men. "Go into the bush and you roll your only dice." How many times had I heard that? Now it made sense! When night fell, we would be game, just like the squirrel, and hardly the best equipped. How quickly the sunshine expired. There would be rain too, even I sensed it, a noticeable cooling of the air, a slight twirl in the uppermost leaves.

Kwokwoiyea stopped. We must make shelter, he said quietly. I would have preferred higher ground but didn't argue. He chose a spot at the back of a heavily buttressed bombax tree reeking with decay. It looked wet, dreary, alien. After pointing it out, he and Moses went back up the trail to cut thatch. Mulba, Akwoi, and I began clearing the site; we hacked off branches, loose roots, saplings, beat back the underbrush and raked the ground as best we could. In ten minutes, we had a space the size of a small room. Then John disappeared after giving Akwoi a low command that he obeyed without a word, quite unusual for him. I climbed around one of the buttresses and peed in the dead leaves. The ground needed more raking. They returned before I finished; Akwoi with an armful of fire starter, which he covered with a tepee of glossy leaves. We spread the remainder over the bare floor. No sooner had Moses and Kwokwoiyea finished lashing the thatch to the buttress fins than the first drops began to fall. No wind, just a light, steady drizzle that was going to last a while, probably all night. The world never looked so bleak. We might as well have been on another planet.

Night fell quickly. But during a rain it came with remarkable stealth. It filled the thick gloom in the distance, destroyed the individuality of leaves changing them to a solid black cloud, covered the ground with an opaque carpet. Soon the smaller branches disappeared as if by the wave of a magician's hand. Then the trunks across the path became vague upright forms looking down at us, not really trees. The only sound came from the quiet drizzle on the broadleaves, like the hissing of a snake. We huddled under our shelter peering out into the dark. No one spoke. I could feel Akwoi shivering. There was no stretching out. My muscles ached, my feet were cold inside water-logged boots and I wasn't taking them off. I was scared. And scared to let them know it.

The rain lasted half the night. When it stopped and the afterdrip subsided to the occasional plunking of heavy drops, we carefully uncovered our sleeping places. Akwoi lit the fire but it only hissed. I was hoping for a feeling of safety but it wasn't that kind of fire. Would it scare off animals? Or would the scent of smoke attract them? It gave no warmth. I suggested one of us stay awake to keep watch and they agreed. Kwokwoiyea would be first; he sat with his back to one of the buttresses and his blanket drawn around his shoulders. The others smoothed out their places. I saw Moses take a leather medicine pouch out of his pack and tie it to a wet branch at the edge of our clearing. No one seemed to notice. I was pleased to see him do it. Another of my kind shared a sense of need. We had a bond. It made sense.

Pitch black. Quiet. Getting chilly. Zip up. No, I want my arms free. Something in my pocket. Damn scout knife. Can't cut bananas. The ground's damp but not cold—warm in fact after lying in one spot. Don't shift. Smells of rot. Never took time to smell the earth. Mostly decay. The silence is awful. It says things. The fire. Should we build it up? No. Crackling would drown out the other sounds, and sound is the only contact we've got with whatever's out there. Try to get some sleep. What a powerful stillness beyond the fringe of our camp. You can feel it with a sixth sense. Crickets of course, only it's not music in here, more like a cat scratching a screen door. Each cry, a distinct being. Close. So close. What's that! I never heard anything like that. Now it's humming. A sorcerer working his grindstone.

"So. You come among us? Very well, but the rules are of a different hue. Surely your friends have warned you, your fair-eyed friends who now lie safe and warm in velvet beds. Will you sleep your cultured sleep tonight? We think not. You thought you knew this woodland song. Alas, we sing it in a different key. It has a verse or two you've yet to learn. 'Go to sleep. Go to sleep. Softly as a black snake sliding down a tree.'"

What's that! A twig! I heard it snap!...Now I'm not sure. Why's my breath so quick? Can't see. Can't see my own hand! Fire's out. Can't hear them. Are they asleep? "Hey!" This is silly. Morning will make it laughable. Moses? Mulba? You asleep? What was that! It sounded like a baby crying. There it is again! An owl, it has to be an owl. Jesus it sounds just like a baby. Some kind of monkey. Why won't it...shhh. Something else! I can feel it moving. Something big. Quiet. Why's it so quiet all of a sudden. Kwokwoiyea? That you?

332

CHAPTER 29

CALL OF THE *PORO*

"It is time."

"What?"

"To go hunting. You may bring two things that are sacred to you. Your scout knife and your copy of Thoreau."

"The Poro? Oh no. I'm an American citizen. Persona non juris. This is the twentieth century for Chrissakes!"

"If you do not come with us tonight, your twentieth century will be the end of you."

The path to the sacred grove. How'd I get here? Who's this? The little ones. Jallah, Daydobah, Johnson Kwiogi, Ramses Tokenu. And Dwoiyou. Slow witted Dwoiyou practically dancing in delight.

"Do not be afraid," Ramses said touching my arm.

"They will frighten you to make you unafraid," Daydobah added. They're speaking like adults.

"You must never speak of this," Kwiogi whispered. "When the Great One comes, touch its face,"

"How will I know it's him?"

"You will know," Jallah advised. "You must touch it."

"You will be a man at last!" Telleywoiyea cried.

"I always knew they'd come for you," John Mulba beamed catching my elbow. "Now you'll be one of us."

"Aren't you coming?"

"We've already been; you must go alone."

"Everything of import—" Dwoiyou! He's found speech! "—transpires in the solitude of the human heart. Do not sacrifice the possibility of enlightenment to Madison Avenue expediency. Beware the siren song."

"Take this," Moses whispered. *"Psittacus Erithacus.* The rare bird you once released to the astonishment of an entire village. We will communicate through it in times of peril."

So quiet. Only a rustle of raffia in a sea of darkness. Voices. A bullroarer! But this is madness!

"Perhaps." Old Fawkpa. "But there's method in it. If madness is a flight from reality has not the madman 'seen' where others refuse to look? For one night let go the mask of reason. Come. The drums call. These trees shall be our books."

Everything's alive. The air, the leaves. Birds. Each voice—like old friends. Everything's familiar. The scent of home. "Stay awhile. Take your shoes off." The moon's fallen out the sky, there, half buried in the sand, quivering like a fish. A lazy river rolls over and yawns, "So you've come at last." Butterflies glide in and out, crimson and yellow, spiders string sparkling pearls from branch to branch. The Forest herself is at her mirror. She calls softly from the next room, "How was school? There's milk in the kitchen."

There they are! All masked. One, two…eight. A buffalo man, Sioux; an Egyptian, Horus in a falcon head; Dionysus with a garland of fruit; Shiva with jets of flame; a round Oriental face smeared with white clay; a South American with brilliant red and blue feathers; and Pacific Island, Maori; and one African, probably Loma, a serene face framed in monkey hair and embedded with cowrie shells with slanted eye slits over an equally tiny mouth. One's missing. There should be nine. What do they want?

"We are the vessels of your past, the heritage of the sleeping earth."

"We are the aspirations of the species."

"We are conversations long forgotten, now remembered."

"The future in gestation, the answers you've yet to learn."

"We are the immortal fruit of mortal brains long since drained to dust."

"Though your godless age has relegated us to the role of villains in third-rate cinema, tonight we forego our prop department shelves and deign to orchestrate a cinema of our own. Perhaps cast a third-rate actor as a statesman, a goddess in a cheap burlesque. Things will no longer appear as they are, but only to show you what they are not."

"Do not underestimate our resolve; our species did not prevail for want of it, nor want of daring in the face of darkness."

"Nature and Reason are parents of us all. Honor both."

"Logic is their daytime child. We come at night."

"We neither endorse nor condemn what you will see. We merely spin the reels another speed."

"We traverse the ages as chambers in a dream."

"Tonight we speak. You listen."

"You who pile the bodies at Austerlitz, make mountains at Verdun, stain the sky at Stalingrad. Hear us."

"You who turn hell green with envy at the very thought of Auschwitz. Hear us."

"Who sicken every sunrise with the cloud of Hiroshima. Hear us."

"We, your savage past, have come to instruct."

"Our schooling is not for the faint of heart."

"A true man is companion to these dark forebodings; they steel his spirit through."

"For this brief night, our savage rites shall course your veins as conduit to your children."

"Understand the ideals we live by are lies, but a worse lie is to think we can live without them."

"You cannot command the flow of time."

"But you can master your place within."

"Know that if you fail, life does not."

"Be steadfast."

"We speak no more."

CHAPTER 30

COUNTRY CLUB FETE

Bach. String quartet. Musicians on a raised platform festooned with crepe, two vases of cut flowers, red, white, and blue bunting. Waiters in tuxedos weaving in and out with silver platters. Cocktails and hors d'oeuvres. Early evening. Elegance, refinement, an atmosphere of cultured ease. Poodles and ermine. Limousines with chauffeurs in white gloves opening their doors to a gleaming white mansion fronted with Grecian columns, a full veranda with an ornate balustrade, guests casually emptying down wide steps onto the green lawn trimmed with clipped shrubbery, gravel walks and brick patios, trellised wisteria, flowering dogwoods and Spanish moss. A winged cherub over a trickling fountain in low floodlight. Granite goddesses—Victory, Harvest, Fatherland. A bar in the gazebo, dancing inside. Gentlemen in tuxedos, bejeweled ladies in long gowns adrift in the garden beneath lines of Japanese lanterns. Expensive perfume. The talk is of the theater and seventeenth century French furniture.

"Can I get you a drink, sir?"

These people act like they know me.

"How's school?"

I've never seen them in my life.

"I dropped out."

"You! A dropout!"

What am I doing here? It's a black tie affair.

"No offense," says the bartender leaning close, "Get a haircut, people'll think you're somekinna o' queer."

"What are your plans now?"

"You're going to like it here at the country club. No niggers or Puerto Ricans."

There's the monkey wrench man. He looks kind o' sad, like somebody stole his girl.

336

"Hi. Remember me? From the carrousel? You gave me a ride once."

"Don't get caught up in the side shows. You're here for the main event."

"Plastics," whispers a chubby gent behind his hand.

Who in the hell was that?

"Creighton Industries. Ready to take off."

"Watch out or you'll wind up in some damn rice paddy."

"Damn reds. Half the world's theirs and the other half negotiable. What t' hell do they want with Vietnam? If we don't stop 'em now they're gonna be in San Diego. And these goddamn hippies protesting. If George Patton were alive today everyone of those long haired sons of bitches would be over there in a foxhole and thankful for it."

"Have you thought about law school?"

"Remember Curly Peterson, scourge of the Delt House? Saw him last week in Philly, says he got the inside track on a slot with American International, pussy job—sixty grand."

"He must have laid the boss's wife."

Gunshots!

"Champagne corks. Relax. We haven't executed anyone here at the country club for some time now. Won't you have one? Fifty-seven I believe."

"Watch the dress fella! Shit! That stain'll never come out. Were ya born in a barn!"

"I beg your pardon. I've been...away."

"Well, maybe it's time to get back into things," says another invitingly, "Isn't this a smashing idea for a class reunion? And wait till you see, out back, later. Lillian darling! Love and kisses. You're adorable."

"MANDY!"

They screamed, looked at each other in disbelief, screamed again, hugged, then got down to business. "Have you seen Wendy she looks absolutely ghastly four kids three marriages I don't know how she does it..."

"How *do you do it?* Let me look at you. Love your new hair. This is Lillian Reilly, an old chum—still on the prowl—excuse me it's Goldfarb isn't it?"

"Vescaccio," smiles the prowler.

"Carleton you're killing me!"

"Carleton Raines, pleased to meet you."

"Mandy darling. Here's someone I want you to meet. He's just back from—where was it dear?"

"Gbanga."

"Isn't that a coincidence," says the prowler drawing near. "I was in Arizona last winter. My ex has a ranch outside Tucson, only fifty acres, the cheap SOB, I just love it but all my friends are back east. Can't very well talk to the cacti. Now I remember, you were working on your…"

"Circumcision."

"Well," she gasped, "you'll have to share your results with me someday OH! Oh, I'm sorry, here let me get that."

"It's only corduroy."

"But it stains, trust me, I've had exper—you've got a nice tan, you didn't get that in the library, there we are, you're really sweet, are you married? Who cares? I know what you're thinking, what a dumb broad, oh well, tell me about your thesis, I'm really very interested—"

"I don't want to talk about it."

"I know just how you feel," she whispers twisting her heel into the ground. "There are some things you don't feel comfortable talking about, you remember Shelia Sylvester—bleached blond, legs from the armpits down—sure you doooo, well, she had hers taken care of in New York—those little things that grow in your stomach—at this live-in clinic, five thousand per diem, but they're real professionals, no questions, no publicity, my ex paid for it too, the prick, just check in for a weekend and fly to Jamaica on Monday. Montego Bay! Have you ever been to the islands? They're marvelous! I just adore the place. They got my diamond though, the bastards. I left it on my dresser, went out to the pool for a quick dip, came back and sure enough, gone. And the police! What a circus, they went through everything. My dainties! Looking for the diamond. Sure fella. Oh well, don't know what the world's coming to. Jim Farmer—tall, glasses, sharp dresser, drives a Porsche—got me this darling little neck piece when he heard what happened. Do you like it? He's in marketing, hated the lab, no money in it; he sent a note too, 'Just a little something to make you forget Jamaica and remember me.' Isn't that sweet? I can't imagine what he paid for it. Sandra darling! Sock it to me BABY! Excuse me just one minute dear, haven't seen her for ages, I still want to hear about your thesis. Ta ta."

"What's going on out back?"

"A little patriotic exercise shall we say."

"On the golf course?"

"Is Brecht existentially plausible?"

"I dunno."

"But don't you see, now that God is dead, law for sale, the electoral process consigned to soap opera, the theater is all we have, all that is brave, inviolate. Do you agree?"

"I dunno."

"Plausibility is of course *passe complet*. Brecht knows this. But he doesn't give a damn. Isn't that exquisitely absurd? Perhaps one has to give a damn not to give a damn. Can one claim authenticity in an age of decadence? Or is decadence itself the sine qua non of the authentic man? I'm so glad I spoke with you. It is always well to learn what the proletariat is thinking."

There she is! The lady from the carrousel. The gleam of satin, the carriage of her head, elegant neck, twinkling jewels, the edge of her skirt dances when she walks. But the tinge of sorrow. The night opens to her. Everything fine emanates from her.

She's with someone. Forrester! That son of a...He sees me. Smiling publicly but mad as hell—excuses himself, "Hi Jess. Hear you're expanding," drapes one arm around my shoulder, smiling, "Good to see you Frank. How's Audrey?" Then as if a friendly chat, "Jeans and corduroy. Stunning."

"Damn it! I didn't know—"

"And a stalemate with the barber's union. In the depths of your oafish provincialism, can you possibly imagine my embarrassment?"

"Cut the crap Everett! Have you any idea what's happening in the real world. They're killing people in the streets. Four students at Kent and you sit here clicking champagne glasses."

"You think I'm having fun? I fancied you my protégé."

"Who is she?"

"An actress."

"Introduce me."

"Dressed like that?"

A bonfire on the green. Crates, chairs, an old sofa. Some kind of war dance, crouching low then vaulting skyward, a howling fury of naked muscles and glistening war paint. Two circles moving in opposite directions around the fire mumbling a low chant. They're armed! Golf clubs, telephones, attache cases.

> *Hiroshima Nagasaki*
> *Cook 'em up like suki yaki*

Those bearing golf clubs are of a higher caste. The best and the brightest. They shriek the loudest, their savage leaps carry them closest to the flames. Elder members in business suits carry putters, but naked young braves are wielding shiny driving irons raising them to the sky in perfect time.

> *Drink no barley*

> *Talk no parley*
> *We want blood of Victor Charlie*

A War Chant! Here at the country club? But they're good Republicans? A few theologians.

> *Praise the prophet,*
> *Praise the Tao*
> *Do it do it do it now*

Columnists and bankers down on all fours barking like dogs, howling, biting, tearing each other's clothes, guzzling a red liquid, suggestive hip thrusts—

> *Raise the profit,*
> *Raise the Dow*
> *Do it do it do it now*

Housewives in hair rollers, hawk-faced hags with sunglasses and plastic flags, fat bank clerks dressed like cowboys, frail librarians tossing books into the flames, all chanting as they circle, an English butler doing the Watusi, a concert musician smashing his cello, a fat soprano hurling her stays, a society page editor who doesn't know where to begin, poseurs and pop stars, a happy hooker and a mad hatter, a psychoanalyst and an inflatable doll, the police chief and the parson's wife.

> *No pink no red*
> *Better dead better dead*

Special personages. A medicine man, his head painted blue with two white stars for eyes and red and white stripes downward. A retired general in a wheelchair waving a cap pistol with a plastic flag in the end. A man in thick lenses and a black robe sitting atop a pole borne by a circus strongman, swaying through the throng, twirling a set of fish scales at the end of a rope. A mysterious on-looker—the only one not dancing—with dark glasses and a miniature radio receiver in his ear. Snarling young witches with red nails and liquid lips dancing lasciviously, whirling animal furs and throbbing to the chant.

"Somebody's gonna get in a lot o' trouble for this!"

"Com'on. Where's the old school spirit!"

"This has gone too far!"

"Relax, it's a publicity stunt."

> *Iffy wary he be fairy*
> *Shoot 'em dead and do not bury*

"Now what are they doing? Why's that kid tied up—THIS IS AGAINST THE LAW!"

"It's an effigy ya dumb hick!"

"Effigy my foot! It's a human sacrifice!"

"It's only theater."

"Like hell! She's fighting back!"

Vietnamese. Black pajamas. Blindfold.

"We can't let them think we're weak. Our national prestige—"

"LOOK WHAT YOU'RE DOING! WARMONGERS!"

"Okay that's enough buddy."

"MURDERERS!"

"Godammit! My wife happens to be present!"

"Your wife's back in the bushes takin' up astronomy!"

"HEY! Watch your gaddamn mouth!"

"THEY'RE FRYIN' THAT KID!"

"We have to burn it to save it."

"Will you open your goddamn eyes!"

"Who da hell is this guy?"

"Some goddamn hippie."

"You're getting rich on this! YOU BASTARDS!"

"Okay that's it!"

"Get your hands off me!"

"He's gotta be on drugs."

"I'm not on drugs dammit!"

"All right! We'll do it the old fashioned way!"

"You're outta here PUNK!!"

"GET A HAIRCUT HIPPIE!"

"DON'T WORRY ABOUT MY HAIR! Worry about why it freaks you out!"

CHAPTER 31

O SHENANDOAH

New York State Thruway East. No Hitchhiking. A VW bus. Banged up but still runnin'. Psychedelic colors. The peace sign, a mandala revolving around a golden Buddha, "Peace" and "Love" interlaced with floating cherubs, the blue earth at the center of a detached eye. Yin Yang. Fishes sporting with a centaur under the Age of Aquarius. Bumper stickers too. "Don't Walk on the Grass." "Another Mother for Peace." California plates.

"Where ya headin'?" A bunch o' hippies.

"East."

"Wanna lift?"

It felt good to be moving again. Summer fields careened past the windows like squares on a quilt. The driver looked bored, wore a red handkerchief twisted into a headband, sunburn on his neck. His bearded face saw a sad world but in quiet acquiescence. Tools littered the floor, a surveyor's transit, monkey wrench, a lead pencil in his front pocket. He wasn't one of them. A little older.

Four more sprawled out in back. Dirty cushions and a makeshift bunk, clothes strewn all over the place, military boots, a sick plant in a cracked pot, album covers, Janis Joplin, the Doors, a battered poster, "Make Love not War" with two naked people doing it. The scent of marijuana.

"Come on back man," a voice said, slow and dreamy. "He don't talk much…juss driiives…readin' the little white lines…some kind o' celestial code…where she stops nobody knooows."

A fresh faced boy in wire rim glasses, shoulder length hair, khaki jacket, sat with his back to a cushion deep in a smile of oblivion. Bobby. That was Turk asleep on the bunk, a lanky light-complected black in sandals, tie died T-shirt, and Grimes on his back staring at the ceiling, a wiry kid with straight blond hair and jeans that had seen the underside of many a car. And Rae, his chick, with her arms around a dirty pillow hugging it like a teddy bear humming to herself, men's overalls, no bra, hair a mess—flower child gone to seed.

"What's your sign?" she asked sullenly.

"I beg your pardon?"

"She means...out in the zodiac, maaan."

"Leo."

"You don't look like a Leo." And she went back to her own world. They didn't trust me.

"Wanna smoke?" he asked relighting a joint.

"No thanks."

"Go to school?"

"Dropped out."

"Me too. Ya might say I took up botany. Grow my own."

"Where from?"

"Ann Arbor...On a Fullbright...Physics. Kept a lot o' bad company...You sure? Dynamite shit, man."

"What are you doing now?"

"'I...celebrate myself...at my ease, observing a spear of summer grass. Creeds and schools in abeyance, Nature without check, every atom belonging to me as good belongs to you...I know the amplitude of time.'" He smiled softly. "Whitman."

"I love Whitman."

"Far out, maaan."

"If they knew how far, they wouldn't let us read him."

"Might as well get it while we can."

"...What exactly?"

"Whatever...What your own soul craves...Someday it's all goin' up in smoke man...a mushroom cloud. Big Mamma. I don't want to be the one to press the button...that's all I know. I've thought about it, maan...The guy who finally pushes the button isn't gonna be some kind o' psycho. It takes real effort to be a psycho, eighty per cent of your brain energy to keep up the delusion of being Jesus Christ or Napoleon or somebody. There's nothin' left, maan. The real probabilities...whoever pushes the button...it'll be some regular Joe like you or me. After the fact...they'll decide he's psycho. Poof...the whole shit and shabang. All I know's it's not gonna be me, man...cuz I'm already gonna be sky high."

"What you know 'bout hell, man?" Turk moaned. "You think you gots some kin' o' cawner on the market? Hell's for real, man, none o' this symbolism shit. You ask Grimes. He been tha. An' that ain't nothin', man. Inside the sun it sixteen million degrees. Celsius. You ionized...just like that. An' they gots betta. You watch yo frien' get ionized. Yeah. Now that's class. He die. You watch. You think they don' make mistakes? Half the people down tha by mistake. Somebody typed the wrong name, the radio operator gets the wrong co-ordi-nates, all of a sudden wooshhhh. You ask Grimes. He been tha."

"Shuch yer trap, man."

"Little place called Dak To."

"Shut up ya fu—" Grimes was crying all of a sudden.

"Saw his bes' frien' step in some shit. Antipersonnel mine. Right in fron' of 'm. Wooshhh. Splashed all over 'im. Hey, Grimes, that why you never take a bath, 'fraid o' washin' off yer bes' frien'? So now he come home an' what he do? He go straight to L.A...t' see the dude's girl...t' make it awll right. Only she already been through three guys by now. Did't wanna hear 'bout it. Had a date that night. All painted up purddy as a pussy cat. You think they gonna let you in out tha Grimes? Out tha in L.A. You'd o' lef' a ring 'round the swimmin' pool. Lil ole hillbilly boy. Tar paper shack, twenny kids runnin' aroun', half got a daddy, half got momma's word. Wha cha gonna do out tha Grimes? Stan' aroun' in them greasy jeans watchin' them slick dudes come cruisin' roun' in them shiny new spawts cars. Couldn't even fin' the bus station."

"Shud up ya fuckin' nigger—"

"Hillbilly boy. Saved my black ass." Now they were both crying. "Naw, you betta off in hell man. It ain't such a bad place. You free down heah. You can shake yer fis' at God Hisself. What He gonna do? You already down in the hole. Now somebody gwone an' stole 'is modasacko. Ain't that the laaas' straw. Hey Grimes—"

"SHUT UP! SHUT UP! I'm sick o' this shit! Both of you! You're fucked up! And your fucked up too for listening!" Rae. Looking at me. She ended up throwing a boot but it only tumbled into some dirty clothes.

"They're both vets," Bobby said concentrating on rolling a another joint. "They do this all the time. It's some kind of cleansing rite...only it doesn't seem to be working. They're great guys...Really."

"How long have you know them?"

"...Two daays. They picked me up. I'm hitchin' jus' like you. Rae's van. She's from California...Long Beach...Turk's from Cajun country...Grimes doesn't know where t' hell he's from."

"I been t' L.A., man," Grimes said without moving. "I guess thass where I'm from."

"Oh no, you're NOT!" Rae snapped viciously. "You're from some shithole in Tennessee! You LOOK like a hillbilly, you TALK like a hillbilly, you BALL like a—"

"Wess Virginia, dammit!"

"Ain't what she said lass night," Turk moaned. "Chattnooga Chattnooga woo woooooo."

"Oh, hell yes, Polecat Holler, I suppose. This is unreal this is so fucking incredible man—"

"Wells Holla."

"Wells Holler! Oh, that's even better, Jesus Christ! I don't believe it! What t' hell am I doing I must o' dropped bad acid I'm not in this fucking van you people are unreal who's the cat drivin'! Where'd we pick him up! I could o' been in Malibu this is so fucking incredible…"

She faded out, grabbed both knees under her chin and buried her face under a cloud of hair.

"High strung," Bobby whispered.

"What you lookin' at?" Grimes snarled. Confederate flag, dirty white T-shirt, Harley tattoo, he fixed his clear eyes on something over my head.

"Sorry. I didn't mean to stare." Christ they were all stoned.

"Yer not better than me man."

"No. I'm not."

"He's okay, man," Bobby smiled. Grimes rolled over, fumbled under a mattress, came back with a harmonica. Rae put her head in his lap and looked up at him, closed her eyes. He started to play *O Shenandoah* and we drove a long time without talking.

"I hope you get your bike back," I said after he stopped."

"Oh, I'm agonna git it back, aw raght," he said angelically.

"I'm glad you can smile about it."

"Well, I'm smilin' cuz whoever dunnit's gonna git messed up…Hay's dawg mate."

"Excuse me?"

"Euuuuu!" Rae grimaced. Dog mate!" She shrieked clinching her fists. "M-e-a-t! MATE! Jesus CHRIST! Are you DENSE! How can you be so fucking dense! You fucking love bikes, somebody fucking steals your bike, the fucking pigs don't give a shit, that's like that's like somebody fucking burns every fucking poem Whitman ever WROTE! You dig it man!"

"I dig it." For some reason that got a laugh and we relaxed a bit while Grimes played another tune and Turk worked on his Chianti bottle.

"You dig rock?" Bobby asked as he rolled another one and passed it to Rae.

"I prefer Bach." (Shouldn't have said that.)

"Far out, maaan," he grinned. "Wanna come anyway?"

"Where?"

"Woodstock."

"Where's that?"

"Be a lot o' people...few hundred maybe."

"But where is it?"

"Well...We're not real sure," he paused. "It's a farm," he paused again. "Someplace." And after another long effort, "Someplace in New York. Wanna come?"

"You can find somebody to ball," Rae snapped.

I never saw such a mess in my life. We got there late afternoon, parked in a field, walked across two others; no one seemed concerned whose property—cars, vans, people, kids, dogs, frisbees, love and friendliness, a camaraderie that wasn't strained, a mellow acceptance of complete strangers, quiet conviction, something deeply American though their elders would have balked. All trying to be different but in the same way. Some went to considerable expense to look poor, the highest value to a generation that never saw real poverty. Bearded gents at ease under a sugar maple passed the pipe of peace—a hundred years before, they would have passed a jug of ginger beer and perhaps talked about the recent war. And there were girls— young, vibrant, with long hair and painted skin, sunglasses, beads and bandannas, in jeans and khaki and makeshift tops—some without tops. I saw them dancing barefoot in the backyard of a school bus, each in her own world but in time to the same music like tribal celebrants at a harvest rite. One had a garland in her hair, daisies, black-eyed Susans, a stem of timothy, lustrous golden hair gleaming in the sun, she radiated the serenity of a Hindu goddess, closed-eyed, supple-armed, full breasts, fine nipples like red raspberries. We stopped and watched. I couldn't help staring..."Far out, maaan," was all Bobby could say. Grimes, the perfect gentleman, "Ain't she somethun." And Turk, somewhere out in orbit, "Now somebody gwone an' stole 'is modasacko. Ain' tha' the lass straw."

Soon we got separated. The driver and I found ourselves along a back trail.

"Let's split," he whispered.

He wheeled over a crushed fence, down a lane, a back road for five miles, finally a highway. Soon we were on the road again; the fresh air felt good. He draped his wrist over the wheel and resumed his private thoughts.

"What's the purpose of all this?"

"The purpose of the young is God's purpose."

"And that of the old?"

"To become young again."

"They're rebelling against everything in sight."

"But there's something healthy in their ardor."

"A bunch of drug addicts thumping guitars?"

"Let them be. Find rebellion of your own."

"Where?"

"The Holy City."

"But we're going to New York."

"It'll have to do."

"Help me, will you?"

"The only help I can offer is to avoid peddlers of help, likewise vendors of truth and decency. Disregard neon signs, avoid loud noises, especially those emanating from the human throat."

"I didn't ask for a disser—say don't I know you?"

"You hardly know yourself."

"Where you from?"

"Massachusetts."

"What's your name?"

"Henry."

"Henry who?"

"Thoreau."

"Henry...*David* Thoreau?"

"The same."

"WOW! You—I, I can't—right here in—I, I'm, you—"

"If you can't speak, shut up."

"The monkey wrench man! I—I've read all your books."

"Have you read the book of Nature?"

"I'm afraid it's out of print."

"Out of style."

"Wilderness just isn't wilderness anymore."

"Oh but it is."

"You need a reservation for a campsite."

"Not where we're going."

Broadway! Wow! Look at the lights. Bright as daytime. Waterfalls of flashing bulbs. There's one dancing! It's Fred Astaire! Top hat and cane. I never saw so many people. Cars like ants. Have you ever heard such a racket? WATCH THAT BUS! Uptown traffic keep right. Why are they all blowing their horns? Rockefeller Plaza, exit parking only. What the hell is that supposed to mean. Billboards. Fly Pan Am to Rio. Drink Coca Cola. See the USA in your Chevrolet. Catch the Channel One Evening News, Cheryl Huneycutt and Broderick Breenbane. Clark Gable and Vivian Leigh, *Gone with the Wind.* Nonstop to Los Angeles, five flights daily, Devlon Airlines Red Carpet Service. Radio WELL, the smoothest sound around. Times Square. All the news that's fit to print. Uncle Sam wants you. Forty-Second Street. Adult books. Those people don't look like bookworms. Solve your accounting problems fast, call Yachusumu today. No Parking. Violators will be towed. Curb your dog. Smoke Camel. Uh oh. Queens Midtown Tunnel, next left. No U-Turn. Yield for pedestrians. No stopping during rush hour. No left any time. Jesus Henry. "Goddammit can't ya see the sign says WALK!" People are so rude. Avenue of the Americas! Greenwich Village. I've read about these places. Bellevue Hospital. Brooklyn Bridge, outbound, two lanes, six to nine a.m., in bound, four lanes, as marked. Brooklyn! We're going the wrong way! "That was a red light Henry."

He careened into a dark side street, pulled up in front of a dark building. Ornate facade. Gold lettering on the window. The Thoreau Society. "How 'bout that Henry? There's your picture in the window." Members only. "Champagne. Nice thought."

He dashed in, came right out, jumped in and squealed away just as the lights came on. Then we stopped in front of another building. Saloon Des Beaux Arts. Must be French. Same thing. He must have had a lot of stops so I got the next bottle ready. Green with white labels, each with a red ribbon and a little inscription. "Best Wishes to The Ministry of Truth." *Mis En Bouteilles au chateau de V.M. Molotov.* Molotov…the name rings a bell—

"Did you know Mr. Molotov?"

"Shut! Up!"

"What was that?"

"I can't believe it, a pup to parley a pack o' wolves."

More champagne. Two cases. The Hall of Certainty. Journal of Vested Interests. House of Political Patronage. Bank of Granite Indifference. Wow! I didn't know all these places existed. The Theater of High Conceit. "There goes a fire truck Henry." The Legion of Beer Hall Patriotism.

"Wait a minute. This doesn't smell like champagne."

"SHUT! UP!"

"Gasoline...what to hell do you think you're doing Henry? You've got the whole damn street on fire!"

"That's it."

"THIS IS AGAINST THE LAW!"

"LOOK! If you don't start shapin' up—"

"I know you set the woods on fire once; that was an accident—"

"And I mean fast—"

"Let go o' my shirt. What do you think you're OUCH!"

"Okay Junior, get this down and get it good. It's us or them. You're either for us or you're against—"

"You don't believe tha—"

"The only law is the law of might. The only truth comes at the point of a gun. Violence—"

"You're chok—"

"VIOLENCE...is the necessary and efficient cause of all social change."

"BullshOOWWW!"

"Revolution...is a mathematical certainty."

"You need a rest Henry, you've been working too—"

"It is not ours to choose, the Revolution has chosen us. We live for it, we die for it; we follow its dictates unquestioningly. We fight...BY-ANY-MEANS-POSSIBLE!"

"THAT'S NOT WHAT YOU SAID!"

"Now get your ass in the truck and deal the champagne."

"I'm exercising my prerogative of civil disobedience."

He jumped out and went to work slinking along the street, smashing windows, breaking off antennas, a moustache on an art poster, spray paint, "Power to the People, Stop the Pigs," street lights "clink," windows—

"Henry. Let's think this over."

Coke bottles, right through the—

"There's a better way Henry. A walk in the woods. A weekend in Maine."

The College of Refined Speech. Wofff.

"Henry! What's come over you? Perhaps you...you've had too much of your own tonic."

The School of Applied Hypocrisy. Right down the corridor. Smooth as a bowling ball. Woooof.

Sirens!

"NOW LOOK WHAT YOU'VE DONE! Disobey, yes! But civil Henry. *Civil!* That's what made it work!"

HUBCAPS! Say it ain't so Joe. Now what? Frisbee. With a hubcap? Renée's French Furs. Regular damn discus thrower. Nice follow through. Bull's-eye! Look at the little suckers scatter! HOW'D YOU DO THAT! They're alive! The Mannikins! NAKED! HERE COME THE COPS! Run Henry!

"Nyamu!…You startled me."

"Indeed."

"I found the bridge but lost *Psittacus Erithacus,* hitched a ride, bunch o' hippies, Henry driving, now he's stealing hubcaps, ducked into Central Park, he's dawg mate in there, that's a colloquialism—"

"Cease! Your venerable ancestor can well take care of himself. It is you! Who are in danger. The salient purpose of this little exercise is your finding direction, not asking it. Yes, you! Your mates are satisfied with a rock concert and a kilo of grass, your elders with a orgy of conspicuous consumption. Sorry times indeed. Small wonder your friend is out of sorts. They have robbed his world of concord and he cannot abide the loss. In happier times he would have spoken a more familiar vein. 'Hoe your own row of beans,' I can hear him say. 'Listen to the wind, mark the solitude of the loon, imbue its commentary on the majesty of night. These are friends you can trust; they will never betray a true companion.' Go now. Go to the country club. See what you can learn."

"But I've been to the country club."

"So you have. I seem to be confused. Well then, what if we ask teacher? Ah, but you are the teacher."

"We need to get back to our beginnings."

"But the signs are so confusing. One way. No standing."

"Back to what made us strong."

"Right turn only, seven to nine a.m., four to six p.m."

"Something firm."

"Ask the taxi driver. Alas he's Pakistani."

"Back where I started."

"A letter to Dear Abby."

"I need to go home."

"But is it existentially plausible?"

"Grandma's."

"Grandma wore a burlap sack."

"But there were stories in the pockets."

"She might let you go to the carnival."

"There's a shortcut through the woods."

"Perhaps they'll have a carrousel."

"Oh for a ride on the carrousel."

"But you don't have a ticket. What will you do? Thrust your fists in your pockets? Fight back the tears?"

"She'll be there."

CHAPTER 32

POMP AND CIRCUMSTANCE

Graduation. *Pomp and Circumstance.* Bright faces, sunny hats, beaming parents, graduates in caps and gowns, embraces and good-byes. A lectern on a makeshift stage, rows of empty chairs, decorations, flowers, loud speakers strung to stately trees. Green grass. A beautiful June day. But I'm not graduating.

Here comes the grand procession. Mortarboards and tassels, gowns trimmed in school colors, faculty forward. Two columns. Wait a minute! They're marching! Military formation. They're old, bespectacled, gray beards and shoulder length hair…but all in step.

"Hope. Hope. Hope toop threep fope. Hope."

A drill sergeant! Barking cadence.

"Aren't they wonderful!"

"But they're not *supposed* to—Forrester!"

"Sign off! One Two! Sign off! Free Faw!"

They can count.

"Sing off one two! FREE FAW!"

All the way to four.

"AH doe know but AH been TODE!"

Oh God. It's going to be poetry.

"AH DOE KNOW BUT AH BEEN TODE!"

Subtle mastery of feeling and form.

"GA trude Stein is Passé CHAUD!"

That was French.

"Wassa mean?"

"I fink it's some kinna French pastry wit cold cheese on top."

"GA TRUDE STEIN IS PASSÉ CHAUD!"

"Who *is* he?"

"Dr. Everett Forrester. *Tres distingue.*"

"If Ah die in a bombast POEM!"

352

"Those sideburns just give me the goose bumps."

"IF AH DAA IN A BOMBAST POEM!"

"Married?"

"Who cares."

"BURY my ass in a tenured HOME!"

"Who's that guy in the corduroy jacket?"

"Some damn hippie."

"Why they got 'im blindfolded?

"He didn't finish his thesis."

"You can't shoot a man for—"

"Rat O BLEEK! Hotch!"

"Flintlocks! Where'd they get—"

"Dee TAIL! OLT! Pot! HARMS!"

"Must be a college prank."

The library. Right on the front steps. Now he's reading from the Book of Joyce, Chap. 1, Verse 1.

"And when you wet the bed…first it is warm…then it gets cold."

"Just what ta hell do you think you're doing Forrester!"

"Red! DAY!"

"Some kind of theater."

"HAIM!"

"They're going to scare the birds away."

"FIE! YAH!"

They did it! I can't belie—Right on campus! Who gave 'em live ammo? Forrester! You're dawg mate Forrester! In his office. Smash the goddamn Bruegel! HAI! The philodendron! HAI!…Oh no. Faculty meeting. Whole damn department.

"Coffee?"

"Damn you Forrester."

"Surely we can be civil about this little foray into adolescent *angst.*"

"Will you look at what you've done!"

They dart knowing glances, wry smiles, some sympathetic, some—

"I'm not on drugs dammit!"

"No one said you were. Have you had these feelings of persecution before?"

"No—yes. That's a loaded question dammit! I know I'm unprepared, I only want to say…the country club—not what it seems—out on the steps—they just shot—"

"Try to speak in coherent sentences please."

"Da...danger, I—you—there's—"

"Someone's in danger? Source please?"

"Why...the spirits."

"You've been talking to the spirits?"

"Damn you Forrester."

"I'm afraid it's already been done."

"Yes, for centuries, maybe that's why there's something to it."

"What...did the spirits have to say?"

"We're in danger."

"Who?"

"All of us. The whole planet." I knew I shouldn't have trusted them. "Okay. Forget about the spirits, you're not ready for that part yet."

"Where are these spirits?"

"All around us. Inside us. You and—Why are you looking at me?"

"Please continue."

"The human spirit is a simple thing...but it needs care. It remains a mystery but opens the universe—stop looking at each other like that."

"What else did the spirits have to say?"

"Life is better than death. Love is stronger than hate. Peace takes more courage than war. Nature is big, and silent, but it's not our enemy. Right and wrong are stilts to help us see over the horizon. Death is not our master—PAY ATTENTION!—art is the speech of the gods; the gods are the human spirit reflected on the face of heaven, the human spirit is a spark of heaven caught in living flesh. When they respond in kind, there's music. Music, is the sound of the universe expanding. Laughter is the water of life smoothing over the rough spots. Fear is the only—"

"In here doctor. Thank you for coming personally."

"You son of bitch Forrester."

"No one's going to harm you."

"I'm gonna mess you up real bad Forrester."

"Try to relax."

"White jacket huh? Then you're—"

"Oh no. I just run rats in the psych department."

"White rats huh?"

"Some gray, a few black. Pigeons too, they're more amiable to conditioning. Wanna candy bar."

"I'm not done with you Forrester!"

"How long's it been since you've been to a ball game?"

"A long time...not since high school."

CHAPTER 33

OUT BEHIND THE BLEACHERS

"Watch that milk shake!"

"Did I glitch ya?"

"These are my good pants dammit!"

"Looks like ya—"

"Shut up!"

Washington Senior High. Homecoming. Car horns, cowbells, whistles, catcalls. The band down front, majorettes warming up. The Homecoming Queen and her court on a small platform. The scoreboard clock counting down. Field lights on telephone poles, faded chalk lines, goal posts decorated red, white, and blue. And there's our mascot, Evel Eagle—Fortney Clinkscale, the student body president who looked more like a mascot out of costume.

The bleachers. Rowdies. My buddy Boomer, an obese eighth grader who should have been a year ahead of me, got his nickname from a chronic problem with flatulence, the terror of fifth period study hall, tonight all decked out in a greasy DA and black leather jacket over a pink V-neck sweater sprinkled with pretzels and coke. Loud, obnoxious, spewing popcorn in your face everytime he opened his fat trap and now he dropped his damn milk shake. Right in my lap.

"FreshMUN FreshMUN, nothin' in the water GUN!"

"POW!" Another paper bag. Popcorn over everybody.

"Hey kid! Ya wanna try a knuckle sam'wich!"

"Shod op!"

"Shod op yersowf!"

"Mommy why does the eagle have a zipper on his back?"

"EY! I had t'ree canny bars! 'Oo tookit!"

"You little creep! Ya got it all over my dress!"

"Sooo I'm rea' sca'ed."

"Mommy why is that man's head painted blue?"

"When's the game start?"

"Tomorrow, this's the pep rally."

"Mommy what's that man got in the brown bottle?"

"POW!"

"Okay you little shit!"

"Haaalp, get er off me, she got cutties ow ow!"

"Eeyuu, he's got grease on his—"

"Mommy what are those people doing under the blanket?"

"Who we playing?"

"The Reds," says the fife player in a sparkling new band uniform.

"Why aren't you with the rest of the band?"

"I got a doctor's excuse."

"Too bad. What's your name?"

"Bertrand Clinkscale. Call me Birdie."

"Fortney's brother?"

"POW!! Did I sca' ya? Did I sca' ya?"

"Why's everybody going crazy Birdie?"

"Becuz we're two touchdown favorites, becuz, becuz our tough defense. Nobody can score on us. It should be a real barn burner."

"Yeah," Boomer belched. "De Reds 're murder on 'ere home fiel'."

"But this is our field."

"Dey go crazy man. Every game, four five fights. Out na parkin' lot. Knifes. Boddoes. Cops 'fraid a come aroun'. Pow! Brass knuccoes. Pow! Pow! Pow! Pow! Pow! Here comes da cheerleaders! Yeaaaa!"

"Jay! Zuss!! KAY!! RICE!!!!"

They came running past the bleachers, two cartwheeling, the others clapping. Bright smiles.

"Wow! Check out the—"

"UuuuuGH!"

"I'll check 'er oil. POW!"

"Watch that milk shake! Oh no not again. These are my good pants dammit!"

"You're gonna be spittin' teet' in a minute kid."

"Tough titty little kitty."

"Act your age ya dumb freshman."

"Humpa humpa!"

"Who's the big one?"

"She's da cap'n."

"Well, how come—"

"Shh. Don't ask."

"Isn't she just a little bit—"

"Shhhh!"

"How'd she get to be Captain? She can't even—"

"Shut up!"

White uniforms, blue trim, varsity letters on their chests, red "A"s trimmed in gold. They run with stiff elbows, bells and white snowballs on their shoestrings, stop, neat right face, winning smiles, hands to their hips looking at each other, now cupped for the first number. Heads atilt. Cute.

"Sidown!"

"SIDOW' YERSE'F! Pinkie pants."

"If you don' yell yer guts out you ain' sittin' wid us!"

All together now. Fists up. Chests out. Jump. Kick. Aaaand…Red tights.

> *READY! LET'S! YELL!*
> *We're the Yanks, We got the tanks!*
> *We got the brains, We got the planes!*
> *They're the gooks, They got the flukes!*
> *Got no dollar, Got no Beau!*
> *If they holler, Let 'em go!*
> *Down the hatch and hello Ho!*

"I never heard that cheer before."

"Just shut up, don't—"

"Well, I didn't think that was appropriate—"

"Hey kid wha' grade you in?"

"Ninth."

"Ee's okay."

"What difference does it make what grade I'm in?"

"Knock it off! The upper classmen'll take ya out behind the bleachers."

"Ya gonna be hearin' some chin music KID!"

"Let's go (BOOM BOOM) let's go!"

"Jiss don't say nuttin' 'bout de cap'n o' de cheerleaders o-KAY?"

> *READY! LET'S! YELL!*
> *Keep the peace, the status quo!*
> *Yell with us and let 'em know!*
> *Slanted eyes and teeth are sin!*

Blood's not blue in yellow skin!
So come on team let's do like Sioux!
Mouth Tse Tung and Food Man Chu!
"Now that cheer definitely had racist ramifications!"
"Shut...up."
"Sue who?"
"It had absolutely nothing to do with school spirit! Good sportsmanship! Or the principles this—"
"Principal! Where?"
"Sidown, ya dumb freshmun!"
"This is NOT what we stand for! The cheerleaders are wrong! Racism and violence are symptomatic of moral decay! We can overcome both. The Constitution has weathered worse storms; it is strong enough to bear dissent, humble enough to withstand contempt; it's the better part of ourselves; if we trust it, it will guide us but we must sustain it by giving it our faith. We can't win with guns alone. It is NOT Un-American to question—"
"IF YOU DON' SHUD UP DA UPPERCLASSMUNS IS GONNA BEAT DA PISS OUT OF US!"
"Look a' da freshmun, he pee peed his pants!"
"It's a milk shake dammit!"
"Pee PEE pee PEE, should a' wore a tee PEE!"
"We're better than this! We're a decent people! A moral people! Our foreign policy should reflect our best—"
"Police! Where?"
"We cannot expect to secure the future with—"
"Boom Boom Rah Rah Boom Boom!"
"With a nineteenth century posture based on—"
"We're number one! We're number one!"
"Ethnocentrism and superiority. The Constitution does not sanction hatred and dirt; its purpose is to overcome them. Its light will show the way, it's power reaches to the darkest alley but we have to embrace it. Freedom isn't diminished in the sharing, we defend it best by practicing it, every act of freedom enacts—" Toilet paper. Great.
"FreshMUN FreshMUN, can't fill up a hot dog BUN!"
"Don't pop yer falsies ya four-eyed hussies!"
READY! LET'S! YELL!
Law and Order, Peace with Honor
Drop a quarter in the slot, sir

Crack the night stick, make 'em beller
Keep the Faith or you are yeller
If you're in a moral pickle
That'll be another nickel

"Stuff that damn cowbell! If we cheapen the life of others, we—"

"FreshMUN FreshMUN, powder sugar on his BUNS!"

"The cheerleaders don't know what t' hell they're talking about! Stop ogling their underpants and listen to what they're saying! DAMMIT how'd she get to be captain of the cheerleaders she can't even get 'er fat ass off the **AHHH!** All right lemme rephrase the ques—"

"FreshMUN FreshMUN, mama's on a diaper RUN!"

"Now we gonna git ut—I tol' ya t' shud up!—"

"Stop your damn bawl—"

Behind the bleachers. Tough guys. Leather jackets. Joe's Texaco, American Legion, Central Catholic. Gave up soap for Lent. We've had it. Nine, ten, if they're so tough, how come it's twelve against—swaggering, heads boppin', match sticks in their teeth, DA's, Luckies rolled up in T-shirt sleeves, garden hose stretched over their biceps. Tattoos—Big Rosie, Sweet Hellion. I knew I should've stayed home tonight.

"MARAUDERS!"

What t' hell? Looka tha' boy sprint! Over the hood, six guys in one—peel out baby!

Vrooommmmmmmmmmmm-m-m-m-m.

What t'hell?

"Ooooo looka d'arley."

"Harley who?"

VmmVmmVrummmmmmm-m-m-m-m-m-m-m.

Two, three, four. Circling. Roaring. Dust swirling. Big bikes. Shiny gas tanks, chrome spokes, steel studded saddle bags, silver handle bars, tassels. Grim riders on a grim errand—greasy jeans, black leather jackets, boots, earrings, gold tooth.

"We 'ad it now. Thems was nuttin', 'eese is—"

"Don't start bawlin'."

Whoa! There she is. On back of the lead bike. Golden hair flitting in the breeze, delicate neck, fine forehead, straight back, doeskin jacket with matching high heeled boots, jeans, nice fit—

"If she 'ad a nickel in 'er bocket you could—"

"Shut up!"

"'eads."

A tiny diamond in her ear. The carriage of her head, the smile. It's *her!* She's looking at me. What does she want?

"Don't look at the drags," Birdie whispered.

"Drags?"

"De chicks man! Don' eeben look at 'em."

Shoulders back, hands on the grips, she looks you straight on, no airs, no pretense—"

"Don' eeben fink abou' wookin at 'em!"

The faint smile. The night goes gentle to her touch.

"Yer still lookin'. Bieee doe wanna die!"

The carrousel! She gave me a ticket. She doesn't get old. How her hair dances on the wind.

"Don't say nuttin' neidder."

She's not like the other girls. I'd like to speak to her but what would I say? I'm only a freshman.

"Now he gettin' off da bike. We bote gonna dieee!"

"Shut up!"

"Birdie, toooo."

"Don't let 'em know you're scared."

"Sooo Jiss looka d'og."

"What?"

"Sooo I wanna sit on da big ole 'og jiss once."

"Hog?"

"Before I dieee—"

"HOG?"

"Go fer a lil' ride before I diieeee!"

"You *filthy* minded—"

"Let him go!"

"Back off Birdie I just about had it with this two ton fart tank one more crack I'm gonna rip yer tongue out and dump ya in a milk shake factory!"

"Le' go my t'roat Yie dint do nuttin—"

"He's talking about—"

"DA BIKE!"

"The bike?…Oh."

"Ereee comes. I wassn' lookin miss'er BAAAAA—"

"Forrester!"

"Yie doe wanna dieee."

"Spill yer milk shake?"

"It can happens when you slit in the blitches sit in the bleachers! Dammit."

"Relax Tiger. Those big shakes must be hard to handle."

"You're not so tough Forrester, I'm not afraid o' your SWITCHBLADE! Oh real cute WATCH IT! DAMN you that was close!"

"Wanna hear it twang?"

"If this gets back to the faculty lounge, you're through!"

"How 'bout a little tune fifer?"

"Leave 'im alone, can't ya see he's got asthma?"

"Ain't that too bad. How 'bout a little Yankee Doodle?"

"Don't play it Birdie!"

"Hear about the fife player up at Central Catholic?"

"He's got a doctor's excuse *Forrester.*"

"Had an unfortunate accident—"

"He's got a big brother *Forrester.*"

"Walked straight into a closed fist."

"His dad's a councilman."

"Fife got jammed right down his throat."

"His mom works for school board!"

"Every time he burps...out comes Dixie. Off key. What about you big guy? Wanna sing it for me?"

"Don't do it Boomer!"

"Way down yonner inna lan' o' gotten—"

"Don't let him intimidate you!"

"Dem dat plants 'em is soon frogotten—"

"What's a matter malt pants, don't like good music?"

"Watch your mouth Forrester!"

"...Your Gramma wore a burlap sack."

"NO SHE DIDN'T...show some courtesy to the lady."

"She's my lady. I guess I'll show 'er what I want."

"She's NOT yours! You don't own—"

"Yes, she is—and yes, I do. You better show *her* some courtesy. She asked to drop in, wants to know if these are your friends. Noblesse oblige."

"Looka WAAAY, looka way, Dixie—"

Good God. Boomer and Birdie. Birdie and Boomer. Either way...What am I gonna...What'll she think?

"Well?"

"Wipe that damn grin—"

"No law against smilin' is there?"

"…Yes…they're my friends."

"Real good. Mama's proud. He-he-he."

"What a' you laughin' at? You don't have any friends!"

"See ya around Tiger."

He turned his back. DA. Lot o' grease. Chains. Bandanna. Skull and crossbones on a shiny leather vest, two rows of steel studs encircling it, dark red gems in the eye sockets. Probably glass. Faded crimson lettering. "Marauders." "Harvard."

"You stole that motorcycle!"

"BAAAAAA—"

He's circling back, swaggering, real cool, head boppin,' smiling delicately.

"I'm afraid I didn't catch that."

"I said…Mr. Harley and Mr. Davidson have obviously *lapsed* into bourgeois lassitude apropos—

"Lassy what?"

"Are ya gonna poun'm inna groun'?"

"Of course not. Marauders don't get mad. Marauders get even."

"OUCH! That was below the Ahh! Ohhh!"

"What d' ya say Slim? Like that bike?"

"I hate bikes!"

"Good. Keep blowin' that fife, and watch out for those blitches."

"Did he crack yer coconuts?"

"I hate that son of a bitch."

Vroommmmmmmm.

Straight up! Ascending into the sky! Front wheel spinning slow. Up, up. She's still there. Hang on.

"BAAA!"

Higher. Over the field lights. Up through the smog. Into the clouds. Don't let go. Please don't let go."

"BAAAAAAAAAA!"

"Stop your damn bawling! You're gonna be okay Birdie, take a deep—He can't *do* that! He's not better than us!"

"Yiii doe wanna diiie!"

"Get hold of yourself! It's an optical illusion! Some kind o' cheap circus trick!"

There she goes. Up and away. If only I could tell you…always the wrong time, the wrong place.

"Thems was angels!"

"Marauders! Read the label. And get off your knees. That's just where they want us. Charisma. Fancy suits. That's all they got. Pull up your pants! I can see your—"

"Now I went an' squash my canny BAAA!"

"I'm gonna get you Forrester."

What does she see in him? What t' hell does she see in him?

CHAPTER 34

UNDER THE KNIFE

A doctor's office. Diplomas on the wall, bookcase, dispensary with a red cross. He's sitting in a high topped chair with his back to his desk where someone's file lies open next to a fish hook and a scalpel. A polished wooden box to one side, something thumping inside, red and yellow wires issue out a brass keyhole rising to an overloaded outlet pulling out of the wall, blood oozing down. And a bust of a human head staring into space with penciled-in regions, Sorrow, Guilt, Fear, and a large area, Unknown. Some damn shrink. Sure enough, there's a couch. He'll wanna trot out his butterflies, I'm supposed to see inkblots! Well, I'm not telling him my dreams.

"Nyamu!"

"Indeed."

"You startled me."

"Small wonder. It is my unhappy duty to inform you you have once again managed to botch your assignment beyond recognition. The idea was to salvage grace, not savage it. I am much distressed with your paltry efforts in the light of so grand an enterprise, one we have had the apparent misfortune to entrust to you in the absence of more viable candidates so sadly wanting in this age of material ease. Where to begin. There is more to life than cheerleaders, motorcycles, and clean pants. To put it in language you can understand, 'tis the fourth quarter and the clock runneth.

"Soon your manhood will be tested. You will come to a dark cave overgrown with luxuriant foliage trickling to the music of a small fountain. You will recall the sound of the owls and the swallows in the umbrage of a dark sycamore by a quiet lake. You will see a 'No Admittance' sign with a red light over the entrance. Ignore the sign. Go in to the cave. Is that clear enough?

"Good. This is the last time I can be of assistance. If you have further need you must create me in the deep of your heart. Go then. Unborn generations

wait the outcome of this little play so absurdly cast on a minuscule planet slung to a wayward star. But remember, there is nothing in the universe without a purpose. A chance mutation of a single gene may send waves of welcome to the faintest galaxy a million years hence."

A giant door. Oak. Wrought iron straps, no knocker, locked tight as a drum, the whole thing set in a massive arch, Gothic circa 1180 southern France, with delicate floral designs carved into the limestone by a master hand, gargoyle heads spouting water trickling down the sides to a clear pool at the base. Lily pads, gold fish, birds singing. No Admittance. A blinking red light. They said to go in. Can't budge it.

"Password please."

"Oh no."

"The X-6000 biospace guidance mechanism is preprogrammed to commence operation pursuant to correct precoded aura stimulus analog. End transmission."

"A damn computer."

"Your response is incorrect. Please try again."

"Psittacus Erithacus!"

"Your response is incorrect. Please try again."

"I'm sick of these childish GAMES!"

Clink. Just a crack. Red light inside. Weighs a ton. What's holding it? Once more…this time everything I got.

After a superhuman effort I managed to squeeze in but failed to notice two large oxygen tanks leaning precariously against the radiator behind the door; it gave way just as I lunged forward, a cloud of hot steam escaped, a flock of cackling hens rent the air with feathers flying, sparks sizzling, a loud clang, then the tanks toppled over into a glass medicine cabinet knocking down a row of blue bottles. The big one splattered all over the floor. Milk of Amnesia.

"Don't anybody light a match!"

Laughter. People all around. Down below, up in galleries. A theater!

"They'll never get it back in the bottle."

What are they laughing at?

"Here's Rosemary for remembrance!"

A parrot. What an incredible place. Dark. Damp. Cobwebs. An eerie sense of deja vu. A reddish glow like a dark room. People working over a table, early American with eagle talons over mahogany balls, fluted legs hiding a neat row of rubber galoshes. TV cameras, electric wires, something dripping.

An overhead fan stirring cigarette smoke. A clock on the wall, eleventh hour. Miss October, surgical diagrams on her navel. Rubble on floor, peanut shells, candy wrappers. Two pin ball machines, a jukebox, Coke cooler, fishing rod and wicker basket, a stack of golf clubs, TV over the bar. *Search for Tomorrow.* "Veronica, I'm your best friend and I feel I should tell you…"

Dusty pickle jars on sagging shelves. Look at 'em. Positivists, Behaviorists, Supremacists, Fundamentalists. They must use a lot of formaldehyde down here. *"Crock!"* A bird cage. Dangling from a cloth cord trying to pull 220 off an overhead 110, the entire system jerry-rigged to a fuse box hammered to the wall.

Who's that on the table? I don't have a twin bro—there's some mistake, you have the wrong what are the straps for?

"Pomp and Circumcision."

"No! I'm already—I can prove it!"

Masks. Narrow eye slits, cowrie shells, raffia, white lab jackets and clip boards, one in a welding helmet. These aren't this isn't a proper hospital! Plasma bottles tied to the nine iron, plastic tubes in and out the Coke machine, through the bird cage, colored liquid pulsating up and down, into a computer terminal with a black cat stretched out licking her chops. Busy nurses…odd uniforms, leather miniskirts, high heel boots. Lot o' make-up.

"Where am I?"

"In the operating room."

"What's that?"

"Essence of Lethe."

"From a whiskey bottle?"

"Put a bottle in front o' me for a frontal lobotomy. Crock."

"Lobotomy! Then why are you shaving my abdomen?"

"Men. You're all alike, you think your brains are in your—"

"Are you a real nurse?"

"Yes. Try to relax."

"Then why are you wearing—"

"I moonlight at the *Roxy* to enhance my income. As you know nursing is a critically underpaid profession. In your future endeavors please do not fail to mention this egregious injustice at any and every opportunity."

"What's in the crock?"

"Spare parts."

"I'm outta here!"

"Shall I zurrow zee zwitch Doktore—"

"Not yet Igor."

"Somebody change the station."

"Welcome to another episode of, Young Dr. Forrester."

"FORRESTER! Help! Police!"

"Good morning gentlemen. Ladies. We are about to witness an extraordinary medical phenomenon. The patient is in his mid twenties, a former graduate fellow, now a dropout, undirected, uncommitted, an unbeliever with no visible means of support and a credit rating of zero, none of which is fatal in these enlightened times; however we are not looking at a simple case of alienation nor this generation's lamentable inability to overcome puberty. I'm afraid it's worse. The polarities of his psychoresponse system have been reversed. In fine, the thought processes are functioning in the present but his feelings are antediluvian. The more he tries to cope with the present, the deeper he regresses into the past. Gentlemen, what you see is a living anachronism. Moreover his condition is complicated by the most malodorous of all diseases—idealism. No outward symptoms, no apparent pain, he could pass for a Republican. I'll never understand it. After two years in hopeless poverty with some first hand experience of dictatorial methods, after Mississippi, Mai Lai, watching his friends bullied and beaten in Chicago, the patient, for lack of a better term, still believes in the innate goodness of his fellow man—"

"Wrong—"

"Although he will not admit it."

"I believe in the possibility of—"

"The beneficence of Nature—"

"The endurance of Nature!"

"Recently, this most heinous condition has taken a turn for the worse complicated by psychotic phenomena. The patient claims to be hearing voices—the wind whispering, birds rehearsing their parts, underground radio broadcasts, flight schedules to Los Angeles—let us hope the hippopotami have yet to discover Verdi. Given this incorrigible tendency to fanta—"

"Nonprofit ontological ruminations."

"We have no alternative. Surgery."

"NO! He's no damn doctor!"

"Let's get to work."

"He's a quack!"

"We will attempt a bilateral abdominal aphrodectomy."

"He's mad!"

"The operation itself is experimental but the technique is well known. Okay let's open him up."

"ALL RIGHT I'LL GET A HAIRCUT!"

"Are we ready then? Good. Scalpel. Clamp. Larger. Thank you. Suction. Lower. And again. *If I were a rich man, if I were a rich man, Yah da da da da da da da daa.* Are the vital signs holding? Brace. Thongs."

"Tongs, Doctor?"

"Yes, tongs. Can you get the cat away—"

"That's an awfully wide incision isn't it?"

"Hickle trickle true."

"Damn thing's dull as a butter knife! Oh...Thank you nurse. Deeper. Suction. Get that crap out of there. Where's the trouble light? Well, who unplugged the stereo?"

"I don't think I wanna see—"

"Bloodnot blue. Bloodnot blue."

"Just as I thought...all red inside."

"Fickle clue, fickle clue."

"I think I'm going to be ill."

"Ah ha."

"I'm not supposed to see this, am I?"

"Crock!"

"Ah HA!"

"There's a word..."

"Drill. Double flanged. Seven-eights."

"'Pathetic.'"

"Okay let 'er rip!"

"'Aesthetic.'"

"We're going in through the outer wall of the moral filament...kind o' sloppy."

"'Anna—'"

"We're penetrating the outer wall of the ego defen—"

"Anesthetic! You forgot the ANESTHETIC!"

"'Yeeess!'"

"Dammit I'm supposed to be asleep!"

"Gentlemen...our long labors are nearly over. We are on the verge of a major scientific breakthrough. You are about to see what no human eyes have ever seen. Are we together then?"

"Shall we inform the Nobel Committee Doctor?"

"Let them wait. Now then, we're going directly into the subconscious, no need of lengthy psychoanalysis, a simple twist of the switchblade."

"OUCH!"

"Let him gush a little, we'll mop up later."

"The AMA's gonna hear about this Forrester!"

"I'm flicking away a few chips of ego shell. Notice how hard, one of nature's toughest excretions. Probe."

"He's insane!"

"Notice the excessive concentrations of Dostoevsky and Nietzsche. Kierkegaard. Kafka. Bernard Shaw. Oscar Wilde—interesting. Euripides. Dante. Goethe. All foreign matter. Rabelais. Marquis de Sade."

"Everett this is humiliating."

"Karl Marx. Note that please. Lord Byron. James Joyce, undigested. Amos Tutuola. Hermann Hesse. Melville. Don't they give them Jonathan Edwards anymore? What's this! Up against the spleen. Ah HA! Just as I thought! Thoreau! And it's inflamed! It'll have to come out!"

"No! Never!"

"Doctor he's hemorrhaging."

"Now then, we're near the end of our long quest."

"Everett. Perhaps you should go on sabbatical."

"Nylon line please. Nine pound."

"A semester in Saskatoon."

"In my tackle box!"

"Yes. A little fishing."

"Thank you. This is going to be a rather delicate affair. He's a slippery little sucker. Thinks he can evade the limelight. This is somewhat like trying to capture a recalcitrant turd with a spinster's darning needle—"

"You should know Everett."

"A little bit to the…patience is our indubitable GOTCH YA!"

"OW!"

"Ladies and Gentlemen…the human spirit. Yes! A worm on a fish hook. See how it squirms. Doesn't like the glare of reality. Hear it respond to sharp stimuli. Tweezers please."

"AHHHH!"

"Hardly poetry, but empirically veritable. Nonetheless these infantile utterances are somehow retained in the jelly where they grow to monstrous proportions thus begetting the definitive human characteristic—"

"I'm gonna get you you son of a—"

"Revenge. It's all in the memory—God, love, patriotism—control what goes in and the organism will dance to whatever tune we play. See how it fights; it doesn't want to remember but oh it must. The pain is excruciating. Observe how valiantly it struggles, this mindless revolting worm born in the world's offal impaled on a cosmic fish hook. How freedom loves pain. The raw dialectic of history. Thus it comes, bare-assed into a cold universe, this slimy clop of fish bait, and it would be a man. It's not satisfied being a worm, do you hear? This disgusting piece of PROTOPLASM! Has the GALL! To think it can be something better! And if a man, why not a gentleman, a Lord, God Himself? And if it were free, what then? Love? Marriage? More worms? Note how exquisitely the steel of reality pierces the flesh of the spirit. The pain is delicious. Observe the shaft penetrate the groin and emerge through the heart—how poetic—how it would curse if only it had a tongue. What a babble of puerile obscenity would greet our ears. What can it hope for?—this worthless piece of squirming slime—comfort? Love? Bourgeois respectability? Better it were never born. Just a pinch of the tweezers to abort an existence as meaningless as this. But not this time. Let's throw it back. Why? Bait. This one carries a fine specimen of the disease—idealism—the sweet cancer of youth, invisible, incurable, seemingly harmless. Hopefully it will spread to epidemic proportions. Imagine the carnage! WARS! RAPINE! DEATH AND DESTRUCTION!! Why the munitions production alone is too staggering to think about, and WE! Gentlemen, stand to reap the profits! UNHEARD OF! OBSCENE! GIGANTIC! PROFITS! **Enoff to r-r-rule zee VARLT!** And why? Because one small worm…wasn't satisfied being a worm."

"You've lost it Everett! You have finally irrevocably LOST IT! Get those damn tweezers out o' my face! You're not aborting me you son of a bitch! I can too scream! Don't pretend you can't hear me **LOOK AT WHAT YOU'RE DOING!**"

CHAPTER 35

DESCENT INTO HELL

"Where am I?"

"Post Op Recovery."

Well-lit. Clean. White sheets, curtains, a vase of cut flowers. Everything perfect, peaceful. The operation! Here's a doctor, another studying a clipboard, a man in a business suit, a trim little nurse. Very serious. The first clears his throat.

"The operation," a deep monotone, "was not a success."

"So what happens now?"

A long pause. Each seemed to be waiting for the other to speak. The nurse leaned close to whisper.

"You're going to hell."

"…I beg your pardon."

They looked at each other in embarrassment, then the second doctor, the one with the clip board, enunciated his words very carefully.

"She said…you are going…to hell."

"But I'm not dead."

"A common myth," avoiding eye contact. "They have a strong PR department."

"Is it possible there's been a mistake?"

No answer.

"I don't recall doing anything that bad, I…ah, that picture I busted up in Forrester's office, a cheap print, I'm thoroughly ashamed…that time with Jenny, we were consenting adults…well…teenagers, she's on the school board now…true I was a bit idealistic—consider my genetic inheritance, peer pressure. I DIDN'T DO ANYTHING THAT BAD!"

"It's not a question of what you did," the nurse smiled tucking in my blanket. "Your spirit was severely weakened due to repeated failures, lack of

371

exercise, impoverished diet. Don't feel bad," she leaned over and pinched my cheek. Nice perfume.

"We tried a surgical bypass," the second doctor continued, "but it went haywire. We couldn't find an electrician."

"After that unfortunate oversight," the first said rather sheepishly, "we had no choice but to go ahead with a direct transplant from a primitive source. It looked good on paper. We don't know what went wrong."

"I'm very sorry," said the man in the suit.

"Can I get a second opinion?"

"We've already talked to specialists. They all agree transplanting the human spirit is not an exact science."

"Can I call my congressman?"

"Your *congressman?* The entire United States Government will shortly be at your disposal."

"With no red tape," the nurse added. "Sorry, sir."

"Can I call an attorney?"

Sideward glances. A long pause. The first came forward, this time with a little more conviction.

"As a lifelong member of the AMA, it is my bittersweet duty to inform you, you will not have difficulty finding legal counsel...good legal counsel...ever again."

"At reasonable prices. Sorry, sir."

"Which brings us to a little matter of a few papers to sign," said the third doctor, the one in the business suit, "and we can wrap this one up."

The first looked at him harshly and he caught himself.

"Figuratively speaking of course. Can you sit up, that's fine, right here on the bottom line then, thank you, and again please, press down hard, I'm afraid they're all in quadruplicate, very well, and once more at the X, aaand again here below—"

"Is all this really necessary?"

"I'm afraid so, initial here please...and here, very good. This is the last one now, you have a fine hand, and one more at the bottom, yes. There, that wasn't so bad."

"What is it?"

"A release," said the second doctor, "We can't afford another class action suit."

"Which reminds me, if they ask you what you do, lie, say you're a data processing trainee; you'll find the accommodations more amiable."

"You always wanted to be an explorer," the nurse winked. "This is the chance of a lifetime."

"How will I know when I'm there?"

"Just open your eyes."

"...And?"

"Follow the crowd."

"But how do I get there...physically?"

"Oh we've made amazing progress this century," she smiled pleasantly. "You can fly nonstop from L.A."

"Devlon Airlines Champagne Flight 969 nonstop from Los Angeleeze now preparing for final descent. All passengers please remain seated, extinguish all comfortable memories and refrain from hoping. Customs and Immigration officials remind you to have your indoctrination papers in order and be prepared to declare all sins and follies in excess of two dollars. Forms are available fore and aft. As we bank into our final turn, may I call your attention to the starboard windows where your captain will shortly give you a breathtaking view of your permanent new home; local weather conditions remain cloudy with increasing smog, seasonal heat lightening in the distance, and a one hundred percent chance of acid rain. Do not be alarmed by the bright flames in the outlying suburbs; these are only small grass fires caused by careless weekend campers, the Forest Service reports they are under control and will be liquidated shortly. To help you acclimate to your new environment our orientation staff is eagerly waiting to answer any and all questions. For further assistance dial H at the nearest red courtesy telephone. Smoking is of course permitted on all levels including the cancer ward. We hope you've enjoyed our in-flight movies, *Mr. Smith Goes to Washington* and *Beat the Devil,* and thank you for flying Devlon."

"Oh Miss! Excuse me. There's been a mistake. I'm going *to* Los Angeles. I'm on the wrong flight."

"I'm sorry, sir, your ticket clearly specifies your final destination."

"Well the ticket's wrong."

"I'm afraid that's not possible, sir."

"Tell the pilot to turn around."

"I'm sorry, sir, that is not possible. Can I get you a cocktail?"

"No. I wanna go to Los Angeles. Disneyland. I wanna ride the carrousel."

"Try to remain calm, sir, I'll see if we have any tranquilizers."

"I don't want a tranquilizer."

"Can I turn on some inspirational music?"

"No."

"There's nothing to worry about, sir, everyone's a little nervous at first. Try this pillow. Think of Devlon Acres as a quiet retirement community. Of course if you're more affluent you'll prefer Devlon Estates: condominiums with whirlpools, massage parlors, shuffleboard, group therapy on Thursdays, and don't tell anyone I told you but don't miss the midnight show at the *Roxy*. And we have a professional football franchise, the True-blue Demons. We're hosting the Monday Nighter this season! Think of it this way—no one has ever come back. Doesn't that speak well of our community?"

"Why are those people singing in the back of the airplane?"

"Businessmen. They think they're going to Vegas for a sales conference; it's the easiest way to get them aboard. May I suggest our in-flight video courtesy of our Division of Human Resources, it documents the many and marvelous job opportunities waiting for persons with…the right stuff."

DEVLON ASSOCIATES
PERSONNEL CONSULTANTS

Air Conditioning: *sales, maintenance, all phases, all expenses paid*
Power Brokers: *knowledge of king making, smoke-filled rooms, bribes, blackmail*
Munitions Procurement: *design, manufacture, marketing*
Network Programming Executive: *visual acuity green, tastes negotiable, family values X-rated*
Image Makers: *turn black into white*
Lobbyists: *no morals necessary*
Racists: *pick your color*
Fundamentalists: *no experience necessary*
Psychopaths: *find your niche*
Terrorists: *must speak Arabic*
Dirty Tricksters: *unlimited opportunity*
Welfare Cheats: *full benefits*
Drug Dealers: *try a new habit*
Pro Athletes: *knoluge of beer cummershuls*
Mafiosoes: *pasta juss like a you mama*
Money Launderers: *a clean start*
Evangelists: *past sins waived*
Demagogues: *rabble rousing a must*

Missile Mechanic: *the sky's the limit*
Arsonists: *self starters*
Call Girls: *hot numbers only*
Rock Musicians: *eternal amplifications*
Third-rate Actors: *must read idiot cards*

IMMEDIATE OPENINGS

Drunks, liars, thieves, punks, bullies, thugs, goons, brigands, boobies, scoundrels of all denominations, statisticians, opinion makers, experts, spies, miscellaneous nonentities, university presidents, do-gooders, idealists.

UNCONDITIONAL DEFERMENTS
In the National Interest
by Order of the President

ALL CHILD ABUSERS

DEVLON ASSOCIATES
An Affirmative Action
Equal Opportunity Employer

lovers, puppy dogs, and children over eighty need not apply

"Excuse me, sir, I think we've found something for you. You are currently unemployed, a nonbeliever, no personal attachments, is that correct?"

"Not exactly—"

"And a liar. Perfect. A HIEROMA Operator."

"What's that?"

"DASA terminology. High Intensity Extrarational Reorientation Machine."

"I don't think I—"

"Relax, let's tighten up that seat belt just a tad."

"I haven't had any train—"

"Everything's on CRAP. Computerized Retroactive Predestination."

"Well, how do I—"

"Hang on to your stick and watch the flames go by."

"Hellar Excursion Module (HEM) maintaining high intensity orbit, visibility good, attitude 10,000 feet and holding. All systems go. Observation

Module (OM) has achieved full separation. Switching to eternal power. You're lookin' good Vulture."

"I've never flown a—"

"Prepare for final descent. Altitude 2000 feet. Trajectory looking good, pressure normal, temperature rising. G-forces, stronger than expected. Fire reverse thrusters, full power."

"Reverse thrusters, full power."

"Altitude 1500 feet."

"They're burnin' bright Houston."

"1200 feet. All systems go. Lateral guidance thruster, east nor' east, one zero degrees."

"I can see Mire Tranquility. Baby it's big."

"Aim for the edge little bird. You don't want to plop down in the middle of that."

"Rrroger."

"Lookin' good, just like a Sunday drive down US-1. 400 feet. Extend landing pods. Pitch 5.5 degrees. 300 feet. Right downtown, Manual Pilot engaged, steady she goes. Deploy heat shields. 200 feet."

"Shields deployed. I sure hope they work this time."

"We've got our fingers crossed. Continuing deceleration. 100 feet. Prepare for touchdown. Landing pods extended. 60 feet and closing. All readings normal. 40 feet. 30. 20. Ten. Nine. Eight."

"We're kickin' up a little dust Houston."

"All engines stop. Three. Two. One. We have touchdown! We have touchdown! The Vulture...has landed!"

"Wow. Here I am. I didn't think we could do it Houston. Houston? Over."

"We read you loud and clear Tranquility. Prepare for EVA immediately."

"Okay, I'll see if I can open the WHOA, it's warm out there Houston."

"Thaaat's right. Okay, just below the hatch you'll see a ladder, three rungs, a TV camera—"

"There he is! Faaantastic. The whole world's watchin' Tranquility."

"There's one giant step for me, one small step for mankind. Over."

"We read and copy Tranquility. Now we want you to unfurl the flag, on the pod bay door below the fire extinguisher, just pull the pin. Plant it...that's it. In front of the camera please, hands out of your pockets. How about a smart salute?

"Isn't this just a little—"

"The taxpayers wanna see where their money's going."

"Are you watchin' my body temperature Houston?"

"Your temperature's lookin' good Tranquility. Try to relax, take a look around. Over."

"Rrroger Houston. My boots are sinking in about a quarter inch, sandy soil. I can see several dry gulleys, some barren hills, not much vegetation—burdock, tumbleweed—rolls of barb wire down in some old canal works; I'm catching an organic fragrance, something like an Arkansas manure pile after a March shower. Over."

"Very good Tranquility, we read and copy."

"No sign of life Houston. Wait! There's a stone column half submerged in the muck, it's pretty well-encrusted with slime, but I can see floral patterns on the cornice, Hellenistic period. It looks like the outlines of a submerged city. There's a bombed out cathedral, a German Panzer. And a carrousel! Smashed horses. I have the feeling I've been here before, over."

"Negative Tranquility, keep moving."

"I'm walking east, I can see sheets of shimmering light in the atmosphere, a little bit like northern lights only brown, there's a slight breeze at my back. Heavy smog—I guess we expected that—can't see the sun, only a greenish glow straight overhead. Mostly brown clouds. Activity off in the distance…they look like flares—there goes another one! Faaantastic. Can't tell if they're natural or man-made. The grass fires seem to be a lot larger than they looked during descent. Over."

"Roger Tranquility. We read and copy."

"There seem to be sulfureous eruptions bubbling out of the ground, a few geysers, brownish green with yellow steam that ignites the minute it touches something. Debris blowing along the surface—"

"Roger Tranquility. We're reading you loud and clear. Can you give us a bearing on those geysers?"

"They're all around Houston. They seem to be worse up by the lake, flames fifty, sixty feet high, burning quite vigorously, wait a min—the water too! The whole damn thing! A Lake of Fire!…just like Cleveland. No big trick."

"This is Mission Control, twenty-seven years, five months, two days into the flight of Hades Eleven. EVA has begun, the mission is on schedule, all systems go. We will shortly have a taped message from the President."

"I seem to be on the outskirts of a large slum with low-rent tenements, boarded windows, TV antennas, lines of laundry strung to crumbling fire escapes. A foul vapor seems to be emanating from the city itself, there's an elevated freeway with heavy traffic—speed limit's still 55, radar enforced—some of the spurs appear to go nowhere, others drop off into the bubbling mud. Acres of free parking. Lot o' big cars—Caddies, Lincolns—crazy drivers, worse than Boston."

"Roger Tranquility. Here's the director."

"Good work TQ-1. I know it's tough but can you leave off your exploring a few seconds to effect a direct temperature reading? The boys down at the Divinity School are really excited. Over."

"...Ahh...negative Houston. I'm afraid, ah, I seem to have forgotten my thermometer. It's warm Houston. A little like an asphalt parade ground at a Texas army base in July. Okay...it's hot. There, I said it. Empirically, unequivocally...pretty warm. Remember to bring some light socks, Hawaiian shirts. Over. Houston? You still there Houston? Sorry about the thermometer. I must have left it on the bathroom sink with my toothbrush. Tell the boys at Divinity School I'll make it up to 'em."

"Roger. Forget the thermometer TQ-1, we've got another little item on the books. Can you get downtown? "

"That'll be tough Houston."

"Hot wire one of the cars!"

"...Ah, I don't know how to tell you this Houston. I'm afraid I don't know how to hotwire an automobile. But I haven't lost confidence in myself. I think...I know I can get the job done. I'm going to try to improve my performance and...and if you stick with me I'm certain I can do acceptable work. I've got my beginners handbook...here it is—foreword by Bill Clinton—first aid kit, I feel I'm ready...Houston? Can you hear me Houston?"

"Hotwire! In your handbook! Under Hillbilly Operations! Right after Intern Management!"

"That would be a misdemean—"

"What t' hell does it matter now!"

"Do I have authorization?"

"Affirmative! Get one with a radio!"

"Are we off the public frequency? Where did we get this guy? Is he gonna be smart enough to open a bird cage?"

"Water service to Devlon Heights and surrounding communities has been temporarily disrupted due to lobbyists clogging the main intake valves. Workmen are wrestling with the problem round the clock and expect to have service restored by early next century. Aaand to you early birds just tuning in, good morning, don't touch that dial, this is Underground Radio WELL, News, Weather and Wombah twenty-four hours a day, your alternative listening style at the far end of your dial. I'm Kit Chillenbraugh and I'll be with you until...what's today? Rrright, the first day of the rest of eternity. Thanks Eddie. When in doubt ask your engineer. So-okay. Weather conditions remain unchanged with a stationary high pressure front driving temperatures into the high 190's, that's 92 to 95 Celsius, smoke direction southeast, 5 knots, winds aloft westerly and holding, the Stench Factor Index on the Nielsen Scale, plus 154 and rising. The forecast for the next five millennia, continued high pressure, unseasonably hot, humid, scattered electric storms, dense smoke concentrations, increasing darkness and zero per cent chance of salvation. Aaand for you commuters on your way to the pits, we have this traffic advisory, a lime truck has overturned on the Dungbridge Overpass; traffic is being redirected via Potsdam Boulevard. Movin' right along...at 5:03 DST, we see our old buddy Howard Stern looking dapper as ever in hip boots and gas mask ready to expose the latest celebrity flap or possibly Madonna's octuplicate implant while I play some old favorites and perhaps a surprise or two for the boys down at Divinity School. Why die boys? You know you can't win. Why all the pain and depravation, lonely nights and empty promises? Give up before it's too late. The Devlon Imperial Army will graciously welcome your surrender and provide for your material comfort. Come on home boys. You've always belonged down here. Hugs and kisses.

"And now the news, brought to you by Devlon Airlines with five flights daily from Los Angeleeze. Despite high level assurances to the contrary, WELL News has learned the prestigious Union of Concerned Satanists is preparing to release a highly damaging report supporting widespread claims of increased and unsafe swamp levels. According to informed sources the report contains documentary evidence of particulate matter in the nation's water supply. Although officials at Redhall have declined comment, a spokesman who asked not to be identified called the story, quote, 'the inflatulation of an over jealous press corps.' On the local front, the Vice President was in town to dedicate the new ultramodern Berkeley People's Park. Calling for increased educational spending and drastically lower taxes, he told a crowd of enthusiastic supporters, 'Why not both? Why not now? Don't let nobody tell you higher education can't open no doors.' Do we have time?—no? Okay, a quick look at *What's Happenin' in Our Town*, tonight's guest lecturer at the Town Forum is former Secretary of the Inferno, Dr.

Henry Kissinger, his topic, 'The Menace of Free Elections in Third World Diplomacy.' And across town at the coliseum, ooooo, bad news, Oakland— excuse me, Rangoon Raiders 27, Demons 24. Tough luck guys. We'll get 'em next time, which is…on the road, the Washington Whiteskins and I don't have to tell you what it's like goin' in there and tryin' t' win one. What's the line Eddie? Skins by 21. Ouch! Well then, we're off to another glorious start on this perfectly luminous morning. For my first selection then, and this is for all you commuters fighting the rush hour madness and especially my old roommates back at Radcliffe, Boopsie, Bubbles, and Bang Bang, here he is just as I promised, old blue eyes himself, Frank Sinatra and…*Fools…Rush In.* Kit loves you."

CHAPTER 36

THE COLUD ENTRANCE

So this is it. No granite portals, words of wisdom, only a putrid ditch with a rotten plank. Steaming slime. Poopy on the sidewalk.

And a dirty ticket booth. Squeaky turnstile, beat-up port o' john, an old wino with a tin cup and a girly mag. Odd place to panhandle. A crooked signpost stuck in the mud, Seoul, Anchorage, Los Angeles. Thick smog. Smoke stacks in the distance. Sickly sky. And hot. Real hot. In the distance the Capitol. Its golden dome sinking in the quagmire but aglow in the spotlights.

High fence. Banged-up zinc, barb wire. Graffiti. No trespassing. A swastika. Uncle Sam Wants You. Kilroy Was Here. Impeach Earl Warren. Nixon-Agnew 68. And Smokey the Bear! Only YOU can prevent Eternal Fire.

A Billboard! Sunshine Village. Urban Renewal Project. Devlon Development Corp. in partnership with The DevlonBank and Sunshine Landscaping Inc., Garden City, N.J. Gaylord P. Sittrich, Commissioner. Your tax dollars at work.

Another billboard: Welcome to Devlon Estates, the Ultramodern Warm Springs Retirement Community, a tropical paradise you'll never want to leave.

I'm not sure they're telling the complete truth down here. Here comes an old Southern gentleman, Confederate jacket, scarlet sash.

"I beg yo poddon suh, this is the colud entrance. Whot folk go in up yonda, Maddox Avenoo an' Wallace Boulevaad."

Across the street another parking lot. 57 Chev. Pickets! Jim Crow must go. Equal Rights NOW.

A limousine. Real quiet. A tuxedoed chauffeur is opening the back door. A lady inside. It's *her!* Oh my. White satin, diamond earrings, flawless coiffure, sparkling jewels around a delicate neck, the carriage of her head. She's crossing the plank. Don't go in there! Effortless, the edge of her skirt dancing as she walks, not a smudge on her fine shoes, stops, removes a ticket from her purse, smiles to the attendant, even the wino, but always the touch of sorrow. She's disappearing behind the fence. Another smile! This time for me! Wants me to follow. She's in some kind of trouble. I don't want to go in there. I could make up a story—about going in. Nobody would know.

But the kids would know. There they are playing Keep-Away, the tallest dancing over the ball, challenging all comers. A skinny waif watches intently, understands at once, darts into the game, comes away with the ball, aims, shoots, BANG off the front of the ticket booth. A beer belly with a black cigar waddles out cursing, flood lights come on. The wino throws a bottle. Now's my chance. Jump the ditch.

WHOA! Nice doggie. Nice—three heads! Cerberus! A piece o' cake. Wonder if he'll take WATCHIT! Cash. Just like meat. The times they are a changin'.

A bus!...dilapidated but still runnin'. Excuse me? The rear...of course. Good morning Father. Rabbi. What's with him, bad karma? Ah! Idealists to the back of...that's cool, history balances its books—

"So this is a bazaar? You wanna trade gimmicks? Father O'Flattery sold out on miracles three centuries now. I can't get Notre Dame tickets for a kosher ham. Harry Quichena here was *this* close to enlightenment, then he wins the New Delhi lottery and blows it on a beauty queen, Miss Pollution Control, now look at him, an air conditioning repairman in the Offal Office. Don't trust anyone! Keep your hand on your wallet!"

Wow! Downtown! Skyscrapers! Traffic! Noise! Advertising everywhere. Catch the Evening News with Broderick Breenbane and Cheryl Honeycutt. Visit Sulfur Springs Natural Baths. Taxis. Follow me to The Rock Music Hall of Fame. The first mile free. More billboards. Adult bookstores. Neon lights. All thrusting skyward, fighting for attention, even in the graveyard: Get out and vote, Citizens for Vito Mozzarella, Chicago City Alderman, Democrat. Dine above the smog: The Condor Room high atop the Devlon Hilton. This week only, Burghers and Dogs, ten per cent off with coup on, Mamma Minsky's Meat Market. El Spoor Lager Beer, brewed from naturally foaming water deep in Nature's source, The U.G. Schmaltz Brewing Co., a Division of Devlon Spirits and Potables. Ride Elijah's Chariot at the New Old Testament Theme Park. SwampSong, The Natural Cologne for Men: One squirt and she'll drop at your feet. Bahamas, Puerto Prince, Paradise, Montana: Let us fly you there, Devlon Airlines.

Look! An electronic ticker-tape! Clear across the building. Market data. North Alaska Refrigeration and Air: n.a., Hollywood Enterprises: up one eighth, National Firearms: up one quarter, Hard Rock Electronics: up three eighths, International Dictatorial Machines: up one half, Nuclear Deterrents: up three quarters.

And a Directory! How convenient.

The Richard Nixon School of Government Ethics. The Kennedy Institute of Moral Superiority. Right across the street from each other. How about that? Lyndon Johnson Commission for National Quagmires. J. Edgar Hoover Center for Racial Equality. Richard J. Daley Memorial Stockyards. Malcolm X Blood Bank. The Dick Clark Conservatory of Music. The Warhol Gallery. The Barbara Walters Charm School. The Ronald Reagan School of Somnambulism. Jimmy Hoffa Bureau of Missing Persons. Norman Mailer Parole Review Board. Edward M. Kennedy Driver Training Academy. Giraldo Rivera School of Journalism. John Wayne Center for Gay Rights. Howard Hughes Shelter for the Homeless. Abbie Hoffman Pharmacy. The Allen Ginsberg Logorrhea Society. Woody Allen Symposium for Nervous Transcendence. Albort Shanker Refirm Skol. The Hugh Hefner Home for Unwed Mothers.

And further down the street: The Museum of Modern Art, National Warehouse of Television Commercials, Hollywood Screenwriters House of Procurement, CIA Experiment Station, KKK Laundry, white sheets only. The Devlon Savings and Loan Association: Why put off that dream? Interest free loans. Let us show you how.

Shops: Fonda Fashions, Designer jeans from the House of Hanoi. McCarthy, Kunstler, & Bailey, Suits for every occasion. GunsGalore, Saturday Night Specials, easy terms, NRA financing on request.

Services: Daly, Yorty, & Rizzo, Windy City Snow Blowers, Sales & Service from names you can trust. Hunt, Mitchell, & McCord, Hotel Security Systems. Morrison, McCartney, & Jagger, Consultants, Grass Care & Weed Control.

Professional offices: John Dean and Associates, Attorneys at Heart. Dr. Charles W. Colson, M.D., Hearts, Minds, and Testes. R. J. Reynolds Cancer Clinic. G. Gordon Liddy, Psychiatric Counseling Services. Eldridge Cleaver, Rape Crisis Intervention, political rapes only. Dulles, Kissinger, and Rusk, Dealers in Clandestine Affairs.

A Public Notice: All persons without valid documentation due to computer error report to Central Processing, Bureau of Emigrations, 101 Infinity Street. Bring Red Card, plus proof of recent immolation.

And the voice of televised confidence: "Why be uncertain? Try Miasma, the new underarm deodorant tested in the pits. Combat nausea, nervousness, indecision. Feel cool, confident, otherworldly. Just one squirt. Miasma. For stamina."

"Put a little fun in your life. Come on down and test drive the new DMC Detroiter, gas guzzling luxury on a suspension of hot air; and for the young at heart, the sporty new DMC DreemCat, four on the floor and backseat galore. The Devlon Motors Corporation."

"Hot? Itchy? Burning hemorrhoids? Feeling tired and run down as though eternity will never end? Missing something in life? Try End-O-Crime, the balm of extinction."

Everything's so strange. Nobody talks, no eye contact. Just like New York. I suppose you get used to it.

A junk yard! A bulging fence and mountains of dead cars sliding away into the swamp, half submerged with smashed fenders and hollow headlights, springs ripping through musty seats, moldy upholstery, an old shoe, broken bottles, a spent condom, beer cans, hills of old tires, stacks of axles, a gutted school bus, an airplane fuselage, tail fin intact, dogs chained to steel drums, no grass, no wind, yet agitation in the brackish water and a smokey sky crisscrossed with search lights, a freeway with a stream of red taillights going nowhere, a line of WWII boxcars, Dachau, Buchenwald, a yard engine on a cluttered track. Clean Fill Wanted. No Swimming. Now a crane with an electromagnet at the end of a greasy cable towering over a mound of scrap, a dirty water tower, Eagles 68, hills of smoking offal, sickly dogs and filthy waifs picking through it, the stink of scorched earth, a black ditch trickling green slime, mounds of plastic statuary, Madonnas, Christs risen, Elvises, a mangled organ, a whore in a dim doorway applying lipstick, more graffiti— Lords, Slicks, no niggers, pussy, Satan lives—a flattened teddy bear in a Mickey Mouse shirt, then another dismal street, and another, and off to the side an artist at an easel faithfully reproducing a billboard classic, *Supermodel with Whiskey Glass,* in black velvet with diamond studded cigarette holder, "For an elegant way to end an evening. Why be old and grave? Drink Eau de Lethe." Devlon Bros. Distilleries. What's this? The Old Saigon Bar and Grill.

"What you lookin' at?"

"Grimes? Is that you?"

"What of it?"

"How ya doin'?"

"Sh...it."

"Ever find your bike?"

"Hell no."

"It was a bad war."

"Yeah. It was bad...I killed her...little girl. Had a face like a pup. I had rear, it was gettin' dark. They come out at night. I heard this sound down in the ditch. How d'hell did I know? It's just one of those things, you can feel their eyes on you. I turned and let go. Young, twelve maybe thirteen, creeping along in the ditch probably afraid to walk on the road, skinny, big eyes. I didn't mean...I saw her a split second before I...her head jerked like some kind o' wild dance, then she turned all red. Next thing I saw was a puddle o' guts down in the mud. Then it stopped. It's never quieter than after a...even the damn insects stop buzzin'. I wanted somebody to scream at me, but nobody said nothin'. My buddies just looked at her an' kept goin'. Nobody gave a shit. I don't know what t' hell she was doin' down in that ditch, probably afraid to walk in the road. What t' hell do you know about it? Where d' hell were you? In some damn college gettin' laid every night? You're one o' them goddamn protesters. Don't lie to me you son of a bitch, I can smell it. You always had it made, brown nosin' you're way through school. What you lookin' at? Yeah. Needle marks. None o' your goddamn business. You're not better than me. Fuck you. Get out o' my goddamn sight."

Across the street, Valhalla Lounge. Officers Only.

"Damn it! We could have won! We should have won! If it wasn't fer those pussy-footed politicians in Wawsh'tun who wouldn't let us do the job. Shit. Saturate the DMZ, put a lid on infiltration routes, eliminate local oppozition, a few little pops up nawth around the hawbor. I don't mean big ones, tactical stuff, Hiroshima weight, just enough to make the little dinks see they can't win. So what we git, pop guns and hippie protests. We should o' took every damn one o' those long haihed bastuds and put 'em in combat ready, six weeks, socko, you're unda fire, protest all the hell you wawnt. They prolonged the damn thing with all those peace demonstrations while we were losin' good min. And our own damn press stabbin' us in the back, the fifth column sons o' bitches, all that coverage to a few shit ass friendlies without enough goddamn sense t' duck. Not one hot damn tom did they show our boys goin' in an' kickin' ass. Not one. Gendlemun, we must be ce'tun we do not make those same unfawchanut miscalculations in the futcha. If we eva have to do it again, and pray to God we do not, we must take a few...precautions, unpleasant though they may be, in the vera beginnin'. Fust the effectuv neutralization of all commanusts and commanust sympathozzas in our own countra, the secured cooperation of the press by whateva means necessara, the total diversion of congressional opposition into acceptable channuls, the elimunation of ani and all need fo' protestin', afta which we can go ova tha and do the job the way it s'pposed to be done. Waw ain't no parla game. You eitha go all out, aw stay home an' play haw'shoes."

"For jobs too tough for the Human Constitution. Bugs, human implants, liquidations extraordinaire. When National Security becomes too sensitive to trust to the people, call Devletron Research & Development Corp. Offices in Moscow, Peking, and Langley, Virginia. Devletron. A name you'll only say once."

"Tired, run down, overcome with stress, anxiety, aching muscles? Stand tall with Spiritol. Take as directed, now in the new tamper proof container available at your loco neighborhood drug dealer. Not recommended for adults."

"In a quandary over dinner? Why not stop in at Mamma's for some exciting new suggestions sure to surprise your guests? That's Mamma Minsky's Meat Market at the corner of Fifth Avenue and Fin de Cheval. Let our professional staff help you choose from a wide variety of recent arrivals, everything from chuck to chops, heartstrings to headcheese, and for a special treat with that old world flavor, be sure to try our new, chile con condor."

"The ultimate in driving luxury is here at last, the all new Devlon Sayaton, the automobile engineered for people going places. Elegance at a glance, eminence on wheels, Sayaton, the accent is on privilege. Now with Devlaire All Climate Control as standard equipment, also ThermoStream styling, HydraDrive, antiLocke brakes, pin cushion ride, and leatherworker interior. Sleek, sublime, 400 Whorse Power in silent submission. Sayaton. You can't afford to ask the price."

CHAPTER 37

STATE OF THE UNION

Coolies. Caucasian! Humpin' it. Barefoot, conical hats, shouldering baskets of fresh dirt into smoking bomb craters half filled with...body parts. They're sure doing it the hard way. It's gonna take—

"Five thousand three hundred and twenty six years plus or minus two per cent if we continue our present rate of 16.9 cubic meters per man per day presuming the availability of clean fill fluctuates no more than—"

"Bob. Not now. Allow me to introduce ourselves, I'm Mr. Schlesinger, former mouthpiece of a former idol of yours, may I present Mr. Lodge, Mr. Rostow, Mr. Taylor, Mr. Rusk, Mssrs. Bundy and Bundy, Allen Dulles, our spiritual father, and of course Bob McNamara on the adding machine."

"If we could increase daily production 5—"

"Bob...Please. We're working 24 hour shifts."

"More helicopters—"

"Bob. Try to look at the big picture."

"Okay. C-130's. From Guam. We could fly 'em—"

"Bob! Crunch the numbers again. That'll keep him busy. Say could you be a real pal? See that Coke machine?"

"I see it's off limits."

"Right. Could you bend the rules a little. It's awfully warm and the work is rather demanding—"

"I haven't got a quarter."

"Only a dime. 1960 prices!"

"Thanks Bob."

"I can't spare a dime."

"No problem. It's broken. Just whack it on the side."

"Does the Coca Cola Company know about this?"

"They'll never find out."

"But we'll know, won't we?"

"Yes, but we can keep it under wraps. Washington's the other side of the world, Congress out to lunch, the public satisfied with bread and circuses."

"I'll need to run a systems analysis."

"It's already been done. The Coca Cola Company can absorb the loss, claim a fourth quarter tax break and not even wink at the IRS."

"It'll be warm as piss."

"For old times sake. You supported us once, rather enthusiastically I recall—the spring of 1960, your senior year at Washington High. The future looked so bright back then, we promised you the moon. Remember the euphoria, that little speech at Ann Arbor, the inaugural—how did it go? Pay any price, bear any burden...heady stuff. So here we are. Not quite Camelot—for all the Calibans. Come on. Hey! Where you goin'? There's no way out!"

"You haven't looked hard enough."

Out in the swamp. Look at 'em. Screwing around, fighting over girly magazines, lighting fire crackers under each other—on company time. Two others off behind a trailer purchasing a pound of sugar, another roasting hot dogs on a pitch fork. Not much enthusiasm for work. Others knee deep in floating sewage shoveling partially coagulated substances into large burlap bags. The beach crew heaving them into dump trucks, missing with regularity. A tally-taker asleep at his clipboard. Overseers sprawled out drunk. These guys have definitely been out in the sun too long. Make that the smog.

Another billboard. "Welcome to Operation Sandbag. We're doing our part." A tough foreman barking orders, the light on his hard hat a bit dim, gas mask hanging on his chest.

"What are we doing? The gentleman wants to know what we're doing. Why we're having a group discussion on environmental safety. We're the sandbag crew! Graveyard shift! Nelson, Hubert, Spiro, George, Henry, Elvis, that's Nikita over there pissing in the wind. I'm Jack! Pleasant outdoor work, just like the ad said. The Water Treatment Plant? Right—fifty yards downstream. The background noise? A little bit like coyotes on a lonely night? 435 public employees cryin' fer a raise. What's that? You don't think you're gonna like it down here? Aw, shucks, sure ya will. We're the elite! We don't even wear our gas masks if we don't want. The pretty boys give us some lip but they can't do without us. The swamp's a risin' m' boy. Shhhh. Don't tell nobody. Sandbags is worth their weight in gold. We can't have swamp water comin' up the windows in the hoity-toity suburbs now could we? Why's the swamp risin'? Oooh tough question. Ever been to the big city? Ever wonder how many johns they got in New York? Los Angeles? All over the world? What would happen if they all flushed at once? It's a mathematical certainty that's gonna happen someday. Ever wonder where it all goes? Some of the things people try to flush away? Did ya see the pink foam on the beach, the yellow crust on break wall? All those pipes comin' in but none goin' out? Did ya notice a slight pungency on the air? Think mebbee these gas masks is the latest fashion statement? Stick around son, you'll get a first class education. No cover ups down here. A sandbag's a sandbag. What we putin' in 'em? Why anything comes down the pipe. The little fishes is nice, pack tight, 'bout two dozen a bag. Humans? Too big. Haff t' cut 'em up. Ever try cuttin' up a New York taxi driver? Tough as nails, worse'n a Chicago probation officer, of course nothin's as bad as an army drill sergeant, 'cept maybe a Washington columnist. Had a whole truck load last week. Noisy suckers, kept squawkin' 'bout government red tape. Had t' bottle 'em. Then they tried the one about takin' the wrong flight—how's that? You too? Computer mis—Hear that Bobby? Bah ah! We got another one...Awww, he fails to see the humor. You know how many people down here by computer mistake? You know who invented computer logic? TV? Angel dust? See-through bras? Guaranteed condoms? **WE DID!** We got the hottest R&D this side o' the Pentagon! Say hey! What's that? An ecological disaster? Awww shucks, we feel badly about—what? Writing your congressman? YOUR CONGRESSMAN! BAAAA AH! He's writing his...stop it! Yer killin' me—Who d' ya think...Computer mis—I haven't laughed so hard since Bill Buckley tried to plead diplomatic immunity, thought he's in East Berlin. Hey! If ya see the Good Humor man tell 'em the clock's runnin'! NIKKY! Haul it in, here's the chief."

Roar of rushing water. A huge pipe. Glutinous substances splash onto a steaming pile of offal in the middle of a sludge pool draining into the swamp. Little fish, twitching and flipping, slip down the pile. A huge bucket crane drops with a thud, closes, a squeaky cable drawing it up, liquid draining out as it swings over a flat car. Nofolk and Sufferin. A manager approaches. Hard hat, nice suit.

"We gotta pick up the pace. Who's he? The little fish? You want to know about the little fish? Aborted foetuses. Welcome to the big city kid. What department? Data processing. What are we doing with them? Fill! The magic word. We're extending the runway over the swamp to accommodate heavier aircraft—you gonna be okay? Well, what t' hell am I supposed to do with 'em? They keep pilin' up. No market value, I can't dump 'em, can't burn 'em, the goddamn EPA'll be down my throat, can't leave 'em layin' around, people don't want to be reminded. Hey you don't look too good. Say, you're not from the EPA? Good, but if you don't mind we're real busy right now. By the way this is a hard hat area, what t' hell you doing in a tuxedo? Your first day. Great. Okay if you're going to be sick—"

"They're still alive."

"The fish? Yeah, that's the idea. When you're alive up there, you're dead down here and vice versa. Fundamental law of the Universe. Hey don't go near 'em, they can give you a nasty bite. Maybe you better check in at the first aid station. Look, lemme give ya a friendly piece of advice. If you expect to get anywhere in this organization, don't come around asking dumb ass questions. Get the drift. Say...ah...you're not with the...CIA? Oh yeah, high finance to day care. The KGB? Same company, send their laundry the same place. Mao's. East side. Next door to El Arabica, the nitrate shop. Expect anything. Perambulators with tank tracks, lollipops with fuses, Russian Easter eggs that go bang in the night—get the picture? And don't touch the sausage at Mamma Minsky's! Thaaat's right...can't even trust mamma."

An old rattletrap missing on one cylinder, soft tires, one headlight, Italian flag on the antenna, ice chest in the trunk. And a music box. *O sole mio.* The Good Humor man!

"Hey buddy, you see the sandbag crew?"

"Down in the swamp. Should I know you, sir?"

"I'm Dante."

"Alighieri?"

"Danny the Torch."

"It's a pleasure to meet you, sir."

"Some people wouldn't say so."

"Then it didn't go well—in the end?"

"Can't complain. Business ain't bad, got two cars, one runnin' one ain't, trailer's paid for, do a little fishin', play a little golf, Beatrice comes over once in awhile."

"That's wonderful."

"She moved back, didn't like it up in Paradise Valley, had it nice too, condo, swimmin' pool, valet service, women's group on Thursday. Why she come back? I dunno. Guess there's no place like home."

"Perhaps to be with you, sir."

"I'd like t' think so."

"I'll bet she's still beautiful."

"She's somethin' lemme tell ya. A few wrinkles but she only gets better, keeps findin' new ways t' stay young. Makes me furgit I'm gettin' old. My little girl's in college, fashion design. Alighieri di Roma. M' boy went into the ministry. Unitarian. Dunno what got into 'm."

"I wish we could have met another place."

"Another time, another place. But the same story; make the best of where you are."

"I'll remember that, sir."

"And never abandon hope. Abandon Hope and you'll never smile again, just like the song says."

"Have you seen Virgil recently?"

"Wyatt's brother? *Gunfight at the OK Corral?* Great flick, better'n *High Noon.* They don't make Westerns like they used t'."

"No, sir. They do not."

"Mamma mia, gotta run."

"May I be of assistance, sir?"

"You? You wanna go in the good humor business?"

"Yes, sir."

"Okay. But lemme tell ya it's dog eat dog. Better men than you have gone under, but if ya work hard, study the classics, ya might make it. There's still opportunity in this country but'cha gotta hustle, good things melt fast. Remember that. Above all, treat all your customers alike, however!—pay attention now—if they don't appreciate good humor, whether they're peons or Popes…show-them-no-mercy."

"We've got quite a few peons who think they're Popes."

"Then may I suggest…whitehouse. *Capisce?*"

"Yes, sir."

"For the boys down at sewage treatment."

"I understand, sir."

"Okay buddy. You're on your own."

"My pleasure, sir."

"Hey, if you're ever up town gimmie a call, VATican 1300. *Ciao.*"

There they are. Look at 'em. Wallowing in it.

"Lying! Swimming! Copulating in it! **Everything but WORK!** This's a **disGRACE!** Look at you! Your dis**GUSTING!"**

"Save your goddamn state of the union address pal. We want our ice cream!"

"**SHUT UP!** You call yourselves public servants! I could find better public service under a dead opossum! At least **maggots** keep the highway clean! At least vultures **PUKE** before they devour somebody! You want a state o' the—I'll give you—**the State of the Union STINKS!** You call yourselves leaders? You couldn't lead a drunken Russian into a Georgetown whorehouse! And don't try financing your visit with deficit spending! If you guys sailed the *Mayflower,* the Red Sox 'd be playin' home games in Vladivostok! Lazy! Lying! No good! Muck raking! Butt kissing! Filibustering! **BUMS!** All ya gotta do is hold the bag! Face upstream! Gravity'll bring it to ya! Any **MORON** can do your job! Now ya want another raise! That's all t' hell your good for! Voting yourselves **PAY RAISES!** Look where the last one gotch ya! Where'd it go? I'll tell ya where, junk bonds! Dirty tricks! Cash payoffs, covert operations! Junkets to Monaco! Fund raisers at a Hollywood tit farm and the whole damn country goin' down the tubes in the meantime! Over stuffed wind bags! Ya look like diarrhea cases at the funny farm! Like you've been buried in horse manure two hundred years...All right! That's your job! So let's see some professionalism! When yer kid asks ya what you did in the Great War, you won't hafta say I was shovelin' red tape in the District of Columbia! **You're United States Congressmen for God sake! Get off your fat asses!** The taxpayers expect a day's labor for a day's wages! Pull up your pants! Change your underwear every term! **Lead by example!** That's exactly what Confucius told the Duke of Lu pursuant to his appointment as Acting Superintendent of Public Works in the town of Chung-tu, Shantung Province, at the dawn of the fifth century B.C.! **DO YOUR HOMEWORK!** Read something besides the polls! And balance the **BUDGET!** Ya cain't hunt possum with yer mother-in-law's dawg! This is a **DEMOCRACY!** Your job's t' clean it up! So pay attention! I'm gonna make ya an offer ya can't refuse. Fill up your bag...**OR GET IN IT!**"

"Who in the *hell* was that!"

"Some squeaky clean—Bobby! That's my fudge bar! You had two! Yes, you did—Gimme that!"

"**HEY!**" These boys have definitely been out in the swamp too long. "I don't wanna come down here to talk to you people again. *Capisce?"*

Mozzarella's Wharf. Cement Block & Necktie Co., Vito Mozzarella, President. Custom block for any occasion. Guaranteed never to resurface. Prices you can't refuse.

Rotten planks, broken rails, a crooked boardwalk over black water, flotsam, slime encrusted posts each with a vulture, the whole affair collapsing under its own weight, and further out a diving board with a burlap bag. The ole swimmin' hole. But foul vapors and flitting specters, stench, thick bubbles splattering putrid mud, hungry foam at the edges, acres of brown scum then a muffled scream, a lazy swirl, and…and someone tied to a post. Forrester!

"O mighty Caesar, dost thou lie so low? Why do I smile? Under these somewhat strained circumstances? Have I gone mad? *Moi?*"

"Hugh Seton-Ramsey, Scotland Yard, Try-To-Be-Calm."

"How'd he—what was—some kinda incendiary—"

"Lilies and Lace."

"How's that?"

"Girl Scouts gone bad."

"Girl scouts?"

"The notorious feminist underground, perpetrators of the nastiest cricket from Saskatoon to Singapore, they've a penchant for the refined male chauvinist, we've beene hot on their trail for some time, a hop and a skip as it were, my associate Chauncey McDowell, RCMP."

"The girl scouts got him?"

"With an Easter egg. And yourself? Ah, yes, petrol works best. Your friend may not be so fortunate, should be resurfacing momentarily."

"He always does."

"I say would you care to see one of the culprits. Russian wouldn't you say?"

"Ukrainian."

"How did you know that?"

"I…I'm a casual student of Orthodox Ovagraphy."

"I say, have I had the pleazhah?"

"Jack Smith, Geothermal Energy Concepts, Dallas, Texas."

"Jolly Good. My associate—but you've already—I'm afraid you're wrong, about the egg, this little gem is not quite…orthodox. Sublime forgery, small firm in Virginia actually, low profile, notice the exquisite detail on the floral motif, a flair for impressionist tonality on a field of Dostoevskian black. Packs a wallop too."

"Ev! No bottom huh? Gee I don't see a life preserver. How 'bout a cement block!…Awww, doesn't float. Dah, didn't know dat Ev. Goin' down again? That's twice!"

"Glup…glup…glup."

"How's 'at? Can't make the waters part? Wanna nother Easter egg?

Should I call a Girl Scout? Three! That's it! Ya only get three chances sucker! Who ya gonna sneer at now? Who ya **SCREW** this time?"

He surfaced unexpectedly, "swamp water" streaming from his face, particulate matter congealed to his hair, lips twisted into a critical frown.

"…'Whom'…The objective…case…please."

CHAPTER 38

SAY IT AIN'T SO JOE

A bombed-out cathedral. Roof fallen in but walls intact. Broken statuary, campfires and lepers, a one-eyed urchin patiently chiseling an embedded jewel out of the altarpiece. Skinny waifs in burlap rags huddled around a fire. Something cooking in a dirty pot. White smoke. A single strand of witch's hair. Rubble in the pews. A row of barefoot angels hanging from the transept, their necks cracked, wings trailing in the dirt. A snake coiled in the baptismal font. Smoldering rubbish. Sick dogs slinking away. A pipe organ twisted into spaghetti—a direct hit. Bach. Where's it coming from? The south transept. A footpath winding through the debris. I've been here before.

There's been an accident. A pickup truck up on blocks. Huge cross overhead. Massive, oak, like a ship's mast, strapped together with wrought iron; but top heavy, creaking, slight sway, the vertical member cracked at the base, crossbeam detached from the wall, buttressed with new 2 x 4's but sagging under the weight of an automobile engine twisting from a taut chain. Greasy block and tackle. Trouble light swinging back and forth in the smoke. Workman pulling violently. One man wedged to the wall like a spider, a burly foreman guzzling beer. They mean to steady it but each heave sets the whole thing twisting. They're not working together. The props aren't gonna hold. Can't take the weight. Advertising—Winters for Governor, a Rebel With a Cause. Smoke Virginettes, Less Tar, No Nicotine. A round Coke sign at the crux. The whole thing's coming down if they don't do something.

It's cracking! Someone shrieked, the engine crashed into the front fender, the whole assembly swinging one eighty the other way. As it came around, a man was clinging to it, entangled in the chains, one arm pinned like a talon, a broken bone jutting out of the flesh, his T-shirt and jeans splattered red. Skinny kid. Blond hair, tattoo, rebel flag. Grimes! Oh my god! Struggling to free himself, workmen cursing, heaving, but they're only...And a cinematography class watches disinterestedly as their instructor administers color to his face.

"Somebody call a doctor for Christ sake!"

"Let him down first! He can't free himself till you let him down!"

"Get an electrician!"

"Secure the base!"

"Over here dammit!"

"You'll never get it that way!"

"Get that damn spotlight out of his face!"

"I'm not an electrician!"

Now a TV crew. They're here before the ambulance. Workmen are lowering him into the bed of the pickup, the plank floor cluttered with chains, oil. Pulleys squeaking like banshees. Photo flashes.

It's *her!* Plain cotton dress, knit shawl, man's boots—*she's not an actress*—up in the truck, whispering to him, kissing his face, his wounds. Only nobody's listening. Confusion, conflicting orders, people running into each other in the frantic rush to beat Channel Seven.

"What began as a routine drive along a secluded coastal highway ended in near tragedy this afternoon for forty-eight year old actress and former exotic dancer, Charity Tryst. Losing control of her new Ferrari before careening into a nearby churchyard and overturning the recently completed *Crux Appalachia* by noted Italian sculptor Alfredo Finnito, the recently divorced, one time academy award nominee was uninjured but later got into a shouting match when workmen tried to extricate her passenger, twenty-two year old Beau Grimes with whom she denies any involvement. This is Cheryl Honeycutt, DBC News."

"Thank you Cheryl. How many husbands does that make? Five! You might say Charity loves company. Ho-kay. More at eleven on that one. Well, it was a real barn burner down at the coliseum—"

"Where am I? How'd I get here? What's happened to—"

The Peoria Palace. It's seen better days. Must have been classy too. Paint pealing off the cherubs, the supple arms of a Grecian goddess beckoning from a dirty niche. Cigarette butts, peanut shells on the floor. Yellow newspapers. A gentleman in a trench coat; two others with sunglasses and hearing aids, a bag of cash, someone called Deep Throat. Well then. How did it play in Peoria?

Opening Night! Spotlights! People! Excitement! A marquee with bright lights bubbling down. A mitered figure blessing a kneeling suppliant, over and again in perfect sync. This place used to be a church, Gothic. Well, can't fight progress. Live Entertainment Nightly. Direct from Las Vegas: Exotic dancers. One Week Only: SOLD OUT. Chicago's all new Policeman's Revue: the Lady Clubbers in *Transvestite Blues.* ALSO: The number one rock band back from their Royal Command Performance in England, THE TURDLES. Coming Soon: *Executive Rex,* Uncut, Rated PG-X.

Dirty tables, smell of liquor, cigarette smoke. A grim bartender and a greasy bouncer, bored bar girls and stoned clientele. Small stage. One spotlight. A stand-up comedian coming to the punch line.

"And the rector said, 'No but I play the organ.' Nothin'. Zilch. What I gotta do t' get a laugh down here? Expire on stage? Sire on stage? Now that's a thought. You people just off the plane? Thought you were headed for Rio? L.A.! The Universal Studio tour? Took a wrong turn at Disneyland? Okay let's go, A rabbi, bookie, lawyer cash in, hop the elevator, St. Peter sez Wha'da ya got? The rabbi sez Here's the winner at Aqueduct. Marketable data, you're in. The bookie sez Here's some insider stock. Convertible paper, he's in. The lawyer sez Cun I predate a check? Come on folks, ya gotta help me out. You people are about as loose as nonunion morticians at a Mafia funeral. Yes, ma'am, they're called jokes. No ma'am, they're not a social disease. Okay let's try again. A playmate, feminist, lady lawyer expire, hop on a broom, blast off. St. Peter sez Show me sum'un? The playmate's confused. Cun ya bake brownies? You're in. The feminist sez I clean house. She's in. The lawyer sez I cun make a Harvey Wallbanger. Mama don' 'low no wall bang playin' up heah, No, mama don'…it's a song, no a drink. That's right, somethin' hard to swallow like a surtax on halos. They frisked ya at the door? Ya thought yer being fitted for wings? What cun I say? Welcome to *J. Edgar's,* formerly the *Blue Bijoux,* formerly the *Peoria Palace* where the show never stops and the customers never show. What? Prejudice against minorities? Nonsense, this's the only place you'll ever be equal. Quota? Fifty per cent's a goal. Could be worse. What if ya got elected? Won a fellowship? Inherited a legacy? Some of us got here the old-fashioned way—hard work! Dedication! Attention to detail! Back where I come from a farmative action meant just what it says, shovelin' horse manure for minimum wage! Okay, one more time. Three persons of unspecified ethnic origin pass out, git in a Cadillac, drive uptown. St. Peter sez Wuzz happenin' man. The first dude sez I gots the sweetes' chitlins you ever et. You're in. The sax player sez I gots the sweetes' blues this side o' New Awluns. He's in. The dude in the brown suit sez As a civil rights attorney, I hope to work for racial integration. St. Peter sez We gots no white folk up heah. Okay, where's the canned laughs? This's worse than workin' the Playboy Club at the NOW Convention. You folks from Iowa? That explains it. Had enough corn. A busman's holiday. Okay tell ya what I'm gonna do. I'm gonna introduce you to a new mode of human intercourse. It's called laughing. No, it won't get you out of here. What's that? It *will!* If you do it religiously. Divine comedy, the road to paradise— you read that in a book. What t' hell, let's try. Imagine you're at the dentist. Open wide, he puts in the tongue depressor, now say Ahhhh! See. Nothin' to it. Now repeat. Ahhh! Again. Ahhh! Now all together. Ah! Ah! Ah! Come on people! This just might work! **There's gotta be a way outta here!** Aw right! Put some feeling into it! Concentrate! Think of an evangelist stepping off the plane asking for the pearly gate. Let's go! The old college try! **Ah! Ah! Ah!** Did it work? Somebody hit the lights. Shit. We're back in Reno. So you *can* get a laugh down here, painful but not impossible. You've been a wonderful audience."

"Ladies and gentlemen…Nerv Bennett! He'll be right back! Let's give him a nice round of applause, not easy comin' down here on such short notice. And he thought Reno was hell. Movin' right along…You're kidding! She's here! After her agent put out a contract on me. Lemme tell ya this guy's somethin' else, J. Edgar Hoover with iridescent canines. Just kidding. Everett…you know I'm kidding. Oh, right, first let me remind you, tonight's late movie held over for two weeks, Cinema Classique, *Executive Rex,* a spine tingling docudrama of naked ambition and political intrigue—uncut, including the eighteen minute gap. Whoa! I'm not touchin' that one with a ten foot pole. What's that ma'am? Never seen a ten foot Pole? How 'bout a twelve inch Italian? Mama mia. Watch it lady, you'll get stuck with the Czech. And now! Direct from the windy city where they brought the house down at the Democratic National Convention, that wild and zany potpourri of synchronized mayhem! Gentlemen in the front row watch out for stray falsies, I give you…the Lady Clubbers!"

> *Shee-ca-go Shee-ca-go*
> *That cudgelin town*
> *She can't go, she can't go*
> *I will knock you a round*
> *You bet your bloody collar*
> *You'll taste some club*
> *In Shee-ca-go*
> *The town that Billy Club Day*

Could not shut down
"We paid two dollars for—"
"They didn't even shave their—"
"How'd he get into those spikes?"
"Eeeew God!"
"Let's hear it for—"
> *We're purr-verts we're purr-verts*
> *What can we say*
> *On Hate Street that lame street*
> *We do things they don't do*
> *In Nazi Ger-man-nay*
> *I saw a man he thumped on a maid*
> *Five'll getch ten he never gets laid*
> *That's why he gets his thrills that way*
> *In Shee-ca-go. Shee-ca-go U! S! A!*

"Hokay! Wasn't that exhilarating? She's really here? Her agent too? With a little gift for me? A Russian Easter egg. The guy's all class. Well then, here's what we've all been waiting for, ladies and gentlemen here she is now, just back from two weeks at the Sunset Strip in Hollywood, that delectable little dish to titillate your palates, or your plowshares if you're from Iowa, Gentlemen I know you'll get the point when I tell you she's in the class of forty eight, I give you…the sedulous siren of scintillating silicone, WILL you welcome! **Miss!…Cherry!…TWIIIIIST!**"

Bach Requiem! Something's wrong. That's not the usual music for—there she is! Gray cowl, shredded burlap, head bowed in utter defeat. No make-up. Color of polished marble. But tears! A dim radiance. Oh my God. What's she doing in a place like this? *Can't they see who she is?* Cat calls. Whistles…she's gotten older but the same carriage, grace in the…but sad. She looks embarrassed to be…

Center stage. Eyes downcast. *It's her.* It's been her all along. Why doesn't she tell us who she is? More cat calls. They came for something else. They're never going to—**NO!** Rotten eggs! Apples! Rocks! They're going ape! A beer bottle! Her right eye. She's bleeding, reeling back, but there's nothing…no one, what's the matter with these people? They're howling delight every time something—a knife! In the breast. Burlap turning red. They're screaming for blood. A spear! Oh my God! Her eyes crying out in disbelief, falling to her knees. No one to help. A gunshot! Silence. Rich blood in a widening circle.

Shouldn't someone…a decent burial? It's the least we can…Have you *any idea* who she is? Easy. Down into—such a dirty hole—don't they have a cemetery? Yes, fold her arms. Cover her with something. Burlap! **Burlap is scratchy!**

"They've killed her."

"They kill her twice every night. It's an act! Next week she's at the *Roxy*— **She's a stripper!** Not some goddamn goddess! Get with it! We pay three bucks, she takes it off, we—"

"She's not an actress. She's somebody's—"

"Art, culture, religion—three bucks."

"She smiled at me once."

"No civilization in history can make that statement."

"A long time ago at a country carnival."

"Two-fifty on Thursday afternoon, ten percent off for seniors."

"Say it ain't so Joe."

CHAPTER 39

EXECUTIVE REX

trident pictures presents

EXECUTIVE REX

A Tragedy in One Act

PG-X

(Some material may not be suitable for some adults)

Dramatis Personae

THE PRESIDENT, *a lame duck*
RIGHT HAND MAN, *Ram*
MAKE-UP ARTIST, *Damage Control Specialist*
NIGHT CLUB COMEDIAN, *Speech Writer*
GOSSIP COLUMNIST, *Press Secretary*
PAPER SHREDDER OPERATOR, *National Security Advisor*
CHIEF POLLSTER, *Human Waste Analyst*
GENERAL MAX BRAINEDORQ, *Pentagon Intellectual*
MARINE COLONEL I.I.GALWORTHY, *a rising star*
SENATOR ON THE LEFT, *the Honorable Seymour Goldburn IV (D) New York, a limousine liberal with an ultraliberal portfolio*
SENATOR ON THE RIGHT, *the Honorable Robert Lee Culpepper (R) S. Carolina, Charter Member, Sons of Scarlett O'Hara*
GENERAL LUDWIG WILHELM VON KRANKENSTRASSER, *WW II Tank Commander, North Africa, the famed Ruby Pantsers, monocle, moustache, black leather glove, known to intimates as 'Fritz'*

MADAM LUDMILLA IVANOLAYEVNA ZUBOVSKY, *Fashion Consultant, matronly coquette, dark glasses, charming Hungarian accent, Ph.D., the Potemkin Institue, flaunts a ruby-studded cigarette holder engraved, 'Toujours Amour, Fritz'*

STONEWALL M. PEACHEM, *key government witness, chronic amnesia, severe speech impediment*

ALFRED X. PECKENPEI, *think tank barracuda, economic guru, man about town, reputed lady killer*

TANYA DE VEALE, *Miss Pollution Control, blond bombshell with a heart of gold*

BILLY BOB BEAUCHANT, *off-the-road stock car driver turned Evangelist*

RABBI YASHAR SHIMUSHI, *got lost on his way to the Deli*

SAJYATIT Y. HARRY QUICHENA, *air conditioning engineer, suspiciously radiant, flirting with enlightenment*

PHYLLIS WHIPPLY, R.N., *physical therapist, prominent socialite, the President's consultant on body awareness*

HUGH SETON-RAMSEY, *Chief Inspector, Scotland Yard*

CHAUNCEY MCDOWELL, *RCMP, and his horse, Roger*

H.F. SMILEY, *eccentric industrialist, king maker*

CLAIRE CLEAVAGE, *Marxist-Leninist ideologue*

DR. BENJAMIN SPINN, *Beltway Alchemist, successfully orchestrated the transmutation of a load of Texas horse manure into a bottle of French perfume before a live television audience*

VITO MOZZARELLA, *trouble shooter*

SLIM SLEAZE, *media consultant*

ORPHEUS, *the bloodhound asleep on the hearth*

FOOL, *acting chairman*

SOUVENIR VENDORS, CITIZENS, LOST SOULS

THE VICE PRESIDENT

THE MYSTERIOUS DR. LA FLEUR

CHORUS OF GENETIC MUTANTS

THE SCENE

An office suite atop the Empire Building rising majestically above the Richard Nixon Pavilion at the heart of the busy capital. From this point the vista opens onto a vast industrial complex sprawling to the four quarters, giant smokestacks pump dense clouds of orange smoke into a pink sky, shrill whistles underscore the continuous drone of monstrous machinery, all in furious but lumbering activity like an anthill in slow motion. To the south, a dismal swamp teems with oil derricks on rotting pylons, well-lit with raging flames atop naked standpipes, defiant against the foul night, brighter than the searching red eye of the beacon on the control tower at the end of the runway. Beyond the suburbs, themselves overcome by sludge, a great river pours civilization's effluvium into the everlasting pit, laden with refuse and sinful bodies, some impaled on scraps of steel, some afloat, others thrashing in the muck, reaching for a handhold, a dead log, crawling over each other, cursing, howling piteously, slime dripping from their faces, some wild with terror clutching flags or crosses, others locked in mortal combat or unnatural acts; and beyond, huge drain pipes discharge thick substances under tremendous pressure, soon intermixed with the contents of a mountainous land fill split asunder by the weight of overloaded garbage trucks disgorging an affluent society while bulldozers try to push it back, some of it catching fire and tumbling over the surface with a suffocating stench. A milky poison trickles from tank cars onto the ground—where carrion dogs lap it up but fall dead, their teeth frozen in a last hideous snarl— smoking as it forms a ditch that eventually finds its way to the edge of the swamp where green sludge creeps up a flimsy break wall, itself crumbling over an oil-stained beach where a carcass of a beached whale lays half open with vultures and crazed humans frantically tearing it apart in hopes of finding what? A lost chance? A way out?

PROLOGUE

NIGHTLY NEWS COMMENTATOR *[A distinguished gray haired gentleman turns to the camera]* From the ninety-second floor of the Empire Building the crisis that stalks a nervous nation is only too apparent. The swamp is rising. The long suppressed Army Corps of Engineers Field Study, recently leaked to the *New York Times,* clearly reveals a sad legacy of irresponsible land use, misappropriated funds, and political payoffs. We read of outlying regions inundated, buildings, vehicles, livestock, half-submerged, schools and hospitals abandoned, people living on roof tops, a stray cat clinging to a light pole too weak to climb up, too terrified to look down. On land, what's left of it, frantic round the clock activity in the critical race against time to win back a dry place to stand in the ongoing battle of the rising "waters." For the time being, sandbags, break walls, makeshift piers, all under various stages of construction stand bravely against the pressures from below while heavy equipment in endless convoy, splattered and overloaded, donated or commandeered, bring ton after ton of precious fill, a commodity worth its weight in gold, one for which the most creative solutions have been proffered from the nation's most creative minds. From hard hats to hairdressers, uptown intellectuals to Motown stranglers pressed into service working shoulder to shoulder, comrades in arms sharing hope, fear, a swig off a stale canteen, oblivious to fame, fatigue, or divine fulmination, heroes and heroines of a malodorous order. Unfortunately for every inch of dry land reclaimed, pressure on subterranean forces increases geometrically; add today's quota (goal if you like) of raw sewage and it hardly takes a genius to see our best efforts quickly and irrevocably lost. After strenuous review of our strategic interests, the safety of our trading partners, and of course with a wary eye on Wall Street not to mention the fast approaching New Hampshire primary, the highest levels of government have responded to the crisis by drawing on the expertise of academia, industry, and the vast human resources that remain the backbone of this country, deciding, after years of debate, commissions, think tank evaluations, to once again attack the problem with yet another public relations initiative. Thus, as the nation anxiously awaits its hour of trial; as rumors abound of an experiment gone wrong, a fumbled cover-up, Soviet subversion, genetic mutations in the suburbs—the tabloids providing photographs, the President himself in chummy confab with the Martians; as its chosen leaders gather in secret session just across the mezzanine where only moments from now thanks to the miracle of modern television, you will be transfixed; these facts remain: one, the swamp cannot be drained, there being no lower lying region in which to drain it; two, the inflow of foreign substances cannot be shut off; three, time…is running out. Now this.

ANGELIC VOICE For Radiance Laboratories here is Actress Charity Tryst.

MISS TRYST Hi. If you're like me you probably enjoy swimming, riding, or just taking in the great outdoors with your family or friends. Unfortunately pain and discomfort due to low level infiltration can bring a sudden end to summertime fun. But now there's help. End-O-Crime. The new, nuclear solution to the pressures of today's increasingly competitive world. In capsule or suppositories, End-O-Crime is the perfect answer to the anxieties of modern living. For freedom, confidence, and the courage to face the unknown, reach for the box with the mushroom on top. For that radiant feeling, try End-O-Crime. Now in lemon, floral, or mountain pine.

ANNOUNCER Also available for persons suffering from Red Syndrome if palpitation and redness persist see your local patrician.

RADIANCE LABORATORIES

a division of Devlon International

[stage lights]

A crimson glow suggesting an eternal flame. A far off roll of thunder. A dark and stormy night.

[Enter Chorus of Genetic Mutants]

CHORUS
Sing no more sweet Muse on lofty themes,
Thy flights are snake eyes in the lowly genes,
Nor pluck that damn Aeolian lyre;
Heroic cause is food for fire.
Reptilian tongues we wag today
To reveal what's writ in the DNA.
O bold experiment! What might have been!
But someone dropped the acid in the gin.
Out came human locomotives, an engineering dream,
Rockin' rollin' smokin' sex machines;
O Fate most cruel!
O untried, inhuman tool!
No sooner wooed than won,
Now we are bland, blue, and undone.
Sing we then of Pride! Pigheaded Flaws!
Saber-toothed kisses and Tragic Claws!
Beauty we bartered for biceps of steel,
Sultry young thighs sleek as an eel,
Honey-filled breasts to defy the breeze
...We never considered bees.
O Gods! O Demons! Ye are defied!

Inalienable rights we cried!
All for Future! Seize the hour!
Now we are neuter. Our Knighthood flour.
And somewhat sour we must descend
To decidedly an unromantic end:
Adieu. Our pickle jars we fain assume.
The fit is tight, but Thought finds room.
The view's not bad! The glass is clean!
Behold! The First Amendment's sunny beam!
Its broad and ample scope!
Wisdom, compassion, and hope!
Let it shine! Sing! Multiply!
From temple, tavern, and sarcophagi!
Throughout the wide elated universe!
To beings everywhere, no matter how diverse!
Yea! A healthy Constitution to hold and keep
Needs more than Doktor Politik to pinch a cheek.
Freedom's Child needs now and then—a little test,
Shortly to be administered—hee hee—with zest;
For we from this sequestered point espy
All that is or ever was and why,
Who's a man and who's a flea,
Who would squat, who would be free,
Why the president sounds like a pimp,
Where an evangelist resembles a chimp,
How to know a statesman from a fool,
A modern poet from a mule.
Ask the ladies in the opera boxes,
They know mink from foxes,
A tenor from a tramp,
Even tho he pisses in his pants.
This, they muse, is simply debonaire;
Thus! Gentlepersons everywhere.
Pray, our humble play attend.
Be certain we mean no one to offend;
If the seeming gods we seem to chasten,
We only mean to mirror the underglow of heaven;
And subluminaries who ascend to celestial blue,

Chivalry ordains help down—a notch or two.
Therefore send not to know
For whom thy attorney tolls,
He tolls within as you shall see
His clapper goes clang to the clink of the fee.

[Exit in parts]

CURTAIN UP

[the set]

A lush office with an elegant crystal chandelier suspended above a highly polished oval table strewn with reports, nameplates, memo pads. Sumptuous surroundings. Red carpet, rose colored walls, fluted pilasters between arched French windows draped in floor length maroon velure. Framed portraits on the walls, Ngo Dinh Diem, Fulgencio Batista, Pinochet, many others, ebony busts in a niches, Niccolo Machiavelli, J. I. Guillotin, etc. Over the ornate black marble mantle, a huge bronze caste of the Devlon logo, the famed "D" in Gothic script within a stylized yellow triangle symbolizing the eternal flame which burns steady but without an apparent source of fuel in the fireplace below and in the hearts of patriots everywhere. On the opposite wall, Andy Warhol's "Aerosol Bomb." A little drop'll do ya. Beneath it the flag hangs deathly still, a red trident on a field of dark stars. The Constitution is prominently displayed on an antique lectern precariously close to the intake bin of an office-sized paper shredder, the power button showing "on." Three telephones, red, black, and yellow, are wired to a self-illuminated, faintly pulsating globe, the oceans showing black, continents red, with countless pinpoints of light pricking through a thin husk of fine wiring collected into a rude assembly resembling a heavy umbilical cord, itself leading to an overloaded fuse box hammered into the wall—the three-pronged switch in the "up" position—where a small colony of quivering bats feed on the seepage of blood. Technicians monitor the situation. They look concerned. The actors are seated in high leather chairs, distinguished looking, at ease with power—civilians in stylish suits, military personnel in full dress. The drapes are drawn, no one can see in, or out, yet a crimson glow somehow enters defusing into a low but pervasive atmosphere. Two MP's at attention at opposite sides of the door, an officer with briefcase handcuffed to

407

his wrist stares blandly ahead. In back, gagged and strapped to a chair, a mad woman rumored to be the president's ex-wife, possibly his mother. Enter, a sleek electric wheelchair flanked by two aides and a white-haired Senator. It pauses under a metal detector. The band strikes up *Hale is the Chief.* All stand. "Ladies and Gentlemen…the President." The chair glides silently to the head of table. In it, a dwarf with an enlarged pear-shaped head, pock-marked purple complexion, numerous pustules, flaky scalp, scant red hair, one walleye, glass, canine dentures, a loud rasping breath, reptilian tongue, and on his nose, a prominent wart with a single bristle, gray at the base, then blond; mucus drains from his good eye, a nervous twitch in the right side of his face is immediately aggravated at the sight of the press corps. Plastic tubes issue to and from all portals of his body, an oxygen tank hisses behind his chair; above, an upright steel rack holds two plastic bags containing yellow and cobalt blue liquids entering him intravenously; a stainless steel tube bends around to the front of his face automatically spraying breath freshener into his mouth at timed intervals; electronic sensors monitor his entire body, a steel plate surgically implanted in his right temple holds a spidery collection of wires merging into a overheated cable leading down to a car battery beneath his seat. DieHard. A chipped porcelain poopy pot rests unsteadily atop its terminals. (The honor of "Cupbearer" belonging to the largest contributor of soft money to the previous campaign.) Despite reports to the contrary, the President is obviously in ill health, possibly senile, emitting foul vapors and deadly gases but nonetheless tenderly squeezing an inflatable doll when insecure, all the time mumbling gibberish with black bile dribbling down a hair lip onto a stained lapel then to a sterling silver platter poised deftly on the white glove of a smart steward who conveys the issue to a prominent think tank. At the president's side stands his Right Hand Man, a seasoned diplomat of overbearing demeanor, severe, deadly, but ready to patiently interpret the stammerings of his president when summoned by a silk cord attached to his sleeve. Someone kicks the Teleprompter. Cheerful platitudes begin to roll. Large print. A secretary begins taking minutes. The members retake their seats. Photographers vying for one last shot are hustled out. A woman in cold cream and hair curlers is ushered to the door by a suave looking gentleman with his hand on the back of her flowery house coat; someone removes a yelping dog from her arms. An aide brings the vice president his model airplane. The door closes, a cloud of cigarette smoke hovers over a somber mood, a sense of urgency settles in.

"An informed electorate being the backbone of our democracy, The Devlon Broadcasting Corporation in cooperation with the National

Endowment for the Eumenides is pleased to bring you the following live telecast of tonight's National Security Council closed hearings. At Devlon...Pride...is our most important product. First, an important message."

"I know! We're runnin' late. Ready on the set! Okay baby. Sell it to me."

"Welcome to the world of Itchyoumama—"

"Cut! That's Yachusumu. Let's try it again."

"Welcome to the world of Yissuesumma—"

"Cut! Tanya...Sweetheart. It's the name of the company. We gotta get it right. What? I know. I'd rather be doing hair color too. Now watch my lips: Yah—chew—sue—moo. Okay? One more time. Love your new face. READY ON—your neckline? Just fine dear. Not at all. Are we ready then? Take a deep breath. Shoulders back, aaand straight into the camera, shhh, low and seductive, just like dinner with your best beau, candle light, music...talk to me."

"Ready Miss De Veale, take twenty-two."

"Welcome to the world of Yachusumu, now introducing the Galaxie 2000 Series laser operated document and paper shredder. Fast, efficient, easy to use. Compact design for home or office, in mahogany or teak to match any decor. Safe for personal diaries, correspondence, old address books. Why worry about Swiss Bank accounts or embarrassing tax records? The Yachusumu model 2000 Deluxe is also effective for newsprint, novels, plays, poems, or anything deemed subversive by higher authority. With minor modifications this state of the art technology can also accommodate legal contracts, court records, political pamphlets, scientific journals, religious scriptures of all denominations, the Magna Charta, the Bill of Rights, and every known form of republican constitution. Remember. At Yachusumu...today's desire is tomorrow's technology."

YACHUSUMU INDUSTRIES
A SUBSIDIARY OF DEVLON ORIENTAL

[[[[[[gong]]]]]]

"And now you can charge it on your DevlonKard, accepted at five million locations world wide. Don't miss the good things in life, just say, 'SinCharge.' And pay later."

APPLY NOW AT YOUR LOCAL DEVLONBANK

NIGHTLY NEWS COMMENTATOR This is DBC News at the Oval Room where the gavel is about to fall.

UNDER SECRETARY The meeting will come to order. Billy Bob.

CHAPLAIN Fo the graaave undatakin' befoe us—

GENERAL BRAINEDORQ *[Clearing his throat]* That'll do padray. We ain't got all night.

FOOL Mr. Secretary.

MR. SECRETARY Mr. Chairman.

FOOL Well, I didn't call this meeting. I'm as much in the dark as you.

MR. SECRETARY Well, who called it then? *[Silence]* Does anyone have any idea?

FINANCIAL CONSULTANT *[Arriving late]* My apologies gentlemen, I just birdied the ninth hole at Brimstone. Sweet little chip shot, you had to be there—

DIRECTOR OF NATURAL RESOURCES Excuse me Mr. Chamun, I don't mean to innarrup', but will somebudda please tun on the ai' conditionin'.

ENERGY CZAR Well, who da hell turned it OFF!

AIDE Sir, we are observing energy conservation measures—

SECRETARY OF CONSERVATION Conservation be damned! I want that air conditioner on when I'm—when Mr. President is in this room!

MR. SECRETARY Thank you Mr. Czar.

DIRECTOR OF ENVIRONMENTAL SAFETY Thank you Mr. Secretary.

MR. HARRY QUICHENA Mr. Secretary, thank you, energy very precious, thank you, must conserve, thank you—

GENERAL BRAINEDORQ Wait a minute! Just wait a goddamn minute! What ta hell's he doin' in here?

PSYCHIC READER He's with the air conditioning people, Brahaminaire. Pompano Beach.

GENERAL BRAINEDORQ This is supposed to be a secret session!

ADVICE COLUMNIST He has full clearance General.

GENERAL BRAINEDORQ Well, who da hell cleared him?

HAIR STYLIST You did, sir.

GENERAL BRAINEDORQ A greasy little wop? Like hell I did!

SECRETARY OF EDUCATION He's Indian, sir.

GENERAL BRAINEDORQ Oh yeah! What tribe?

MR. HARRY QUICHENA I am Hindu, thank you, from New Delhi, thank you.

GENERAL BRAINEDORQ Will somebody better tell him t' stay t' hell on the goddamn reservation!

FOOL Gentlemen could we—

GENERAL BRAINEDORQ And just what t' hell's he smilin' for?

PSYCHIC READER He's very close to enlightenment.

GENERAL BRAINEDORQ Well, the last time we trusted an Indian they lost the whole damn country to the British!

ADVICE COLUMNIST You wanna turn off the air conditioner? Thank yoooou.

FOOL Thank you Veronica. Gentlemen! Can we please—

LEGAL COUNSEL Right. Wha' da we got? *[Silence]*

FOOL *[The members look around uneasily. The chairman begins in an upbeat tone.]* Can someone tell us why we've convened? Speak up. Anyone. David? Walter?

AIDE *[Stepping forward]* Let me preface my remarks with a short excerpt from the dissenting opinion, Clinton vs. Clinton, New York Superior Court of—

LEGAL COUNSEL Not here Freddy!

FOOL Just tell us what happened.

AIDE In my own words, sir?

FOOL What are we doing here?

AIDE *[Thinks carefully, then begins nervously.]* One of the data processing trainees has apparently run amok…Sir.

MR. PEACHEM *[Shifts his weight ominously]*

MR. SECRETARY And?

PUBLIC RELATIONS EXPERT I'm sure it's nothing serious, sir.

NIGHT CLUB COMEDIAN Ha!

DAMAGE CONTROL SPECIALIST We've dealt with this sort of thing before.

SENATOR FROM THE SOUTH *[The Honorable Robert B. Lee Culpepper, a distinguished southern gentleman exuding southern comfort]* I hope yawl didn't call me up heah just 'cause you got one mo' looney runnin' roun' loose!

SECRETARY OF HEALTH We can always use another volunteer for the IQ experiments.

COMMISSIONER OF PUBLIC WORKS Put 'em on a san'bag crew.

DIRECTOR OF PUBLIC SAFETY Can't we hire somebody to beat him up?

LEGAL COUNSEL Technically he's on federal property. We'd be liable.

SECRETARY OF DEFENSE You mean if somebody accidently walks into a closed fist we're RESPONSIBLE?

LEGAL COUNSEL Depends on whom you have for counsel. My card, sir.

JUNIOR OFFICER Excuse me, sir. *[His elders yield]* What my friend seems unable to say *[he exhales nervously]* we're not dealing with just another psych case. *[The tension mounts]* I'm afraid it's more serious this time *[he pauses becoming visibly contrite]* preliminary reports indicate *[he wipes his brow]* it appears that we've had *[his lips quiver]* we have had *[he comes to attention]* a breach of security. Sir.

[A palpable silence descends on the room. Madam Zubovsky exhales a plume of cigarette smoke. Mr. Peachem's stomach rumbles. Thunder in the distance. The lights flicker.]

GENERAL KRANKENSTRASSER *[Begins rigor mortis]*

THE PRESIDENT *[Gags. A substantial glob of white bile runs down his chin to the silver platter.]*

SENIOR INTELLIGENCE OFFICER *[Hurriedly scribbles a note "For Your Eyes Only," shoves it toward Dr. La Fleur, "This's our chance. Ram's history."]*

DR. LA FLEUR *[Also writes a note, discreetly folds it, passes it to gossip columnist, "Dinner at Sans Merci. As planned."]*

GOSSIP COLUMNIST Shh. *[Winks]*

FOOL *[Breaking the silence]* Are you certain?

JUNIOR OFFICER Yes.

PROFESSOR OF CLASSICAL LANGUAGES Shit.

PSYCHIC READER Can it be a malfunction of the surveillance system?

JUNIOR OFFICER No.

SPEECH WRITER A Hippie prank?

JUNIOR OFFICER Afraid not.

SKI INSTRUCTOR I never expected this.

FOOL Ben. Can you help us with this one?

DR. SPINN I'm thinkin'. I'm thinkin'.

SENATOR FROM THE SOUTH Well, Hod Dayum!

NATIONAL SECURITY ADVISOR That makes TWO this century.

PRESS SECRETARY And just what is that supposed to mean?

SENIOR INTELLIGENCE OFFICER It means, sir, *two* too many.

FOOL Gentlemen. We are convened here tonight to address ourselves to the question of whether or not the territorial integrity of our country is inviolate, therefore in my capacity as acting chairman may I strenuously request we confine ourselves to that issue and that issue only.

DAMAGE CONTROL SPECIALIST Does anyone outside this room know? *[No answer.]*

PRESS SECRETARY Mr. Chairman! It is absolutely essential the press not be informed.

SENIOR INTELLIGENCE OFFICER I completely agree. The polls are showing a significant drop in credibility—

PUBLIC RELATIONS EXPERT And we've got the New Hampshire thing coming up—

MAKE-UP ARTIST New Hampshire! We've gotta bury it till November!

FOOL *[Pensively]* How'd he get in? Why would anyone want to get it?

RABBI SHIMUSHI Why would anyone want to get out?

JUNIOR OFFICER Preliminary reports indicate entry Friday 0400 hours Wallace Boulevard South. Sir.

FOOL Isn't that the colored entrance?

LEGAL COUNSEL You mean—

SECRETARY OF HEALTH Is he—

GOSSIP COLUMNIST Could he pass—

SECRETARY OF DOMESTIC RELATIONS Has he had—

JUNIOR OFFICER He's Caucasian, a bit spacey, listens to Bach. There's a good chance he just wandered in. *[The President coughs yellow bile]*

RABBI SHIMUSHI Looking for an honest man.

FOOL Ben. Have you got anything?

DR. SPINN I'm thinkin'. I'm thinkin'.

SENATOR FROM THE SOUTH *[With clinched fists]* Ma fellow Senatas! This!…is an outrage! A damnable, incombustible out…How many toms have I stood up heah befo' this O-gust bodda and pleaded, nay begged, on these wawn old knees…we got to keep up with the toms. Separate entrances? Tha' went out with minstrel shows! Ma honorable colleagues, once agin may I most sinsally, most humbly, ask, that in the futcha, we send evrabudda, regodless of…of—

AIDE *[in a hurried whisper]* Race, creed, or color—

SENATOR FROM THE SOUTH Regodless of race, creed, etc., just send 'em all on down t' central processin', give 'em all a lil ole numba, plug 'em into a GREA' big computa—

413

SENATOR FROM THE NORTH *[The Honorable Seymour Goldburn, urbane, cosmopolitan, well-heeled. Double breasted suit, silk shirt, engraved cuff links, scented hair combed straight back.]* My distinguished colleague from the South benignly refrains from mentioning his own repeated efforts to attract Devlon Data Processing to his home constituency. I only wish to clarify the record, thank you Mr. Chairman.

THE HONORABLE SENATOR FROM THE SOUTH Suuh! I beg yo poddon! I have the flow!

THE HONORABLE SENATOR FROM THE NORTH *[removing his glasses]* Nor does the Senator care to disclose his personal holdings in said corporation.

THE HONORABLE SENATOR FROM THE SOUTH Mr. Chamun I obe-ject!

THE HONORABLE SENATOR FROM THE NORTH Nor understand-ably has he a plausible explanation for his recent junket to Taiwan.

THE HONORABLE SENATOR FROM THE SOUTH You wokin' on thin oss boy.

THE HONORABLE SENATOR FROM THE NORTH *[Sweetly]* Who could have picked up the tab?

THE HONORABLE SENATOR FROM THE SOUTH Go'bun you unda ma skin an' ma tempacha's ROZZIN!

THE HONORABLE SENATOR FROM THE NORTH *[Theatrically]* Frankly my dear, I don't give a damn.

THE HONORABLE SENATOR FROM THE SOUTH Watch yo mouf, boy!

JUNIOR OFFICER Oh God not again.

NATIONAL SECURITY ADVISOR For godsake Goldburn! This is not a partisan issue!

FOOL I'm afraid I have to agree. We've apparently…we've actually had a breach of authority excuse me security. Can we please deal with the situation at hand? Thank you gentlemen. Wha' da ya got Ben?

DR. SPINN I'm thinkin'. I'm thinkin'. Pay yer bills, I could think a little faster.

THE HONORABLE SENATOR FROM THE SOUTH If we locate up thaya in Noo Yoke with all that yoonyun activata the entiah pro-ject will be up shit crik in six weeks tom!

THE HONORABLE SENATOR FROM THE NORTH *[Uncharacteris-tically severe]* And just where do you propose to come up with the skilled labor to "count" all those lil ole computa chips—

FOOL Seymour, please—

THE HONORABLE SENATOR FROM THE NORTH *[Unaccountably irritable]* You rednecks couldn't organize a pony ride on Jeb Stuart's birthday!

THE HONORABLE SENATOR FROM THE SOUTH *[Removing his coat]* Cease and Desist! Those are fatten wuds Suuh! Fatten wuds!

JUNIOR OFFICER *[Aside]* I could have been surfing in Malibu.

SENIOR INTELLIGENCE OFFICER *[Restraining him]* Beauregard! For Chrissakes! *[They struggle. A dueling pistol falls to the floor. All pretend not to notice. In sotto voce:]* Jesus Christ Beauregard. How'd ya get it past the metal detector? *[Madam Zubovsky twists the barrel of her cigarette holder with an audible "click."]*

FOOL Seymour. You know how easily he gets emotional.

THE HONORABLE SENATOR FROM THE SOUTH *[Resumes his attack, beside himself]* You Yankees wouldn't know a computa chip from a buffalo chip!

THE HONORABLE SENATOR FROM THE NORTH *[Rising to the occasion]* But we do know a conflict of interest!

FOOL That does it…all right who's got the gavel? *[General Brainedorq wrests it angerly from the Vice President who's toying with a model airplane.]*

THE HONORABLE SENATOR FROM THE NORTH *[With theatrical flourish]* Let the SuePreem Coat de Sod—

GOSSIP COLUMNIST *[Popping her bubble gum]* Knock it off SeeMORE! Nobody's makin' fun o' the way you talk!

THE HONORABLE SENATOR FROM THE SOUTH *[Furious!]* You Suuh are a no good, teetotalin', son of a polecat communust sypathozzin' no good an' you don't love this cuntra—

THE HONORABLE SENATOR FROM THE NORTH *[Livid!]* You rancid tub of ignorance! The lies come out o' yer fat head like green apples out of a hog's ass fer two cents I'd take that pop gun and—

TECHNICIAN Excuse me, sir, I have to change the tape.

ALL **TAPES!**

DAMAGE CONTROL SPECIALIST **IDIOT!**

PLUMBER What MORON authorized a recording device in this room!

THE PRESIDENT *[Gags. Red. The steward deftly whisks away the dripping platter and clicks his fingers for another.]*

MR. PEACHEM *[Contemplates the ceiling impetuously]*

ROGER *[Snorts]*

GENERAL KRANKENSTRASSER *[Stiffens]*

RIGHT HAND MAN *[With extreme delicacy]* The President himself authorized it. *[Embarrassed silence]* Relax. We've nothing to hide. We're making history. School children will want to read what happened here. *[He checks his watch]* Besides. We're going to edit the tapes.

THE HONORABLE SENATOR FROM THE NORTH As I was saying, *[composing himself]* my colleague's statement…is no longer operative.

PUBLIC RELATIONS COORDINATOR *[Quickly taking advantage]* What my friend from the South is trying to say, if you'll indulge me, sir, is something even more fundamental. Gentlemen. It's our image. There I've said it. The "I" word. People are not perceiving us the way we would like. We're no longer the dreaded superpower. The polls are showing a significant drop in the president's popularity. Last month's news conference— clobbered again by *I Love Lucy* reruns. And the alleged rendezvous with the movie starlet at Caesar's Palace? *60 Minutes* sends its top crew to the dog sled races. **WHY?** *[He pounds the table]* This is indubitably the most dynamic president of the millennium. Let me share some figures with you. Our projected application pool next quarter, down 6%; share of the domestic market lost to foreign competition, up 11%; letters of intent from prospective superstars, down 18%; direct cash purchases of naked souls, down 24%; and of course the bellwether figure, the conversion rate per capita in the key district of West Hollywood, adjusted for fundamentalist defections, down a whopping 43%. And the result? Choirboys have moved into our territory, TV evangelists, morning inspiration with Billy Sunshine, in California, where else?, they've opened a drive-in confessional…bought out a car wash; and just last week, you'll love this one, last week the Gambino Family called, two o'clock in the morning they know where to find you, can we see about Junior getting into Law School? They can't even find Hoffa for us! Last month we practically had to go begging to get the president on the cover of *Time*. Not photogenic enough. So who do they use? J. Edgar Hoover. People aren't afraid of us anymore. That's the bottom line. Case in point, the Duchy of Grand Lipswich by way of the Philippine delegation has formally requested us to withdraw our submarines from Pubic Bay. Let me assure you it's no isolated event. Oh where have all the young men gone? Marching for peace at the Pentagon, registering voters in Mississippi, planting trees in Oregon. Meanwhile our barstools are empty, our brothels vacant, our lobbies silent. My own kid wants to be in a rock band—after five years at M.I.T. Gentlemen, *[he lowers his voice]* and I won't take up more of your valuable time; we've basically got a sound product, the hottest little item on the shelf, the same formula, the same down home appeal that's made us number one ever since Eve bought the first apple and there's no reason **we can't be number one AGAIN!** All we've got to do...is put it in a package people will buy.

PSYCHIC READER It's not the packaging, leave that to the television people.

NETWORK EXECUTIVE We're not here to sell soap. Let's talk product.

USED CAR SALESMAN *[Taking the challenge]* All right! Let's talk product! Where is it? Our celebrated product? In people's homes? On the shelves? Hell no it's rotting in some damn warehouse out it the swamp, and the swamp, as Professor La Fleur assures us, is rising.

PIMP IN RESIDENCE We're not selling a product! We're providing a service!

HAIR STYLIST We're creating a persona...CHARISMA—

EVANGELIST It's awwwl economics. Co'moe people.

MR. PECKENPEI Id ain' all eca-nomics! I always said dat!

MISS POLLUTION CONTROL Well, in my opinion, we're here to formulate policy.

SENATOR GOLDBURN Tanya darling. Tsk tsk.

ARTIST IN RESIDENCE *[Highly excited]* Policy! What policy! We haven't got a policy!

DR. LA FLEUR Zhentlemen. *[Dr. La Fleur clears his throat in majestic solemnity. All listen. Madam Zubovsky prims her hair.]* Zhentlemen. Forgid aboud bolizy.

ARTIST IN RESIDENCE *[Extremely aroused]* Oh, hell yes! Foreign imports up the ass! GNP down the crapper! Japs buyin' Palm Beach. Forget about policy! Forget about your French chauffeur!

DR. LA FLEUR *[Kissinger Professor of Rhetoric at the Harvard School of Advanced Terminology]* Young man, *[Clearing his throat]* innerubt me onze again and you vill be out in zee zwamp zandbagging it wid zee coolies. Now zen. Zhentlemen. We are an intellizensia. Vee cannot affort anozzer orgy ov emozhionalizm, nor bozzer wid zee romandazizm ov demograzy. Ven our anzestors zwept down from Asia into Ainshunt Greeze, zey did not zit around debading bolizy. Zey did it...becuss zey knew ZEY COULD GID AVAY VID IT! Now zen, zee zwamp is lizing, more rabidly zan we andizibaded. Left ving schlocks are zbray painding bublic buildings "Heil no vee von't go." An underground radio zdation broadgazts zee airline zchedule to Loz Angelust. Zee black markut iz zelling Norse Vietnameze gaz masks at brizes infladed zurteen hundurd ber zent. Needless to zay zee coolies are getting rezluss. We cannot exbect to keep zem oggupied wid Rog 'n' Roll indevanutly. And now an unauzzorized perzon has gained entry to glazzivied invormation.

FOOL Thank you Professor La Fleur. I'm sure we all appreciate the gravity of the situation, but I'm afraid National Security considerations have rendered this entire discussion academic.

DR. SPINN Okay! How 'bout this!…nah.

FOOL Ben! We're paying you ten million dollars! Does that jog the brain cells?

DR. SPINN Ah come on. That's countin' stock options, company car, after taxes I'm down t' nine five. Chicken feed! By the way, they got chickens down at Mama Minsky's?

FOOL **Ben!**…Your country needs you.

MISS POLLUTION CONTROL Well, in my opinion we're completely overreacting to a relatively innocuous development. *[General Krankenstrasser's monocle fogs]* If one insists on going after small game half-cocked one can surely expect to have his perceptive apparatus called into question if not his manhoo—

MR. PECKENPEI, COL. GALWORTHY, DR. LA FLEUR *[in unison]* **TANYA SHUT UP!**

SENATOR GOLDBURN *[Very gently with a fatherly smile]* Tanya. Sweetheart. Remember what we said. You can come and watch…but you can't talk.

RIGHT HAND MAN *[After glaring viciously at Senator Goldburn resumes coldly]* Who the hell is he?

SPIRITUAL ADVISOR Better yet, who's payroll?

SPEECH WRITER Is he…*[loses his nerve]*

RIGHT HAND MAN Russian? *[A nervous silence. Madam Zubovsky removes her compact, checks her make-up.]*

COL. GALWORTHY *[Sweetly]* No. Apparently one of ours.

MR. PEACHEM *[Experiences momentary spasms in the larynx]*

ALL What! *[Tense silence]*

RIGHT HAND MAN On the yellowjacket list?

MR. PEACHEM *[Experiences slight palpitations in the lower tongue]*

COL. GALWORTHY *[With affected nonchalance]* Apparently not.

RIGHT HAND MAN Political influence?

COL. GALWORTHY *[Returning a scented silk handkerchief to his sleeve]* None.

SENIOR INTELLIGENCE OFFICER Did you check our contacts on the far left?

MR. PEACHEM *[Clears his throat expectantly]*

COL. GALWORTHY Yes. Nothing.

SENIOR INTELLIGENCE OFFICER Impossible. How can anybody...be such a nobody?

FOOL Ben. We need somethun.

PRESS SECRETARY What's his name?

COL. GALWORTHY We're not certain of the pronuncia—

RIGHT HAND MAN *[Pounding the table]* What t' hell can he be doing down—

GENERAL BRAINEDORQ *[In pained anger]* Some goddamn pinko wimp! On some half-assed goodie-two-shoe mission!

ALL Mission!

MR. PEACHEM *[Grimaces sullenly]*

COL. GALWORTHY *[Blithely]* Yes. Are you ready for this? Someone gave him a bird, *Psittacus Erithacus,* supposedly an endangered species, find a place to let it go. Cute, *n'est-ce pas?*

GENERAL BRAINEDORQ Thumb sucking! Candy ass! Walks right in to a restricted area! We're testin' everaday now—

CARDINAL MALSANTINI *[Ecumenical envoy]* And let us once again remind our brethren-in-arms, though morally repugnant we deem these underground tests absolutely essential to the preservation of Christian civilization.

GENERAL BRAINEDORQ No authorization. No game plan. He ain't even in uniform—you there! Steward! Mr. President wants somethun, look alive boy!—

COL. GALWORTHY *[With airy detachment]* Never applied for admission, no references, no connections—

GENERAL BRAINEDORQ We checked his superiors, he's supposed to be some damn place in Africa breedin' chickens.

MR. SECRETARY What's he know so far?

DAMAGE CONTROL SPECIALIST More specifically, what does he know and when did he know it?

NATIONAL SECURITY ADVISOR Can we maintain plausible deniability? *[He makes at note for his memoirs]*

PLUMBER Has he seen the water treatment plant?

SECRETARY OF WELFARE The meat packing facilities?

SECRETARY OF HEALTH The pump house at the fire station?

SENIOR INTELLIGENCE OFFICER The laboratory? *[Madam Zubovsky contemplates her manicure]*

SCIENCE ADVISOR The genetic experiments? *[Madam Zubovsky removes a scented appointment book from her alligator bag]*

MUNITIONS LOBBY The Bacterial Combat Division? *[Madam Zubovsky makes a brief notation]*

[The clock strikes eleven]

[General Krankenstrasser's monocle falls]

MASSEUSE Has he seen the midnight show at the *Roxy*?

[The masseuse glares at the gossip columnist who glares severely at Dr. La Fleur who glares viciously at Senator Goldburn who glares diplomatically at the hair stylist who glares dumfoundedly at Col. Galworthy who glares embarrassingly at the masseuse]

MR. PEACHEM *[Breaks wind…audibly]*

MR. SECRETARY Well?

JUNIOR OFFICER I don't know, sir.

FOOL Ben. The clock's runnin'.

DR. SPINN *[Far away, quizzical, then a million dollar smile]* Right. What'a they do with the chicken feathers down at Mama Minsky's?

MEAT INSPECTOR Put 'em in da sausage.

PSYCHIC READER 'Tell 'em it's angel hair pasta.' That was YOU! Ding dong! I can't believe Nader bought it!

DR. SPINN Ya never paid me fer that'n neither! But never mind, I'm on a roll. Okay *[rubbing his hands together]* we buy some time, make a few phone calls, dip our boy in a little swamp tar, roll 'im in chicken feathers, dab a little gold paint on the edges, Presto! A fallen angel! TV'll love it! Piece o' cake!

RABBI SHIMUSHI Perhaps some French perfume.

GENERAL BRAINEDORQ That! Is the most ridiculous goddamn thing I ever heard! **Chicken feathers!**

DR. SPINN Wha' da ya want fer a lousy ten mil? The second coming? I don't have to work fer you guys! I wanch ya t' know that! I'm doin' YOU a favor! Ten mil! That's an insult! I could be on Madison Avenue! Network TV! The soaps know a good idea when they hear it! Even the liberals pay their bills!

COL. GALWORTHY Can it Spinny! And by the way, we know how you pulled off that little caper with the French perfume. Liquid mescaline in the air conditioner. Real cute. Fooled Larry King—not us!

MR. HARRY QUICHENA Hari Hari! Not to put masculine in hair conditionings, thank you, bad for kar thank you ma will born to dog life thank you—

GENERAL BRAINEDORQ Will somebody tell tha' boy t' shut t' hell up!

TANYA DE VEALE Harry darling. We'll talk about it in the next life.

[Mr. Harry Quichena resumes his place more radiant than ever]

COL. GALWORTHY Thank you sweetheart. Love your new hair.

GENERAL BRAINEDORQ I jus' don't trust tha' boy! What's he got under tha' orange dress?

DIRECTOR OF POPULATION MANAGEMENT Well, chicken feathers or no, our friend came in from the south so he must have seen the sandbagging operation.

SECRETARY OF DEFENSE He's a fairy, first bag o' fish he'll run.

COL. GALWORTHY *[Haughtily sardonic]* But one can never be certain, can one?

SENIOR INTELLIGENCE OFFICER Has he seen the Day Care Centers?

JUNIOR OFFICER Negative. We've gottem covered.

MASSEUSE The Abortion Clinics?

JUNIOR OFFICER All disguised as Day Care Centers.

RIGHT HAND MAN Well, WHAT T' HELL HAS HE SEEN!

JUNIOR OFFICER He hasn't *seen* anything, sir. He doesn't seem to know where he is, thinks there's a way out. Obviously he's heard the underground radio broadcasts, he's using an alias, claims to have a box at the opera, tried to contact the ACLU.

SPEECH WRITER And he's been overheard haranguing the inmates down at the funny farm as if it's a joint session of congress. A veritable State of the Union Address.

GENERAL BRAINEDORQ And he destroyed an ambulance!

COL. GALWORTHY The *ambience* of a poetry reading was somewhat compromised; he swung in on a vine screaming savagely until he was driven off but not before smashing a vaze and two Warhols.

GENERAL BRAINEDORQ The drift being we can't let him out, he knows too much.

GOSSIP COLUMNIST And he's been hanging around the *Roxy*.

MAKE-UP ARTIST And he's running around practically naked!

COL. GALWORTHY Except for some perfectly hideous leaves around his *derriere—*

FASHION CONSULTANT Leafs?

GENERAL BRAINEDORQ Madam Zubovsky PLEASE!

COL. GALWORTHY Yes, dear. Leaves. White chalk on his face. A homemade spear. So far he hasn't found a dragon. *Mal acquis, mal arriver, mal a la—*

GENERAL BRAINEDORQ *[Brandishing a big cigar]* That's exactly what your counterpart in the Kremlin wants you to think Sonny.

DAMAGE CONTROL SPECIALIST Well, even if he's a Soviet plant, he can't hurt us unless he gets out. *[Madam Zubovsky smiles demurely]*

THE HONORABLE SENATOR FROM THE NORTH Well, if he got in, he can get out! Perhaps down South they have colored exits, as well!

THE HONORABLE SENATOR FROM THE SOUTH Suuh, Ah take O-Fence.

THE HONORABLE SENATOR FROM THE NORTH Or perhaps he can leave in the same manner as our classified secrets—

THE HONORABLE SENATOR FROM THE SOUTH A verra seriyuss charge Suuh!

THE HONORABLE SENATOR FROM THE NORTH *[Greasy with sarcasm]* In the "southun comfort" of a lil' ole co-pritt aircraff with a lil' ole southun belle t' sit bah his sahde.

THE HONORABLE SENATOR FROM THE SOUTH *[Standing]* Suuh! You have impugned! The honah! Of the southun WOEMAN!

RIGHT HAND MAN **SHUT UUUUP!** *[The chandelier tingles. After a tense pause he continues, enunciating his words one at a time through clinched teeth.]* If either of you dung bags opens your fat trap again…THE BRICK WORKS! HUMAN WASTE RECYCLING DIVISION! **NO GAS MASKS!** *[Both resume their places meekly]*

DAMAGE CONTROL SPECIALIST Even if he were to get out, sir, it wouldn't necessarily be a problem.

PRESS SECRETARY We could easily counter anything he might leak to the press.

GOSSIP COLUMNIST We could say he went native.

SLIM SLEAZE Plant a mike in 'is underwear.

PUBLIC RELATIONS EXPERT History of mental problems. Social maladjustment.

SLIM SLEAZE A camera! They make 'em small.

LEGAL COUNSEL Say he's a hippie. You got credible deniability up the wazoo.

SPEECH WRITER Give him some acquaintances on the left—the far left.

THE GHOST OF SENATOR JOSEPH McCARTHY *[Far away, eerie, spine tingling]*...known cumnusts and cumnust sympathozzas...

PUBLIC RELATIONS EXPERT He took things too seriously—the sit-ins, the demonstrations, flirted with Marxism.

GENERAL BRAINEDORQ Why not a Marxist flat out? He wasn't tough! They got him!

SPEECH WRITER Even drugs! We could say—

DIRTY TRICKSTER Better yet! We could plant—

SENIOR INTELLIGENCE OFFICER Have him volunteer? Mind altering drugs! A posthumous award!

TAX CONSULTANT Do a tax audit. Everybody cheats.

PUBLIC RELATIONS EXPERT Or we could say—*[A telephone rings. Yellow.]*

AIDE CIA. Line one, sir.

RIGHT HAND MAN Cut the tape.

TECHNICIAN It's voice activated, sir.

RIGHT HAND MAN Then put a gap in it! Tell 'em your (expletive deleted) secretary pushed the wrong (expletive deleted) button! *[He picks up the phone with a savage glance at the technician]* Ram here...yes...right...got it. *[To the Junior Intelligence Officer]* Has he seen the nuclear facility back east? *[No one dares move a muscle.]*

THE PRESIDENT *[Begins coughing lightly]*

JUNIOR OFFICER You mean the land fill?

THE PRESIDENT *[Continues gagging. Red.]*

RIGHT HAND MAN That's a dummy operation! *[Madam Zubovsky smiles...covertly!]* I'm talking about the plutonium enrichment experiments. Pollywoddle Street! Code name! TOYS FOR TOTS! *[Madam Zubovsky coughs violently! One false eyelash spirals outward alighting on General Krankenstrasser's cheek, now showing some color. The masseuse gasps. Dr. La Fleur turns white.]* HAS HE BEEN WITHIN FIVE MILES OF IT?!

THE PRESIDENT *[His condition worsens, now having severe nervous attack, copious discharge of red and yellow bile, facial twitch; smoke, sparks, electrical static issue from his head plate. The battery cable begins melting. His personal physician rushes to his side with a horoscope but his agony continues until the curtain falls.]*

JUNIOR OFFICER *[Shaken]* I don't know anything about it!
RIGHT HAND MAN Well, he must NOT…see it!
JUNIOR OFFICER How can he, sir, if we can't?
RIGHT HAND MAN IDIOTS! MORONS! Do I have to draw **pictures!**
[He pounds the table upsetting the silver platter. Calming himself, he looks down at his President for inspiration, then continues amicably] Wouldn't it be…unfortunate, if our friend were to have a little "accident?" A slip on the catwalk down at the Brick Works, a rotted plank way out at the end of Mozzarella's Wharf—just thinking aloud—an error…on the sausage grinder down at Mamma Minsky's. Or a nice, Russian, Easter egg…with **his morning COFFEE!** Do I need to be more **EXPLICIT! YOUR COMMANDER IN CHIEF HAS GIVEN YOU AN ORDER!**
GOOD SOLDIERS *[Snapping to attention]* **Yes, SIR!** *[The abrupt movement creates a slight jolt in the atmosphere. The Constitution slips quietly off the lectern into the intake hopper of the paper shredder. Yachusumu Galaxie 2000 Deluxe. Patented Samurai Blades. Streams of shredded waste rain down on the scene like clouds of confetti at a Fourth of July parade. Madam Zubovsky makes a brief notation; General Krankenstrasser moans; Senator Goldburn checks his portfolio; Dr. La Fleur exudes the ambience of French cologne; Miss Whipply twinges with excitement; the vice president, manning his toy airplane, mouths the sound of an imaginary bomb run at an enemy ashtray, the president's ex-wife (mother?) struggles furiously in her chair, Tanya wipes away a tear, Orpheus howls. The fuse box on the wall begins to detach, the overhead lights flick on and off signaling an imminent brownout. Meanwhile the President's condition deteriorates rapidly, his headplate crackles, the breath freshener goes berserk, choo choo choo choo, the liquid in the intravenous feeding bottles begins boiling furiously; stench, sparks, electrical smoke explode under his chair. The President bellows savagely, a deafening metallic clang shatters the poopy pot resonating throughout the four quarters like a good rock band hitting its stride at the last gig. Gutterdammerdung! Numerous species are released into the atmosphere: myotis lucifugus, oryzomys argentatus, dugesiella hentzi, scatophaga stercoraria, intellectualis liberalis—all robust specimens screaming hellishly as they fly to their assignments while the president levitates over a flaming rocket thrust. No one moves. Wise men look upward for guidance. The eternal flame in the fireplace continues without a flicker. Low flashes of crimson lightening off stage. Thunder roll in the distance. Squeaking wings. Baying hounds. And*

from an open window across the alley, the ghostly glow of an abandoned television, "Don't go away folks, Johnny'll be right back."]

CURTAIN

[house lights]

[Enter Chorus of Genetic Mutants]

EPILOGUE

The play is done.
The empty stage once more has won.
We come to put the matter in perspective,
Forgive us use of slight invective:
O Infamy! Damnation! Deeds most foul!
Over the barrel! Prepare to howl!
Crime Undercover! Uncover your ass!
Yea the strap! The strap at last!
How sweet the pink skin meets the leather,
Each lash a raindrop, 'tis monsoon weather.
Yea! A field so wide! So lily white!
Make it RED! Till it GLOWS! In the NIGHT!
How did it play in PEORIA?
Ad dementis GLORIA!!
Come ye thunderbolts, come down,
Aim for where the buns abound;
All their sins on tape provided.
Sweet thunderbolts. Be laser guided.
Bring up the rear!
Blow the bugle out thine ear!
Sound the savage battle cry!
Rock 'n' roll can never die!
Follow Sweet Liberty's bust!
Friends! Countrymen! Whom do you trust?
Square-jawed network anchors stinking of cologne
Or hybrid country yokels raised on pone de cone?
...But we digress.

Let us return to the decline of the West.
Rome...and succeeding Houses of Ill Repute
Since bought out, boarded, or mute,
Fell not to soldiers' sharp pricks from without
But to malaise, bad water, and gout.
History thus proffers a lesson:
Love horses, sip wine, avoid indiscretion.
A sad day indeed when nature's pickled mistakes
Must ope up their jars to tutor the gentry on Fate.
Fools! Mortals! Fate made ye such.
Gave ye Galahad, gonad, and lust!
In time these twisted ends shall meet
To weave a waltz for three left feet,
Meanwhile—Patriots please listen—
Thy pistol sha'n't rust in the kitchen.
Justice shall rule! Truth prevail!
Impeachable crimes unpardoned to jail!
Hides to outhouse walls emphatically!
Stapled! Forthwith! Pneumatically!
Rot ye villains as villains must!
Fouler rat fiends ne'er bit nobler dust!
Thy sacred trust, a hill of dung
Where Freedom's anthem should've sung.

a trident release

Filmed on location at the Royal Devlon National Preserve

Madam Zubovsky's evening wear............Paul Chauvin, Paris

Hair Styles.......................by LaChien, Beverly Hills

The President's make-up.....................Dye SchnozVart

Script...........................U.S. Gov't Printing Office

Technical Assistance...Congress of Fundamentalist Ministers

The Vice President's hobby-horse...............KiddyMan Toys

Stand-in for Dr. La Fleur.......................Clark Kent

Travel Arrangements by Devlon Airlines

trident pictures

A DIVISION OF THE DEVLON COMMUNICATIONS GROUP

CHAPTER 40

THE MONDAY NIGHTER

Central Command. Twirling reels and twinkling lights, a gigantic electronic brain humming with savage efficiency, our entire civilization on tape, every conversation that ever was, recorded, sanitized for television. Banks of monitors. The afternoon soaps, a golf tournament, the French chef, children's story hour, the academy awards. Wow. American culture on a platter. One saboteur could do a lot of damage.

"Welcome back. We're here on the fabled ninth hole at the Brimstone Fire and Country Club. Jimmy McPhee, dean of the circuit, is lining up a fairly routine chip shot notwithstanding the jets of hot gas and mucus substances gurgling churlishly out of the fairway. To break par he must blast out of an abandoned privy pit, across a flaming inferno avoiding several lines of rather second class laundry, as well as the nasty smelling carcass to the right of the green about thirty yards from the pin. The gallery is respectfully silent and somewhat thin after yesterday's unfortunate crocodile attack. Bob Hillary whom you recall was only two under par at the time is recovering nicely at his home and we send along our best wishes. Hope to see you back on the tour real soon Bob.

"The main difficulty here on the ninth is not so much the crocodiles, mad dogs, or frequent sulphuric eruptions, rather the unnerving fact the entire green, this entire leg of the course to be exact, is built, somewhat precipitantly, over a nuclear waste dump at one time well out in the swamp but thanks to the wilderness reclamation project at present some six inches above the danger level although the crocodiles don't know it, the upshot of which, you just don't feel like digging in, putts tend to wander, chips usually slice."

"The French Chef is made possible by a grant from the Devlon Brotherhood of Amalgamated Meat Grinders. Here now is Monsieur Le Chef."

"Bonjour!…et goot aftairenoo. I am Chef McDonald Legumes, ant totay I haff a very speshall treat to share wiss you. Ash you know, zee correct hors d'oeuvre eess essential to zee educated palate. Do not efen sink to do wissout. Sacre moi, how you zay, comme les femmes sans l'amour."

"The following is made possible by a grant from Devletex, makers of fine feminine products including the Spirit of 38, the new scientifically tested see-through bra. Devletex and Delisex are registered trademarks of Devlon Cosmetics & Pharmaceuticals."

"Good morning boys and girls and welcome to *Story Hour*. I'm Miss Cleavage and this morning I'd like to read to you from one of my favorite stories and I hope yours, as well, *Mrs. Trotsky and the Ginger Red House*. Are you ready boys and girls? Very goood."

"Bon. Ajourd'hui, I haff for you, an old world favoreete, mais! Wiss a new twist zat will sooprice your friences. Chauve-souris…en grille."

"Yesterday boys and girls, you remember we left the Jefferson children, Pasha, Fifi, Leroy, and little Tommy, out in the hallway with their fingers pressed to their ears after Pasha had deftly placed a gaily colored Russian Easter egg in Mrs. Trotsky's diaper bag. 'Do you think it will work? Will it? Will it? Will it?' Fifi whispered in gleeful anticipation. 'Shhh,' Pasha commanded while little Tommy clutched Teddy tightly to his breast.

"As we know boys and girls Mrs. Trotsky was old and forgetful and somewhat frigid in her stays…let's try that again boys and girls…somewhat rigid in her ways. But she had many children, so many she often misplaced them or inadvertently dropped them in her diaper bag. Can you imagine Mrs. Trotsky's astonishment when she reached into the diapers, and what did she find? Yessss. An Easter egg! 'Look. Lenny. Look,' she exclaimed, momentarily forgetting her old lover left her in 1924 after an ideological schism long before she married Crazy Joe who treated her very harshly as we saw in the last chapter. But just then…she heard something. Shhh. Maybe we can hear it too. Tick…tock…tick…tock. Yesss. The Easter egg was ticking. Now it's your turn boys and girls. When I go, tick tock, sway back and forth, thaaat's right, varrry goood, just like the pendulum on Uncle Karl's big…clock.

"As you remember boys and girls, Uncle Karl was mean and grumpy and no one loved him. He lived alone with mice and old newspapers forever racking his brains trying to purify an ideology so pure it liquidated anyone who touched it. But when he heard the ticking, he came back to life, stormed out of his workshop, grabbed the Easter egg and threw it in the alley where there was a loud thump. 'Dummkopf!' he cried as he looked around. Uncle

Karl was suspicious by nature. Just then, though pressing her hand fervently to her lips, Fifi could no longer repress one last giggle. 'Vhat vuss zat?' he growled. Yes, Uncle Karl. Here are your children huddling in terror. Pointing to the diaper bag, he ominously removed his belt. Uncle Karl was fuuurious. His nose turned red, his moustache quivered, his voice roared. Little Tommy started to cry. Poor Pasha. Poor Fifi. What were they to do? What would you do boys and girls?"

"The Devlon Academy of Arts and Sciences proudly welcomes you to tonight's Academy Awards Show. Here to present the next award are Tanya De Veale and Country Music Idol, Fats Hogreffe."

"You know Rock, winning an Oscar is a lot like having sex—"

"Psst, not yet—"

"...I don't get it."

"Tanya. Sweetheart. Just read the cards."

"Well, Marlon, I guess it's time to present Hollywood's prestigious Launcelot Snopes Artistic Achievement Award to the person most responsible for elevating slymbles into he-roses try it again Tanya—"

"Tell her to put on her glasses—"

"Tell him to suck it in—"

"Not that one—"

"Well, Fats, I guess it's time to present Hollywood's prestigious Launcelot Snopes Artistic Achievement Award to the person most responsible for elevating...slime balls into heroes."

"The nominees are..."

"Maintenant! Wiss zee tip of zee fork, press zhently into zee zhuice. Viola! C'est fini! Clip zee winks? Jamais! Absolument non! Spread zee winks, comme ca, decorateefli around zee edges of zee plattaire, garneesh corelorefolly wiss zee green leaf, membe zee rat cerise, en forme naturelle...comme ca, ant...Regardez la. C'est la poesie. A pinch of rossmarie, a splosh uf cognac. C'est tout! I guarantee, zey will melt in your mouse. Ziss is Chef McDonald Legumes, see you zoon at zee Sans Merci. Et bon appetit."

"And the winner is: Ford Francis Coppola for *The Godfather.*"

"THANK you Jesus. Thank you. Ah'm happi! AW YEAH and Ah'm may-ud at the devil tanoght."

"Welcome to Morning Inspiration with the Reverend Billy Bob Beauchant, live from the Church of Ultra Righteousness."

"And now boys and girls...the story gets a little bit scary. Shall I go on? Or shall I stop?"

"The devil he betta watch out tanoght. Now the devil he varra cleva. He gots many a henchmun, many a cleva trap. An' don'ch you thank you gonna git away, you tha! With them dezonnah jeans an' Hi-talyun sunglassuz. YOU tha sippin' Perry Hay Watta, dravin' one o' them Jap-O-neeze sin wagons, YOU up tha in them panthouses sittin' in a Jack Woozy bathtub big enough fo fahv people...Now wha' they need a bathtub big enough fo' fahv people? **FAHV!** You thank the LAWD cain't count? He uns cun count evathang you eva thunk on one hayund while He playin' *Dixie* on the trombone with th' otha un."

"While Uncle Karl took Fifi over his knee to exercise his prerogative of party discipline, Little Tommy went to the diaper bag and what did he find? Yesss, another Easter egg. He wanted to see what made it go tick tock. But as he examined the lovely painted flowers, he saw something written on the bottom. 'Look Pasha! Look!' cried little Tommy who was learning to read very well indeed. 'Made in Langley, Virginia. It's not a Russian Easter egg at all!' Uncle Karl gasped. His eyes popped, his cheeks turned red. 'Das vuss mein inwenchen! Capitalist schwein! Zey haff shtolen ut!' But just then boys and girls...the ticking...stopped. 'Mien Gott!' implored Uncle Karl somewhat belatedly...Have you ever taken something that didn't belong to you? Have you ever played with something you shouldn't have? Can you imagine how little Tommy feels? How do you feel...boys and girls?"

"The DAY is at hayund! HAY men! Let me tell ya brethren, the TROOTH stands nekid outside the kitchen doe! Repent sinna! You in great travail. You walkin' a thin line oba the evalastin' fiah of eetunnel pa-dition. You walkin' a tot rope ova Niagga Falls. You gonna git flushed down sinna! Only JEEzus can save you. Onla Jeezus cares. Not that you da-zuv ut sinna, not that yo' lie-un deceitful life is wurth a plug nickel. But the Lawd has infunut murcy, infunut come-passion, infunut fie-nan-shul ree-sauces fo depraved, disgustin', creapin', crawlin' varmin LIKE YOU! This may be yo lass chance. An' when the day arrahves, when the roulette wheel of yo' life winds down an' yo soul clinks into the slot...what will it be sinna? Red o' Black? Both glitch yew eetunnel DAMNATION! Why? You wawnt t' axe WHY? Becuzz the Lawd done rigged the game. Becuzz He love yew. Cuzz when yew look down an' see evalastin' damn-nation, you will change yo eevil, lustful, revoltin' ways and come to the Heavenly Casino in the skah wha nobody loses. BEE-LEEVE an' the taght rope oba the howlin' pit will be a six lane freeway to the panthouse in the skah!"

"Buck Runonski! Rahib von Chitterling! Walter O'Malley Memorial Coliseum the fans are going wild!"

431

"Welcome home everybody! It's Monday Night Madness a la mode!"

"Make mine inna watta bucket! Is's da big one baby! Wassa been now? Five hunner' year since dey had a legitamut contenner down 'ere in Swamptown. An' it's fer da 'hole ball a wax. You can trow out da book! Expect anyfing! Dey're sweatin' bullets in Vegas tonight I cun tell ya dat!"

"That's right Buck. The atmosphere is eee-lectric. From barstool to boardroom, day care to death row, one burning question. Can he do it? The hometown boy on a hometown quest. If you think this's just another game, well, maybe you better drink your gruel and get t' bed; we got ourselves a big league dragon slaying, a must win situation, packed house, national television, stars, celebrities, has-beens and wanna-bes, Tanya De Veale, the vice president looking for a photo op, Jack Nicholson at his courtside seat— they're called razor blaces Jack! UUUSE EM! It doesn't get better than this and DBC Sports is bringing it to you LIVE thanks to the nice people at El Spoor Beer, El Spoor! The only truly fire brewed beer, look for the label with the lady on top. We'll be getting under way shortly, I see the band is preparing to leave the field after a sterling run through *A Hot Time in the Old Town Tonight;* the hundred piece ensemble in traditional red and black with gold trim is led by drum major Farleigh F. Pimpleton III, Strutter to his friends, a product of America's heartland, Peoria, Illinois, where from the time he was old enough to walk he wanted no more than to lead a band, no matter how, no matter where. How about that Buck?"

"Well, if dey don' git dat ban' off a fiel', yer gonna see some purtty flat fife players I cun tell ya dat."

"Meanwhile the young rookie looks healthy enough wouldn't you say Buck?"

"Yeah but dat arm ain't gonna gittem t' Canton."

"That's CanTON Buck. Kwangchow Province. Back where it all began—"

"Our next category is for best actor appearing in a serious role. The nominees are: Edward Kennedy in *A Girl Called Sobriety.* Dan Quayle in *Thirty Seconds Over Kokomo.* William Clinton in *Inhale the Wind.* Michael Jackson in *Mondo Bizzaro.* And Ronald Reagan in *Happy Daze.* "

"How do AH know? How do a lil ole countra boy frum back woods o' Carolana KNOW? Well, lemme tell ya…the Lawd SPOKE t' mi! Back when ah'z a young 'un. Ah waw'unt so uprot. Oh no! Ah'z a sinna sunk in the bawnyod of bodily pleazha, racin' poe-leece caws, drankin' frum fobidden bottles, chasin' lash-ee-vious wimmin, treein' 'em in the back seat o' the Chev-O-lay like a coon dawg in possum season! An' the Lawd saw. An' the

Lawd wept. But He had murcy own my lewdful ways. 'Billy Bob.' An' Ah said, 'Don' botha me Ah'm a greazin' my Chev-O-lay'—faw barra, fuel injection vee-hate, outrun annathang in the state—an' the Lawd was moved. 'Billy Bob,' He said in a whispah. 'Ah gots betta f' you.' 'You mean a Cad-O-lack Lawd?' 'Eeben betta, Billy Bob.' 'You mean a Cad-O-lack with ova drahve?' An' the Lawd shook His head. He give Hisself a pinch a snuff. 'Ah ain't talkin' no uthly means of trans-poe-tation, Billy Bob.' An' ma hawt froze. 'Tha mo ways t' git wha you goin' than a Cad-O-lack, Billy Bob.' 'Oh yeah, Hay men.' 'Do you wawnt t' do the Lawd's work Billy Bob, no matta wha it take yew?' 'Oh yessuh, Lawd, no matta.' 'Then prepare fo a long journey Billy Bob.' 'My Chev-O-lay hittin' on all eight Lawd!' An' the Lawd was vexed with mi. 'Fu-git the Chev-O-lay!' 'Ah take the truck, Lawd!' An' the Lawd wuz WROTH with mi. 'Fu-git the truck!' An' the Lawd composed Hisself. 'Billy Bob…I gots little job f' you, juss the place f' you, a noss wome place, hit wome in summa, hit wome agin in winna. An' the Lawd smiled a miss-teary-ous smile. An' heah Ah am! HAY MEN!"

"Jimmy McPhee will have to settle for yet another double bogey here on the ninth, his putt having activated a small land mine to the right of the pin, the detonation triggering a cache of subterranean ordnance, the green itself smoking lavishly, wounded spectators attended to, an uplifted manhole cover nowhere in sight, the liberated sewage taxing everyone's ingenuity, and now as the smoke is clearing we can see the flag floating in a pool of stagnant foam at the bottom of a rather substantial crater off to the right, Jimmy McPhee's caddy clinging, perhaps impaled, to the lower limb of a shattered billboard prop—good caddies increasingly rare these days—the clubs strewn haphazardly in all directions, the gallery uncharacteristically edgy. The shot itself appears to have careened off a television cameraman before coming to rest about six feet out in the swamp under several inches of what one might call very thick water. Medics are at this time strapping Jimmy onto a stretcher; from our somewhat removed vantage point we can see a plasma bottle strung to…a four iron wouldn't you say? Possibly a five. He's conscious and alert, cradling his putter to his breast, questioning the officials about replaying the shot but I'm afraid the rules here at Brimstone are quite specific, he will have to continue from the final lay, not the point of impact. Tough luck old chum, I'm sure I speak for us all, we hope to see you in your old form real soon. Well then, tradition once again holds here on Brimstone's fabled ninth hole where no one has ever birdied and lived to tell about it; Bogey City as it's fondly recalled, Dante's End for the artistically inclined, either way the nemesis of many a fine player, the last chance so to speak where an aura of disbelief haunts the faint of heart and a twist of the unexpected attends the steadiest stroke."

"The following is made possible by a grant from the Bolles Foundation."

"Good evening. And welcome. I'm C. Ransome Savage, and this is *Book Beat.* It's been said…old friends, like old wine, never waste their vintage on wasted praise. Tonight then, it is my happy circumstance to introduce, once again, without a breath of wasted praise nor a drop of needless badinage, my very special guest, as always, Miss Helen Headley-Bolles, author, philanthropist, social activist, past president of the National Endourment of the Arts, political *agent provocateur* for various and sundry women's groups, indeed the editorial conscience of the so-called Nyet Set, and if I may indulge a secret, soon to be named chairperson of Activists for a Stable Swamp, an ad hoc environmental group, I'm told, recently formed to once and for all lay to rest all this business about rising swamps, cover-ups, political footballs, and so forth.…Her…most recent book—a reminiscence really, structurally a collage of poetry, prose, character studies, with the added panache of a marvelous travel sketch or two thrown in for good measure, Paris under the occupation comes to mind at once—in part phantasmagorial, otherwise *roman a clef,* has won instant critical acclaim, the *TLS* calling it, and I quote, 'A bittersweet concupiscence of tenor and twang,' and no, I'm not going to forget to mention the title, *Soeur du Mal,* from Cerebral House, an imprint of Devlon Publishing. Well, then, Helen, what a pleasure to have you back."

"Thank you Charlie."

"How long's it been now?"

"Oh. Too. Too long."

"Helen, can you tell us a little bit about your new book?"

"Well, it all began in a little café in the Village, they were redoing the interior at the time, Fauve was in, art deco out; one of the workmen, a swarthy fellow with a five o'clock shadow, unlaundered coveralls, a stunted El Ropo clamped in his teeth, mused aloud to his cohorts, why couldn't someone make…one of those little contrivances that whirls around…a widget or—"

"A screwdriver I presume—"

"How?"

"A machine for embedding ferrous projectiles into processed cellulose…how does one put it…screws, the sticky little gismos for cementing the social apparatus as it were, the furniture one might say."

"Whatever. The driver mused aloud, as I said, why couldn't someone make a…screw that lasts and my friend, an actore, countered, somewhat jejunely to be sure, why couldn't someone write a play that lasts."

"But the title, it seems so...so extraneous to your, how shall I put it...your...yeomen effervescence."

"Well, the title, of course, I owe to an offhand remark some years ago at *Renaldo's,* in Napoli, by my old chum Fritz Krankenstrasser who has an astonishing sensibility to the more delicate nuances between feeling and form being active as he was in the Fauve movement before it fizzled out so unaccountably."

"What exactly did he say?"

"Fleur du Bal—Soeur du Mal."

"Which means?"

"Nothing, only Fritzy's devil-may-care way of discharging his spleen at the difficulty of maintaining traditional standards on army rations, this being postwar Vienna of course—did I say Napoli? That comes later—with the Russians just down the street and the price of knockwurst somewhere in the stratosphere."

"What were you doing in Vienna just then?"

"I was an army-air force nurse attached to the Four Corps and Fritz was working with the OSS, something about rehabilitation of former artists as he was fond of putting it. We spent many enchanting evenings in an abandoned convent, huddled in the vestry with a bottle of *Chateau Bravache, vingt-trois,* a last stub of candle, reading Goethe, he the Faustian, me the incurable Romantic, ruing the passing of the old order, but always hopeful, intrepid, making plans for the future even as the last wave of allied bombers droned their melancholy odium, me for my first book, I could feel the milk rising, and Fritzy, irrepressible playboy that he was, for a short vacation to the Argentine."

"It sounds like you were young and very much in love."

"Oh, yes."

"Where do people like you and Fritz get the inspiration?"

"From each other. Naturally."

"Naturally. As a special treat then Helen, won't you read for us tonight...from your poetry?"

"You're very sweet."

"What's it going to be then?"

"Ruby Panthers. What else?"

"The very choice we were all hoping for."

> *tortured chasms yawn*
> *white ennui*

prodigal might
careening
despair
desolation
chaste passion
naked puritans
black vortices
apocalypse

"THANK you Jesus. Thank you. Ah'm happi! AW yeah Ah'm happi. An' Ah'm mayud at the devil. Ah ame pos-i-tively fa-row-shus mayud! HAY MEN! An' Ah'm happi…that Ah'm mayud."

dark dank
dreamless
transcending
la monde manque
sans amour

"Spawts Hotline, you're on n'air!"

savage transfiguration
mummified
reeling vertigo
giddy
I assent
the Bacchic rite
virginal bath
transmogrified

"Say Buck, is 'ere ah any trut' to da rumor da Demons is movin' ta L.A.?"

"No way Baby! SQUASH DAT ONE! Why we wanna move? We in na league wit' Washington, New York. Da Demons is stayin' put! You cun take dat t' da BANK!"

dripping tongues
fire maidens
mourning
Teutonic Night
armour piercing saint
breed damnation
crimson geysers
gushing
blood red sunsets

brazen arias
proud titans
ruby panthers
toujours amour

"Miss Helen Headley-Bolles from *Soeur du Mal.* This is C. Ransome Savage...good night."

"ISSUZ IT! EE'S BREAKIN' LOOSE! EE'S GOIN' FER DA JAGULAR! ONE GUY T' BEAT! TWENNY! TEN!—"

"For that time of the month when nature cramps an active life style, let Devlatex Sanitary Tampkins dissolve your anxiety. Soft, absorbent, easy to install. Complete freedom for today's feminine spirit. Why be late for a very important date? Also Junior Tampions for the active teenage miss. Some assembly required."

"We interrupt our regularly scheduled program to bring you this DBC News Bulletin. There has been an attempted dragon slaying at the Hydraelectric Plant in Diablo Canyon. Further details are unavailable at this time, however we hope to have a live on-the-scene report momentarily. This is Broderick Breenbane, DBC News, the Capitol."

"MEDIC!"

"Huuuh ahhh huuuh ahhh huuuh—"

"Hugh Seton-Ramsey, Scotland Yard, Try-To-Be-Calm."

"Huuuh ahhh huuuh ahhh."

"Miss Bolles, what happened?"

...informed sources—

...deranged data processing—

...loner—

...whom neighbors described—

...left wing radical—

...known to have consorted—

...demanding to be flown—

...los angeles—

...terse statement—

...kremlin angrily denied—

...quote—

...capitalist paranoi—

"I was reading my poe-em when this ghastly aboriginal person came smashing through the wall upturning a vaze and frightening poor Charlie out of his wits—Charlie dear, you can come out now."

PLEASE STAND BY

frequency check—one zero niner
cherokee—eakins—antietam
puritan—homer—appomattox
go ahead puritan
?go channel secure
affirmative
?what t' hell's going on down there
situation unresolved
?is he one of ours
unknown
?can he get out
unknown—could afford desired window
?has Swampfire II been damaged
negative—Swampfire II fully operational
goto condition orange
operation yellowjacket—condition orange

"Okay, we're back. We're not! **WHAT!** Cut to a tamp—"

"I don' believe ut! Ee did ut! Da fans'z goin ape! D're streamin on na fiel'! De cops can' hol 'em back. Look out! POW! Da ban's on na field! 'Ere goes da goal pos'! Crunch! POW! Watch dat umbrella lady! WHOA! Welcome t' da DSL! Look ud 'em! Beer's gonna be knee deep ta-night! I cun tell ya dat!"

"A tampon commercial—Cut to a—THE WHOLE DAMN NETWOR—WHAT IDIOT…Network decision—next booth—are we on the—Let's take another look Buck."

"'Ere 'e is 'ittin da 'ole, little head juke, not a lotta fancy moves but fer a puny little white guy who can't run very fass, he gits da job done; 'ere it is again in slow mo, you cun see fer yerself, he really doesn't have a lotta at'letic ability."

"Don't forget Buck he's given away a few tons."

"So da lizard's got a few pounds on 'm, dat means ya make it up wit technique. Okay, 'ere it is from groun level **POW!** Right in yer livin' room! See dat! Gimme da chalk! Dat angle should be t'irty degrees from da vertigul, you git hit runnin' straight up SPLAT! Yer a bird drop on da fron' of a bus! Okay, 'ere it is again, see what I mean! No ummmph! You gotta hit da sucker like ya mean it!"

"Perhaps his strategy called for—"

"Fergit stragedy! Fergit eversing yer mudder ever learned ya! Issuz

438

basically a simple game! 'Ere's da lizard! 'Ere's you! Somebuddy sez 'Hup.' You eat lizard! Er lizard eats you!"

"But he gets the job done Buck."

"Ahh dat's right Tyrone I mean Rawhide, a dead dragon's a dead dragon. Dat's da name o' da game! It ain't purtty but—hole da phone! 'Ere's what I'm talkin' 'bout, ya cun see ut on da reverse angle camera, he fergits to shut his mout'. **A typical rookie mistake!** POW! Right na kisser! I love it! Da green stuff, da yellow stuff, God knows what else sloshin' aroun' down in na bottom of a dragon. Da boys out na truck did a nummer on 'issun. Looks like a psychedelic tar baby at a hippie weddin', a little celerbation inna en' zone but altogetter a real spunky effort. Coaches like t' see dat!"

"That's right Buck, and for all you youngsters who think you might want to play this game—"

"Keep dat mout' shut if yer gonna punchure a dragon! Wade a minute! Hole da phone! We got a flag on na fiel'! **T'ere bringin' it back! I don' believe ut!** Now d'ere tryin' a git da fans back in 'eir seats! Good luck! Da band's onna field! It's pannamodium city! Some'ody's gonna be eatin' trombone fer supper! Watch dat water cooler! T'ere makin' toot picks outta da goal post! T'ere trowin' beer bottoes! Snowballs! Anyfing 'ey cun—"

"Those can't be snowballs Buck!"

"Eastah eggs! Ba stools! Da livin' room sofer. Right na midsection! Dat 'adda 'urt!"

"It looks like the banderillas for fan appreciation day weren't a good idea Buck."

"Typeriders! Beer kegs! Medium size ultity poles! Wuss at? A pianna! Muss a come from da blimp! Zapped a photogafer! One o' da papanazis! Spread-egoed unner'neat 'bout two foot deep! Ee ain't gonna be feelin' too chipper in da mornin, I cun tell ya dat!"

"Paparazzis Buck. And his camera's still clicking! What are these guys made of?"

"An' da boo-birds are out. 'Ese gotta be da mos' rapid fans in da league! Wassat? Morgatrof cocktrails! Han' granais! Brazukas! Meanwhiya da commissiona's on na phone upstai's. If dey git dis 'un fingered out I'll have fait' in govamunt bureaucracy, I'll go back t' my ex-wife, I'll—"

"Excuse me Buck, we're going down to the field where referee Tommy Tubbs will hopefully clarify the situation—"

"If he cun rememmer t' flip on his mike, co'ma Tommy—Look out! We got a little extracurricular activity. O yeah! It wouldn't be Monday Night!

Bote benches! Wha' cun I say? Ya gotta love 'em! Can't see oo's on da bottom o' da pile, d're tryin' na pull 'em off, now da cheerleadas! I don' believe ut! She go' some kinna potata masha!"

"Those are numchuks, Buck."

"Watch dat stogy lady!"

"It's going to take a few minutes to cool things down."

"Gimme a fire 'ose, I'll cool 'em down. WA'CH OUT! Da sucka's still got some propane in 'um!"

"That's right Buck. These fire breathers never go down easy."

"Cooked some tail feadders."

"Fortunately cooler heads prevail. The girls are being led back to the bullpen area while the officials try to restore order. We'll be—uh oh, got his cap knocked off."

"Git dat cap on! Atta boy, Tommy!"

"He still hasn't turned on his—"

"C'mon Tommy, da liddo button on da—"

"WOPE YO WASS!—"

"Whoa-kay, som'ony gimme a new pair o' heardrums—"

"Ewe wawnt a run awn mae!"

"Wha? Wha? Why can'nay speak Inglish?"

"Ewe wawnt a pace o' mae!"

"Forrester **SHUT UP!**"

"It's poetry Buck, we're not supposed to understand."

"Ewe thank Eye wawnt yore ottergiraffe!"

"Ee wen' ta Hereford, dinny?"

"Okay that's it! We have offsetting penalties. 76 Defense: entrenchment, unsportsmanlike conduct. 17 Offense: illegal penetration of the neutral zone."

"How about that Buck?"

"Wha' cun I say? Ee's a rookie, dudder one's a schmo."

"The play…is being reviewed."

"WHA!"

"It looks like there going to review the play upstairs, Buck."

"I don' believe ut! Wha' da dey want! Juss open yer eyes!"

"Remember Buck, Instant Replay has to be conclusive before the ruling on the field can be overturned."

"Conclucid! Juss looka da sucka! Ee's belly up! Dragon guts all ova da carpet, tail section someplace in da two dolla seats! Slop gushin' out like

Texas crude! Smoke blowin' out 'is teet! I'd say dat's one purtty dead dragon! I ain't no doctor ner nuttin!"

"After further review—"

"Yer dawg mate, Forrester!"

"Here we go again."

"Okay! Dey bote got da heave ho!"

"It's about time!"

"Atta boy Tommy! Don't take nuttin from nobody!"

"And they can both expect to have their wallets lightened in the very near future. I had lunch with the commissioner and he assured me he's dead serious about putting an end to these ugly altercations."

"Dat's an AUTOMATIC fifteen dollah fine! Ya gotta ittem where ut urts! Wha kinna message we sendin da kids? I git a bag o' mail from da schoo teachas. Deir a'ways knockin my grammar. She never did nuttin' t' nobody."

"After further review, the perceiver was not out of bounds. *Dragonis Pyropneumius ex spiritus est, sub specie aeternitatis, de generis del mundus expandex; ergo habeus corpus ex nihilo nulla necessitas; mortuem dragonum esse BONUM.*"

"THANK you Jesus. Thank you. Ah'm happi! Aw yeah Ahem happi. An' Ah'm happi, that Ah'm mayud."

CHAPTER 41

SWAMPFIRE

"Good evening. This is *Week in Review* made possible by a grant from the Devlon Oil Corporation and your local Devoco Dealer.

"And a wild week it was. Suburban brush fires out of control, a critical shortage of sandbags at the water treatment plant, a 1.2 million dollar port o' john at the Pentagon, yet another call for volunteer blood donors at Marquis de Sade Charity Hospital, an unnatural birth at the genetics lab—what's that make? Three?—Ralph Nader ready to blow the whistle on the meat packers, troops loyal to General Frank Zappa in de facto control of the countryside, threats of a wildcat walkout in the air conditioning industry, more student demonstrations at the nation's top day-care centers, continuing uncertainty on Wall Street, and now another dragon slaying. How about that Bob?"

"Some people just don't give up, do they?"

"Why now? At this juncture?"

"Why climb Everest? Why invest in thermal underwear?"

"Well, what Bob is saying—"

"I'm not saying anything, I'm asking!"

"I've heard it's a rather puny specimen this time."

"The thing at the lab?"

"No the dragon."

"Any comment on that? Anyone?"

"Well, David, it's not that modern dragons have gotten smaller, the universe has gotten larger."

"Thank you for that bit of relativity theory—"

"And you heard it right here on DBC."

"Is it going to catch on? Another passing fad?"

"The underwear?"

"No. The dragon. Can we confine ourselves—"

"Speaking of which, did you hear the call? *Aeternitatis del mundus expandex.* How can you have permanence in an expanding universe? Un-ba-lievable! This isn't rocket science, elementary Einstein! Where do they git these guys? Instant Replay my foot! They couldn't replay *Debbie Does Dallas* at a Brooklyn stag party. What's St. Peter got that we ain't got? I'll tell ya—"

"Could we not go into—"

"PR! They got the lobbies, the speech writers, influence peddlers. They're not better than us. How'd they get where they are? Daddy paid their way!"

"If we go into that, we'll be here all night."

"We're already gonna be here—"

"Seven days!"

"Could we please not go—"

"Seven days to create the universe! Fifteen billion light years across and they made it in seven days—with PR like that I'd be rich, I'd get a date with Madonna!"

"You couldn't get a date with her agent."

"Which tells ya something about the way they do business up there. I'm sorry David, I had to say it."

"Meanwhile the dragon's probably died of boredom."

"Alfred. This one's right up your alley. First let me introduce my special guest this evening, Alfred X. Peckenpei, senior fellow at the Brookings Institute, guru of fiscal reform, knight-errant of the past five administrations, author of numerous articles, everything from Martin Heidegger to the latest dance craze—what is it this time? The Wombpa?—last of the New Deal intellectuals although he won't admit it, and, I must add, a perfectly horrendous squash partner. Alfred, you can't go on hiding in a think tank forever."

"Where da ya want me t' stot?"

"How about in your field of expertise. Economics."

"Well, David, some of our problems aren't really economic. I always said that."

"Is it going to help? Will another dead dragon change things?"

"I don't know, David. As the parakeet said to the pussy cat, the *Times* they are a changin'. To answer your original question, no, it's probably not going to catch on. We're not talkin' about swallowing gold fish or piling into a Volkswagen; it takes a special kind of person to want to penetrate the heart of society's darkest uncertainty. Dragon slaying ain't exactly surfing at Malibu.

There's a complicated selection process, a rigorous training period, postgraduate examinations, field study some place in Louisiana, everything's hush hush, six weeks at Fort Bragg, the hours are long, the wages low, no guarantee of hitting pay dirt, they don't have a union, even the Teamsters don't want 'em, unemployment's at unacceptable levels—dragons like rabbits and unemployed dragon slayers—does that tell ya somethin'? Now the Japanese wanna play, rumor has it they're getting in in a big way with robotics. And don't forget the ladies, they wanna take a stab at it. What a' we gonna do? We gotta give 'em equal opportunity. That means two sets o' port-o-johns at every training facility at 1.2 million dollars a unit. How did they arrive at that figure? The answer's in committee. The romance is gone David. For godsake if your kid says he wants to be a dragon slayer, tell 'im to go t' law school, at least he'll have a pay check. A 5000 year backlog in the criminal courts and not enough good lawyers. I never thought I'd live t' say it. And that ain't all, you gotta pass an in-service practicum in the House Ethics Committee. Not lawyers! Dragon slayers! PAY ATTENTION! In effect you gotta have a LICENSE ta squash a reptile! It's hell out there David. Read the entrails yourself. Sheep! But save the chops. $3.99 a pound! Highway robbery. At Mamma Minsky's and yer not even sure they're sheep. So along comes the EPA. Guess what? Dragons are an endangered species. Why? Nobody knows. Might as well ask the sphinx, better yet ask Peachem. Stonewall's got a lot in common with the sphinx, except he passes gas. So now it's dragon season. Ya gotta get a variance from the nearest jurisdiction even if it's fifty miles away; the affluent communities downwind are sure to be up in arms, they got connections up on the Hill, more red tape, you gotta file an environmental impact analysis with NADS, and that ain't good enough for the state o' New York, they gotta have their own. In California!—where else!—you gotta prove you're socially sensitive! To do that, you gotta have a stable psychological profile—they interview your playmates, your poker buddies, expect a tax audit, any subversive political organizations? All the way back to your college days, homosexual tendencies? Dijya love your mother? Dijya fight with your father? I tell ya David this country's got some problems an' they ain' all economic! Next time ask me some'un easy, corporate tax law, Chinese crosswords."

"Spawts Hotline, you're on n'air."

"Ah...yeah. Okay. Ah...well...ah...wha' da ya think o' da Demons?"

"Good stot fer an expansion franchise, no place to go but up. Spawts Hotline, you're on n' air."

"Hi Buck. How 'bout this for a trade? Even up. Mohammed Ali for ah…ah Emily Dickin—"

"Spawts Hotline, you're on n'air."

"God dammit Buck what t' hell's—"

"Whoa! We're on n'air. Wash yer langage."

"We missed the whole goddamn thing! Preempted for a Tampoon commercial! Whole east side don't blame it on yer dumb ass affiliate major league butt kicking first time in five hunner year whole damn world watchin'—"

"CEASE! Okay! Slow down. Wasyer name?"

"Roland Studstil, *Studstil's Bar and Grill,* busted up my memorabillia, makin' chopsticks outta the furniture, smashed Pete Rose's autographed bookfinder—"

"ROLAN! Count t' ten."

"Becuzz some DICKHEAD—"

"Rolan! We're gonna make it up t'ya. How bout a mont's supply o'—"

"Tampoons! You know what YOU cun do with—"

"Dat's it. Yer outta 'ere! Spawts Hotline, you're on n'air."

"How ya doin' Buck?"

"Juss fine. How's yerself?"

"Can't complain. Gettin' a little older, maybe a little wiser. Say Buck, I was havin' a beer with the guys down at *Mickey's* and we were havin' a little discussion—no busted bottles, cracked noggins—hey! We're scholars and gennelmen, right? Who, in yer opinion was the best all around heavyweight—ever?"

"Teddy Dostoevsky! An' I'll fight anybuddy 'hoo says he ain't! Sports Hotline, you're on n'air."

"Uuuuuh huuh uuuuuh huuh—"

"Spawts Hotline, you're on n'air."

"Hi Buck, how ya doin'?"

"Well, I see we got a lady caller this evenin'. Wus yer name sweethot?"

"Rosie Reckenball from St. Claire Wisconsin."

"Okay Rosie, don' talk too much."

"Sure Buck. Why don't you ever talk about women's sports?"

"Ah co'ma Rosie! Dat's a innalectshul question! Go pump some iron! When ya fink yer big enuff ta boogie wit da big boys CALL ME BACK!"

—WELL! Hot and sultry, down and dirty, we're on the air! The swamp is a rizin' baby, you betch yer uppers. Wombpa till ya womit, wha'cha got to lose? For Sonny from Barb, Suzie from Sal, Missy from Duke and all the limey lackeys at the FCC—eenee nee nee na na—it's The Beatles! We're havin' a revolution! YEAH!—

"You hypocrite! You fat tub o' stupid. Intellectual question my FOOT!"

"Ah cum'ma Rosie, dat's a dummy q'estion—"

"You wanna DUMMY question? Okay! Why aren't there any women running for the Presidency?"

"Rosie! Yer mudder spit rivets! Yer grammar skinned oxes! What makes ya fink you cun rassle alligatas? Spawts Hotline, you're on n'air."

"Professor Runonski. T.R. Dumalot, Urbana, Indiana. Pronounced do-may-LOW. Ya know I'm getting a little tired of these high priced bonus babies that never seem to pan out. Why don't we chuck the draft and try to sign some established veterans? Ya can't beat experience."

"I agree one hunner per cent. Got anybody in mind?"

"Somebody who cun lead us outta the doledrums."

"Somebody wit' a NAME maybe!"

"Somebody who's been arou—"

"Okay, when 'is mudder calls 'im, wha' she say?"

"Somebody like ah…Jimmy Joyce."

"…'Hoo?"

"James…Joyce…from Dublin."

"Double wha'?"

"Dublin!…IRELAND! Some little island over there in England. They chug their whiskey out o' soup pots and pitch the bottles at passing tanks."

"Oh DAT Jimmy Joyce! Jimmy da lip! My art goes where da wild goose goes!"

"Yeah, he's got a few years left, doesn't like it in Dublin, he might go for a little change o' venue."

"Ah. Dat's not bad T.R. but lemme put it dis way, Jimmy's got some big league 'ead problems, can't seem t' fin' 'iz way 'ome at night, downtown Dublin, an' dat's s'pose' ta be a gimme, in utter words he's got da 'ome fiel' a'vannage but finks he's on da road, can't tell a cathouse from a Catlick Church, tries t' lead a bunch a drunks down da primrose pat' but no good, dey can' even sing let alone walk, gits lost goin' to 'iz own funeral, at leas' he finks it's 'iz own, so betta stop fer anudder roun' o' soup, now he's too pooped t' percipitate so let's talk politics, nobody knows who's on firs', Bloom's out ta lunch, da stiff ain't talkin', so back t' da cathouse, only dis time it's 'is own apotment an' guess what? Sommony's on na rug talkin' gibberish yas yas yas a hunderd times but wh's da question! Besides, da patata mashas 'll never let 'm go. Spawts Hotline, you're on n'air."

"...It's gonna happen Buck..."

"Wha's gonna happen."

"We're gonna do it Buck—"

"Psssst. Talk a little louder, I can't heah ya."

"...It's gonna happen."

"Ya awready said dat!"

"We're goin' all the way."

"Wai' da minute! Whoa!"

"We can take 'em Buck."

"CEASE! WHA' YA TALKIN' ABOUT! COME IN MARS!"

"This time...we do it right."

"Okay. Square one! Wuss yer name?"

"Ron."

"Ron 'hoo?"

"Reagan."

"Okay Ron. Juss as' me a question."

"...Do you think we can do it Buck?"

"DO WHAT!"

"Armageddon...The Evil Empire."

"Wha? Who?"

"We've been eating their dirt a long time. Now's the time for all good men to—excuse me I dropped my cue card—come to the aid of their country. They got the guns, the money, the glamour boys...we only got ourselves Buck. You gotta want it Buck. Down in your socks you gotta believe. We're gonna do it. I guarantee it!"

"Okay. Don' git 'cited. I don' wanna hurt nobody's feelin's ner nuttin'. I'm gonna give ya a little piece of advice, are ya listenin'? Before ya go t' bed t'night, do me a little favor, do yerself a favor, firs' brush yer teet, say yer prayers, hug yer teddy, den go stick yer 'ead 'n a bottle o' prune juice. Spawts Hot—"

"Huuh uuh huuh uuuh—"

"You! YOU! Are an ignoramus! Ya got da brains of a cockroach! Gitch yerself a head transplant if ya cun fin' a gorilla dumb enough t' trade! Spawts Hotline, you're on n'air. Wassat, Eddie? Nexx call's dynami—"

"Hi, Buuuck."

"Hi ya, little girl, wha'ch ya doin'?"

"I'm doin' my nails, Buuck."

"Yer mama know yer not in bed?"

"I am in bed, Buuck. I practically live in bed if ya know what I mean."

"Yeah—No! Wha'd ya mean?"

"I mean it's so hard for a girl these days, gee with my teddies and my tiny red jammies and the lights and the photographers—"

"Look, I don' have time t' play games. As' me a question 'bout spawts."

"Gee, Buck, don't get sore. A girl's gotta try."

"SO TRY!"

"Well, Buck—gee you're cute when your mad—I was sittin' here wonderin'…you ever do that, Buck, sit around wonderin'?"

"Oh, yeah! Allatime!"

"I was wonderin'…well, ya think I should do it, Buck?"

"DO WHAT!"

"Gee, Buck, donch ya read those classy mags at the supermarket? You know, *Fortune, New Yorker?* Now they want me to do the centerfold in *The National Review.* I just don't know, Buck. I mean, how far should a girl go?"

"Daa—dat's a tough one."

"To tell the truth, Buck—and I know I can confide in you—I just don't feel comfortable, they keep asking me, you know, to do more with less—"

"Wha?"

"They want me to wear less clothing."

"Daa…It's da IRS again! Dey already got da shirt off my back, what else dey want?"

"That's not what I mean, Buck. Gee, can't you use your imagination?"

"My maji wha? I'm tryin'. Don' go way, I wish I studied 'arder in schoo'. Tell ya what, if 'ey don' pick up da gahbage, don' pay yer taxes!"

"Well, it's not that easy, Buck. This is so confusing. I've got to do what's best for the country."

"Oh, yeah! I almos' fu'got. Wassa matta wit me?"

"Should I, Buck? I mean, a girl can only go so far. I'm already down to the bare bones, if ya know what I mean."

"Ya mean dey wan' us ta pay taxes on our bones?"

"Nooo. To put it in a nutshell—if I go all the way, what's left for the honeymoon?"

"Nuttin! Dey awready went ta da moon!"

"The other day I agreed to do a spot in *The New Republican* and they don't even pay minimum wage. That's—"

"Zoweee! Tanyer De Ville—why dinch ya—Eddie hit da lights! Sweethot you're my—we gotch yer pitcher right 'ere in da studio! Gee Miss De Ville you're da greatess."

"Thanks Buuck, it's not easy being centerfold of the century. It's actually very demanding, there are lots of responsibilities."

"Oh yeah, I cun imagine—"

"Work, work, work. The bigger the better, ha cha cha."

"'Ats right! I always said dat!"

"Why are we so obsessed with being number one?"

"But Baby, yer awready packin' t'irdy yates."

"Yes, but nothing gold can stay. A famous poet said that. It's symbolic of what's happening to our society. Complacency has set in, the national malaise is epidemic, the deficit is outta sight. Thirty trillion! How much debt can the GNP absorb? Can we assume a constant growth rate in the foreseeable future? What can those turkeys be thinking? What do we have to do to get their attention?"

"Daa—"

"I'm sorry Buck, I had to get it off my chest. The taxpayers have a right to be heard. Don't you see we're losing it Buck. Do you ever worry about losing it?"

"Oh yeah—No! Wha' da we losin'?"

"Our youth. Our stature. Our moral fiber. Time is passing us by. I've read all the deep thinkers on the subject, everything from Royko to George Will, none of 'em knows Buck, they're too busy talking baseball. How do you think that makes a girl feel? Whatever happened to serious philosophical dialogue in this country? Doesn't anyone read Dostoevsky anymore?"

"Ah...yeah. Sweethot, I'd do anyfing—I'd trade my mudder! I'd go ta da moon! But lemme tell ya som'un, someday sommony smarta 'an me's gonna come along an' he's gonna setch ya straight. Baby. You ain't losin' nuttin', I cun tell ya dat! Spawts Hotline, you're on n'air."

"Buck, is it possible the dragon died of a heart attack?"

"No way! It's a stupid lizard! Only one gonna git a 'art attack is ME lis'nun ta bozos like YOU!"

"Gut evening."

"Okay. Gotch yer clothes on?"

"Maaa..."

"Wuss yer name?"

"Albert?"

"Albert who?"

"Einstein."

"Hinestye?"

"Shhtein!"

"Like a chug a beer? Lemme see. Ya use t' play fer da Giants?"

"I did some field work."

"Okay, back t' baseball. I dunno 'ow t' thank ya Al."

"In response to the young lady who's worried about the deficit, I'd like to suggest she take up the violin. I suffered the same insecurity over the efficacy of mathematics in my younger days until I learned to assuage the paradox of its apparent nonreality with the certainty of music."

"...Play da fiddle in cennerfiel'! REAL GOOD AL! Now go play wit yer trains! If a train's goin' hunnert mile a hour, how fass's da pressdunt goin' chasin' a intern up da aisle? Spawts Hotline, you're on n'air."

"Juss tell me one thing, where they git these wimp dragon slayers? Skinny enough fer a ballet dancer! What's this country comin' to? PINK TIGHTS!"

"Ahh, 'e wasn't wearin'—wha'd ya say yer—"

"Ed McNuttley, Ypsilanti, Michigan—"

"At's 's natchl color Ed. Maybe yer TV's outta wack."

"So wha' ditty do? Shave his legs? Back in the good old days, ya chugged a few beers, grabbed yer shotgun, if ya got wasted, ya dragged yer carcass t' the nearest bar, try again tomorrah, no big bucks, no endossments, ya sharpened yer spear on yer own backside."

"He got da job done, dinny?"

"Cu'ma, Buck. Some pussy who listens t' Botch. Who d'hell's Botch, anyway? Some cat in panny hose an' a powdered wig. Does that tell ya somethun?"

"Da lizard's dog meat! Da fans's goin' ape! Botch's playin' Dixie! You make da call!"

"All right Buck. I'll call it."

"Wai' da minute! Wha's goin' on! Who a' you?"

"Ya pushed the wrong button mutton-head! My name is Wilson O. Dimwitz, West Palm Beach, I used t' be in the publishing business in New Jersey, you know, where they ah...make books—"

"Yeah! Yeah! I got da pi'ture Wilson! Ya make book!"

"Fer the kids t' read. An' by the way Buck if yer lookin' fer a good business investment—"

"Oh yeah, I know juss where t' fin' ya! Behin' da blackes' cigar in—"

"Luigi's Health Club, North Miami. Ask the hat check girl. Okay Buck, I'll call it. Class. Look at the great ones. They all had it, that certain somethin'. You cun count 'em on one hand. Hercules the Greek, Gil Gamesh, B.A. Wulf, Sigfried Whasisname, even St. George—he was a saint already!—never went t' college! And Captain Ahab. So he lost a tough one. Did he argue the call? No! He went down with the ship! Like a man!"

"Ya want points fer style? Dis ain't figure skatin!"

"It just ain't the same anymore. Ya git what I'm sayin Buck?"

"Well, Ed, Irvin', all you regalers…da times, 'ey are a changin'. Spawts Hotline, you're on n'air."

"This ain't no tea party! It's a liberal conspiracy! They're takin' over, them pinko perfessers an' wimmen faminists, they emanskillated us. We suppose t' stay home and knit doilies? So the dragon can get equal opportunity? Whose side they on? How we s'ppose t' show 'em what we're made of? Pretty soon ya won't be able to squash a roach in yer own toilet widout readin'm his rights."

"I don' know what t' tell ya…"

"Norman Bellewikki."

"Norman. Pour yerself a stiff one, turn on a old John Wayne movie, hug yer dog, tell da little woman she's lookin' good. Spawts—

"All rat! Mah name is Helsworth P. Humpdinger, the boys call me Splash, an' I cun tell y'all a thang er two bout readin' people thur rats. We calls ut the Miranda Statemunt an' lemme tell ya it's a mouthful. Ah wurk down in the pits, pon tar prep, Soul Scrubbers Local 102, mu job's ta paint the bottoms o' sinners befur they goes inta the kiln. We's already wurkin' 18 air shifts—an' we cain't take a break, the lon keeps ta movin; if'n ya gits behond they piles up lak horse minure at a race track, ore unions's in Lass Vegus at a tragedy session. Bu' we still gats ta read'um thur rats. You try readin' the Miranda Statemunt 48 toms a minute? You cain't do ut. A used cur salesmun cain't do ut. You gats the rat ta ramain solunt. Well, lemme tell y'all whun that 'ere kiln gits ta cracklin' roun' 'bout 400 dagrees Fairnhot an' the pon tar starts ta cookin', ah guruntee thur not gonna wanna ramain solunt."

"Yo-kay. Spawts Hotline, you're on n'air."

"Buck! Capt. Ahab did NOT go down with his ship! He went down with the FISH!"

"Ahhh…"

"Buck, wedder ya go down wit da ship, er da fish. What's da big diff?"

"I fink what da Cap'n meant…goin' down wit da fish, dat ain't class. Spawts Hotline, you're on n'air."

"Good EVENING, sir. My name is Gwendolyn Mandergelt-O'Roarke, I am currently editor of *Feminism Today,* chairperson of the Alliance for Decency in Broadcasting, professor of English Diction at Stanford University and I am active on the North American Save the Whales Committee—"

"Uhhh—Eddie do som'un—Ahh gee Gwenalun, ya soun' a little pissed."

"Excuse me, sir, I neither appre—"

"Sounds like yer loaded fer bare Gwennalun."

"APPRECIATE nor CONDONE your raw style of humor vis-a-vis the gravity of the critical issues facing not only women but caring individuals everywhere; your program regrettably and all too frequently alludes to or alights upon the anatomy, status, and position of persons less 'substantial' than yourself in terms of vulgarity well outside the norms of accepted political and social correctness without the **slightest** effort as to fairness, objectivity, etiquette, or concern for the rights of others; MOREOVER, your egregious and WELL-EARNED reputation of provincialism, chauvinism, ethnic insens—"

"Da clock's runnin' Gwenalun—"

"Has been WELL-DOCUMENTED by a citizens watch group monitoring aberrant behavior on the air ways, your program having been cited for thirty-six separate instances of sexist allusion, racial slur, and/or inappropriate reference to persons of alternative life styles, I therefore—"

"Ya gotta point Gwenalun—ON NA TOP A YER 'EAD!"

"HAVE NO ALTERNATIVE but to inform you, SIR, of our watch group's intention of filing a brief—"

"Yer breakin' my hot Gwenalun—"

"Furthermore I am not amused—"

"Aroused maybe?"

"By unwarranted interruptions, sexual innuendo, your casual unconcern for anyone's feelings but your own—"

"Eddie, tell dat queer hillbilly to git in 'ere wit da pizza 'r I'll snatch 'iz chassity belt."

"MAY I remind you, sir, your license to broadcast is up for renewal, my organization has the wherewithal AND the moral obligation to flood your switchboard on a nightly basis, boycott your sponsors locally and nationwide, and to TERMINATE YOUR CONTRACT with DBC Sports via its parent company DBC News with whose board of directors I am in constant contact in my capacity as ombudsperson for the Committee for the Physically

Handicapped. NOW THEN! May I take this occasion to acquaint you with a small geographical detail, to WIT, the REPUBLIC...OF IRELAND...is NOT...**AN ISLAND IN ENGLAND!"**

"Gee Gwenalun, don' pop yer—"

"MOREOVER! I should like to call your attention to the biological fact! A WHALE...**IS NOT...A FISH!"**

"Sounds like it's time ta feed yer tarantula Gwenna—"

"The order Cetacea includes all large marine mammals commonly known as whales including *Physeter catodon macro-cephalus,* also known as the sperm whale—"

"A wha? Wha' kinna whale—"

"VALUED for its oil, spermaceti—"

"Sperma wha—"

"The species most—"

"I'll have mine wit' meat balls Gwenalun, an' don' fergit da gahlick—"

"Prized by the whaling industry which historically and down to the present day continues the brutal murder of these gentle creatures, the largest and most graceful of our mammal cousins, AND the most communicative, as well; perhaps more so than some of our bygone! Overweight! SPORTS LEGENDS **TURNED COMMENTATORS!"**

"An' dey cun talk better too...ah...yeah...ah Gwenalun...'anks fer callin', yer da ulta mutt. Betta take yer pill now, an' don't furgit yer yoga menstrations, chug some milk shakes, GO eat some raw meat GWENALUN! When ya fink yer big enough t' handle a king-size Hungarian sausage wit 'ossrattish on top call me BACK! **DAT'S POETRY GWENALUN!** Deconstruct it anyhow ya want! **YER OUTTA HA!** Yer mudder humps 'er buns at da Roxy! **YER PAPA PINS 'IZ PANNY HOSE WIT BUBBA GUM!** You may not be da biggest bozo ever called up **YER IN DA TOP TEN I CUN TELL YA DAT! Spawts Hotline, you're on n'air."**

"Hey! Watch 'ow ya talk to a lady ya fordy acre gut farm! If ya can't say sum'un' nice shu'ch yer fat trap!"

"Okay ya soun' familyer, wha's yer name?"

"Familyer am I? **I'm yer mutter-in-law ya—"**

"Spawts Hotline, you're on n'air."

"DON'CH yew try hangin' up on me ya good-fer-nuttin' blowed up beer blimp!"

"Cu'ma, Mama—"

"It's MISS Minsky! **SHAD AP WHILE I'M TALKIN'!"**

"Mama da guys is lis'nun—"

"I don' care 'ooze lissnun! Sell yer own mutter fer dat blond boobie trap **I'LL SEN' YA T' DA MOON!** Yu'll be da firs' Ungarian Assernaut!"

"MAMA! Now looka, ya broke down da door"

"Quitch yer bawlin' before I trow up!"

"Ya broke down da door, Mama."

"An' don' fergit t' pick up ten poun' o' kabassa on yer way home, tell Olga my private stock—"

"Ten poun' gonna be nuff, Mama?"

"An' keep yer paws outta da cash regisser I catch ya in n'ere I'll use yer gonads fer golf balls!"

"Mama yer drivin' me nuts—"

"An' don' stop no place neidder, I smell liquor on yer dog breat'—"

"Mama, juss as' me a quess'ion 'bout spawts?"

"An' don' lemme catch ya comin' outta no hootchy-kootch joint neidder—Ya wa' wimmin libernation! I'LL GIVE YA—ah ah—"

"Mama! Mama! Y'okay?"

"AH AH HRRRR—"

"Da docta said don't git 'cited, Mama! Where's yer bottoe?"

"KEEP YER FAT MITS OFF MY LIQER I'll putch ya t'rough da sassage grinner! Loo' katch ya! Why donch ya git a job!"

"I gotta job, Mama! Dose educated ladies is alweez pickin' on me how'z I s'ppose t' know a whale ain' no FISH?"

"YA WANNA WHALE! Go look inna mirror! An' don' fall inna watta! Dey'll fink it's two humpbacks goin' tagedder! If ya 'ad two pints less booze in yer brain I'd use what's lef' fer headcheese—An' anudder fing, Olga better not be missin' no more work Sairdy night! Headache my foot! Mess aroun' wit' my Olga—STAN' STILL—"

"Bu' mama we're—"

"Married my foot! Da bar tenner 'uz too drunk ta fin' na ring finiger—"

"Ow! Mama! I ain' na punchin' ba—"

"Cook wit da leff!"

"Cu'ma, Mama, I di'n't do nuttin—"

"Clean wit da righ'! Cook wit da leff—"

"Mama 'at 'urt!"

"Clean wit da—**GIMME DA**—Wha' ya hidin' I' nere!"

"NUTTIN', MAMA!"

"GIRLY MAG—look atch ya! Stuck like a—"

"Mama my fly's cot inna dess draw—"

"Wha' ya needa—ya can' even—gimme da key—"

"I ain' go' no key."

"Okay stan' back."

"Mamma no! No' da mea' cleava! Mama, please!"

"Shad ap! I ain' gonna touch ya."

"No, Mama, please. Please, Mama, promise."

"Okay, I promise."

"Ya sure, Mama, ya wouldn't—"

"YEAOWWW! Mama, **ya kilt me!** Oh, Mama! Mama!"

"Tabasca sauce!"

"Fer my pizza. I putta boddoe in my pocket. Oh, Mama ya scairt me."

"Now looka yer shirt. Dat stain'll never come out. Dey'll fink it's mod'n art er lass week's booze pardy. 'Ow many time I gotta tell ya **clean unnerwear inna mornin'!** 'Hoo ever 'eard a 'earts o' nis unnerwear WASSAT? **RABBUTS!** O' nis slippas! If I 'ad a shotgun WASSA MATTA NOW? Aw, don' cry, li'l Buggie! Mommy's torry. **AAH MY BABY'S NOT GITTIN' NUFF T' EEAT!** My li'l piggie pie! Looka dose tiny teeks my baby's no' gittin' nuff t' **eeea' AAAR!"**

"After a hard day in the pits, come on in to El Spoor Red Label Beer bottled by master brewers fermented in Germany; also El Spoor Lite for great taste and half the calories. Have an El Spoor. You've earned it."

"Anks, Eddie. Yer a pal."

"Hi, Buck, I just had t' tell ya you're the greatest, a scholar and a gentleman, the Renaissance man incarnate."

"Talkin' like dat's like makin' love to an old maid. Ya can't overdo it. Wha's yer name?"

"H.F. Smiley. The boys call me Hi Fi. I'm calling from the Nuclear Weapons Research Center in Menlo Park, California."

"Whoa! California! I didn't know we got dat far."

"Delayed broadcast. We pick you up at four in the morning. Down here in the basement we lose track of time anyway, what with the walls eight foot thick and the Public Policy boys at their all night poker game. As you know Buck nuclear weapons research is pretty serious business. But boring. We need to break up the monotony once in awhile, hear some new jokes. We can't afford to lose contact with the real world. See that sucker over there? Swampfire II. Six million megaton. We call it the ultimate detergent."

"Yer a gas, Hi Fi, I cun tell ya dat."

"That's right, Buck. You're our man! Our cult hero! Your face should be on a dollar bill, the face that stopped a thousand hockey pucks."

"Dat's nuttin'! You shou'da see Mama's right han'—"

"And you're her number one sparring partner! How many times have you two gone around? Why you're a national instition, Buck. Motherhood and the Monday Night Fights.

"I took a few hits, I cun tell ya dat."

"And…expanded in the experience as we say out here in California. As a matter of fact your name came up just the other day at an informal strategy meeting, a bull session to tell the truth, that's where we do all our heavy duty brain bustin', the theoretical stuff, who t' nuke, who t' juke. So then, I'm gonna ask ya a little question. Take your time now. I'm not gonna throw ya a curve, just fishin', a little wager with the boys. Buck. Have you ever thought of running for political office?"

"Da's a good one Hi Fi. Sommony slip some Mad Dog in yer mint julep?"

"Ha ha. That's great Buck. Love ya. The boys are on the floor. Watch that plutonium bucket! Oh no, the old confetti trick. Sucker! These guys are a riot Buck. Let me tell ya. Look out! A rubber snake in the ignition system! I'm splittin' a gut. Gotta catch my breath. Whew! A laugh a minute. Are ya still there? Let's see where were we? Oh yeah, politics. Let me assure you Buck we're a thousand per cent, irrevocably…where d' all those wires go? The clock's runnin' guys—"

"Wha' kinna poli—"

"As far as you can carry the ball Buck. The governor, the Senate. Who knows? The presidency."

"I don' know nuttin' 'bout politics."

"There's nothin' to it Buck. All you gotta do is read the idiot car—I mean the teleprompter. Just like doin' a beer commercial. You'll be great at it Buck! Maybe a little hair color, a little body work on the old schnoz—"

"Wha? Who?"

"That's show biz Buck! Don't worry about the PR, the boys in the back room'll take care of anything comes down the chute. I can see it now. The cover of *Time*. 'Devlon's Runonski. New Fire from the Old Guard.' You're a household name Buck! Down home appeal, rugged good looks! The people love you. They trust you."

"My t'ird grade teacha ussa say—"

"Of course we'll have to plant a little headplate in yer noggin."

"I could be pussedunt if I cleaned up my gramma, t'ere bote in na sanitarium."

"Think about it. And for heaven sake Buck, don't let anybody tell you bigger ain't better."

"I dunno 'bout da headplate business."

"Nothin' to it Buck. They knock ya out, punch a hole in yer head—"

"A 'ole in yer 'ead?"

"So we can ring yer bell when we need ya, yer back on the tee by four o'clock."

"'Ow big a 'ole in yer 'ead?"

"Just a small hole Buck."

"I don' fink I like it Hi Fi."

"Just a small headplate."

"Dats what dey said 'bout da 'ockey puck."

"No bigger than a horseshoe."

"I'll hafta fink about ut."

"A small horseshoe."

"I don' fink I wanna be no pussedunt."

"Sure ya do, it's the greatest job in the world. All ya do is make promises and pinch bottoms, the boys in the back room'll clean 'em up for ya—the promises."

"Wassa 'orse gonna do wit' one shoe?"

"Just one more thing Buck—did you ever hear of an aphrodectomy?"

"Wassat?"

"Ah…a weight loss technique."

"Why can't da VP do ut?"

"He's got to go around the country breeding good will. Let me explain. You're a hard nut to crack Buck."

"Do I git a tax break?"

"No but you get a depreciation allowance on domestic futures—it's the IRS Buck, don't try to figure it out."

"I dunno Hi Fi—"

"We've got to tailor you to the job."

"Wid anudder operation—"

"Relax. You'll like being a eunuch."

"Wassa ewe-notch?"

"Ah…it's like a beatnik without the bongos, a liberal without a lost cause, a feminist without a filibuster—"

"I'm gittin' confused."

"Technically it's called the Clinton Caveat—so the country won't get caught with its pants down so to speak. Here's how it works. Remember when

457

you were a kid and your Mama had a Christmas tree with an angel on top and big red balls so shiny you could count your teeth and if you dropped one it broke in a million pieces? And after Christmas she verrry carefully…ah…*removed* them from the tree and put them in a hat box up in the attic?"

"I don' fink I like da general idea High Fi."

"We're gonna be real careful Buck."

"Deir Mama's hairlooms. She brought 'em all da way from Hungaria in na darnin' basket."

"All we're gonna do is take 'em off the tree awhile, and when you're done being president, we'll put 'em back."

"Dey cun do dat?"

"Another miracle of modern science."

"Oh yeah, how?"

"By adding water. Then you're a reconstituted Republican—ever wonder why they start saying intelligent things after they leave office?"

"What if I don' git 'lected?"

"Oh there are numerous opportunities out there Buck. You could be the CEO of a large corporation, the president of a prestigious university, a network executive, a Hollywood mongul, a campaign strategist, a beltway lobbist, the list is endless, we'd be here all night—what the heck, I guess we are here all night, a supreme court justice, a drug lord, a pro wrestler, the president of a Uni—I already said that, a Madison Avenue heavyweight, an art critic, a rock star, a rap artist, or you could underwrite the Rush Limbaugh Show."

"My name is Paul Chauvin, chairman, Runonski for President; Paris, Tennessee. Why there are no women candidates for President is a complex and involuted question. To be sure there are many capable and deserving women, all of whom would bring honor and innovation to the highest office of this grand old Republic, BUT, can they take the heat? Let me remind the ladies we're not talking about slaving over another hot stove; we're talking prime time in the big kitchen."

"Hole it rat tha! I sayed fa-REEZE! Yeah. You! Skinny butt. You in vi-O-lation of City Orda-Nance 101-D, impropah dis-posul of taxic bi-O-cahcass, two ton an' ovah, hunting sayed creature widou' valid license, willful destruction of endaggered species, *dragonis pie-row-panumis,* inciting to public excitement, failya to obey a law enfoecement officah!…honey, you in a deep pile."

"Roight. An amphibious marine reptile is it? Fine specimen, very like a whale."

"Who he?"

"Hugh Seton-Ramsey, Scotland Yard, Try-To-Be-Calm."

"You woik in the yawd?"

"I don't believe I've had the pleazhah—"

"Somebody collah tha' boy! He gittin' away!"

"Heading for the swamp I see?"

"Shee! We nevah gittem in tha!"

"Roight. I do regret to intercede but the extreme delicacy of the situation requiahs—could you come a little closer please...Officer Vickers. Mavis is it? Jolly good. May I present my partner, Chauncey McDowell, RCMP."

"He gwone now."

"But in the right direction. Scotland Yard has beene anticipating such a contingency for some time now. Legend has it there's a way out. Recent satellite observations have confirmed a dirth of sunspot activity, Jupiter unaligned with Mars, children obeying their elders. As the grim Irish poet put it, 'The sinner cannot hold.'"

"Wha' chew been drinkin' boy? Whey you wearin' tha' raincoa'? Wha' chew got unna tha—"

"Clever disguise, don't you think?"

"Wor you gitch you tha' mumbrella? He ain' nevah gonna rain down heah!"

"Precisely. But the swamp continues to rise."

"An' whey you a'wuz smilin'? Ain' noboda a'wuz smilin' down heah! Dey's sum'un **w-r-r-r-ronge** wich you, boy!"

"Actually...yes. For some time now we've beene itching to have someone...take the plunge, but alas, no volunteers, until our young friend happened along, delightful chap. Do you get the drift, Miss Vickers? I say, would you care to join me for a cup of tea? Should anyone osk, it would be best if nyether of us had any recollection of this little affair. You're hoping to advonce to detective? This way, the carcass won't mind."

"Won't mind at all. Yet I bleed a thousand years."

"*You!* Look at you! You're hideous! Slain! Hide your face in shame."

"Slain again and crawled in a ditch to die, the fate of fallen foes...I am the paragon of fallen foes, yet I ask a boon."

"A boon?"

"Understanding."

"What's to understand? You're ugly, slimey, disgus—"

"Yet I die of a broken heart."

"…And a rather high pitched voice. Almost—"

"A contralto."

"You mean you're—Oh God."

"And do you wonder I have no mate, fight like a man, prefer the company of dames?"

"Oh no."

"There is a word in your language—"

"What have I done?"

"My lineage runs to the isle of Lesbos."

"A fem…les…from Lesbos. I'm going to be—"

"The laughing stock of the generation you so despise. But do not give up. The ugliness you would have slain is coiled in your heart; you must overcome it with understanding, for true beauty is more than absence of ugliness; it is the understanding that all that breathes is worthy of love. You will win her not with killing but with unassuming love. Farewell, small brother."

CHAPTER 42

THE HEART OF DARKNESS

How now my wayward? Alone and fearful lost? Amid the foul contagion of pride run riot? The rank surfeit of fear too bold to bear? The worst is now to come. Brave once more the smithy of thy soul, one more naked dream deep in the natal swamp where mortal mud and sacred fire entwine. Be strong. You have slain your dragon and won your freedom. Know that freedom is by far more dire. This tortured world awaits another tortured birth. Cry loud, but come you must into this tragic scene, if only to forget your solitary line and die somewhere in shame. Let demons rage and crack their cheeks; they cannot touch the secret of thy soul. Listen to the drums, let morning birdsong guide the peregrinations of thy brain. The rising sun is yet to kiss thy cheek.

The swamp! Fire's out. Quiet. So quiet. Damn it, who let the fire go out! Dark. Something moved! Kwoikwoiyea? Moses? Drums! Can't be. A footstep. Close. Real close.

Run my darling run
Run to the chimney
Under the grate
Into the ashes
Head down and wait

I'm so sleepy. Mustn't sleep. I can hear it. Something trickling. No…creaking. Like a door opening. So dark. Cold.

Then take my hand.
I am Death.
I am warmth to all that's cold,
Ease to all that's old,
I am balm to where it hurts,
Calm to these that
NO!

All flights to Seoul, Anchorage, and Los Angeleeze have been cancelled indefinitely. They were never scheduled due to lies, deceit, cowardice, and pride. Furthermore this airplanet is not equipped with auto pilot, the navigator is dead, the radio out, the passengers near panic, and fossil fuel in limited supply. This is not a recording.

A drum—voices swimming in a sea of—simple rhythm, lulling, immanent—but no words, only whispers slipping through the memory like tiny snakes.

Night time right time might bite right NOW!
What!
Night right. Might light. Sight NOW!
Nothing there.
*Sight RIGHT bite LIGHT might FIGHT right **NOW!***
Must be dreaming.
Meat retreat. Meat retreat.
Birds—
Creep creep creep creep creep
Fire's out. Mulba? You awake?
Sleep seep. Three deep. Meet meet meet meet meet
Damn birds. Mustn't sleep.
Peep deep. Creep leap. See see see see see
Something out there. Black. Heavy. Like a—
Mort de lit. Mort de lit. Oui oui oui oui oui
Can't remember—
Deep resleep. Be discreet.
What? The instant I open—
Beat retreat. Beat retreat.
Closer. It's coming—
Tout de suite. Tout de suite. Oui oui oui oui oui
Mustn't fall asleep.
Saw paw. Raw paw. Claw paw. LAW! LAW! LAW! LAW! LAW!
That one…wasn't one of us.
Ram town. Lamb drown. Man crown. See ya downtown.
Something trying to…no shape. Never a—
Sing song SWEET
That one's different—
Sweet song SLEEP
So close! It can't be more than a few feet—

Sweet wrong KEEP
Got to restart the fire.
Heat strong DEEP
Got to get out of here.
Thee reTREAT
But where?
Sweet throng SEE. Thee thee thee thee thee
There on the weather vane! Gone. Even the birds abandoned the old place. Look how empty. A farmstead without…all that makes a home a home…the windmill ready to tumble into the weeds, torn burlap over the barn window, gray siding, rusted door rails, naked beams, the whole damn thing ready to collapse, sumac in the silo, an old reaper sunk in the grass, windows boarded shut, porch gone, the living room wall exposed to the elements, crumpled plaster, bare lathing, stained wall paper—it seems indecent to look into someone's—a bird's nest on the mantel, rotted floors, rat holes, a smashed toy drum under the staircase, water dripping on a tin can. Die. Die. Die. Die.

Somebody lived here once. The walls knew the sound of evening grace. Children ran in the yard. Back in the Depression. Squatters. The sheriff ran 'em off. Hillbillies with a house full of kids, dirt poor but too proud to surrender. The father fighting mad, the mother wore men's work shoes and a shabby cotton dress that dragged in the mud, but she left with her head up whispering lovingly to the two-year-old who cried in her arms clinging to her hair with his tiny fists.

I was playing trains with Samuel and Luke and a man came and he was bigger and bigger and a shiny on his pocket and Papa wanted angry but Joshua came and holding his arms and Ezra fell down and Mommy said now we have to go away and Rachael and Sarah started to cry and Mommy said not to cry but water filled up my mouth and she kissed me and the house is crying too.

Nobody ever lived there again. The dogs came back a week later. What was the name? Green? Graves? Even Grandma can't remember. People around here don't like to talk about it. The sheriff said he was real sorry. Grimes. That's it. The Christmas season too. Ugly wallpaper. To roving boys twenty years later the old place became a haunted castle. You could tell by the way the wind moaned in the empty barn…like the mouth of a giant sleeping. Dare ya t' go in. A great place to play explorer. Double dare ya. There's a secret map under the—
Run my darling run
Run to the burrow

Under the well
Then to the furrow
Deep down don't tell

A junk yard. I've been here before. But not like this. It's come to life. The same landmarks…schoolyard, carrousel, church. The kid pinned to the crossbeam. *La Pieta* in the back seat of a limo contemplating a child. Pure white. Tears down the granite. She's got a switchblade. What do I care if some damn actress is hooked on drugs! Side shows! It's close. I can smell the damn thing. Something bad is going to happen.

Traffic control tower. Blue field lights. A red beacon sweeping a deserted runway. They're on emergency power. Something went wrong at the electric plant. Search lights. It won't be coming from out there! It's in here!

Swampfire II clear for take off—vector two one niner—ceiling 100 feet—cloud cover dense to heavy evade as needed—condition red—good hunting

Somebody took out Central Command. One damn terrorist with a homemade…They've panicked. Confusion. Wild shouts. All monitors suddenly eerie yellow. Hum of insects—helicopter—no! Bull roarer! People running. Technicians in white jackets screaming, fighting to disengage smoking electrical cords, their navels red. Radar dishes spinning frantically. Soldiers in battle gear taking up positions behind disabled cars, sandbags, some digging in, others slashing through the swamp. Rattle of small arms. What are they shooting at? Men in gas masks, like prehistoric insects, racing against traffic, heavy backpacks, yellow rubber suits. Mortar blasts, billows of smoke. An official car slides up. Men in business suits hurry to the radar consoles, one takes a headset, two others begin photographing everything in sight. Now they're studying a computer readout. More gunfire. Tracers. Flares. Falling debris. What are they shooting at? There's nothing there. Houses bursting into flame. An inhuman wailing, bleeding civilians crawling for cover, ripped flesh stuck to their clothing, nauseated survivors heaving in agony. People in dumb stupor walking into oncoming traffic. A laughing madman. Savage machine gunfire. Exploding artillery. People running, fighting to get on trucks, motor bikes, children thrown off to make room. Riot! Someone's trying to hot wire a car. Four others beating him with tire irons. They're…now a gang…but the car's stalled, they're still…can't they…don't…now a terrier pup racing after a pickup, a bawling boy reaching back; it jumps into the tail gate, falls back, its final yelp crushed in the horn blast of the next truck. Last minute looting in the business district. Medics running. Stretchers. Yells. This way! Have you seen my daughter! Blond hair! School clothes! Get t' hell out o' the way! Check the church basement! No it's been hit! Get 'er out o' here!

Puffs of red mist, floating, foul smelling. Scent of spring butchering. An alien specter drifting across the swamp, settling like glue on windshields, cars, jeeps, the yard engine's wipers smear it back and forth beating it into a red gum. Burns like tar. Eats your skin. People running. Handkerchiefs over their faces, coughing, vomiting. The earth soaked red, buzzing flies, carrion dogs testing then attacking warm corpses, red jaws pulling at shreds of flesh, intestines, snarling at each other, eyeing competitors. Men beating them back with clubs. Rows and rows of plastic bags. Some leaking. The swamp choked. Weary soldiers. Heave! Some sink. Some don't.

A red faced torso practically swimming in the slippery mud. Can't move. Give me a knife. My legs. Cover me up. I don't want…Please.

we got a bogey at five o'clock—confirm

confirmed—two zero niner and closing—speed twelve knots—under navigation

under what—repeat

under navigation—confirmed

ours

negative

origin

unknown

South! The sneaky bastards!

Beep rePEAT. Beep rePLETE. See see see see see

It's not from this goddamn planet!

Knock it off! We don't need panic. It's not one of ours, it beeps, we damn well know where it's from.

Beep be GREET. Be disCREET. Thee thee thee thee thee

A star. Bright as Venus. But sickly yellow in the southern sky. Descending in deathly silence, dropping out of the black clouds towards the blue runway lights. Cut the lights for Chrissakes! Not the radar damn it! Closer. One by one technicians break for the parking lot. The phone booth—one last—someone frantically pounding the glass. Forget it Frank! Get out! Get to hell out!

puritan to cherokee—respond

appomattox open—antietam go

commence operation yellowjacket stop go to condition red phase one all systems stop notify all units via closed channel stop confirm via code 12—may god be with us gentlemen

The eye of the storm. Slow descent. Final approach. People kneeling in alleys, beside cars, holding their heads, a rosary. The crane! Raises its electromagnet over its cab like a cobra ready to strike. The yard engine! Wheels in reverse, crashes through an overgrown fence, overturns on its side in a muddy lot, one wiper frantically clacking back and forth fighting the red mist, the other stuck closed, red spray spurting from exhaust vents. One headlight, eerie yellow like all the rest. The row of smoke stacks bent towards the source belching red steam, power lines twitching under tremendous force. Crackling static. Antennas quivering, forelegs rubbing each other like insects. Carrion dogs slinking under the flat cars, tails between their legs. Give me a gun. Somebody give me a gun.

Now it comes. First the junk cars, hollow headlight sockets come to life, then the airplane, the rectangular eyes of the yard engine, street lights, windows of abandoned buildings, monitors, radar screens—the same ungodly glow, pale yellow with a hint of green, unnatural, faint, barely enough to define the vessel that holds it. Neon signs, computer screens. The same pale cast. Tornado sky.

It's not an aircraft! It's not from this planet! But unexpectedly graceful, weightless. You can sense it eyeing the runway, picking its spot, touching down with scarcely a whisper. Don't look! You'll go mad.

Jet blast. Tremendous power shaking flat cars, toppling buildings. Something's wrong. It's implosive—a shrieking wind pulling everything in, loose debris, dust, smoke. The crane's electromagnet horizontal.

I can see it. The far end of the runway, a half pirouette, two pricks of piercing light in a fiendish halo like stars in a nebula. An alien consciousness, dumb animality. It's come for me.

No more side shows. Find it. Kill it. Get out.

But why kill it? Can it be that bad? Can any living thing be so bad?

Somebody give me a knife!

A simple virus. Remove it. Recover. Go home.

The simplest creatures have their secrets.

It's alien. Evil. Destroy it.

How do we know it's evil?

Orders from above. Do not question authority.

Has anyone tried to…

Find it. Kill it. Get out. Do not toy with the—

Speak to it?

Complete the mission.

Night right, sight might, light blight, deep deep deep deep deep
It's near. I can feel it.
Little baBOON. Fiddle till NOON. See ya real SOON.
It's close. Moving in. Premeditated stealth. A primordial nightmare waking to devour its children. The swamp. They think it's alien but they're wrong. It's in the swamp. That's where it lives.

The deeper into the swamp, the shallower the water. Doesn't stink so bad away from human habitation. Not so many corpses. Very quiet. Eerie. Yellowish heat lightening. Sonic rumble. I've been here before. It's different, submerged but familiar. Schoolyard. Carrousel. Dead horses. There's been an accident. Flares. They're trying to communicate.

It's close.

Wake up!

Wake up you die!

There. Feel it moving. How fast it fits the frame of Night. Not a glimmer, not a whisper. Now drums. Far away.

Afraid o' thee, not me, not me.
Closer.
Come unsee, come unsee.
A 57 Chev. Water up to the fender skirts. Something in the back seat…a teddy bear. No! A boy. How beautiful. Bright, wholesome, angelic hair. What's your…oh no…He's playing with a knife. Oh God no. Eyes like…oh no. Please no. No. No. No.

Sweet boy SLEEP
I don't have a name. I live under the water. They came and took me away when I was very small.

Deep boy KEEP
Mommy said not to cry but my mouth filled up with water.

Meat boy REAP
Now I'm an aborted boy and nobody to play with me.

Sleep boy WEEP
Jenny said it doesn't hurt anymore.

Sweet boy KEEP
You would have been my daddy.

Secret SLEEP
It wasn't her fault. Her mama made her do it.

Thee boy MEET
You weren't good enough for them. Your name sounds funny.

Sweet boy FREE
Now you're not allowed to play with me.
Sweet boy SLEEP
I have to play with snakes.
Free boy KEEP
I can't find Teddy and it's getting nighttime.
Keep boy WEEP
Don't cry. Don't cry my boy.
Free thee WEEP
My boy. My sweet boy.
Dry cry CREEP. Weep weep weep weep weep
An orchid. Out in the swamp. Growing on something dead. Look! The water's clear! There must be a spring. Out here! In the middle of...Faces under the water. Hundreds. Well-preserved. Hair floating. They want to speak. Can't. Mouths full of water. The words are floating away. What do they want? Something's wrong. There's been an accident.

Run my darling run
Run to the cellar
Hide in the sackcloth
Under the butter
Stay. Analyze the problem. What tools do you need? What options are open?
It's coming. It's big. It wants to bite.
Stay. All is not lost.
Mommy I don't want to play this game.
The situation is manageable if you work, think, analyze.
You must my darling.
Not to play is to die. You must act with conviction.
Do what you know is right my darling, what your heart whispers true.
Not to act is to—
They said it would come by air, it rose from the swamp; the radar pointed north, it came from the south; we expected something foreign, it spoke our native tongue. An armed invasion? It was more an internal hunger. Supernatural? Definitely of this earth, intelligent, refined, frightened. It simply lifted its head and began to breathe like a confused animal rising from primordial sleep in a backwoods swamp where no one was looking, there to be confronted by the first unfortunate soul who happened to stumble in its path.

May I have your attention please. We are currently experiencing atomsfearic turbulence due to moral trepidations in the intestinal corridor. All passengers prepare for direct inner face.

The orchid. It's moving. Clear water. Some kind of fountain. Shooting up. Higher. Silky phantoms with sinuous tails. Faces of sorrow, anger, ugliness. Everything foul and disgusting. Hideous deformities. Snarling demons. Gnarled limbs and dirty scales. Clear-eyed malevolence. Essence of evil. Perfidious, rotten, damned by all that's decent. Now blood. Gushing outward in full eruption.

Nyamu! Without a mask! Now I know you! Yes, the fountain's bubbling down. It's come for me. There it is. Revealed. A black tree stump carved into human form. Wet. Slimy. Like a foetus. Only old. Something out of the rag heap of the past, a noise in the basement, a relic that moans once a thousand years. Large head, too big for the trunk. Smells of rotten meat, burnt wiring. A trace of blood. But the face! A haunting sense of someone familiar. The scent of the species. Neither Negroid nor Caucasian, but something ancestral, a prodigal animality come home, dark, demonic, predatory. Feral force in a protruding snout, bovine muzzle, high forehead, a delicate eyebrow, one immense eye formed from a camera lens but off center, white slashes on the perimeter, Nikon, staring blankly to the side, the pale glow within, the source of a consuming abyss, magnetic, horrid, then a mechanical clicking as it tries to focus, some kind of remote control, it's looking for something, the other eye lid sewn partially shut with nylon fish line, the loose end floating weightlessly in space, the eye within steady, red, terror struck, like a beast with a spear in its neck waiting to be put out of its misery. Rows of pin-sized lights embedded in the temple and cheekbones, green, yellow, red, blinking on and off, musical dial tones, rusty steel spikes hammered through the jaw from under the chin at odd angles, through swollen lips like tusks, a red serpent's tongue dancing in and out, cleft and lambent like a tiny flame. Wrinkled human skin, definitely human, straight brown hair neatly parted, oiled, brushed but untrimmed, laced with cobweb, like a mummy. Its left ear missing, shot off or surgically removed, in its place a jumble of electrical wiring stuffed into the temple, red, yellow, white, the operation incomplete, a three-fingered copper circuit breaker with a red plastic handle in the open position hanging half way out the incision as if in birth, primitive brain surgery, loose wires floating in zero gravity, but sparking when they touch, blood trickling out the burlap gauze and down the side of the neck, thickening into black grease on silvery green scales, then into open gills dilating for air, a stone arrowhead embedded within. And a leather neck piece! A compass. Two hands. Pointing opposite directions. Ticking. Flies orbiting the head, settling on strings of ripped flesh, its good eye immobile, a faint rasp of expiring breath…but at the bridge of the eyes, the place where you recognize someone…someone I know…in mute agony, near death but emitting radio transmissions—

swampfire to cherokee—maintaining attack speed—two zero niner—all units red—over

And soft whispers—gentle, feminine, refined—

Run my darling run
Run to the kitchen
Under the sink
Never a whimper
Never a blink

And a fatherly voice, soft but firm—

Stay. Analyze the problem. Do you need an electrician, a counselor, a savior?

And a clock ticking. Intense heat. Drums. Voices. A low chant—

Witch witch
Burn a witch
Close your eyes
Bite the switch

But its breathing. Where there's breath there's…

Do not panic. How much time do you have?

There's a rational explanation. This is not the—

Creep…Creep…Leopard feat.

Middle Ages. Witches don't—

Softly as a black snake sliding down a stem.

It's still breathing.

appomattox to swampfire stop commence address verification stop cowboy—sunfire—beatrice

After all these centuries—

Spear back. Spear look.

Don't touch it. For God sake don't touch it.

Do not approach the—

It now. It look.

All unauthorized personnel—

Fear bite. Near site.

Do not attempt to make contact! You are in a restricted area! Repeat! You are in—

Fear sight. Might bite.

You are NOT authorized—

Fear stink. It link.

Do not go near it you dumb bastard!

Touch it and your through! You'll never work here again!

Touch it and you're dead! We're all dead! Hey! The joke's over! Get away from the goddamn console! That's an order!

Fear bite. Sight night. It rite.

This building is off limits to all! Repeat! ALL—

Look now. It make. Fear make.

You must touch it.

Look make. It make look make.

You will be afraid but you must touch it.

charlie—oscar—whiskey—bravo—oscar—yankee

Repeat! All unauthorized persons—

Teeth down. It look.

On the side of the bulkhead!

Bite not. Run not. Fear down.

Right in front of the goddamn—

Talk not. Teeth down.

You are in direct violation—

Look to. Look wait.

Don't build a wall between us Hon.

Thing keep DEEP

You take things so literally.

Hair stand. It look.

Direct violation of a police order!

Ring sing SWEET

Loosen up. Let your hair down.

Creep round. It keep.

Perhaps if you came in out of left field.

Red down. Bite not

Pry prong DEEP

This is the Commissioner of Police, we have the entire area surrounded! You have no avenue of egress!

Spear down. Bite not.

471

Marksmen are standing by. They will only be called in if you—
Red rot SEEP
Red bite. Teeth cry.
Come out now and—
Strike not. Run not.
You listen to too much Bach. Get hip man.
Thing sing BEEP
You take things too seriously. People are going to fuck up. Face it.
Look round. All see.
I always knew you'd be one of us.
Fear down. Fear down look. Fear down look now.
Is he on drugs?
sierra—uniform—november
Okay buddy ya wanna talk about it?
Spear down. Spear down look. Spear down look stay.
Okay, let's talk. I'm usin' the bullhorn so ya can hear me! I'm not mad at ya!
Breathe come. It make breathe make.
We don't wanna hurt ya.
Breathe make. Breathe make wind talk. Wind talk sing make.
Okay I'm pullin' back the guns. I gave 'em the day off. Maybe when this's all over we can all have a beer together. Wha' da ya say?
Wind sing bird make. Bird sing it make.
We, your father and I, cannot relate to you anymore. You're drifting farther and farther away. What's happening to you? Ever since you got back—
It make song make.
He's been hanging around those goddamn hippies!
Song make free make.
He could get his damn hair cut for one thing!
Free make bird fly.
What t' *hell* makes him think he can shit on every goddamn thing we ever fought for? He's gotta be on drugs.
Bird fly free come. It make free make.
He needs to get some counseling.
Good morning, my name is General John Crogan, Commandant, First Battalion, Third Wing, Air National Guard. You are hereby ordered to cease and desist! Evacuate the area NOW! That is an order!

Thing rePLETE.

How in the hell did the son of a bitch get in!

Sing bring SLEEP. Song sing SWEET.

Why in the hell can't a goddamn civilian follow orders like everybody else?

Night bite. Fight light. Bright rite. Sight might. Try try try try try

I don't believe I've had the pleasure, sir. My name is Father Conlan, Rector at St. Anthony's.

Rector Rector dead as Hector!

The Governor has asked me to inform you he has ordered the Commissioner to withdraw all police units from the immediate area. No one wants to hurt you. We can walk out of here right now, you and I.

Magnum Rectum ergo Sanctum!

Ah yes, I see someone has hidden a tape recorder on the premises, an old trick we wore out at St. Anthony's long ago. It's as simple as that. The voices. You're not imagining them. It's the Devil. I'm afraid he's got all the latest technology.

Magnum Sanctum ergo Rankum!

All the old temptations in living High Fidelity. Fight it my son. You can beat him. Fight the good fight. Come with me, we'll fight him together.

foxtrot—india—romeo—echo

I have some good news for you. Someone you care about is coming. It'll only be a few minutes.

Bird ring FREE

I don't even know his name Father.

Free ring THEE

Can I be alone with him? One minute. Can you ask those people—one minute!

Thee ring ME

Hi. My name's Michael. I teach electronics at the Community College. Can you hear me? I don't think you know me, we may have met a long time ago. There's no tape recorder like the man said, he brought it with him—tried to deceive you and the police haven't really pulled back. In fact two more SWAT teams are on the way and they're heavily armed. They're scared. So am I. Nobody can figure out what happened. They assured us…Can you hear me? I'm not going to lie to you I promise.

bravo—echo—alpha—tango

We don't have much time. We've…we've all been under a lot of stress. But we're going to get you out of here. I know how you must feel. They

473

laughed at me too. Don't let them tell you you're…different. Please listen to me it's not too late no matter how…unpopular…I was never one of the gang either. Back in high school I wanted to sit with the cool kids at the back table. I wanted it so bad it hurt but they only ignored me. Called me Nerdo. Kids. They don't realize…

Tree branch. Tree branch head grow.

What? What are you trying to say?

Tree branch head grow. Tree branch head grow red rot. Head grow tree branch. Head grow red rot.

What did you say?

Head branch red bite. Head branch red bite FIX.

Speak up. Don't be afraid. I'd like to get to know you better. Maybe we can be friends.

"Sing song SWEET! Ring wrong SUITE! Bring long SLEEP!"

Oh God. I'm an electrician not a psychologist! Okay. I'm sorry. I didn't mean to yell. I…I teach elec…commun…college. I have a wife and two beautiful daughters I love very much. I…I…Please. Please for them…think of…think of…

Tree branch it not. Tree branch bite. Tree branch it bite.

Two daughters. Small house…dog…Samson. On weekends we like to go to the mountains, I like the Kingston Trio, my hobby's woodcraft theoretically this should not have happened the system's not supposed to arm itself somehow it did, we know you didn't do it, you couldn't have done it alone one person can't, all commands have to be crossverified but once verified the computer is programmed to read any further instructions as a command to fire…to prevent enemy interfer…Please don't touch it. I beg you. I know…in your heart you're trying to help.

Tree branch lick. Tree branch fix.

romeo—india—charlie—echo

Leave him alone. He's going to be all right.

Red rot bite. Red rot fix.

GET T' HELL OUT OF THE GODDAMN—

You **must** touch it.

That's an order Pilgrim!

Ever been to the Rockies in summer when the wild flowers are on? I know this place in the Tetons, Idaho side, I've been going there since I was a little boy. There's a high meadow that turns into a lake of purple and white, all flowers, they only last a couple weeks up there, you can wade through 'em and not leave a path, they close in behind you like surf at the beach—

Swampfire to cherokee—address code—confirmed
The geeks don't have souls.
The best damn thing you can do is put 'em out o' their goddamn misery.
I'd like to take you there someday. We could hike up to the snow line.
Build a campfire. Cook up some trout.
Tree branch red bite. Tree branch red bite fix.
I know you don't want to hurt anyone. But you've got to help me. I think
I can fix it.
Kill 'em all! Let God sort 'em out.
cherokee to appomattox
I'll bring along my wife's sister—
address verification complete
Regular tomboy, you'll like her.
She touch sweet touch.
If you don't come with us tonight—
Tree branch fix sweet. Tree branch fix touch.
Your twentieth century will be the end of—
Red rite. Red rite fix. Red rite sweet make. Red rot fix make.
Better dead than red—
commence address code imprint
You better believe it.
Man hand. Man hand reach. Man hand reach bright.
That's just a Geiger counter, it does that when you go near it. It's not going
to hurt you.
cowboy sunfish beat rice
We feel you have a bright future in data processing.
Touch. Touch branch. Man hand touch branch.
Beatrice! Beatrice! What idiot read Beat Rice!
Read wrong BEEP
Strike my darling Strike
Bite in the bite place
Under the face
Down in the neck place
No wait for grace
We have an overload! Cut power! Red alert! Red—
I can't hold 'er! Sweet Jesus I can't—
Tree branch break. Tree branch break down. It break out down.
Fire in the cockpit! Mayday! Mayday!

Tree man BREECH

She's goin' down! Bail out! Aban—

appomattox to Swampfire—mission abort—mission abort

Arc in the silo! We've got an arc in the—

Fire bite Fire bite Fire bite Fire bite!

I didn't do it! The handle broke! Just when I—I didn't do it!

Sing song SWEET. Leap rePEAT. Bye rye WHEAT. Feat comPLETE.
Weep weep weep weep weep

Fire Ball Fire Ball Fire Ball!

I'm sorry. I'm so sorry.

Cry hi HEAT

Pasha! Moja Cbihya!

Jean Pierre! T'enfuis!

Yisang! YISANG!!

Bao! Bao! Bao! Bao!

BILLY! Hold your brother's hand! BILLY!

Static. A spark. Promethean fire. Spikes, scales, wadding, fragments of a three-pronged switch spiralling outward. Suffocating stench. A filament of rising smoke, a single strand of witch's hair curling upward like an umbilical cord with an embryo forming on top, whirring insects, bull roarers, helicopters, tanks, jets, thousands, full throttle, thunderous roar, a ball of light, a primeval sun, a column of rising smoke, expanding, thickening, a tree, a tower, twisting, billowing upward, penetrating the dome of heaven, blinding bright, turning inward, a rising cumulus cloud, growing, rolling under into itself, mountainous mushroom brown, noonday sun in deepest night, now a halo racing beyond the smoke, godly brilliance from ungodly light, the sickly glow, devouring night—

Night bite Site bright Fright rite sight Might, See see see see see

Our monster baby come home at last, Death's fairest daughter smiling bright. Fret no more sweet mother, Hell has signed its name on hills and fields, come home to claim it's own.

BASTARDS! Arrogant, egotistical bas—Look what you've done! Is your ideology pure enough now? Did you cover yourselves with glory?

Knock it off!

Idiots! Well, who won? Tell us who won?

Now by God we'll see what our boys are made of, hey?

Bastards! Look at what you've done.

And there was a big light in the sky and it was bigger and bigger like sunshine only sleeptime and there was a big fire truck and two more fire trucks and a policeman and going faster and faster and their lights turning faster and faster and people running and two cars went together and a man got out and shouting and people shouting and two men fighting and the houses burning and falling down and a man ran in and another man his pants burning and people crying and a big fire came out and very hot like summertime and a lady her hair all messed up and she was running and she grabbed me and pushed me away and running I want my mommy I can't find mommy—

Six children, holding hands on a smoking rubbish heap, a small black boy in the center, defiant, proud, bright smile; oriental girl, downcast, shy; blond caucasian boy, hair combed, neat shirt, tie, fine shoes; tall, slim, dark skinned waif, any shantytown, any continent, scavenged shoes, toothy smile; Latin American girl, turned sideways, empty cup in hand, frightened; Indian boy, long pants, barefoot, small rib cage, penetrating eyes, an old man in a ten year old body. Holding hands. They mean to put on a school play.

The Grosse Pointe Rotary and Garden Club biweekly luncheon has been canceled until further notice.

Algonquin Airlines Charter Flight 192 to Palm Beach has been delayed due to mechanical difficulties. All passengers please report to the decontamination center in the main lobby. This is a routine check only. There is no danger to the public.

Due to unacceptable radiation levels, the following schools will not hold classes this morning: Camden Elementary School, Firelands Junior High School, Washington Senior High, Tri-County Joint Vocational School, St. Mary's School for Girls, The Wayne County School for the Retarded, Southern Ontario Community College, The Indianapolis Christian Bible School, The Malcolm X Academy, The Helen Keller Center, The New York School of Cosmetology at Buffalo, Penn State University, all branches.

The Governor has declared a state of emergency in the following…

The following hospitals are no longer accepting…

The Surgeon General has requested all municipal authorities to suspend pumping fresh water from the following sources: southern Lake Michigan, Lake Huron below Saginaw Bay, Lake St. Clair, Lake Erie, western Lake Ontario and the Finger Lakes Region of New York. This is a precautionary measure until further testing is completed.

Liars!

Tryouts for the Kennsington Community Players' spring production of *The Unsinkable Molly Brown* have been temporarily canceled due to…

Pumping will resume as soon as safe radiation levels can be verified. To apply for safe water ration books, call any one of the following 800 numbers. This is a standby program only; there is no cause for public alarm.

Liars! Bastards!

Power is being restored to the following communities pending emergency...

A spokesman for Northern Bell said full service will be resumed in about a week. Persons without access to working phone lines are encouraged to use the portable facilities at their local police stations. These units will be in place as soon as possible.

This evening's performance of *Swan Lake* will not...

The AMA has advised all expectant mothers in their first trimester to call their attending physicians. This is a voluntary procedure only, your local hospital will advise you of your options.

Work on the People's Monument to World Peace has been temporarily suspended. Construction will continue as soon as radiation levels have fallen within acceptable limits. We repeat, there is no threat to public safety, this is a precautionary procedure only.

Oh, hell yes!

The Department of Transportation has issued the following traffic advisory: all interstate highways have been closed to civilian and nonemergency vehicles; if you must travel keep on designated federal routes. Do not attempt long trips without local authorization.

The Commandant of the National Guard has ordered all Army and Navy Surplus outlets to suspend the sale of contamination suits. Violations will be prosecuted.

Auxiliary military personnel will begin collecting excess canned goods at private homes in the Worthington area for distribution to—

Distribution my ass!

Citizens will be issued government vouchers in full payment.

The acting Surgeon General has requested all homes to limit their consumption of water to five gallons per day. This is for temporary conservation purposes only, full availability will be—

The Red Cross has suggested the following procedure for the home treatment of first and second-degree burns. Prepare an unguent of mustard, flour—

What about a treatment for—

The following is a National Security Bulletin. Due to widespread civil disturbances, the looting of private enterprises, and the mounting threat to public safety, the Pentagon in cooperation with the National Security Council has ordered martial law effective immediately. This is a temporary measure only—

Bull SHIT!

taken to insure—

Liars! Morons!

Operation Yellowjacket Phase III will commence at 0300 hours, all participatory units are ordered to report to debarkation centers immediately. Code Green. There is no cause for public alarm, citizens are asked to cooperate by staying in their homes. You will be fully informed of all further developments.

Bullshit! Why weren't we informed before—What t' hell's Operation Yellowjacket!

Operation Yellowjacket is proceeding on schedule. Phase III, Code Blue will commence 0600 hours.

All owner operators of commercial freight vehicles, five tons and over, are hereby ordered to appear at the following staging areas for the transport of emergency food pending—

In compliance with Operation Yellowjacket, Code White, the following persons are hereby ordered to report to the National Induction Center for per-term loyalty testing. Full compliance is mandatory. Violators will be subject to immediate house arrest—

Emergency medical attention can be obtained at the following churches. Bring all available health and biographical documents—

To alleviate unwarranted public concern, the acting Lieutenant Governor has issued the following statement: Operation Yellowjacket is the emergency distribution of medicine and food stuffs to schools, hospitals, and—

Aren't they passing out lollipops!

What in the hell is going on!

THIS IS A MILITARY COUP! WAKE UP!

Where the hell's the damn government anyway!

The government! The entire east coast...

That's not possible—

Try gettin' through—

The lines are down, that's all.

No...No radio. Short wave. Nothin.

Those bastards—

We've just about had enough of your stupid questions! Just SHUT T' HELL UP!

No I won't shut up!

Somebody said some damn data processing trainee went berserk, that's all I know.

Oh, hell yes! Blame it on—

Hey, buddy. You better back off. My brother-in-law says they're pickin' up dangerous elements.

Hell yes! Round 'em up! What t' hell's a dangerous element? Somebody who—

Puttin' 'em in vans and takin' 'em away. Got the picture? Now shut t' hell up or we're all—

Fuck 'em! What's Code Orange? What's Code Green? Why distribute foodstuffs to schools if they're closed. I got a shitload o' stupid questions!

In compliance with Operation Yellowjacket and in order to facilitate more effective communications, this station has been ordered to temporarily suspend all broadcasting operations. For further information tune to your Conelrad stations, 640 or 1240 on your A.M. frequency. This is not a test. We will resume broadcasting as soon as conditions permit.

Horseshit!

St. Paul's A Cappella Boy's Choir will now sing *America the Beautiful.*

That's it! There goes the first amen...we're...

Purple mountain majes—

So fast...it came so...there was nothing I could...I didn't...the handle...something must have...everything was fun and games then...

Amber waves of—

Damn you! Damn your flags! Your parades! Your—

God shed His grace—

Your MACHO CRAP! Here's your goddamn Sunday school patriotism! Truckin' people away! Fighting in the streets! You stupid, pompous, arrogant sons o' bitches! Look at what you've done!

Across the fruitful—

LOOK AT WHAT YOU'VE DONE! LOOK AT...Look at...

America, America—

What you...what you...what you...made me do. You bastards! You filthy Bastards!

From sea to—

Look at what you...

shining—

What you made me...

shining—
What you...
shining—
What...I...
shining—
Look at what I've done.

CHAPTER 43

THE WISDOM OF A CHIPMUNK

"We go now." Kwokwoiyea!

I woke in a sea of gray mist. Lush green leaves squirted out of the mist like tongues dripping clear water back to earth, seemingly unattached to anything in the murky background. The air damp, musty; visibility maybe twelve yards. Wet tree trunks glistened, lianas dropped out of gloom like ropes, a chill hung on the air; but a pot of soup bubbled merrily over a smoking fire. I sat up rubbing my eyes. I'd been up most of the night. When I fell off, I must have slept straight through. After a pee in the mud I toweled off my hands and face with a wide leaf. The clink of a pot led me back the fire. Without thinking I drew up my blanket and sat close while Moses added some fuel. John offered a steaming cup from the palms of his hands, like a priest.

Alphabet soup. Akwoi studied his letters. If you got a word and swallowed it, it would come true. Moses searched intently. We knew he wanted a bicycle so I suggested "bike"—whoever monitored these things would know. John as always had a disadvantage, all the things he wanted were big words— education, scholarship. Akwoi of course had no trouble. "Tits." (I don't know where he was getting it; he wasn't getting it from me.) Kwokwoiyea too, he silently arranged his word with a leaf stem but kept it to himself. What could it be? First in the hunt, a chiefdom? I didn't have much. "Nut." "Guts." Finally I got s-u-n, but that was cheating; *son* needed an o. Then I found one, but decided to keep *sun*. Yes, sweet sunshine. What could be finer after a long night? Once you swallowed, you couldn't change. How seriously they took these things.

"I' we no reash toni'," Kwokwoiyea suggested, "we slee' two ti' i' de bwush oh." He had the quietest way of winning arguments, our leader; never a sharp word, only a reminder what we already knew. I knew one damn thing. I wasn't sleeping in the bush again.

A few steps down the trail and my old friends were back, the stiffness in my legs and the rash on my shoulder. I looked back. Save for a single strand of smoke rising off the dead fire, the place looked more like an animal lair, smashed leaves and the imprints of our bodies in the earth.

A little later Moses confided to us his dream of unexpectedly coming on an entire village of white people out in the bush, fine people in fine clothes going about their business, automobiles, bicycles, radios, twist dancing. He'd always wanted a bicycle. Now he was certain to get one. If you dreamt something in the bush, it was supposed to come true. He leaped in triumph.

I dreamed too. But something awful. I'd never been so scared in my life. Pure fear. Bestial silence. It gripped you by the arms and shook you but you couldn't scream. You could feel its wet tongue on your neck. To give it a human face in the form of a mask had been the most ingenious invention of all.

Now I remember. A tiny bell, it wakened me within my dream like a telephone in the inner ear. I reached for the receiver but it fell before I touched it, then a sigh, and a woman's lips pressed to my ear, "Come ride the merry-go-round...with me." Then a click and the buzzing of insects. I'd had a line out but lost it. Could this be the beginning of religion? A workable fiction to get through the night? A bedtime story? Could it be that simple?

"There it goes." They stopped in their tracks. "That bird. Hear it?" We all looked. "It sounds like: 'Sing song SWEET.' I kept hearing it all night."

"I can hear it," John said, his eyes searching.

"Teacha, yes," Kwokwoiyea smiled.

"It has green feathers," John added as he mimicked its whistle. "And no larger than a baby's hand. The people say it is a spirit looking for its shadow; that's because they cannot see it. I have seen it many times. It's song is bigger than its mouth."

"Give me PEACE." And we smiled.

After a couple hours we rose to the base of a sandy ridge—a subtle shift in the tint of the leaves, a higher pitch to echoes told us we were rising. Soon we found ourselves walking through heavy, untouched forest; each hardwood a colossus testifying the region was little used by men save the solitary hunters who hardly stirred the mists. Not so many ferns, more creepers. A high canopy screened out whatever breezes may have visited the upper world leaving perfect motionlessness down on the ground, the effect was that of passing through a great indoor corridor, a past age preserved in ruin, unmolested as though locked in a vault. Even the thinnest wisps of moss recorded no drift of time. A deceptive calm became a working silence, an exquisite equilibrium held sway between the monstrous force thrusting tons of lumber into the sky and the soft silence resonating in the sunlight. The air radiated warmth on everything it touched. The very hang of the leaves suggested eternal fertility; their plump hearts burst from invisible stems like opulent fruit in a childhood dream. The weakest hint of red spawned a feeling for life as though the forest bled, and we, mere parasites picking our way through. Now it slept. Not an echo of last night's terrible voices. Vines like great cables fell to earth in sweeping arcs, laced with moss, now and then caught in a mesh before leaping skyward like festoons to suggest a bacchanalia somewhere in the sky. When a half-fallen tree got caught, they pulled taut. Dead logs lay half deformed but with a profusion of new tentacles growing out their sides, tenderness reaching upward like clean flames from the side of a black corpse. From time to time, a dot of brilliant color: yellow, orange, orchid, deep crimson.

I looked up. The mists had lifted. The sun hovered overhead playing hide and seek in the leaves, first in stealth sliding over the backs of heavy limbs, then bounding to the next refuge where it followed our sluggish movement along the faint trail through the fetid perma-rot until we came to one of the rare cracks in the ceiling; there it broke through the embroidery in a sudden shower of thin revolving spindles that fell to earth, revolved in the spotted branches, then reappeared, a delighted dance on the faces of wide boughs or in undulating rhythms on black leaves at the bottom of a clear pool. When it touched a green tendril, the tone of the receptacle at once changed to a soft vigor in contrast to the solemn immobility of the heavy forms simmering in the background. But the interlude ended and she quickly changed complexion in the mirror of her longing; no more the impetuous sprite teasing a timid age-mate, but a young mother glowing over her child. One splash of sunshine and the world smiles.

Save for Moses telling us his dream, we went on without much talk, only the squish of our footsteps. Occasionally someone kicked a pebble up the path where it diced against another, the sound resonating off the wide tree trunks as though inside a drum; this and the drone of insects beneath a continual undercurrent of birdsong. Then a clamor of monkeys like a heated argument up in the balcony. To experienced hunters it was all language. Within hundreds of species, they could detect the absence of one, much as a conductor misses a single note in a symphony. The sudden loss carried a ciphered message, the proximity of a certain predator which in turn meant the possibility of another if a second set of conditions correlated. All interwove like voices in a grand opus. Knowing the parts inspired an intimate feeling for the entire system—trees, wind, clouds—all moved in unison like a school of fish responding to an invisible bond. Feeling these rhythms separated the real hunters from those who told tales.

After the first day and without much thought, we'd fallen into a regular order—Kwokwoiyea first, then Moses, Mulba, Akwoi, and me. Akwoi said he didn't mind being last as long as I came after him. I was getting used to the way he walked, a quick light step that stretched into a longer stride when the trail permitted. He swatted at flies with a wand of braided leaves, hummed to himself or upbraided the meanness of the trail when it bit his foot. Sweat trickled down my face. Depending on the depth of shade, daytime temperatures shot into the mid-nineties without much ado. It wasn't so bad if a breeze moved. Moses taught me how to use the slightest breath of air. Listen for a light exhale in the leaves, turn in that direction at once, catch it directly in the face for a quick refresher, an old hunter's trick. He'd learned it from a man who claimed to have been taught by animals.

All at once he threw back his head and let go a wild yell. "Woi!" No meaning, no reason. Then Akwoi in response. "Oodwoiyoooooh!" He drew it out into song. Animal cries! They marked the boundary between empty gulfs of silence, made us feel each other. I knew they'd laugh but what to hell. "Haaaaaaaaayah!" I surprised myself. Eddies went rippling through the birdsong. Akwoi staggered in disbelief. John Mulba answered in kind. It took a few minutes for the forest to absorb a foreign language, but its murmurings soon came back, without comment.

Slowly, we rose out of the deep forest onto higher terrain where drainage and a change in the soil brought still a lighter shade of green, more variety, stranglers and oil palms, denser entanglement, but fewer giant hardwoods, less dampness, no more veils of hanging moss, and a noticeable absence of swamp grass. For the first time we felt a weak current of air. Flakes of blue sky sparkled in the leaves. Before long we came to an abandoned clearing where the remains of a shelter, maybe Moonface's hermitage, had long ago collapsed under the weight of young saplings shooting out the rotten thatch. Nearby, a dead trunk shot straight up with only a single sideward limb; ivy engulfed the entire skeleton bubbling out the top like a fountain.

A heron! It sailed across the dark backdrop in majestic solemnity, rose as it neared its perch, alighted, two flaps, then stretched its wings for a curtain call before assuming camouflage in the purple shadows. Moses took a shot but didn't have the distance; the arc of his pebble and the flight of the bird went their separate ways.

By mid-afternoon we came to the outlying farms of Kpodokpodo. A footpath showing signs of upkeep jumped a ravine. Soon it led past two well-maintained coffee groves and later on, cultivated cacao, both cash crops indicating the stories of Kpodokpodo's wealth had foundation. Then we saw the first inhabitants, women in a shelter, children outside spreading palm nuts over drying mats. They paused in their work to look us over. They called out the customary greeting, "What news?" Moses returned the standard response, "No news. Friends passing."

We were getting near. The trail began to cut back on the return of a wide semicircle that kept us off their sacred mountain, a low Appalachian affair without peaks, completely overgrown. Rumor had it no one was allowed to go near. It wasn't clear why. The village lay on its northeastern base overlooking a second, oblong cousin somewhat lower in elevation, situated beyond a wide basin of untouched forest further to the east. This afforded a magnificent view, rare in the interior, and probably the source of Kpodokpodo's reputation.

The last half mile! The trail turned into a sandy dirt track wide enough to walk abreast. In the leaves to one side, the head of a cow stopped browsing long enough to watch us pass. Soon we caught the first glimpse of Kpodokpodo's thatched rooftops adrift in a green sea and within minutes stepped out into the direct sunlight, the forest ending abruptly at the medicine posts. A few more steps and we were in the middle of town. We looked at each other. Hardly a spectacular entrance—but we made it! One of the sleeping dogs managed to lift an ear. That was it.

The remembered maps of the old men turned out to be accurate, remarkably accurate come to think of it—six days of sweat—and the bridge, exactly where they said it would be. And the stories were true. Kpodokpodo was beautiful, clean, open, a magnificent view, splendid houses, white as milk in the brilliant sunshine, shaded porches, paca nuts drying in the sun, chickens scratching in the dirt, banana and papaya groves on the outskirts. Old style circular dwellings clustered around the newer, rectangular shapes taking over in the center, but even these despite zinc roofing and screened windows displayed traditional tribal designs carved into wooden frames around the doorways or painted black over the whitewash. What had to be the chief's house caught my eye at once; besides the traditional light blue shutters, it sported a factory made door complete with polished brass doorknob, a slit bamboo sun blind guarding the eastern opening of a grand veranda furnished with two painted chairs, a coffee table, of course a hammock, and two carved pillars with figurines supporting the world.

We just stood there looking at each other, tired, sweaty. The children were the first to notice, eyeing us cautiously from the distance like timid wildlife. Then two boys came forward, about twelve, dressed in worn khaki shorts belted with strings of vine; they showed no fear as they shook hands with each of us in turn. Even the young exchanged their first greetings in grave formality, but once dispensed with, a barrage of excited questions followed. Where from? What clan? Anything to trade? Slingshot rubber? Peanut butter? Soon the throng of curious boys surrounded us excitedly, hand shakes all around, bright smiles, and old home week before we knew it. Even the very young who kept their distance at first, finally lost their fear and joined the fun. The ease of conversation indicated no problem with dialect.

The worst of the midday heat forced people into shade where they caught up on small jobs, like repairing the hand bellows in the blacksmith kitchen. Two worked and two sat on the ledge with their backs to the village, absorbed in conversation. As soon as they saw us, a stalwart, middle-aged man in a leather apron emerged from inside and came forward calmly. Poised, dignified in bearing, he greeted us cordially, sent a boy for water, and invited us to rest ourselves in the palaver kitchen until the chief returned from his farm.

In most towns a palaver kitchen meant a much abused meeting place hanging together out of necessity, but here! A show place! New, the size of two houses, open to all sides with fat posts planted in thick clay, a squared ledge, crisp palm thatch neatly trimmed at the eaves, low enough to keep out the sun but not the view. A cement step graced the entry, the floor swept clean despite roving goats. We threw down our gear. I thought I caught a whisper about juju on the mountain. The boy who first saw us motioned me to an elaborate hammock slung invitingly in the corner only inches off the ground. I took off my boots and swung in. Tan and maroon raffia woven in an intricate design, bead-like ornaments dangling from the edges, it fairly caressed the small of your back. Akwoi was already sprawled out in another at the opposite corner, Kwokwoiyea on the floor with his back to a post, Moses who could sleep anywhere, flat on his back staring at the ceiling in dumb exhaustion. John Mulba wandered off somewhere, probably to inquire about the local taboos. Soon the novelty of our presence wore off and the kids returned to their play. I was really tired. Didn't sleep well last night.

Beyond the underside of the roofline, the village sloped away towards the basin. A light push of the foot put everything in motion to the soft creaking in the support ropes, the pendulous rising and falling of the pointed rooftops, their gradual coming to rest, and the southerly mountain in the distance like the hump of a grazing bull. Behind the immediate detail of houses and fences, the forest faded into succeeding shades of grayer green each marking its distance from the other by the loss of color until a purplish overcast melted into an indistinct horizon. From up above pure sunlight fell into the village. It dazzled in the heat shimmer above the zinc roofs, trickled down the skin of sweaty inhabitants, bleached the whitewashed walls that looked even brighter from the shade, enough to hurt if you didn't squint. It baked the ground into hard pavement. But is was a healing heat—peaceful, serene, cleansing the village of noise, settling over things like a soft blanket. No shadows. Every object—tools, rocks, a loom, people hurrying from one pool of shade to another—everything in the deep bath of sunlight stood out in relief, sharp in detail as if under strong scrutiny. By turning my neck, I could see the better part of the uphill side of town, randomly spaced houses, some with fenced-in yards, but no more than thirty in all. A flagpole planted in a small pyramid of rocks bore a bleached white cloth in mute stillness. The entrance we'd crossed was no more than an opening in the underbrush darkened by shadows from a giant cottonwood towering behind a cluster of small round buildings and nearly as big around. Fruit trees too—lemon, grapefruit, a small cacao grove, the ground beneath cleared off to facilitate the harvest. A carpenter had taken advantage of the same shade and pitched his sawhorses under lengths of board that served as a table; he rocked back and forth over his work, a steady, relaxed rhythm, no more than the heat allowed. On a nearby porch, an obese woman lay on her side with her heavy breasts spilling onto the raffia mat, her knees drawn up, feet together, probably a headwife, snoring in sumptuous contentment while two girls knelt behind quietly chatting to themselves as they braided her hair. But their words ran together joining the drone of far off voices under the trees. The thick heat muffled every sound into a singular monotone as though the town were mumbling to the sky about the unrelenting heat. If there were clocks in Kpodokpodo, they too would have fallen in step with the sweep of the carpenter's arm, and he to the circles of a sailing hawk.

Soon the calm of the brilliant afternoon worked its spell; the village became a daydream. The blacksmith's hammer became a school bell, the creak of a hammock the winding of a new toy, the flow of time like turning the pages of a family album, watching old snapshots come to life, the way they looked at you, the way they smiled, so real you think you can speak to them. Don't cry Jenny. Old memories, clear as a bell, spoken long ago, intact but without a frame of reference. Did you ride the merry-go-round? Did you tell the lady thank you?

Dismembered sounds began revolving a little faster—shouts, the thumping of rice mortars, a gust of air in the leaves, the bark of a dog—then a quick jerk of my head and the entire village came to life bustling in the late afternoon shadows in preparation for the evening meal. The sun had fallen behind the giant cottonwood, a magnificent umbrella shading half the village this time of day. I sat up—alone in the palaver kitchen a bit embarrassed at having dozed off in the chief's hammock. No one seemed to notice. People went about their business with hardly a glance; I felt a bit ridiculous as I walked through town looking for my companions. People strained under their headloads, a small boy in a game of tag veered off shyly. Three men ignored me as they bickered over the price of two grouse lying in the dust. Surveying the open eyes and limp necks, a hunter stood to the side with his arm over the barrel of a shot gun like a shoulder yoke. In silent assent he took payment from a stout bronze-skinned man and walked away. On passing behind a woman pounding rice, his free hand gave her a soft caress. She turned and taunted him for not bringing her something but he only laughed.

Akwoi and Mulba met me coming the other way.

"Why didn't you wake me?"

"He said to leave you."

"I'm embarrassed, we don't even know these people."

Akwoi cleared his throat, terribly delighted, brimming with important news.

"The chief would like you to join him for tea," he said gravely, then in his usual up-tempo, "Did I say it right?"

"He told us to bring you to his porch when you are awake," John said, a little uncertain of himself. Then it dawned on me. After six days in the bush, three without a bath, the avowed purpose of finding an untouched village, barging in unannounced, falling asleep in the chief's hammock…we were being invited…to tea.

"Did I say it right?" Akwoi pestered. "Is that how an English butler can say it?"

"I guess so. I never met an English butler," I said tiredly. "Where are the others?"

"Heah me," Moses said right behind me.

"What have you been up to?"

"We have been looking for a girl friend for you," Akwoi answered with a leery smile.

"De ma' lie oh."

"He's been looking for a girl for himself," Mulba scoffed, "but people are laughing at him."

"No! Nevah! You think I am greedy? I take care of my friend first, I don't care for my own!"

"Then where's the girl?" I said. Moses snickered.

"You do not worry! I will find you! I know where to look!"

"You couldn't find meat on market day."

"Wha' you do da one loffing on me?" he retorted falling into country English. "We wi' fi' yah!" And he put up his fists in a comic boxing stance, dancing backward, showing off to everyone's delight.

When he saw us, the old man sprang to his feet and hurried across the porch with real delight. His fatherly smile at once eased my embarrassment. He stood before me pumping my hand looking me straight in the eye with a low humming grunt until it ended in three clicks. Three! He didn't even know me. He eagerly repeated the whole thing with each of my friends—the whole show for my benefit, they'd already met—inquiring after their fathers although he knew no one from our village. After hearing that we bore no urgent news, he said matter-of-factly he'd been expecting us. We shot glances at each other. He resumed his seat. Instantly he was up again directing curious children to bring chairs. In his sixties at least, slim but muscular, distinguished by very thin white hair, high-tempoed and unusually active for his age, he reminded me of a chipmunk. His name was Kobwoi.

When the chairs arrived I gave the first one to John but the old man clicked his fingers, "No." He meant me to have it. Still he eyed me intensely. What was he so pleased about? Practically squatting in his low hammock, knees at chest level, he kept in constant motion, first kicking the rump of an intruding goat, flicking flies with a hand broom, now sending a child for his fly swatter, rapidly firing directions as she ran, gesturing as he spoke, then up to see what was taking so long, clapping his hands to set the pace, then down again, maintaining a child-like delight in everything he did. He reveled in conversation. Unfortunately it was as hot paced as the rest of his activity and I couldn't follow. Now he jumped up to brush a horse fly off my shoulder. He resumed his seat again catching the corner of a brown store-bought robe before squatting with an assertive grunt. We must see his coffee farm, he said, feeling the ground for his rubber sandals. The farm we saw wasn't his but his son's. His was even larger. With great pleasure he told us he had twenty eight sons and so-so daughters, and many of these had fine sons of their own. Now he had his yellow plastic fly swatter which in his infrequent moments of quiet, rested across his lap like an official baton. If the fly happened to alight on a child—too bad. He ordered them still. They grimaced but knew better than to move. Splat! At once his conversation resumed as he wiped the sore spot with his own sleeve and if the child were very young, added a soft squeeze. Too many flies this time of year, then to me gravely, 'They carry disease.' Why the old devil. Was it his way of teaching them to keep flies off themselves? When his conversation began to lose steam, he revived it with questions. How long would we stay? Only until tomorrow. He seemed genuinely grieved. Did we have need of anything? Only rest. He assented with a low humming grunt, his favorite expression, then casually observed, 'You come the long way.' His head jerked with another short grunt, he issued an order over his shoulder, turned and made to speak but shot up abruptly to shoo away some chickens, called to someone inside, then once again resumed his seat much pleased with himself.

Well, how did I like sleeping in the bush? He was going to have a little fun with me. I looked at Mulba whose glance said, "no diplomacy." Right. I wasn't going to lie. I said I was frightened. I kept hearing things all night, probably birds but they sounded human. (Laughter.) Mulba's eyes told me to be careful. 'Well, tonight you sleep here,' he countered, 'that's why we have houses.' (Loud laughter.) We'd attracted a crowd by now. When it died down, he asked abruptly why I'd come to his village. I groped, but finally told him to see the sunrise. He cut off further explanation with a gesture of approval and at once flew into a long fiery speech directing it at John Mulba sensing I couldn't follow. The idea of slowing down didn't occur to him.

What luck! We'd walked in on a festive event. The day after tomorrow the girls would be coming to town from the bush school to visit their parents. In the old days it wasn't permitted but now they did it twice a session. There would be dancing, enjoyment, plenty to eat. Perhaps Nyamu would come. We must stay to see. The word "must" was an invitation. We were his personal guests. Before I figured out what transpired, John was thanking him for me. This wasn't an occasion to miss! One look at the faces of my friends and I knew it was something special; they couldn't hide their delight. I repeated our thanks. What luck! What an incredible piece of luck! We were not to take pictures however. Kobwoi clicked an imaginary camera. So it was true. No cameras. "I have no"—I turned to John for help…"camera" didn't translate easily, finally in desperation—"Cam-rah-bwoi," meaning "Camera friend," which should have worked. (I was to learn later there was no such construction, but it was close enough to "Keh-nah-bwi," initiated, hence newly circumcised, friends. God what a language.) The place went crazy. John and Moses stared at the dirt in utter embarrassment. Akwoi, too. They were all at that delicate age…and there were ladies present. Fortunately Kobwoi caught what I meant and gleefully clicked his fingers.

When it quieted down, I noticed we'd gathered quite a crowd, maybe twenty people, most of them laughing brightly. They were returning from their farms for the evening meal. Kobwoi scattered the small boys who were inching too close, two hanging on his hammock and one under my chair. Why weren't pictures allowed? He answered in a barrage. "Pictures are not allowed," John relayed, "because if your people see what a fine, beautiful town is here, they would all want to come. Then too many people." The sudden change of mentality caught me off guard. Of course. There had to be something behind that child-like demeanor.

His senior wife nudged through the crowd carrying a steaming pot—her indifference identified her. As soon as he saw, Kobwoi shot up from his seat to take it from her but she warned him off. A very young helper, perhaps a granddaughter, handed him a tin box and a roll of white cloth that he took to his hammock and unwound, carefully removing a delicate pair of round, wire rimmed spectacles. After unfolding the frames he drew them to his temples with both hands allowing the lenses to settle over the end of his nose. Why he needed glasses to serve tea was to remain a mystery. Another girl brought six cups, four porcelain and two dainty Victorian specimens with a picture of the Prince of Wales. Saucers too. He took one of the cups by the handle, dipped it in the pot and set it on the ground. This little ritual obviously gave him great pleasure. When all five were filled, he pried the lid off the tin box with the tip of his hunting knife—an instrument that would have drawn considerable attention at more refined afternoon tea parties—took out two tea bags and began dunking them vigorously, lifting them high in the air without losing a drop. The children watched in awe. Now we must wait. It was necessary that the tea "sleep" in the water a short time. He had learned this a long time ago, he explained, from an Englishman. Every afternoon about this time this man took tea—no matter what. Even when he went hunting! Can you imagine? And he would share it with his porters. "Heah you a' Jack!" (This sentence he recited in English.) He called everyone "Jack." Perhaps they didn't have other names where he came from. Just then a child hardly old enough to walk, spied the colorful cups, crawled forward to see, but Kobwoi's fly swatter switched his bare butt and sent him scurrying under the hammock.

When the tea was ready, he raised the first cup to his lips and drew in noisily, observing the Loma custom of a host serving himself first to make certain everything was right. He put the cup down. Did I take sugar? Someone handed him a strip of raw cane; he held it over the cups squeezing it between his knife and thumb. Then he handed the cups around one at a time, me, Kwokwoiyea, Moses, Mulba, and Akwoi—our marching order in the bush. This was not without meaning. How did he know? He'd hardly noticed Kwokwoiyea, yet he knew he was our leader. They had a rapport I'd never enter. I could imagine Akwoi's tirade had I served him last. Despite the afternoon temperature, the hot tea went down real easy, altogether a pleasure though not as much as our host. Before we finished a small girl in braids, slippers, and a simple wrap around skirt tied at the side came in with a dish of unsweetened wafers which she held out to each of us, a little shy but unafraid. She must have been his favorite judging from the affection he showed her. Her task done, she stood at his knee fidgeting with the hammock while his old hand encircled her arm.

"The first time I made a long bush trip," Kobwoi began, "I was about Akwoi's age. Do you have ears?" (That meant a story was coming.) Everyone went silent, a few hummed approval, John drew near to translate. Kobwoi leaned forward, holding the girl to his side much pleased with the opportunity. "There was this old Englishman, you see, not the one that called us Jack, another one; he didn't hunt or trade, couldn't even smile, can you imagine? I remember him well. He was the first white man I ever saw up close. He, this English, had spectacles; he used them to look in a book and to write. We thought it some kind of magic, he said 'yes' and took me by the hand and held the glass to the sun, it made a spot on my skin, at first nothing, then 'Yeii!' We thought lightning lived in those glasses—but more of that later—and when I carried them to him I carried them like a deadly poison.

"In those times there were no motor roads and very few foreigners, usually Mandingo traders from the north. Well, this man was going here and there in the bush looking for a place to make a Mission, but he wasn't a man of God, himself, only a scout. He did bear the image of your dead ancestor carved on a tiny cross; he wore it around his neck on a gold chain. Our images upset him, but he bore one of his own. But no mind. Well, Dogbwazi was chief at that time, did you know? He is dead now, but remains near. When Dogbwazi learned what the white man was up to, he immediately offered his assistance in the persons of porters and guides, of which I was one—and I felt honored because I was so young, newly come from bush school. Of course, the real reason we went was to keep the man away from our sacred groves and we were given secret instructions, accordingly. This wasn't very difficult because white men like him are very clever here in town but have no sense in the bush. Most of the time they take the long way without even trying—unlike yourself. (Here Kobwoi slapped his hands together in sheer delight.) So we went all over the bush with the man, first here, there, back again. Finally, he hammered four sharp sticks in the ground, tiny ribbons tied around. Some kind of medicine, we thought.

"When he finished, he took us all the way to Freetown, my age-mates and myself. I was young as I said, untutored in the way of the world. Well! Every afternoon—tea; every morning—shave. Never miss. But he did not share his tea with us like the hunter, the one who called us 'Jack.' And when he shaved, one of us had to sit right up in front of him, like this, to hold the mirror. Eh yah! He was ugly. He had a big red nose and brown teeth and whiskers, like a porcupine. As I would be holding the mirror, my friends would be singing, in Loma, of course, "See the monkey in the water." We had no mirrors of our own, but we knew our reflections from clean water, of course. It was all I could do to keep from laughing; sometimes my hands would shake it was so funny. Then he would look up, very serious, and my friends would begin singing again, 'See the monkey in the water, see another holding the water.' And he would be turning his face around and making faces, like this. Now! Are you listening? My friends and I believed that if lightning flashed in the mirror and you saw, a terrible disease would come. Of course, it is not true, but we were untraveled in those days. None of us had ever seen such a mirror with glass and shiny metal all around. Well, one morning, hear this, it began to rain…and lightning. My friend, Frofulu, was holding the mirror that day, but the others of us, we were not singing, be certain. We were anxiously watching the clouds. Sure enough. Bdoooo-Pah! A lightning flash. The man twitched and cut himself. Frofulu naturally thought he had seen the dreaded reflection and there was blood on his face. He dropped the mirror and fled in terror. We others followed. The man stood up in surprise, shouting after us, the shaving soap on his face. At first, he used angry words. We remained in the bush. Then he used gentle words. When he called my name, I went back, then the others. Frofulu came last; he'd had a terrible fright; so had the

Englishman; he must have thought we were abandoning him. Of course, we were not; we had our instructions. He must have thought us terribly superstitious. Actually, we were not afraid of lightning, or thunder, or the mirror, or him—only the thought of seeing lightning *in the mirror* because that was something we had never seen.

"Well, he took us to Freetown, part way by lorry. It bounced terribly. I thought we would fall out for sure, but we didn't. The first thing I remember was the sea. I had never seen it in my life. What a magnificent being. Sparkling blue. And so very great. I cannot begin to tell of it, or of my feelings, my heart was drumming in excitement. I thought it was a great river, greater than I'd ever seen. But where was the other side? And the waves! Talking. Poosh. Poosh. They chased us up the beach, then back in their house again.

"The old man didn't seem to notice the sea, but he was very happy to be in Freetown. He bought us many fine things, bread, sweets, shoes. Shoes! We had never worn shoes before. We carried our feet high in the air like walking through tall grass. And he took us to a strange smelling place with bells in the rooftop. I never heard such fine bells. They sang in your ear after they stopped ringing. Then they poured water on our heads to make us worthy. One of my mates thought the water was for drinking and they were not pleased when he tried. I did not understand at the time it meant we were giving up our Loma beliefs, otherwise I would not have allowed and neither would my mates.

"Well, he paid us in tiny coins. At first we thought he cheated us because the money was so small, but when we came to the market place we soon found it bought more than all our wire money together. I bought many fine things; fine cloth, a sterling knife—I still have it—a Panama hat. And the food, fish in cans, smoked bacon, jellies, horseradish, candies, tins of pudding, gin— but I was unable to drink the entire bottle—no matter, it all came up; English food is the sweetest on earth if only it would stay in the stomach.

"Two of my mates soon parted and we never saw them again, two others stayed in Freetown to work for round money and three of us started for home. One died on the way. Of seven two came home, myself and Gbegi. He lives to Gbunde. If you pass that way you must carry to him my warmest greetings, we hunted together some time ago."

As soon as he finished, Kobwoi jumped up and hurried into the house to see about dinner. "We are going to eat chicken," Akwoi whispered. The minute he returned, he was at it again. He said he could always tell an American from an Englishman. When he saw my interest, he beamed with pleasure. "Well then." He paused for attention. "Hear this. If you put food before white people and they cannot eat it, the Englishman will say, 'I am not hungry,' even if he is. Later on when no one is looking he will be chewing candies. But the American, he will take the food and taste it even if it does not agree with him and, later, when he thinks no one is looking he will throw it away. I have seen this! Throwing away food! Do you believe?

"Not long ago," he said changing his tone to one of serious intent—how quickly he went from the jovial storyteller to the diplomat—"the rainy season last, two American men, and one other who was white, but neither American nor English, came here wanting to dig on our mountain, only little bottles they said. Of course, we could not allow." Again, he sent a little girl in the house for something. "We gave them samples of earth, from our mountain, just to get rid of them." The child returned with a laboratory test tube. "Do you know what this is?" he asked. "They were pouring a sickly water into it and shaking it and watching it. Then last dry season they returned. What do you think they want?"

"Iron," I said.

"In little bottles?"

"The bottles are only samples. They will test the sample to see how rich— how strong the ore is."

"And if it is strong?"

"…They will be back."

"Pah!" He emitted another low grunt, not in pleasure this time, eyeing me intently, then hit the heels of his hands together in an *I told you so* gesture that, for the first and only time, betrayed anxiety. They'd assured him they wouldn't be back.

The mountain, their sacred mountain, was one of the richest deposits in the country. And it was no longer a secret, bush pilots had been reporting their compasses going haywire for some years now and the mining companies were already jockeying for position. It was only a matter of time. These latest tests were a postscript. He'd find out soon enough.

By now it was clear Kobwoi was going to go on half the night. He had yet to get to his hunting stories. One episode led to the next, all through dinner which turned out a real delight. After his reference to American manners, I was a little uneasy but without cause. They served it in assembly line fashion, first a girl with a pan of water and soap, then a boy with a towel, a second girl with bowls, then spoons, drinking water, followed by young women with the main course. Each came before us in turn, bearing herself in the fashion befitting a Loma woman, poised, aloof, seemingly unconcerned while we served ourselves, not a hint of anxiety there might not be enough left at the end of the line. Chicken in palm oil and cassava greens, seasoned with peppers and okra, served over steaming rice. Papaya and pineapple for dessert.

It was late when they showed us to our sleeping places. Stars sparkled in a clear sky. A refreshing nighttime air soothed the discomfort of the afternoon heat. A bed! And a straw mattress! What luxury after last night. And the sunrise tomorrow promised to be clear. We would be paid, after all, for our pains.

CHAPTER 44

MR. SUN AND LADY MOON

Next morning we rose early. Only a hint of purple in the east, ebony sky, stars etched in a grainy mirror. No moon. At the edge of town Kwokwoiyea and Mulba ambled up without a sound.

"Shh. The sunrise. Remember?"

They looked tired but followed in silence.

"It'll be better from the pasture."

Before long three others slipped out of the shadows: Moses, Akwoi, and a third boy from the village. The morning felt chill. Akwoi folded his arms to keep warm.

"Where's your shirt?

"He giff to de womah," Moses snickered.

"You lie!" Then to me, "Is cold. You stupi'."

No more than an oval clearing on the low side of town, the pasture retained a slight luminance in the surrounding cavern. I hadn't guessed what it was until I overheard some kids arguing whether an airplane could land there. Not quite. But it offered a fairly uncluttered view to the east, a clearing of any kind being rare in the jungle—this no more than a football field, its grass grazed low. A lake of dew settled in, a few steps along the trail and my pants were soaked to the knees. We stopped next to an old stump; Moses propped himself on the down side, feet together, back square, calmly chewing a strip of sugar cane, Kwokwoiyea crouched, Akwoi jumped up and down to keep warm. After a bit John and I decided to look for a better place. When the village boy understood, he motioned us to a break in the trees higher up.

It began in silence. Tomb-like, palpable, an immense gloom dropped a thick cloak over every thought, devoured every breath. Now and then the flitting bird or the creak of a limb stirred the air but only to feed dreamy phantoms yawning in a slumbering brain. And Night herself? Not a ripple in her silk.

Then the heavy world listed in the darkness. Something seemed to moan, an old memory murmured something faint. A tremor shook a half-opened eye, a breath expired, a mirror opened. A slight displacement shifted the solid black below the horizon, the mountain began to separate from the sky, the grazing bull took shape. At once the earth responded, the air came to life, the first faint glow smiled in the east. Morning came like a wet calf rising to its feet, feeling for its mother. The forest began to materialize out of cool vapors softly slipping through layers of impenetrable leaves, pockets of fog formed over low depressions in the hills, white serpents rose from the swamps. But not a sigh of breeze. The world paused to think. Broad leaves hung mute under the ponderous weight of pure water soon to bathe the bright earth with glistening fingers.

Now color! A pink tint in the breech. Violet embers on the undersides of cirrus clouds. Rose breast-feathers. Vermilion scarves rolled into glowing streamers. Now crimson! Orange! Bright ribbons splashing the face of heaven! Powerful eruptions shooting bold wheel spokes into retreating violet! Deep purple melting black. Stars winking out. Furious activity below the horizon, a sweating smithy in last minute preparation for the sacred event.

And the forest. Bowed, silent, but struck to the sap, each tree afire with life, each leaf opening, lifting its face to feel the first finger of light.

And music! A heart begins to beat, countless eyes reopen, a million throats find voice. On the tongue of dawn a song is formed. Torrents of birdsong! A clamoring ovation! Growing! Pounding! A deafening sea storm raging upward! Each branch bursting with song! Waves of wild delight! All the passions of all our lifetimes brazenly unleashed! Naked revelry! A mad Bacchanalia gone berserk! Sky and earth married to the god of joy! All the gods in gallant chorus! Crimson heavens. Innocence and omniscience in bright embrace, a pagan conception in rapturous flight! Behold! The fire birth from the belly of the Night! Rejoice! Shout! One last Te Deum to the black silence! To the drunken dancer reeling to the riot of birdsong gushing out the trees. A world rejoices. Hear. Music. Joy. Throbbing rhythm, wild warbling cries, deep gutturals, shrill whistles, enough to pierce the hardest soul, triumphant, overpowering, pulsating with life. Brilliant birds atop the world, alight the thinnest branches, defying gravity, swaying over the edge of the abyss, their ugly heads slit half-open in song. Psalms from carrion throats. Beauty from bestial terror. Now monkey clatter, dogs, braying goats, domestic roosters, a human voice too—somewhere back in the village.

It peaked just as the first fire began to quiver in the trees. A brilliant crescent on the bull's back. An ocean of orange flame lifted its face from prayer, turning to meet the warm glow of a new born eye. Now the sweating smithy threw all his weight into one last effort and the swollen sphere rose into the radiant air, free at last, spewing waterfalls of sunlight back to earth. A thousand Niagaras pouring mighty rivers of birdsong into the thundering cascade. And a thousand more! Surely the birth of a god. But a natural birth, and a natural response, the simple wonder in a child's eye. In the west, deep oceans of blue spreading wide, the last morning stars retire as though in blessing. The promise of something fine.

For every nightmare, a sunrise. That awful night in the bush. Did early men go through the same terror? And the joy of being alive the next morning? Surely they knew. Even the birds know. Why hadn't we thought of telling stories back there?

"It is beautifu' t'ing to see." Kwokwoiyea! A whole sentence! Two this week!

Now I could feel its warmth on my face, the urge to stretch out, to jump and tumble and call out to my kind. At least a shout—I'd often heard grown men give a shout to the first ray of light.

"Why do the birds sing at sunrise?" I asked as it ebbed away, now resembling the laughter of a delighted audience after the last curtain call. No one answered. "You have a story about it. I know you do." Akwoi leered.

"Teacha, it is not a good story," Moses smiled.

"Then it's about sex, is it?" More embarrassment. "Let me tell you something. When you learn to talk about these things without making monkey, then you will be a proper man. You understand? Now tell me the story."

"Why?"

"Because when I'm old I want to remember this trip, the story will be my water jar."

"Teacha, I cannot," Akwoi mumbled.

"Oh, yes, you can. And do not sell me trinkets or you will pay."

"They will be laughing on me."

"That's their problem." Still embarrassed, Moses said something addressing him by his bush name but he kept staring at the ground. "Let me tell you something else my friend. Your storyteller is old; Kpoodu, he coughs blood. When he is gone who will tell stories? You! You must remember them. I will share you a secret. This has been a hard trip for me; I was afraid, afraid to sleep in the bush, afraid you would laugh at me. But now I feel better. Tell me a story. I earned it."

By now we were comfortably sprawled out on a bare rock. A breath of freshness came off the earth, the grass sparkled with dew, the low hills began emerging from the mists like a school of whales in a gray sea. Akwoi continued staring at his toes, fidgeting with a fly whip. After some time he looked away and began.

"Mr. Sun…Teacha, I cannot."

"Yes, you can. I *will* hear it, or we will wait here all day. Then what will these people think; they already think we're crazy, we come the long way."

"Mr. Sun was sleeping down. He was…in his house. Lady Moon…"

"It was what you call an eclipse," Mulba broke in. "Like the one we saw last May."

"I am telling!" Akwoi snapped. All he needed was help from his rival. "It was long time now. Before people could read in books, before they knew eclipse. Mr. Sun was sleeping down…eh yah…they cannot be sleeping—"

"We have a word for it in our language," I said. Moses leaped up and spun around, clicking his fingers to suppress laughter. Kwokwoiyea beamed inwardly. "Go on. You're doing fine."

"Mr. Sun was sleeping down with Lady Moon. Their arms were holding strong—like the men when they come to wrestle in the marketplace. Mr. Sun was burning big fire and he could not let go. Lady Moon could not speak. It was sweet so. And then she is singing, only it is not singing, it is not words, it is like Nyamu's wife when it comes into town at night. If you remember that one you will know. And then Mr. Sun told her, 'Is sweet so.' Well, it was long time that night. And when…when they finish, they are tired and go to sleep.

"When it is time to wake up for morning, Mr. Sun was sleeping down behind the trees. The sky did not wake up. Night would not go away. The people were afraid. It was time to get up and go to work but daytime did not come. People could not see to walk and soon their stomachs were angry. No one knew what to do. Small children started to cry. After while the old men went to look for God but they could not find Him. He could not see to find His sandals and He could not go to the palaver kitchen to make judgments without His sandals. Meantime people were crying and stumbling over things, all the animals ran to hide in the bush and the wind stopped talking to the trees. And it came very quiet. Even the snakes crawled back in the ground and baby monkeys ran to their mothers' backs. People asked of the cowrie shells. Nothing. Old men tried to make medicine. Nothing. And the BBC man said it was appalling conditions—"

"That is not in the story!" Mulba cried.

"I am telling yah!"

"He is adding water in the soup!"

"It is fine soup! You will eat!"

"You will spoil—"

"It cannot spoil, I will cook my own!"

How they worked themselves up over stories. If we were back at school, a half dozen different versions would be raging by now.

"Let him tell it the way he wants," I said.

"Was appalling conditions yah! Vaddy bat! So the people went to the spirit place and made sacrifice. The spirit came and told them, 'Mr. Sun is sleeping. That is all. Do not disturb him, he will wake up soon.' So the people came back. But they are still afraid. Then Mr. Dog said, 'Listen to me. We need helpers. My own, I can bark when strangers come into the village or when something makes noise in the bush. That is my job. Now we will go and ask our brothers, the Birds. Let it be their job to waken Mr. Sun in the morning. They must call him so he cannot be sleeping too late. As soon as they see his forehead they must call louder and louder until he comes out of his house. Then everything will be all bright.' So that is why the birds can sing in the morning, and sometimes when you see the red clouds growing up in the sky before the sun comes, that is Lady Moon pulling her fine expensive blanket over herself. And the next time you see her in the sky, she will be smiling with her fine white teeth."

By now the village rooftops were awash in bright sunshine. The great cottonwood standing sentinel reflected white from its gray bark. There was something uncanny about the way these giants worked the light into different moods: bleak in the morning mists, shimmery in rain, a hint of Grecian columns in the brilliance of noon. Further up the mountainside the higher branches shone in the direct sunlight like a thicket of polished ivory flung onto a green mat. The village came to life. The sounds of morning rang like bells. The clank of pots, the rattle of tools, all measured the drift of the rising day. Men slowly filed out of their houses, dreamlike on their way to their farms, the ever present machete at their hips. Women shooed away goats or swept off porches. Roosters pranced and trumpeted. An old man relieved himself by a compost heap. Children were up and chasing each other. Three teenagers came out to meet us on the way back. Some good natured banter soon followed.

"You nevah befo' see de su'?" one of the newcomers said in English.

"You nevah befo' see de whi' ma'?" Moses countered.

"You moof fro' da ma'," the first snapped. "I talk-eeng to de ma'. You no' go' de su' fo' yo' country?"

"We have the same sun as you," I said, "but it doesn't sing so loud." Moses and Akwoi grinned in anticipation.

"You t'eenk da one de su' singing?" he asked in disbelief.

"Da one de bar'," his companion said.

"You no' go' de bar' fo' yo' country?" the first asked. Akwoi was fighting to hold it in.

"Yes, we have birds."

"But he can't see the birds," John Mulba protested, "so he must hear the sun!" This put them in convulsions.

"There you are," I said.

"You boy!" Akwoi burst out a mile a minute, "I talking to you yah! De ma' know yah! He canno' see de bir' no bir' he pu' de gloss o' heez eye, he loo' see, no bir', who da one talking? Ah you zee, Mistah Su', heah he, he be singing, I finish wi' you ma' no mo' palabah." He ended in a wild flurry that sent them staggering. Then to me, "You loffing on me. You will pay."

CHAPTER 45

THE DRUMS OF KPODOKPODO

The day of the grand celebration we expected to see Kobwoi decked out in his finest robe, but to our surprise he made his appearance in a nineteen-thirties-style pin stripe suit, white shirt with a soft collar, slightly yellowed, lavender and maroon floral tie, red suspenders and point-toed Italian shoes— no socks. And topped off with a felt fedora. The jacket was beginning to show signs of the climate, lapels turning up, a button missing. Back home it could have been the costume of a vaudeville comedian; here it was the privilege of a chief, a wealthy one at that. Kobwoi wore it with style. He stepped smartly off his front porch pointing an ivory-handled walking cane in his intended direction, not unaware of the eyes that followed his every movement, the click of his fingers, the casual swing of his free hand as it slipped into his pocket and came out with sweets for the children, while his young attendant, a boy of ten, marched in front solemnly elevating the bright red umbrella. He conferred some business, directed the palaver kitchen swept, shook hands with new arrivals, checked the sun's height, looked every bit the man in charge. A last he made his way back to his porch, a brood of small fry in tow, a curious dog to the rear, at once began fidgeting with the raffia sun shade, forever the chipmunk, arranging chairs, shooing goats, questioning his senior wife, emitting low grunts as she answered. Ordering water, he retired to his hammock, drew his hunting knife from a holster in his jacket and began slicing limes. When he saw us, he eagerly motioned us in. The sun wouldn't be so hot on the porch and he promised we would see all. The cool drink hit the spot.

No significant event in a tribal village could transpire without the sanction of *the Poro;* today was no exception. Something like the archbishop blessing the opera house. It came abruptly. First the adolescent boys stopped in their tracks. Everyone strained to hear, then their faces lit into smiles. "It is

504

coming!" Soon we could hear it—drums, whistle, cowbell. "It," referred to Nyamu, the spirit of *the Poro*. As schoolchildren became more adept at English, they began calling him "it." But it had a wife. Again no gender, another "it." If confronted with this seeming contradiction, they shrugged it off; perhaps everyday language could only approximate the realities of the spiritual world.

Now we could all hear it. Young men and boys jostled for the best view but no one dared get too close. It carried a small whip and did not hesitate to strike if not given wide berth.

It came on apace. Small boys retreated screaming. Adults smiled. It swept into the nearest open space and went straight into a vigorous dance, whirling, caressing the earth, round and around in ecstatic delight, but always a subdued grace within the naked rhythms. A retinue of six cult men came in tow, two drummers, a rattle shaker, a cowbell player—he held it on the end of stick above his head and struck it from below—wood block player and a singer (interlocutor). They all sang and danced in place, each in his own orbit but bound to the gravity of the mask. The whistle must have been inside. The mask itself was prominent, oblong, black, a yard in length. Weighty and grotesque it covered the entire front hanging nearly to the ground over a wide raffia skirt that whispered to the earth as it swirled. The feet and legs were tightly wrapped in cloth, a blue embroidered shawl circled the shoulders and a three pronged iron hand emerged from one sleeve—to catch boys and take them to the bush. A hand whip, the symbol of *Poro* discipline—perhaps akin to the gavel—hung from the other. It didn't look human. The glare of its countenance conjured something not of this world. But the dance, the dance spanned the ages, married the supernatural to the mundane world.

And how it danced. Liquid motion, sensuous rhythm, leaps, whirls, flourishes into animal life then back again, but always centered on the mask, the sacred object, the revelation. Then it dropped to its knees, rested its chin on the ground looking from side to side in constant rapport with the leitmotif that emerged when the louder rhythm abated, sometimes emitting deep guttural utterances, far away cries, moans and whispers, archaic words to be translated by the interlocutor who acted as town crier.

Then it would rise and repair to another part of town to take care of business, usually things esoteric that had no meaning to the uninitiated, but sometimes clear promises, *"Where are my babies? I will see you in the bush oh."* And the young boys would retreat squealing. But soon they came back like birds to a favorite perch, the bolder ones inching closer, pushing, straining to see, hanging on to a comrade but always on the lookout for a quick retreat.

Suddenly it stopped before a closed door. One of the poorer houses on the edge of town. It seemed to know where to go. Sure enough, the door opened and two women dragged out an old cripple on a flimsy mat. She had leprosy scars on her ankles and her jaw hung open in the agony of heavy breathing. She seemed to be in a trance herself, but understood the situation, who was before her. It knelt on the ground, its raffia skirt spread out, head tilted like a pup inquiring of its master. The six attendants stopped playing, squatted or rested on one knee. The old woman asked after the well being of a deceased ancestor, presumably someone dear. Miraculously the answer came from within the mask, in the very words of that ancestor, whispered in complete intimacy through the art of a ventriloquist. The woman rocked back and forth in a complete trance, the conversation taking her back to her childhood. There was no doubt the ancestor was "there." When the session ended they took her back inside and it rose to dance again, a pensive floating affair, a reminiscence of things past. This was the only serious moment of its visit. Otherwise the mood was entirely festive.

Later on as it passed the chief's porch, it stopped abruptly in front of me. Everything went silent. It stared at me. What magnetism. I didn't dare look away.

At last it spoke, short snappy utterances as though a bother. The interlocutor conveyed its words, the whole exchange to be translated later.

"What…is that?"

"That, O Nyamu, is a white man."

An awful silence followed, as though a mummy sat up and pointed.

"What's he doing here?"

The empty eye sockets, the wild visage, the aura of immeasurable age. These people understood fear.

"He has come to teach the children book."

Another silence. They were playing with me. I tried to be cool but couldn't; they wanted me to sweat a little. The old chief, absorbed in peeling limes.

"Well, go tell him hello."

Instantly it fell back into rhythm and proceeded on its way. Kids came running up to convey the message, delighted with the whole affair. I'd caught the word *whaneii,* "hello" in Loma. Mulba beamed and Akwoi grinned rakishly as if to say, "Scared the pants off you, didn't it?" What a strange transaction. Communication with the spiritual world. Me? A naturalist through and through. In some mysterious way they'd accepted me. As though the forest itself had opened up to reveal a path I'd never seen. But why? There were so many things I didn't understand.

It disappeared as quickly as it came, the whisk of raffia over the ground, the receding chant, a clank of a cowbell. The branches on the path closed in behind it and the sun beat down in the village square as if nothing had transpired. Gone. Like a gust of wind.

After its departure there was a lull. Musicians began carrying in their instruments setting up under a temporary thatch awning with a plastic flag at each end. The scent of meat and palm oil drifted out from a cook kitchen. The smithy deserted. Kids and dogs ran in and out.

The ceremony we were about to witness was to take place in the village "square" bordered by the chief's front porch, the medicine rock across town, the musicians' orchestra, and the palaver kitchen jutting in from the side. The remaining space was roughly an oval, the center of which would be the stage, now empty save for scratching chickens and a game of tag. The participants and their audience would be feeling the full glare of the midday sun; it hammered down unimpeded by thin layers of transparent cloud.

Musicians began limbering up. A young boy beat a play rhythm on his father's drum while the latter conversed with a friend. People waited on porches, under the eaves or whatever shade they could find. A red umbrella floated above the crowd like a kite. The palaver kitchen overflowed. Children, goats, cripples. Women dressed in their finest, babies tied to their backs, moved about with ease; others sat on ledges, stools, young people leaned on each other or against posts. Dozens of eager conversations fought for attention. Young dandies in store-bought shirts vied for the best vantage points. One straddled a bicycle, a pure status symbol, there being no place to ride. Now and then children interrupted their play to cast an eye in the direction of the women's grove.

Sande was the women's counterpart of *The Poro,* the sacred cult that conducted initiation rites and held a heavy hand in tribal governance. I never learned much about it; it was indecent for men to inquire. The head *zo* woman was greatly revered for her magic, as well as secular powers. She played an important role in the intricate power structure and there were enterprises that could not be undertaken without her direct participation; for example she had to be present when the boys swore they'd abstained from sex during their stay in the bush—if they lied, she would know, and the penalty was severe, death in the old days.

The *Sande's* basic purpose was simple, the magic transformation of a child into an adult, ritualized of course—tribal people ritualized everything, even tasks as mundane as iron smelting to insure the same result since they didn't understand the chemistry, and who after all understands the chemistry of human metamorphosis, the giggling little girl flowering into a woman?

I heard a shout. There followed some good natured scuffling, course laughter. A young man in his early twenties swaggered up and down before the onlookers. To their delight he suddenly went dead serious strutting pompously, shoulders back, marching forward as he stepped in place or jumped to avoid imaginary goat droppings. Some kind of pantomime. He rudely pushed people aside, gestured wildly, scolded. No one was safe. And he threatened his elders! A young person *did not* do that in Loma society. Something was up. Now he shoved a distinguished middle aged man from behind! Then he turned and pointed a warning finger. No way. He brandished a polished sardine can tied to the end of a short stick, like a mirror, aiming the reflected sun straight into peoples' eyes. Now he put it before his face and seemed to be looking for something, eyes popped, mouth agape. Then the reflection chased people. Perhaps a game of tag. If that didn't work, he chased them half way across town until he cornered them. One of the victims tried to beat off the glare with an empty shirt. The little spot of light took on a personality of its own looking into houses, beckoning people, hiding in their hair, soon it caught a man urinating in the weeds a hundred yards off. When it got lost, he ordered the sun not to move and sure enough, it came dancing across the rooftops, swooping down on people, tickling them under their chins. The more obnoxious he became, the better they liked it. Some kept taking sideward glances at me. When he came by the chief's porch, he stopped and flashed it straight in my eyes. I squinted and drew a roar of laughter. I didn't get it. Moses and Akwoi grinned wickedly. Kwokwoiyea smiled warmly, a bit embarrassed. John Mulba bent over and whispered in English, "He is what you call a mime. *White Man Come to Take Pictures.* The sardine can is his camera."

Wow! What a commentary! But what was the message? Yankee go home? Maybe not. Just a reminder there's such a thing as manners even if you're wealthy enough to own a camera. Kobwoi was in on it too. The old devil! There he sat, a picture of nonchalance, the modernized chief thoroughly enjoying this little episode of tribal comedy.

The young mime continued showboating, now looking into people's mouths, waving them out of the way, kicking a stool aside, forcing a man to hold a knife in his teeth while he adjusted the "camera." Then he got to the women, examining them like fish in the marketplace, rejecting the fairest, which brought down a torrent of protest, giving them belly (pregnancy) denying it while making more. They must have sensed I wasn't a very important white man. They usually weren't this open. Now he bent forward at the waist with one buttock pointed grotesquely to the side and rooster-strutted before his audience taking their picture. Nosing in on the musicians, he treated them to a clumsy dance but walked off in a parody of sophistication, arms akimbo, pondering the sky, deep in thought until he checked an imaginary watch, cartwheeled, came up popeyed, ran back and forth thrashing the air and fell spread-eagled in front of his friends. Soon they were mimicking him. When he revived he discovered a bevy of young women his own age who'd been taunting him all along. Joining them on the pretense of taking their picture, his stealthy fingers soon found the side of a well-formed breast. They screamed in mock outrage driving him away in a barrage of abuse. A stout woman kicked him square in the pants. But he'd worked his magic. The festive mood had taken hold.

The music helped too. At full intensity the drums could drive a dancer to delirium. But for the time being they played mildly, separate turns or tuning checks, occasionally an amusing attempt to mimic the mime. A complete family of drums began to assemble in the square, everything from improvised cook pots to kerosene cans, relics to renowned heirlooms, these bearing proper names, even titles. I could see two *fanga,* singing drums, several *badigi,* multi-headed drums, an hourglass, a kettle, bongos, something resembling an anvil, plus some interesting variations, water gourds with the drumsticks inside. The largest instrument took four men to carry; a hollow log, they set it under a matted awning festooned in lengths of orange and yellow cloth, decorated with fresh palm branches and the national flag lashed to a pole. Two men squatted behind it, each with pair of unequal sticks nearly the size of baseball bats. They could play singly or in tandem. An apprentice kneeled at the right hand of the muscular lead drummer who sported sunglasses and a colorful embroidered Mandingo hat cocked deftly to one side. On his left, his six year old son, same hat, same angle. Behind him another man tightened the heads of a second log drum decorated with cowrie shells and monkey hair and lengths of fine ribbon. A wood xylophone lay on the ground nearby; as he approached it, its master inquired, "Well, are you ready to play?" Two more drummers—the same who appeared earlier with Nyamu—carried their instruments on shoulder straps enabling them to move through the crowd dancing in place as they went. Another rode his like a hobby horse bobbing up and down from the hips, alternating from finger tips to the heels of his hands while his face turned up and away as if from a hot anvil. Women played a series of rattles, shakers, grating slats, wood blocks, and calabash gourds strung over with loose nets of beads. They too danced as they played shifting their feet or doing half turns. One backpacked a baby who looked unimpressed with the whole affair. There were Western influences too—a length of iron pipe struck with a metal rod, a "can-can," two tin cans with a shirt sleeve over the open ends for pouring pebbles back and forth, and an automobile radiator, Ford, struck on the side or scraped across the fins with a flat stick. A cowbell finished the collection, and of course human hands and voices. No one had a clay pipe though, probably because they were nocturnal. A pity too. Contrary to popular belief tribal music isn't all percussion; these exquisite pipes carried a feeling for soft lyric—forerunner of the blues—low and seductive, particularly at night when the still air accentuated the suggestive voices adrift in the dark, one of which was said to be the voice of Nyamu's wife, Wai.

Now they began in earnest. He, the head man, started simply with his left hand, two taps of the forefinger, a slap of the open hand, repeated softly, all the while conversing with someone as his son followed every movement. Then he rapped out a phrase without interrupting the conversation:

Look around downtown look around.
Look around downtown look around.

And the large tree drum broadcast to the surrounding hills:

LOOK AROUND DOWNTOWN LOOK AROUND!!!
LOOK AROUND DOWNTOWN LOOK AROUND!!!

A visible electricity buzzed through the crowd. The hobby horse drummer called out:

Drumcall drumcall all come home.

And a another continued:

Come a drum come come Come an' drum
Drum a drum from home Loma come home.

And the two in tandem:

Come drum come drum come drum home.
Come drum come drum drum from home.

Tribal music is built on the belief that all things have an animality, a spirit that makes them what they are, waits to be inflamed by the right words, moved by the right rhythms. It longs for release. This of course includes drums, many of which were treated as more than mere instruments. They were living beings and answered in the only language they knew, soon taking possession of *their* instruments, the musicians, then the dancers, invariably the audience. When music possessed them, it was impossible for tribal people to sit still as every missionary knew.

The music never really began or ended, it came in gusts with short lulls. Nor did all the instruments play at once. If one or two players dropped out for a breather, others filled in. The intricate rhythmic patterns seemed childishly repetitive at first—and that was exactly the intention, to lure the brain into a waking sleep so "the hunter could catch him." A subtle variation in each repeated phrase carried the prey into the next rhythmic pattern, again childishly repetitive and likely to change at once, but always under the influence of a living thing seeking freedom. Thus benevolent spirits came to town and took human form. This music was never formally studied or taught; it moved under its own power carrying people along with it—or as Louis Armstrong said of jazz, "Nobody writes this stuff, it just happens." It lived on vigor and joy and the smell of sweat. And it was impossible to escape. Only when I noticed Akwoi nudging Moses did I realize my own head was keeping time. Kobwoi grunted approval.

At last they were coming! Some hadn't been home for months judging from their parents' faces. The musicians went silent as people strained to hear. Broad white smiles flashed across eager faces. A murmur rose. Then the children bolted for the makeshift blind at the edge of town, green palm fronds staked in the ground to shield the view to the women's grove. They waited on tiptoes. They weren't to go any further. The initiates would emerge from behind it.

Faint and far away, the sound of distant voices grew to a familiar chant filtering through the forest. High pitched, youthful, it came closer, across a creek, up a bank, clearer with each step. *"Sabi! Sabi!"* A headdress! In the leaves behind the fence! See it…gently rising and dipping in cadence. And another! Four, five, a whole line, each about eighteen inches high, elaborately wound with cloth, deep purple, black, interwoven into braids of hair, draped with strings of scarlet beads and shiny thread with white cowrie shells dangling like earrings. The lead headdress bore the sacred mark of the *Sande,* and the face beneath the look of authority. *"They've come!"* someone cried. The trail skirted a patch of corn stalks—the blind wasn't very effective— avoided a compost heap and emerged from a papaya grove on the downhill side of town opposite the route to the men's grove. When the procession reached the fence, it stopped. So did the singing. The head matron moved down the file checking the beadwork, perhaps whispering a final word of encouragement. After she passed, two older girls stole glances around the blind. Then a younger sister, all arms and legs, leaned way out to get a good look while her smaller mates, some no more than six, held back in wide-eyed wonder. But then came one of those little scenes that bring a grand event back down to earth, the definitive human signature in the right-hand corner. One of the old dogs, not realizing the initiates were now new persons, or perhaps a bit forgetful, picked up the scent of a former acquaintance and sought her out wagging his tail.

At a renewed burst of music they filed out from behind the fence and began a long zigzagging course in and out among the houses singing and clapping in unison with smaller brothers and sisters running alongside. I counted twenty-six plus the four matrons, three of whom were hardly older than the oldest of their charges. After setting it in motion, the head matron left the procession and went directly to the square where she took her place behind the head drummer, a severe woman with an intelligent bearing but a steel expression—at least here in town where she received not so much as a passing nod. Everyone gave her wide berth including the young dandies in store-bought shirts who stopped their chatter at her approach. Meantime the initiates undid their fine headdresses for the coming dance. Most had braided hair; a few did not. No jewelry. They wore only leaves, the fresh green leaves of the forest strung to a cord around the waist, another around each ankle, sometimes with bells. That was all, save for a an arm bracelet, again of grass or leaf, or a straw garland. Some had their skin scarifications; some did not. Several older girls had red beads or cowrie shells in their hair; whether these denoted rank, I couldn't tell. All had their faces smeared with white clay, the color of death, death of the child in this case for they were now women, Loma women, proud, secure, refined in bearing with a measured grace that would carry them into old age. They looked nimble, quick. Probably fast runners. Those of marriageable age had a look of savoir-faire; they walked with a superior air oblivious to all eyes which must have been devastating to the hopeful young men whispering in shaded doorways.

By the time they wove their way into the square, the tempo picked up. They bent forward at the hips with their arms in front, palms up, in a half-walk half-dance mode, undulating, synchronized. As the crowd closed in around them, the procession disintegrated and they went straight into a spirited dance, each dancing in place facing where she wished, doing her own variation of the pounding drumsong that soon reached a deluge checked only by the counterbeat of the woodblock that seemed to bide time in a world of its own. Musicians called out encouragement or shouted refrains to which the women's chorus answered spontaneously, first in words then song. Wheels of rhythm began turning. The cricket roll gave way to daring leaps of fancy inspired by sheer exuberance. Neither musician nor dancer led; each answered a singular call camouflaged in the event. Something forgotten fought to break loose. Now the hobby horse drummer came near one of the younger dancers to give her some personal encouragement. It wasn't long before the dance began to entice the crowd. People standing perfectly still suddenly snapped their necks or elbows, some spun around several times then resumed as spectators. The cowbell player seemed to have his instrument strung from above on an invisible cord; he trotted around it as he played and sang. Others stepped forward and back as they worked their instruments as if trying to scare up game. Women shook their rattles furiously, screaming song. Brazen sunshine poured down into the dense thicket of flickering arms and feet, the whole scene played to the speed of an old silent movie but splashed with a dab of color, a bright shirt or a head-tie, the red umbrella dancing too. Aware only of themselves, the dancers saw nothing, knew nothing save the music. In wild fury they beat the earth, caressed the air, celebrated life. Just once a look of acquaintance passed from one face to another as two leaping forms came down eye to eye. Hands shot into the sky, then to their ankles, then sideward as they whirled. Knees kicked upward and out, elbows made triangles behind their backs, heads panned from side to side in mock bird motion as their feet stepped and stepped and side stepped. Anklets whirled. Flat out. A leaf or two flew off. They were birds, serpents, spirits, human torsos all at once.

After a twenty minute run, the tempo relaxed a bit. A few weaker dancers nearly stopped but continued keeping time. All were drenched with sweat, discolored from the knees down by the ankle-deep dust now drifting off to the side. The music rested, like dripping water after a storm. A very old, diseased woman unable to stand watched from a mat in a doorway. She seemed to be crying. The lull was brief. The head drummer rapped out another call to dance and the women echoed in response. Then it hit again. A downpour! Drowning everything, every word, every worry. The entire world awash in music. The pure sunshine felt so good you wanted to yell.

A spirit found a body. Dance was just that, pure spirit touching the clay of life as in the fingers on the Sistine Chapel. Deep in the human core a tiny cog clicked, just as it was meant to, and the whole day blossomed into a stunning display of animality reaching beyond itself. The worm began to feel the butterfly. Within the stomping and swimming and prancing, they turned in place, fingers in flight, elbows high in the small of the back, shoulders undulating, moving forward on invisible wheels, modulating from sky to earth, from human to spirit and back again; within the outward form an inward mystery unfolded, as though the person who danced was the repertoire of memories so old human understanding had no words. "There is something inside me not myself."

Not in the Greek sense, an *ekstasis* or stepping out of oneself, a separation of the soul from its mooring and a taste of pure freedom thus forming an ideal to be remembered; but in the tribal sense, a return, a stepping *in* to oneself, rediscovering the animal origin of the human spirit. "To dance" and "to see" was the same word, *ka*. To be an explorer meant to dance. To dance meant to see new territories.

Just how it happened I couldn't tell, but before anyone realized, a solo dancer was emerging. The ensemble continued, all twenty-six, no center stage or staged choreography, but things began to revolve around a nucleus. A lithe girl just beginning to fill out began to catch people's attention. Sixteen, maybe older, she had fine nipples on full round breasts, smooth shoulders, lanky arms, serenity of bearing—and stunning beauty, even in clay face which added a feeling of pathos. Her eyes fell to the earth like sunshine, to the side and down, in complete innocence but in full rapport with her heritage. No superiority, no airs, she danced and laughed and sang, imbued with a child's delight in other children, a new woman flowering, memorizing the laughter of childhood, the essence that would define womanhood in the heart of her soul the rest of her days.

The lead drummer spoke of her softly,
Look around look around look around downtown
And the hip drum forbade all sorrow,
Don't frown around downtown don't frown
Then in tandem they addressed her formally,
Come drum drum see
Drum come from thee
Some drum from me
Drum'll come, come an' see
Sun'll sun for thee

And an invitation,
Like a lily lovely lady like to DANCE?
Even the cowbell,
Tell bell pell-mell rang CLANG!
Then, in a deep resonating roll like distant thunder, which surely meant something to the men, some of whom checked their own steps to take a steadier look, for here was refreshment for a burning day,
Come town come down DRUM DOWNTOWN!
Come drum come drum DROWN DOWNTOWN!
She'd been chosen for this, surely, by the perceptive eye of the old *zo* woman who looked on dispassionately. There may well have been more going on than met the eye of an outsider; this could be a subtle reminder to the elder men of the village their power was by no means total. They could only look on in silent admiration as the young neophyte began to respond to the music, imperceptibly at first, then with feeling, discovery, even satiety, a yearling browsing in sunlight unaware of the hunter's stealth. The woodblock jumped in delight. The xylophone cried for her.
Come along a long song belong to me.
Please belong to me
Her disciplined gaze saw nothing. She answered only the eyes of her age-mates as she turned in place beginning to twitch in the wrists and shoulders, a wading flamingo flexing her wings but not ready to fly. A call to dance from the lead drummer. She ignored it! Not an eyelash moved! She kept turning, searching. Another call to dance, more modest this time. No! Not a trace of interest! Total command. Damn if the old *zo* woman wasn't giving us all a lesson. Wield the reins, Sir Patriarch, the heart of beauty you cannot touch. Now she turned her back on the musicians and bent forward passing word glances to her age-mates who answered eagerly, thrilled to be in her constellation. Some were ready to race ahead but she checked them. Not the faintest smile. Complete serenity. Everyone in the crowd came alert. When she satisfied herself her mates were with her, she looked away, at ease with herself, chin back, absorbing music, building energy, the butterfly stretching wet wings. An elbow shot up behind her, then fell back into place. A slight keeping of time in the neck and one shoulder. The musicians continued their enticement with mellow runs on the xylophone, a sharp strike on the pipe, and occasional burst of rattles like gusts in the leaves. Nothing. The drummers retreated, playing half-heartedly. All eyes fixed on her. She and no one else was going to pick the time—her time. Another half turn, a caress of the earth,

a quizzical head gesture, a meaningful glance to an imaginary partner—then the explosion. It came from deep within, pure, sensuous, uninhibited, with an intensity straight from the tribal heart. The musicians answered in kind, inspired. Full volume. A torrential outburst of beating hands! Thunderous resonance! Robust shouts! Wild jubilation! In nimble grace she twisted, whirled, dipped, jumped impossible jumps, violent movements cut clean. Her muscles trembled, her feet beat an additional drum pattern, her face turned to one side, arms swinging freely, lower, lower, at her ankles, then they found the sky, then back, then up. Floating hands, leaves swirling, arms flying out as she whirled, now on one foot, faster, faster. She seemed to challenge the drums,

Dumb drum dumb drum come drum SPEAK!

They tried to restrain her,

Thus thus
Mustn't rush it
Easy does it
Trust trust

But no,

Old men told men cold men SHEEP!
Old men mold men fold then SLEEP!

They cautioned,

Hush girl shush girl as is meet
Seek clique, meek street, be discreet

She challenged,

Come drum GUSH
Drum some LUSH
Some'll drum thus
Some'll drum summer drum as is MEAT

Wow! Right back in their teeth. They responded,

Summer found bound
Summer found sound
Some are found run aground round about town

But faster,

Come a drum drum come
Come a drum come a drum come a drum
Drum a drum drum from a drum drummer LOOK!

And faster,

Loma Lady make a ready

Make a dumb drum SPEAK!
But she prevailed,
Dumber drummer dumb drum no go way
Some'll drum some'll run some'll come n' STAY!

This brief encounter ended in a flurry of sound and motion, louder and livelier than ever, the whole town catching the upbeat, drums and dance in complete harmony. The repeated appearance of her placid clay face became a flickering apparition on a black background. The rustling leaves on her ankles danced a dance of their own. She was nature's prodigy; she pulsed with the throbbing music, wheeled outward, then back, writhing, twisting into fierce contortions, breaking free, but all the while her inward radiance held firm; her wet face, sublimely undisturbed though the dance carried her to near frenzy. Beads of sweat flew off her supple skin. But something inside supplied new strength. The act of discovery carried its own momentum.

That she would lead a life of toil and pain and unremitting labor, that disease and too frequent childbirth would scar this splendid form, that she would be old by her thirties was something people forgot for the moment, for it was her moment, a time to blossom in the sun. She danced in full innocence of the ageless human drama she performed, of the memories she rekindled in old men's hearts. There were things she was yet to learn. Soon she would hold a lover, perhaps her first. For the present there was no medicine in the world that could match the delicacy of this supreme moment, this brief sunrise that would never come again. Maybe that's why the old woman in the doorway wept.

Drenched with sweat, breathing like an athlete, she at last retired among her age-mates who picked up the pace where she left off. Now she clapped time for them. There was no applause; they showed approval by joining in. Inwardly they danced with her. The crowd had become a sea of bobbing heads. Every able body responded in its own way. Moses and Akwoi jumped in earlier, now Kwokwoiyea and John, like fish to water, in a thicket of flying arms and stomping feet, cries and shouts. Kobwoi too. In his suit and red suspenders. Luckily he'd kicked off his Italian shoes. Finally I tried. I learned a few steps, but the exuberance—that was all theirs. I never learned her name. Maybe it was best. I knew at once how I'd remember her. *Gbwolu.* The face that launched a thousand dance steps.

It went on intermittently all afternoon. At one point when things seemed to have died down, a small gathering formed outside an open doorway. An elderly woman, a grandmother surely, hardly able to lift herself from her drudgery, had come forward to greet one of the girls, a ten-year old, not with words but with dance. And there she stood, a withered old crone with dangling flaps at her breast, a toothless smile, arthritic hands, sickly ribs, ugly enough to be the butt of rude jokes. She sagged under the weight of her own frame and we could hear the rasping of her difficult breath. I expected something ludicrous. Miraculously, without apparent effort, she drew an eternal flame out of her old bones; in the agony of age and disease, her spirit soared. A heavenly smile beamed, soft, gentle. Though restricted in movement, she made her statements in slow simple motions that seemed to be off in the distance. The sweep of her open palms, a simple leaning to one side, the bird-like turning of the head, flowing hands—all spoke the feelings of youth but from the other side of a lifetime. An easy rising and turning forward of the shoulders suggested the flapping of a sailing hawk lazily lifting to a new height. She achieved soaring ballet leaps simply by inhaling air and then coming down. By a mere widening of the eyes, she spoke to the girl, *"Are you come home my child?"* And the answer, *"I am here sweet mother."* They circled facing each other, inch by inch, the old woman nudging the young into taking its first steps. Simple three beat rhythm. No music, just a low humming chant. *Kra kra koo.* Her head followed turning from side to side accenting the end of each phrase with a blink of the eyes, panning from side to side, the chin and neck searching, then only the neck moved, then stillness, dance in demeanor alone. She withdrew into herself but it somehow magically transferred to the child who picked it up swinging her gangly arms, same time, same space. Their eyes met. The old woman swayed from side to side. One last time she raised her eyes and the girl's response reflected in her swimming eyes. When she finished, she shuffled back into the darkened doorway like an old animal returning to the safety of its lair.

CHAPTER 46

A SECOND KIND OF COURAGE

"I wanna hold your hand."

"JAMESON!"

"Damn it Jameson, are we going to the United States tonight!"

Our last night. Mass confusion, the Beatles all but drowned out, Jameson nowhere in sight, the drunken bellow receding in the din. My flight wasn't till next morning but most of us were going to the airport tonight, just in case.

We met at the *Moby Dick* for one last binge. The place was packed. A blaring jukebox, clinking beer bottles, spilt drinks, but it didn't matter; a jubilant young crowd and its well-wishers refused to let sorrow spoil a farewell. A dozen spirited conversations vied with the music, only the cigarette smoke remained immobile. Some tried to exchange addresses, others jammed together in small knots or spilled into the street, newcomers piled out of cabs with awkward bundles of luggage, themselves trying to catch someone's attention, hand shakes ending in bear hugs, at least as far as the bar where another gang, arms draped around each other, swayed back and forth thundering our marching song:

Amoeba!

I think I just swallowed...a moeba!

"We're goin' home baby! We're GOIN'...HOME!"

"That great big beautiful bird's leavin' woo woo faw New Yawk—"

"Hey Reilly! If I ever see ya back in the states, how my gonna know ya without a Guinness in your hand?"

"He'll have his—"

"Anybody know what time we get t' New York?"

"Hey! Where'd Jameson go?"

"I'm right here dammit. I need some money for gas. Gas! The stuff that makes the motor go." Jameson. Old reliable.

"Jasemun. Juss gimmie the keys."

"Yeah. Right."

"Jamezun," Rick drew himself up mimicking LBJ, "We wawnt yew t' know we're proud of yew. Ameriga is proud of yew."

"Take the night off Jamie. Gitch yourself a little—"

"You wanna go home tonight!" Jameson snapped. "Wanna run out half way t' the airport?…That's right, five big ones, say good-bye to Uncle George."

"Hey! Where you goin'!"

"T' get gas damn it!"

"Don't you run out on me Jameson!"

"Just try t' stay on your feet another twenty minutes."

"I'll hunt you down Jameson!"

"TWENTY MINUTES!"

And suddenly I'm on

The pathway to the john…all daaaay

(Two years ago these guys were supposed to save the world. Well…we tried.)

"Sophia Loren? Here?"

"Not *here* jackass! Back in the bush."

"What t' hell's she doin' back in the bush?"

"Just shut up!"

"This is modrunized Ahfrican folk tale, you see," an African pal in a Hawaiian shirt explained. "To exercise the…ahmagination. Allow the gentleman to proceed."

"There's this evil spirit. It's been documented."

"It's not his imagination needs exercise Tumboe!"

"Be patients, if you please."

"Right. It can change itself into any form. Every Christmas it assumes a Sophia Loren-type appearance and goes around biting its victims in the neck."

"But it's not Christmas!"

"It is if she bites ya!"

"Once you're bitten, you got thirty seconds to live—"

"'Ats no' very go'am mush."

"That's right. It's not very much, BUT, you can do anything you want…for thirty seconds. Then…you die."

"Hey! Richardson wants to see you!" the assistant Rep clapped my back, then offered his hand smiling, "Something about an unauthorized field trip. I guess we can forget it now."

"Good luck," someone whispered.

"Maggie. Is that you?"

"Sure 'nough."

"You're lookin' good." She'd lost weight.

"You too," she said on the point of tears. I hardly knew her but felt like hugging her. So I did.

"I'm sorry I didn't get around to see you Maggie."

"That's all right. If you're ever down Missouri way, look me up. Springfield." Then a warm kiss on the cheek.

"Hi stranger."

"Alice?"

"How 'bout a smooch? Ummm—YEOW!"

It took an effort just to get near enough the bar to shout. After three times I gave up on creme de menthe, asked for rum and coke, came away with a beer. People I hadn't seen in two years offered a last hand shake. The jukebox launched into a country tune, the bar girls mouthing the words as they gyrated in place flashing five dollar smiles. I squeezed past and made my way to the far corner where Chris shared a separate table with a elegant young woman.

Our age, tall, long neck, gold earrings, the same diameter as a matching arm band, she had a proud forehead held back in a manner that suggested tribal origins. She wore a simple yellow blouse, dark skirt, sandals, slight make-up, but her hair—luxurious ebony in shining folds with a single braid worked into a coil at one side, pinned with a hand-carved wooden comb. A tiny gold cross danced in the nape of her neck. Even in the frail light, her dark features ripened with expression, no hidden feelings, a silent longing altogether out of place in the surroundings. I sat on my suitcase against the wall. Another quiet embrace, their lips hardly moved, her thumb caressing his neck. When they released, she kissed him once on the chin, looked for something in his eyes, then clasped her hand over his. So it was true.

"Didn't I tell you?" he said to her as though confirming a wager. Then to me, "Sir. You stink of wood smoke."

I sniffed my sleeve. "I'll get it cleaned first thing I get home."

"There's a dry cleaner just up the street."

"I didn't know that."

"You didn't get that thing cleaned in two years? That's right, how would you know two years have passed?"

521

"It's been at the bottom of my footlocker. My roof leaked. I had termites."

"Did you consider carving notches on your staff? Who cut your hair?"

"A guy in my village. He hasn't had a lot of experience with white people."

He smiled delicately, "Somehow you're the one person I'd never worry about." He beamed as he looked me over. "Allow me to present Miss Jeanetta Khanu-Diggs, originally from Robertsport, formerly employed at USIS. Sir Caliban of the Gola Forest."

She reached across the table and squeezed my hand with unexpected warmth. "I am so pleased you came to say good-bye," she said putting me at ease at once. "We saw you come in. Chris was hoping to see you one last time." She spoke in deep tones, perfect enunciation, elongating vowels, knoow and caame. Definitely out of place. Then she returned her hand to his and began quietly quizzing me about my family, assuring me I was in for a happy reunion. Chris stared at his glass as she spoke. "Why don't you find a chair?" she said at last.

"This is fine," I said edging a little closer. Then I remembered a book he'd loaned me.

"Did you read it?" he asked.

"Yeah."

"And?"

"And what?"

"Do you still think we can't bridge the gap?"

"Can we avoid an intellectual—"

"But he became a Buddhist."

"Could we please not—"

"You still think people are islands? You with the medicine around your neck?"

"It's an European's conception of Buddhism. To a Buddhist it may be something different."

"Oh yeah. What?"

"Something he wouldn't have to write about."

"How can you say that without being a Buddhist?"

"By knowing my heart."

"How do you say this word?" Jeanetta said looking over the cover.

"Siddhartha," he answered softly. "You keep it darling. I hope it brings you peace."

"I will read it too," she said brightly, "and I will know you the better." She kissed him.

Things were worse than I thought. I'd heard of his affair with an African girl but chose not to ask questions—what are you going to do when it's time to go home? Maybe I should've. He was avoiding something.

"Cheer up," I said lifting my beer bottle half-heartedly. "The troops are going home. Well done, good sport and all that crap."

"I'm tired of being a good sport, the troops are pigs and I'm not going home." This last almost under his breath.

"Do naught talk that way about your friends," Jeanetta pleaded straight into his eyes, then kissed him again to make sure. We sat in silence a little while, he staring at his glass, she bearing her burden. The crowd kept up the festive pace, the jukebox blared. Something was wrong. Doc had given a hint mumbling something about our generation going to hell and his having led the way, then practically ordered me to look him up before I left.

"Not going home," I said. Now Jeanetta stared at her glass.

"I'm refusing to bear arms for my country. Is that clear enough?"

"Vietnam?"

He didn't move.

"I didn't realize how bad things were till I picked up a paper the other day. Jesus. I don't like it."

"Don't you?" he smiled. "It's very simple really. We're bestowing democracy on that country in the most original method in history—supporting a military dictatorship." Then he changed his tone, "Why do we always support the dictators?"

"I don't know. I can't believe it's on purpose—"

"Oh you can't! Maybe you *have* been up in the bush too long." He paused then continued, quietly but firmly. "The thought of being shot at isn't what scares me...but when I think of shooting someone else, actually squeezing the trigger and watching a human body fly to pieces, somebody I don't even know...I couldn't do it. If I'm going to die for something, it's not going to be looking down the end of a barrel. When I was a kid, I got an air rifle for my birthday. We were out shooting, another kid and I; we saw a robin sitting on a fence. He took a shot and missed, then again, kept missing. The stupid bird wouldn't move. Then I took a shot—from the hip—didn't really want to hit it—but did, right in the eye. It fell in the dirt, flapping its wings, the eye bashed in, its beak open, the tongue trying to come out. But not a sound. I can still remember the tongue, stretching out in the dirt, trying to get out of the body. I could never go to war...after that I got a regular rifle, then another. Dad liked guns. I learned to shoot so I could miss on purpose."

"What will you do?"

"My flight's via Lisbon. That's where I get off. Me and my trusty guitar. What else should I want? I think I'll hole up in Spain for awhile. Might go to Sweden if I have to. I've thought about it. It's not a matter of courage, it's a matter of will; the will to overcome the blind impulse of the pack. No matter how strong the arguments there's always that war mentality menacing the better part of ourselves."

"You'll have second thoughts."

"I've already had second thoughts—third thoughts. They all say the same thing. What morality allows this? Be damned if I can find any."

"If you're sure you're right," I said, "but if there's any doubt, it'll come back to haunt you."

I think there are two kinds of courage," he said. "Holding your ground in the face of flying bullets is one, but there's another, the courage to do what you know is right in the face of fools who would have you do otherwise…even if the fools happen to be—"

"Do naught do this. Your own father. I cannot understand how you can be so unrespecting. You must ask Gawd to guide you."

"Knowing which to follow when," he concluded, "that's the trick."

"When I was a small girl and something was troubling me," Jeanetta continued, "I would go to my grandmother. Even after she is died, I would go to her and ask. But you think this is—"

"No darling," he said lifting her fingers to his lips. "No we don't."

By now the place was quieting down. Some had gone up the street to another bar. One of our buddies, a towel around his waist, helped out behind this one. The door was wide open. Outside white streaks of rain slashed across the dim streetlight. Kids ran up and down the gutter looking for a frog, or a fortune should one of the drunks lose his wallet. A man leaned against the fender of a taxi cupping his hands to light a cigarette before turning to watch two bar girls run across the street shielding their heads under newspapers. The noise inside made it a complete pantomime.

"But how can you be so certain you'll be drafted?" I said. "The doc says they'll probably consider our service, put us at the bottom of the list. You can always get a job teaching school."

"Me! Teach school?" He looked around as if to see if anyone were listening. "God you are naive." He stopped, stared at his glass again, looked at me…"You really don't…" Then he exhaled and began a low but steady explanation, almost a monologue. "Remember Maureen Brubaker? Miss

Personality Plus. Ever wonder why she took a shine to me, why the good congressman just happened to stop in one day, why I didn't get kicked out for that little caper with the motorcade? You're a gem. Didn't you even figure out why we were supposed to be incompatible roommates?" He smiled awkwardly. Then with his eyes on the ashtray continued softly, "My father chairs a corporation with operations on four continents; my mother's active in DAR, Boston Chapter. You're quite right, I don't have to worry about getting drafted. Creightons never get drafted…they volunteer. Ever hear of Creighton Industries? AmeriNard? Solid little company. A little rat's nest inside a big rat's nest all connected by an endless chain of dollar bills. Good investment. Want the address? Early American furniture, a Remington on the wall—Frederic, we have a collection of the other Remingtons as well—a photogenic receptionist, she can type too; we like style, but no gum chewing. Guys in uniform, you feel real safe. Flag a mile high on a silver pole inside a bed of red geraniums, a circle of white stones around the edge, gold eagle on top. Real traditional. What do they make? Electronics mostly, the kind of things you usually don't find at your neighborhood hardware store."

"What kind of electronics?"

"Gadgets. Thingamajigs."

"What kind of gadgets?"

"Component parts to be more precise. We have to be precise. Component parts to what? The gentleman is asking himself. Component…the major component parts…to missile guidance systems."

He finished losing eye contact in spite of himself, then to Jeanetta like a kindergarten teacher, "And what does your daddy do?"

"Do naught do this," she pleaded. "Do naught pain yourself so. Your oown father. You must honor him no matter what he's done. It is the way of sons to their fathers. It is not yours to choose; to hate him so is to hate yourself. And you. Shame on you, to make your friend talk of such things when you see it pains his only heart."

"Cheer up! You're goin' home!" A hand with a shiny watch clapped down on his shoulder. A bald American bent over grinning drunkenly. "Me, I got another year in this armpit. Here's t' the States." He had a week off next month, he explained to Jeanetta, draping his arm around Chris, and was planning a short outing, a little hunting, a little this, a little that. But reliable guides, that was the real problem. "The chap at the bar said one of your oddball friends," he coughed, "I gotta have a reliable guide. I'll pay top dollar."

"I can't imagine to whom he's referring," Chris answered with feigned delicacy.

"Well, I guess there's only one kind o' bush you guys are interested in," and he clapped him on the back again with a quick leer at Jeanetta. "I wish you guys could come along but you'll be back home with all the broads by then. Say hello t' Lady Bird."

"Delightful fellow," Chris said.

"A little less hair, he'd pass for a tapeworm."

"Shoo! Both of you," Jeanetta whispered. "It is very bad to disrespect your elders you know. You must always show respect. It makes you stronger." Then in a softer tone she turned to me, "And what about you? What will you do when you go home?"

"I got a fellowship."

Mark kept glaring at the drunk. After his anger passed he came back to his old self. "Graduate school?"

"Yeah."

"You!"

"Yes. Me. What's so damn—"

"I know I'm going to regret asking," he said savoring the moment, "in what field of endeavor?"

"American Studies."

His sneer changed to a wicked grin.

"I fail to see the humor." He kept grinning. "Damn you then. I hope you choke on those perfect teeth."

"You with your...you know what this is?" he said to Jeanetta.

"It's a leopard's tooth," I said. "A gift."

"It is very nice," she smiled.

"Ha!"

He sat back grinning. "American Studies. That's precious. Your American associates seem to think you prefer the company of tribesmen to themselves."

"I don't see where—"

"Oh but I'd love to take you to one of my mother's social functions."

"I could handle it."

"Did you include any spirits in your dossier? What about professional references? Your medicine man? The witch?"

"You have absolutely no faith in the pliability of the human soul."

He leaned over and whispered something in Jeanetta's ear while she kept looking at me dreamily. Then he drew back and she smiled shyly.

"Will you do something very special for me?" she asked.

"Sure."

He drew her close and whispered again as though giving directions.

"Something personal?" she confided, then smiled as he gave her boost in my direction.

"Shoot."

"Tonight, you are leaving my country for the last time. Perhaps I will never see you again. Before you go, won't you please tell me...I will be favored if you can tell me...how do you pronounce...your last naame? I would be pleased to knoow."

All of a sudden it got quiet, even the damn jukebox. Uncanny. The party had passed its peak but people were still enjoying themselves, drinks all around, intimate couples at the other tables, bar girls cruising.

"Watch my lips." Outside the rain was letting up. "War! Like ven you shooting people. Gin! Like ven you have too much for drink ant vant to fall down on floor. Zhin! Like ven you do sometink bat ant dewelop a zbeech imbediment. Ski! Like when you slite down mountain. Wor-gin-zhin-ski. Only V make like W for some strench reason, like two drunken Cossacks when they try to figure out why they look alike. Ant 'gin' becomes 'yin' after you wake up in ditch. Zo! Ve haff! Vorjinzhinski! **EEZ RAWSHYUN!** Amerikanski ozzwole!! You dawn't know Rawshyun ven you zee vun! So you see my deah, I simply con't go the boooll, I con't donce in skis."

Now it really got quiet, but people were looking at Creighton for some reason. Then he let go.

"She asked for your name! Not a psychoanalysis!"

Then someone popped another quarter in the jukebox and the Beatles were back at it. "Eez olt Rawshyun fulk sonk," I said.

"I thought it might be Polish," he added after a bit. "Your name! Polish names usually end in 'I' don't they?"

"Yeah but the immigrants didn't know that."

"Then your father—"

"Was an immigrant. Came on a tub. 1912. He used to say if he were rich he would have taken the *Titanic*. She sailed that spring."

"I never knew anyone who's parents were immigrants. Not too many Vorjinzhinskis where I prepped."

"Not too many Creightons at the Orthodox Church Bazaar. Great piroshki. I...I wish I could have gotten to know you better. When's your flight?"

"Twelve thirty," he said sullenly.

"Shouldn't you—"

"Jameson's supposed to pick me up. Yours?"

"Tomorrow morning. We're going out tonight just in case. Too bad Orley's not here, we'd all be home by now."

"He's gone. He has 'driven,' if you'll pardon the expression, his last jeep for the United States Government. Andersen and Gaines finagled a flight through Paris."

"I hope they're whoopin' it up, too," I said. "I wonder if we'll ever see each other again? Any of us."

"You never know."

The rest of the time passed as slow as the smoke drifting for the doorway. I began to feel the tension of waiting. Upcountry it was never a problem; now all I knew was if I missed my flight, I'd be off schedule. How fast we fall back to our old ways. No one said anything for a long time. Jeanetta's long fingers rested on his arm; her face, pure sorrow. She looked out the window at the empty street, then to him, then me, as if for help although she knew none was coming. Now a nervous gesture, checking her bag, a glance, a heavy inward breath as she fought to hold it in; her people weren't good at hiding their feelings under false pretensions. Chris wasn't much better under the circumstances. I felt awkward. Now and then some friends came over to say a last good-bye and, "Look me up sometime." Charley #6 slipped in and out between people displaying gold chains and ivory jewelry. Two beggar kids snuck in and began working the crowd.

"Creighton! For Chrissakes get a move on!" Jameson's square frame shouldered through some tables then stopped well out of range. Chris rose awkwardly, bent down and kissed her, first on the forehead, the cheek, then the lips. She kissed him back, long and with feeling, a good-bye that begged for anything but good-bye, while his fingers drew away from her cheek. Jameson paused, embarrassed, "Everybody's in the truck,"

Chris stood up and slung his duffel bag over his shoulder. Her eyes followed him in unflinching pain.

"And you," Jameson said to me. "Don't move! I don't have time for one of your little excursions tonight."

Chris said something to her in a dialect and she responded in kind. I stood up to let him pass. He clasped his hand to the side of my neck drawing my forehead to his, "Good luck in grad school," he smiled. "And don't start going by the book, you'll always be stronger that way."

"The second kind of courage," I whispered. "Good-bye."

He took up his guitar, clutching it with both arms and awkwardly pushed his way through the crowd.

Jeanetta stared after him, then into space for a long time keeping up a fierce effort to hold back the tears. "I'm sorry," I said. After awhile the crowd thinned out, the juke box stopped, the place became an empty tenement after an eviction. Now you noticed the cracked walls, litter on the floor. "Would you like me to see you home?"

"No thank you," she answered with some composure. "It is naught necessary. Do you care if I stay with you for a time? I can naught to go home yet."

"Of course not."

"I do naught live far."

"You're tribal aren't you?"

"My mother was Vai, my father Americo-Liberian. I saw very little of him but he did help me into University. I studied there for two years, I wanted to be a pharmacist but lost my funding." Once she started speaking it came easier. "I took employment first with the USIS, then a German company as a stenographer but after some months they discontinued their services. After that I looked for temporary jobs, the last at *The Alcove,* on U.N. Boulevard. They told me I was to be hostess. I was only two nights. I never want to go again. I am a stenographer. Do you understand? It is so difficult to find lasting employment—and honest dealings. I...I am so ashamed. I am naught...*The Alcove*...I had to find work you see, I went to school, I am preferred by...how could I have married him?"

"He asked you to marry him?"

"Yes. But how could I?"

"As easy as finding a pastor."

"You talk just like him," and she tried to smile. "We've been through this...many time. I wish I never came here. I wish I never saw him." She couldn't hold back the tears anymore. "Gawd knows I love him. But how could I? To go home with him, to meet his parents? I would be so afraid."

"Why?"

"It is a long story."

"Tell me."

She sighed. "I am Roman Catholic. He is naught."

"Is that all?"

"Yes." Then in a lower tone, "I do not think he beliefs in Gawd. How can anyone naught belief in Gawd? He does naught love his family. He is naught

529

going home to them like the rest of you. I worry about him, he is only a child. I will never understand you…you Americans. You have everything but you are such children. You talk so badly of your elders. Such angry words. When I asked him why he does not worship, he said because God is too busy counting His money. Is nothing sacred to you?"

"We have our problems too. Try to understand."

"Forgive me," she cried, wiping back the tears. "I do naught mean to be rude. You have such strange ways. I could never be like you," she looked away calling on all her strength. "Now I do naught know what is to become of me."

"Ask your grandmother."

"Please do naught make jokes."

"No joke," I smiled. She looked at me intensely, desperate want on the face of defiance. Emergent Africa. What were we doing to them? "Tell me your tribal name."

"Zihanu." And she beamed a child's delight. "Zee—ah—noo."

"That's beautiful."

"Thank you."

"I think God will favor you…Someday." I lied.

"How do you know this?"

"Because…the meek shall inherit the earth." I didn't believe that either.

"I do naught think that you know this. But you are very kind."

"May I walk you home? It would be my pleasure."

"Your friend said to stay."

"He won't be back for awhile."

"It is naught far. I have small apartment, but how long I don't know, the rent is too dear."

Outside she hiked up the shoulder strap of her bag and stepped along briskly. It was raining again. Steady, forlorn, sweet desolation. There was something reassuring about rain, its certainty, sadness, but also its cleansing power, it seemed to bring back the old tribal toughness, wash the tears and bow the head to bolder tasks.

"Can you lend me some money?" she asked with downcast eyes. "I am short this month—until I get another job. I do naught want to worry him so. It is too difficult finding…good work. Do you understand? I am a stenographer."

"Sure." I took out my wallet. Sixty two bucks. All I had left. "Take it."

"Thank you very much," she said removing a slip of paper from her bag.

"Write me please your address here. I will send you remittance as soon as I find work."

"It's not necessary."

"You must."

"No, please. Forget it."

"I can naught," she said defiantly. "I am a stenographer."

CHAPTER 47

A LAST FAREWELL

Twenty to three. Empty terminal. Dreary lights. My friends sprawled out on the floor like straw dummies. The ride to the airport had been uneventful; rain all the way, appropriately, just as it had that first night two years ago. Someone remarked how quickly the time passed. The place looked utterly desolate—stained walls, dripping flag, two guards asleep standing up, the potholes in the crumbling pavement—nothing had changed. Jameson circled the lot twice, picked one, and driving straight for it sang a lusty war cry until we bounced out of our seats to a collective cheer. The last jolt. We piled out and he gave her a final pat on the fender, our trusty jeep. Surprisingly we got through customs without the usual delays. Was I taking anything out of the country surpassing a hundred dollars? I said No. Then we plopped down and tried to get some sleep—everybody but me.

After walking the length of the building two times, I stretched out against a post and gave up. Quarter of four. Tense. Couldn't relax, a fuzzy uneasiness made me keep checking the clock. It seemed there were clocks everywhere, like cats with big white eyes trying to trick me with their clever hands. Twelve to four.

Going home. But it wouldn't be the same—or so we'd been warned. And now a war going on, demonstrations on college campuses, riots in the ghettoes. But how could it not be the same? Home isn't a place, it's a state of the soul, the glow of remembered love by which all things are judged same or false. If you've really got a home, you take it with you. It's the one thing that does stay the same. Then why so uncertain?

I walked outside and leaned on the fence. There she sat, a prehistoric bird materializing out of the mist, wet skin and a row of tiny teeth along the side, four yellow pods like egg sacks tucked under her wings. A monster with square nostrils in its forehead. I'd have to stop thinking like this. An airplane is an airplane. My world allows no such imaginings.

Dawn began to break. Attendants in yellow coveralls swarmed over it, several gathered on a platform beneath one engine, a man in a white shirt and headset watched as a second service truck pulled up. At the edge of the runway the forest began to separate from the sky, an ocean of mist languished on the points of thatched rooftops; beyond, native workmen filed along a footpath in front of women pounding rice in wooden mortars. It didn't seem so monstrous in the natural light; its smooth curves flexed in the gray drizzle like shiny muscles, steel wings swept back, sculptured shoulders bent forward—and the yellow egg sacks had become plastic engine covers.

Jet aircraft and car horns. My world was coming back with a vengeance, a world of number and necessity where U-235 splits with ease and virgins don't have babies, where dreams don't count nor evening breezes whisper fertile secrets.

I never had that little talk with John Mulba. I left him with his mad dream of going to America to study medicine. Saying good-bye had been sheer agony. He looked into my eyes blinking dumbly, asked if I'd remember him. I tried to embrace him but it was awkward, real awkward. Words wouldn't come. Then he took my hand and walked me to the jeep. I never got used to holding hands as a sign of masculine friendship. The others saw—and smiled—Moses, Kwokwoiyea, Akwoi, Telleywoiyea, Fdumo James, Peter Kpudumah, Taanu, David Beyan, Isaac Kezelee, we shook hands, three clicks all around, Old Fawkpa, several elders, Gburulu, deathly sober, two senior women, the chief himself. The rest of the village watched from a distance, my school girls ladylike, demure, but all smiles when I waved, small fry under foot as usual. Ramses Tokenu asked if he could go with me and I wasn't sure but his mother would've allowed. The jeep took forever getting up speed. I looked back. There they where in a cloud of dust in the middle of the road, John Mulba standing off to the side staring after me. What could he be thinking? He *knew* I'd go home some day! They all did. Would the timelessness of their days return? Or had the ring been broken? I thought about it all the way to the coast. Had I interfered where I shouldn't have? They didn't seem to think so, wanted to know when I was coming back as if I could come at the drop of a hat. In two years I never got it across to them I wasn't rich.

A little later Larry came out for a look. "Hey Baby," he sighed to the airplane. "We're goin' home." Then to me. "You keep an eye on it now."

"Okay."

"Get any sleep?"

"Nah."

"Me neither. What time you got?"

"'Bout six thirty." Two crewman from what had to be our flight hurried past in the matter-of-fact way of airmen.

"Can we get on yet?" Larry asked.

"Afraid not," the first answered. "We won't be getting under way for another five, maybe six hours. Flight delay."

"You're kidding!"

"Nope," the second added. "We're looking over one of the engines right now. Nothing serious, but the airplane has to be a hundred percent before we take off."

"Relax," the first smiled, "we're gonna get you home."

"What's the matter," Larry ribbed him, "won't she start? Need a pair o' jumper cables?"

"Sounds like ya got a girl waitin'," he grinned.

"Man," Larry kept at him, "I'm so high for gettin' out o' here I'll get out an' push."

"I got a better idea," he laughed. "Why don't you go have some breakfast on us. Just sign your flight number."

The restaurant was deserted save for a young steward inside the door. A tribal boy eager at his new job, he snapped to attention but relaxed when he saw who we were, his ritual scarifications visible in the open neck of his white uniform. He wasn't afraid of us. I felt good about that. Watching intently as we seated ourselves by the window—so Larry could keep an eye on the airplane—he promptly passed out dinner menus. Jameson whispered something, then a word of encouragement in dialect and he began taking them up, a bit confused.

All at once Clark Reardon stepped through the door rubbing his hands in anticipation. "Well, gentlemen. I see we're in for breakfast and a skip across the lake. My compliments to your hairdressers." Junior consul at the Embassy, only a few years our senior, he looked like a young lawyer, confident, brisk, sharp with enthusiasm. He introduced Dr. Van Meter, a trouble shooter from the State Department doing the SubSahara before returning to the Middle East, his wife, Lucille, and Mr. Ashir, a Lebanese businessman bound for Dakar. The courtesies were brief. "So the junket's over," Van Meter said drawing up a chair. "Almost," Larry smiled. He ignored the answer, unfolded his napkin and began wiping the silverware, at the same time launching into a renewed conversation with Mr. Ashir just as the steward returned with the breakfast menus. "You must have had a wonderful experience," Mrs. Van Meter smiled sweetly, "and now you can look forward to seeing your families." Clark and Scot returned her smile. Van Meter was pumping the Lebanese mercilessly. The Middle East was ready to blow up, the slightest provocation, etc. Mr. Ashir sadly agreed but remained hesitant on details. "What about Vietnam?" Jameson asked. "That's not the problem," Van Meter scowled, perturbed at the interruption. "We'll have that situation wrapped up in six months." But the Middle East? There were ominous signs and he meant to get to the bottom of it before returning to Washington. What, if war broke out tomorrow, would be the Lebanese posture? Mr. Ashir shrugged his shoulders. Passions were older than politics. But Van Meter insisted on specifics. The two of them moved to the next table for privacy. Poor Mr. Ashir.

"You guys look like you slept here," Clark said, as congenial as he was nattily dressed.

"We did."

"You *slept* in the terminal?"

"Clark. Don't repeat yourself," Greg scolded.

"That's insane," he continued. "All you had to do was check with me. You could have stayed at the Embassy, rode out with us, enjoyed a leisurely breakfast and zip across the lake." He ended in a said-and-done tone, the flat of his hand taking off.

"My dear Clark," Scot began with extreme relish. "Allow me to inform you your zipping plans are somewhat premature."

"Flight delay," Larry added.

"You're kidding," he said flabbergasted. "Don't do this to me. You know—"

"They're working on the plane right now." Sure enough, there they were right outside the window.

"Shit."

"Clark PLEASE." Greg gasped.

"You should have checked with us Clark."

He looked perplexed, turned to Mrs. Van Meter who was tasting her juice as if it were medicine, then to his boss, "Dr. Van Meter. Excuse me, sir. A slight problem. There's been a departure change."

"Damn it!" Van Meter exclaimed throwing his napkin to the table. "Doesn't anything run on time in this country?" He looked at his watch. "Can I get to Monrovia and back before take off?"

535

"I'll check, sir," Clark said.

"No. Let's get going." He brusquely pushed himself from the table just as the steward began serving him. "Reardon, stay here and stall 'em if I'm late." They hurried out, Van Meter and Mr. Ashir leading, Mrs. Van Meter fumbling in her purse.

"It could be worse Clark," Greg smiled. "You could be stranded in an elevator with Sophia Loren."

"Do you guys have any idea who he is?"

"We really don't give a damn Clark."

"…Slept in the terminal?"

"Only one night," Jameson said. "Larry wanted to come out last week but we wouldn't let him."

We began breakfast in good spirits. Bacon, eggs, milk, buttered pastries— things we hadn't seen much upcountry. At one point Jameson picked up his bacon with his fingers but remembered where he was. "Hell of a lot easier their way." Then four stewardesses came in, sleepy-eyed but carefully made up, probably from our flight. Real neat. White blouses, navy flight jackets, shoulder bags. A hint of perfume followed them across the room where they seated themselves without breaking off their easy conversation. The uncomfortable breakfast steward approached cautiously.

"Stop gawking," Clark whispered.

"He's not gawking, he's leering," Larry explained.

"It's been a long dry season," Scot observed.

"And it's taken its toll on man and beast alike," Greg added.

"They look—" Jameson paused rolling a country cigar, a loose collection of leaves bound with string.

"You're not going to—"

"Clean." He shook his match. "Real clean."

"Ignite—"

"Probably had a bath every day of her life," Greg mused.

"You guys are in a lot o' trouble, you know that?" Clark mumbled but managed a glance of his own.

"Healthy!" Jameson coughed, "That's the word I want."

"Bet they never heard of elephantiasis," Scot mused.

"That's disgusting!" Clark snapped. "What is that thing? It smells like—"

"Upcountry…it's called a cigar," Larry explained.

"Spheroid?"

"Fertile!" Jameson pondered trying his luck at smoke rings. "That's the word I want."

"Sometimes they come with a little Negro to carry them around," Larry added. "The cigar."

"Probably paint their toenails every night," Greg surmised.

"Why don't you go ask?" Clark snapped.

"My good man," Scot answered severely, "one does not probe too deep, too soon. Diplomacy."

"Why don't you go ask?" Larry grinned. "I see you've got the Old Spice workin'."

Clark thought a minute, straightened his tie. "Look. If I ask them to join us...do you...just try to act civilized." He folded his napkin, rose from the table. "Extinguish the compost."

Crossing the room he casually buttoned his jacket, went straight to their table, placed his hand on the back of a chair and began a lengthy explanation they seemed to enjoy. He had a gift. They returned his easy smile answering questions in detail, encouraging him with quiet body language. He listened to each in turn then cracked a joke, probably at our expense, and they were already old friends. One more question and to our amazement they got up leaving the confused steward holding a pitcher of orange juice.

"I don't believe it!" Greg whispered.

"He did it! They're actually..." And they were, all four followed by the steward who looked utterly lost.

"I'm not sure I'm ready for this," Scot mumbled.

"Just act natural," Larry suggested. Jameson rubbed out his cigar.

They were pretty too. One blond, one dark and outgoing, the third business-like, the last reserved but inquisitive with tiny earrings and her hair bobbed. All four greeted us pleasantly when we rose, Clark watching like a schoolmarm.

"Oh don't bother," the dark one smiled.

"You'll have to excuse the rusticity," Clark said, "they've been up in the bush twenty years."

"That sounds exciting," the blond smiled, crossing her legs. We couldn't believe our eyes.

"Yes," Scot stammered after an embarrassing pause. "Yes, it was."

"The jungle always looks so green flying over," she added. "I've always wondered what's inside."

"Hot. Sweaty. Lot o' bugs," Larry said. "You wouldn't like it."

"Maybe not," the dark one said, "Just the same I'd like to see for myself, it must be lovely to get away from all the hustle and bustle."

No one could think of anything to say.

"Right." Clark cried rubbing his hands together after an awkward pause. "Young man! Right this way!" He caught the steward retreating to the kitchen. "That's right! Orange juice for everybody!" He wasn't half serious but the steward, by now totally confused, dutifully refilled everyone's glass. "Now then. How about introductions?" So with Clark presiding we went around the table, each saying his or her name and trying to remember the others, but afterwards things went silent again so he suggested another round, this time our home towns. It worked. Somehow the names of those far-off places broke the ice—Altoona, P.A., Traverse City, Sioux Rapids, Fort Worth, Greenville, Santa Clara, Oak Park, Delray Beach, Kipton, Los Angeles—each sounding a chord that whispered "home." Before we knew it several lively conversations got going and we quite forgot ourselves. Eunice grew up on a farm in Iowa and Diane collected antiques. They were really nice, interested in what we did though surprised to learn we had so little contact with the outside world.

"That's an interesting neckpiece," Diane said to me.

"Thank you," I said.

"A toast! A toast!" Clark cried lifting his orange juice over the chatter.

"To the end of the dry season," Greg offered.

"I give up," Clark sighed, "Why do I try?"

"To airplanes, to the trade winds, to South Carolina," Larry beamed. "Bet you never thought you'd live to hear a Negro toast a southern state."

"How about…to new acquaintances and old towns?" Janet suggested.

"To apple pie, mama, and southern fried chicken."

"To going home."

"What's so bad about the dry season anyway?" Terri asked. None of us dared look at each other. "I think I'd prefer it to constant rain every day."

"It's difficult to keep clean," Scot finally answered, with effort. "Hot and dusty. The rainy season's really more pleasant once you get used to it. The afternoon showers cool things off."

"I don't think they're telling us everything." Janet smiled.

"Yes. Do tell us everything," Clark insisted.

"I have a feeling we're not talking about the weather," Eunice cautioned in Terri's direction.

"We're really not as bad as we look." Jameson smiled. He took a photo out of his wallet and passed it around. "See, that's what I used to look like. It's hard to keep clean upcountry, that's all."

"Is that you Jameson?" Clark sneered. "In a suit?"

"Tell us about it," Diane laughed. "Sometimes you can't even get a hot shower—at the airport."

"But you can wash your hair in a two gallon bucket," Terri broke in. "There's a trick to it—like this," and she demonstrated to everyone's amazement.

"And if you want a shower," Scot added, "all you do is hammer some nail holes in the bottom, hang it over your head. Presto."

"Hey! I never thought of that," she laughed.

"We know all the tricks," Jameson sighed.

"Yeah," Larry chuckled. "Tell 'em about the time you pulled the bridge down. With his winch."

"Oh no," Clark groaned.

"It's not what you think," Scot said.

"A winch—"

"Yes, perhaps you'd better explain."

"We know what a winch is," Diane laughed.

"Ha!" Jameson scolded. "Well then, for Clark's benefit—a rising young diplomat should know a winch from a wench, don't you agree ladies?"

"Yes, definitely," Diane beamed.

"One's to pull you out of the mud, the other's to pull you in," Scot suggested.

"Are you writing this down Clark?"

"A winch, my dear sir, is a powered cable on the front end of a jeep. Normally when you hook on to something solid, like a bridge, you don't expect it to move, right? Wrong. Not in this country."

Jameson's story turned out to be quite entertaining, especially the part about filing a written report to an engineer who couldn't read. Afterwards they began filling us in on what was happening back home. The Yankees finally lost, color TV everywhere, business booming, the Beatles still on top. Janet and Diane really did want to visit the African wilds but were skeptical about some of the stories they heard. How could they find a reliable guide? What were the natives really like?

"They're just like us," Larry said. "They laugh and cry and enjoy their friends. Only they don't dress Madison Avenue."

"Or paint their toenails," Greg added.

"I don't know these guys," Clark groaned, looking to the heavens for help.

"So that's what you're worried about," Eunice glared.

"Well, yeah," Greg admitted. "We were sitting here filing our teeth, wondering—"

"Observe," Eunice said removing her shoe. "The little piggy who stayed home. You guys are gonna do just fine."

"You won't have any trouble catching up on your girl watching," Janet added, "now that miniskirts are in style."

"Are they really?" Clark asked regaining his composure.

"Haven't you heard! That's right, you guys—"

"I thought it was some kind of gimmick," Scot said.

"Oh no," Terri smiled. "Everyone's wearing them, the shorter the better. Eight inches above the knee, can you imagine?"

"Unfortunately we can," Jameson said dryly.

"How do you sit down in them?" Larry asked.

"You have to learn to sit all over again," Janet said.

"Back to the basics," Greg added.

"Something like that," Diane smiled. "You know," she continued thinking aloud, "I've always wanted to see a native market place. I know there's one nearby and now that we've got some time—"

She didn't have far to look for an escort. It felt good to get outside but the marketplace was unbearable. I slipped away the first chance I got. Had to walk.

Soon the clatter of the airport died away, the road skirted the edge of town and began winding through a rubber plantation. After a bit, I found a tractor trail into the man-made jungle, each tree bent to the same arc, secreting the same sap, forming sections and areas and farms, numbered and recorded somewhere in a ledger stretching all the way to Wall Street. In a country without enough to eat, the best soil grew rubber. It was starting to bother me—something a Marxist would notice. And that bothered me too.

So my world would be ordered again. Someday soon I'd have to sit down and plan my career. The romantic interlude was over, like a strict parent the real world was calling me back. But you can't go home again. Maybe not, but we can avoid a homeless future. The river runs one way but the water keeps coming back. Eternal Recurrence. It didn't jive with the death of God. I'd have to reread Nietzsche. I sniffed my sleeve, wood smoke, I'd have to get it cleaned first thing, a haircut too, maybe a new suit. Why couldn't I share the jubilance of my friends?

I felt a growing impatience for people like Van Meter. They came looking for poverty, found it, and now went home thinking they'd seen the real Africa when in fact "the real Africa" remained invisible right under their noses, incommunicado in the silent faces who watched them wheeling through dusty villages scattering kids and chickens, cursing it all in a language as discordant as the sound of the motor. What they didn't understand, the hard drivers, was that the Africa they hated—the corruption and cruel dictators, fast buck artists and begging Uncle Toms—was no more than a macabre parody, and in hating it they were in fact hating themselves, for they looked in a mirror. But what of it? They'd return to their cocktail parties where the myths they entertained would make witty conversation pieces.

Two years ago I'd been one of them, secure, confident, clicking off the same cliches. Now I saw my world not as the shiny package of peace and prosperity but rather a sham, an escape from the really important things. And I'd come to educate them, the infant culture instructing the grandsire. I grimaced at the thought of it.

They were dying. That was no myth. Each day the motor road brought something new and took back a small parcel of tribal independence in exchange. Soon radios would overwhelm the storyteller and the strong young men would drift down to the coast where they'd learn new skills—like trying to serve breakfast to a bunch of foreigners who can't sit still long enough to eat. "Old things die," Old Fawkpa lamented one gentle evening on the way home from his farm in an uncharacteristic lapse into emotion which he considered womanish. Yet that one phrase, one flare that somehow escaped the calloused exterior of the old tribesman stuck to me and I saw him for the first time as his glaucous eyes scanned the treetops where he knew the same roosting birds would find the same sunset he knew as a boy. It spoke of an entire way of life. The great tribal experiment begun at the dawn of humanity would soon close, perhaps in my lifetime. Yet they hung on. If forbearance in the face of a certain end makes a thing heroic, then Old Fawkpa and his peers were just that.

In a way I was glad my work turned out as ineffectual as it had. Of that I had no illusions. True, a few of them could read. But where would it lead? The principles of the two-cycle engine would replace the speech of the evening breeze. The Faustian trade. But they made it eagerly, just as we had a few centuries past.

Yet there were victories, small ones, and savoring them staved off the cynicism that comes of losing the big ones: the trip to Kpodokpodo, Nyamu telling me hello, the witch at Dawawoli (she died shortly after our trip, one evening a traveler appeared at my door with a soft knock and the bad news,

"Da o' womah. She die-oh.") small Zeezee's first kill, a yearling bush hog strung to a pole and carried to town in sweet triumph. That day we were Caesar's legions returning from Gaul victorious.

Maybe it's the little things that count after all—songs and sunrises, trinkets and friendships; though grains of sand they hold fast the grand edifices we live by. It was something to grasp.

And there were memories—clear as photographs: pot-bellied kids sucking the last drops of nourishment from discarded beer cans, the weathered mud huts with thatched caps atilt in the sun, the deadening spell of the noonday heat, the reprieve of the afternoon rain, the smell of burnt palm oil, the old women crouched in darkened doorways spinning cotton. They were great ladies, the old women. The more the burden, the greater their bearing. They forced their old bones into tasks that seemed beyond endurance, yet they somehow bore up, their smiles more precious for the undercurrent of pain. Their wrinkled faces and diseased bodies managed to belie just the opposite, a healthy *joie de vivre* that echoed in their toothless laughter like music in a morgue. I'd never understand how they could laugh in the face of such squalor. I came expecting poverty pure and dismal but found something else, a masterpiece in a broken-down pawn shop.

I'd learned a few things. Poverty is a dedicated teacher. Simplicity is eternal. Silence is grace. Untouched wilderness is pure nature and pure nature well met becomes what it's always been, the supernatural. But to touch it is to make it natural again; it must remain unknown, we must keep our distance but imbibe when we can. We need this tonic of the wilderness, as our venerable ancestor said, to set limits on what we know, to curb the excesses of reasoned nonsense.

By now my village would be awake, astir from its sleep just as the morning light began to creep through the forest. The first sign of life would be the women going down to the creek. They would slip through the mist, single file, the earthen jars erect on their heads, down to the riverbank in silent ease, now remounting the winding path in subdued grace like devout pilgrims ascending the steps of a magnificent cathedral. Then the rice mortars would begin to beat. The wind would speak up. Tongues of dry rice would leap from the winnowing baskets. A cock would declare day, beams of sunlight bathe the whitewashed walls, windows fly open, the murmur of neighbors growing on the air; Jacob and Daydobah would be playing in the dirt out back, their chatter rising to the momentous transactions of childhood. Now the slam of a screen door, running feet, the cackle of scattering hens. A shout. The bark of a dog. The far off staccato of a wild bird…and the soft tapping on my back window with the first question of the day. "Did Geronimo really ride into battle naked?"

Kids. They made it worth while. As long as there are children there's hope.

Soon they'd be making their way to their farms. The forest would seal them into their small world leaving them to their solitude and whatever they made of it, their time measured out in the constant flow of birdsong, or the rhythmic clinking of their hoes striking pebbles in the soft earth. Women and girls did the hoeing. They worked in small knots away from the profane ears of men where their uninhibited chatter could go on save for pauses of rest and occasional peels of laughter. They worked in spurts hoeing feverishly to the rhythm of a work chant, their wet backs dipping in unison until they pulled up out of breath. A burst of energy spent, the head woman would straighten up, look back over the fresh earth, draw new wind and perhaps comment on the eternal menace of aching backs. But not without a dose of encouragement. "Look you! My sisters! I am older than you, therefore my back pains me the greater. But no matter, I will not cry. It is a small burden. Surely no greater than bearing a lover aloft in the night." They'd scream in unison and dip into the next spurt with renewed strength, taking up a new chant as their hoes sprayed loose soil over their feet. "Surely no greater! No greater!" So they worked, without much notice to a passing white man who didn't speak much Loma anyway. I'd miss my morning walks. The work chants. The lush mists. The immensity of the jungle's silence. I'd never known such peace.

"Indeed."

"Nyamu?"

"No longer startled?"

"Guess not."

"Going home then?…Vorjinzhinski—a fine American name, and not so hard to pronounce. Godspeed. You had the right idea but the wrong continent, found your name but lost your innocence. Now regain it. Innocence lost is but a shedding of the childhood skin, regained it is the essence of true manhood. Without it there can be no fusion of human hearts, no conviction we are beings of a common clay. Do not mistake it for weakness. But take care. Things will be different now. You will find a wasteland so vast your wise men tremble. Culture will be an aimless degeneracy, art will wear the smile of a whore, loud profanity the banner of freedom, brazen liars shall bellow the truth, former heroes will have sold their names. The best will be forgotten; the worst televised. Your taste for something better will drown in a sea of smut; you will see your own generation as a pack of undisciplined brats. Sex, drugs, and rock 'n' roll shall be their childish mantra. You will be a freak among them. Yes, these little talks are not without a price. Now you've tasted the elixir of my spirit, savor it but do not intoxicate yourself; it will succor you through darker times than these. Your country will lose an ill-starred war; thereafter you will witness its long and graceless decline. Steel your heart to the knowledge this too will pass, that that matters will endure. All is NOT vanity. Truth and beauty yet abide even in a world as crass as this, and honor resides where it always has, in the hearts of those who bear its scars. Keep clean the lamp of remembrance. Cherish the chance of something good. Do not despair. Despair is the bastard child of fear; fear is the only enemy a man must face; it is the dragon within. You must slay it and all its hideous progeny—apathy, arrogance, cynicism, selfishness, nihilism, terror."

"Slay a dragon? How does one—"

"By giving me life."

"But you are dying."

"I die...and I do not die...as the occasion requires. It is you who hold the balance."

"Me?"

"Yes. You have seen into the hollow of my face; it is yours to rekindle my flame. You must make me live, if not in name, in joy! Laughter! Love of life!"

"But I'm the weakest of all. You said so yourself."

"Indeed. But weakness is sire of imagination, nature's invitation to use your brains. Our species would have expired for want of it. Examine the nail on your hand and that of the leopard. Who has the advantage? One night in the bush has taught you as much. You have thus bridged the chasm from modern thought to me; now jump back again. Do not quail before this godless revelation; the harshest truth is beauty to a placid eye. If God is dead, inspire another. Indeed our ancestors invented me to counter nature's injustice. I am but a child of imagination, a stepping stone to a higher species, a real advantage if I breed results. There can be no strength without weakness, no courage without fear, no god without an alien universe; these apparent anomalies are children of a destined marriage, they bear fruit for those who dare."

"I...I can't tell them I've been talking to you."

"You will find a way."

"I can't."

"You must. I wish I could tell you this little task is but an exercise in make-believe but I'm afraid the future is woven of today's imaginings and therein lies the resurrection of our kind. What I set you to is life and death. Do not abandon your own."

"They will laugh at me."

"Good. Laughter is fair beginning, the magic elixir to save us from ourselves. The mad man and the hardened criminal know it not, the fool in his wisdom drinks deep. Do not underestimate its power. To cause another human face to soften into human joy is to do the work of peace. To find peace is to possess my very wife. Do you quite understand? I speak not of human flesh. She is not of earthly matter."

"She doesn't speak to me."

"She will. Hold your peace and she will favor you as she did at the carrousel so long ago."

"Surely that's a challenge."

"A challenge? So be it. I have danced my dance. May its vigor excite a smile in my Lady's heart. Your penchant for forbidden fruit will guide you now."

"I will miss you."

"You will endure."

"Why is good-bye so hard?"

"A hard good-bye is the price of a new beginning. You will find a way."

"Good hunting old friend."

"Beware of the jungle you call civilization."

CHAPTER 48

SUNRISE

"Good afternoon ladies and gentlemen and welcome aboard Pan American Flight 521, Monrovia to New York via Dakar. We will be getting under way shortly pending ground clearance. Your captain is Mr. Grimes, your co-pilot, Mr. Reichert, your flight engineer, Mr. Stenowizc; I'm Miss Ritenour, your head stewardess. We will be flying at thirty-three thousand feet, weather conditions are cloudy with intermittent rain, our air time to Dakar will be two hours and thirty-five minutes approximately. On behalf of your captain and crew I would like to wish you a very good day and if there's anything we can do to make your trip more pleasant, please don't hesitate to call on us. Fasten your seat belts and please observe the 'No Smoking' warning lamp."

I must have dozed off. Dreaming. I met an old friend. Couldn't place him but we had a long chat about old times. He'd given me an unexpected vote of confidence, someone I'd never given much credence.

"No she didn't."

"She did."

"You're hearing things."

"You're crazy."

"What *is the problem?*" Clark asked loosening his tie.

"It's in your head."

"It's not in my head."

"You've been up in the bush too long."

"She has to know we're destitute."

"That's the point. Would she purposely aggravate an inflamed condition?"

"What's not in his head?"

"'Anything.'"

"What on *earth* are you talking about?" Clark said in complete exasperation.

"Our associate is of the opinion the lady emphasized the word 'anything' in her rendering of, 'Anything we can do to make your trip more pleasant,'" Scot explained.

"It's standard procedure." Clark pleaded. "They read it off a card!"

"Then it's false advertising," Jameson said from the next seat in front.

"Write your congressman," Clark snapped.

"I knew you'd understand, Jameson," Greg sighed and Larry gave a thumbs up from across the aisle.

Clark took up a magazine, began leafing through it, very professional, then stopped and looked at me. "What...is that garish object around your neck?"

"A leopard's tooth."

"Brown?"

"Dried blood."

"Gots t' hab blood on it," Larry whispered. "Oddahwise...no oomph."

"That's disgusting," he winced.

"Just precocious," Larry reassured him. "Take it easy. You goin' home Baby." He clasped him around the shoulder. "Any minute now. Any minute." Then he kissed him.

"You guys are sick," Clark whispered, "Not only sick, diseased."

The terminal started to move. Ever so slow. Turning, receding, then bumping along. Now we were at the end of the runway, turning a half pirouette, slow, deliberate. We stopped again. Now what? Another long pause. At last. I could feel the thrust of the engines, rising speed—I remembered naked children running alongside trucks as long as they could keep up—faster and faster, then the ground fell away as though it were dropped from a window. Down below the forest looked calm but uninviting, not a hint of human trespass. The great cottonwood trees were no more than green goose bumps on a wrinkled skin. Soon a cloud layer intervened and everything disappeared as though a witch's hand passed over a smoking cauldron. I kept hearing that drunken voice in the bar last night, "Are we going to the United States tonight?" Tonight! All this time the fast cars and miniskirts had been that close, a nine hour flight. The entire two years had been like a half sleep where sounds of one world invade another—so close yet so far away.

I felt tired. Soon we leveled off and the engines relaxed into a low whine. Now and then we felt the bump of an air pocket, otherwise smooth sailing through a sea of clouds, billowy, bridal white. Then another bump, muffled, like a heavy crate dropping to the ground far away. Another bump. It cracked open. A statue inside, white marble with shreds of burlap coming undone. It's her! A masterpiece coming to life, you can see her smile, that unmistakable smile.

Dreaming again. Before leaving for Africa, I'd spent my last day at the New York World's Fair. I'd seen *La Pieta* there. I remember passing before it on a moving sidewalk thinking how absurd to get a two minute glimpse of something eternal.

I looked out the window. A new day dawned. The clouds seemed to float in timeless radiance, white and feathery, as though beyond the breath of gravity. And the sun! Twice risen, beaming bright over a teeming earth kicking in its swaddling clothes.

The stewardess. Where had I heard that voice before? In the dream telling me my flight was cancelled. I kept seeing some kind of actress, only she wasn't an actress, rather a haunting vision, dark, chthonic, like the earth herself in all her infinite variety—forests, fields, faint moonlight on a shimmering sea, maiden-mother, the primal remembrance that wakens the best in us. The Holy Mother! I didn't recognize her in the flesh, she'd always been…polished marble. But in a way she really was an actress; she appeared in so many epiphanies. And so many voices. Longing breezes, whispers in the gathering dusk, raindrops kissing wet clay. Lady Night, unveiling her face to consummate her marriage to the sunrise, here in the shining temple of earth and water with all the world's forests singing joyous praise. Listen!

"I am maiden; I am mother"

Another smile.

"I am laden. I am other."

Deeper.

She makes satin out of burlap. Grandma's apron. A feed sack with big pockets in front and she filled them with corn when we went to feed the ducks. She fed them by hand with calloused hands that gripped like a vise and she waddled when she walked with her feet sticking out the sides of men's shoes. She wore a babushka and a black sweater with a hole in the elbow. The kids laughed at her. She smelled funny too and the apron was scratchy. But she took me on her lap and kissed me and sang to me in the old country language, the forbidden language because I was to be an American. *Moiyea Mallo Kashka.* And when she died one of the fine ladies said, "Let's hope they buried that apron with her," and I cried because I thought the burlap would be scratchy down in the ground.

Deeper.

A black leopardess. Licking her cubs, butterflies orbiting her head and leafy breezes dancing in the grass. She stays their wobbly balance with her loving tongue, her warmth whispering in their ears.

"Hungry? Suckle then and be content. How your tail tells your story. Did you find game at the waterhole? Did you vanquish all those dragons made of air? Stretch those mighty claws, call out to your kind, but next time don't stray so far from home. The day will come the world will waken to your cry, the night go silent at your passing. Here's a mother's kiss, and once again and yet another. Come let me wash your ears. So like your father. In joy of being so like me."

Deeper.

Here in the wild. All this time as simple as an animal's love for its young. What else is the human spirit but love that's born in savage flesh then grows to forms more fitting to its purpose? How it flows from mold to mold like blood through a thousand species. From animal to mother, mistress, lover—finally to she of the dreams. The devil's wife! The marriage of Heaven and Hell! Yes! How did I miss it? That one night with all the windows boarded shut while the whole earth shivered in excitement. The dreamy solo afloat on the silky air, so out of place yet so intimate, like wet lips pressed to your ear whispering wild desire. See her as you may. Black if you wish. Or White, brown, yellow, red. She's all of them at once. And fertile. See her round hip; her soft hair caressing her nipple; her smile, her enchanting music none other than the revealed presence of a virgin Earth humming in the joy of expectant motherhood. A gift from Heaven. Like a ride on the carrousel! Why had she given me that ticket? She must have lost a child. She definitely lost a child, I know that now with certainty. See the horses rearing, the lights flashing and the ump pah pah machine…only it sounds like a grand orchestra on a grand occasion. The royal bearing, the tilt of her head, shimmering silk, sparkling jewels, a tiny diamond at the center of her forehead. A single daisy in her hair. The immense love within. But she never speaks. If only…just once. Please just once. Oh for a ride on the—

"How now my Wayward? Home at last? How my dawn rekindles at the sight of thee. My sunlight dances, my seas leap up in wild delight, in red excitement I scarce control. How my love could bathe this little earth of every tear, every hurt but give me one sweet smile of my sweet child's lips. Come let me look thee in the eye, brush your hair, kiss an eyelid too. Did you dream an impossible dream? Dreams are tomorrow's harvest; plant them deep and give them credence, they will blossom in a better world. Did you defy your elders? Remember it well. It will echo when yours come rebel-mouthed to you. Make love not war they will seem to say. Tell them love alone is love enough, it need not make war on war. Have you tasted forbidden fruit? Now pay the price. Forgo the wealth of Eden and look to the future, you are yet to taste its unforbidden bounty. Have you faltered when you should have led the way? There is room in heaven for error, a niche in hell for hope. Think how small an errant human step, how miscue breeds discovery, how truth revolves within the amplitude of time until today's plateaus become tomorrow's primer. And did you preach the death of God? Gods die too, and their mothers. Is not every death snuffed out in an infant's cry? Every night in another sunrise? Have you played with nuclear fire? Do you remember how you cried when you burnt your fingers? Are human fingers meant to burn? And so you lost a war? What is a war either lost or won within the compass of my smile? What is ever lost but what we throw away? In bitterest defeat we find our bravest friends. Weep then at your wall of fallen friends; my love is closer than you think. Find one fatherless child to kiss and I am your friend come home. When all the world turns away, when none would have us in his prayers, humility spreads its wings. Know now and never once forget, it, and none other, is the key to my heart, the unpolished jewel that centers my heavenly crown. Without it none can savor joy nor master shame. Accept it and you are not alone. In the memory of those you've lost, think what better may come. Repeat a thousand times, better is yet to come. Let me see your face, your child's heart. There I dwell. Do not misuse a single hour nor regret a passing age. Take this kiss, it's but a droplet in my ocean's love. Welcome. Welcome home. A thousand kisses welcome. Come let me squeeze your neck. Like raindrops let these kisses splash, let blue skies burst, rainbows blush, the bright and teeming future can wait another day. This dance is mine! These joyous tears cannot obey, they rush to consecrate a son's return. Surely I have love enough and more, for every heart, every face this little earth lifts upward to my grace. And you, my wayward, my prince of causes…not lost, incomplete; let me look you in the heart. Lost, alone, I love you not one kiss less. Come bask with me now in the beautiful sun. In childhood the man is made; his soul is centered on a mother's joy. Remember me. All things must pass but love is time's companion. In the depth of thy soul's most savage wilderness remember me; in the terror of thy darkest desperation look to me. There is no wound so deep nor grief so wide this smile cannot heal. There is nothing in this world so foul this kiss can't save, nor anything so brave."